# HARRY POTTER

## AND THE GOBLET OF FIRE

BY

## J.K. ROWLING

ILLUSTRATIONS BY MARY GRANDPRÉ

SCHOLASTIC INC.

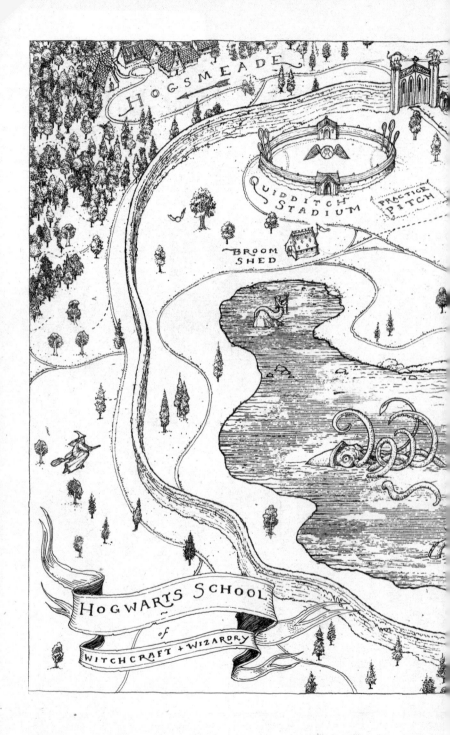

To Peter Rowling,

in memory of Mr. Ridley

and to Susan Sladden,

who helped Harry

out of his cupboard

Text © 2000 by J.K. Rowling
Interior illustrations by Mary GrandPré © 2000 by Warner Bros.
Excerpt from *Harry Potter and the Order of the Phoenix*, text © 2003 by J.K. Rowling;
illustration by Mary GrandPré © 2003 by Warner Bros.
Cover illustration by Brian Selznick © 2018 by Scholastic Inc.
Map illustration by Levi Pinfold © 2017 by Bloomsbury Publishing Plc.
Wizarding World and Harry Potter Publishing Rights © J.K. Rowling
Wizarding World TM & © Warner Bros. Entertainment Inc.
Wizarding World and Harry Potter characters, names, and related indicia are TM
and © Warner Bros. Entertainment Inc. • All rights reserved. Published by Scholastic Inc.,
*Publishers since 1920.* SCHOLASTIC, the LANTERN LOGO, and associated logos are
trademarks and/or registered trademarks of Scholastic Inc.

Arthur A. Levine Books hardcover edition art directed by David Saylor,
published by Arthur A. Levine Books, an imprint of Scholastic Inc., July 2000.

ISBN 978-1-338-29917-5

10 9 8 7 6 5 4 3 2 1     18 19 20 21 22

Printed in the U.S.A.   40
This edition first printing 2018

# CONTENTS

# HARRY POTTER

## AND THE GOBLET OF FIRE

# THE RIDDLE HOUSE

The villagers of Little Hangleton still called it "the Riddle House," even though it had been many years since the Riddle family had lived there. It stood on a hill overlooking the village, some of its windows boarded, tiles missing from its roof, and ivy spreading unchecked over its face. Once a fine-looking manor, and easily the largest and grandest building for miles around, the Riddle House was now damp, derelict, and unoccupied.

The Little Hangletons all agreed that the old house was "creepy." Half a century ago, something strange and horrible had happened there, something that the older inhabitants of the village still liked to discuss when topics for gossip were scarce. The story had been picked over so many times, and had been embroidered in so many places, that nobody was quite sure what the truth was anymore. Every version of the tale, however, started in the same place: Fifty years before, at daybreak on a fine summer's morning, when the

Riddle House had still been well kept and impressive, a maid had entered the drawing room to find all three Riddles dead.

The maid had run screaming down the hill into the village and roused as many people as she could.

"Lying there with their eyes wide open! Cold as ice! Still in their dinner things!"

The police were summoned, and the whole of Little Hangleton had seethed with shocked curiosity and ill-disguised excitement. Nobody wasted their breath pretending to feel very sad about the Riddles, for they had been most unpopular. Elderly Mr. and Mrs. Riddle had been rich, snobbish, and rude, and their grown-up son, Tom, had been, if anything, worse. All the villagers cared about was the identity of their murderer — for plainly, three apparently healthy people did not all drop dead of natural causes on the same night.

The Hanged Man, the village pub, did a roaring trade that night; the whole village seemed to have turned out to discuss the murders. They were rewarded for leaving their firesides when the Riddles' cook arrived dramatically in their midst and announced to the suddenly silent pub that a man called Frank Bryce had just been arrested.

"Frank!" cried several people. "Never!"

Frank Bryce was the Riddles' gardener. He lived alone in a run-down cottage on the grounds of the Riddle House. Frank had come back from the war with a very stiff leg and a great dislike of crowds and loud noises, and had been working for the Riddles ever since.

There was a rush to buy the cook drinks and hear more details.

"Always thought he was odd," she told the eagerly listening villagers, after her fourth sherry. "Unfriendly, like. I'm sure if I've offered him a cuppa once, I've offered it a hundred times. Never wanted to mix, he didn't."

"Ah, now," said a woman at the bar, "he had a hard war, Frank. He likes the quiet life. That's no reason to —"

"Who else had a key to the back door, then?" barked the cook. "There's been a spare key hanging in the gardener's cottage far back as I can remember! Nobody forced the door last night! No broken windows! All Frank had to do was creep up to the big house while we was all sleeping. . . ."

The villagers exchanged dark looks.

"I always thought he had a nasty look about him, right enough," grunted a man at the bar.

"War turned him funny, if you ask me," said the landlord.

"Told you I wouldn't like to get on the wrong side of Frank, didn't I, Dot?" said an excited woman in the corner.

"Horrible temper," said Dot, nodding fervently. "I remember, when he was a kid . . ."

By the following morning, hardly anyone in Little Hangleton doubted that Frank Bryce had killed the Riddles.

But over in the neighboring town of Great Hangleton, in the dark and dingy police station, Frank was stubbornly repeating, again and again, that he was innocent, and that the only person he had seen near the house on the day of the Riddles' deaths had been a teenage boy, a stranger, dark-haired and pale. Nobody else in the village had seen any such boy, and the police were quite sure that Frank had invented him.

Then, just when things were looking very serious for Frank, the report on the Riddles' bodies came back and changed everything.

The police had never read an odder report. A team of doctors had examined the bodies and had concluded that none of the Riddles had been poisoned, stabbed, shot, strangled, suffocated, or (as far as they could tell) harmed at all. In fact (the report continued, in a tone of unmistakable bewilderment), the Riddles all appeared to be in perfect health — apart from the fact that they were all dead. The doctors did note (as though determined to find something wrong with the bodies) that each of the Riddles had a look of terror upon his or her face — but as the frustrated police said, whoever heard of three people being *frightened* to death?

As there was no proof that the Riddles had been murdered at all, the police were forced to let Frank go. The Riddles were buried in the Little Hangleton churchyard, and their graves remained objects of curiosity for a while. To everyone's surprise, and amid a cloud of suspicion, Frank Bryce returned to his cottage on the grounds of the Riddle House.

"'S far as I'm concerned, he killed them, and I don't care what the police say," said Dot in the Hanged Man. "And if he had any decency, he'd leave here, knowing as how we knows he did it."

But Frank did not leave. He stayed to tend the garden for the next family who lived in the Riddle House, and then the next — for neither family stayed long. Perhaps it was partly because of Frank that the new owners said there was a nasty feeling about the place, which, in the absence of inhabitants, started to fall into disrepair.

The wealthy man who owned the Riddle House these days neither lived there nor put it to any use; they said in the village that he kept it for "tax reasons," though nobody was very clear what these might be. The wealthy owner continued to pay Frank to do the gardening, however. Frank was nearing his seventy-seventh birthday now, very deaf, his bad leg stiffer than ever, but could be seen pottering around the flower beds in fine weather, even though the weeds were starting to creep up on him, try as he might to suppress them.

Weeds were not the only things Frank had to contend with either. Boys from the village made a habit of throwing stones through the windows of the Riddle House. They rode their bicycles over the lawns Frank worked so hard to keep smooth. Once or twice, they broke into the old house for a dare. They knew that old Frank's devotion to the house and grounds amounted almost to an obsession, and it amused them to see him limping across the garden, brandishing his stick and yelling croakily at them. Frank, for his part, believed the boys tormented him because they, like their parents and grandparents, thought him a murderer. So when Frank awoke one night in August and saw something very odd up at the old house, he merely assumed that the boys had gone one step further in their attempts to punish him.

It was Frank's bad leg that woke him; it was paining him worse than ever in his old age. He got up and limped downstairs into the kitchen with the idea of refilling his hot-water bottle to ease the stiffness in his knee. Standing at the sink, filling the kettle, he looked up at the Riddle House and saw lights glimmering in its upper windows. Frank knew at once what was going on. The boys had broken into the house again, and judging by the flickering quality of the light, they had started a fire.

Frank had no telephone, and in any case, he had deeply mistrusted the police ever since they had taken him in for questioning about the Riddles' deaths. He put down the kettle at once, hurried back upstairs as fast as his bad leg would allow, and was soon back in his kitchen, fully dressed and removing a rusty old key from its hook by the door. He picked up his walking stick, which was propped against the wall, and set off into the night.

The front door of the Riddle House bore no sign of being forced, nor did any of the windows. Frank limped around to the back of the house until he reached a door almost completely hidden by ivy, took out the old key, put it into the lock, and opened the door noiselessly.

He let himself into the cavernous kitchen. Frank had not entered it for many years; nevertheless, although it was very dark, he remembered where the door into the hall was, and he groped his way toward it, his nostrils full of the smell of decay, ears pricked for any sound of footsteps or voices from overhead. He reached the hall, which was a little lighter owing to the large mullioned windows on either side of the front door, and started to climb the stairs, blessing the dust that lay thick upon the stone, because it muffled the sound of his feet and stick.

On the landing, Frank turned right, and saw at once where the intruders were: At the very end of the passage a door stood ajar, and a flickering light shone through the gap, casting a long sliver of gold across the black floor. Frank edged closer and closer, grasping his walking stick firmly. Several feet from the entrance, he was able to see a narrow slice of the room beyond.

The fire, he now saw, had been lit in the grate. This surprised him. Then he stopped moving and listened intently, for a man's voice spoke within the room; it sounded timid and fearful.

"There is a little more in the bottle, my Lord, if you are still hungry."

"Later," said a second voice. This too belonged to a man — but it was strangely high-pitched, and cold as a sudden blast of icy wind. Something about that voice made the sparse hairs on the back of Frank's neck stand up. "Move me closer to the fire, Wormtail."

Frank turned his right ear toward the door, the better to hear. There came the clink of a bottle being put down upon some hard surface, and then the dull scraping noise of a heavy chair being dragged across the floor. Frank caught a glimpse of a small man, his back to the door, pushing the chair into place. He was wearing a long black cloak, and there was a bald patch at the back of his head. Then he went out of sight again.

"Where is Nagini?" said the cold voice.

"I — I don't know, my Lord," said the first voice nervously. "She set out to explore the house, I think. . . ."

"You will milk her before we retire, Wormtail," said the second voice. "I will need feeding in the night. The journey has tired me greatly."

Brow furrowed, Frank inclined his good ear still closer to the door, listening very hard. There was a pause, and then the man called Wormtail spoke again.

"My Lord, may I ask how long we are going to stay here?"

"A week," said the cold voice. "Perhaps longer. The place is moderately comfortable, and the plan cannot proceed yet. It would be foolish to act before the Quidditch World Cup is over."

Frank inserted a gnarled finger into his ear and rotated it. Owing, no doubt, to a buildup of earwax, he had heard the word "Quidditch," which was not a word at all.

"The — the Quidditch World Cup, my Lord?" said Wormtail.

(Frank dug his finger still more vigorously into his ear.) "Forgive me, but — I do not understand — why should we wait until the World Cup is over?"

"Because, fool, at this very moment wizards are pouring into the country from all over the world, and every meddler from the Ministry of Magic will be on duty, on the watch for signs of unusual activity, checking and double-checking identities. They will be obsessed with security, lest the Muggles notice anything. So we wait."

Frank stopped trying to clear out his ear. He had distinctly heard the words "Ministry of Magic," "wizards," and "Muggles." Plainly, each of these expressions meant something secret, and Frank could think of only two sorts of people who would speak in code: spies and criminals. Frank tightened his hold on his walking stick once more, and listened more closely still.

"Your Lordship is still determined, then?" Wormtail said quietly.

"Certainly I am determined, Wormtail." There was a note of menace in the cold voice now.

A slight pause followed — and then Wormtail spoke, the words tumbling from him in a rush, as though he was forcing himself to say this before he lost his nerve.

"It could be done without Harry Potter, my Lord."

Another pause, more protracted, and then —

"Without Harry Potter?" breathed the second voice softly. "I see . . ."

"My Lord, I do not say this out of concern for the boy!" said Wormtail, his voice rising squeakily. "The boy is nothing to me, nothing at all! It is merely that if we were to use another witch or wizard — any wizard — the thing could be done so much more quickly! If you allowed me to leave you for a short while — you know that I can disguise myself most effectively — I could be back here in as little as two days with a suitable person —"

"I could use another wizard," said the cold voice softly, "that is true. . . ."

"My Lord, it makes sense," said Wormtail, sounding thoroughly relieved now. "Laying hands on Harry Potter would be so difficult, he is so well protected —"

"And so you volunteer to go and fetch me a substitute? I wonder . . . perhaps the task of nursing me has become wearisome for you, Wormtail? Could this suggestion of abandoning the plan be nothing more than an attempt to desert me?"

"My Lord! I — I have no wish to leave you, none at all —"

"Do not lie to me!" hissed the second voice. "I can always tell, Wormtail! You are regretting that you ever returned to me. I revolt you. I see you flinch when you look at me, feel you shudder when you touch me. . . ."

"No! My devotion to Your Lordship —"

"Your devotion is nothing more than cowardice. You would not be here if you had anywhere else to go. How am I to survive without you, when I need feeding every few hours? Who is to milk Nagini?"

"But you seem so much stronger, my Lord —"

"Liar," breathed the second voice. "I am no stronger, and a few days alone would be enough to rob me of the little health I have regained under your clumsy care. *Silence!*"

Wormtail, who had been sputtering incoherently, fell silent at once. For a few seconds, Frank could hear nothing but the fire crackling. Then the second man spoke once more, in a whisper that was almost a hiss.

"I have my reasons for using the boy, as I have already explained to you, and I will use no other. I have waited thirteen years. A few more months will make no difference. As for the protection surrounding the boy, I believe my plan will be effective. All that is needed is a little courage from you, Wormtail — courage you will find, unless you wish to feel the full extent of Lord Voldemort's wrath —"

"My Lord, I must speak!" said Wormtail, panic in his voice now. "All through our journey I have gone over the plan in my head — my Lord, Bertha Jorkins's disappearance will not go unnoticed for long, and if we proceed, if I murder —"

"If?" whispered the second voice. "If? If you follow the plan, Wormtail, the Ministry need never know that anyone else has died. You will do it quietly and without fuss; I only wish that I could do it myself, but in my present condition . . . Come, Wormtail, one more death and our path to Harry Potter is clear. I am not asking you to do it alone. By that time, my *faithful* servant will have rejoined us —"

"*I* am a faithful servant," said Wormtail, the merest trace of sullenness in his voice.

"Wormtail, I need somebody with brains, somebody whose loyalty has never wavered, and you, unfortunately, fulfill neither requirement."

"I found you," said Wormtail, and there was definitely a sulky edge to his voice now. "I was the one who found you. I brought you Bertha Jorkins."

"That is true," said the second man, sounding amused. "A stroke of brilliance I would not have thought possible from you, Wormtail — though, if truth be told, you were not aware how useful she would be when you caught her, were you?"

"I — I thought she might be useful, my Lord —"

"Liar," said the second voice again, the cruel amusement more pronounced than ever. "However, I do not deny that her information was invaluable. Without it, I could never have formed our plan, and for that, you will have your reward, Wormtail. I will allow you to perform an essential task for me, one that many of my followers would give their right hands to perform. . . ."

"R-really, my Lord? What — ?" Wormtail sounded terrified again.

"Ah, Wormtail, you don't want me to spoil the surprise? Your part will come at the very end . . . but I promise you, you will have the honor of being just as useful as Bertha Jorkins."

"You . . . you . . ." Wormtail's voice suddenly sounded hoarse, as though his mouth had gone very dry. "You . . . are going . . . to kill me too?"

"Wormtail, Wormtail," said the cold voice silkily, "why would I kill you? I killed Bertha because I had to. She was fit for nothing after my questioning, quite useless. In any case, awkward questions would have been asked if she had gone back to the Ministry with the news that she had met you on her holidays. Wizards who are supposed to be dead would do well not to run into Ministry of Magic witches at wayside inns. . . ."

Wormtail muttered something so quietly that Frank could not hear it, but it made the second man laugh — an entirely mirthless laugh, cold as his speech.

"*We could have modified her memory?* But Memory Charms can be broken by a powerful wizard, as I proved when I questioned her. It would be an insult to her *memory* not to use the information I extracted from her, Wormtail."

Out in the corridor, Frank suddenly became aware that the hand gripping his walking stick was slippery with sweat. The man with the cold voice had killed a woman. He was talking about it without any kind of remorse — with *amusement*. He was dangerous — a madman. And he was planning more murders — this boy, Harry Potter, whoever he was — was in danger —

Frank knew what he must do. Now, if ever, was the time to go to the police. He would creep out of the house and head straight for the telephone box in the village . . . but the cold voice was speaking again, and Frank remained where he was, frozen to the spot, listening with all his might.

"One more murder . . . my faithful servant at Hogwarts . . . Harry Potter is as good as mine, Wormtail. It is decided. There will be no more argument. But quiet . . . I think I hear Nagini. . . ."

And the second man's voice changed. He started making noises such as Frank had never heard before; he was hissing and spitting without drawing breath. Frank thought he must be having some sort of fit or seizure.

And then Frank heard movement behind him in the dark passageway. He turned to look, and found himself paralyzed with fright.

Something was slithering toward him along the dark corridor floor, and as it drew nearer to the sliver of firelight, he realized with a thrill of terror that it was a gigantic snake, at least twelve feet long. Horrified, transfixed, Frank stared as its undulating body cut a wide, curving track through the thick dust on the floor, coming closer and closer — What was he to do? The only means of escape was into the room where two men sat plotting murder, yet if he stayed where he was the snake would surely kill him —

But before he had made his decision, the snake was level with him, and then, incredibly, miraculously, it was passing; it was following the spitting, hissing noises made by the cold voice beyond the door, and in seconds, the tip of its diamond-patterned tail had vanished through the gap.

There was sweat on Frank's forehead now, and the hand on the walking stick was trembling. Inside the room, the cold voice was continuing to hiss, and Frank was visited by a strange idea, an impossible idea. . . . *This man could talk to snakes.*

Frank didn't understand what was going on. He wanted more than anything to be back in his bed with his hot-water bottle. The problem was that his legs didn't seem to want to move. As he stood there shaking and trying to master himself, the cold voice switched abruptly to English again.

"Nagini has interesting news, Wormtail," it said.

"In-indeed, my Lord?" said Wormtail.

"Indeed, yes," said the voice. "According to Nagini, there is an old Muggle standing right outside this room, listening to every word we say."

Frank didn't have a chance to hide himself. There were footsteps, and then the door of the room was flung wide open.

A short, balding man with graying hair, a pointed nose, and small, watery eyes stood before Frank, a mixture of fear and alarm in his face.

"Invite him inside, Wormtail. Where are your manners?"

The cold voice was coming from the ancient armchair before the fire, but Frank couldn't see the speaker. The snake, on the other hand, was curled up on the rotting hearth rug, like some horrible travesty of a pet dog.

Wormtail beckoned Frank into the room. Though still deeply shaken, Frank took a firmer grip upon his walking stick and limped over the threshold.

The fire was the only source of light in the room; it cast long, spidery shadows upon the walls. Frank stared at the back of the armchair; the man inside it seemed to be even smaller than his servant, for Frank couldn't even see the back of his head.

"You heard everything, Muggle?" said the cold voice.

"What's that you're calling me?" said Frank defiantly, for now that he was inside the room, now that the time had come for some sort of action, he felt braver; it had always been so in the war.

"I am calling you a Muggle," said the voice coolly. "It means that you are not a wizard."

"I don't know what you mean by wizard," said Frank, his voice growing steadier. "All I know is I've heard enough to interest the police tonight, I have. You've done murder and you're planning more! And I'll tell you this too," he added, on a sudden inspiration, "my wife knows I'm up here, and if I don't come back —"

"You have no wife," said the cold voice, very quietly. "Nobody knows you are here. You told nobody that you were coming. Do not lie to Lord Voldemort, Muggle, for he knows . . . he always knows. . . ."

"Is that right?" said Frank roughly. "Lord, is it? Well, I don't think much of your manners, *my Lord*. Turn 'round and face me like a man, why don't you?"

"But I am not a man, Muggle," said the cold voice, barely audible now over the crackling of the flames. "I am much, much more than a man. However . . . why not? I will face you. . . . Wormtail, come turn my chair around."

The servant gave a whimper.

"You heard me, Wormtail."

Slowly, with his face screwed up, as though he would rather have done anything than approach his master and the hearth rug where the snake lay, the small man walked forward and began to turn the chair. The snake lifted its ugly triangular head and hissed slightly as the legs of the chair snagged on its rug.

And then the chair was facing Frank, and he saw what was sitting in it. His walking stick fell to the floor with a clatter. He opened his mouth and let out a scream. He was screaming so loudly that he never heard the words the thing in the chair spoke as it raised a wand. There was a flash of green light, a rushing sound, and Frank Bryce crumpled. He was dead before he hit the floor.

Two hundred miles away, the boy called Harry Potter woke with a start.

# THE SCAR

Harry lay flat on his back, breathing hard as though he had been running. He had awoken from a vivid dream with his hands pressed over his face. The old scar on his forehead, which was shaped like a bolt of lightning, was burning beneath his fingers as though someone had just pressed a white-hot wire to his skin.

He sat up, one hand still on his scar, the other reaching out in the darkness for his glasses, which were on the bedside table. He put them on and his bedroom came into clearer focus, lit by a faint, misty orange light that was filtering through the curtains from the street lamp outside the window.

Harry ran his fingers over the scar again. It was still painful. He turned on the lamp beside him, scrambled out of bed, crossed the room, opened his wardrobe, and peered into the mirror on the inside of the door. A skinny boy of fourteen looked back at him, his bright green eyes puzzled under his untidy black hair. He examined the lightning-bolt scar of his reflection more closely. It looked normal, but it was still stinging.

Harry tried to recall what he had been dreaming about before he had awoken. It had seemed so real. . . . There had been two people he knew and one he didn't. . . . He concentrated hard, frowning, trying to remember. . . .

The dim picture of a darkened room came to him. . . . There had been a snake on a hearth rug . . . a small man called Peter, nicknamed Wormtail . . . and a cold, high voice . . . the voice of Lord Voldemort. Harry felt as though an ice cube had slipped down into his stomach at the very thought. . . .

He closed his eyes tightly and tried to remember what Voldemort had looked like, but it was impossible. . . . All Harry knew was that at the moment when Voldemort's chair had swung around, and he, Harry, had seen what was sitting in it, he had felt a spasm of horror, which had awoken him . . . or had that been the pain in his scar?

And who had the old man been? For there had definitely been an old man; Harry had watched him fall to the ground. It was all becoming confused. Harry put his face into his hands, blocking out his bedroom, trying to hold on to the picture of that dimly lit room, but it was like trying to keep water in his cupped hands; the details were now trickling away as fast as he tried to hold on to them. . . . Voldemort and Wormtail had been talking about someone they had killed, though Harry could not remember the name . . . and they had been plotting to kill someone else . . . *him*!

Harry took his face out of his hands, opened his eyes, and stared around his bedroom as though expecting to see something unusual there. As it happened, there were an extraordinary number of unusual things in this room. A large wooden trunk stood open at the foot of his bed, revealing a cauldron, broomstick, black robes, and assorted spellbooks. Rolls of parchment littered that part of his desk that was not taken up by the large, empty cage in which his snowy owl, Hedwig, usually perched. On the floor beside his bed a book lay open; Harry had been reading it before he fell asleep last night. The pictures in this book were all moving. Men in bright orange robes were zooming in and out of sight on broomsticks, throwing a red ball to one another.

Harry walked over to the book, picked it up, and watched one of the wizards score a spectacular goal by putting the ball through a fifty-foot-high hoop. Then he snapped the book shut. Even Quidditch — in Harry's opinion, the best sport in the world — couldn't distract him at the moment. He placed *Flying with the Cannons* on his bedside table, crossed to the window, and drew back the curtains to survey the street below.

Privet Drive looked exactly as a respectable suburban street would be expected to look in the early hours of Saturday morning. All the curtains were closed. As far as Harry could see through the darkness, there wasn't a living creature in sight, not even a cat.

And yet . . . and yet . . . Harry went restlessly back to the bed and sat down on it, running a finger over his scar again. It wasn't the pain that bothered him; Harry was no stranger to pain and injury. He had lost all the bones from his right arm once and had them painfully regrown in a night. The same arm had been pierced by a venomous foot-long fang not long afterward. Only last year Harry had fallen fifty feet from an airborne broomstick. He was used to bizarre accidents and injuries; they were unavoidable if you attended Hogwarts School of Witchcraft and Wizardry and had a knack for attracting a lot of trouble.

No, the thing that was bothering Harry was that the last time his scar had hurt him, it had been because Voldemort had been close by. . . . But Voldemort couldn't be here, now. . . . The idea of Voldemort lurking in Privet Drive was absurd, impossible. . . .

Harry listened closely to the silence around him. Was he half-expecting to hear the creak of a stair or the swish of a cloak? And then he jumped slightly as he heard his cousin Dudley give a tremendous grunting snore from the next room.

Harry shook himself mentally; he was being stupid. There was no one in the house with him except Uncle Vernon, Aunt Petunia, and Dudley, and they were plainly still asleep, their dreams untroubled and painless.

Asleep was the way Harry liked the Dursleys best; it wasn't as though they were ever any help to him awake. Uncle Vernon, Aunt Petunia, and Dudley were Harry's only living relatives. They were Muggles who hated and despised magic in any form, which meant that Harry was about as welcome in their house as dry rot. They had explained away Harry's long absences at Hogwarts over the last three years by telling everyone that he went to St. Brutus's Secure Center for Incurably Criminal Boys. They knew perfectly well that, as an underage wizard, Harry wasn't allowed to use magic outside Hogwarts, but they were still apt to blame him for anything that went wrong about the house. Harry had never been able to confide in them or tell them anything about his life in the Wizarding world. The very idea of going to them when they awoke, and telling them about his scar hurting him, and about his worries about Voldemort, was laughable.

And yet it was because of Voldemort that Harry had come to live with the Dursleys in the first place. If it hadn't been for Voldemort, Harry would not have had the lightning scar on his forehead. If it hadn't been for Voldemort, Harry would still have had parents. . . .

Harry had been a year old the night that Voldemort — the most powerful Dark wizard for a century, a wizard who had been gaining power steadily for eleven years — arrived at his house and killed his father and mother. Voldemort had then turned his wand on Harry; he had performed the curse that had disposed of many full-grown witches and wizards in his steady rise to power — and, incredibly, it had not worked. Instead of killing the small boy, the curse had rebounded upon Voldemort. Harry had survived with nothing but a lightning-shaped cut on his forehead, and Voldemort had been reduced to something barely alive. His powers gone, his life almost extinguished, Voldemort had fled; the terror in which the secret community of witches and wizards had lived for so long had lifted, Voldemort's followers had disbanded, and Harry Potter had become famous.

It had been enough of a shock for Harry to discover, on his eleventh birthday, that he was a wizard; it had been even more disconcerting to find out that everyone in the hidden Wizarding world knew his name. Harry had arrived at Hogwarts to find that heads turned and whispers followed him wherever he went. But he was used to it now: At the end of this summer, he would be starting his fourth year at Hogwarts, and Harry was already counting the days until he would be back at the castle again.

But there was still a fortnight to go before he went back to school. He looked hopelessly around his room again, and his eye paused on the birthday cards his two best friends had sent him at the end of July. What would they say if Harry wrote to them and told them about his scar hurting?

At once, Hermione Granger's voice seemed to fill his head, shrill and panicky.

"*Your scar hurt? Harry, that's really serious.* . . . *Write to Professor Dumbledore! And I'll go and check* Common Magical Ailments and Afflictions. . . . *Maybe there's something in there about curse scars.* . . . "

Yes, that would be Hermione's advice: Go straight to the headmaster of Hogwarts, and in the meantime, consult a book. Harry stared out of the window at the inky blue-black sky. He doubted very much whether a book could help him now. As far as he knew, he was the only living person to have survived a curse like Voldemort's; it was highly unlikely, therefore, that he would find his symptoms listed in *Common Magical Ailments and Afflictions.* As for informing the headmaster, Harry had no idea where Dumbledore went during the summer holidays. He amused himself for a moment, picturing Dumbledore, with his long silver beard, full-length wizard's robes, and pointed hat, stretched out on a beach somewhere, rubbing suntan lotion onto his long crooked nose. Wherever Dumbledore was, though, Harry was sure that Hedwig would be able to find him; Harry's owl had never yet failed to deliver a letter to anyone, even without an address. But what would he write?

*Dear Professor Dumbledore, Sorry to bother you, but my scar hurt this morning. Yours sincerely, Harry Potter.*

Even inside his head the words sounded stupid.

And so he tried to imagine his other best friend, Ron Weasley's, reaction, and in a moment, Ron's red hair and long-nosed, freckled face seemed to swim before Harry, wearing a bemused expression.

*"Your scar hurt? But . . . but You-Know-Who can't be near you now, can he? I mean . . . you'd know, wouldn't you? He'd be trying to do you in again, wouldn't he? I dunno, Harry, maybe curse scars always twinge a bit. . . . I'll ask Dad. . . ."*

Mr. Weasley was a fully qualified wizard who worked in the Misuse of Muggle Artifacts Office at the Ministry of Magic, but he didn't have any particular expertise in the matter of curses, as far as Harry knew. In any case, Harry didn't like the idea of the whole Weasley family knowing that he, Harry, was getting jumpy about a few moments' pain. Mrs. Weasley would fuss worse than Hermione, and Fred and George, Ron's sixteen-year-old twin brothers, might think Harry was losing his nerve. The Weasleys were Harry's favorite family in the world; he was hoping that they might invite him to stay any time now (Ron had mentioned something about the Quidditch World Cup), and he somehow didn't want his visit punctuated with anxious inquiries about his scar.

Harry kneaded his forehead with his knuckles. What he really wanted (and it felt almost shameful to admit it to himself) was someone like — someone like a *parent*: an adult wizard whose advice he could ask without feeling stupid, someone who cared about him, who had had experience with Dark Magic. . . .

And then the solution came to him. It was so simple, and so obvious, that he couldn't believe it had taken so long — *Sirius.*

Harry leapt up from the bed, hurried across the room, and sat down at his desk; he pulled a piece of parchment toward him, loaded his eagle-feather quill with ink, wrote *Dear Sirius,* then paused, wondering how best to phrase his problem, still marveling at the fact that he hadn't thought of Sirius straight away. But then, perhaps it wasn't so surprising — after all, he had only found out that Sirius was his godfather two months ago.

There was a simple reason for Sirius's complete absence from Harry's life until then — Sirius had been in Azkaban, the terrifying wizard jail guarded by creatures called dementors, sightless, soul-sucking fiends who had come to search for Sirius at Hogwarts when he had escaped. Yet Sirius had been innocent — the murders for which he had been convicted had been committed by Wormtail, Voldemort's supporter, whom nearly everybody now believed dead. Harry, Ron, and Hermione knew otherwise, however; they had come face-to-face with Wormtail only the previous year, though only Professor Dumbledore had believed their story.

For one glorious hour, Harry had believed that he was leaving the Dursleys at last, because Sirius had offered him a home once his name had been cleared. But the chance had been snatched away from him — Wormtail had escaped before they could take him to the Ministry of Magic, and Sirius had had to flee for his life. Harry had helped him escape on the back of a hippogriff called Buckbeak, and since then, Sirius had been on the run. The home Harry might have had if Wormtail had not escaped had been haunting him all summer. It had been doubly hard to return to the Dursleys knowing that he had so nearly escaped them forever.

Nevertheless, Sirius had been of some help to Harry, even if he couldn't be with him. It was due to Sirius that Harry now had all his school things in his bedroom with him. The Dursleys had never allowed this before; their general wish of keeping Harry as miserable as possible, coupled with their fear of his powers, had led them to lock his school trunk in the cupboard under the stairs every summer prior to this. But their attitude had changed since they had found out that Harry had a dangerous murderer for a god-father — for Harry had conveniently forgotten to tell them that Sirius was innocent.

Harry had received two letters from Sirius since he had been back at Privet Drive. Both had been delivered, not by owls (as was usual with wizards), but by large, brightly colored tropical birds. Hedwig had not approved of these flashy intruders; she had been most reluctant to allow them to drink from her water tray before flying off again. Harry, on the other hand, had liked them; they put him in mind of palm trees and white sand, and he hoped that, wherever Sirius was (Sirius never said, in case the letters were intercepted), he was enjoying himself. Somehow, Harry found it hard to imagine dementors surviving for long in bright sunlight; perhaps that was why Sirius had gone south. Sirius's letters, which were now hidden beneath the highly useful loose floorboard under Harry's bed, sounded cheerful, and in both of them he had reminded Harry to call on him if ever Harry needed to. Well, he needed to now, all right. . . .

Harry's lamp seemed to grow dimmer as the cold gray light that precedes sunrise slowly crept into the room. Finally, when the sun had risen, when his bedroom walls had turned gold, and when sounds of movement could be heard from Uncle Vernon and Aunt Petunia's room, Harry cleared his desk of crumpled pieces of parchment and reread his finished letter.

*Dear Sirius,*

*Thanks for your last letter. That bird was enormous; it could hardly get through my window.*

*Things are the same as usual here. Dudley's diet isn't going too well. My aunt found him smuggling doughnuts into his room yesterday. They told him they'd have to cut his pocket money if he keeps doing it, so he got really angry and chucked his PlayStation out of the window. That's a sort of computer thing you can play games on. Bit stupid really, now he hasn't even got* Mega-Mutilation Part Three *to take his mind off things.*

*I'm okay, mainly because the Dursleys are terrified you might turn up and turn them all into bats if I ask you to.*

*A weird thing happened this morning, though. My scar hurt again. Last time that happened it was because Voldemort was at Hogwarts. But I don't reckon he can be anywhere near me now, can he? Do you know if curse scars sometimes hurt years afterward?*

*I'll send this with Hedwig when she gets back; she's off hunting at the moment. Say hello to Buckbeak for me.*

*Harry*

Yes, thought Harry, that looked all right. There was no point putting in the dream; he didn't want it to look as though he was too worried. He folded up the parchment and laid it aside on his desk, ready for when Hedwig returned. Then he got to his feet, stretched, and opened his wardrobe once more. Without glancing at his reflection, he started to get dressed before going down to breakfast.

# THE INVITATION

**B**y the time Harry arrived in the kitchen, the three Dursleys were already seated around the table. None of them looked up as he entered or sat down. Uncle Vernon's large red face was hidden behind the morning's *Daily Mail,* and Aunt Petunia was cutting a grapefruit into quarters, her lips pursed over her horselike teeth.

Dudley looked furious and sulky, and somehow seemed to be taking up even more space than usual. This was saying something, as he always took up an entire side of the square table by himself. When Aunt Petunia put a quarter of unsweetened grapefruit onto Dudley's plate with a tremulous "There you are, Diddy darling," Dudley glowered at her. His life had taken a most unpleasant turn since he had come home for the summer with his end-of-year report.

Uncle Vernon and Aunt Petunia had managed to find excuses for his bad marks as usual: Aunt Petunia always insisted that Dudley was a very gifted boy whose teachers didn't understand him, while Uncle Vernon maintained that "he didn't want some swotty little nancy boy for a son anyway." They also skated over the accusations of bullying in the report — "He's a boisterous little boy, but he wouldn't hurt a fly!" Aunt Petunia had said tearfully.

However, at the bottom of the report there were a few well-chosen comments from the school nurse that not even Uncle Vernon and Aunt Petunia could explain away. No matter how much Aunt Petunia wailed that Dudley was big-boned, and that his poundage was really puppy fat, and that he was a growing boy who needed plenty of food, the fact remained that the school outfitters didn't stock knickerbockers big enough for him anymore. The school nurse had seen what Aunt Petunia's eyes — so sharp when it came to spotting fingerprints on her gleaming walls, and in observing the comings and goings of the neighbors — simply refused to see: that far from needing extra nourishment, Dudley had reached roughly the size and weight of a young killer whale.

So — after many tantrums, after arguments that shook Harry's bedroom floor, and many tears from Aunt Petunia — the new regime had begun. The diet sheet that had been sent by the Smeltings school nurse had been taped to the fridge, which had been emptied of all Dudley's favorite things — fizzy drinks and cakes, chocolate bars and burgers — and filled instead with fruit and vegetables and the sorts of things that Uncle Vernon called "rabbit food." To make Dudley feel better about it all, Aunt Petunia had insisted that the whole family follow the diet too. She now passed a grapefruit quarter to Harry. He noticed that it was a lot smaller than Dudley's. Aunt Petunia seemed to feel that the best way to keep up Dudley's morale was to make sure that he did, at least, get more to eat than Harry.

But Aunt Petunia didn't know what was hidden under the loose floorboard upstairs. She had no idea that Harry was not following the diet at all. The moment he had got wind of the fact that he was expected to survive the summer on carrot sticks, Harry had sent Hedwig to his friends with pleas for help, and they had risen to the occasion magnificently. Hedwig had returned from Hermione's house with a large box stuffed full of sugar-free snacks. (Hermione's parents were dentists.) Hagrid, the Hogwarts gamekeeper, had obliged with a sack full of his own homemade rock cakes. (Harry hadn't touched these; he had had too much experience of Hagrid's cooking.) Mrs. Weasley, however, had sent the family owl, Errol, with an enormous fruitcake and assorted meat pies. Poor Errol, who was elderly and feeble, had needed a full five days to recover from the journey. And then on Harry's birthday (which the Dursleys had completely ignored) he had received four superb birthday cakes, one each from Ron, Hermione, Hagrid, and Sirius. Harry still had two of them left, and so, looking forward to a real breakfast when he got back upstairs, he ate his grapefruit without complaint.

Uncle Vernon laid aside his paper with a deep sniff of disapproval and looked down at his own grapefruit quarter.

"Is this it?" he said grumpily to Aunt Petunia.

Aunt Petunia gave him a severe look, and then nodded pointedly at Dudley, who had already finished his own grapefruit quarter and was eyeing Harry's with a very sour look in his piggy little eyes.

Uncle Vernon gave a great sigh, which ruffled his large, bushy mustache, and picked up his spoon.

The doorbell rang. Uncle Vernon heaved himself out of his chair and set off down the hall. Quick as a flash, while his mother was occupied with the kettle, Dudley stole the rest of Uncle Vernon's grapefruit.

Harry heard talking at the door, and someone laughing, and Uncle Vernon answering curtly. Then the front door closed, and the sound of ripping paper came from the hall.

Aunt Petunia set the teapot down on the table and looked curiously around to see where Uncle Vernon had got to. She didn't have to wait long to find out; after about a minute, he was back. He looked livid.

"You," he barked at Harry. "In the living room. Now."

Bewildered, wondering what on earth he was supposed to have done this time, Harry got up and followed Uncle Vernon out of the kitchen and into the next room. Uncle Vernon closed the door sharply behind both of them.

"So," he said, marching over to the fireplace and turning to face Harry as though he were about to pronounce him under arrest. "*So.*"

Harry would have dearly loved to have said, "So what?" but he didn't feel that Uncle Vernon's temper should be tested this early in the morning, especially when it was already under severe strain from lack of food. He therefore settled for looking politely puzzled.

"This just arrived," said Uncle Vernon. He brandished a piece of purple writing paper at Harry. "A letter. About you."

Harry's confusion increased. Who would be writing to Uncle Vernon about him? Who did he know who sent letters by the postman?

Uncle Vernon glared at Harry, then looked down at the letter and began to read aloud:

*Dear Mr. and Mrs. Dursley,*

*We have never been introduced, but I am sure you have heard a great deal from Harry about my son Ron.*

*As Harry might have told you, the final of the Quidditch World Cup takes place this Monday night, and my husband, Arthur, has just managed to get prime tickets through his connections at the Department of Magical Games and Sports.*

*I do hope you will allow us to take Harry to the match, as this really is a once-in-a-lifetime opportunity; Britain hasn't hosted the Cup for thirty years, and tickets are extremely hard to come by. We would of course be glad to have Harry stay for the remainder of the summer holidays, and to see him safely onto the train back to school.*

*It would be best for Harry to send us your answer as quickly as possible in the normal way, because the Muggle postman has never delivered to our house, and I am not sure he even knows where it is.*

*Hoping to see Harry soon,*
*Yours sincerely,*

*Molly Weasley*

*P.S. I do hope we've put enough stamps on.*

Uncle Vernon finished reading, put his hand back into his breast pocket, and drew out something else.

"Look at this," he growled.

He held up the envelope in which Mrs. Weasley's letter had come, and Harry had to fight down a laugh. Every bit of it was covered in stamps except for a square inch on the front, into which Mrs. Weasley had squeezed the Dursleys' address in minute writing.

"She did put enough stamps on, then," said Harry, trying to sound as though Mrs. Weasley's was a mistake anyone could make. His uncle's eyes flashed.

"The postman noticed," he said through gritted teeth. "Very interested to know where this letter came from, he was. That's why he rang the doorbell. Seemed to think it was *funny.*"

Harry didn't say anything. Other people might not understand why Uncle Vernon was making a fuss about too many stamps, but Harry had lived with the Dursleys too long not to know how touchy they were about anything even slightly out of the ordinary. Their worst fear was that someone would find out that they were connected (however distantly) with people like Mrs. Weasley.

Uncle Vernon was still glaring at Harry, who tried to keep his expression neutral. If he didn't do or say anything stupid, he might just be in for the treat of a lifetime. He waited for Uncle Vernon to say something, but he merely continued to glare. Harry decided to break the silence.

"So — can I go then?" he asked.

A slight spasm crossed Uncle Vernon's large purple face. The mustache bristled. Harry thought he knew what was going on behind the mustache: a furious battle as two of Uncle Vernon's most fundamental instincts came into conflict. Allowing Harry to go would make Harry happy, something Uncle Vernon had struggled against for thirteen years. On the other hand, allowing Harry to disappear to the Weasleys' for the rest of the summer would get rid of him two weeks earlier than anyone could have hoped, and Uncle Vernon hated having Harry in the house. To give himself thinking time, it seemed, he looked down at Mrs. Weasley's letter again.

"Who is this woman?" he said, staring at the signature with distaste.

"You've seen her," said Harry. "She's my friend Ron's mother, she was meeting him off the Hog — off the school train at the end of last term."

He had almost said "Hogwarts Express," and that was a sure way to get his uncle's temper up. Nobody ever mentioned the name of Harry's school aloud in the Dursley household.

Uncle Vernon screwed up his enormous face as though trying to remember something very unpleasant.

"Dumpy sort of woman?" he growled finally. "Load of children with red hair?"

Harry frowned. He thought it was a bit rich of Uncle Vernon to call anyone "dumpy," when his own son, Dudley, had finally achieved what he'd been threatening to do since the age of three, and become wider than he was tall.

Uncle Vernon was perusing the letter again.

"Quidditch," he muttered under his breath. "*Quidditch* — what is this rubbish?"

Harry felt a second stab of annoyance.

"It's a sport," he said shortly. "Played on broom —"

"All right, all right!" said Uncle Vernon loudly. Harry saw, with some satisfaction, that his uncle looked vaguely panicky. Apparently his nerves couldn't stand the sound of the word "broomsticks" in his living room. He took refuge in perusing the letter again. Harry saw his lips form the words "send us your answer . . . in the normal way." He scowled.

"What does she mean, 'the normal way'?" he spat.

"Normal for us," said Harry, and before his uncle could stop him, he added, "you know, owl post. That's what's normal for wizards."

Uncle Vernon looked as outraged as if Harry had just uttered a disgusting swearword. Shaking with anger, he shot a nervous look through the window, as though expecting to see some of the neighbors with their ears pressed against the glass.

"How many times do I have to tell you not to mention that unnaturalness under my roof?" he hissed, his face now a rich plum color. "You stand there, in the clothes Petunia and I have put on your ungrateful back —"

"Only after Dudley finished with them," said Harry coldly, and indeed, he was dressed in a sweatshirt so large for him that he had had to roll back the sleeves five times so as to be able to use his hands, and which fell past the knees of his extremely baggy jeans.

"I will not be spoken to like that!" said Uncle Vernon, trembling with rage.

But Harry wasn't going to stand for this. Gone were the days when he had been forced to take every single one of the Dursleys' stupid rules. He wasn't following Dudley's diet, and he wasn't going to let Uncle Vernon stop him from going to the Quidditch World Cup, not if he could help it. Harry took a deep, steadying breath and then said, "Okay, I can't see the World Cup. Can I go now, then? Only I've got a letter to Sirius I want to finish. You know — my godfather."

He had done it. He had said the magic words. Now he watched the purple recede blotchily from Uncle Vernon's face, making it look like badly mixed black currant ice cream.

"You're — you're writing to him, are you?" said Uncle Vernon, in a would-be calm voice — but Harry had seen the pupils of his tiny eyes contract with sudden fear.

"Well — yeah," said Harry, casually. "It's been a while since he heard from me, and, you know, if he doesn't, he might start thinking something's wrong."

He stopped there to enjoy the effect of these words. He could almost see the cogs working under Uncle Vernon's thick, dark, neatly parted hair. If he tried to stop Harry writing to Sirius, Sirius would think Harry was being mistreated. If he told Harry he couldn't go to the Quidditch World Cup, Harry would write and tell Sirius, who would *know* Harry was being mistreated. There was only one thing for Uncle Vernon to do. Harry could see the conclusion forming in his uncle's mind as though the great mustached face were transparent. Harry tried not to smile, to keep his own face as blank as possible. And then —

"Well, all right then. You can go to this ruddy . . . this stupid . . . this World Cup thing. You write and tell these — these *Weasleys* they're to pick you up, mind. I haven't got time to go dropping you off all over the country. And you can spend the rest of the summer there. And you can tell your — your godfather . . . tell him . . . tell him you're going."

"Okay then," said Harry brightly.

He turned and walked toward the living room door, fighting the urge to jump into the air and whoop. He was going . . . he was going to the Weasleys', he was going to watch the Quidditch World Cup!

Outside in the hall he nearly ran into Dudley, who had been lurking behind the door, clearly hoping to overhear Harry being told off. He looked shocked to see the broad grin on Harry's face.

"That was an *excellent* breakfast, wasn't it?" said Harry. "I feel really full, don't you?"

Laughing at the astonished look on Dudley's face, Harry took the stairs three at a time, and hurled himself back into his bedroom.

The first thing he saw was that Hedwig was back. She was sitting in her cage, staring at Harry with her enormous amber eyes, and clicking her beak in the way that meant she was annoyed about something. Exactly what was annoying her became apparent almost at once.

"OUCH!" said Harry as what appeared to be a small, gray, feathery tennis ball collided with the side of his head. Harry massaged the spot furiously, looking up to see what had hit him, and saw a minute owl, small enough to fit into the palm of his hand, whizzing excitedly around the room like a loose firework. Harry then realized that the owl had dropped a letter at his feet. Harry bent down, recognized Ron's handwriting, then tore open the envelope. Inside was a hastily scribbled note.

*Harry — DAD GOT THE TICKETS — Ireland versus Bulgaria, Monday night. Mum's writing to the Muggles to ask you to stay. They might already have the letter, I don't know how fast Muggle post is. Thought I'd send this with Pig anyway.*

Harry stared at the word "Pig," then looked up at the tiny owl now zooming around the light fixture on the ceiling. He had never seen anything that looked less like a pig. Maybe he couldn't read Ron's writing. He went back to the letter:

> *We're coming for you whether the Muggles like it or not, you can't miss the World Cup, only Mum and Dad reckon it's better if we pretend to ask their permission first. If they say yes, send Pig back with your answer pronto, and we'll come and get you at five o'clock on Sunday. If they say no, send Pig back pronto and we'll come and get you at five o'clock on Sunday anyway.*
>
> *Hermione's arriving this afternoon. Percy's started work — the Department of International Magical Cooperation. Don't mention anything about Abroad while you're here unless you want the pants bored off you.*
>
> *See you soon —*
> *Ron*

"Calm down!" Harry said as the small owl flew low over his head, twittering madly with what Harry could only assume was pride at having delivered the letter to the right person. "Come here, I need you to take my answer back!"

The owl fluttered down on top of Hedwig's cage. Hedwig looked coldly up at it, as though daring it to try and come any closer.

Harry seized his eagle-feather quill once more, grabbed a fresh piece of parchment, and wrote:

> *Ron, it's all okay, the Muggles say I can come. See you five o'clock tomorrow. Can't wait.*
> *Harry*

He folded this note up very small, and with immense difficulty, tied it to the tiny owl's leg as it hopped on the spot with excitement. The moment the note was secure, the owl was off again; it zoomed out of the window and out of sight.

Harry turned to Hedwig.

"Feeling up to a long journey?" he asked her.

Hedwig hooted in a dignified sort of a way.

"Can you take this to Sirius for me?" he said, picking up his letter. "Hang on . . . I just want to finish it."

He unfolded the parchment and hastily added a postscript.

*If you want to contact me, I'll be at my friend Ron Weasley's for the rest of the summer. His dad's got us tickets for the Quidditch World Cup!*

The letter finished, he tied it to Hedwig's leg; she kept unusually still, as though determined to show him how a real post owl should behave.

"I'll be at Ron's when you get back, all right?" Harry told her.

She nipped his finger affectionately, then, with a soft swooshing noise, spread her enormous wings and soared out of the open window.

Harry watched her out of sight, then crawled under his bed, wrenched up the loose floorboard, and pulled out a large chunk of birthday cake. He sat there on the floor eating it, savoring the happiness that was flooding through him. He had cake, and Dudley had nothing but grapefruit; it was a bright summer's day, he would be leaving Privet Drive tomorrow, his scar felt perfectly normal again, and he was going to watch the Quidditch World Cup. It was hard, just now, to feel worried about anything — even Lord Voldemort.

# CHAPTER FOUR

# BACK TO THE BURROW

By twelve o'clock the next day, Harry's school trunk was packed with his school things and all his most prized possessions — the Invisibility Cloak he had inherited from his father, the broomstick he had gotten from Sirius, the enchanted map of Hogwarts he had been given by Fred and George Weasley last year. He had emptied his hiding place under the loose floorboard of all food, double-checked every nook and cranny of his bedroom for forgotten spellbooks or quills, and taken down the chart on the wall counting down the days to September the first, on which he liked to cross off the days remaining until his return to Hogwarts.

The atmosphere inside number four, Privet Drive was extremely tense. The imminent arrival at their house of an assortment of wizards was making the Dursleys uptight and irritable. Uncle Vernon had looked downright alarmed when Harry informed him that the Weasleys would be arriving at five o'clock the very next day.

"I hope you told them to dress properly, these people," he

snarled at once. "I've seen the sort of stuff your lot wear. They'd better have the decency to put on normal clothes, that's all."

Harry felt a slight sense of foreboding. He had rarely seen Mr. or Mrs. Weasley wearing anything that the Dursleys would call "normal." Their children might don Muggle clothing during the holidays, but Mr. and Mrs. Weasley usually wore long robes in varying states of shabbiness. Harry wasn't bothered about what the neighbors would think, but he was anxious about how rude the Dursleys might be to the Weasleys if they turned up looking like their worst idea of wizards.

Uncle Vernon had put on his best suit. To some people, this might have looked like a gesture of welcome, but Harry knew it was because Uncle Vernon wanted to look impressive and intimidating. Dudley, on the other hand, looked somehow diminished. This was not because the diet was at last taking effect, but due to fright. Dudley had emerged from his last encounter with a fully-grown wizard with a curly pig's tail poking out of the seat of his trousers, and Aunt Petunia and Uncle Vernon had had to pay for its removal at a private hospital in London. It wasn't altogether surprising, therefore, that Dudley kept running his hand nervously over his backside, and walking sideways from room to room, so as not to present the same target to the enemy.

Lunch was an almost silent meal. Dudley didn't even protest at the food (cottage cheese and grated celery). Aunt Petunia wasn't eating anything at all. Her arms were folded, her lips were pursed, and she seemed to be chewing her tongue, as though biting back the furious diatribe she longed to throw at Harry.

"They'll be driving, of course?" Uncle Vernon barked across the table.

"Er," said Harry.

He hadn't thought of that. How *were* the Weasleys going to pick him up? They didn't have a car anymore; the old Ford Anglia they had once owned was currently running wild in the Forbidden Forest at Hogwarts. But Mr. Weasley had borrowed a Ministry of Magic car last year; possibly he would do the same today?

"I think so," said Harry.

Uncle Vernon snorted into his mustache. Normally, Uncle Vernon would have asked what car Mr. Weasley drove; he tended to judge other men by how big and expensive their cars were. But Harry doubted whether Uncle Vernon would have taken to Mr. Weasley even if he drove a Ferrari.

Harry spent most of the afternoon in his bedroom; he couldn't stand watching Aunt Petunia peer out through the net curtains every few seconds, as though there had been a warning about an escaped rhinoceros. Finally, at a quarter to five, Harry went back downstairs and into the living room.

Aunt Petunia was compulsively straightening cushions. Uncle Vernon was pretending to read the paper, but his tiny eyes were not moving, and Harry was sure he was really listening with all his might for the sound of an approaching car. Dudley was crammed into an armchair, his porky hands beneath him, clamped firmly around his bottom. Harry couldn't take the tension; he left the room and went and sat on the stairs in the hall, his eyes on his watch and his heart pumping fast from excitement and nerves.

But five o'clock came and then went. Uncle Vernon, perspiring slightly in his suit, opened the front door, peered up and down the street, then withdrew his head quickly.

"They're late!" he snarled at Harry.

"I know," said Harry. "Maybe — er — the traffic's bad, or something."

Ten past five . . . then a quarter past five . . . Harry was starting to feel anxious himself now. At half past, he heard Uncle Vernon and Aunt Petunia conversing in terse mutters in the living room.

"No consideration at all."

"We might've had an engagement."

"Maybe they think they'll get invited to dinner if they're late."

"Well, they most certainly won't be," said Uncle Vernon, and Harry heard him stand up and start pacing the living room. "They'll take the boy and go, there'll be no hanging around. That's if they're coming at all. Probably mistaken the day. I daresay *their kind* don't set much store by punctuality. Either that or they drive some tin-pot car that's broken d — AAAAAAAARRRRRGH!"

Harry jumped up. From the other side of the living room door came the sounds of the three Dursleys scrambling, panic-stricken, across the room. Next moment Dudley came flying into the hall, looking terrified.

"What happened?" said Harry. "What's the matter?"

But Dudley didn't seem able to speak. Hands still clamped over his buttocks, he waddled as fast as he could into the kitchen. Harry hurried into the living room.

Loud bangings and scrapings were coming from behind the Dursleys' boarded-up fireplace, which had a fake coal fire plugged in front of it.

"What is it?" gasped Aunt Petunia, who had backed into the wall and was staring, terrified, toward the fire. "What is it, Vernon?"

But they were left in doubt barely a second longer. Voices could be heard from inside the blocked fireplace.

"Ouch! Fred, no — go back, go back, there's been some kind of mistake — tell George not to — OUCH! George, no, there's no room, go back quickly and tell Ron —"

"Maybe Harry can hear us, Dad — maybe he'll be able to let us out —"

There was a loud hammering of fists on the boards behind the electric fire.

"Harry? Harry, can you hear us?"

The Dursleys rounded on Harry like a pair of angry wolverines.

"What is this?" growled Uncle Vernon. "What's going on?"

"They — they've tried to get here by Floo powder," said Harry, fighting a mad desire to laugh. "They can travel by fire — only you've blocked the fireplace — hang on —"

He approached the fireplace and called through the boards.

"Mr. Weasley? Can you hear me?"

The hammering stopped. Somebody inside the chimney piece said, "Shh!"

"Mr. Weasley, it's Harry . . . the fireplace has been blocked up. You won't be able to get through there."

"Damn!" said Mr. Weasley's voice. "What on earth did they want to block up the fireplace for?"

"They've got an electric fire," Harry explained.

"Really?" said Mr. Weasley's voice excitedly. "Eclectic, you say? With a *plug*? Gracious, I must see that. . . . Let's think . . . ouch, Ron!"

Ron's voice now joined the others'.

"What are we doing here? Has something gone wrong?"

"Oh no, Ron," came Fred's voice, very sarcastically. "No, this is exactly where we wanted to end up."

"Yeah, we're having the time of our lives here," said George, whose voice sounded muffled, as though he was squashed against the wall.

"Boys, boys . . ." said Mr. Weasley vaguely. "I'm trying to think what to do. . . . Yes . . . only way . . . Stand back, Harry."

Harry retreated to the sofa. Uncle Vernon, however, moved forward.

"Wait a moment!" he bellowed at the fire. "What exactly are you going to —"

BANG.

The electric fire shot across the room as the boarded-up fireplace burst outward, expelling Mr. Weasley, Fred, George, and Ron in a cloud of rubble and loose chippings. Aunt Petunia shrieked and fell backward over the coffee table; Uncle Vernon caught her before she hit the floor, and gaped, speechless, at the Weasleys, all of whom had bright red hair, including Fred and George, who were identical to the last freckle.

"That's better," panted Mr. Weasley, brushing dust from his long green robes and straightening his glasses. "Ah — you must be Harry's aunt and uncle!"

Tall, thin, and balding, he moved toward Uncle Vernon, his hand outstretched, but Uncle Vernon backed away several paces, dragging Aunt Petunia. Words utterly failed Uncle Vernon. His best suit was covered in white dust, which had settled in his hair and mustache and made him look as though he had just aged thirty years.

"Er — yes — sorry about that," said Mr. Weasley, lowering his hand and looking over his shoulder at the blasted fireplace. "It's all my fault. It just didn't occur to me that we wouldn't be able to get out at the other end. I had your fireplace connected to the Floo Network, you see — just for an afternoon, you know, so we could get Harry. Muggle fireplaces aren't supposed to be connected, strictly speaking — but I've got a useful contact at the Floo Regulation Panel and he fixed it for me. I can put it right in a jiffy, though, don't worry. I'll light a fire to send the boys back, and then I can repair your fireplace before I Disapparate."

Harry was ready to bet that the Dursleys hadn't understood a single word of this. They were still gaping at Mr. Weasley, thunderstruck. Aunt Petunia staggered upright again and hid behind Uncle Vernon.

"Hello, Harry!" said Mr. Weasley brightly. "Got your trunk ready?"

"It's upstairs," said Harry, grinning back.

"We'll get it," said Fred at once. Winking at Harry, he and George left the room. They knew where Harry's bedroom was, having once rescued him from it in the dead of night. Harry suspected that Fred and George were hoping for a glimpse of Dudley; they had heard a lot about him from Harry.

"Well," said Mr. Weasley, swinging his arms slightly, while he tried to find words to break the very nasty silence. "Very — erm — very nice place you've got here."

As the usually spotless living room was now covered in dust and bits of brick, this remark didn't go down too well with the Dursleys. Uncle Vernon's face purpled once more, and Aunt Petunia started chewing her tongue again. However, they seemed too scared to actually say anything.

Mr. Weasley was looking around. He loved everything to do with Muggles. Harry could see him itching to go and examine the television and the video recorder.

"They run off eckeltricity, do they?" he said knowledgeably. "Ah yes, I can see the plugs. I collect plugs," he added to Uncle Vernon. "And batteries. Got a very large collection of batteries. My wife thinks I'm mad, but there you are."

Uncle Vernon clearly thought Mr. Weasley was mad too. He moved ever so slightly to the right, screening Aunt Petunia from view, as though he thought Mr. Weasley might suddenly run at them and attack.

Dudley suddenly reappeared in the room. Harry could hear the clunk of his trunk on the stairs, and knew that the sounds had scared Dudley out of the kitchen. Dudley edged along the wall, gazing at Mr. Weasley with terrified eyes, and attempted to conceal himself behind his mother and father. Unfortunately, Uncle Vernon's bulk, while sufficient to hide bony Aunt Petunia, was nowhere near enough to conceal Dudley.

"Ah, this is your cousin, is it, Harry?" said Mr. Weasley, taking another brave stab at making conversation.

"Yep," said Harry, "that's Dudley."

He and Ron exchanged glances and then quickly looked away from each other; the temptation to burst out laughing was almost overwhelming. Dudley was still clutching his bottom as though afraid it might fall off. Mr. Weasley, however, seemed genuinely concerned at Dudley's peculiar behavior. Indeed, from the tone of his voice when he next spoke, Harry was quite sure that Mr. Weasley thought Dudley was quite as mad as the Dursleys thought *he* was, except that Mr. Weasley felt sympathy rather than fear.

"Having a good holiday, Dudley?" he said kindly.

Dudley whimpered. Harry saw his hands tighten still harder over his massive backside.

Fred and George came back into the room carrying Harry's school trunk. They glanced around as they entered and spotted Dudley. Their faces cracked into identical evil grins.

"Ah, right," said Mr. Weasley. "Better get cracking then."

He pushed up the sleeves of his robes and took out his wand. Harry saw the Dursleys draw back against the wall as one.

"Incendio!" said Mr. Weasley, pointing his wand at the hole in the wall behind him.

Flames rose at once in the fireplace, crackling merrily as though they had been burning for hours. Mr. Weasley took a small drawstring bag from his pocket, untied it, took a pinch of the powder inside, and threw it onto the flames, which turned emerald green and roared higher than ever.

"Off you go then, Fred," said Mr. Weasley.

"Coming," said Fred. "Oh no — hang on —"

A bag of sweets had spilled out of Fred's pocket and the contents were now rolling in every direction — big, fat toffees in brightly colored wrappers.

Fred scrambled around, cramming them back into his pocket, then gave the Dursleys a cheery wave, stepped forward, and walked right into the fire, saying "the Burrow!" Aunt Petunia gave a little shuddering gasp. There was a whooshing sound, and Fred vanished.

"Right then, George," said Mr. Weasley, "you and the trunk."

Harry helped George carry the trunk forward into the flames and turn it onto its end so that he could hold it better. Then, with a second whoosh, George had cried "the Burrow!" and vanished too.

"Ron, you next," said Mr. Weasley.

"See you," said Ron brightly to the Dursleys. He grinned broadly at Harry, then stepped into the fire, shouted "the Burrow!" and disappeared.

Now Harry and Mr. Weasley alone remained.

"Well . . .'bye then," Harry said to the Dursleys.

They didn't say anything at all. Harry moved toward the fire, but just as he reached the edge of the hearth, Mr. Weasley put out a hand and held him back. He was looking at the Dursleys in amazement.

"Harry said good-bye to you," he said. "Didn't you hear him?"

"It doesn't matter," Harry muttered to Mr. Weasley. "Honestly, I don't care."

Mr. Weasley did not remove his hand from Harry's shoulder.

"You aren't going to see your nephew till next summer," he said to Uncle Vernon in mild indignation. "Surely you're going to say good-bye?"

Uncle Vernon's face worked furiously. The idea of being taught consideration by a man who had just blasted away half his living room wall seemed to be causing him intense suffering. But Mr. Weasley's wand was still in his hand, and Uncle Vernon's tiny eyes darted to it once, before he said, very resentfully, "Good-bye, then."

"See you," said Harry, putting one foot forward into the green flames, which felt pleasantly like warm breath. At that moment, however, a horrible gagging sound erupted behind him, and Aunt Petunia started to scream.

Harry wheeled around. Dudley was no longer standing behind

his parents. He was kneeling beside the coffee table, and he was gagging and sputtering on a foot-long, purple, slimy thing that was protruding from his mouth. One bewildered second later, Harry realized that the foot-long thing was Dudley's tongue — and that a brightly colored toffee wrapper lay on the floor before him.

Aunt Petunia hurled herself onto the ground beside Dudley, seized the end of his swollen tongue, and attempted to wrench it out of his mouth; unsurprisingly, Dudley yelled and sputtered worse than ever, trying to fight her off. Uncle Vernon was bellowing and waving his arms around, and Mr. Weasley had to shout to make himself heard.

"Not to worry, I can sort him out!" he yelled, advancing on Dudley with his wand outstretched, but Aunt Petunia screamed worse than ever and threw herself on top of Dudley, shielding him from Mr. Weasley.

"No, really!" said Mr. Weasley desperately. "It's a simple process — it was the toffee — my son Fred — real practical joker — but it's only an Engorgement Charm — at least, I think it is — please, I can correct it —"

But far from being reassured, the Dursleys became more panic-stricken; Aunt Petunia was sobbing hysterically, tugging Dudley's tongue as though determined to rip it out; Dudley appeared to be suffocating under the combined pressure of his mother and his tongue; and Uncle Vernon, who had lost control completely, seized a china figure from on top of the sideboard and threw it very hard at Mr. Weasley, who ducked, causing the ornament to shatter in the blasted fireplace.

"Now really!" said Mr. Weasley angrily, brandishing his wand. "I'm trying to *help*!"

Bellowing like a wounded hippo, Uncle Vernon snatched up another ornament.

"Harry, go! Just go!" Mr. Weasley shouted, his wand on Uncle Vernon. "I'll sort this out!"

Harry didn't want to miss the fun, but Uncle Vernon's second ornament narrowly missed his left ear, and on balance he thought it best to leave the situation to Mr. Weasley. He stepped into the fire, looking over his shoulder as he said "the Burrow!" His last fleeting glimpse of the living room was of Mr. Weasley blasting a third ornament out of Uncle Vernon's hand with his wand, Aunt Petunia screaming and lying on top of Dudley, and Dudley's tongue lolling around like a great slimy python. But next moment Harry had begun to spin very fast, and the Dursleys' living room was whipped out of sight in a rush of emerald-green flames.

# WEASLEYS' WIZARD
# WHEEZES

Harry spun faster and faster, elbows tucked tightly to his sides, blurred fireplaces flashing past him, until he started to feel sick and closed his eyes. Then, when at last he felt himself slowing down, he threw out his hands and came to a halt in time to prevent himself from falling face forward out of the Weasleys' kitchen fire.

"Did he eat it?" said Fred excitedly, holding out a hand to pull Harry to his feet.

"Yeah," said Harry, straightening up. "What *was* it?"

"Ton-Tongue Toffee," said Fred brightly. "George and I invented them, and we've been looking for someone to test them on all summer. . . ."

The tiny kitchen exploded with laughter; Harry looked around and saw that Ron and George were sitting at the scrubbed wooden table with two red-haired people Harry had never seen before, though he knew immediately who they must be: Bill and Charlie, the two eldest Weasley brothers.

"How're you doing, Harry?" said the nearer of the two, grinning at him and holding out a large hand, which Harry shook, feeling calluses and blisters under his fingers. This had to be Charlie, who worked with dragons in Romania. Charlie was built like the twins, shorter and stockier than Percy and Ron, who were both long and lanky. He had a broad, good-natured face, which was weather-beaten and so freckly that he looked almost tanned; his arms were muscular, and one of them had a large, shiny burn on it.

Bill got to his feet, smiling, and also shook Harry's hand. Bill came as something of a surprise. Harry knew that he worked for the Wizarding bank, Gringotts, and that Bill had been Head Boy at Hogwarts; Harry had always imagined Bill to be an older version of Percy: fussy about rule-breaking and fond of bossing everyone around. However, Bill was — there was no other word for it — *cool*. He was tall, with long hair that he had tied back in a ponytail. He was wearing an earring with what looked like a fang dangling from it. Bill's clothes would not have looked out of place at a rock concert, except that Harry recognized his boots to be made, not of leather, but of dragon hide.

Before any of them could say anything else, there was a faint popping noise, and Mr. Weasley appeared out of thin air at George's shoulder. He was looking angrier than Harry had ever seen him.

"That *wasn't funny*, Fred!" he shouted. "What on earth did you give that Muggle boy?"

"I didn't give him anything," said Fred, with another evil grin. "I just *dropped* it. . . . It was his fault he went and ate it, I never told him to."

"You dropped it on purpose!" roared Mr. Weasley. "You knew he'd eat it, you knew he was on a diet —"

"How big did his tongue get?" George asked eagerly.

"It was four feet long before his parents would let me shrink it!"

Harry and the Weasleys roared with laughter again.

"It *isn't funny*!" Mr. Weasley shouted. "That sort of behavior seriously undermines wizard–Muggle relations! I spend half my life campaigning against the mistreatment of Muggles, and my own sons —"

"We didn't give it to him because he's a Muggle!" said Fred indignantly.

"No, we gave it to him because he's a great bullying git," said George. "Isn't he, Harry?"

"Yeah, he is, Mr. Weasley," said Harry earnestly.

"That's not the point!" raged Mr. Weasley. "You wait until I tell your mother —"

"Tell me what?" said a voice behind them.

Mrs. Weasley had just entered the kitchen. She was a short, plump woman with a very kind face, though her eyes were presently narrowed with suspicion.

"Oh hello, Harry, dear," she said, spotting him and smiling. Then her eyes snapped back to her husband. "Tell me *what,* Arthur?"

Mr. Weasley hesitated. Harry could tell that, however angry he was with Fred and George, he hadn't really intended to tell Mrs. Weasley what had happened. There was a silence, while Mr.

Weasley eyed his wife nervously. Then two girls appeared in the kitchen doorway behind Mrs. Weasley. One, with very bushy brown hair and rather large front teeth, was Harry's and Ron's friend, Hermione Granger. The other, who was small and red-haired, was Ron's younger sister, Ginny. Both of them smiled at Harry, who grinned back, which made Ginny go scarlet — she had been very taken with Harry ever since his first visit to the Burrow.

"Tell me *what,* Arthur?" Mrs. Weasley repeated, in a dangerous sort of voice.

"It's nothing, Molly," mumbled Mr. Weasley, "Fred and George just — but I've had words with them —"

"What have they done this time?" said Mrs. Weasley. "If it's got anything to do with Weasleys' Wizard Wheezes —"

"Why don't you show Harry where he's sleeping, Ron?" said Hermione from the doorway.

"He knows where he's sleeping," said Ron, "in my room, he slept there last —"

"We can all go," said Hermione pointedly.

"Oh," said Ron, cottoning on. "Right."

"Yeah, we'll come too," said George.

*"You stay where you are!"* snarled Mrs. Weasley.

Harry and Ron edged out of the kitchen, and they, Hermione, and Ginny set off along the narrow hallway and up the rickety staircase that zigzagged through the house to the upper stories.

"What are Weasleys' Wizard Wheezes?" Harry asked as they climbed.

Ron and Ginny both laughed, although Hermione didn't.

"Mum found this stack of order forms when she was cleaning

Fred and George's room," said Ron quietly. "Great long price lists for stuff they've invented. Joke stuff, you know. Fake wands and trick sweets, loads of stuff. It was brilliant, I never knew they'd been inventing all that . . ."

"We've been hearing explosions out of their room for ages, but we never thought they were actually *making* things," said Ginny. "We thought they just liked the noise."

"Only, most of the stuff— well, all of it, really — was a bit dangerous," said Ron, "and, you know, they were planning to sell it at Hogwarts to make some money, and Mum went mad at them. Told them they weren't allowed to make any more of it, and burned all the order forms. . . . She's furious at them anyway. They didn't get as many O.W.L.s as she expected."

O.W.L.s were Ordinary Wizarding Levels, the examinations Hogwarts students took at the age of fifteen.

"And then there was this big row," Ginny said, "because Mum wants them to go into the Ministry of Magic like Dad, and they told her all they want to do is open a joke shop."

Just then a door on the second landing opened, and a face poked out wearing horn-rimmed glasses and a very annoyed expression.

"Hi, Percy," said Harry.

"Oh hello, Harry," said Percy. "I was wondering who was making all the noise. I'm trying to work in here, you know — I've got a report to finish for the office — and it's rather difficult to concentrate when people keep thundering up and down the stairs."

"We're not *thundering,*" said Ron irritably. "We're walking. Sorry if we've disturbed the top-secret workings of the Ministry of Magic."

"What are you working on?" said Harry.

"A report for the Department of International Magical Cooperation," said Percy smugly. "We're trying to standardize cauldron thickness. Some of these foreign imports are just a shade too thin — leakages have been increasing at a rate of almost three percent a year —"

"That'll change the world, that report will," said Ron. "Front page of the *Daily Prophet,* I expect, cauldron leaks."

Percy went slightly pink.

"You might sneer, Ron," he said heatedly, "but unless some sort of international law is imposed we might well find the market flooded with flimsy, shallow-bottomed products that seriously endanger —"

"Yeah, yeah, all right," said Ron, and he started off upstairs again. Percy slammed his bedroom door shut. As Harry, Hermione, and Ginny followed Ron up three more flights of stairs, shouts from the kitchen below echoed up to them. It sounded as though Mr. Weasley had told Mrs. Weasley about the toffees.

The room at the top of the house where Ron slept looked much as it had the last time that Harry had come to stay: the same posters of Ron's favorite Quidditch team, the Chudley Cannons, were whirling and waving on the walls and sloping ceiling, and the fish tank on the windowsill, which had previously held frog spawn, now contained one extremely large frog. Ron's old rat, Scabbers, was here no more, but instead there was the tiny gray owl that had delivered Ron's letter to Harry in Privet Drive. It was hopping up and down in a small cage and twittering madly.

"Shut *up*, Pig," said Ron, edging his way between two of the four beds that had been squeezed into the room. "Fred and George are in here with us, because Bill and Charlie are in their room," he told Harry. "Percy gets to keep his room all to himself because he's got to *work*."

"Er — why are you calling that owl Pig?" Harry asked Ron.

"Because he's being stupid," said Ginny. "Its proper name is Pigwidgeon."

"Yeah, and that's not a stupid name at all," said Ron sarcastically. "Ginny named him," he explained to Harry. "She reckons it's sweet. And I tried to change it, but it was too late, he won't answer to anything else. So now he's Pig. I've got to keep him up here because he annoys Errol and Hermes. He annoys me too, come to that."

Pigwidgeon zoomed happily around his cage, hooting shrilly. Harry knew Ron too well to take him seriously. He had moaned continually about his old rat, Scabbers, but had been most upset when Hermione's cat, Crookshanks, appeared to have eaten him.

"Where's Crookshanks?" Harry asked Hermione now.

"Out in the garden, I expect," she said. "He likes chasing gnomes. He's never seen any before."

"Percy's enjoying work, then?" said Harry, sitting down on one of the beds and watching the Chudley Cannons zooming in and out of the posters on the ceiling.

"Enjoying it?" said Ron darkly. "I don't reckon he'd come home if Dad didn't make him. He's obsessed. Just don't get him onto the subject of his boss. *According to Mr. Crouch . . . as I was saying to Mr. Crouch . . . Mr. Crouch is of the opinion . . . Mr. Crouch was telling me . . .* They'll be announcing their engagement any day now."

"Have you had a good summer, Harry?" said Hermione. "Did you get our food parcels and everything?"

"Yeah, thanks a lot," said Harry. "They saved my life, those cakes."

"And have you heard from — ?" Ron began, but at a look from Hermione he fell silent. Harry knew Ron had been about to ask about Sirius. Ron and Hermione had been so deeply involved in helping Sirius escape from the Ministry of Magic that they were almost as concerned about Harry's godfather as he was. However, discussing him in front of Ginny was a bad idea. Nobody but themselves and Professor Dumbledore knew about how Sirius had escaped, or believed in his innocence.

"I think they've stopped arguing," said Hermione, to cover the awkward moment, because Ginny was looking curiously from Ron to Harry. "Shall we go down and help your mum with dinner?"

"Yeah, all right," said Ron. The four of them left Ron's room and went back downstairs to find Mrs. Weasley alone in the kitchen, looking extremely bad-tempered.

"We're eating out in the garden," she said when they came in. "There's just not room for eleven people in here. Could you take the plates outside, girls? Bill and Charlie are setting up the tables. Knives and forks, please, you two," she said to Ron and Harry, pointing her wand a little more vigorously than she had intended at a pile of potatoes in the sink, which shot out of their skins so fast that they ricocheted off the walls and ceiling.

"Oh for heaven's *sake,*" she snapped, now directing her wand at a dustpan, which hopped off the sideboard and started skating across the floor, scooping up the potatoes. "Those two!" she burst out savagely, now pulling pots and pans out of a cupboard, and Harry knew she meant Fred and George. "I don't know what's going to happen to them, I really don't. No ambition, unless you count making as much trouble as they possibly can. . . ."

Mrs. Weasley slammed a large copper saucepan down on the

kitchen table and began to wave her wand around inside it. A creamy sauce poured from the wand-tip as she stirred.

"It's not as though they haven't got brains," she continued irritably, taking the saucepan over to the stove and lighting it with a further poke of her wand, "but they're wasting them, and unless they pull themselves together soon, they'll be in real trouble. I've had more owls from Hogwarts about them than the rest put together. If they carry on the way they're going, they'll end up in front of the Improper Use of Magic Office."

Mrs. Weasley jabbed her wand at the cutlery drawer, which shot open. Harry and Ron both jumped out of the way as several knives soared out of it, flew across the kitchen, and began chopping the potatoes, which had just been tipped back into the sink by the dustpan.

"I don't know where we went wrong with them," said Mrs. Weasley, putting down her wand and starting to pull out still more saucepans. "It's been the same for years, one thing after another, and they won't listen to — OH NOT *AGAIN!*"

She had picked up her wand from the table, and it had emitted a loud squeak and turned into a giant rubber mouse.

"One of their fake wands again!" she shouted. "How many times have I told them not to leave them lying around?"

She grabbed her real wand and turned around to find that the sauce on the stove was smoking.

"C'mon," Ron said hurriedly to Harry, seizing a handful of cutlery from the open drawer, "let's go and help Bill and Charlie."

They left Mrs. Weasley and headed out the back door into the yard.

They had only gone a few paces when Hermione's bandy-legged

ginger cat, Crookshanks, came pelting out of the garden, bottle-brush tail held high in the air, chasing what looked like a muddy potato on legs. Harry recognized it instantly as a gnome. Barely ten inches high, its horny little feet pattered very fast as it sprinted across the yard and dived headlong into one of the Wellington boots that lay scattered around the door. Harry could hear the gnome giggling madly as Crookshanks inserted a paw into the boot, trying to reach it. Meanwhile, a very loud crashing noise was coming from the other side of the house. The source of the commotion was revealed as they entered the garden, and saw that Bill and Charlie both had their wands out, and were making two battered old tables fly high above the lawn, smashing into each other, each attempting to knock the other's out of the air. Fred and George were cheering, Ginny was laughing, and Hermione was hovering near the hedge, apparently torn between amusement and anxiety.

Bill's table caught Charlie's with a huge bang and knocked one of its legs off. There was a clatter from overhead, and they all looked up to see Percy's head poking out of a window on the second floor.

"Will you keep it down?!" he bellowed.

"Sorry, Perce," said Bill, grinning. "How're the cauldron bottoms coming on?"

"Very badly," said Percy peevishly, and he slammed the window shut. Chuckling, Bill and Charlie directed the tables safely onto the grass, end to end, and then, with a flick of his wand, Bill reattached the table leg and conjured tablecloths from nowhere.

By seven o'clock, the two tables were groaning under dishes and dishes of Mrs. Weasley's excellent cooking, and the nine Weasleys,

Harry, and Hermione were settling themselves down to eat beneath a clear, deep-blue sky. To somebody who had been living on meals of increasingly stale cake all summer, this was paradise, and at first, Harry listened rather than talked as he helped himself to chicken and ham pie, boiled potatoes, and salad.

At the far end of the table, Percy was telling his father all about his report on cauldron bottoms.

"I've told Mr. Crouch that I'll have it ready by Tuesday," Percy was saying pompously. "That's a bit sooner than he expected it, but I like to keep on top of things. I think he'll be grateful I've done it in good time, I mean, it's extremely busy in our department just now, what with all the arrangements for the World Cup. We're just not getting the support we need from the Department of Magical Games and Sports. Ludo Bagman —"

"I like Ludo," said Mr. Weasley mildly. "He was the one who got us such good tickets for the Cup. I did him a bit of a favor: His brother, Otto, got into a spot of trouble — a lawnmower with unnatural powers — I smoothed the whole thing over."

"Oh Bagman's *likable* enough, of course," said Percy dismissively, "but how he ever got to be Head of Department . . . when I compare him to Mr. Crouch! I can't see Mr. Crouch losing a member of our department and not trying to find out what's happened to them. You realize Bertha Jorkins has been missing for over a month now? Went on holiday to Albania and never came back?"

"Yes, I was asking Ludo about that," said Mr. Weasley, frowning. "He says Bertha's gotten lost plenty of times before now — though I must say, if it was someone in my department, I'd be worried. . . ."

"Oh Bertha's *hopeless,* all right," said Percy. "I hear she's been shunted from department to department for years, much more trouble than she's worth . . . but all the same, Bagman ought to be trying to find her. Mr. Crouch has been taking a personal interest, she worked in our department at one time, you know, and I think Mr. Crouch was quite fond of her — but Bagman just keeps laughing and saying she probably misread the map and ended up in Australia instead of Albania. However" — Percy heaved an impressive sigh and took a deep swig of elderflower wine — "we've got quite enough on our plates at the Department of International Magical Cooperation without trying to find members of other departments too. As you know, we've got another big event to organize right after the World Cup."

Percy cleared his throat significantly and looked down toward the end of the table where Harry, Ron, and Hermione were sitting. "*You* know the one I'm talking about, Father." He raised his voice slightly. "The top-secret one."

Ron rolled his eyes and muttered to Harry and Hermione, "He's been trying to get us to ask what that event is ever since he started work. Probably an exhibition of thick-bottomed cauldrons."

In the middle of the table, Mrs. Weasley was arguing with Bill about his earring, which seemed to be a recent acquisition.

". . . with a horrible great fang on it. Really, Bill, what do they say at the bank?"

"Mum, no one at the bank gives a damn how I dress as long as I bring home plenty of treasure," said Bill patiently.

"And your hair's getting silly, dear," said Mrs. Weasley, fingering her wand lovingly. "I wish you'd let me give it a trim. . . ."

"I like it," said Ginny, who was sitting beside Bill. "You're so old-fashioned, Mum. Anyway, it's nowhere near as long as Professor Dumbledore's. . . ."

Next to Mrs. Weasley, Fred, George, and Charlie were all talking spiritedly about the World Cup.

"It's got to be Ireland," said Charlie thickly, through a mouthful of potato. "They flattened Peru in the semifinals."

"Bulgaria has got Viktor Krum, though," said Fred.

"Krum's one decent player, Ireland has got seven," said Charlie shortly. "I wish England had got through. That was embarrassing, that was."

"What happened?" said Harry eagerly, regretting more than ever his isolation from the Wizarding world when he was stuck on Privet Drive.

"Went down to Transylvania, three hundred and ninety to ten," said Charlie gloomily. "Shocking performance. And Wales lost to Uganda, and Scotland was slaughtered by Luxembourg."

Harry had been on the Gryffindor House Quidditch team ever since his first year at Hogwarts and owned one of the best racing brooms in the world, a Firebolt. Flying came more naturally to Harry than anything else in the magical world, and he played in the position of Seeker on the Gryffindor House team.

Mr. Weasley conjured up candles to light the darkening garden before they had their homemade strawberry ice cream, and by the time they had finished, moths were fluttering low over the table, and the warm air was perfumed with the smells of grass and honeysuckle. Harry was feeling extremely well fed and at peace with the world as he watched several gnomes sprinting through the rosebushes, laughing madly and closely pursued by Crookshanks.

Ron looked carefully up the table to check that the rest of the family were all busy talking, then he said very quietly to Harry, "So — *have* you heard from Sirius lately?"

Hermione looked around, listening closely.

"Yeah," said Harry softly, "twice. He sounds okay. I wrote to him yesterday. He might write back while I'm here."

He suddenly remembered the reason he had written to Sirius, and for a moment was on the verge of telling Ron and Hermione about his scar hurting again, and about the dream that had awoken him . . . but he really didn't want to worry them just now, not when he himself was feeling so happy and peaceful.

"Look at the time," Mrs. Weasley said suddenly, checking her wristwatch. "You really should be in bed, the whole lot of you — you'll be up at the crack of dawn to get to the Cup. Harry, if you leave your school list out, I'll get your things for you tomorrow in Diagon Alley. I'm getting everyone else's. There might not be time after the World Cup, the match went on for five days last time."

"Wow — hope it does this time!" said Harry enthusiastically.

"Well, I certainly don't," said Percy sanctimoniously. "I *shudder* to think what the state of my in-tray would be if I was away from work for five days."

"Yeah, someone might slip dragon dung in it again, eh, Perce?" said Fred.

"That was a sample of fertilizer from Norway!" said Percy, going very red in the face. "It was nothing *personal*!"

"It was," Fred whispered to Harry as they got up from the table. "We sent it."

# THE PORTKEY

Harry felt as though he had barely lain down to sleep in Ron's room when he was being shaken awake by Mrs. Weasley.

"Time to go, Harry, dear," she whispered, moving away to wake Ron.

Harry felt around for his glasses, put them on, and sat up. It was still dark outside. Ron muttered indistinctly as his mother roused him. At the foot of Harry's mattress he saw two large, disheveled shapes emerging from tangles of blankets.

"'S' time already?" said Fred groggily.

They dressed in silence, too sleepy to talk, then, yawning and stretching, the four of them headed downstairs into the kitchen.

Mrs. Weasley was stirring the contents of a large pot on the stove, while Mr. Weasley was sitting at the table, checking a sheaf of large parchment tickets. He looked up as the boys entered and spread his arms so that they could see his clothes more clearly. He was wearing what appeared to be a golfing sweater and a very old pair of jeans, slightly too big for him and held up with a thick leather belt.

"What d'you think?" he asked anxiously. "We're supposed to go incognito — do I look like a Muggle, Harry?"

"Yeah," said Harry, smiling, "very good."

"Where're Bill and Charlie and Per-Per-Percy?" said George, failing to stifle a huge yawn.

"Well, they're Apparating, aren't they?" said Mrs. Weasley, heaving the large pot over to the table and starting to ladle porridge into bowls. "So they can have a bit of a lie-in."

Harry knew that Apparating meant disappearing from one place and reappearing almost instantly in another, but had never known any Hogwarts student to do it, and understood that it was very difficult.

"So they're still in bed?" said Fred grumpily, pulling his bowl of porridge toward him. "Why can't we Apparate too?"

"Because you're not of age and you haven't passed your test," snapped Mrs. Weasley. "And where have those girls got to?"

She bustled out of the kitchen and they heard her climbing the stairs.

"You have to pass a test to Apparate?" Harry asked.

"Oh yes," said Mr. Weasley, tucking the tickets safely into the back pocket of his jeans. "The Department of Magical Transportation had to fine a couple of people the other day for Apparating without a license. It's not easy, Apparition, and when it's not done properly it can lead to nasty complications. This pair I'm talking about went and Splinched themselves."

Everyone around the table except Harry winced.

"Er — *Splinched*?" said Harry.

"They left half of themselves behind," said Mr. Weasley, now spooning large amounts of treacle onto his porridge. "So, of course, they were stuck. Couldn't move either way. Had to wait for the Accidental Magic Reversal Squad to sort them out. Meant a fair old bit of paperwork, I can tell you, what with the Muggles who spotted the body parts they'd left behind. . . ."

Harry had a sudden vision of a pair of legs and an eyeball lying abandoned on the pavement of Privet Drive.

"Were they okay?" he asked, startled.

"Oh yes," said Mr. Weasley matter-of-factly. "But they got a heavy fine, and I don't think they'll be trying it again in a hurry. You don't mess around with Apparition. There are plenty of adult wizards who don't bother with it. Prefer brooms — slower, but safer."

"But Bill and Charlie and Percy can all do it?"

"Charlie had to take the test twice," said Fred, grinning. "He failed the first time, Apparated five miles south of where he meant to, right on top of some poor old dear doing her shopping, remember?"

"Yes, well, he passed the second time," said Mrs. Weasley, marching back into the kitchen amid hearty sniggers.

"Percy only passed two weeks ago," said George. "He's been Apparating downstairs every morning since, just to prove he can."

There were footsteps down the passageway and Hermione and Ginny came into the kitchen, both looking pale and drowsy.

"Why do we have to be up so early?" Ginny said, rubbing her eyes and sitting down at the table.

"We've got a bit of a walk," said Mr. Weasley.

"Walk?" said Harry. "What, are we walking to the World Cup?"

"No, no, that's miles away," said Mr. Weasley, smiling. "We only need to walk a short way. It's just that it's very difficult for a large number of wizards to congregate without attracting Muggle attention. We have to be very careful about how we travel at the best of times, and on a huge occasion like the Quidditch World Cup —"

"George!" said Mrs. Weasley sharply, and they all jumped.

"What?" said George, in an innocent tone that deceived nobody.

"What is that in your pocket?"

"Nothing!"

"Don't you lie to me!"

Mrs. Weasley pointed her wand at George's pocket and said, *"Accio!"*

Several small, brightly colored objects zoomed out of George's pocket; he made a grab for them but missed, and they sped right into Mrs. Weasley's outstretched hand.

"We told you to destroy them!" said Mrs. Weasley furiously, holding up what were unmistakably more Ton-Tongue Toffees. "We told you to get rid of the lot! Empty your pockets, go on, both of you!"

It was an unpleasant scene; the twins had evidently been trying to smuggle as many toffees out of the house as possible, and it was only by using her Summoning Charm that Mrs. Weasley managed to find them all.

*"Accio! Accio! Accio!"* she shouted, and toffees zoomed from all sorts of unlikely places, including the lining of George's jacket and the turn-ups of Fred's jeans.

"We spent six months developing those!" Fred shouted at his mother as she threw the toffees away.

"Oh a fine way to spend six months!" she shrieked. "No wonder you didn't get more O.W.L.s!"

All in all, the atmosphere was not very friendly as they took their departure. Mrs. Weasley was still glowering as she kissed Mr. Weasley on the cheek, though not nearly as much as the twins, who had each hoisted their rucksacks onto their backs and walked out without a word to her.

"Well, have a lovely time," said Mrs. Weasley, "and *behave yourselves,*" she called after the twins' retreating backs, but they did not look back or answer. "I'll send Bill, Charlie, and Percy along around midday," Mrs. Weasley said to Mr. Weasley, as he, Harry, Ron, Hermione, and Ginny set off across the dark yard after Fred and George.

It was chilly and the moon was still out. Only a dull, greenish tinge along the horizon to their right showed that daybreak was drawing closer. Harry, having been thinking about thousands of wizards speeding toward the Quidditch World Cup, sped up to walk with Mr. Weasley.

"So how *does* everyone get there without all the Muggles noticing?" he asked.

"It's been a massive organizational problem," sighed Mr. Weasley. "The trouble is, about a hundred thousand wizards turn up at the World Cup, and of course, we just haven't got a magical site big enough to accommodate them all. There are places Muggles can't penetrate, but imagine trying to pack a hundred thousand wizards into Diagon Alley or platform nine and three-quarters. So we had to find a nice deserted moor, and set up as many anti-Muggle precautions as possible. The whole Ministry's been working on it for months. First, of course, we have to stagger the arrivals. People with cheaper tickets have to arrive two weeks be-forehand. A limited number use Muggle transport, but we can't have too many clogging up their buses and trains — remember, wizards are coming from all over the world. Some Apparate, of course, but we have to set up safe points for them to appear, well away from Muggles. I believe there's a handy wood they're using as the Apparition point. For those who don't want to Apparate, or can't, we use Portkeys. They're objects that are used to transport wizards from one spot to another at a prearranged time. You can do large groups at a time if you need to. There have been two hundred Portkeys placed at strategic points around Britain, and the nearest one to us is up at the top of Stoatshead Hill, so that's where we're headed."

Mr. Weasley pointed ahead of them, where a large black mass rose beyond the village of Ottery St. Catchpole.

"What sort of objects are Portkeys?" said Harry curiously.

"Well, they can be anything," said Mr. Weasley. "Unobtrusive things, obviously, so Muggles don't go picking them up and play-ing with them . . . stuff they'll just think is litter. . . ."

They trudged down the dark, dank lane toward the village, the silence broken only by their footsteps. The sky lightened very slowly as they made their way through the village, its inky black-ness diluting to deepest blue. Harry's hands and feet were freezing. Mr. Weasley kept checking his watch.

They didn't have breath to spare for talking as they began to climb Stoatshead Hill, stumbling occasionally in hidden rabbit holes, slipping on thick black tuffets of grass. Each breath Harry took was sharp in his chest and his legs were starting to seize up when, at last, his feet found level ground.

"Whew," panted Mr. Weasley, taking off his glasses and wiping them on his sweater. "Well, we've made good time — we've got ten minutes. . . ."

Hermione came over the crest of the hill last, clutching a stitch in her side.

"Now we just need the Portkey," said Mr. Weasley, replacing his glasses and squinting around at the ground. "It won't be big. . . . Come on . . ."

They spread out, searching. They had only been at it for a couple of minutes, however, when a shout rent the still air.

"Over here, Arthur! Over here, son, we've got it!"

Two tall figures were silhouetted against the starry sky on the other side of the hilltop.

"Amos!" said Mr. Weasley, smiling as he strode over to the man who had shouted. The rest of them followed.

Mr. Weasley was shaking hands with a ruddy-faced wizard with a scrubby brown beard, who was holding a moldy-looking old boot in his other hand.

"This is Amos Diggory, everyone," said Mr. Weasley. "He works for the Department for the Regulation and Control of Magical Creatures. And I think you know his son, Cedric?"

Cedric Diggory was an extremely handsome boy of around seventeen. He was Captain and Seeker of the Hufflepuff House Quidditch team at Hogwarts.

"Hi," said Cedric, looking around at them all.

Everybody said hi back except Fred and George, who merely nodded. They had never quite forgiven Cedric for beating their team, Gryffindor, in the first Quidditch match of the previous year.

"Long walk, Arthur?" Cedric's father asked.

"Not too bad," said Mr. Weasley. "We live just on the other side of the village there. You?"

"Had to get up at two, didn't we, Ced? I tell you, I'll be glad when he's got his Apparition test. Still . . . not complaining . . . Quidditch World Cup, wouldn't miss it for a sackful of Galleons — and the tickets cost about that. Mind you, looks like I got off easy. . . ." Amos Diggory peered good-naturedly around at the three Weasley boys, Harry, Hermione, and Ginny. "All these yours, Arthur?"

"Oh no, only the redheads," said Mr. Weasley, pointing out his children. "This is Hermione, friend of Ron's — and Harry, another friend —"

"Merlin's beard," said Amos Diggory, his eyes widening. "Harry? Harry *Potter*?"

"Er — yeah," said Harry.

Harry was used to people looking curiously at him when they met him, used to the way their eyes moved at once to the lightning scar on his forehead, but it always made him feel uncomfortable.

"Ced's talked about you, of course," said Amos Diggory. "Told us all about playing against you last year. . . . I said to him, I said — Ced, that'll be something to tell your grandchildren, that will. . . . *You beat Harry Potter!*"

Harry couldn't think of any reply to this, so he remained silent. Fred and George were both scowling again. Cedric looked slightly embarrassed.

"Harry fell off his broom, Dad," he muttered. "I told you . . . it was an accident. . . ."

"Yes, but *you* didn't fall off, did you?" roared Amos genially, slapping his son on his back. "Always modest, our Ced, always the gentleman . . . but the best man won, I'm sure Harry'd say the same, wouldn't you, eh? One falls off his broom, one stays on, you don't need to be a genius to tell which one's the better flier!"

"Must be nearly time," said Mr. Weasley quickly, pulling out his watch again. "Do you know whether we're waiting for any more, Amos?"

"No, the Lovegoods have been there for a week already and the Fawcetts couldn't get tickets," said Mr. Diggory. "There aren't any more of us in this area, are there?"

"Not that I know of," said Mr. Weasley. "Yes, it's a minute off. . . . We'd better get ready. . . ."

He looked around at Harry and Hermione.

"You just need to touch the Portkey, that's all, a finger will do —"

With difficulty, owing to their bulky backpacks, the nine of them crowded around the old boot held out by Amos Diggory.

They all stood there, in a tight circle, as a chill breeze swept over the hilltop. Nobody spoke. It suddenly occurred to Harry how odd this would look if a Muggle were to walk up here now . . . nine people, two of them grown men, clutching this manky old boot in the semidarkness, waiting. . . .

"Three . . ." muttered Mr. Weasley, one eye still on his watch, "two . . . one . . ."

It happened immediately: Harry felt as though a hook just behind his navel had been suddenly jerked irresistibly forward. His feet left the ground; he could feel Ron and Hermione on either side of him, their shoulders banging into his; they were all speeding forward in a howl of wind and swirling color; his forefinger was stuck to the boot as though it was pulling him magnetically onward and then —

His feet slammed into the ground; Ron staggered into him and he fell over; the Portkey hit the ground near his head with a heavy thud.

Harry looked up. Mr. Weasley, Mr. Diggory, and Cedric were still standing, though looking very windswept; everybody else was on the ground.

"Seven past five from Stoatshead Hill," said a voice.

# BAGMAN AND CROUCH

Harry disentangled himself from Ron and got to his feet. They had arrived on what appeared to be a deserted stretch of misty moor. In front of them was a pair of tired and grumpy-looking wizards, one of whom was holding a large gold watch, the other a thick roll of parchment and a quill. Both were dressed as Muggles, though very inexpertly: The man with the watch wore a tweed suit with thigh-length galoshes; his colleague, a kilt and a poncho.

"Morning, Basil," said Mr. Weasley, picking up the boot and handing it to the kilted wizard, who threw it into a large box of used Portkeys beside him; Harry could see an old newspaper, an empty drinks can, and a punctured football.

"Hello there, Arthur," said Basil wearily. "Not on duty, eh? It's all right for some. . . . We've been here all night. . . . You'd better get out of the way, we've got a big party coming in from the Black Forest at five-fifteen. Hang on, I'll find your campsite. . . . Weasley . . .

Weasley . . ." He consulted his parchment list. "About a quarter of a mile's walk over there, first field you come to. Site manager's called Mr. Roberts. Diggory . . . second field . . . ask for Mr. Payne."

"Thanks, Basil," said Mr. Weasley, and he beckoned everyone to follow him.

They set off across the deserted moor, unable to make out much through the mist. After about twenty minutes, a small stone cottage next to a gate swam into view. Beyond it, Harry could just make out the ghostly shapes of hundreds and hundreds of tents, rising up the gentle slope of a large field toward a dark wood on the horizon. They said good-bye to the Diggorys and approached the cottage door.

A man was standing in the doorway, looking out at the tents. Harry knew at a glance that this was the only real Muggle for several acres. When he heard their footsteps, he turned his head to look at them.

"Morning!" said Mr. Weasley brightly.

"Morning," said the Muggle.

"Would you be Mr. Roberts?"

"Aye, I would," said Mr. Roberts. "And who're you?"

"Weasley — two tents, booked a couple of days ago?"

"Aye," said Mr. Roberts, consulting a list tacked to the door. "You've got a space up by the wood there. Just the one night?"

"That's it," said Mr. Weasley.

"You'll be paying now, then?" said Mr. Roberts.

"Ah — right — certainly —" said Mr. Weasley. He retreated a short distance from the cottage and beckoned Harry toward him. "Help me, Harry," he muttered, pulling a roll of Muggle money from his pocket and starting to peel the notes apart. "This one's a — a — a ten? Ah yes, I see the little number on it now. . . . So this is a five?"

"A twenty," Harry corrected him in an undertone, uncomfortably aware of Mr. Roberts trying to catch every word.

"Ah yes, so it is. . . . I don't know, these little bits of paper . . ."

"You foreign?" said Mr. Roberts as Mr. Weasley returned with the correct notes.

"Foreign?" repeated Mr. Weasley, puzzled.

"You're not the first one who's had trouble with money," said Mr. Roberts, scrutinizing Mr. Weasley closely. "I had two try and pay me with great gold coins the size of hubcaps ten minutes ago."

"Did you really?" said Mr. Weasley nervously.

Mr. Roberts rummaged around in a tin for some change.

"Never been this crowded," he said suddenly, looking out over the misty field again. "Hundreds of pre-bookings. People usually just turn up. . . ."

"Is that right?" said Mr. Weasley, his hand held out for his change, but Mr. Roberts didn't give it to him.

"Aye," he said thoughtfully. "People from all over. Loads of foreigners. And not just foreigners. Weirdos, you know? There's a bloke walking 'round in a kilt and a poncho."

"Shouldn't he?" said Mr. Weasley anxiously.

"It's like some sort of . . . I dunno . . . like some sort of rally," said Mr. Roberts. "They all seem to know each other. Like a big party."

At that moment, a wizard in plus-fours appeared out of thin air next to Mr. Roberts's front door.

"*Obliviate!*" he said sharply, pointing his wand at Mr. Roberts.

Instantly, Mr. Roberts's eyes slid out of focus, his brows

unknitted, and a look of dreamy unconcern fell over his face. Harry recognized the symptoms of one who had just had his memory modified.

"A map of the campsite for you," Mr. Roberts said placidly to Mr. Weasley. "And your change."

"Thanks very much," said Mr. Weasley.

The wizard in plus-fours accompanied them toward the gate to the campsite. He looked exhausted: His chin was blue with stubble and there were deep purple shadows under his eyes. Once out of earshot of Mr. Roberts, he muttered to Mr. Weasley, "Been having a lot of trouble with him. Needs a Memory Charm ten times a day to keep him happy. And Ludo Bagman's not helping. Trotting around talking about Bludgers and Quaffles at the top of his voice, not a worry about anti-Muggle security. Blimey, I'll be glad when this is over. See you later, Arthur."

He Disapparated.

"I thought Mr. Bagman was Head of Magical Games and Sports," said Ginny, looking surprised. "He should know better than to talk about Bludgers near Muggles, shouldn't he?"

"He should," said Mr. Weasley, smiling, and leading them through the gates into the campsite, "but Ludo's always been a bit . . . well . . . *lax* about security. You couldn't wish for a more enthusiastic Head of the sports department though. He played Quidditch for England himself, you know. And he was the best Beater the Wimbourne Wasps ever had."

They trudged up the misty field between long rows of tents. Most looked almost ordinary; their owners had clearly tried to make them as Muggle-like as possible, but had slipped up by adding chimneys, or bellpulls, or weather vanes. However, here and there was a tent so obviously magical that Harry could hardly be surprised that Mr. Roberts was getting suspicious. Halfway up the field stood an extravagant confection of striped silk like a miniature palace, with several live peacocks tethered at the entrance. A little farther on they passed a tent that had three floors and several turrets; and a short way beyond that was a tent that had a front garden attached, complete with birdbath, sundial, and fountain.

"Always the same," said Mr. Weasley, smiling. "We can't resist showing off when we get together. Ah, here we are, look, this is us."

They had reached the very edge of the wood at the top of the field, and here was an empty space, with a small sign hammered into the ground that read WEEZLY.

"Couldn't have a better spot!" said Mr. Weasley happily. "The field is just on the other side of the wood there, we're as close as we could be." He hoisted his backpack from his shoulders. "Right," he said excitedly, "no magic allowed, strictly speaking, not when we're out in these numbers on Muggle land. We'll be putting these tents up by hand! Shouldn't be too difficult. . . . Muggles do it all the time. . . . Here, Harry, where do you reckon we should start?"

Harry had never been camping in his life; the Dursleys had never taken him on any kind of holiday, preferring to leave him with Mrs. Figg, an old neighbor. However, he and Hermione worked out where most of the poles and pegs should go, and though Mr. Weasley was more of a hindrance than a help, because he got thoroughly overexcited when it came to using the mallet, they finally managed to erect a pair of shabby two-man tents.

All of them stood back to admire their handiwork. Nobody looking at these tents would guess they belonged to wizards, Harry thought, but the trouble was that once Bill, Charlie, and Percy arrived, they would be a party of ten. Hermione seemed to have spotted this problem too; she gave Harry a quizzical look as Mr. Weasley dropped to his hands and knees and entered the first tent.

"We'll be a bit cramped," he called, "but I think we'll all squeeze in. Come and have a look."

Harry bent down, ducked under the tent flap, and felt his jaw drop. He had walked into what looked like an old-fashioned, three-room flat, complete with bathroom and kitchen. Oddly enough, it was furnished in exactly the same sort of style as Mrs. Figg's house: There were crocheted covers on the mismatched chairs and a strong smell of cats.

"Well, it's not for long," said Mr. Weasley, mopping his bald patch with a handkerchief and peering in at the four bunk beds that stood in the bedroom. "I borrowed this from Perkins at the office. Doesn't camp much anymore, poor fellow, he's got lumbago."

He picked up the dusty kettle and peered inside it. "We'll need water. . . ."

"There's a tap marked on this map the Muggle gave us," said Ron, who had followed Harry inside the tent and seemed completely unimpressed by its extraordinary inner proportions. "It's on the other side of the field."

"Well, why don't you, Harry, and Hermione go and get us some water then" — Mr. Weasley handed over the kettle and a couple of saucepans — "and the rest of us will get some wood for a fire?"

"But we've got an oven," said Ron. "Why can't we just —"

"Ron, anti-Muggle security!" said Mr. Weasley, his face shining with anticipation. "When real Muggles camp, they cook on fires outdoors. I've seen them at it!"

After a quick tour of the girls' tent, which was slightly smaller than the boys', though without the smell of cats, Harry, Ron, and Hermione set off across the campsite with the kettle and saucepans.

Now, with the sun newly risen and the mist lifting, they could see the city of tents that stretched in every direction. They made their way slowly through the rows, staring eagerly around. It was only just dawning on Harry how many witches and wizards there must be in the world; he had never really thought much about those in other countries.

Their fellow campers were starting to wake up. First to stir were the families with small children; Harry had never seen witches and wizards this young before. A tiny boy no older than two was crouched outside a large pyramid-shaped tent, holding a wand and poking happily at a slug in the grass, which was swelling slowly to the size of a salami. As they drew level with him, his mother came hurrying out of the tent.

"*How* many times, Kevin? You *don't — touch — Daddy's — wand —* yecchh!"

She had trodden on the giant slug, which burst. Her scolding carried after them on the still air, mingling with the little boy's yells — "You bust slug! You bust slug!"

A short way farther on, they saw two little witches, barely older than Kevin, who were riding toy broomsticks that rose only high enough for the girls' toes to skim the dewy grass. A Ministry wizard had already spotted them; as he hurried past Harry, Ron, and Hermione he muttered distractedly, "In broad daylight! Parents having a lie-in, I suppose —"

Here and there adult wizards and witches were emerging from their tents and starting to cook breakfast. Some, with furtive looks around them, conjured fires with their wands; others were striking matches with dubious looks on their faces, as though sure this couldn't work. Three African wizards sat in serious conversation, all of them wearing long white robes and roasting what looked like a rabbit on a bright purple fire, while a group of middle-aged American witches sat gossiping happily beneath a spangled banner stretched between their tents that read: THE SALEM WITCHES' INSTITUTE. Harry caught snatches of conversation in strange languages from the inside of tents they passed, and though he couldn't understand a word, the tone of every single voice was excited.

"Er — is it my eyes, or has everything gone green?" said Ron.

It wasn't just Ron's eyes. They had walked into a patch of tents that were all covered with a thick growth of shamrocks, so that it looked as though small, oddly shaped hillocks had sprouted out of the earth. Grinning faces could be seen under those that had their flaps open. Then, from behind them, they heard their names.

"Harry! Ron! Hermione!"

It was Seamus Finnigan, their fellow Gryffindor fourth year. He was sitting in front of his own shamrock-covered tent, with a sandy-haired woman who had to be his mother, and his best friend, Dean Thomas, also of Gryffindor.

"Like the decorations?" said Seamus, grinning. "The Ministry's not too happy."

"Ah, why shouldn't we show our colors?" said Mrs. Finnigan. "You should see what the Bulgarians have got dangling all over *their* tents. You'll be supporting Ireland, of course?" she added, eyeing Harry, Ron, and Hermione beadily. When they had assured her that they were indeed supporting Ireland, they set off again, though, as Ron said, "Like we'd say anything else surrounded by that lot."

"I wonder what the Bulgarians have got dangling all over their tents?" said Hermione.

"Let's go and have a look," said Harry, pointing to a large patch of tents upfield, where the Bulgarian flag — white, green, and red — was fluttering in the breeze.

The tents here had not been bedecked with plant life, but each and every one of them had the same poster attached to it, a poster of a very surly face with heavy black eyebrows. The picture was, of course, moving, but all it did was blink and scowl.

"Krum," said Ron quietly.

"What?" said Hermione.

"Krum!" said Ron. "Viktor Krum, the Bulgarian Seeker!"

"He looks really grumpy," said Hermione, looking around at the many Krums blinking and scowling at them.

"*Really grumpy*?" Ron raised his eyes to the heavens. "Who cares what he looks like? He's unbelievable. He's really young too. Only just eighteen or something. He's a *genius,* you wait until tonight, you'll see."

There was already a small queue for the tap in the corner of the field. Harry, Ron, and Hermione joined it, right behind a pair of men who were having a heated argument. One of them was a very old wizard who was wearing a long flowery nightgown. The other was clearly a Ministry wizard; he was holding out a pair of pin-striped trousers and almost crying with exasperation.

"Just put them on, Archie, there's a good chap. You can't walk around like that, the Muggle at the gate's already getting suspicious —"

"I bought this in a Muggle shop," said the old wizard stubbornly. "Muggles wear them."

"Muggle *women* wear them, Archie, not the men, they wear *these*," said the Ministry wizard, and he brandished the pinstriped trousers.

"I'm not putting them on," said old Archie in indignation. "I like a healthy breeze 'round my privates, thanks."

Hermione was overcome with such a strong fit of the giggles at this point that she had to duck out of the queue and only returned when Archie had collected his water and moved away.

Walking more slowly now, because of the weight of the water, they made their way back through the campsite. Here and there, they saw more familiar faces: other Hogwarts students with their families. Oliver Wood, the old Captain of Harry's House Quidditch team, who had just left Hogwarts, dragged Harry over to his parents' tent to introduce him, and told him excitedly that he had just been signed to the Puddlemere United reserve team. Next they were hailed by Ernie Macmillan, a Hufflepuff fourth year, and a little farther on they saw Cho Chang, a very pretty girl who played Seeker on the Ravenclaw team. She waved and smiled at Harry, who slopped quite a lot of water down his front as he waved back. More to stop Ron from smirking than anything, Harry hurriedly pointed out a large group of teenagers whom he had never seen before.

"Who d'you reckon they are?" he said. "They don't go to Hogwarts, do they?"

"'Spect they go to some foreign school," said Ron. "I know there are others. Never met anyone who went to one, though. Bill had a penfriend at a school in Brazil . . . this was years and years ago . . . and he wanted to go on an exchange trip but Mum and Dad couldn't afford it. His penfriend got all offended when he said he wasn't going and sent him a cursed hat. It made his ears shrivel up."

Harry laughed but didn't voice the amazement he felt at hearing about other Wizarding schools. He supposed, now that he saw representatives of so many nationalities in the campsite, that he had been stupid never to realize that Hogwarts couldn't be the only one. He glanced at Hermione, who looked utterly unsurprised by the information. No doubt she had run across the news about other Wizarding schools in some book or other.

"You've been ages," said George when they finally got back to the Weasleys' tents.

"Met a few people," said Ron, setting the water down. "You not got that fire started yet?"

"Dad's having fun with the matches," said Fred.

Mr. Weasley was having no success at all in lighting the fire, but it wasn't for lack of trying. Splintered matches littered the ground around him, but he looked as though he was having the time of his life.

"Oops!" he said as he managed to light a match and promptly dropped it in surprise.

"Come here, Mr. Weasley," said Hermione kindly, taking the box from him, and showing him how to do it properly.

At last they got the fire lit, though it was at least another hour before it was hot enough to cook anything. There was plenty to watch while they waited, however. Their tent seemed to be pitched right alongside a kind of thoroughfare to the field, and Ministry members kept hurrying up and down it, greeting Mr. Weasley cordially as they passed. Mr. Weasley kept up a running commentary, mainly for Harry's and Hermione's benefit; his own children knew too much about the Ministry to be greatly interested.

"That was Cuthbert Mockridge, Head of the Goblin Liaison Office. . . . Here comes Gilbert Wimple; he's with the Committee on Experimental Charms; he's had those horns for a while now. . . . Hello, Arnie . . . Arnold Peasegood, he's an Obliviator — member of the Accidental Magic Reversal Squad, you know. . . . and that's Bode and Croaker . . . they're Unspeakables. . . ."

"They're what?"

"From the Department of Mysteries, top secret, no idea what they get up to. . . ."

At last, the fire was ready, and they had just started cooking eggs and sausages when Bill, Charlie, and Percy came strolling out of the woods toward them.

"Just Apparated, Dad," said Percy loudly. "Ah, excellent, lunch!"

They were halfway through their plates of eggs and sausages when Mr. Weasley jumped to his feet, waving and grinning at a man who was striding toward them. "Aha!" he said. "The man of the moment! Ludo!"

Ludo Bagman was easily the most noticeable person Harry had seen so far, even including old Archie in his flowered nightdress. He was wearing long Quidditch robes in thick horizontal stripes of bright yellow and black. An enormous picture of a wasp was splashed across his chest. He had the look of a powerfully built man gone slightly to seed; the robes were stretched tightly across a large belly he surely had not had in the days when he had played Quidditch for England. His nose was squashed (probably broken by a stray Bludger, Harry thought), but his round blue eyes, short blond hair, and rosy complexion made him look like a very over-grown schoolboy.

"Ahoy there!" Bagman called happily. He was walking as though he had springs attached to the balls of his feet and was plainly in a state of wild excitement.

"Arthur, old man," he puffed as he reached the campfire, "what a day, eh? What a day! Could we have asked for more perfect weather? A cloudless night coming . . . and hardly a hiccough in the arrangements. . . . Not much for me to do!"

Behind him, a group of haggard-looking Ministry wizards rushed past, pointing at the distant evidence of some sort of a magical fire that was sending violet sparks twenty feet into the air.

Percy hurried forward with his hand outstretched. Apparently his disapproval of the way Ludo Bagman ran his department did not prevent him from wanting to make a good impression.

"Ah — yes," said Mr. Weasley, grinning, "this is my son Percy. He's just started at the Ministry — and this is Fred — no, George, sorry — *that's* Fred — Bill, Charlie, Ron — my daughter, Ginny — and Ron's friends, Hermione Granger and Harry Potter."

Bagman did the smallest of double takes when he heard Harry's name, and his eyes performed the familiar flick upward to the scar on Harry's forehead.

"Everyone," Mr. Weasley continued, "this is Ludo Bagman, you know who he is, it's thanks to him we've got such good tickets —"

Bagman beamed and waved his hand as if to say it had been nothing.

"Fancy a flutter on the match, Arthur?" he said eagerly, jingling what seemed to be a large amount of gold in the pockets of his yellow-and-black robes. "I've already got Roddy Pontner betting me Bulgaria will score first — I offered him nice odds, considering Ireland's front three are the strongest I've seen in years — and little Agatha Timms has put up half shares in her eel farm on a week-long match."

"Oh . . . go on then," said Mr. Weasley. "Let's see . . . a Galleon on Ireland to win?"

"A Galleon?" Ludo Bagman looked slightly disappointed, but recovered himself. "Very well, very well . . . any other takers?"

"They're a bit young to be gambling," said Mr. Weasley. "Molly wouldn't like —"

"We'll bet thirty-seven Galleons, fifteen Sickles, three Knuts," said Fred as he and George quickly pooled all their money, "that Ireland wins — but Viktor Krum gets the Snitch. Oh and we'll throw in a fake wand."

"You don't want to go showing Mr. Bagman rubbish like that —" Percy hissed, but Bagman didn't seem to think the wand was rubbish at all; on the contrary, his boyish face shone with excitement as he took it from Fred, and when the wand gave a loud squawk and turned into a rubber chicken, Bagman roared with laughter.

"Excellent! I haven't seen one that convincing in years! I'd pay five Galleons for that!"

Percy froze in an attitude of stunned disapproval.

"Boys," said Mr. Weasley under his breath, "I don't want you betting. . . . That's all your savings. . . . Your mother —"

"Don't be a spoilsport, Arthur!" boomed Ludo Bagman, rattling his pockets excitedly. "They're old enough to know what they want! You reckon Ireland will win but Krum'll get the Snitch? Not a chance, boys, not a chance. . . . I'll give you excellent odds on that one. . . . We'll add five Galleons for the funny wand, then, shall we. . . ."

Mr. Weasley looked on helplessly as Ludo Bagman whipped out a notebook and quill and began jotting down the twins' names.

"Cheers," said George, taking the slip of parchment Bagman handed him and tucking it away carefully. Bagman turned most cheerfully back to Mr. Weasley.

"Couldn't do me a brew, I suppose? I'm keeping an eye out for Barty Crouch. My Bulgarian opposite number's making difficulties, and I can't understand a word he's saying. Barty'll be able to sort it out. He speaks about a hundred and fifty languages."

"Mr. Crouch?" said Percy, suddenly abandoning his look of poker-stiff disapproval and positively writhing with excitement. "He speaks over two hundred! Mermish and Gobbledegook and Troll . . ."

"Anyone can speak Troll," said Fred dismissively. "All you have to do is point and grunt."

Percy threw Fred an extremely nasty look and stoked the fire vigorously to bring the kettle back to the boil.

"Any news of Bertha Jorkins yet, Ludo?" Mr. Weasley asked as Bagman settled himself down on the grass beside them all.

"Not a dicky bird," said Bagman comfortably. "But she'll turn up. Poor old Bertha . . . memory like a leaky cauldron and no sense of direction. Lost, you take my word for it. She'll wander back into the office sometime in October, thinking it's still July."

"You don't think it might be time to send someone to look for her?" Mr. Weasley suggested tentatively as Percy handed Bagman his tea.

"Barty Crouch keeps saying that," said Bagman, his round eyes widening innocently, "but we really can't spare anyone at the moment. Oh — talk of the devil! Barty!"

A wizard had just Apparated at their fireside, and he could not have made more of a contrast with Ludo Bagman, sprawled on the grass in his old Wasp robes. Barty Crouch was a stiff, upright, elderly man, dressed in an impeccably crisp suit and tie. The parting in his short gray hair was almost unnaturally straight, and his narrow toothbrush mustache looked as though he trimmed it using a slide rule. His shoes were very highly polished. Harry could see at once why Percy idolized him. Percy was a great believer in rigidly following rules, and Mr. Crouch had complied with the rule about Muggle dressing so thoroughly that he could have passed for a bank manager; Harry doubted even Uncle Vernon would have spotted him for what he really was.

"Pull up a bit of grass, Barty," said Ludo brightly, patting the ground beside him.

"No thank you, Ludo," said Crouch, and there was a bite of impatience in his voice. "I've been looking for you everywhere. The Bulgarians are insisting we add another twelve seats to the Top Box."

"Oh is *that* what they're after?" said Bagman. "I thought the chap was asking to borrow a pair of tweezers. Bit of a strong accent."

"Mr. Crouch!" said Percy breathlessly, sunk into a kind of half-bow that made him look like a hunchback. "Would you like a cup of tea?"

"Oh," said Mr. Crouch, looking over at Percy in mild surprise. "Yes — thank you, Weatherby."

Fred and George choked into their own cups. Percy, very pink around the ears, busied himself with the kettle.

"Oh and I've been wanting a word with you too, Arthur," said Mr. Crouch, his sharp eyes falling upon Mr. Weasley. "Ali Bashir's on the warpath. He wants a word with you about your embargo on flying carpets."

Mr. Weasley heaved a deep sigh.

"I sent him an owl about that just last week. If I've told him once I've told him a hundred times: Carpets are defined as a Muggle Artifact by the Registry of Proscribed Charmable Objects, but will he listen?"

"I doubt it," said Mr. Crouch, accepting a cup from Percy. "He's desperate to export here."

"Well, they'll never replace brooms in Britain, will they?" said Bagman.

"Ali thinks there's a niche in the market for a family vehicle," said Mr. Crouch. "I remember my grandfather had an Axminster that could seat twelve — but that was before carpets were banned, of course."

He spoke as though he wanted to leave nobody in any doubt that all his ancestors had abided strictly by the law.

"So, been keeping busy, Barty?" said Bagman breezily.

"Fairly," said Mr. Crouch dryly. "Organizing Portkeys across five continents is no mean feat, Ludo."

"I expect you'll both be glad when this is over?" said Mr. Weasley.

Ludo Bagman looked shocked.

"Glad! Don't know when I've had more fun. . . . Still, it's not as though we haven't got anything to look forward to, eh, Barty? Eh? Plenty left to organize, eh?"

Mr. Crouch raised his eyebrows at Bagman.

"We agreed not to make the announcement until all the details —"

"Oh details!" said Bagman, waving the word away like a cloud of midges. "They've signed, haven't they? They've agreed, haven't they? I bet you anything these kids'll know soon enough anyway. I mean, it's happening at Hogwarts —"

"Ludo, we need to meet the Bulgarians, you know," said Mr. Crouch sharply, cutting Bagman's remarks short. "Thank you for the tea, Weatherby."

He pushed his undrunk tea back at Perey and waited for Ludo to rise; Bagman struggled to his feet, swigging down the last of his tea, the gold in his pockets chinking merrily.

"See you all later!" he said. "You'll be up in the Top Box with me — I'm commentating!" He waved, Barty Crouch nodded curtly, and both of them Disapparated.

"What's happening at Hogwarts, Dad?" said Fred at once. "What were they talking about?"

"You'll find out soon enough," said Mr. Weasley, smiling.

"It's classified information, until such time as the Ministry decides to release it," said Percy stiffly. "Mr. Crouch was quite right not to disclose it."

"Oh shut up, Weatherby," said Fred.

A sense of excitement rose like a palpable cloud over the campsite as the afternoon wore on. By dusk, the still summer air itself seemed to be quivering with anticipation, and as darkness spread like a curtain over the thousands of waiting wizards, the last vestiges of pretense disappeared: The Ministry seemed to have bowed to the inevitable and stopped fighting the signs of blatant magic now breaking out everywhere.

Salesmen were Apparating every few feet, carrying trays and pushing carts full of extraordinary merchandise. There were luminous rosettes — green for Ireland, red for Bulgaria — which were squealing the names of the players, pointed green hats bedecked with dancing shamrocks, Bulgarian scarves adorned with lions that really roared, flags from both countries that played their national anthems as they were waved; there were tiny models of Firebolts that really flew, and collectible figures of famous players, which strolled across the palm of your hand, preening themselves.

"Been saving my pocket money all summer for this," Ron told Harry as they and Hermione strolled through the salesmen, buying souvenirs. Though Ron purchased a dancing shamrock hat and a large green rosette, he also bought a small figure of Viktor Krum, the Bulgarian Seeker. The miniature Krum walked backward and forward over Ron's hand, scowling up at the green rosette above him.

"Wow, look at these!" said Harry, hurrying over to a cart piled high with what looked like brass binoculars, except that they were covered with all sorts of weird knobs and dials.

"Omnioculars," said the saleswizard eagerly. "You can replay action . . . slow everything down . . . and they flash up a play-by-play breakdown if you need it. Bargain — ten Galleons each."

"Wish I hadn't bought this now," said Ron, gesturing at his dancing shamrock hat and gazing longingly at the Omnioculars.

"Three pairs," said Harry firmly to the wizard.

"No — don't bother," said Ron, going red. He was always

touchy about the fact that Harry, who had inherited a small fortune from his parents, had much more money than he did.

"You won't be getting anything for Christmas," Harry told him, thrusting Omnioculars into his and Hermione's hands. "For about ten years, mind."

"Fair enough," said Ron, grinning.

"Oooh, thanks, Harry," said Hermione. "And I'll get us some programs, look —"

Their money bags considerably lighter, they went back to the tents. Bill, Charlie, and Ginny were all sporting green rosettes too, and Mr. Weasley was carrying an Irish flag. Fred and George had no souvenirs as they had given Bagman all their gold.

And then a deep, booming gong sounded somewhere beyond the woods, and at once, green and red lanterns blazed into life in the trees, lighting a path to the field.

"It's time!" said Mr. Weasley, looking as excited as any of them. "Come on, let's go!"

# THE QUIDDITCH
# WORLD CUP

Clutching their purchases, Mr. Weasley in the lead, they all hurried into the wood, following the lantern-lit trail. They could hear the sounds of thousands of people moving around them, shouts and laughter, snatches of singing. The atmosphere of feverish excitement was highly infectious; Harry couldn't stop grinning. They walked through the wood for twenty minutes, talking and joking loudly, until at last they emerged on the other side and found themselves in the shadow of a gigantic stadium. Though Harry could see only a fraction of the immense gold walls surrounding the field, he could tell that ten cathedrals would fit comfortably inside it.

"Seats a hundred thousand," said Mr. Weasley, spotting the awestruck look on Harry's face. "Ministry task force of five hundred have been working on it all year. Muggle Repelling Charms on every inch of it. Every time Muggles have got anywhere near here all year, they've suddenly remembered urgent appointments and had to dash away again . . . bless them," he added fondly, lead-ing the way toward the nearest entrance, which was already sur-rounded by a swarm of shouting witches and wizards.

"Prime seats!" said the Ministry witch at the entrance when she checked their tickets. "Top Box! Straight upstairs, Arthur, and as high as you can go."

The stairs into the stadium were carpeted in rich purple. They clambered upward with the rest of the crowd, which slowly filtered away through doors into the stands to their left and right. Mr. Weasley's party kept climbing, and at last they reached the top of the staircase and found themselves in a small box, set at the high-est point of the stadium and situated exactly halfway between the golden goalposts. About twenty purple-and-gilt chairs stood in two rows here, and Harry, filing into the front seats with the Weasleys, looked down upon a scene the likes of which he could never have imagined.

A hundred thousand witches and wizards were taking their places in the seats, which rose in levels around the long oval field. Every-thing was suffused with a mysterious golden light, which seemed to come from the stadium itself. The field looked smooth as vel-vet from their lofty position. At either end of the field stood three goal hoops, fifty feet high; right opposite them, almost at Harry's eye level, was a gigantic blackboard. Gold writing kept dashing across it as though an invisible giant's hand were scrawling upon the blackboard and then wiping it off again; watching it, Harry saw that it was flashing advertisements across the field.

*The Bluebottle: A Broom for All the Family — Safe, Reliable, and with Built-in Anti-Burglar Buzzer . . . Mrs.*

*Skower's All-Purpose Magical Mess Remover: No Pain, No Stain! . . . Gladrags Wizardwear — London, Paris, Hogsmeade . . .*

Harry tore his eyes away from the sign and looked over his shoulder to see who else was sharing the box with them. So far it was empty, except for a tiny creature sitting in the second from last seat at the end of the row behind them. The creature, whose legs were so short they stuck out in front of it on the chair, was wearing a tea towel draped like a toga, and it had its face hidden in its hands. Yet those long, batlike ears were oddly familiar. . . .

*"Dobby?"* said Harry incredulously.

The tiny creature looked up and stretched its fingers, revealing enormous brown eyes and a nose the exact size and shape of a large tomato. It wasn't Dobby — it was, however, unmistakably a house-elf, as Harry's friend Dobby had been. Harry had set Dobby free from his old owners, the Malfoy family.

"Did sir just call me Dobby?" squeaked the elf curiously from between its fingers. Its voice was higher even than Dobby's had been, a teeny, quivering squeak of a voice, and Harry suspected — though it was very hard to tell with a house-elf — that this one might just be female. Ron and Hermione spun around in their seats to look. Though they had heard a lot about Dobby from Harry, they had never actually met him. Even Mr. Weasley looked around in interest.

"Sorry," Harry told the elf, "I just thought you were someone I knew."

"But I knows Dobby too, sir!" squeaked the elf. She was shielding her face, as though blinded by light, though the Top Box was not brightly lit. "My name is Winky, sir — and you, sir —" Her dark brown eyes widened to the size of side plates as they rested upon Harry's scar. "You is surely Harry Potter!"

"Yeah, I am," said Harry.

"But Dobby talks of you all the time, sir!" she said, lowering her hands very slightly and looking awestruck.

"How is he?" said Harry. "How's freedom suiting him?"

"Ah, sir," said Winky, shaking her head, "ah sir, meaning no disrespect, sir, but I is not sure you did Dobby a favor, sir, when you is setting him free."

"Why?" said Harry, taken aback. "What's wrong with him?"

"Freedom is going to Dobby's head, sir," said Winky sadly. "Ideas above his station, sir. Can't get another position, sir."

"Why not?" said Harry.

Winky lowered her voice by a half-octave and whispered, *"He is wanting paying for his work, sir."*

"Paying?" said Harry blankly. "Well — why shouldn't he be paid?"

Winky looked quite horrified at the idea and closed her fingers slightly so that her face was half-hidden again.

"House-elves is not paid, sir!" she said in a muffled squeak. "No, no, no. I says to Dobby, I says, go find yourself a nice family and settle down, Dobby. He is getting up to all sorts of high jinks, sir, what is unbecoming to a house-elf. You goes racketing around like this, Dobby, I says, and next thing I hear you's up in front of the Department for the Regulation and Control of Magical Creatures, like some common goblin."

"Well, it's about time he had a bit of fun," said Harry.

"House-elves is not supposed to have fun, Harry Potter," said

Winky firmly, from behind her hands. "House-elves does what they is told. I is not liking heights at all, Harry Potter." — she glanced toward the edge of the box and gulped — "but my master sends me to the Top Box and I comes, sir."

"Why's he sent you up here, if he knows you don't like heights?" said Harry, frowning.

"Master — master wants me to save him a seat, Harry Potter. He is very busy," said Winky, tilting her head toward the empty space beside her. "Winky is wishing she is back in master's tent, Harry Potter, but Winky does what she is told. Winky is a good house-elf."

She gave the edge of the box another frightened look and hid her eyes completely again. Harry turned back to the others.

"So that's a house-elf?" Ron muttered. "Weird things, aren't they?"

"Dobby was weirder," said Harry fervently.

Ron pulled out his Omnioculars and started testing them, staring down into the crowd on the other side of the stadium.

"Wild!" he said, twiddling the replay knob on the side. "I can make that old bloke down there pick his nose again . . . and again . . . and again . . ."

Hermione, meanwhile, was skimming eagerly through her velvet-covered, tasseled program.

"'A display from the team mascots will precede the match,'" she read aloud.

"Oh that's always worth watching," said Mr. Weasley. "National teams bring creatures from their native land, you know, to put on a bit of a show."

The box filled gradually around them over the next half hour.

Mr. Weasley kept shaking hands with people who were obviously very important wizards. Percy jumped to his feet so often that he looked as though he were trying to sit on a hedgehog. When Cornelius Fudge, the Minister of Magic himself, arrived, Percy bowed so low that his glasses fell off and shattered. Highly embarrassed, he repaired them with his wand and thereafter remained in his seat, throwing jealous looks at Harry, whom Cornelius Fudge had greeted like an old friend. They had met before, and Fudge shook Harry's hand in a fatherly fashion, asked how he was, and introduced him to the wizards on either side of him.

"Harry Potter, you know," he told the Bulgarian minister loudly, who was wearing splendid robes of black velvet trimmed with gold and didn't seem to understand a word of English. "*Harry Potter . . .* oh come on now, you know who he is . . . the boy who survived You-Know-Who . . . you *do* know who he is —"

The Bulgarian wizard suddenly spotted Harry's scar and started gabbling loudly and excitedly, pointing at it.

"Knew we'd get there in the end," said Fudge wearily to Harry. "I'm no great shakes at languages; I need Barty Crouch for this sort of thing. Ah, I see his house-elf's saving him a seat. . . . Good job too, these Bulgarian blighters have been trying to cadge all the best places . . . ah, and here's Lucius!"

Harry, Ron, and Hermione turned quickly. Edging along the second row to three still-empty seats right behind Mr. Weasley were none other than Dobby the house-elf's former owners: Lucius Malfoy; his son, Draco; and a woman Harry supposed must be Draco's mother.

Harry and Draco Malfoy had been enemies ever since their very first journey to Hogwarts. A pale boy with a pointed face and white-blond hair, Draco greatly resembled his father. His mother was blonde too; tall and slim, she would have been nice-looking if she hadn't been wearing a look that suggested there was a nasty smell under her nose.

"Ah, Fudge," said Mr. Malfoy, holding out his hand as he reached the Minister of Magic. "How are you? I don't think you've met my wife, Narcissa? Or our son, Draco?"

"How do you do, how do you do?" said Fudge, smiling and bowing to Mrs. Malfoy. "And allow me to introduce you to Mr. Oblansk — Obalonsk — Mr. — well, he's the Bulgarian Minister of Magic, and he can't understand a word I'm saying anyway, so never mind. And let's see who else — you know Arthur Weasley, I daresay?"

It was a tense moment. Mr. Weasley and Mr. Malfoy looked at each other and Harry vividly recalled the last time they had come face-to-face: It had been in Flourish and Blotts bookshop, and they had had a fight. Mr. Malfoy's cold gray eyes swept over Mr. Weasley, and then up and down the row.

"Good lord, Arthur," he said softly. "What did you have to sell to get seats in the Top Box? Surely your house wouldn't have fetched this much?"

Fudge, who wasn't listening, said, "Lucius has just given a *very* generous contribution to St. Mungo's Hospital for Magical Maladies and Injuries, Arthur. He's here as my guest."

"How — how nice," said Mr. Weasley, with a very strained smile.

Mr. Malfoy's eyes had returned to Hermione, who went slightly pink, but stared determinedly back at him. Harry knew exactly what was making Mr. Malfoy's lip curl like that. The Malfoys prided themselves on being purebloods; in other words, they considered anyone of Muggle descent, like Hermione, second-class. However, under the gaze of the Minister of Magic, Mr. Malfoy didn't dare say anything. He nodded sneeringly to Mr. Weasley and continued down the line to his seats. Draco shot Harry, Ron, and Hermione one contemptuous look, then settled himself between his mother and father.

"Slimy gits," Ron muttered as he, Harry, and Hermione turned to face the field again. Next moment, Ludo Bagman charged into the box.

"Everyone ready?" he said, his round face gleaming like a great, excited Edam. "Minister — ready to go?"

"Ready when you are, Ludo," said Fudge comfortably.

Ludo whipped out his wand, directed it at his own throat, and said "*Sonorus!*" and then spoke over the roar of sound that was now filling the packed stadium; his voice echoed over them, booming into every corner of the stands.

"Ladies and gentlemen . . . welcome! Welcome to the final of the four hundred and twenty-second Quidditch World Cup!"

The spectators screamed and clapped. Thousands of flags waved, adding their discordant national anthems to the racket. The huge blackboard opposite them was wiped clear of its last message (*Bertie Bott's Every Flavor Beans — A Risk with Every Mouthful!*) and now showed BULGARIA: 0, IRELAND: 0.

"And now, without further ado, allow me to introduce . . . the Bulgarian National Team Mascots!"

The right-hand side of the stands, which was a solid block of scarlet, roared its approval.

"I wonder what they've brought," said Mr. Weasley, leaning forward in his seat. "Aaah!" He suddenly whipped off his glasses and polished them hurriedly on his robes. *"Veela!"*

"What are veel — ?"

But a hundred veela were now gliding out onto the field, and Harry's question was answered for him. Veela were women . . . the most beautiful women Harry had ever seen . . . except that they weren't — they couldn't be — human. This puzzled Harry for a moment while he tried to guess what exactly they could be; what could make their skin shine moon-bright like that, or their white-gold hair fan out behind them without wind . . . but then the music started, and Harry stopped worrying about them not being human — in fact, he stopped worrying about anything at all.

The veela had started to dance, and Harry's mind had gone completely and blissfully blank. All that mattered in the world was that he kept watching the veela, because if they stopped dancing, terrible things would happen. . . .

And as the veela danced faster and faster, wild, half-formed thoughts started chasing through Harry's dazed mind. He wanted to do something very impressive, right now. Jumping from the box into the stadium seemed a good idea . . . but would it be good enough?

"Harry, what *are* you doing?" said Hermione's voice from a long way off.

The music stopped. Harry blinked. He was standing up, and one of his legs was resting on the wall of the box. Next to him, Ron was frozen in an attitude that looked as though he were about to dive from a springboard.

Angry yells were filling the stadium. The crowd didn't want the veela to go. Harry was with them; he would, of course, be supporting Bulgaria, and he wondered vaguely why he had a large green shamrock pinned to his chest. Ron, meanwhile, was absentmindedly shredding the shamrocks on his hat. Mr. Weasley, smiling slightly, leaned over to Ron and tugged the hat out of his hands.

"You'll be wanting that," he said, "once Ireland have had their say."

"Huh?" said Ron, staring openmouthed at the veela, who had now lined up along one side of the field.

Hermione made a loud tutting noise. She reached up and pulled Harry back into his seat. *"Honestly!"* she said.

"And now," roared Ludo Bagman's voice, "kindly put your wands in the air . . . for the Irish National Team Mascots!"

Next moment, what seemed to be a great green-and-gold comet came zooming into the stadium. It did one circuit of the stadium, then split into two smaller comets, each hurtling toward the goalposts. A rainbow arced suddenly across the field, connecting the two balls of light. The crowd oooohed and aaaaahed, as though at a fireworks display. Now the rainbow faded and the balls of light reunited and merged; they had formed a great shimmering shamrock, which rose up into the sky and began to soar over the stands. Something like golden rain seemed to be falling from it —

"Excellent!" yelled Ron as the shamrock soared over them, and heavy gold coins rained from it, bouncing off their heads and seats. Squinting up at the shamrock, Harry realized that it was actually comprised of thousands of tiny little bearded men with red vests, each carrying a minute lamp of gold or green.

"Leprechauns!" said Mr. Weasley over the tumultuous applause of the crowd, many of whom were still fighting and rummaging around under their chairs to retrieve the gold.

"There you go," Ron yelled happily, stuffing a fistful of gold coins into Harry's hand, "for the Omnioculars! Now you've got to buy me a Christmas present, ha!"

The great shamrock dissolved, the leprechauns drifted down onto the field on the opposite side from the veela, and settled themselves cross-legged to watch the match.

"And now, ladies and gentlemen, kindly welcome — the Bulgarian National Quidditch Team! I give you — Dimitrov!"

A scarlet-clad figure on a broomstick, moving so fast it was blurred, shot out onto the field from an entrance far below, to wild applause from the Bulgarian supporters.

"Ivanova!"

A second scarlet-robed player zoomed out.

"Zograf! Levski! Vulchanov! Volkov! Aaaaaaand — *Krum*!"

"That's him, that's him!" yelled Ron, following Krum with his Omnioculars. Harry quickly focused his own.

Viktor Krum was thin, dark, and sallow-skinned, with a large curved nose and thick black eyebrows. He looked like an overgrown bird of prey. It was hard to believe he was only eighteen.

"And now, please greet — the Irish National Quidditch Team!" yelled Bagman. "Presenting — Connolly! Ryan! Troy! Mullet! Moran! Quigley! Aaaaaand — *Lynch*!"

Seven green blurs swept onto the field; Harry spun a small dial on the side of his Omnioculars and slowed the players down enough to read the word "Firebolt" on each of their brooms and see their names, embroidered in silver, upon their backs.

"And here, all the way from Egypt, our referee, acclaimed

Chairwizard of the International Association of Quidditch, Hassan Mostafa!"

A small and skinny wizard, completely bald but with a mustache to rival Uncle Vernon's, wearing robes of pure gold to match the stadium, strode out onto the field. A silver whistle was protruding from under the mustache, and he was carrying a large wooden crate under one arm, his broomstick under the other. Harry spun the speed dial on his Omnioculars back to normal, watching closely as Mostafa mounted his broomstick and kicked the crate open — four balls burst into the air: the scarlet Quaffle, the two black Bludgers, and (Harry saw it for the briefest moment, before it sped out of sight) the minuscule, winged Golden Snitch. With a sharp blast on his whistle, Mostafa shot into the air after the balls.

"Theeeeeeeey're OFF!" screamed Bagman. "And it's Mullet! Troy! Moran! Dimitrov! Back to Mullet! Troy! Levski! Moran!"

It was Quidditch as Harry had never seen it played before. He was pressing his Omnioculars so hard to his glasses that they were cutting into the bridge of his nose. The speed of the players was incredible — the Chasers were throwing the Quaffle to one another so fast that Bagman only had time to say their names. Harry spun the slow dial on the right of his Omnioculars again, pressed the play-by-play button on the top, and he was immediately watching in slow motion, while glittering purple lettering flashed across the lenses and the noise of the crowd pounded against his eardrums.

HAWKSHEAD ATTACKING FORMATION, he read as he watched the three Irish Chasers zoom closely together, Troy in the center, slightly ahead of Mullet and Moran, bearing down upon the Bulgarians. PORSKOFF PLOY flashed up next, as Troy made as though to dart upward with the Quaffle, drawing away the Bulgarian Chaser

Ivanova and dropping the Quaffle to Moran. One of the Bulgarian Beaters, Volkov, swung hard at a passing Bludger with his small club, knocking it into Moran's path; Moran ducked to avoid the Bludger and dropped the Quaffle; and Levski, soaring beneath, caught it —

"TROY SCORES!" roared Bagman, and the stadium shuddered with a roar of applause and cheers. "Ten zero to Ireland!"

"What?" Harry yelled, looking wildly around through his Omnioculars. "But Levski's got the Quaffle!"

"Harry, if you're not going to watch at normal speed, you're going to miss things!" shouted Hermione, who was dancing up and down, waving her arms in the air while Troy did a lap of honor around the field. Harry looked quickly over the top of his Omnioculars and saw that the leprechauns watching from the sidelines had all risen into the air again and formed the great, glittering shamrock. Across the field, the veela were watching them sulkily.

Furious with himself, Harry spun his speed dial back to normal as play resumed.

Harry knew enough about Quidditch to see that the Irish Chasers were superb. They worked as a seamless team, their movements so well coordinated that they appeared to be reading one another's minds as they positioned themselves, and the rosette on Harry's chest kept squeaking their names: *"Troy — Mullet — Moran!"* And within ten minutes, Ireland had scored twice more, bringing their lead to thirty–zero and causing a thunderous tide of roars and applause from the green-clad supporters.

The match became still faster, but more brutal. Volkov and Vulchanov, the Bulgarian Beaters, were whacking the Bludgers as fiercely as possible at the Irish Chasers, and were starting to prevent them from using some of their best moves; twice they were forced to scatter, and then, finally, Ivanova managed to break through their ranks; dodge the Keeper, Ryan; and score Bulgaria's first goal.

"Fingers in your ears!" bellowed Mr. Weasley as the veela started to dance in celebration. Harry screwed up his eyes too; he wanted to keep his mind on the game. After a few seconds, he chanced a glance at the field. The veela had stopped dancing, and Bulgaria was again in possession of the Quaffle.

"Dimitrov! Levski! Dimitrov! Ivanova — oh I say!" roared Bagman.

One hundred thousand wizards gasped as the two Seekers, Krum and Lynch, plummeted through the center of the Chasers, so fast that it looked as though they had just jumped from airplanes without parachutes. Harry followed their descent through his Omnioculars, squinting to see where the Snitch was —

"They're going to crash!" screamed Hermione next to Harry.

She was half right — at the very last second, Viktor Krum pulled out of the dive and spiraled off. Lynch, however, hit the ground with a dull thud that could be heard throughout the stadium. A huge groan rose from the Irish seats.

"Fool!" moaned Mr. Weasley. "Krum was feinting!"

"It's time-out!" yelled Bagman's voice, "as trained mediwizards hurry onto the field to examine Aidan Lynch!"

"He'll be okay, he only got ploughed!" Charlie said reassuringly to Ginny, who was hanging over the side of the box, looking horror-struck. "Which is what Krum was after, of course. . . ."

Harry hastily pressed the replay and play-by-play buttons on his Omnioculars, twiddled the speed dial, and put them back up to his eyes.

He watched as Krum and Lynch dived again in slow motion. *Wronski Defensive Feint — dangerous Seeker diversion* read the shining purple lettering across his lenses. He saw Krum's face contorted with concentration as he pulled out of the dive just in time, while Lynch was flattened, and he understood — Krum hadn't seen the Snitch at all, he was just making Lynch copy him. Harry had never seen anyone fly like that; Krum hardly looked as though he was using a broomstick at all; he moved so easily through the air that he looked unsupported and weightless. Harry turned his Omnioculars back to normal and focused them on Krum. He was now circling high above Lynch, who was being revived by mediwizards with cups of potion. Harry, focusing still more closely upon Krum's face, saw his dark eyes darting all over the ground a hundred feet below. He was using the time while Lynch was revived to look for the Snitch without interference.

Lynch got to his feet at last, to loud cheers from the green-clad supporters, mounted his Firebolt, and kicked back off into the air. His revival seemed to give Ireland new heart. When Mostafa blew his whistle again, the Chasers moved into action with a skill unrivaled by anything Harry had seen so far.

After fifteen more fast and furious minutes, Ireland had pulled ahead by ten more goals. They were now leading by one hundred and thirty points to ten, and the game was starting to get dirtier.

As Mullet shot toward the goalposts yet again, clutching the Quaffle tightly under her arm, the Bulgarian Keeper, Zograf, flew out to meet her. Whatever happened was over so quickly Harry didn't catch it, but a scream of rage from the Irish crowd, and Mostafa's long, shrill whistle blast, told him it had been a foul.

"And Mostafa takes the Bulgarian Keeper to task for cobbing —

excessive use of elbows!" Bagman informed the roaring spectators. "And — yes, it's a penalty to Ireland!"

The leprechauns, who had risen angrily into the air like a swarm of glittering hornets when Mullet had been fouled, now darted together to form the words "HA, HA, HA!" The veela on the other side of the field leapt to their feet, tossed their hair angrily, and started to dance again.

As one, the Weasley boys and Harry stuffed their fingers into their ears, but Hermione, who hadn't bothered, was soon tugging on Harry's arm. He turned to look at her, and she pulled his fingers impatiently out of his ears.

"Look at the referee!" she said, giggling.

Harry looked down at the field. Hassan Mostafa had landed right in front of the dancing veela, and was acting very oddly indeed. He was flexing his muscles and smoothing his mustache excitedly.

"Now, we can't have that!" said Ludo Bagman, though he sounded highly amused. "Somebody slap the referee!"

A mediwizard came tearing across the field, his fingers stuffed into his own ears, and kicked Mostafa hard in the shins. Mostafa seemed to come to himself; Harry, watching through the Omnioculars again, saw that he looked exceptionally embarrassed and had started shouting at the veela, who had stopped dancing and were looking mutinous.

"And unless I'm much mistaken, Mostafa is actually attempting to send off the Bulgarian team mascots!" said Bagman's voice. "Now *there's* something we haven't seen before. . . . Oh, this could turn nasty. . . ."

It did: The Bulgarian Beaters, Volkov and Vulchanov, landed on either side of Mostafa and began arguing furiously with him, gesticulating toward the leprechauns, who had now gleefully formed the words "HEE, HEE, HEE." Mostafa was not impressed by the Bulgarians' arguments, however; he was jabbing his finger into the air, clearly telling them to get flying again, and when they refused, he gave two short blasts on his whistle.

"*Two* penalties for Ireland!" shouted Bagman, and the Bulgarian crowd howled with anger. "And Volkov and Vulchanov had better get back on those brooms . . . yes . . . there they go . . . and Troy takes the Quaffle . . ."

Play now reached a level of ferocity beyond anything they had yet seen. The Beaters on both sides were acting without mercy: Volkov and Vulchanov in particular seemed not to care whether their clubs made contact with Bludger or human as they swung them violently through the air. Dimitrov shot straight at Moran, who had the Quaffle, nearly knocking her off her broom.

"*Foul!*" roared the Irish supporters as one, all standing up in a great wave of green.

"Foul!" echoed Ludo Bagman's magically magnified voice. "Dimitrov skins Moran — deliberately flying to collide there — and it's got to be another penalty — yes, there's the whistle!"

The leprechauns had risen into the air again, and this time, they formed a giant hand, which was making a very rude sign indeed at the veela across the field. At this, the veela lost control. Instead of dancing, they launched themselves across the field and began throwing what seemed to be handfuls of fire at the leprechauns. Watching through his Omnioculars, Harry saw that they didn't look remotely beautiful now. On the contrary, their faces were elongating into sharp, cruel-beaked bird heads, and long, scaly wings were bursting from their shoulders —

"And *that,* boys," yelled Mr. Weasley over the tumult of the crowd below, "is why you should never go for looks alone!"

Ministry wizards were flooding onto the field to separate the veela and the leprechauns, but with little success; meanwhile, the pitched battle below was nothing to the one taking place above. Harry turned this way and that, staring through his Omnioculars, as the Quaffle changed hands with the speed of a bullet.

"Levski — Dimitrov — Moran — Troy — Mullet — Ivanova — Moran again — Moran — MORAN SCORES!"

But the cheers of the Irish supporters were barely heard over the shrieks of the veela, the blasts now issuing from the Ministry members' wands, and the furious roars of the Bulgarians. The game recommenced immediately; now Levski had the Quaffle, now Dimitrov —

The Irish Beater Quigley swung heavily at a passing Bludger, and hit it as hard as possible toward Krum, who did not duck quickly enough. It hit him full in the face.

There was a deafening groan from the crowd; Krum's nose looked broken, there was blood everywhere, but Hassan Mostafa didn't blow his whistle. He had become distracted, and Harry couldn't blame him; one of the veela had thrown a handful of fire and set his broom tail alight.

Harry wanted someone to realize that Krum was injured; even though he was supporting Ireland, Krum was the most exciting player on the field. Ron obviously felt the same.

"Time-out! Ah, come on, he can't play like that, look at him —"

*"Look at Lynch!"* Harry yelled.

For the Irish Seeker had suddenly gone into a dive, and Harry was quite sure that this was no Wronski Feint; this was the real thing. . . .

"He's seen the Snitch!" Harry shouted. "He's seen it! Look at him go!"

Half the crowd seemed to have realized what was happening; the Irish supporters rose in another great wave of green, screaming their Seeker on . . . but Krum was on his tail. How he could see where he was going, Harry had no idea; there were flecks of blood flying through the air behind him, but he was drawing level with Lynch now as the pair of them hurtled toward the ground again —

"They're going to crash!" shrieked Hermione.

"They're not!" roared Ron.

"Lynch is!" yelled Harry.

And he was right — for the second time, Lynch hit the ground with tremendous force and was immediately stampeded by a horde of angry veela.

"The Snitch, where's the Snitch?" bellowed Charlie, along the row.

"He's got it — Krum's got it — it's all over!" shouted Harry.

Krum, his red robes shining with blood from his nose, was rising gently into the air, his fist held high, a glint of gold in his hand.

The scoreboard was flashing BULGARIA: 160, IRELAND: 170 across the crowd, who didn't seem to have realized what had happened. Then, slowly, as though a great jumbo jet were revving up, the rumbling from the Ireland supporters grew louder and louder and erupted into screams of delight.

"IRELAND WINS!" Bagman shouted, who like the Irish, seemed to be taken aback by the sudden end of the match.

"KRUM GETS THE SNITCH — BUT IRELAND WINS — good lord, I don't think any of us were expecting that!"

"What did he catch the Snitch for?" Ron bellowed, even as he jumped up and down, applauding with his hands over his head. "He ended it when Ireland were a hundred and sixty points ahead, the idiot!"

"He knew they were never going to catch up!" Harry shouted back over all the noise, also applauding loudly. "The Irish Chasers were too good. . . . He wanted to end it on his terms, that's all. . . ."

"He was very brave, wasn't he?" Hermione said, leaning forward to watch Krum land as a swarm of mediwizards blasted a path through the battling leprechauns and veela to get to him. "He looks a terrible mess. . . ."

Harry put his Omnioculars to his eyes again. It was hard to see what was happening below, because leprechauns were zooming delightedly all over the field, but he could just make out Krum, surrounded by mediwizards. He looked surlier than ever and refused to let them mop him up. His team members were around him, shaking their heads and looking dejected; a short way away, the Irish players were dancing gleefully in a shower of gold descending from their mascots. Flags were waving all over the stadium, the Irish national anthem blared from all sides; the veela were shrinking back into their usual, beautiful selves now, though looking dispirited and forlorn.

"Vell, ve fought bravely," said a gloomy voice behind Harry. He looked around; it was the Bulgarian Minister of Magic.

"You can speak English!" said Fudge, sounding outraged. "And you've been letting me mime everything all day!"

"Vell, it vos very funny," said the Bulgarian minister, shrugging.

"And as the Irish team performs a lap of honor, flanked by their mascots, the Quidditch World Cup itself is brought into the Top Box!" roared Bagman.

Harry's eyes were suddenly dazzled by a blinding white light, as the Top Box was magically illuminated so that everyone in the stands could see the inside. Squinting toward the entrance, he saw two panting wizards carrying a vast golden cup into the box, which they handed to Cornelius Fudge, who was still looking very disgruntled that he'd been using sign language all day for nothing.

"Let's have a really loud hand for the gallant losers — Bulgaria!" Bagman shouted.

And up the stairs into the box came the seven defeated Bulgarian players. The crowd below was applauding appreciatively; Harry could see thousands and thousands of Omniocular lenses flashing and winking in their direction.

One by one, the Bulgarians filed between the rows of seats in the box, and Bagman called out the name of each as they shook hands with their own minister and then with Fudge. Krum, who was last in line, looked a real mess. Two black eyes were blooming spectacularly on his bloody face. He was still holding the Snitch. Harry noticed that he seemed much less coordinated on the ground. He was slightly duck-footed and distinctly round-shouldered. But when Krum's name was announced, the whole stadium gave him a resounding, earsplitting roar.

And then came the Irish team. Aidan Lynch was being supported by Moran and Connolly; the second crash seemed to have dazed him and his eyes looked strangely unfocused. But he grinned happily as Troy and Quigley lifted the Cup into the air and the crowd below thundered its approval. Harry's hands were numb with clapping.

At last, when the Irish team had left the box to perform another lap of honor on their brooms (Aidan Lynch on the back of Connolly's, clutching hard around his waist and still grinning in a bemused sort of way), Bagman pointed his wand at his throat and muttered, *"Quietus."*

"They'll be talking about this one for years," he said hoarsely, "a really unexpected twist, that. . . . shame it couldn't have lasted longer. . . . Ah yes. . . . yes, I owe you . . . how much?"

For Fred and George had just scrambled over the backs of their seats and were standing in front of Ludo Bagman with broad grins on their faces, their hands outstretched.

# CHAPTER NINE

# THE DARK MARK

Don't tell your mother you've been gambling," Mr. Weasley implored Fred and George as they all made their way slowly down the purple-carpeted stairs.

"Don't worry, Dad," said Fred gleefully, "we've got big plans for this money. We don't want it confiscated."

Mr. Weasley looked for a moment as though he was going to ask what these big plans were, but seemed to decide, upon reflection, that he didn't want to know.

They were soon caught up in the crowds now flooding out of the stadium and back to their campsites. Raucous singing was borne toward them on the night air as they retraced their steps along the lantern-lit path, and leprechauns kept shooting over their heads, cackling and waving their lanterns. When they finally reached the tents, nobody felt like sleeping at all, and given the level of noise around them, Mr. Weasley agreed that they could all have one last cup of cocoa together before turning in. They were soon arguing enjoyably about the match; Mr. Weasley got drawn into a disagreement about cobbing with Charlie, and it was only when Ginny fell asleep right at the tiny table and spilled hot chocolate all over the floor that Mr. Weasley called a halt to the verbal replays and insisted that everyone go to bed. Hermione and Ginny went into the next tent, and Harry and the rest of the Weasleys changed into pajamas and clambered into their bunks. From the other side of the campsite they could still hear much singing and the odd echoing bang.

"Oh I am glad I'm not on duty," muttered Mr. Weasley sleepily. "I wouldn't fancy having to go and tell the Irish they've got to stop celebrating."

Harry, who was on a top bunk above Ron, lay staring up at the canvas ceiling of the tent, watching the glow of an occasional leprechaun lantern flying overhead, and picturing again some of Krum's more spectacular moves. He was itching to get back on his own Firebolt and try out the Wronski Feint. . . . Somehow Oliver Wood had never managed to convey with all his wriggling diagrams what that move was supposed to look like. . . . Harry saw himself in robes that had his name on the back, and imagined the sensation of hearing a hundred-thousand-strong crowd roar, as Ludo Bagman's voice echoed throughout the stadium, "I give you . . . *Potter!*"

Harry never knew whether or not he had actually dropped off to sleep — his fantasies of flying like Krum might well have slipped into actual dreams — all he knew was that, quite suddenly, Mr. Weasley was shouting.

"Get up! Ron — Harry — come on now, get up, this is urgent!"

Harry sat up quickly and the top of his head hit canvas.

"'S' matter?" he said.

Dimly, he could tell that something was wrong. The noises in the campsite had changed. The singing had stopped. He could hear screams, and the sound of people running. He slipped down from the bunk and reached for his clothes, but Mr. Weasley, who had pulled on his jeans over his own pajamas, said, "No time, Harry — just grab a jacket and get outside — quickly!"

Harry did as he was told and hurried out of the tent, Ron at his heels.

By the light of the few fires that were still burning, he could see people running away into the woods, fleeing something that was moving across the field toward them, something that was emitting odd flashes of light and noises like gunfire. Loud jeering, roars of laughter, and drunken yells were drifting toward them; then came a burst of strong green light, which illuminated the scene.

A crowd of wizards, tightly packed and moving together with wands pointing straight upward, was marching slowly across the field. Harry squinted at them. . . . They didn't seem to have faces. . . . Then he realized that their heads were hooded and their faces masked. High above them, floating along in midair, four struggling figures were being contorted into grotesque shapes. It was as though the masked wizards on the ground were puppeteers, and the people above them were marionettes operated by invisible strings that rose from the wands into the air. Two of the figures were very small.

More wizards were joining the marching group, laughing and pointing up at the floating bodies. Tents crumpled and fell as the marching crowd swelled. Once or twice Harry saw one of the marchers blast a tent out of his way with his wand. Several caught fire. The screaming grew louder.

The floating people were suddenly illuminated as they passed over a burning tent and Harry recognized one of them: Mr. Roberts, the campsite manager. The other three looked as though they might be his wife and children. One of the marchers below flipped Mrs. Roberts upside down with his wand; her nightdress fell down to reveal voluminous drawers and she struggled to cover herself up as the crowd below her screeched and hooted with glee.

"That's sick," Ron muttered, watching the smallest Muggle child, who had begun to spin like a top, sixty feet above the ground, his head flopping limply from side to side. "That is really sick. . . ."

Hermione and Ginny came hurrying toward them, pulling coats over their nightdresses, with Mr. Weasley right behind them. At the same moment, Bill, Charlie, and Percy emerged from the boys' tent, fully dressed, with their sleeves rolled up and their wands out.

"We're going to help the Ministry!" Mr. Weasley shouted over all the noise, rolling up his own sleeves. "You lot — get into the woods, and *stick together*. I'll come and fetch you when we've sorted this out!"

Bill, Charlie, and Percy were already sprinting away toward the oncoming marchers; Mr. Weasley tore after them. Ministry wizards were dashing from every direction toward the source of the trouble. The crowd beneath the Roberts family was coming ever closer.

"C'mon," said Fred, grabbing Ginny's hand and starting to pull her toward the wood. Harry, Ron, Hermione, and George followed. They all looked back as they reached the trees. The crowd beneath the Roberts family was larger than ever; they could see the Ministry wizards trying to get through it to the hooded wizards in the center, but they were having great difficulty. It looked as though they were scared to perform any spell that might make the Roberts family fall.

The colored lanterns that had lit the path to the stadium had been extinguished. Dark figures were blundering through the trees; children were crying; anxious shouts and panicked voices were reverberating around them in the cold night air. Harry felt himself being pushed hither and thither by people whose faces he could not see. Then he heard Ron yell with pain.

"What happened?" said Hermione anxiously, stopping so abruptly that Harry walked into her. "Ron, where are you? Oh this is stupid — *Lumos*!"

She illuminated her wand and directed its narrow beam across the path. Ron was lying sprawled on the ground.

"Tripped over a tree root," he said angrily, getting to his feet again.

"Well, with feet that size, hard not to," said a drawling voice from behind them.

Harry, Ron, and Hermione turned sharply. Draco Malfoy was standing alone nearby, leaning against a tree, looking utterly relaxed. His arms folded, he seemed to have been watching the scene at the campsite through a gap in the trees.

Ron told Malfoy to do something that Harry knew he would never have dared say in front of Mrs. Weasley.

"Language, Weasley," said Malfoy, his pale eyes glittering. "Hadn't you better be hurrying along, now? You wouldn't like *her* spotted, would you?"

He nodded at Hermione, and at the same moment, a blast like a bomb sounded from the campsite, and a flash of green light momentarily lit the trees around them.

"What's that supposed to mean?" said Hermione defiantly.

"Granger, they're after *Muggles,*" said Malfoy. "D'you want to be showing off your knickers in midair? Because if you do, hang around . . . they're moving this way, and it would give us all a laugh."

"Hermione's a witch," Harry snarled.

"Have it your own way, Potter," said Malfoy, grinning maliciously. "If you think they can't spot a Mudblood, stay where you are."

"You watch your mouth!" shouted Ron. Everybody present knew that "Mudblood" was a very offensive term for a witch or wizard of Muggle parentage.

"Never mind, Ron," said Hermione quickly, seizing Ron's arm to restrain him as he took a step toward Malfoy.

There came a bang from the other side of the trees that was louder than anything they had heard. Several people nearby screamed. Malfoy chuckled softly.

"Scare easily, don't they?" he said lazily. "I suppose your daddy told you all to hide? What's he up to — trying to rescue the Muggles?"

"Where're *your* parents?" said Harry, his temper rising. "Out there wearing masks, are they?"

Malfoy turned his face to Harry, still smiling.

"Well . . . if they were, I wouldn't be likely to tell you, would I, Potter?"

"Oh come on," said Hermione, with a disgusted look at Malfoy, "let's go and find the others."

"Keep that big bushy head down, Granger," sneered Malfoy.

"Come *on*," Hermione repeated, and she pulled Harry and Ron up the path again.

"I'll bet you anything his dad *is* one of that masked lot!" said Ron hotly.

"Well, with any luck, the Ministry will catch him!" said Hermione fervently. "Oh I can't believe this. Where have the others got to?"

Fred, George, and Ginny were nowhere to be seen, though the path was packed with plenty of other people, all looking nervously over their shoulders toward the commotion back at the campsite. A huddle of teenagers in pajamas was arguing vociferously a little way along the path. When they saw Harry, Ron, and Hermione, a girl with thick curly hair turned and said quickly, *"Où est Madame Maxime? Nous l'avons perdue —"*

"Er — what?" said Ron.

"Oh . . ." The girl who had spoken turned her back on him, and as they walked on they distinctly heard her say, "'Ogwarts."

"Beauxbatons," muttered Hermione.

"Sorry?" said Harry.

"They must go to Beauxbatons," said Hermione. "You know . . . Beauxbatons Academy of Magic . . . I read about it in *An Appraisal of Magical Education in Europe.*"

"Oh . . . yeah . . . right," said Harry.

"Fred and George can't have gone that far," said Ron, pulling out his wand, lighting it like Hermione's, and squinting up the path. Harry dug in the pockets of his jacket for his own wand — but it wasn't there. The only thing he could find was his Omnioculars.

"Ah, no, I don't believe it . . . I've lost my wand!"

"You're kidding!"

Ron and Hermione raised their wands high enough to spread the narrow beams of light farther on the ground; Harry looked all around him, but his wand was nowhere to be seen.

"Maybe it's back in the tent," said Ron.

"Maybe it fell out of your pocket when we were running?" Hermione suggested anxiously.

"Yeah," said Harry, "maybe . . ."

He usually kept his wand with him at all times in the Wizarding world, and finding himself without it in the midst of a scene like this made him feel very vulnerable.

A rustling noise nearby made all three of them jump. Winky the house-elf was fighting her way out of a clump of bushes nearby. She was moving in a most peculiar fashion, apparently with great difficulty; it was as though someone invisible were trying to hold her back.

"There is bad wizards about!" she squeaked distractedly as she leaned forward and labored to keep running. "People high — high in the air! Winky is getting out of the way!"

And she disappeared into the trees on the other side of the path, panting and squeaking as she fought the force that was restraining her.

"What's up with her?" said Ron, looking curiously after Winky. "Why can't she run properly?"

"Bet she didn't ask permission to hide," said Harry. He was thinking of Dobby: Every time he had tried to do something the Malfoys wouldn't like, the house-elf had been forced to start beating himself up.

"You know, house-elves get a *very* raw deal!" said Hermione indignantly. "It's slavery, that's what it is! That Mr. Crouch made her go up to the top of the stadium, and she was terrified, and he's got her bewitched so she can't even run when they start trampling tents! Why doesn't anyone *do* something about it?"

"Well, the elves are happy, aren't they?" Ron said. "You heard old Winky back at the match . . . 'House-elves is not supposed to have fun'. . . that's what she likes, being bossed around. . . ."

"It's people like *you,* Ron," Hermione began hotly, "who prop up rotten and unjust systems, just because they're too lazy to —"

Another loud bang echoed from the edge of the wood.

"Let's just keep moving, shall we?" said Ron, and Harry saw him glance edgily at Hermione. Perhaps there was truth in what Malfoy had said; perhaps Hermione *was* in more danger than they were. They set off again, Harry still searching his pockets, even though he knew his wand wasn't there.

They followed the dark path deeper into the wood, still keeping an eye out for Fred, George, and Ginny. They passed a group of goblins who were cackling over a sack of gold that they had undoubtedly won betting on the match, and who seemed quite unperturbed by the trouble at the campsite. Farther still along the path, they walked into a patch of silvery light, and when they looked through the trees, they saw three tall and beautiful veela standing in a clearing, surrounded by a gaggle of young wizards, all of whom were talking very loudly.

"I pull down about a hundred sacks of Galleons a year!" one of them shouted. "I'm a dragon killer for the Committee for the Disposal of Dangerous Creatures."

"No, you're not!" yelled his friend. "You're a dishwasher at the Leaky Cauldron. . . . but I'm a vampire hunter, I've killed about ninety so far —"

A third young wizard, whose pimples were visible even by the dim, silvery light of the veela, now cut in, "I'm about to become the youngest-ever Minister of Magic, I am."

Harry snorted with laughter. He recognized the pimply wizard: His name was Stan Shunpike, and he was in fact a conductor on the triple-decker Knight Bus. He turned to tell Ron this, but Ron's face had gone oddly slack, and next second Ron was yelling, "Did I tell you I've invented a broomstick that'll reach Jupiter?"

"*Honestly!*" said Hermione, and she and Harry grabbed Ron firmly by the arms, wheeled him around, and marched him away. By the time the sounds of the veela and their admirers had faded completely, they were in the very heart of the wood. They seemed to be alone now; everything was much quieter.

Harry looked around. "I reckon we can just wait here, you know. We'll hear anyone coming a mile off."

The words were hardly out of his mouth, when Ludo Bagman emerged from behind a tree right ahead of them.

Even by the feeble light of the two wands, Harry could see that a great change had come over Bagman. He no longer looked buoyant and rosy-faced; there was no more spring in his step. He looked very white and strained.

"Who's that?" he said, blinking down at them, trying to make out their faces. "What are you doing in here, all alone?"

They looked at one another, surprised.

"Well — there's a sort of riot going on," said Ron.

Bagman stared at him.

"What?"

"At the campsite . . . some people have got hold of a family of Muggles. . . ."

Bagman swore loudly.

"Damn them!" he said, looking quite distracted, and without another word, he Disapparated with a small *pop*!

"Not exactly on top of things, Mr. Bagman, is he?" said Hermione, frowning.

"He was a great Beater, though," said Ron, leading the way off the path into a small clearing, and sitting down on a patch of dry grass at the foot of a tree. "The Wimbourne Wasps won the league three times in a row while he was with them."

He took his small figure of Krum out of his pocket, set it down on the ground, and watched it walk around. Like the real Krum, the model was slightly duck-footed and round-shouldered, much less impressive on his splayed feet than on his broomstick. Harry was listening for noise from the campsite. Everything seemed much quieter; perhaps the riot was over.

"I hope the others are okay," said Hermione after a while.

"They'll be fine," said Ron.

"Imagine if your dad catches Lucius Malfoy," said Harry, sitting down next to Ron and watching the small figure of Krum slouching over the fallen leaves. "He's always said he'd like to get something on him."

"That'd wipe the smirk off old Draco's face, all right," said Ron.

"Those poor Muggles, though," said Hermione nervously. "What if they can't get them down?"

"They will," said Ron reassuringly. "They'll find a way."

"Mad, though, to do something like that when the whole Ministry of Magic's out here tonight!" said Hermione. "I mean, how do they expect to get away with it? Do you think they've been drinking, or are they just —"

But she broke off abruptly and looked over her shoulder. Harry and Ron looked quickly around too. It sounded as though someone was staggering toward their clearing. They waited, listening to the sounds of the uneven steps behind the dark trees. But the footsteps came to a sudden halt.

"Hello?" called Harry.

There was silence. Harry got to his feet and peered around the tree. It was too dark to see very far, but he could sense somebody standing just beyond the range of his vision.

"Who's there?" he said.

And then, without warning, the silence was rent by a voice unlike any they had heard in the wood; and it uttered, not a panicked shout, but what sounded like a spell.

"*MORSMORDRE!*"

And something vast, green, and glittering erupted from the patch of darkness Harry's eyes had been struggling to penetrate; it flew up over the treetops and into the sky.

"What the — ?" gasped Ron as he sprang to his feet again, staring up at the thing that had appeared.

For a split second, Harry thought it was another leprechaun formation. Then he realized that it was a colossal skull, comprised of what looked like emerald stars, with a serpent protruding from its mouth like a tongue. As they watched, it rose higher and higher, blazing in a haze of greenish smoke, etched against the black sky like a new constellation.

Suddenly, the wood all around them erupted with screams. Harry didn't understand why, but the only possible cause was the sudden appearance of the skull, which had now risen high enough to illuminate the entire wood like some grisly neon sign. He scanned the darkness for the person who had conjured the skull, but he couldn't see anyone.

"Who's there?" he called again.

"Harry, come on, *move!*" Hermione had seized the collar of his jacket and was tugging him backward.

"What's the matter?" Harry said, startled to see her face so white and terrified.

"It's the Dark Mark, Harry!" Hermione moaned, pulling him as hard as she could. "You-Know-Who's sign!"

"*Voldemort's—?*"

"Harry, come *on!*"

Harry turned — Ron was hurriedly scooping up his miniature Krum — the three of them started across the clearing — but before they had taken a few hurried steps, a series of popping noises announced the arrival of twenty wizards, appearing from thin air, surrounding them.

Harry whirled around, and in an instant, he registered one fact: Each of these wizards had his wand out, and every wand was pointing right at himself, Ron, and Hermione.

Without pausing to think, he yelled, "DUCK!"

He seized the other two and pulled them down onto the ground.

"*STUPEFY!*" roared twenty voices — there was a blinding series of flashes and Harry felt the hair on his head ripple as though a powerful wind had swept the clearing. Raising his head a fraction of an inch he saw jets of fiery red light flying over them from the wizards' wands, crossing one another, bouncing off tree trunks, rebounding into the darkness —

"Stop!" yelled a voice he recognized. "STOP! *That's my son!*"

Harry's hair stopped blowing about. He raised his head a little higher. The wizard in front of him had lowered his wand. He rolled over and saw Mr. Weasley striding toward them, looking terrified.

"Ron — Harry" — his voice sounded shaky — "Hermione — are you all right?"

"Out of the way, Arthur," said a cold, curt voice.

It was Mr. Crouch. He and the other Ministry wizards were closing in on them. Harry got to his feet to face them. Mr. Crouch's face was taut with rage.

"Which of you did it?" he snapped, his sharp eyes darting between them. "Which of you conjured the Dark Mark?"

"We didn't do that!" said Harry, gesturing up at the skull.

"We didn't do anything!" said Ron, who was rubbing his elbow and looking indignantly at his father. "What did you want to attack us for?"

"Do not lie, sir!" shouted Mr. Crouch. His wand was still pointing directly at Ron, and his eyes were popping — he looked slightly mad. "You have been discovered at the scene of the crime!"

"Barty," whispered a witch in a long woolen dressing gown, "they're kids, Barty, they'd never have been able to —"

"Where did the Mark come from, you three?" said Mr. Weasley quickly.

"Over there," said Hermione shakily, pointing at the place where they had heard the voice. "There was someone behind the trees . . . they shouted words — an incantation —"

"Oh, stood over there, did they?" said Mr. Crouch, turning his popping eyes on Hermione now, disbelief etched all over his face. "Said an incantation, did they? You seem very well informed about how that Mark is summoned, missy —"

But none of the Ministry wizards apart from Mr. Crouch seemed to think it remotely likely that Harry, Ron, or Hermione had conjured the skull; on the contrary, at Hermione's words, they had all raised their wands again and were pointing in the direction she had indicated, squinting through the dark trees.

"We're too late," said the witch in the woolen dressing gown, shaking her head. "They'll have Disapparated."

"I don't think so," said a wizard with a scrubby brown beard. It was Amos Diggory, Cedric's father. "Our Stunners went right through those trees. . . . There's a good chance we got them. . . ."

"Amos, be careful!" said a few of the wizards warningly as Mr. Diggory squared his shoulders, raised his wand, marched across the clearing, and disappeared into the darkness. Hermione watched him vanish with her hands over her mouth.

A few seconds later, they heard Mr. Diggory shout.

"Yes! We got them! There's someone here! Unconscious! It's — but — blimey . . ."

"You've got someone?" shouted Mr. Crouch, sounding highly disbelieving. "Who? Who is it?"

They heard snapping twigs, the rustling of leaves, and then crunching footsteps as Mr. Diggory reemerged from behind the trees. He was carrying a tiny, limp figure in his arms. Harry recognized the tea towel at once. It was Winky.

Mr. Crouch did not move or speak as Mr. Diggory deposited his elf on the ground at his feet. The other Ministry wizards were all staring at Mr. Crouch. For a few seconds Crouch remained transfixed, his eyes blazing in his white face as he stared down at Winky. Then he appeared to come to life again.

"This — cannot — be," he said jerkily. "No —"

He moved quickly around Mr. Diggory and strode off toward the place where he had found Winky.

"No point, Mr. Crouch," Mr. Diggory called after him. "There's no one else there."

But Mr. Crouch did not seem prepared to take his word for it. They could hear him moving around and the rustling of leaves as he pushed the bushes aside, searching.

"Bit embarrassing," Mr. Diggory said grimly, looking down at Winky's unconscious form. "Barty Crouch's house-elf . . . I mean to say . . ."

"Come off it, Amos," said Mr. Weasley quietly, "you don't seriously think it was the elf? The Dark Mark's a wizard's sign. It requires a wand."

"Yeah," said Mr. Diggory, "and she *had* a wand."

"*What?*" said Mr. Weasley.

"Here, look." Mr. Diggory held up a wand and showed it to Mr. Weasley. "Had it in her hand. So that's clause three of the Code of Wand Use broken, for a start. *No non-human creature is permitted to carry or use a wand.*"

Just then there was another *pop,* and Ludo Bagman Apparated right next to Mr. Weasley. Looking breathless and disorientated, he spun on the spot, goggling upward at the emerald-green skull.

"The Dark Mark!" he panted, almost trampling Winky as he turned inquiringly to his colleagues. "Who did it? Did you get them? Barty! What's going on?"

Mr. Crouch had returned empty-handed. His face was still ghostly white, and his hands and his toothbrush mustache were both twitching.

"Where have you been, Barty?" said Bagman. "Why weren't you at the match? Your elf was saving you a seat too — gulping gargoyles!" Bagman had just noticed Winky lying at his feet. "What happened to *her*?"

"I have been busy, Ludo," said Mr. Crouch, still talking in the same jerky fashion, barely moving his lips. "And my elf has been Stunned."

"Stunned? By you lot, you mean? But why — ?"

Comprehension dawned suddenly on Bagman's round, shiny face; he looked up at the skull, down at Winky, and then at Mr. Crouch.

"*No!*" he said. "Winky? Conjure the Dark Mark? She wouldn't know how! She'd need a wand, for a start!"

"And she had one," said Mr. Diggory. "I found her holding one, Ludo. If it's all right with you, Mr. Crouch, I think we should hear what she's got to say for herself."

Crouch gave no sign that he had heard Mr. Diggory, but Mr. Diggory seemed to take his silence for assent. He raised his own wand, pointed it at Winky, and said, *"Rennervate!"*

Winky stirred feebly. Her great brown eyes opened and she blinked several times in a bemused sort of way. Watched by the silent wizards, she raised herself shakily into a sitting position.

She caught sight of Mr. Diggory's feet, and slowly, tremulously, raised her eyes to stare up into his face; then, more slowly still, she looked up into the sky. Harry could see the floating skull reflected twice in her enormous, glassy eyes. She gave a gasp, looked wildly around the crowded clearing, and burst into terrified sobs.

"Elf!" said Mr. Diggory sternly. "Do you know who I am? I'm a member of the Department for the Regulation and Control of Magical Creatures!"

Winky began to rock backward and forward on the ground, her breath coming in sharp bursts. Harry was reminded forcibly of Dobby in his moments of terrified disobedience.

"As you see, elf, the Dark Mark was conjured here a short while ago," said Mr. Diggory. "And you were discovered moments later, right beneath it! An explanation, if you please!"

"I — I — I is not doing it, sir!" Winky gasped. "I is not knowing how, sir!"

"You were found with a wand in your hand!" barked Mr. Diggory, brandishing it in front of her. And as the wand caught the green light that was filling the clearing from the skull above, Harry recognized it.

"Hey — that's mine!" he said.

Everyone in the clearing looked at him.

"Excuse me?" said Mr. Diggory, incredulously.

"That's my wand!" said Harry. "I dropped it!"

"You dropped it?" repeated Mr. Diggory in disbelief. "Is this a confession? You threw it aside after you conjured the Mark?"

"Amos, think who you're talking to!" said Mr. Weasley, very angrily. "Is *Harry Potter* likely to conjure the Dark Mark?"

"Er — of course not," mumbled Mr. Diggory. "Sorry . . . carried away . . ."

"I didn't drop it there, anyway," said Harry, jerking his thumb toward the trees beneath the skull. "I missed it right after we got into the wood."

"So," said Mr. Diggory, his eyes hardening as he turned to look at Winky again, cowering at his feet. "You found this wand, eh, elf? And you picked it up and thought you'd have some fun with it, did you?"

"I is not doing magic with it, sir!" squealed Winky, tears streaming down the sides of her squashed and bulbous nose. "I is . . . I is . . . I is just picking it up, sir! I is not making the Dark Mark, sir, I is not knowing how!"

"It wasn't her!" said Hermione. She looked very nervous, speaking up in front of all these Ministry wizards, yet determined all the same. "Winky's got a squeaky little voice, and the voice we heard doing the incantation was much deeper!" She looked around at Harry and Ron, appealing for their support. "It didn't sound anything like Winky, did it?"

"No," said Harry, shaking his head. "It definitely didn't sound like an elf."

"Yeah, it was a human voice," said Ron.

"Well, we'll soon see," growled Mr. Diggory, looking unimpressed. "There's a simple way of discovering the last spell a wand performed, elf, did you know that?"

Winky trembled and shook her head frantically, her ears flapping, as Mr. Diggory raised his own wand again and placed it tip to tip with Harry's.

*"Prior Incantato!"* roared Mr. Diggory.

Harry heard Hermione gasp, horrified, as a gigantic serpent-tongued skull erupted from the point where the two wands met, but it was a mere shadow of the green skull high above them; it looked as though it were made of thick gray smoke: the ghost of a spell.

*"Deletrius!"* Mr. Diggory shouted, and the smoky skull vanished in a wisp of smoke.

"So," said Mr. Diggory with a kind of savage triumph, looking down upon Winky, who was still shaking convulsively.

"I is not doing it!" she squealed, her eyes rolling in terror. "I is not, I is not, I is not knowing how! I is a good elf, I isn't using wands, I isn't knowing how!"

*"You've been caught red-handed, elf!"* Mr. Diggory roared. *"Caught with the guilty wand in your hand!"*

"Amos," said Mr. Weasley loudly, "think about it . . . precious few wizards know how to do that spell. . . . Where would she have learned it?"

"Perhaps Amos is suggesting," said Mr. Crouch, cold anger in every syllable, "that I routinely teach my servants to conjure the Dark Mark?"

There was a deeply unpleasant silence. Amos Diggory looked horrified. "Mr. Crouch . . . not . . . not at all . . ."

"You have now come very close to accusing the two people in this clearing who are *least* likely to conjure that Mark!" barked Mr. Crouch. "Harry Potter — and myself! I suppose you are familiar with the boy's story, Amos?"

"Of course — everyone knows —" muttered Mr. Diggory, looking highly discomforted.

"And I trust you remember the many proofs I have given, over a long career, that I despise and detest the Dark Arts and those who practice them?" Mr. Crouch shouted, his eyes bulging again.

"Mr. Crouch, I — I never suggested you had anything to do with it!" Amos Diggory muttered again, now reddening behind his scrubby brown beard.

"If you accuse my elf, you accuse me, Diggory!" shouted Mr. Crouch. "Where else would she have learned to conjure it?"

"She — she might've picked it up anywhere —"

"Precisely, Amos," said Mr. Weasley. "*She might have picked it up anywhere.* . . . Winky?" he said kindly, turning to the elf, but she flinched as though he too was shouting at her. "Where exactly did you find Harry's wand?"

Winky was twisting the hem of her tea towel so violently that it was fraying beneath her fingers.

"I — I is finding it . . . finding it there, sir. . . ." she whispered, "there . . . in the trees, sir. . . ."

"You see, Amos?" said Mr. Weasley. "Whoever conjured the Mark could have Disapparated right after they'd done it, leaving Harry's wand behind. A clever thing to do, not using their own wand, which could have betrayed them. And Winky here had the misfortune to come across the wand moments later and pick it up."

"But then, she'd have been only a few feet away from the real cul-prit!" said Mr. Diggory impatiently. "Elf? Did you see anyone?"

Winky began to tremble worse than ever. Her giant eyes flick-ered from Mr. Diggory, to Ludo Bagman, and onto Mr. Crouch. Then she gulped and said, "I is seeing no one, sir . . . no one . . ."

"Amos," said Mr. Crouch curtly, "I am fully aware that, in the ordinary course of events, you would want to take Winky into your department for questioning. I ask you, however, to allow me to deal with her."

Mr. Diggory looked as though he didn't think much of this suggestion at all, but it was clear to Harry that Mr. Crouch was such an important member of the Ministry that he did not dare refuse him.

"You may rest assured that she will be punished," Mr. Crouch added coldly.

"M-m-master . . ." Winky stammered, looking up at Mr. Crouch, her eyes brimming with tears. "M-m-master, p-p-please . . ."

Mr. Crouch stared back, his face somehow sharpened, each line upon it more deeply etched. There was no pity in his gaze.

"Winky has behaved tonight in a manner I would not have believed possible," he said slowly. "I told her to remain in the tent. I told her to stay there while I went to sort out the trouble. And I find that she disobeyed me. *This means clothes.*"

"No!" shrieked Winky, prostrating herself at Mr. Crouch's feet. "No, master! Not clothes, not clothes!"

Harry knew that the only way to turn a house-elf free was to present it with proper garments. It was pitiful to see the way Winky clutched at her tea towel as she sobbed over Mr. Crouch's feet.

"But she was frightened!" Hermione burst out angrily, glaring at Mr. Crouch. "Your elf's scared of heights, and those wizards in masks were levitating people! You can't blame her for wanting to get out of their way!"

Mr. Crouch took a step backward, freeing himself from contact with the elf, whom he was surveying as though she were something filthy and rotten that was contaminating his over-shined shoes.

"I have no use for a house-elf who disobeys me," he said coldly, looking over at Hermione. "I have no use for a servant who forgets what is due to her master, and to her master's reputation."

Winky was crying so hard that her sobs echoed around the clearing. There was a very nasty silence, which was ended by Mr. Weasley, who said quietly, "Well, I think I'll take my lot back to the tent, if nobody's got any objections. Amos, that wand's told us all it can — if Harry could have it back, please —"

Mr. Diggory handed Harry his wand and Harry pocketed it.

"Come on, you three," Mr. Weasley said quietly. But Hermione didn't seem to want to move; her eyes were still upon the sobbing elf. "Hermione!" Mr. Weasley said, more urgently. She turned and followed Harry and Ron out of the clearing and off through the trees.

"What's going to happen to Winky?" said Hermione, the moment they had left the clearing.

"I don't know," said Mr. Weasley.

"The way they were treating her!" said Hermione furiously. "Mr. Diggory, calling her 'elf' all the time . . . and Mr. Crouch! He knows she didn't do it and he's still going to sack her! He didn't care how frightened she'd been, or how upset she was — it was like she wasn't even human!"

"Well, she's not," said Ron.

Hermione rounded on him.

"That doesn't mean she hasn't got feelings, Ron. It's disgusting the way —"

"Hermione, I agree with you," said Mr. Weasley quickly, beckoning her on, "but now is not the time to discuss elf rights. I want to get back to the tent as fast as we can. What happened to the others?"

"We lost them in the dark," said Ron. "Dad, why was everyone so uptight about that skull thing?"

"I'll explain everything back at the tent," said Mr. Weasley tensely.

But when they reached the edge of the wood, their progress was impeded. A large crowd of frightened-looking witches and wizards was congregated there, and when they saw Mr. Weasley coming toward them, many of them surged forward.

"What's going on in there?"

"Who conjured it?"

"Arthur — it's not — *Him*?"

"Of course it's not Him," said Mr. Weasley impatiently. "We don't know who it was; it looks like they Disapparated. Now excuse me, please, I want to get to bed."

He led Harry, Ron, and Hermione through the crowd and back into the campsite. All was quiet now; there was no sign of the masked wizards, though several ruined tents were still smoking.

Charlie's head was poking out of the boys' tent.

"Dad, what's going on?" he called through the dark. "Fred, George, and Ginny got back okay, but the others —"

"I've got them here," said Mr. Weasley, bending down and entering the tent. Harry, Ron, and Hermione entered after him.

Bill was sitting at the small kitchen table, holding a bedsheet to his arm, which was bleeding profusely. Charlie had a large rip in his shirt, and Percy was sporting a bloody nose. Fred, George, and Ginny looked unhurt, though shaken.

"Did you get them, Dad?" said Bill sharply. "The person who conjured the Mark?"

"No," said Mr. Weasley. "We found Barty Crouch's elf holding

Harry's wand, but we're none the wiser about who actually conjured the Mark."

*"What?"* said Bill, Charlie, and Percy together.

"Harry's wand?" said Fred.

*"Mr. Crouch's elf?"* said Percy, sounding thunderstruck.

With some assistance from Harry, Ron, and Hermione, Mr. Weasley explained what had happened in the woods. When they had finished their story, Percy swelled indignantly.

"Well, Mr. Crouch is quite right to get rid of an elf like that!" he said. "Running away when he'd expressly told her not to . . . embarrassing him in front of the whole Ministry . . . how would that have looked, if she'd been brought up in front of the Department for the Regulation and Control —"

"She didn't do anything — she was just in the wrong place at the wrong time!" Hermione snapped at Percy, who looked very taken aback. Hermione had always got on fairly well with Percy — better, indeed, than any of the others.

"Hermione, a wizard in Mr. Crouch's position can't afford a house-elf who's going to run amok with a wand!" said Percy pompously, recovering himself.

"She didn't run amok!" shouted Hermione. "She just picked it up off the ground!"

"Look, can someone just explain what that skull thing was?" said Ron impatiently. "It wasn't hurting anyone. . . . Why's it such a big deal?"

"I told you, it's You-Know-Who's symbol, Ron," said Hermione, before anyone else could answer. "I read about it in *The Rise and Fall of the Dark Arts.*"

"And it hasn't been seen for thirteen years," said Mr. Weasley quietly. "Of course people panicked . . . it was almost like seeing You-Know-Who back again."

"I don't get it," said Ron, frowning. "I mean . . . it's still only a shape in the sky. . . ."

"Ron, You-Know-Who and his followers sent the Dark Mark into the air whenever they killed," said Mr. Weasley. "The terror it inspired . . . you have no idea, you're too young. Just picture coming home and finding the Dark Mark hovering over your house, and knowing what you're about to find inside. . . ." Mr. Weasley winced. "Everyone's worst fear . . . the very worst . . ."

There was silence for a moment. Then Bill, removing the sheet from his arm to check on his cut, said, "Well, it didn't help us tonight, whoever conjured it. It scared the Death Eaters away the moment they saw it. They all Disapparated before we'd got near enough to unmask any of them. We caught the Robertses before they hit the ground, though. They're having their memories modified right now."

"Death Eaters?" said Harry. "What are Death Eaters?"

"It's what You-Know-Who's supporters called themselves," said Bill. "I think we saw what's left of them tonight — the ones who managed to keep themselves out of Azkaban, anyway."

"We can't prove it was them, Bill," said Mr. Weasley. "Though it probably was," he added hopelessly.

"Yeah, I bet it was!" said Ron suddenly. "Dad, we met Draco Malfoy in the woods, and he as good as told us his dad was one of those nutters in masks! And we all know the Malfoys were right in with You-Know-Who!"

"But what were Voldemort's supporters —" Harry began. Everybody flinched — like most of the Wizarding world, the Weasleys always avoided saying Voldemort's name. "Sorry," said Harry quickly. "What were You-Know-Who's supporters up to, levitating Muggles? I mean, what was the point?"

"The point?" said Mr. Weasley with a hollow laugh. "Harry, that's their idea of fun. Half the Muggle killings back when You-Know-Who was in power were done for fun. I suppose they had a few drinks tonight and couldn't resist reminding us all that lots of them are still at large. A nice little reunion for them," he finished disgustedly.

"But if they *were* the Death Eaters, why did they Disapparate when they saw the Dark Mark?" said Ron. "They'd have been pleased to see it, wouldn't they?"

"Use your brains, Ron," said Bill. "If they really were Death Eaters, they worked very hard to keep out of Azkaban when You-Know-Who lost power, and told all sorts of lies about him forcing them to kill and torture people. I bet they'd be even more frightened than the rest of us to see him come back. They denied they'd ever been involved with him when he lost his powers, and went back to their daily lives. . . . I don't reckon he'd be over-pleased with them, do you?"

"So . . . whoever conjured the Dark Mark . . ." said Hermione slowly, "were they doing it to show support for the Death Eaters, or to scare them away?"

"Your guess is as good as ours, Hermione," said Mr. Weasley. "But I'll tell you this . . . it was only the Death Eaters who ever knew how to conjure it. I'd be very surprised if the person who did it hadn't been a Death Eater once, even if they're not now. . . ."

Listen, it's very late, and if your mother hears what's happened she'll be worried sick. We'll get a few more hours sleep and then try and get an early Portkey out of here."

Harry got back into his bunk with his head buzzing. He knew he ought to feel exhausted: It was nearly three in the morning, but he felt wide-awake — wide-awake, and worried.

Three days ago — it felt like much longer, but it had only been three days — he had awoken with his scar burning. And tonight, for the first time in thirteen years, Lord Voldemort's mark had appeared in the sky. What did these things mean?

He thought of the letter he had written to Sirius before leaving Privet Drive. Would Sirius have gotten it yet? When would he reply? Harry lay looking up at the canvas, but no flying fantasies came to him now to ease him to sleep, and it was a long time after Charlie's snores filled the tent that Harry finally dozed off.

# MAYHEM AT THE MINISTRY

M r. Weasley woke them after only a few hours sleep. He used magic to pack up the tents, and they left the campsite as quickly as possible, passing Mr. Roberts at the door of his cottage. Mr. Roberts had a strange, dazed look about him, and he waved them off with a vague "Merry Christmas."

"He'll be all right," said Mr. Weasley quietly as they marched off onto the moor. "Sometimes, when a person's memory's modified, it makes him a bit disorientated for a while . . . and that was a big thing they had to make him forget."

They heard urgent voices as they approached the spot where the Portkeys lay, and when they reached it, they found a great number of witches and wizards gathered around Basil, the keeper of the Portkeys, all clamoring to get away from the campsite as quickly as possible. Mr. Weasley had a hurried discussion with Basil; they joined the queue, and were able to take an old rubber tire back to Stoatshead Hill before the sun had really risen. They walked back through Ottery St. Catchpole and up the damp lane toward the Burrow in the dawn light, talking very little because they were so exhausted, and thinking longingly of their breakfast. As they rounded the corner and the Burrow came into view, a cry echoed along the lane.

"Oh thank goodness, thank goodness!"

Mrs. Weasley, who had evidently been waiting for them in the front yard, came running toward them, still wearing her bedroom slippers, her face pale and strained, a rolled-up copy of the *Daily Prophet* clutched in her hand.

"Arthur — I've been so worried — *so worried* —"

She flung her arms around Mr. Weasley's neck, and the *Daily Prophet* fell out of her limp hand onto the ground. Looking down, Harry saw the headline: *SCENES OF TERROR AT THE QUID-DITCH WORLD CUP,* complete with a twinkling black-and-white photograph of the Dark Mark over the treetops.

"You're all right," Mrs. Weasley muttered distractedly, releasing Mr. Weasley and staring around at them all with red eyes, "you're alive. . . . Oh *boys* . . . "

And to everybody's surprise, she seized Fred and George and pulled them both into such a tight hug that their heads banged together.

"*Ouch!* Mum — you're strangling us —"

"I shouted at you before you left!" Mrs. Weasley said, starting to sob. "It's all I've been thinking about! What if You-Know-Who had got you, and the last thing I ever said to you was that you didn't get enough O.W.L.s? Oh Fred . . . George . . ."

"Come on, now, Molly, we're all perfectly okay," said Mr. Weasley soothingly, prising her off the twins and leading her back toward the house. "Bill," he added in an undertone, "pick up that paper, I want to see what it says. . . ."

When they were all crammed into the tiny kitchen, and Hermione had made Mrs. Weasley a cup of very strong tea, into which Mr. Weasley insisted on pouring a shot of Ogdens Old Firewhisky, Bill handed his father the newspaper. Mr. Weasley scanned the front page while Percy looked over his shoulder.

"I knew it," said Mr. Weasley heavily. "*Ministry blunders . . . culprits not apprehended . . . lax security . . . Dark wizards running unchecked . . . national disgrace . . .* Who wrote this? Ah . . . of course . . . Rita Skeeter."

"That woman's got it in for the Ministry of Magic!" said Percy furiously. "Last week she was saying we're wasting our time quibbling about cauldron thickness, when we should be stamping out vampires! As if it wasn't *specifically* stated in paragraph twelve of the Guidelines for the Treatment of Non-Wizard Part-Humans —"

"Do us a favor, Perce," said Bill, yawning, "and shut up."

"I'm mentioned," said Mr. Weasley, his eyes widening behind his glasses as he reached the bottom of the *Daily Prophet* article.

"Where?" spluttered Mrs. Weasley, choking on her tea and whisky. "If I'd seen that, I'd have known you were alive!"

"Not by name," said Mr. Weasley. "Listen to this: *'If the terrified wizards and witches who waited breathlessly for news at the edge of the wood expected reassurance from the Ministry of Magic, they were sadly disappointed. A Ministry official emerged some time after the appearance of the Dark Mark alleging that nobody had been hurt, but refusing to give any more information. Whether this statement will be enough to quash the rumors that several bodies were removed from the woods an hour later, remains to be seen.'* Oh really," said Mr. Weasley in exasperation, handing the paper to Percy. "Nobody *was* hurt. What was I supposed to say? *Rumors that several bodies were removed from the woods . . .* well, there certainly will be rumors now she's printed that."

He heaved a deep sigh. "Molly, I'm going to have to go into the office; this is going to take some smoothing over."

"I'll come with you, Father," said Percy importantly. "Mr. Crouch will need all hands on deck. And I can give him my cauldron report in person."

He bustled out of the kitchen. Mrs. Weasley looked most upset.

"Arthur, you're supposed to be on holiday! This hasn't got anything to do with your office; surely they can handle this without you?"

"I've got to go, Molly," said Mr. Weasley. "I've made things worse. I'll just change into my robes and I'll be off. . . ."

"Mrs. Weasley," said Harry suddenly, unable to contain himself, "Hedwig hasn't arrived with a letter for me, has she?"

"Hedwig, dear?" said Mrs. Weasley distractedly. "No . . . no, there hasn't been any post at all."

Ron and Hermione looked curiously at Harry. With a meaningful look at both of them he said, "All right if I go and dump my stuff in your room, Ron?"

"Yeah . . . think I will too," said Ron at once. "Hermione?"

"Yes," she said quickly, and the three of them marched out of the kitchen and up the stairs.

"What's up, Harry?" said Ron, the moment they had closed the door of the attic room behind them.

"There's something I haven't told you," Harry said. "On Saturday morning, I woke up with my scar hurting again."

Ron's and Hermione's reactions were almost exactly as Harry had imagined them back in his bedroom on Privet Drive. Hermione gasped and started making suggestions at once, mentioning a number of reference books, and everybody from Albus Dumbledore to Madam Pomfrey, the Hogwarts nurse. Ron simply looked dumbstruck.

"But — he wasn't there, was he? You-Know-Who? I mean — last time your scar kept hurting, he was at Hogwarts, wasn't he?"

"I'm sure he wasn't on Privet Drive," said Harry. "But I was dreaming about him . . . him and Peter — you know, Wormtail. I can't remember all of it now, but they were plotting to kill . . . someone."

He had teetered for a moment on the verge of saying "me," but couldn't bring himself to make Hermione look any more horrified than she already did.

"It was only a dream," said Ron bracingly. "Just a nightmare."

"Yeah, but was it, though?" said Harry, turning to look out of the window at the brightening sky. "It's weird, isn't it? . . . My scar hurts, and three days later the Death Eaters are on the march, and Voldemort's sign's up in the sky again."

"Don't — say — his — name!" Ron hissed through gritted teeth.

"And remember what Professor Trelawney said?" Harry went on, ignoring Ron. "At the end of last year?"

Professor Trelawney was their Divination teacher at Hogwarts. Hermione's terrified look vanished as she let out a derisive snort.

"Oh Harry, you aren't going to pay attention to anything that old fraud says?"

"You weren't there," said Harry. "You didn't hear her. This time was different. I told you, she went into a trance — a real one. And she said the Dark Lord would rise again . . . *greater and more terrible than ever before* . . . and he'd manage it because his servant was going to go back to him . . . and that night Wormtail escaped."

There was a silence in which Ron fidgeted absentmindedly with a hole in his Chudley Cannons bedspread.

"Why were you asking if Hedwig had come, Harry?" Hermione asked. "Are you expecting a letter?"

"I told Sirius about my scar," said Harry, shrugging. "I'm waiting for his answer."

"Good thinking!" said Ron, his expression clearing. "I bet Sirius'll know what to do!"

"I hoped he'd get back to me quickly," said Harry.

"But we don't know where Sirius is . . . he could be in Africa or somewhere, couldn't he?" said Hermione reasonably. "Hedwig's not going to manage *that* journey in a few days."

"Yeah, I know," said Harry, but there was a leaden feeling in his stomach as he looked out of the window at the Hedwig-free sky.

"Come and have a game of Quidditch in the orchard, Harry," said Ron. "Come on — three on three, Bill and Charlie and Fred and George will play. . . . You can try out the Wronski Feint. . . ."

"Ron," said Hermione, in an I-don't-think-you're-being-very-sensitive sort of voice, "Harry doesn't want to play Quidditch right now. . . . He's worried, and he's tired. . . . We all need to go to bed. . . ."

"Yeah, I want to play Quidditch," said Harry suddenly. "Hang on, I'll get my Firebolt."

Hermione left the room, muttering something that sounded very much like *"Boys."*

Neither Mr. Weasley nor Percy was at home much over the following week. Both left the house each morning before the rest of the family got up, and returned well after dinner every night.

"It's been an absolute uproar," Percy told them importantly the Sunday evening before they were due to return to Hogwarts. "I've been putting out fires all week. People keep sending Howlers, and of course, if you don't open a Howler straight away, it explodes. Scorch marks all over my desk and my best quill reduced to cinders."

"Why are they all sending Howlers?" asked Ginny, who was mending her copy of *One Thousand Magical Herbs and Fungi* with Spellotape on the rug in front of the living room fire.

"Complaining about security at the World Cup," said Percy. "They want compensation for their ruined property. Mundungus Fletcher's put in a claim for a twelve-bedroomed tent with en-suite Jacuzzi, but I've got his number. I know for a fact he was sleeping under a cloak propped on sticks."

Mrs. Weasley glanced at the grandfather clock in the corner. Harry liked this clock. It was completely useless if you wanted to know the time, but otherwise very informative. It had nine golden hands, and each of them was engraved with one of the Weasley family's names. There were no numerals around the face, but descriptions of where each family member might be. "Home," "school," and "work" were there, but there was also "traveling," "lost," "hospital," "prison," and, in the position where the number twelve would be on a normal clock, "mortal peril."

Eight of the hands were currently pointing to the "home"

position, but Mr. Weasley's, which was the longest, was still pointing to "work." Mrs. Weasley sighed.

"Your father hasn't had to go into the office on weekends since the days of You-Know-Who," she said. "They're working him far too hard. His dinner's going to be ruined if he doesn't come home soon."

"Well, Father feels he's got to make up for his mistake at the match, doesn't he?" said Percy. "If truth be told, he was a tad unwise to make a public statement without clearing it with his Head of Department first —"

"Don't you dare blame your father for what that wretched Skeeter woman wrote!" said Mrs. Weasley, flaring up at once.

"If Dad hadn't said anything, old Rita would just have said it was disgraceful that nobody from the Ministry had commented," said Bill, who was playing chess with Ron. "Rita Skeeter never makes anyone look good. Remember, she interviewed all the Gringotts Charm Breakers once, and called me 'a long-haired pillock'?"

"Well, it *is* a bit long, dear," said Mrs. Weasley gently. "If you'd just let me —"

"*No,* Mum."

Rain lashed against the living room window. Hermione was immersed in *The Standard Book of Spells, Grade 4,* copies of which Mrs. Weasley had bought for her, Harry, and Ron in Diagon Alley. Charlie was darning a fireproof balaclava. Harry was polishing his Firebolt, the broomstick servicing kit Hermione had given him for his thirteenth birthday open at his feet. Fred and George were sitting in a far corner, quills out, talking in whispers, their heads bent over a piece of parchment.

"What are you two up to?" said Mrs. Weasley sharply, her eyes on the twins.

"Homework," said Fred vaguely.

"Don't be ridiculous, you're still on holiday," said Mrs. Weasley.

"Yeah, we've left it a bit late," said George.

"You're not by any chance writing out a new *order form,* are you?" said Mrs. Weasley shrewdly. "You wouldn't be thinking of restarting Weasleys' Wizard Wheezes, by any chance?".

"Now, Mum," said Fred, looking up at her, a pained look on his face. "If the Hogwarts Express crashed tomorrow, and George and I died, how would you feel to know that the last thing we ever heard from you was an unfounded accusation?"

Everyone laughed, even Mrs. Weasley.

"Oh your father's coming!" she said suddenly, looking up at the clock again.

Mr. Weasley's hand had suddenly spun from "work" to "traveling"; a second later it had shuddered to a halt on "home" with the others, and they heard him calling from the kitchen.

"Coming, Arthur!" called Mrs. Weasley, hurrying out of the room.

A few moments later, Mr. Weasley came into the warm living room carrying his dinner on a tray. He looked completely exhausted.

"Well, the fat's really in the fire now," he told Mrs. Weasley as he sat down in an armchair near the hearth and toyed unenthusiastically with his somewhat shriveled cauliflower. "Rita Skeeter's been ferreting around all week, looking for more Ministry mess-ups to report. And now she's found out about poor old Bertha going missing, so that'll be the headline in the *Prophet* tomorrow. I *told* Bagman he should have sent someone to look for her ages ago."

"Mr. Crouch has been saying it for weeks and weeks," said Percy swiftly.

"Crouch is very lucky Rita hasn't found out about Winky," said Mr. Weasley irritably. "There'd be a week's worth of headlines in his house-elf being caught holding the wand that conjured the Dark Mark."

"I thought we were all agreed that that elf, while irresponsible, did *not* conjure the Mark?" said Percy hotly.

"If you ask me, Mr. Crouch is very lucky no one at the *Daily Prophet* knows how mean he is to elves!" said Hermione angrily.

"Now look here, Hermione!" said Percy. "A high-ranking Ministry official like Mr. Crouch deserves unswerving obedience from his servants —"

"His *slave,* you mean!" said Hermione, her voice rising passionately, "because he didn't *pay* Winky, did he?"

"I think you'd all better go upstairs and check that you've packed properly!" said Mrs. Weasley, breaking up the argument. "Come on now, all of you. . . ."

Harry repacked his broomstick servicing kit, put his Firebolt over his shoulder, and went back upstairs with Ron. The rain sounded even louder at the top of the house, accompanied by loud whistlings and moans from the wind, not to mention sporadic howls from the ghoul who lived in the attic. Pigwidgeon began twittering and zooming around his cage when they entered. The sight of the half-packed trunks seemed to have sent him into a frenzy of excitement.

"Bung him some Owl Treats," said Ron, throwing a packet across to Harry. "It might shut him up."

Harry poked a few Owl Treats through the bars of Pigwidgeon's cage, then turned to his trunk. Hedwig's cage stood next to it, still empty.

"It's been over a week," Harry said, looking at Hedwig's deserted perch. "Ron, you don't reckon Sirius has been caught, do you?"

"Nah, it would've been in the *Daily Prophet*," said Ron. "The Ministry would want to show they'd caught *someone*, wouldn't they?"

"Yeah, I suppose. . . ."

"Look, here's the stuff Mum got for you in Diagon Alley. And she's got some gold out of your vault for you . . . and she's washed all your socks."

He heaved a pile of parcels onto Harry's camp bed and dropped the money bag and a load of socks next to it. Harry started unwrapping the shopping. Apart from *The Standard Book of Spells, Grade 4,* by Miranda Goshawk, he had a handful of new quills, a dozen rolls of parchment, and refills for his potion-making kit — he had been running low on spine of lionfish and essence of belladonna. He was just piling underwear into his cauldron when Ron made a loud noise of disgust behind him.

"What is *that* supposed to be?"

He was holding up something that looked to Harry like a long, maroon velvet dress. It had a moldy-looking lace frill at the collar and matching lace cuffs.

There was a knock on the door, and Mrs. Weasley entered, carrying an armful of freshly laundered Hogwarts robes.

"Here you are," she said, sorting them into two piles. "Now, mind you pack them properly so they don't crease."

"Mum, you've given me Ginny's new dress," said Ron, handing it out to her.

"Of course I haven't," said Mrs. Weasley. "That's for you. Dress robes."

*"What?"* said Ron, looking horror-struck.

"Dress robes!" repeated Mrs. Weasley. "It says on your school list that you're supposed to have dress robes this year . . . robes for formal occasions."

"You've got to be kidding," said Ron in disbelief. "I'm not wearing that, no way."

"Everyone wears them, Ron!" said Mrs. Weasley crossly. "They're all like that! Your father's got some for smart parties!"

"I'll go starkers before I put that on," said Ron stubbornly.

"Don't be so silly," said Mrs. Weasley. "You've got to have dress robes, they're on your list! I got some for Harry too . . . show him, Harry. . . ."

In some trepidation, Harry opened the last parcel on his camp bed. It wasn't as bad as he had expected, however; his dress robes didn't have any lace on them at all — in fact, they were more or less the same as his school ones, except that they were bottle green instead of black.

"I thought they'd bring out the color of your eyes, dear," said Mrs. Weasley fondly.

"Well, they're okay!" said Ron angrily, looking at Harry's robes. "Why couldn't I have some like that?"

"Because . . . well, I had to get yours secondhand, and there wasn't a lot of choice!" said Mrs. Weasley, flushing.

Harry looked away. He would willingly have split all the money in his Gringotts vault with the Weasleys, but he knew they would never take it.

"I'm never wearing them," Ron was saying stubbornly. "Never."

"Fine," snapped Mrs. Weasley. "Go naked. And, Harry, make sure you get a picture of him. Goodness knows I could do with a laugh."

She left the room, slamming the door behind her. There was a funny spluttering noise from behind them. Pigwidgeon was choking on an overlarge Owl Treat.

"Why is everything I own rubbish?" said Ron furiously, striding across the room to unstick Pigwidgeon's beak.

# ABOARD THE
# HOGWARTS EXPRESS

There was a definite end-of-the-holidays gloom in the air when Harry awoke next morning. Heavy rain was still splattering against the window as he got dressed in jeans and a sweatshirt; they would change into their school robes on the Hogwarts Express.

He, Ron, Fred, and George had just reached the first-floor landing on their way down to breakfast, when Mrs. Weasley appeared at the foot of the stairs, looking harassed.

"Arthur!" she called up the staircase. "Arthur! Urgent message from the Ministry!"

Harry flattened himself against the wall as Mr. Weasley came clattering past with his robes on back-to-front and hurtled out of sight. When Harry and the others entered the kitchen, they saw Mrs. Weasley rummaging anxiously in the drawers — "I've got a quill here somewhere!" — and Mr. Weasley bending over the fire, talking to —

Harry shut his eyes hard and opened them again to make sure that they were working properly.

Amos Diggory's head was sitting in the middle of the flames like a large, bearded egg. It was talking very fast, completely unperturbed by the sparks flying around it and the flames licking its ears.

". . . Muggle neighbors heard bangs and shouting, so they went and called those what-d'you-call-'ems — please-men. Arthur, you've got to get over there —"

"Here!" said Mrs. Weasley breathlessly, pushing a piece of parchment, a bottle of ink, and a crumpled quill into Mr. Weasley's hands.

"— it's a real stroke of luck I heard about it," said Mr. Diggory's head. "I had to come into the office early to send a couple of owls, and I found the Improper Use of Magic lot all setting off— if Rita Skeeter gets hold of this one, Arthur —"

"What does Mad-Eye say happened?" asked Mr. Weasley, unscrewing the ink bottle, loading up his quill, and preparing to take notes.

Mr. Diggory's head rolled its eyes. "Says he heard an intruder in his yard. Says he was creeping toward the house, but was ambushed by his dustbins."

"What did the dustbins do?" asked Mr. Weasley, scribbling frantically.

"Made one hell of a noise and fired rubbish everywhere, as far as I can tell," said Mr. Diggory. "Apparently one of them was still rocketing around when the please-men turned up —"

Mr. Weasley groaned.

"And what about the intruder?"

"Arthur, you know Mad-Eye," said Mr. Diggory's head, rolling its eyes again. "Someone creeping into his yard in the dead of night? More likely there's a very shell-shocked cat wandering around somewhere, covered in potato peelings. But if the Improper Use of Magic lot get their hands on Mad-Eye, he's had it — think of his record — we've got to get him off on a minor charge, something in your department — what are exploding dustbins worth?"

"Might be a caution," said Mr. Weasley, still writing very fast, his brow furrowed. "Mad-Eye didn't use his wand? He didn't actually attack anyone?"

"I'll bet he leapt out of bed and started jinxing everything he could reach through the window," said Mr. Diggory, "but they'll have a job proving it, there aren't any casualties."

"All right, I'm off," Mr. Weasley said, and he stuffed the parchment with his notes on it into his pocket and dashed out of the kitchen again.

Mr. Diggory's head looked around at Mrs. Weasley.

"Sorry about this, Molly," it said, more calmly, "bothering you so early and everything . . . but Arthur's the only one who can get Mad-Eye off, and Mad-Eye's supposed to be starting his new job today. Why he had to choose last night . . ."

"Never mind, Amos," said Mrs. Weasley. "Sure you won't have a bit of toast or anything before you go?"

"Oh go on, then," said Mr. Diggory.

Mrs. Weasley took a piece of buttered toast from a stack on the kitchen table, put it into the fire tongs, and transferred it into Mr. Diggory's mouth.

"Fanks," he said in a muffled voice, and then, with a small *pop*, vanished.

Harry could hear Mr. Weasley calling hurried good-byes to Bill,

Charlie, Percy, and the girls. Within five minutes, he was back in the kitchen, his robes on the right way now, dragging a comb through his hair.

"I'd better hurry — you have a good term, boys," said Mr. Weasley to Harry, Ron, and the twins, fastening a cloak over his shoulders and preparing to Disapparate. "Molly, are you going to be all right taking the kids to King's Cross?"

"Of course I will," she said. "You just look after Mad-Eye, we'll be fine."

As Mr. Weasley vanished, Bill and Charlie entered the kitchen.

"Did someone say Mad-Eye?" Bill asked. "What's he been up to now?"

"He says someone tried to break into his house last night," said Mrs. Weasley.

"Mad-Eye Moody?" said George thoughtfully, spreading marmalade on his toast. "Isn't he that nutter —"

"Your father thinks very highly of Mad-Eye Moody," said Mrs. Weasley sternly.

"Yeah, well, Dad collects plugs, doesn't he?" said Fred quietly as Mrs. Weasley left the room. "Birds of a feather . . ."

"Moody was a great wizard in his time," said Bill.

"He's an old friend of Dumbledore's, isn't he?" said Charlie.

"Dumbledore's not what you'd call *normal*, though, is he?" said Fred. "I mean, I know he's a genius and everything . . ."

"Who *is* Mad-Eye?" asked Harry.

"He's retired, used to work at the Ministry," said Charlie. "I met him once when Dad took me in to work with him. He was an Auror — one of the best . . . a Dark wizard catcher," he added, seeing Harry's blank look. "Half the cells in Azkaban are full because of him. He made himself loads of enemies, though . . . the families of people he caught, mainly . . . and I heard he's been getting really paranoid in his old age. Doesn't trust anyone anymore. Sees Dark wizards everywhere."

Bill and Charlie decided to come and see everyone off at King's Cross station, but Percy, apologizing most profusely, said that he really needed to get to work.

"I just can't justify taking more time off at the moment," he told them. "Mr. Crouch is really starting to rely on me."

"Yeah, you know what, Percy?" said George seriously. "I reckon he'll know your name soon."

Mrs. Weasley had braved the telephone in the village post office to order three ordinary Muggle taxis to take them into London.

"Arthur tried to borrow Ministry cars for us," Mrs. Weasley whispered to Harry as they stood in the rain-washed yard, watching the taxi drivers heaving six heavy Hogwarts trunks into their cars. "But there weren't any to spare. . . . Oh dear, they don't look happy, do they?"

Harry didn't like to tell Mrs. Weasley that Muggle taxi drivers rarely transported overexcited owls, and Pigwidgeon was making an earsplitting racket. Nor did it help that a number of Filibuster's Fabulous Wet-Start, No-Heat Fireworks went off unexpectedly when Fred's trunk sprang open, causing the driver carrying it to yell with fright and pain as Crookshanks clawed his way up the man's leg.

The journey was uncomfortable, owing to the fact that they were jammed in the back of the taxis with their trunks. Crookshanks took quite a while to recover from the fireworks, and by the time they entered London, Harry, Ron, and Hermione were all severely scratched. They were very relieved to get out at King's Cross, even though the rain was coming down harder than ever, and they got soaked carrying their trunks across the busy road and into the station.

Harry was used to getting onto platform nine and three-quarters by now. It was a simple matter of walking straight through the apparently solid barrier dividing platforms nine and ten. The only tricky part was doing this in an unobtrusive way, so as to avoid attracting Muggle attention. They did it in groups today; Harry, Ron, and Hermione (the most conspicuous, since they were accompanied by Pigwidgeon and Crookshanks) went first; they leaned casually against the barrier, chatting unconcernedly, and slid sideways through it . . . and as they did so, platform nine and three-quarters materialized in front of them.

The Hogwarts Express, a gleaming scarlet steam engine, was already there, clouds of steam billowing from it, through which the many Hogwarts students and parents on the platform appeared like dark ghosts. Pigwidgeon became noisier than ever in response to the hooting of many owls through the mist. Harry, Ron, and Hermione set off to find seats, and were soon stowing their luggage in a compartment halfway along the train. They then hopped back down onto the platform to say good-bye to Mrs. Weasley, Bill, and Charlie.

"I might be seeing you all sooner than you think," said Charlie, grinning, as he hugged Ginny good-bye.

"Why?" said Fred keenly.

"You'll see," said Charlie. "Just don't tell Percy I mentioned it . . . it's 'classified information, until such time as the Ministry sees fit to release it,' after all."

"Yeah, I sort of wish I were back at Hogwarts this year," said Bill, hands in his pockets, looking almost wistfully at the train.

"*Why?*" said George impatiently.

"You're going to have an interesting year," said Bill, his eyes twinkling. "I might even get time off to come and watch a bit of it. . . ."

"A bit of *what*?" said Ron.

But at that moment, the whistle blew, and Mrs. Weasley chivvied them toward the train doors.

"Thanks for having us to stay, Mrs. Weasley," said Hermione as they climbed on board, closed the door, and leaned out of the window to talk to her.

"Yeah, thanks for everything, Mrs. Weasley," said Harry.

"Oh it was my pleasure, dears," said Mrs. Weasley. "I'd invite you for Christmas, but . . . well, I expect you're all going to want to stay at Hogwarts, what with . . . one thing and another."

"Mum!" said Ron irritably. "What d'you three know that we don't?"

"You'll find out this evening, I expect," said Mrs. Weasley, smiling. "It's going to be very exciting — mind you, I'm very glad they've changed the rules —"

"What rules?" said Harry, Ron, Fred, and George together.

"I'm sure Professor Dumbledore will tell you. . . . Now, behave, won't you? *Won't* you, Fred? And you, George?"

The pistons hissed loudly and the train began to move.

"Tell us what's happening at Hogwarts!" Fred bellowed out of the window as Mrs. Weasley, Bill, and Charlie sped away from them. "What rules are they changing?"

But Mrs. Weasley only smiled and waved. Before the train had rounded the corner, she, Bill, and Charlie had Disapparated.

Harry, Ron, and Hermione went back to their compartment. The thick rain splattering the windows made it very difficult to see out of them. Ron undid his trunk, pulled out his maroon dress robes, and flung them over Pigwidgeon's cage to muffle his hooting.

"Bagman wanted to tell us what's happening at Hogwarts," he said grumpily, sitting down next to Harry. "At the World Cup, remember? But my own mother won't say. Wonder what —"

"Shh!" Hermione whispered suddenly, pressing her finger to her lips and pointing toward the compartment next to theirs. Harry and Ron listened, and heard a familiar drawling voice drifting in through the open door.

". . . Father actually considered sending me to Durmstrang rather than Hogwarts, you know. He knows the headmaster, you see. Well, you know his opinion of Dumbledore — the man's such a Mudblood-lover — and Durmstrang doesn't admit that sort of riffraff. But Mother didn't like the idea of me going to school so far away. Father says Durmstrang takes a far more sensible line than Hogwarts about the Dark Arts. Durmstrang students actually *learn* them, not just the defense rubbish we do. . . ."

Hermione got up, tiptoed to the compartment door, and slid it shut, blocking out Malfoy's voice.

"So he thinks Durmstrang would have suited him, does he?" she said angrily. "I wish he *had* gone, then we wouldn't have to put up with him."

"Durmstrang's another Wizarding school?" said Harry.

"Yes," said Hermione sniffily, "and it's got a horrible reputation. According to *An Appraisal of Magical Education in Europe,* it puts a lot of emphasis on the Dark Arts."

"I think I've heard of it," said Ron vaguely. "Where is it? What country?"

"Well, nobody knows, do they?" said Hermione, raising her eyebrows.

"Er — why not?" said Harry.

"There's traditionally been a lot of rivalry between all the magic schools. Durmstrang and Beauxbatons like to conceal their whereabouts so nobody can steal their secrets," said Hermione matter-of-factly.

"Come off it," said Ron, starting to laugh. "Durmstrang's got to be about the same size as Hogwarts — how are you going to hide a great big castle?"

"But Hogwarts *is* hidden," said Hermione, in surprise. "Everyone knows that . . . well, everyone who's read *Hogwarts: A History,* anyway."

"Just you, then," said Ron. "So go on — how d'you hide a place like Hogwarts?"

"It's bewitched," said Hermione. "If a Muggle looks at it, all they see is a moldering old ruin with a sign over the entrance saying DANGER, DO NOT ENTER, UNSAFE."

"So Durmstrang'll just look like a ruin to an outsider too?"

"Maybe," said Hermione, shrugging, "or it might have Muggle-repelling charms on it, like the World Cup stadium. And to keep foreign wizards from finding it, they'll have made it Unplottable —"

"Come again?"

"Well, you can enchant a building so it's impossible to plot on a map, can't you?"

"Er . . . if you say so," said Harry.

"But I think Durmstrang must be somewhere in the far north," said Hermione thoughtfully. "Somewhere very cold, because they've got fur capes as part of their uniforms."

"Ah, think of the possibilities," said Ron dreamily. "It would've been so easy to push Malfoy off a glacier and make it look like an accident. . . . Shame his mother likes him. . . ."

The rain became heavier and heavier as the train moved farther north. The sky was so dark and the windows so steamy that the lanterns were lit by midday. The lunch trolley came rattling along the corridor, and Harry bought a large stack of Cauldron Cakes for them to share.

Several of their friends looked in on them as the afternoon progressed, including Seamus Finnigan, Dean Thomas, and Neville Longbottom, a round-faced, extremely forgetful boy who had been brought up by his formidable witch of a grandmother. Seamus was still wearing his Ireland rosette. Some of its magic seemed to be wearing off now; it was still squeaking *"Troy — Mullet — Moran!"* but in a very feeble and exhausted sort of way. After half an hour or so, Hermione, growing tired of the endless Quidditch talk, buried herself once more in *The Standard Book of Spells, Grade 4,* and started trying to learn a Summoning Charm.

Neville listened jealously to the others' conversation as they relived the Cup match.

"Gran didn't want to go," he said miserably. "Wouldn't buy tickets. It sounded amazing though."

"It was," said Ron. "Look at this, Neville. . . ."

He rummaged in his trunk up in the luggage rack and pulled out the miniature figure of Viktor Krum.

"Oh *wow*," said Neville enviously as Ron tipped Krum onto his pudgy hand.

"We saw him right up close, as well," said Ron. "We were in the Top Box —"

"For the first and last time in your life, Weasley."

Draco Malfoy had appeared in the doorway. Behind him stood Crabbe and Goyle, his enormous, thuggish cronies, both of whom appeared to have grown at least a foot during the summer. Evidently they had overheard the conversation through the compartment door, which Dean and Seamus had left ajar.

"Don't remember asking you to join us, Malfoy," said Harry coolly.

"Weasley . . . what is *that*?" said Malfoy, pointing at Pigwidgeon's cage. A sleeve of Ron's dress robes was dangling from it, swaying with the motion of the train, the moldy lace cuff very obvious.

Ron made to stuff the robes out of sight, but Malfoy was too quick for him; he seized the sleeve and pulled.

"Look at this!" said Malfoy in ecstasy, holding up Ron's robes and showing Crabbe and Goyle, "Weasley, you weren't thinking of *wearing* these, were you? I mean — they were very fashionable in about 1890. . . ."

"Eat dung, Malfoy!" said Ron; the same color as the dress robes as he snatched them back out of Malfoy's grip. Malfoy howled with derisive laughter; Crabbe and Goyle guffawed stupidly.

"So . . . going to enter, Weasley? Going to try and bring a

bit of glory to the family name? There's money involved as well, you know . . . you'd be able to afford some decent robes if you won. . . ."

"What are you talking about?" snapped Ron.

*"Are you going to enter?"* Malfoy repeated. "I suppose *you* will, Potter? You never miss a chance to show off, do you?"

"Either explain what you're on about or go away, Malfoy," said Hermione testily, over the top of *The Standard Book of Spells, Grade 4.*

A gleeful smile spread across Malfoy's pale face.

"Don't tell me you don't *know?*" he said delightedly. "You've got a father and brother at the Ministry and you don't even *know?* My God, *my* father told me about it ages ago . . . heard it from Cornelius Fudge. But then, Father's always associated with the top people at the Ministry. . . . Maybe your father's too junior to know about it, Weasley . . . yes . . . they probably don't talk about important stuff in front of him. . . ."

Laughing once more, Malfoy beckoned to Crabbe and Goyle, and the three of them disappeared.

Ron got to his feet and slammed the sliding compartment door so hard behind them that the glass shattered.

"*Ron!*" said Hermione reproachfully, and she pulled out her wand, muttered *"Reparo!"* and the glass shards flew back into a single pane and back into the door.

"Well . . . making it look like he knows everything and we don't. . . ." Ron snarled. "*Father's always associated with the top people at the Ministry.'*. . . Dad could've got a promotion any time . . . he just likes it where he is. . . ."

"Of course he does," said Hermione quietly. "Don't let Malfoy get to you, Ron —"

"Him! Get to me!? As if!" said Ron, picking up one of the remaining Cauldron Cakes and squashing it into a pulp.

Ron's bad mood continued for the rest of the journey. He didn't talk much as they changed into their school robes, and was still glowering when the Hogwarts Express slowed down at last and finally stopped in the pitch-darkness of Hogsmeade station.

As the train doors opened, there was a rumble of thunder overhead. Hermione bundled up Crookshanks in her cloak and Ron left his dress robes over Pigwidgeon as they left the train, heads bent and eyes narrowed against the downpour. The rain was now coming down so thick and fast that it was as though buckets of ice-cold water were being emptied repeatedly over their heads.

"Hi, Hagrid!" Harry yelled, seeing a gigantic silhouette at the far end of the platform.

"All righ', Harry?" Hagrid bellowed back, waving. "See yeh at the feast if we don' drown!"

First years traditionally reached Hogwarts Castle by sailing across the lake with Hagrid.

"Oooh, I wouldn't fancy crossing the lake in this weather," said Hermione fervently, shivering as they inched slowly along the dark platform with the rest of the crowd. A hundred horseless carriages stood waiting for them outside the station. Harry, Ron, Hermione, and Neville climbed gratefully into one of them, the door shut with a snap, and a few moments later, with a great lurch, the long procession of carriages was rumbling and splashing its way up the track toward Hogwarts Castle.

# THE TRIWIZARD
# TOURNAMENT

Through the gates, flanked with statues of winged boars, and up the sweeping drive the carriages trundled, swaying dangerously in what was fast becoming a gale. Leaning against the window, Harry could see Hogwarts coming nearer, its many lighted windows blurred and shimmering behind the thick curtain of rain. Lightning flashed across the sky as their carriage came to a halt before the great oak front doors, which stood at the top of a flight of stone steps. People who had occupied the carriages in front were already hurrying up the stone steps into the castle. Harry, Ron, Hermione, and Neville jumped down from their carriage and dashed up the steps too, looking up only when they were safely inside the cavernous, torch-lit entrance hall, with its magnificent marble staircase.

"Blimey," said Ron, shaking his head and sending water everywhere, "if that keeps up the lake's going to overflow. I'm soak — ARRGH!"

A large, red, water-filled balloon had dropped from out of the ceiling onto Ron's head and exploded. Drenched and sputtering, Ron staggered sideways into Harry, just as a second water bomb dropped — narrowly missing Hermione, it burst at Harry's feet, sending a wave of cold water over his sneakers into his socks. People all around them shrieked and started pushing one another in their efforts to get out of the line of fire. Harry looked up and saw, floating twenty feet above them, Peeves the Poltergeist, a little man in a bell-covered hat and orange bow tie, his wide, malicious face contorted with concentration as he took aim again.

"PEEVES!" yelled an angry voice. "Peeves, come down here at ONCE!"

Professor McGonagall, deputy headmistress and Head of Gryffindor House, had come dashing out of the Great Hall; she skidded on the wet floor and grabbed Hermione around the neck to stop herself from falling.

"Ouch — sorry, Miss Granger —"

"That's all right, Professor!" Hermione gasped, massaging her throat.

"Peeves, get down here NOW!" barked Professor McGonagall, straightening her pointed hat and glaring upward through her square-rimmed spectacles.

"Not doing nothing!" cackled Peeves, lobbing a water bomb at several fifth-year girls, who screamed and dived into the Great Hall. "Already wet, aren't they? Little squirts! Wheeeeeeeeee!" And he aimed another bomb at a group of second years who had just arrived.

"I shall call the headmaster!" shouted Professor McGonagall. "I'm warning you, Peeves —"

Peeves stuck out his tongue, threw the last of his water bombs into the air, and zoomed off up the marble staircase, cackling insanely.

"Well, move along, then!" said Professor McGonagall sharply to the bedraggled crowd. "Into the Great Hall, come on!"

Harry, Ron, and Hermione slipped and slid across the entrance hall and through the double doors on the right, Ron muttering furiously under his breath as he pushed his sopping hair off his face.

The Great Hall looked its usual splendid self, decorated for the start-of-term feast. Golden plates and goblets gleamed by the light of hundreds and hundreds of candles, floating over the tables in midair. The four long House tables were packed with chattering students; at the top of the Hall, the staff sat along one side of a fifth table, facing their pupils. It was much warmer in here. Harry, Ron, and Hermione walked past the Slytherins, the Ravenclaws, and the Hufflepuffs, and sat down with the rest of the Gryffindors at the far side of the Hall, next to Nearly Headless Nick, the Gryffindor ghost. Pearly white and semitransparent, Nick was dressed tonight in his usual doublet, but with a particularly large ruff, which served the dual purpose of looking extra-festive, and insuring that his head didn't wobble too much on his partially severed neck.

"Good evening," he said, beaming at them.

"Says who?" said Harry, taking off his sneakers and emptying them of water. "Hope they hurry up with the Sorting. I'm starving."

The Sorting of the new students into Houses took place at the start of every school year, but by an unlucky combination of circumstances, Harry hadn't been present at one since his own. He

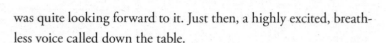

was quite looking forward to it. Just then, a highly excited, breathless voice called down the table.

"Hiya, Harry!"

It was Colin Creevey, a third year to whom Harry was something of a hero.

"Hi, Colin," said Harry warily.

"Harry, guess what? Guess what, Harry? My brother's starting! My brother Dennis!"

"Er — good," said Harry.

"He's really excited!" said Colin, practically bouncing up and down in his seat. "I just hope he's in Gryffindor! Keep your fingers crossed, eh, Harry?"

"Er — yeah, all right," said Harry. He turned back to Hermione, Ron, and Nearly Headless Nick. "Brothers and sisters usually go in the same Houses, don't they?" he said. He was judging by the Weasleys, all seven of whom had been put into Gryffindor.

"Oh no, not necessarily," said Hermione. "Parvati Patil's twin's in Ravenclaw, and they're identical. You'd think they'd be together, wouldn't you?"

Harry looked up at the staff table. There seemed to be rather more empty seats there than usual. Hagrid, of course, was still fighting his way across the lake with the first years; Professor McGonagall was presumably supervising the drying of the entrance hall floor, but there was another empty chair too, and Harry couldn't think who else was missing.

"Where's the new Defense Against the Dark Arts teacher?" said Hermione, who was also looking up at the teachers.

They had never yet had a Defense Against the Dark Arts teacher who had lasted more than three terms. Harry's favorite by far had been Professor Lupin, who had resigned last year. He looked up and down the staff table. There was definitely no new face there.

"Maybe they couldn't get anyone!" said Hermione, looking anxious.

Harry scanned the table more carefully. Tiny little Professor Flitwick, the Charms teacher, was sitting on a large pile of cushions beside Professor Sprout, the Herbology teacher, whose hat was askew over her flyaway gray hair. She was talking to Professor Sinistra of the Astronomy department. On Professor Sinistra's other side was the sallow-faced, hook-nosed, greasy-haired Potions master, Snape — Harry's least favorite person at Hogwarts. Harry's loathing of Snape was matched only by Snape's hatred of him, a hatred which had, if possible, intensified last year, when Harry had helped Sirius escape right under Snape's overlarge nose — Snape and Sirius had been enemies since their own school days.

On Snape's other side was an empty seat, which Harry guessed was Professor McGonagall's. Next to it, and in the very center of the table, sat Professor Dumbledore, the headmaster, his sweeping silver hair and beard shining in the candlelight, his magnificent deep green robes embroidered with many stars and moons. The tips of Dumbledore's long, thin fingers were together and he was resting his chin upon them, staring up at the ceiling through his half-moon spectacles as though lost in thought. Harry glanced up at the ceiling too. It was enchanted to look like the sky outside, and he had never seen it look this stormy. Black and purple clouds were swirling across it, and as another thunderclap sounded outside, a fork of lightning flashed across it.

"Oh hurry up," Ron moaned, beside Harry, "I could eat a hippogriff."

The words were no sooner out of his mouth than the doors of the Great Hall opened and silence fell. Professor McGonagall was leading a long line of first years up to the top of the Hall. If Harry, Ron, and Hermione were wet, it was nothing to how these first years looked. They appeared to have swum across the lake rather than sailed. All of them were shivering with a combination of cold and nerves as they filed along the staff table and came to a halt in a line facing the rest of the school — all of them except the smallest of the lot, a boy with mousy hair, who was wrapped in what Harry recognized as Hagrid's moleskin overcoat. The coat was so big for him that it looked as though he were draped in a furry black circus tent. His small face protruded from over the collar, looking almost painfully excited. When he had lined up with his terrified-looking peers, he caught Colin Creevey's eye, gave a double thumbs-up, and mouthed, *I fell in the lake!* He looked positively delighted about it.

Professor McGonagall now placed a four-legged stool on the ground before the first years and, on top of it, an extremely old, dirty, patched wizard's hat. The first years stared at it. So did everyone else. For a moment, there was silence. Then a long tear near the brim opened wide like a mouth, and the hat broke into song:

> *A thousand years or more ago,*
> *When I was newly sewn,*
> *There lived four wizards of renown,*
> *Whose names are still well known:*
> *Bold Gryffindor, from wild moor,*
> *Fair Ravenclaw, from glen,*
> *Sweet Hufflepuff, from valley broad,*

*Shrewd Slytherin, from fen.*
*They shared a wish, a hope, a dream,*
*They hatched a daring plan*
*To educate young sorcerers*
*Thus Hogwarts School began.*
*Now each of these four founders*
*Formed their own House, for each*
*Did value different virtues*
*In the ones they had to teach.*
*By Gryffindor, the bravest were*
*Prized far beyond the rest;*
*For Ravenclaw, the cleverest*
*Would always be the best;*
*For Hufflepuff, hard workers were*
*Most worthy of admission;*
*And power-hungry Slytherin*
*Loved those of great ambition.*
*While still alive they did divide*
*Their favorites from the throng,*
*Yet how to pick the worthy ones*
*When they were dead and gone?*
*'Twas Gryffindor who found the way,*
*He whipped me off his head.*
*The founders put some brains in me*
*So I could choose instead!*
*Now slip me snug about your ears,*
*I've never yet been wrong,*
*I'll have a look inside your mind*
*And tell where you belong!*

The Great Hall rang with applause as the Sorting Hat finished.

"That's not the song it sang when it Sorted us," said Harry, clapping along with everyone else.

"Sings a different one every year," said Ron. "It's got to be a pretty boring life, hasn't it, being a hat? I suppose it spends all year making up the next one."

Professor McGonagall was now unrolling a large scroll of parchment.

"When I call out your name, you will put on the hat and sit on the stool," she told the first years. "When the hat announces your House, you will go and sit at the appropriate table.

"Ackerley, Stewart!"

A boy walked forward, visibly trembling from head to foot, picked up the Sorting Hat, put it on, and sat down on the stool.

"RAVENCLAW!" shouted the hat.

Stewart Ackerley took off the hat and hurried into a seat at the Ravenclaw table, where everyone was applauding him. Harry caught a glimpse of Cho, the Ravenclaw Seeker, cheering Stewart Ackerley as he sat down. For a fleeting second, Harry had a strange desire to join the Ravenclaw table too.

"Baddock, Malcolm!"

"SLYTHERIN!"

The table on the other side of the hall erupted with cheers; Harry could see Malfoy clapping as Baddock joined the Slytherins. Harry wondered whether Baddock knew that Slytherin House had turned out more Dark witches and wizards than any other. Fred and George hissed Malcolm Baddock as he sat down.

"Branstone, Eleanor!"

"HUFFLEPUFF!"

"Cauldwell, Owen!"

"HUFFLEPUFF!"

"Creevey, Dennis!"

Tiny Dennis Creevey staggered forward, tripping over Hagrid's moleskin, just as Hagrid himself sidled into the Hall through a door behind the teachers' table. About twice as tall as a normal man, and at least three times as broad, Hagrid, with his long, wild, tangled black hair and beard, looked slightly alarming — a misleading impression, for Harry, Ron, and Hermione knew Hagrid to possess a very kind nature. He winked at them as he sat down at the end of the staff table and watched Dennis Creevey putting on the Sorting Hat. The rip at the brim opened wide —

"GRYFFINDOR!" the hat shouted.

Hagrid clapped along with the Gryffindors as Dennis Creevey, beaming widely, took off the hat, placed it back on the stool, and hurried over to join his brother.

"Colin, I fell in!" he said shrilly, throwing himself into an empty seat. "It was brilliant! And something in the water grabbed me and pushed me back in the boat!"

"Cool!" said Colin, just as excitedly. "It was probably the giant squid, Dennis!"

"*Wow!*" said Dennis, as though nobody in their wildest dreams could hope for more than being thrown into a storm-tossed, fathoms-deep lake, and pushed out of it again by a giant sea monster.

"Dennis! Dennis! See that boy down there? The one with the black hair and glasses? See him? *Know who he is, Dennis?*"

Harry looked away, staring very hard at the Sorting Hat, now Sorting Emma Dobbs.

The Sorting continued; boys and girls with varying degrees of fright on their faces moving one by one to the four-legged stool, the line dwindling slowly as Professor McGonagall passed the L's.

"Oh hurry up," Ron moaned, massaging his stomach.

"Now, Ron, the Sorting's much more important than food," said Nearly Headless Nick as "Madley, Laura!" became a Hufflepuff.

" 'Course it is, if you're dead," snapped Ron.

"I do hope this year's batch of Gryffindors are up to scratch," said Nearly Headless Nick, applauding as "McDonald, Natalie!" joined the Gryffindor table. "We don't want to break our winning streak, do we?"

Gryffindor had won the Inter-House Championship for the last three years in a row.

"Pritchard, Graham!"

"SLYTHERIN!"

"Quirke, Orla!"

"RAVENCLAW!"

And finally, with "Whitby, Kevin!" ("HUFFLEPUFF!"), the Sorting ended. Professor McGonagall picked up the hat and the stool and carried them away.

"About time," said Ron, seizing his knife and fork and looking expectantly at his golden plate.

Professor Dumbledore had gotten to his feet. He was smiling around at the students, his arms opened wide in welcome.

"I have only two words to say to you," he told them, his deep voice echoing around the Hall. *"Tuck in."*

"Hear, hear!" said Harry and Ron loudly as the empty dishes filled magically before their eyes.

Nearly Headless Nick watched mournfully as Harry, Ron, and Hermione loaded their own plates.

"Aaah, 'at's be'er," said Ron, with his mouth full of mashed potato.

"You're lucky there's a feast at all tonight, you know," said Nearly Headless Nick. "There was trouble in the kitchens earlier."

"Why? Wha' 'appened?" said Harry, through a sizable chunk of steak.

"Peeves, of course," said Nearly Headless Nick, shaking his head, which wobbled dangerously. He pulled his ruff a little higher up on his neck. "The usual argument, you know. He wanted to attend the feast — well, it's quite out of the question, you know what he's like, utterly uncivilized, can't see a plate of food without throwing it. We held a ghost's council — the Fat Friar was all for giving him the chance — but most wisely, in my opinion, the Bloody Baron put his foot down."

The Bloody Baron was the Slytherin ghost, a gaunt and silent specter covered in silver bloodstains. He was the only person at Hogwarts who could really control Peeves.

"Yeah, we thought Peeves seemed hacked off about something," said Ron darkly. "So what did he do in the kitchens?"

"Oh the usual," said Nearly Headless Nick, shrugging. "Wreaked havoc and mayhem. Pots and pans everywhere. Place swimming in soup. Terrified the house-elves out of their wits —"

*Clang.*

Hermione had knocked over her golden goblet. Pumpkin juice spread steadily over the tablecloth, staining several feet of white linen orange, but Hermione paid no attention.

"There are house-elves *here*?" she said, staring, horror-struck, at Nearly Headless Nick. "Here at *Hogwarts*?"

"Certainly," said Nearly Headless Nick, looking surprised at her reaction. "The largest number in any dwelling in Britain, I believe. Over a hundred."

"I've never seen one!" said Hermione.

"Well, they hardly ever leave the kitchen by day, do they?" said Nearly Headless Nick. "They come out at night to do a bit of cleaning . . . see to the fires and so on. . . . I mean, you're not supposed to see them, are you? That's the mark of a good house-elf, isn't it, that you don't know it's there?"

Hermione stared at him.

"But they get *paid*?" she said. "They get *holidays,* don't they? And — and sick leave, and pensions, and everything?"

Nearly Headless Nick chortled so much that his ruff slipped and his head flopped off, dangling on the inch or so of ghostly skin and muscle that still attached it to his neck.

"Sick leave and pensions?" he said, pushing his head back onto his shoulders and securing it once more with his ruff. "House-elves don't want sick leave and pensions!"

Hermione looked down at her hardly touched plate of food, then put her knife and fork down upon it and pushed it away from her.

"Oh c'mon, 'Er-my-knee," said Ron, accidentally spraying Harry with bits of Yorkshire pudding. "Oops — sorry, 'Arry —" He swallowed. "You won't get them sick leave by starving yourself!"

"Slave labor," said Hermione, breathing hard through her nose. "That's what made this dinner. *Slave labor.*"

And she refused to eat another bite.

The rain was still drumming heavily against the high, dark glass. Another clap of thunder shook the windows, and the stormy ceiling flashed, illuminating the golden plates as the remains of the first course vanished and were replaced, instantly, with puddings.

"Treacle tart, Hermione!" said Ron, deliberately wafting its smell toward her. "Spotted dick, look! Chocolate gateau!"

But Hermione gave him a look so reminiscent of Professor McGonagall that he gave up.

When the puddings too had been demolished, and the last crumbs had faded off the plates, leaving them sparkling clean, Albus Dumbledore got to his feet again. The buzz of chatter filling the Hall ceased almost at once, so that only the howling wind and pounding rain could be heard.

"So!" said Dumbledore, smiling around at them all. "Now that we are all fed and watered," ("Hmph!" said Hermione) "I must once more ask for your attention, while I give out a few notices.

"Mr. Filch, the caretaker, has asked me to tell you that the list of objects forbidden inside the castle has this year been extended to include Screaming Yo-yos, Fanged Frisbees, and Ever-Bashing Boomerangs. The full list comprises some four hundred and thirty-seven items, I believe, and can be viewed in Mr. Filch's office, if anybody would like to check it."

The corners of Dumbledore's mouth twitched. He continued, "As ever, I would like to remind you all that the forest on the grounds is out-of-bounds to students, as is the village of Hogs-meade to all below third year.

"It is also my painful duty to inform you that the Inter-House Quidditch Cup will not take place this year."

"What?" Harry gasped. He looked around at Fred and George, his fellow members of the Quidditch team. They were mouthing soundlessly at Dumbledore, apparently too appalled to speak. Dumbledore went on, "This is due to an event that will be starting in October, and continuing throughout the school year, taking up much of the teachers' time and energy — but I am sure you will all enjoy it immensely. I have great pleasure in announcing that this year at Hogwarts —"

But at that moment, there was a deafening rumble of thunder and the doors of the Great Hall banged open.

A man stood in the doorway, leaning upon a long staff, shrouded in a black traveling cloak. Every head in the Great Hall swiveled toward the stranger, suddenly brightly illuminated by a fork of lightning that flashed across the ceiling. He lowered his hood, shook out a long mane of grizzled, dark gray hair, then began to walk up toward the teachers' table.

A dull *clunk* echoed through the Hall on his every other step. He reached the end of the top table, turned right, and limped heavily toward Dumbledore. Another flash of lightning crossed the ceiling. Hermione gasped.

The lightning had thrown the man's face into sharp relief, and it was a face unlike any Harry had ever seen. It looked as though it had been carved out of weathered wood by someone who had only the vaguest idea of what human faces are supposed to look like, and was none too skilled with a chisel. Every inch of skin seemed to be scarred. The mouth looked like a diagonal gash, and a large chunk of the nose was missing. But it was the man's eyes that made him frightening.

One of them was small, dark, and beady. The other was large, round as a coin, and a vivid, electric blue. The blue eye was moving ceaselessly, without blinking, and was rolling up, down, and from side to side, quite independently of the normal eye — and then it rolled right over, pointing into the back of the man's head, so that all they could see was whiteness.

The stranger reached Dumbledore. He stretched out a hand that was as badly scarred as his face, and Dumbledore shook it, muttering words Harry couldn't hear. He seemed to be making some inquiry of the stranger, who shook his head unsmilingly and replied in an undertone. Dumbledore nodded and gestured the man to the empty seat on his right-hand side.

The stranger sat down, shook his mane of dark gray hair out of his face, pulled a plate of sausages toward him, raised it to what was left of his nose, and sniffed it. He then took a small knife out of his pocket, speared a sausage on the end of it, and began to eat. His normal eye was fixed upon the sausages, but the blue eye was still darting restlessly around in its socket, taking in the Hall and the students.

"May I introduce our new Defense Against the Dark Arts teacher?" said Dumbledore brightly into the silence. "Professor Moody."

It was usual for new staff members to be greeted with applause, but none of the staff or students clapped except Dumbledore and Hagrid, who both put their hands together and applauded, but the sound echoed dismally into the silence, and they stopped fairly quickly. Everyone else seemed too transfixed by Moody's bizarre appearance to do more than stare at him.

"Moody?" Harry muttered to Ron. "*Mad-Eye Moody?* The one your dad went to help this morning?"

"Must be," said Ron in a low, awed voice.

"What happened to him?" Hermione whispered. "What happened to his *face*?"

"Dunno," Ron whispered back, watching Moody with fascination.

Moody seemed totally indifferent to his less-than-warm welcome. Ignoring the jug of pumpkin juice in front of him, he reached again into his traveling cloak, pulled out a hip flask, and took a long draught from it. As he lifted his arm to drink, his cloak was pulled a few inches from the ground, and Harry saw, below the table, several inches of carved wooden leg, ending in a clawed foot.

Dumbledore cleared his throat.

"As I was saying," he said, smiling at the sea of students before him, all of whom were still gazing transfixed at Mad-Eye Moody, "we are to have the honor of hosting a very exciting event over the coming months, an event that has not been held for over a century. It is my very great pleasure to inform you that the Triwizard Tournament will be taking place at Hogwarts this year."

"You're JOKING!" said Fred Weasley loudly.

The tension that had filled the Hall ever since Moody's arrival suddenly broke. Nearly everyone laughed, and Dumbledore chuckled appreciatively.

"I am *not* joking, Mr. Weasley," he said, "though now that you mention it, I did hear an excellent one over the summer about a troll, a hag, and a leprechaun who all go into a bar . . ."

Professor McGonagall cleared her throat loudly.

"Er — but maybe this is not the time . . . no . . ." said Dumbledore, "where was I? Ah yes, the Triwizard Tournament . . . well, some of you will not know what this tournament involves, so I hope those who *do* know will forgive me for giving a short explanation, and allow their attention to wander freely.

"The Triwizard Tournament was first established some seven hundred years ago as a friendly competition between the three largest European schools of wizardry: Hogwarts, Beauxbatons, and Durmstrang. A champion was selected to represent each school, and the three champions competed in three magical tasks. The schools took it in turns to host the tournament once every five years, and it was generally agreed to be a most excellent way of establishing ties between young witches and wizards of different nationalities — until, that is, the death toll mounted so high that the tournament was discontinued."

*"Death toll?"* Hermione whispered, looking alarmed. But her anxiety did not seem to be shared by the majority of students in the Hall; many of them were whispering excitedly to one another, and Harry himself was far more interested in hearing about the tournament than in worrying about deaths that had happened hundreds of years ago.

"There have been several attempts over the centuries to reinstate the tournament," Dumbledore continued, "none of which has been very successful. However, our own Departments of International Magical Cooperation and Magical Games and Sports have decided the time is ripe for another attempt. We have worked hard over the summer to ensure that this time, no champion will find himself or herself in mortal danger.

"The Heads of Beauxbatons and Durmstrang will be arriving with their shortlisted contenders in October, and the selection of the three champions will take place at Halloween. An impartial judge will decide which students are most worthy to compete for the Triwizard Cup, the glory of their school, and a thousand Galleons personal prize money."

"I'm going for it!" Fred Weasley hissed down the table, his face lit with enthusiasm at the prospect of such glory and riches. He was not the only person who seemed to be visualizing himself as the Hogwarts champion. At every House table, Harry could see people either gazing raptly at Dumbledore, or else whispering fervently to their neighbors. But then Dumbledore spoke again, and the Hall quieted once more.

"Eager though I know all of you will be to bring the Triwizard Cup to Hogwarts," he said, "the Heads of the participating schools, along with the Ministry of Magic, have agreed to impose an age restriction on contenders this year. Only students who are of age — that is to say, seventeen years or older — will be allowed to put forward their names for consideration. This" — Dumbledore raised his voice slightly, for several people had made noises of outrage at these words, and the Weasley twins were suddenly looking furious — "is a measure we feel is necessary, given that the tournament tasks will still be difficult and dangerous, whatever precautions we take, and it is highly unlikely that students below sixth and seventh year will be able to cope with them. I will personally be ensuring that no under-age student hoodwinks our impartial judge into making them Hogwarts champion." His light blue eyes twinkled as they flickered over Fred's and George's mutinous faces. "I therefore beg you not to waste your time submitting yourself if you are under seventeen.

"The delegations from Beauxbatons and Durmstrang will be arriving in October and remaining with us for the greater part of this year. I know that you will all extend every courtesy to our foreign guests while they are with us, and will give your whole-hearted support to the Hogwarts champion when he or she is selected. And now, it is late, and I know how important it is to you all to be alert and rested as you enter your lessons tomorrow morning. Bedtime! Chop chop!"

Dumbledore sat down again and turned to talk to Mad-Eye Moody. There was a great scraping and banging as all the students got to their feet and swarmed toward the double doors into the entrance hall.

"They can't do that!" said George Weasley, who had not joined the crowd moving toward the door, but was standing up and glaring at Dumbledore. "We're seventeen in April, why can't we have a shot?"

"They're not stopping me entering," said Fred stubbornly, also scowling at the top table. "The champions'll get to do all sorts of stuff you'd never be allowed to do normally. And a thousand Galleons prize money!"

"Yeah," said Ron, a faraway look on his face. "Yeah, a thousand Galleons . . ."

"Come on," said Hermione, "we'll be the only ones left here if you don't move."

Harry, Ron, Hermione, Fred, and George set off for the entrance hall, Fred and George debating the ways in which Dumbledore might stop those who were under seventeen from entering the tournament.

"Who's this impartial judge who's going to decide who the champions are?" said Harry.

"Dunno," said Fred, "but it's them we'll have to fool. I reckon a couple of drops of Aging Potion might do it, George. . . ."

"Dumbledore knows you're not of age, though," said Ron.

"Yeah, but he's not the one who decides who the champion is, is he?" said Fred shrewdly. "Sounds to me like once this judge knows who wants to enter, he'll choose the best from each school and never mind how old they are. Dumbledore's trying to stop us giving our names."

"People have died, though!" said Hermione in a worried voice as they walked through a door concealed behind a tapestry and started up another, narrower staircase.

"Yeah," said Fred airily, "but that was years ago, wasn't it? Anyway, where's the fun without a bit of risk? Hey, Ron, what if we find out how to get 'round Dumbledore? Fancy entering?"

"What d'you reckon?" Ron asked Harry. "Be cool to enter, wouldn't it? But I s'pose they might want someone older. . . . Dunno if we've learned enough. . . ."

"I definitely haven't," came Neville's gloomy voice from behind Fred and George.

"I expect my gran'd want me to try, though. She's always going on about how I should be upholding the family honor. I'll just have to — oops. . . ."

Neville's foot had sunk right through a step halfway up the staircase. There were many of these trick stairs at Hogwarts; it was second nature to most of the older students to jump this particular step, but Neville's memory was notoriously poor. Harry and Ron seized him under the armpits and pulled him out, while a suit of armor at the top of the stairs creaked and clanked, laughing wheezily.

"Shut it, you," said Ron, banging down its visor as they passed.

They made their way up to the entrance to Gryffindor Tower,

which was concealed behind a large portrait of a fat lady in a pink silk dress.

"Password?" she said as they approached.

"Balderdash," said George, "a prefect downstairs told me."

The portrait swung forward to reveal a hole in the wall through which they all climbed. A crackling fire warmed the circular common room, which was full of squashy armchairs and tables. Hermione cast the merrily dancing flames a dark look, and Harry distinctly heard her mutter *"Slave labor,"* before bidding them good night and disappearing through the doorway to the girls' dormitory.

Harry, Ron, and Neville climbed up the last, spiral staircase until they reached their own dormitory, which was situated at the top of the tower. Five four-poster beds with deep crimson hangings stood against the walls, each with its owner's trunk at the foot. Dean and Seamus were already getting into bed; Seamus had pinned his Ireland rosette to his headboard, and Dean had tacked up a poster of Viktor Krum over his bedside table. His old poster of the West Ham football team was pinned right next to it.

"Mental," Ron sighed, shaking his head at the completely stationary soccer players.

Harry, Ron, and Neville got into their pajamas and into bed. Someone — a house-elf, no doubt — had placed warming pans between the sheets. It was extremely comfortable, lying there in bed and listening to the storm raging outside.

"I might go in for it, you know," Ron said sleepily through the darkness, "if Fred and George find out how to . . . the tournament . . . you never know, do you?"

"S'pose not. . . ."

Harry rolled over in bed, a series of dazzling new pictures forming in his mind's eye. . . . He had hoodwinked the impartial judge into believing he was seventeen . . . he had become Hogwarts champion . . . he was standing on the grounds, his arms raised in triumph in front of the whole school, all of whom were applauding and screaming . . . he had just won the Triwizard Tournament. . . . Cho's face stood out particularly clearly in the blurred crowd, her face glowing with admiration. . . .

Harry grinned into his pillow, exceptionally glad that Ron couldn't see what he could.

# MAD-EYE MOODY

The storm had blown itself out by the following morning, though the ceiling in the Great Hall was still gloomy; heavy clouds of pewter gray swirled overhead as Harry, Ron, and Hermione examined their new course schedules at breakfast. A few seats along, Fred, George, and Lee Jordan were discussing magical methods of aging themselves and bluffing their way into the Triwizard Tournament.

"Today's not bad . . . outside all morning," said Ron, who was running his finger down his schedule. "Herbology with the Hufflepuffs and Care of Magical Creatures . . . damn it, we're still with the Slytherins. . . ."

"Double Divination this afternoon," Harry groaned, looking down. Divination was his least favorite subject, apart from Potions. Professor Trelawney kept predicting Harry's death, which he found extremely annoying.

"You should have given it up like me, shouldn't you?" said

Hermione briskly, buttering herself some toast. "Then you'd be doing something sensible like Arithmancy."

"You're eating again, I notice," said Ron, watching Hermione adding liberal amounts of jam to her toast too.

"I've decided there are better ways of making a stand about elf rights," said Hermione haughtily.

"Yeah . . . and you were hungry," said Ron, grinning.

There was a sudden rustling noise above them, and a hundred owls came soaring through the open windows carrying the morning mail. Instinctively, Harry looked up, but there was no sign of white among the mass of brown and gray. The owls circled the tables, looking for the people to whom their letters and packages were addressed. A large tawny owl soared down to Neville Longbottom and deposited a parcel into his lap — Neville almost always forgot to pack something. On the other side of the Hall Draco Malfoy's eagle owl had landed on his shoulder, carrying what looked like his usual supply of sweets and cakes from home. Trying to ignore the sinking feeling of disappointment in his stomach, Harry returned to his porridge. Was it possible that something had happened to Hedwig, and that Sirius hadn't even got his letter?

His preoccupation lasted all the way across the sodden vegetable patch until they arrived in greenhouse three, but here he was distracted by Professor Sprout showing the class the ugliest plants Harry had ever seen. Indeed, they looked less like plants than thick, black, giant slugs, protruding vertically out of the soil. Each was squirming slightly and had a number of large, shiny swellings upon it, which appeared to be full of liquid.

"Bubotubers," Professor Sprout told them briskly. "They need squeezing. You will collect the pus —"

"The *what?*" said Seamus Finnigan, sounding revolted.

"Pus, Finnigan, pus," said Professor Sprout, "and it's extremely valuable, so don't waste it. You will collect the pus, I say, in these bottles. Wear your dragon-hide gloves; it can do funny things to the skin when undiluted, bubotuber pus."

Squeezing the bubotubers was disgusting, but oddly satisfying. As each swelling was popped, a large amount of thick yellowish-green liquid burst forth, which smelled strongly of petrol. They caught it in the bottles as Professor Sprout had indicated, and by the end of the lesson had collected several pints.

"This'll keep Madam Pomfrey happy," said Professor Sprout, stoppering the last bottle with a cork. "An excellent remedy for the more stubborn forms of acne, bubotuber pus. Should stop students resorting to desperate measures to rid themselves of pimples."

"Like poor Eloise Midgen," said Hannah Abbott, a Hufflepuff, in a hushed voice. "She tried to curse hers off."

"Silly girl," said Professor Sprout, shaking her head. "But Madam Pomfrey fixed her nose back on in the end."

A booming bell echoed from the castle across the wet grounds, signaling the end of the lesson, and the class separated; the Hufflepuffs climbing the stone steps for Transfiguration, and the Gryffindors heading in the other direction, down the sloping lawn toward Hagrid's small wooden cabin, which stood on the edge of the Forbidden Forest.

Hagrid was standing outside his hut, one hand on the collar of his enormous black boarhound, Fang. There were several open wooden crates on the ground at his feet, and Fang was whimpering and straining at his collar, apparently keen to investigate the contents more closely. As they drew nearer, an odd rattling noise reached their ears, punctuated by what sounded like minor explosions.

"Mornin'!" Hagrid said, grinning at Harry, Ron, and Hermione. "Be'er wait fer the Slytherins, they won' want ter miss this — Blast-Ended Skrewts!"

"Come again?" said Ron.

Hagrid pointed down into the crates.

"Eurgh!" squealed Lavender Brown, jumping backward.

"Eurgh" just about summed up the Blast-Ended Skrewts in Harry's opinion. They looked like deformed, shell-less lobsters, horribly pale and slimy-looking, with legs sticking out in very odd places and no visible heads. There were about a hundred of them in each crate, each about six inches long, crawling over one another, bumping blindly into the sides of the boxes. They were giving off a very powerful smell of rotting fish. Every now and then, sparks would fly out of the end of a skrewt, and with a small *phut,* it would be propelled forward several inches.

"On'y jus' hatched," said Hagrid proudly, "so yeh'll be able ter raise 'em yerselves! Thought we'd make a bit of a project of it!"

"And why would we *want* to raise them?" said a cold voice.

The Slytherins had arrived. The speaker was Draco Malfoy. Crabbe and Goyle were chuckling appreciatively at his words.

Hagrid looked stumped at the question.

"I mean, what do they *do*?" asked Malfoy. "What is the *point* of them?"

Hagrid opened his mouth, apparently thinking hard; there was a few seconds' pause, then he said roughly, "Tha's next lesson, Malfoy. Yer jus' feedin' 'em today. Now, yeh'll wan' ter try 'em on a few diff'rent things — I've never had 'em before, not sure what they'll go fer — I got ant eggs an' frog livers an' a bit o' grass snake — just try 'em out with a bit of each."

"First pus and now this," muttered Seamus.

Nothing but deep affection for Hagrid could have made Harry, Ron, and Hermione pick up squelchy handfuls of frog liver and lower them into the crates to tempt the Blast-Ended Skrewts. Harry couldn't suppress the suspicion that the whole thing was entirely pointless, because the skrewts didn't seem to have mouths.

*"Ouch!"* yelled Dean Thomas after about ten minutes. "It got me!"

Hagrid hurried over to him, looking anxious.

"Its end exploded!" said Dean angrily, showing Hagrid a burn on his hand.

"Ah, yeah, that can happen when they blast off," said Hagrid, nodding.

"Eurgh!" said Lavender Brown again. "Eurgh, Hagrid, what's that pointy thing on it?"

"Ah, some of 'em have got stings," said Hagrid enthusiastically (Lavender quickly withdrew her hand from the box). "I reckon they're the males. . . . The females've got sorta sucker things on their bellies. . . . I think they might be ter suck blood."

"Well, I can certainly see why we're trying to keep them alive," said Malfoy sarcastically. "Who wouldn't want pets that can burn, sting, and bite all at once?"

"Just because they're not very pretty, it doesn't mean they're not useful," Hermione snapped. "Dragon blood's amazingly magical, but you wouldn't want a dragon for a pet, would you?"

Harry and Ron grinned at Hagrid, who gave them a furtive smile from behind his bushy beard. Hagrid would have liked nothing better than a pet dragon, as Harry, Ron, and Hermione knew only too well — he had owned one for a brief period during their first year, a vicious Norwegian Ridgeback by the name of Norbert. Hagrid simply loved monstrous creatures, the more lethal, the better.

"Well, at least the skrewts are small," said Ron as they made their way back up to the castle for lunch an hour later.

"They are *now*," said Hermione in an exasperated voice, "but once Hagrid's found out what they eat, I expect they'll be six feet long."

"Well, that won't matter if they turn out to cure seasickness or something, will it?" said Ron, grinning slyly at her.

"You know perfectly well I only said that to shut Malfoy up," said Hermione. "As a matter of fact I think he's right. The best thing to do would be to stamp on the lot of them before they start attacking us all."

They sat down at the Gryffindor table and helped themselves to lamb chops and potatoes. Hermione began to eat so fast that Harry and Ron stared at her.

"Er — is this the new stand on elf rights?" said Ron. "You're going to make yourself puke instead?"

"No," said Hermione, with as much dignity as she could muster with her mouth bulging with sprouts. "I just want to get to the library."

"*What?*" said Ron in disbelief. "Hermione — it's the first day back! We haven't even got homework yet!"

Hermione shrugged and continued to shovel down her food as though she had not eaten for days. Then she leapt to her feet, said, "See you at dinner!" and departed at high speed.

When the bell rang to signal the start of afternoon lessons, Harry and Ron set off for North Tower where, at the top of a tightly spiraling staircase, a silver stepladder led to a circular trapdoor in the ceiling, and the room where Professor Trelawney lived.

The familiar sweet perfume spreading from the fire met their nostrils as they emerged at the top of the stepladder. As ever, the curtains were all closed; the circular room was bathed in a dim reddish light cast by the many lamps, which were all draped with scarves and shawls. Harry and Ron walked through the mass of occupied chintz chairs and poufs that cluttered the room, and sat down at the same small circular table.

"Good day," said the misty voice of Professor Trelawney right behind Harry, making him jump.

A very thin woman with enormous glasses that made her eyes appear far too large for her face, Professor Trelawney was peering down at Harry with the tragic expression she always wore whenever she saw him. The usual large amount of beads, chains, and bangles glittered upon her person in the firelight.

"You are preoccupied, my dear," she said mournfully to Harry. "My inner eye sees past your brave face to the troubled soul within. And I regret to say that your worries are not baseless. I see difficult times ahead for you, alas . . . most difficult . . . I fear the thing you dread will indeed come to pass . . . and perhaps sooner than you think. . . ."

Her voice dropped almost to a whisper. Ron rolled his eyes at Harry, who looked stonily back. Professor Trelawney swept past them and seated herself in a large winged armchair before the fire, facing the class. Lavender Brown and Parvati Patil, who deeply admired Professor Trelawney, were sitting on poufs very close to her.

"My dears, it is time for us to consider the stars," she said. "The movements of the planets and the mysterious portents they reveal only to those who understand the steps of the celestial dance. Human destiny may be deciphered by the planetary rays, which intermingle . . ."

But Harry's thoughts had drifted. The perfumed fire always made him feel sleepy and dull-witted, and Professor Trelawney's rambling talks on fortune-telling never held him exactly spellbound — though he couldn't help thinking about what she had just said to him. *"I fear the thing you dread will indeed come to pass . . ."*

But Hermione was right, Harry thought irritably, Professor Trelawney really was an old fraud. He wasn't dreading anything at the moment at all . . . well, unless you counted his fears that Sirius had been caught . . . but what did Professor Trelawney know? He had long since come to the conclusion that her brand of fortune-telling was really no more than lucky guesswork and a spooky manner.

Except, of course, for that time at the end of last term, when she had made the prediction about Voldemort rising again . . . and Dumbledore himself had said that he thought that trance had been genuine, when Harry had described it to him. . . .

*"Harry!"* Ron muttered.

"What?"

Harry looked around; the whole class was staring at him. He sat up straight; he had been almost dozing off, lost in the heat and his thoughts.

"I was saying, my dear, that you were clearly born under the baleful influence of Saturn," said Professor Trelawney, a faint note of resentment in her voice at the fact that he had obviously not been hanging on her words.

"Born under — what, sorry?" said Harry.

"Saturn, dear, the planet Saturn!" said Professor Trelawney, sounding definitely irritated that he wasn't riveted by this news. "I was saying that Saturn was surely in a position of power in the heavens at the moment of your birth. . . . Your dark hair . . . your mean stature . . . tragic losses so young in life . . . I think I am right in saying, my dear, that you were born in midwinter?"

"No," said Harry, "I was born in July."

Ron hastily turned his laugh into a hacking cough.

Half an hour later, each of them had been given a complicated circular chart, and was attempting to fill in the position of the planets at their moment of birth. It was dull work, requiring much consultation of timetables and calculation of angles.

"I've got two Neptunes here," said Harry after a while, frowning down at his piece of parchment, "that can't be right, can it?"

"Aaaaah," said Ron, imitating Professor Trelawney's mystical whisper, "when two Neptunes appear in the sky, it is a sure sign that a midget in glasses is being born, Harry. . . ."

Seamus and Dean, who were working nearby, sniggered loudly, though not loudly enough to mask the excited squeals from Lavender Brown — "Oh Professor, look! I think I've got an unaspected planet! Oooh, which one's that, Professor?"

"It is Uranus, my dear," said Professor Trelawney, peering down at the chart.

"Can I have a look at Uranus too, Lavender?" said Ron.

Most unfortunately, Professor Trelawney heard him, and it was this, perhaps, that made her give them so much homework at the end of the class.

"A detailed analysis of the way the planetary movements in the coming month will affect you, with reference to your personal chart," she snapped, sounding much more like Professor McGonagall than her usual airy-fairy self. "I want it ready to hand in next Monday, and no excuses!"

"Miserable old bat," said Ron bitterly as they joined the crowds descending the staircases back to the Great Hall and dinner. "That'll take all weekend, that will. . . ."

"Lots of homework?" said Hermione brightly, catching up with them. "Professor Vector didn't give *us* any at all!"

"Well, bully for Professor Vector," said Ron moodily.

They reached the entrance hall, which was packed with people queuing for dinner. They had just joined the end of the line, when a loud voice rang out behind them.

"Weasley! Hey, Weasley!"

Harry, Ron, and Hermione turned. Malfoy, Crabbe, and Goyle were standing there, each looking thoroughly pleased about something.

"What?" said Ron shortly.

"Your dad's in the paper, Weasley!" said Malfoy, brandishing a copy of the *Daily Prophet* and speaking very loudly, so that everyone in the packed entrance hall could hear. "Listen to this!

### FURTHER MISTAKES AT THE MINISTRY OF MAGIC

It seems as though the Ministry of Magic's troubles are not yet at an end, *writes Rita Skeeter, Special Correspondent.* Recently under fire for its poor

crowd control at the Quidditch World Cup, and
still unable to account for the disappearance of one
of its witches, the Ministry was plunged into fresh
embarrassment yesterday by the antics of Arnold
Weasley, of the Misuse of Muggle Artifacts Office."

Malfoy looked up.

"Imagine them not even getting his name right, Weasley. It's
almost as though he's a complete nonentity, isn't it?" he crowed.

Everyone in the entrance hall was listening now. Malfoy straightened the paper with a flourish and read on:

Arnold Weasley, who was charged with possession
of a flying car two years ago, was yesterday involved
in a tussle with several Muggle law-keepers
("policemen") over a number of highly aggressive
dustbins. Mr. Weasley appears to have rushed to
the aid of "Mad-Eye" Moody, the aged ex-Auror
who retired from the Ministry when no longer able
to tell the difference between a handshake and attempted murder. Unsurprisingly, Mr. Weasley
found, upon arrival at Mr. Moody's heavily
guarded house, that Mr. Moody had once again
raised a false alarm. Mr. Weasley was forced to
modify several memories before he could escape
from the policemen, but refused to answer *Daily
Prophet* questions about why he had involved the
Ministry in such an undignified and potentially
embarrassing scene.

"And there's a picture, Weasley!" said Malfoy, flipping the paper over and holding it up. "A picture of your parents outside their house — if you can call it a house! Your mother could do with losing a bit of weight, couldn't she?"

Ron was shaking with fury. Everyone was staring at him.

"Get stuffed, Malfoy," said Harry. "C'mon, Ron. . . ."

"Oh yeah, you were staying with them this summer, weren't you, Potter?" sneered Malfoy. "So tell me, is his mother really that porky, or is it just the picture?"

"You know *your* mother, Malfoy?" said Harry — both he and Hermione had grabbed the back of Ron's robes to stop him from launching himself at Malfoy — "that expression she's got, like she's got dung under her nose? Has she always looked like that, or was it just because you were with her?"

Malfoy's pale face went slightly pink.

"Don't you dare insult my mother, Potter."

"Keep your fat mouth shut, then," said Harry, turning away.

BANG!

Several people screamed — Harry felt something white-hot graze the side of his face — he plunged his hand into his robes for his wand, but before he'd even touched it, he heard a second loud BANG, and a roar that echoed through the entrance hall.

"OH NO YOU DON'T, LADDIE!"

Harry spun around. Professor Moody was limping down the marble staircase. His wand was out and it was pointing right at a pure white ferret, which was shivering on the stone-flagged floor, exactly where Malfoy had been standing.

There was a terrified silence in the entrance hall. Nobody but Moody was moving a muscle. Moody turned to look at Harry —

at least, his normal eye was looking at Harry; the other one was pointing into the back of his head.

"Did he get you?" Moody growled. His voice was low and gravelly.

"No," said Harry, "missed."

"LEAVE IT!" Moody shouted.

"Leave — what?" Harry said, bewildered.

"Not you — him!" Moody growled, jerking his thumb over his shoulder at Crabbe, who had just frozen, about to pick up the white ferret. It seemed that Moody's rolling eye was magical and could see out of the back of his head.

Moody started to limp toward Crabbe, Goyle, and the ferret, which gave a terrified squeak and took off, streaking toward the dungeons.

"I don't think so!" roared Moody, pointing his wand at the ferret again — it flew ten feet into the air, fell with a smack to the floor, and then bounced upward once more.

"I don't like people who attack when their opponent's back's turned," growled Moody as the ferret bounced higher and higher, squealing in pain. "Stinking, cowardly, scummy thing to do. . . ."

The ferret flew through the air, its legs and tail flailing helplessly.

"Never — do — that — again —" said Moody, speaking each word as the ferret hit the stone floor and bounced upward again.

"Professor Moody!" said a shocked voice.

Professor McGonagall was coming down the marble staircase with her arms full of books.

"Hello, Professor McGonagall," said Moody calmly, bouncing the ferret still higher.

"What — what are you doing?" said Professor McGonagall, her eyes following the bouncing ferret's progress through the air.

"Teaching," said Moody.

"Teach — Moody, *is that a student?*" shrieked Professor McGonagall, the books spilling out of her arms.

"Yep," said Moody.

"No!" cried Professor McGonagall, running down the stairs and pulling out her wand; a moment later, with a loud snapping noise, Draco Malfoy had reappeared, lying in a heap on the floor with his sleek blond hair all over his now brilliantly pink face. He got to his feet, wincing.

"Moody, we *never* use Transfiguration as a punishment!" said Professor McGonagall weakly. "Surely Professor Dumbledore told you that?"

"He might've mentioned it, yeah," said Moody, scratching his chin unconcernedly, "but I thought a good sharp shock —"

"We give detentions, Moody! Or speak to the offender's Head of House!"

"I'll do that, then," said Moody, staring at Malfoy with great dislike.

Malfoy, whose pale eyes were still watering with pain and humiliation, looked malevolently up at Moody and muttered something in which the words "my father" were distinguishable.

"Oh yeah?" said Moody quietly, limping forward a few steps, the dull *clunk* of his wooden leg echoing around the hall. "Well, I know your father of old, boy. . . . You tell him Moody's keeping a close eye on his son . . . you tell him that from me. . . . Now, your Head of House'll be Snape, will it?"

"Yes," said Malfoy resentfully.

"Another old friend," growled Moody. "I've been looking forward to a chat with old Snape. . . . Come on, you. . . ."

And he seized Malfoy's upper arm and marched him off toward the dungeons.

Professor McGonagall stared anxiously after them for a few moments, then waved her wand at her fallen books, causing them to soar up into the air and back into her arms.

"Don't talk to me," Ron said quietly to Harry and Hermione as they sat down at the Gryffindor table a few minutes later, surrounded by excited talk on all sides about what had just happened.

"Why not?" said Hermione in surprise.

"Because I want to fix that in my memory forever," said Ron, his eyes closed and an uplifted expression on his face. "Draco Malfoy, the amazing bouncing ferret . . ."

Harry and Hermione both laughed, and Hermione began doling beef casserole onto each of their plates.

"He could have really hurt Malfoy, though," she said. "It was good, really, that Professor McGonagall stopped it —"

"Hermione!" said Ron furiously, his eyes snapping open again, "you're ruining the best moment of my life!"

Hermione made an impatient noise and began to eat at top speed again.

"Don't tell me you're going back to the library this evening?" said Harry, watching her.

"Got to," said Hermione thickly. "Loads to do."

"But you told us Professor Vector —"

"It's not schoolwork," she said. Within five minutes, she had cleared her plate and departed. No sooner had she gone than her seat was taken by Fred Weasley.

"Moody!" he said. "How cool is he?"

"Beyond cool," said George, sitting down opposite Fred.

"Supercool," said the twins' best friend, Lee Jordan, sliding into the seat beside George. "We had him this afternoon," he told Harry and Ron.

"What was it like?" said Harry eagerly.

Fred, George, and Lee exchanged looks full of meaning.

"Never had a lesson like it," said Fred.

"He *knows*, man," said Lee.

"Knows what?" said Ron, leaning forward.

"Knows what it's like to be out there *doing* it," said George impressively.

"Doing what?" said Harry.

"Fighting the Dark Arts," said Fred.

"He's seen it all," said George.

"'Mazing," said Lee.

Ron dived into his bag for his schedule.

"We haven't got him till Thursday!" he said in a disappointed voice.

# THE UNFORGIVABLE CURSES

The next two days passed without great incident, unless you counted Neville melting his sixth cauldron in Potions. Professor Snape, who seemed to have attained new levels of vindictiveness over the summer, gave Neville detention, and Neville returned from it in a state of nervous collapse, having been made to disembowel a barrel full of horned toads.

"You know why Snape's in such a foul mood, don't you?" said Ron to Harry as they watched Hermione teaching Neville a Scouring Charm to remove the toad guts from under his fingernails.

"Yeah," said Harry. "Moody."

It was common knowledge that Snape really wanted the Dark Arts job, and he had now failed to get it for the fourth year running. Snape had disliked all of their previous Dark Arts teachers, and shown it — but he seemed strangely wary of displaying overt animosity to Mad-Eye Moody. Indeed, whenever Harry saw the two of them together — at mealtimes, or when they passed in the corridors — he had the distinct impression that Snape was avoiding Moody's eye, whether magical or normal.

"I reckon Snape's a bit scared of him, you know," Harry said thoughtfully.

"Imagine if Moody turned Snape into a horned toad," said Ron, his eyes misting over, "and bounced him all around his dungeon. . . ."

The Gryffindor fourth years were looking forward to Moody's first lesson so much that they arrived early on Thursday lunchtime and queued up outside his classroom before the bell had even rung. The only person missing was Hermione, who turned up just in time for the lesson.

"Been in the —"

"Library." Harry finished her sentence for her. "C'mon, quick, or we won't get decent seats."

They hurried into three chairs right in front of the teacher's desk, took out their copies of *The Dark Forces: A Guide to Self-Protection,* and waited, unusually quiet. Soon they heard Moody's distinctive clunking footsteps coming down the corridor, and he entered the room, looking as strange and frightening as ever. They could just see his clawed, wooden foot protruding from underneath his robes.

"You can put those away," he growled, stumping over to his desk and sitting down, "those books. You won't need them."

They returned the books to their bags, Ron looking excited.

Moody took out a register, shook his long mane of grizzled gray hair out of his twisted and scarred face, and began to call out names, his normal eye moving steadily down the list while his magical eye swiveled around, fixing upon each student as he or she answered.

"Right then," he said, when the last person had declared themselves present, "I've had a letter from Professor Lupin about this class. Seems you've had a pretty thorough grounding in tackling Dark creatures — you've covered boggarts, Red Caps, hinkypunks, grindylows, Kappas, and werewolves, is that right?"

There was a general murmur of assent.

"But you're behind — very behind — on dealing with curses," said Moody. "So I'm here to bring you up to scratch on what wizards can do to each other. I've got one year to teach you how to deal with Dark —"

"What, aren't you staying?" Ron blurted out.

Moody's magical eye spun around to stare at Ron; Ron looked extremely apprehensive, but after a moment Moody smiled — the first time Harry had seen him do so. The effect was to make his heavily scarred face look more twisted and contorted than ever, but it was nevertheless good to know that he ever did anything as friendly as smile. Ron looked deeply relieved.

"You'll be Arthur Weasley's son, eh?" Moody said. "Your father got me out of a very tight corner a few days ago. . . . Yeah, I'm staying just the one year. Special favor to Dumbledore. . . . One year, and then back to my quiet retirement."

He gave a harsh laugh, and then clapped his gnarled hands together.

"So — straight into it. Curses. They come in many strengths and forms. Now, according to the Ministry of Magic, I'm supposed to teach you countercurses and leave it at that. I'm not supposed to show you what illegal Dark curses look like until you're in the sixth year. You're not supposed to be old enough to deal with it till then. But Professor Dumbledore's got a higher opinion of your nerves, he reckons you can cope, and I say, the sooner you know what you're up against, the better. How are you supposed to defend yourself against something you've never seen? A wizard who's about to put an illegal curse on you isn't going to tell you what he's about to do. He's not going to do it nice and polite to your face. You need to be prepared. You need to be alert and watchful. You need to put that away, Miss Brown, when I'm talking."

Lavender jumped and blushed. She had been showing Parvati her completed horoscope under the desk. Apparently Moody's magical eye could see through solid wood, as well as out of the back of his head.

"So . . . do any of you know which curses are most heavily punished by Wizarding law?"

Several hands rose tentatively into the air, including Ron's and Hermione's. Moody pointed at Ron, though his magical eye was still fixed on Lavender.

"Er," said Ron tentatively, "my dad told me about one. . . . Is it called the Imperius Curse, or something?"

"Ah, yes," said Moody appreciatively. "Your father *would* know that one. Gave the Ministry a lot of trouble at one time, the Imperius Curse."

Moody got heavily to his mismatched feet, opened his desk drawer, and took out a glass jar. Three large black spiders were scuttling around inside it. Harry felt Ron recoil slightly next to him — Ron hated spiders.

Moody reached into the jar, caught one of the spiders, and held it in the palm of his hand so that they could all see it. He then pointed his wand at it and muttered, *"Imperio!"*

The spider leapt from Moody's hand on a fine thread of silk and began to swing backward and forward as though on a trapeze. It stretched out its legs rigidly, then did a back flip, breaking the thread and landing on the desk, where it began to cartwheel in circles. Moody jerked his wand, and the spider rose onto two of its hind legs and went into what was unmistakably a tap dance.

Everyone was laughing — everyone except Moody.

"Think it's funny, do you?" he growled. "You'd like it, would you, if I did it to you?"

The laughter died away almost instantly.

"Total control," said Moody quietly as the spider balled itself up and began to roll over and over. "I could make it jump out of the window, drown itself, throw itself down one of your throats . . ."

Ron gave an involuntary shudder.

"Years back, there were a lot of witches and wizards being controlled by the Imperius Curse," said Moody, and Harry knew he was talking about the days in which Voldemort had been all-powerful. "Some job for the Ministry, trying to sort out who was being forced to act, and who was acting of their own free will.

"The Imperius Curse can be fought, and I'll be teaching you how, but it takes real strength of character, and not everyone's got it. Better avoid being hit with it if you can. CONSTANT VIGILANCE!" he barked, and everyone jumped.

Moody picked up the somersaulting spider and threw it back into the jar.

"Anyone else know one? Another illegal curse?"

Hermione's hand flew into the air again and so, to Harry's slight surprise, did Neville's. The only class in which Neville usually volunteered information was Herbology, which was easily his best subject. Neville looked surprised at his own daring.

"Yes?" said Moody, his magical eye rolling right over to fix on Neville.

"There's one — the Cruciatus Curse," said Neville in a small but distinct voice.

Moody was looking very intently at Neville, this time with both eyes.

"Your name's Longbottom?" he said, his magical eye swooping down to check the register again.

Neville nodded nervously, but Moody made no further inquiries. Turning back to the class at large, he reached into the jar for the next spider and placed it upon the desktop, where it remained motionless, apparently too scared to move.

"The Cruciatus Curse," said Moody. "Needs to be a bit bigger for you to get the idea," he said, pointing his wand at the spider. *"Engorgio!"*

The spider swelled. It was now larger than a tarantula. Abandoning all pretense, Ron pushed his chair backward, as far away from Moody's desk as possible.

Moody raised his wand again, pointed it at the spider, and muttered, *"Crucio!"*

At once, the spider's legs bent in upon its body; it rolled over and began to twitch horribly, rocking from side to side. No sound came from it, but Harry was sure that if it could have given voice, it would have been screaming. Moody did not remove his wand, and the spider started to shudder and jerk more violently —

"Stop it!" Hermione said shrilly.

Harry looked around at her. She was looking, not at the spider, but at Neville, and Harry, following her gaze, saw that Neville's hands were clenched upon the desk in front of him, his knuckles white, his eyes wide and horrified.

Moody raised his wand. The spider's legs relaxed, but it continued to twitch.

"*Reducio*," Moody muttered, and the spider shrank back to its proper size. He put it back into the jar.

"Pain," said Moody softly. "You don't need thumbscrews or knives to torture someone if you can perform the Cruciatus Curse. . . . That one was very popular once too.

"Right . . . anyone know any others?"

Harry looked around. From the looks on everyone's faces, he guessed they were all wondering what was going to happen to the last spider. Hermione's hand shook slightly as, for the third time, she raised it into the air.

"Yes?" said Moody, looking at her.

"*Avada Kedavra*," Hermione whispered.

Several people looked uneasily around at her, including Ron.

"Ah," said Moody, another slight smile twisting his lopsided mouth. "Yes, the last and worst. *Avada Kedavra* . . . the Killing Curse."

He put his hand into the glass jar, and almost as though it knew what was coming, the third spider scuttled frantically around the bottom of the jar, trying to evade Moody's fingers, but he trapped it, and placed it upon the desktop. It started to scuttle frantically across the wooden surface.

Moody raised his wand, and Harry felt a sudden thrill of foreboding.

"*Avada Kedavra!*" Moody roared.

There was a flash of blinding green light and a rushing sound, as though a vast, invisible something was soaring through the air — instantaneously the spider rolled over onto its back, unmarked, but unmistakably dead. Several of the students stifled cries; Ron had thrown himself backward and almost toppled off his seat as the spider skidded toward him.

Moody swept the dead spider off the desk onto the floor.

"Not nice," he said calmly. "Not pleasant. And there's no counter-curse. There's no blocking it. Only one known person has ever survived it, and he's sitting right in front of me."

Harry felt his face redden as Moody's eyes (both of them) looked into his own. He could feel everyone else looking around at him too. Harry stared at the blank blackboard as though fascinated by it, but not really seeing it at all. . . .

So that was how his parents had died . . . exactly like that spider. Had they been unblemished and unmarked too? Had they simply seen the flash of green light and heard the rush of speeding death, before life was wiped from their bodies?

Harry had been picturing his parents' deaths over and over again for three years now, ever since he'd found out they had been murdered, ever since he'd found out what had happened that night: Wormtail had betrayed his parents' whereabouts to Voldemort, who had come to find them at their cottage. How Voldemort had killed Harry's father first. How James Potter had tried to hold him off, while he shouted at his wife to take Harry and run . . . Voldemort had advanced on Lily Potter, told her to move aside so that he could kill Harry . . . how she had begged him to kill her instead, refused to stop shielding her son . . . and so

Voldemort had murdered her too, before turning his wand on Harry. . . .

Harry knew these details because he had heard his parents' voices when he had fought the dementors last year — for that was the terrible power of the dementors: to force their victims to relive the worst memories of their lives, and drown, powerless, in their own despair. . . .

Moody was speaking again, from a great distance, it seemed to Harry. With a massive effort, he pulled himself back to the present and listened to what Moody was saying.

"*Avada Kedavra*'s a curse that needs a powerful bit of magic behind it — you could all get your wands out now and point them at me and say the words, and I doubt I'd get so much as a nosebleed. But that doesn't matter. I'm not here to teach you how to do it.

"Now, if there's no countercurse, why am I showing you? *Because you've got to know.* You've got to appreciate what the worst is. You don't want to find yourself in a situation where you're facing it. CONSTANT VIGILANCE!" he roared, and the whole class jumped again.

"Now . . . those three curses — *Avada Kedavra,* Imperius, and Cruciatus — are known as the Unforgivable Curses. The use of any one of them on a fellow human being is enough to earn a life sentence in Azkaban. That's what you're up against. That's what I've got to teach you to fight. You need preparing. You need arming. But most of all, you need to practice *constant, never-ceasing vigilance.* Get out your quills . . . copy this down. . . ."

They spent the rest of the lesson taking notes on each of the Unforgivable Curses. No one spoke until the bell rang — but when

Moody had dismissed them and they had left the classroom, a torrent of talk burst forth. Most people were discussing the curses in awed voices — "Did you see it twitch?" "— and when he killed it — just like that!"

They were talking about the lesson, Harry thought, as though it had been some sort of spectacular show, but he hadn't found it very entertaining — and nor, it seemed, had Hermione.

"Hurry up," she said tensely to Harry and Ron.

"Not the ruddy library again?" said Ron.

"No," said Hermione curtly, pointing up a side passage. "Neville."

Neville was standing alone, halfway up the passage, staring at the stone wall opposite him with the same horrified, wide-eyed look he had worn when Moody had demonstrated the Cruciatus Curse.

"Neville?" Hermione said gently.

Neville looked around.

"Oh hello," he said, his voice much higher than usual. "Interesting lesson, wasn't it? I wonder what's for dinner, I'm — I'm starving, aren't you?"

"Neville, are you all right?" said Hermione.

"Oh yes, I'm fine," Neville gabbled in the same unnaturally high voice. "Very interesting dinner — I mean lesson — what's for eating?"

Ron gave Harry a startled look.

"Neville, what — ?"

But an odd clunking noise sounded behind them, and they turned to see Professor Moody limping toward them. All four of them fell silent, watching him apprehensively, but when he spoke, it was in a much lower and gentler growl than they had yet heard.

"It's all right, sonny," he said to Neville. "Why don't you come up to my office? Come on . . . we can have a cup of tea. . . ."

Neville looked even more frightened at the prospect of tea with Moody. He neither moved nor spoke. Moody turned his magical eye upon Harry.

"You all right, are you, Potter?"

"Yes," said Harry, almost defiantly.

Moody's blue eye quivered slightly in its socket as it surveyed Harry. Then he said, "You've got to know. It seems harsh, maybe, *but you've got to know.* No point pretending . . . well . . . come on, Longbottom, I've got some books that might interest you."

Neville looked pleadingly at Harry, Ron, and Hermione, but they didn't say anything, so Neville had no choice but to allow himself to be steered away, one of Moody's gnarled hands on his shoulder.

"What was that about?" said Ron, watching Neville and Moody turn the corner.

"I don't know," said Hermione, looking pensive.

"Some lesson, though, eh?" said Ron to Harry as they set off for the Great Hall. "Fred and George were right, weren't they? He really knows his stuff, Moody, doesn't he? When he did *Avada Kedavra,* the way that spider just *died,* just snuffed it right —"

But Ron fell suddenly silent at the look on Harry's face and didn't speak again until they reached the Great Hall, when he said he supposed they had better make a start on Professor Trelawney's predictions tonight, since they would take hours.

Hermione did not join in with Harry and Ron's conversation during dinner, but ate furiously fast, and then left for the library again. Harry and Ron walked back to Gryffindor Tower, and Harry, who had been thinking of nothing else all through dinner, now raised the subject of the Unforgivable Curses himself.

"Wouldn't Moody and Dumbledore be in trouble with the Ministry if they knew we'd seen the curses?" Harry asked as they approached the Fat Lady.

"Yeah, probably," said Ron. "But Dumbledore's always done things his way, hasn't he, and Moody's been getting in trouble for years, I reckon. Attacks first and asks questions later — look at his dustbins. Balderdash."

The Fat Lady swung forward to reveal the entrance hole, and they climbed into the Gryffindor common room, which was crowded and noisy.

"Shall we get our Divination stuff, then?" said Harry.

"I s'pose," Ron groaned.

They went up to the dormitory to fetch their books and charts, to find Neville there alone, sitting on his bed, reading. He looked a good deal calmer than at the end of Moody's lesson, though still not entirely normal. His eyes were rather red.

"You all right, Neville?" Harry asked him.

"Oh yes," said Neville, "I'm fine, thanks. Just reading this book Professor Moody lent me. . . ."

He held up the book: *Magical Water Plants of the Mediterranean.*

"Apparently, Professor Sprout told Professor Moody I'm really good at Herbology," Neville said. There was a faint note of pride in his voice that Harry had rarely heard there before. "He thought I'd like this."

Telling Neville what Professor Sprout had said, Harry thought, had been a very tactful way of cheering Neville up, for Neville very rarely heard that he was good at anything. It was the sort of thing Professor Lupin would have done.

Harry and Ron took their copies of *Unfogging the Future* back down to the common room, found a table, and set to work on their predictions for the coming month. An hour later, they had made very little progress, though their table was littered with bits of parchment bearing sums and symbols, and Harry's brain was as fogged as though it had been filled with the fumes from Professor Trelawney's fire.

"I haven't got a clue what this lot's supposed to mean," he said, staring down at a long list of calculations.

"You know," said Ron, whose hair was on end because of all the times he had run his fingers through it in frustration, "I think it's back to the old Divination standby."

"What — make it up?"

"Yeah," said Ron, sweeping the jumble of scrawled notes off the table, dipping his pen into some ink, and starting to write.

"Next Monday," he said as he scribbled, "I am likely to develop a cough, owing to the unlucky conjunction of Mars and Jupiter." He looked up at Harry. "You know her — just put in loads of misery, she'll lap it up."

"Right," said Harry, crumpling up his first attempt and lobbing it over the heads of a group of chattering first years into the fire. "Okay . . . on Monday, *I* will be in danger of — er — burns."

"Yeah, you will be," said Ron darkly, "we're seeing the skrewts again on Monday. Okay, Tuesday, *I'll* . . . erm . . ."

"Lose a treasured possession," said Harry, who was flicking through *Unfogging the Future* for ideas.

"Good one," said Ron, copying it down. "Because of . . .

erm . . . Mercury. Why don't you get stabbed in the back by some-one you thought was a friend?"

"Yeah . . . cool . . ." said Harry, scribbling it down, "because . . . Venus is in the twelfth house."

"And on Wednesday, I think I'll come off worst in a fight."

"Aaah, I was going to have a fight. Okay, I'll lose a bet."

"Yeah, you'll be betting I'll win my fight. . . ."

They continued to make up predictions (which grew steadily more tragic) for another hour, while the common room around them slowly emptied as people went up to bed. Crookshanks wandered over to them, leapt lightly into an empty chair, and stared inscrutably at Harry, rather as Hermione might look if she knew they weren't doing their homework properly.

Staring around the room, trying to think of a kind of misfortune he hadn't yet used, Harry saw Fred and George sitting together against the opposite wall, heads together, quills out, poring over a single piece of parchment. It was most unusual to see Fred and George hidden away in a corner and working silently; they usually liked to be in the thick of things and the noisy center of attention. There was something secretive about the way they were working on the piece of parchment, and Harry was reminded of how they had sat together writing something back at the Burrow. He had thought then that it was another order form for Weasleys' Wizard Wheezes, but it didn't look like that this time; if it had been, they would surely have let Lee Jordan in on the joke. He wondered whether it had anything to do with entering the Triwizard Tournament.

As Harry watched, George shook his head at Fred, scratched out something with his quill, and said, in a very quiet voice that nevertheless carried across the almost deserted room, "No — that sounds like we're accusing him. Got to be careful . . ."

Then George looked over and saw Harry watching him. Harry grinned and quickly returned to his predictions — he didn't want George to think he was eavesdropping. Shortly after that, the twins rolled up their parchment, said good night, and went off to bed.

Fred and George had been gone ten minutes or so when the portrait hole opened and Hermione climbed into the common room carrying a sheaf of parchment in one hand and a box whose contents rattled as she walked in the other. Crookshanks arched his back, purring.

"Hello," she said, "I've just finished!"

"So have I!" said Ron triumphantly, throwing down his quill.

Hermione sat down, laid the things she was carrying in an empty armchair, and pulled Ron's predictions toward her.

"Not going to have a very good month, are you?" she said sardonically as Crookshanks curled up in her lap.

"Ah well, at least I'm forewarned," Ron yawned.

"You seem to be drowning twice," said Hermione.

"Oh am I?" said Ron, peering down at his predictions. "I'd better change one of them to getting trampled by a rampaging hippogriff."

"Don't you think it's a bit obvious you've made these up?" said Hermione.

"How dare you!" said Ron, in mock outrage. "We've been working like house-elves here!"

Hermione raised her eyebrows.

"It's just an expression," said Ron hastily.

Harry laid down his quill too, having just finished predicting his own death by decapitation.

"What's in the box?" he asked, pointing at it.

"Funny you should ask," said Hermione, with a nasty look at Ron. She took off the lid and showed them the contents.

Inside were about fifty badges, all of different colors, but all bearing the same letters: S.P.E.W.

"'Spew'?" said Harry, picking up a badge and looking at it. "What's this about?"

"Not *spew*," said Hermione impatiently. "It's S-P-E-W. Stands for the Society for the Promotion of Elfish Welfare."

"Never heard of it," said Ron.

"Well, of course you haven't," said Hermione briskly, "I've only just started it."

"Yeah?" said Ron in mild surprise. "How many members have you got?"

"Well — if you two join — three," said Hermione.

"And you think we want to walk around wearing badges saying 'spew,' do you?" said Ron.

"S-P-E-W!" said Hermione hotly. "I was going to put *Stop the Outrageous Abuse of Our Fellow Magical Creatures and Campaign for a Change in Their Legal Status* — but it wouldn't fit. So that's the heading of our manifesto."

She brandished the sheaf of parchment at them.

"I've been researching it thoroughly in the library. Elf enslavement goes back centuries. I can't believe no one's done anything about it before now."

"Hermione — open your ears," said Ron loudly. "They. Like. It. They *like* being enslaved!"

"Our short-term aims," said Hermione, speaking even more

loudly than Ron, and acting as though she hadn't heard a word, "are to secure house-elves fair wages and working conditions. Our long-term aims include changing the law about non-wand use, and trying to get an elf into the Department for the Regulation and Control of Magical Creatures, because they're shockingly underrepresented."

"And how do we do all this?" Harry asked.

"We start by recruiting members," said Hermione happily. "I thought two Sickles to join — that buys a badge — and the proceeds can fund our leaflet campaign. You're treasurer, Ron — I've got you a collecting tin upstairs — and Harry, you're secretary, so you might want to write down everything I'm saying now, as a record of our first meeting."

There was a pause in which Hermione beamed at the pair of them, and Harry sat, torn between exasperation at Hermione and amusement at the look on Ron's face. The silence was broken, not by Ron, who in any case looked as though he was temporarily dumbstruck, but by a soft *tap, tap* on the window. Harry looked across the now empty common room and saw, illuminated by the moonlight, a snowy owl perched on the windowsill.

"Hedwig!" he shouted, and he launched himself out of his chair and across the room to pull open the window.

Hedwig flew inside, soared across the room, and landed on the table on top of Harry's predictions.

"About time!" said Harry, hurrying after her.

"She's got an answer!" said Ron excitedly, pointing at the grubby piece of parchment tied to Hedwig's leg.

Harry hastily untied it and sat down to read, whereupon Hedwig fluttered onto his knee, hooting softly.

"What does it say?" Hermione asked breathlessly.

The letter was very short, and looked as though it had been scrawled in a great hurry. Harry read it aloud:

> *Harry —*
>
> *I'm flying north immediately. This news about your scar is the latest in a series of strange rumors that have reached me here. If it hurts again, go straight to Dumbledore — they're saying he's got Mad-Eye out of retirement, which means he's reading the signs, even if no one else is.*
>
> *I'll be in touch soon. My best to Ron and Hermione. Keep your eyes open, Harry.*
>
> *Sirius*

Harry looked up at Ron and Hermione, who stared back at him.

"He's flying north?" Hermione whispered. "He's coming *back*?"

"Dumbledore's reading what signs?" said Ron, looking perplexed. "Harry — what's up?"

For Harry had just hit himself in the forehead with his fist, jolting Hedwig out of his lap.

"I shouldn't've told him!" Harry said furiously.

"What are you on about?" said Ron in surprise.

"It's made him think he's got to come back!" said Harry, now slamming his fist on the table so that Hedwig landed on the back of Ron's chair, hooting indignantly. "Coming back, because he thinks I'm in trouble! And there's nothing wrong with me! And I haven't got anything for you," Harry snapped at Hedwig, who was clicking her beak expectantly, "you'll have to go up to the Owlery if you want food."

Hedwig gave him an extremely offended look and took off for the open window, cuffing him around the head with her outstretched wing as she went.

"Harry," Hermione began, in a pacifying sort of voice.

"I'm going to bed," said Harry shortly. "See you in the morning."

Upstairs in the dormitory he pulled on his pajamas and got into his four-poster, but he didn't feel remotely tired.

If Sirius came back and got caught, it would be his, Harry's, fault. Why hadn't he kept his mouth shut? A few seconds' pain and he'd had to blab. . . . If he'd just had the sense to keep it to himself. . . .

He heard Ron come up into the dormitory a short while later, but did not speak to him. For a long time, Harry lay staring up at the dark canopy of his bed. The dormitory was completely silent, and, had he been less preoccupied, Harry would have realized that the absence of Neville's usual snores meant that he was not the only one lying awake.

# BEAUXBATONS AND DURMSTRANG

Early next morning, Harry woke with a plan fully formed in his mind, as though his sleeping brain had been working on it all night. He got up, dressed in the pale dawn light, left the dormitory without waking Ron, and went back down to the deserted common room. Here he took a piece of parchment from the table upon which his Divination homework still lay and wrote the following letter: .

> *Dear Sirius,*
>
> *I reckon I just imagined my scar hurting, I was half asleep when I wrote to you last time. There's no point coming back, everything's fine here. Don't worry about me, my head feels completely normal.* Harry

He then climbed out of the portrait hole, up through the silent castle (held up only briefly by Peeves, who tried to overturn a large vase on him halfway along the fourth-floor corridor), finally arriving at the Owlery, which was situated at the top of West Tower.

The Owlery was a circular stone room, rather cold and drafty, because none of the windows had glass in them. The floor was entirely covered in straw, owl droppings, and the regurgitated skeletons of mice and voles. Hundreds upon hundreds of owls of every breed imaginable were nestled here on perches that rose right up to the top of the tower, nearly all of them asleep, though here and there a round amber eye glared at Harry. He spotted Hedwig nestled between a barn owl and a tawny, and hurried over to her, sliding a little on the dropping-strewn floor.

It took him a while to persuade her to wake up and then to look at him, as she kept shuffling around on her perch, showing him her tail. She was evidently still furious about his lack of gratitude the previous night. In the end, it was Harry suggesting she might be too tired, and that perhaps he would ask Ron to borrow Pigwidgeon, that made her stick out her leg and allow him to tie the letter to it.

"Just find him, all right?" Harry said, stroking her back as he carried her on his arm to one of the holes in the wall. "Before the dementors do."

She nipped his finger, perhaps rather harder than she would ordinarily have done, but hooted softly in a reassuring sort of way all the same. Then she spread her wings and took off into the sunrise. Harry watched her fly out of sight with the familiar feeling of unease back in his stomach. He had been so sure that Sirius's reply would alleviate his worries rather than increasing them.

"That was a *lie,* Harry," said Hermione sharply over breakfast, when he told her and Ron what he had done. "You *didn't* imagine your scar hurting and you know it."

"So what?" said Harry. "He's not going back to Azkaban because of me."

"Drop it," said Ron sharply to Hermione as she opened her mouth to argue some more, and for once, Hermione heeded him, and fell silent.

Harry did his best not to worry about Sirius over the next couple of weeks. True, he could not stop himself from looking anxiously around every morning when the post owls arrived, nor, late at night before he went to sleep, prevent himself from seeing horrible visions of Sirius, cornered by dementors down some dark London street, but betweentimes he tried to keep his mind off his godfather. He wished he still had Quidditch to distract him; nothing worked so well on a troubled mind as a good, hard training session. On the other hand, their lessons were becoming more difficult and demanding than ever before, particularly Moody's Defense Against the Dark Arts.

To their surprise, Professor Moody had announced that he would be putting the Imperius Curse on each of them in turn, to demonstrate its power and to see whether they could resist its effects.

"But — but you said it's illegal, Professor," said Hermione uncertainly as Moody cleared away the desks with a sweep of his wand, leaving a large clear space in the middle of the room. "You said — to use it against another human was —"

"Dumbledore wants you taught what it feels like," said Moody, his magical eye swiveling onto Hermione and fixing her with an eerie, unblinking stare. "If you'd rather learn the hard way — when someone's putting it on you so they can control you completely — fine by me. You're excused. Off you go."

He pointed one gnarled finger toward the door. Hermione went very pink and muttered something about not meaning that she wanted to leave. Harry and Ron grinned at each other. They knew Hermione would rather eat bubotuber pus than miss such an important lesson.

Moody began to beckon students forward in turn and put the Imperius Curse upon them. Harry watched as, one by one, his classmates did the most extraordinary things under its influence. Dean Thomas hopped three times around the room, singing the national anthem. Lavender Brown imitated a squirrel. Neville performed a series of quite astonishing gymnastics he would certainly not have been capable of in his normal state. Not one of them seemed to be able to fight off the curse, and each of them recovered only when Moody had removed it.

"Potter," Moody growled, "you next."

Harry moved forward into the middle of the classroom, into the space that Moody had cleared of desks. Moody raised his wand, pointed it at Harry, and said, *"Imperio!"*

It was the most wonderful feeling. Harry felt a floating sensation as every thought and worry in his head was wiped gently away, leaving nothing but a vague, untraceable happiness. He stood there feeling immensely relaxed, only dimly aware of everyone watching him.

And then he heard Mad-Eye Moody's voice, echoing in some distant chamber of his empty brain: *Jump onto the desk . . . jump onto the desk. . . .*

Harry bent his knees obediently, preparing to spring.

*Jump onto the desk. . . .*

Why, though? Another voice had awoken in the back of his brain.

Stupid thing to do, really, said the voice.

*Jump onto the desk. . . .*

No, I don't think I will, thanks, said the other voice, a little more firmly . . . no, I don't really want to. . . .

*Jump! NOW!*

The next thing Harry felt was considerable pain. He had both jumped and tried to prevent himself from jumping — the result was that he'd smashed headlong into the desk, knocking it over, and, by the feeling in his legs, fractured both his kneecaps.

"Now, *that's* more like it!" growled Moody's voice, and suddenly, Harry felt the empty, echoing feeling in his head disappear. He remembered exactly what was happening, and the pain in his knees seemed to double.

"Look at that, you lot . . . Potter fought! He fought it, and he damn near beat it! We'll try that again, Potter, and the rest of you, pay attention — watch his eyes, that's where you see it — very good, Potter, very good indeed! They'll have trouble controlling *you*!"

"The way he talks," Harry muttered as he hobbled out of the Defense Against the Dark Arts class an hour later (Moody had insisted on putting Harry through his paces four times in a row, until Harry could throw off the curse entirely), "you'd think we were all going to be attacked any second."

"Yeah, I know," said Ron, who was skipping on every alternate step. He had had much more difficulty with the curse than Harry, though Moody assured him the effects would wear off by lunchtime. "Talk about paranoid . . ." Ron glanced nervously over his shoulder to check that Moody was definitely out of earshot and went on. "No wonder they were glad to get shot of him at the Ministry. Did you hear him telling Seamus what he did to that witch who shouted 'Boo' behind him on April Fools' Day? And when are we supposed to read up on resisting the Imperius Curse with everything else we've got to do?"

All the fourth years had noticed a definite increase in the amount of work they were required to do this term. Professor McGonagall explained why, when the class gave a particularly loud groan at the amount of Transfiguration homework she had assigned.

"You are now entering a most important phase of your magical education!" she told them, her eyes glinting dangerously behind her square spectacles. "Your Ordinary Wizarding Levels are drawing closer —"

"We don't take O.W.L.s till fifth year!" said Dean Thomas indignantly.

"Maybe not, Thomas, but believe me, you need all the preparation you can get! Miss Granger remains the only person in this class who has managed to turn a hedgehog into a satisfactory pincushion. I might remind you that *your* pincushion, Thomas, still curls up in fright if anyone approaches it with a pin!"

Hermione, who had turned rather pink again, seemed to be trying not to look too pleased with herself.

Harry and Ron were deeply amused when Professor Trelawney told them that they had received top marks for their homework in their next Divination class. She read out large portions of their predictions, commending them for their unflinching acceptance of the horrors in store for them — but they were less amused when she asked them to do the same thing for the month after next; both of them were running out of ideas for catastrophes.

Meanwhile Professor Binns, the ghost who taught History of Magic, had them writing weekly essays on the goblin rebellions of the eighteenth century. Professor Snape was forcing them to research antidotes. They took this one seriously, as he had hinted that he might be poisoning one of them before Christmas to see if their antidote worked. Professor Flitwick had asked them to read three extra books in preparation for their lesson on Summoning Charms.

Even Hagrid was adding to their workload. The Blast-Ended Skrewts were growing at a remarkable pace given that nobody had yet discovered what they ate. Hagrid was delighted, and as part of their "project," suggested that they come down to his hut on alternate evenings to observe the skrewts and make notes on their extraordinary behavior.

"I will not," said Draco Malfoy flatly when Hagrid had proposed this with the air of Father Christmas pulling an extra-large toy out of his sack. "I see enough of these foul things during lessons, thanks."

Hagrid's smile faded off his face.

"Yeh'll do wha' yer told," he growled, "or I'll be takin' a leaf outta Professor Moody's book. . . . I hear yeh made a good ferret, Malfoy."

The Gryffindors roared with laughter. Malfoy flushed with anger, but apparently the memory of Moody's punishment was still sufficiently painful to stop him from retorting. Harry, Ron, and Hermione returned to the castle at the end of the lesson in high spirits; seeing Hagrid put down Malfoy was particularly satisfying, especially because Malfoy had done his very best to get Hagrid sacked the previous year.

When they arrived in the entrance hall, they found themselves unable to proceed owing to the large crowd of students congregated there, all milling around a large sign that had been erected at the foot of the marble staircase. Ron, the tallest of the three, stood on tiptoe to see over the heads in front of them and read the sign aloud to the other two:

### TRIWIZARD TOURNAMENT

THE DELEGATIONS FROM BEAUXBATONS AND
DURMSTRANG WILL BE ARRIVING AT 6 O'CLOCK
ON FRIDAY THE 30TH OF OCTOBER. LESSONS WILL
END HALF AN HOUR EARLY —

"Brilliant!" said Harry. "It's Potions last thing on Friday! Snape won't have time to poison us all!"

STUDENTS WILL RETURN THEIR BAGS AND BOOKS
TO THEIR DORMITORIES AND ASSEMBLE IN FRONT
OF THE CASTLE TO GREET OUR GUESTS BEFORE
THE WELCOMING FEAST.

"Only a week away!" said Ernie Macmillan of Hufflepuff, emerging from the crowd, his eyes gleaming. "I wonder if Cedric knows? Think I'll go and tell him. . . ."

"Cedric?" said Ron blankly as Ernie hurried off.

"Diggory," said Harry. "He must be entering the tournament."

"That idiot, Hogwarts champion?" said Ron as they pushed their way through the chattering crowd toward the staircase.

"He's not an idiot. You just don't like him because he beat Gryffindor at Quidditch," said Hermione. "I've heard he's a really good student — *and* he's a prefect."

She spoke as though this settled the matter.

"You only like him because he's *handsome,*" said Ron scathingly.

"Excuse me, I don't like people just because they're handsome!" said Hermione indignantly.

Ron gave a loud false cough, which sounded oddly like *"Lockhart!"*

The appearance of the sign in the entrance hall had a marked effect upon the inhabitants of the castle. During the following week, there seemed to be only one topic of conversation, no matter where Harry went: the Triwizard Tournament. Rumors were flying from student to student like highly contagious germs: who was going to try for Hogwarts champion, what the tournament would involve, how the students from Beauxbatons and Durmstrang differed from themselves.

Harry noticed too that the castle seemed to be undergoing an extra-thorough cleaning. Several grimy portraits had been scrubbed, much to the displeasure of their subjects, who sat huddled in their frames muttering darkly and wincing as they felt their raw pink faces. The suits of armor were suddenly gleaming and moving without squeaking, and Argus Filch, the caretaker, was behaving so ferociously to any students who forgot to wipe their shoes that he terrified a pair of first-year girls into hysterics.

Other members of the staff seemed oddly tense too.

"Longbottom, kindly do *not* reveal that you can't even perform a simple Switching Spell in front of anyone from Durmstrang!" Professor McGonagall barked at the end of one particularly difficult lesson, during which Neville had accidentally transplanted his own ears onto a cactus.

When they went down to breakfast on the morning of the thirtieth of October, they found that the Great Hall had been decorated overnight. Enormous silk banners hung from the walls, each of them representing a Hogwarts House: red with a gold lion for Gryffindor, blue with a bronze eagle for Ravenclaw, yellow with a black badger for Hufflepuff, and green with a silver serpent for Slytherin. Behind the teachers' table, the largest banner of all bore the Hogwarts coat of arms: lion, eagle, badger, and snake united around a large letter H.

Harry, Ron, and Hermione sat down beside Fred and George at the Gryffindor table. Once again, and most unusually, they were sitting apart from everyone else and conversing in low voices. Ron led the way over to them.

"It's a bummer, all right," George was saying gloomily to Fred. "But if he won't talk to us in person, we'll have to send him the letter after all. Or we'll stuff it into his hand. He can't avoid us forever."

"Who's avoiding you?" said Ron, sitting down next to them.

"Wish you would," said Fred, looking irritated at the interruption.

"What's a bummer?" Ron asked George.

"Having a nosy git like you for a brother," said George.

"You two got any ideas on the Triwizard Tournament yet?" Harry asked. "Thought any more about trying to enter?"

"I asked McGonagall how the champions are chosen but she

wasn't telling," said George bitterly. "She just told me to shut up and get on with Transfiguring my raccoon."

"Wonder what the tasks are going to be?" said Ron thoughtfully. "You know, I bet we could do them, Harry. We've done dangerous stuff before. . . ."

"Not in front of a panel of judges, you haven't," said Fred. "McGonagall says the champions get awarded points according to how well they've done the tasks."

"Who are the judges?" Harry asked.

"Well, the Heads of the participating schools are always on the panel," said Hermione, and everyone looked around at her, rather surprised, "because all three of them were injured during the Tournament of 1792, when a cockatrice the champions were supposed to be catching went on the rampage."

She noticed them all looking at her and said, with her usual air of impatience that nobody else had read all the books she had, "It's all in *Hogwarts: A History*. Though, of course, that book's not *entirely* reliable. *A* Revised *History of Hogwarts* would be a more accurate title. Or *A Highly Biased and Selective History of Hogwarts, Which Glosses Over the Nastier Aspects of the School*."

"What are you on about?" said Ron, though Harry thought he knew what was coming.

"*House-elves!*" said Hermione, her eyes flashing. "Not once, in over a thousand pages, does *Hogwarts: A History* mention that we are all colluding in the oppression of a hundred slaves!"

Harry shook his head and applied himself to his scrambled eggs. His and Ron's lack of enthusiasm had done nothing whatsoever to curb Hermione's determination to pursue justice for house-elves.

True, both of them had paid two Sickles for a S.P.E.W. badge, but they had only done it to keep her quiet. Their Sickles had been wasted, however; if anything, they seemed to have made Hermione more vociferous. She had been badgering Harry and Ron ever since, first to wear the badges, then to persuade others to do the same, and she had also taken to rattling around the Gryffindor common room every evening, cornering people and shaking the collecting tin under their noses.

"You do realize that your sheets are changed, your fires lit, your classrooms cleaned, and your food cooked by a group of magical creatures who are unpaid and enslaved?" she kept saying fiercely.

Some people, like Neville, had paid up just to stop Hermione from glowering at them. A few seemed mildly interested in what she had to say, but were reluctant to take a more active role in campaigning. Many regarded the whole thing as a joke.

Ron now rolled his eyes at the ceiling, which was flooding them all in autumn sunlight, and Fred became extremely interested in his bacon (both twins had refused to buy a S.P.E.W. badge). George, however, leaned in toward Hermione.

"Listen, have you ever been down in the kitchens, Hermione?"

"No, of course not," said Hermione curtly, "I hardly think students are supposed to —"

"Well, we have," said George, indicating Fred, "loads of times, to nick food. And we've met them, and they're *happy*. They think they've got the best job in the world —"

"That's because they're uneducated and brainwashed!" Hermione began hotly, but her next few words were drowned out by the sudden whooshing noise from overhead, which announced the arrival of the post owls. Harry looked up at once, and saw Hedwig soaring toward him. Hermione stopped talking abruptly; she and Ron watched Hedwig anxiously as she fluttered down onto Harry's shoulder, folded her wings, and held out her leg wearily.

Harry pulled off Sirius's reply and offered Hedwig his bacon rinds, which she ate gratefully. Then, checking that Fred and George were safely immersed in further discussions about the Triwizard Tournament, Harry read out Sirius's letter in a whisper to Ron and Hermione.

> *Nice try, Harry.*
>
> *I'm back in the country and well hidden. I want you to keep me posted on everything that's going on at Hogwarts. Don't use Hedwig, keep changing owls, and don't worry about me, just watch out for yourself. Don't forget what I said about your scar.*
>
> *Sirius*

"Why d'you have to keep changing owls?" Ron asked in a low voice.

"Hedwig'll attract too much attention," said Hermione at once. "She stands out. A snowy owl that keeps returning to wherever he's hiding . . . I mean, they're not native birds, are they?"

Harry rolled up the letter and slipped it inside his robes, wondering whether he felt more or less worried than before. He supposed that Sirius managing to get back without being caught was something. He couldn't deny either that the idea that Sirius was much nearer was reassuring; at least he wouldn't have to wait so long for a response every time he wrote.

"Thanks, Hedwig," he said, stroking her. She hooted sleepily, dipped her beak briefly into his goblet of orange juice, then took off again, clearly desperate for a good long sleep in the Owlery.

There was a pleasant feeling of anticipation in the air that day. Nobody was very attentive in lessons, being much more interested in the arrival that evening of the people from Beauxbatons and Durmstrang; even Potions was more bearable than usual, as it was half an hour shorter. When the bell rang early, Harry, Ron, and Hermione hurried up to Gryffindor Tower, deposited their bags and books as they had been instructed, pulled on their cloaks, and rushed back downstairs into the entrance hall.

The Heads of Houses were ordering their students into lines.

"Weasley, straighten your hat," Professor McGonagall snapped at Ron. "Miss Patil, take that ridiculous thing out of your hair."

Parvati scowled and removed a large ornamental butterfly from the end of her plait.

"Follow me, please," said Professor McGonagall. "First years in front . . . no pushing. . . ."

They filed down the steps and lined up in front of the castle. It was a cold, clear evening; dusk was falling and a pale, transparent-looking moon was already shining over the Forbidden Forest. Harry, standing between Ron and Hermione in the fourth row from the front, saw Dennis Creevey positively shivering with anticipation among the other first years.

"Nearly six," said Ron, checking his watch and then staring down the drive that led to the front gates. "How d'you reckon they're coming? The train?"

"I doubt it," said Hermione.

"How, then? Broomsticks?" Harry suggested, looking up at the starry sky.

"I don't think so . . . not from that far away. . . ."

"A Portkey?" Ron suggested. "Or they could Apparate — maybe you're allowed to do it under seventeen wherever they come from?"

"You can't Apparate inside the Hogwarts grounds, how often do I have to tell you?" said Hermione impatiently.

They scanned the darkening grounds excitedly, but nothing was moving; everything was still, silent, and quite as usual. Harry was starting to feel cold. He wished they'd hurry up. . . . Maybe the foreign students were preparing a dramatic entrance. . . . He remembered what Mr. Weasley had said back at the campsite before the Quidditch World Cup: "always the same — we can't resist showing off when we get together. . . ."

And then Dumbledore called out from the back row where he stood with the other teachers —

"Aha! Unless I am very much mistaken, the delegation from Beauxbatons approaches!"

"Where?" said many students eagerly, all looking in different directions.

"*There!*" yelled a sixth year, pointing over the forest.

Something large, much larger than a broomstick — or, indeed, a hundred broomsticks — was hurtling across the deep blue sky toward the castle, growing larger all the time.

"It's a dragon!" shrieked one of the first years, losing her head completely.

"Don't be stupid . . . it's a flying house!" said Dennis Creevey.

Dennis's guess was closer. . . . As the gigantic black shape skimmed over the treetops of the Forbidden Forest and the lights shining from the castle windows hit it, they saw a gigantic, powder-blue, horse-drawn carriage, the size of a large house, soaring toward them, pulled through the air by a dozen winged horses, all palominos, and each the size of an elephant.

The front three rows of students drew backward as the carriage hurtled ever lower, coming in to land at a tremendous speed — then, with an almighty crash that made Neville jump backward onto a Slytherin fifth year's foot, the horses' hooves, larger than dinner plates, hit the ground. A second later, the carriage landed too, bouncing upon its vast wheels, while the golden horses tossed their enormous heads and rolled large, fiery red eyes.

Harry just had time to see that the door of the carriage bore a coat of arms (two crossed, golden wands, each emitting three stars) before it opened.

A boy in pale blue robes jumped down from the carriage, bent forward, fumbled for a moment with something on the carriage floor, and unfolded a set of golden steps. He sprang back respectfully. Then Harry saw a shining, high-heeled black shoe emerging from the inside of the carriage — a shoe the size of a child's sled — followed, almost immediately, by the largest woman he had ever seen in his life. The size of the carriage, and of the horses, was immediately explained. A few people gasped.

Harry had only ever seen one person as large as this woman in his life, and that was Hagrid; he doubted whether there was an inch difference in their heights. Yet somehow — maybe simply because he was used to Hagrid — this woman (now at the foot of the steps, and looking around at the waiting, wide-eyed crowd) seemed even more unnaturally large. As she stepped into the light flooding from the entrance hall, she was revealed to have a handsome, olive-skinned face; large, black, liquid-looking eyes; and a rather beaky nose. Her hair was drawn back in a shining knob at the base of her neck. She was dressed from head to foot in black satin, and many magnificent opals gleamed at her throat and on her thick fingers.

Dumbledore started to clap; the students, following his lead, broke into applause too, many of them standing on tiptoe, the better to look at this woman.

Her face relaxed into a gracious smile and she walked forward toward Dumbledore, extending a glittering hand. Dumbledore, though tall himself, had barely to bend to kiss it.

"My dear Madame Maxime," he said. "Welcome to Hogwarts."

"Dumbly-dorr," said Madame Maxime in a deep voice. "I 'ope I find you well?"

"In excellent form, I thank you," said Dumbledore.

"My pupils," said Madame Maxime, waving one of her enormous hands carelessly behind her.

Harry, whose attention had been focused completely upon Madame Maxime, now noticed that about a dozen boys and girls, all, by the look of them, in their late teens, had emerged from the carriage and were now standing behind Madame Maxime. They were shivering, which was unsurprising, given that their robes seemed to be made of fine silk, and none of them were wearing cloaks. A few had wrapped scarves and shawls around their heads. From what Harry could see of them (they were standing in Madame Maxime's enormous shadow), they were staring up at Hogwarts with apprehensive looks on their faces.

"'As Karkaroff arrived yet?" Madame Maxime asked.

"He should be here any moment," said Dumbledore. "Would you like to wait here and greet him or would you prefer to step inside and warm up a trifle?"

"Warm up, I think," said Madame Maxime. "But ze 'orses —"

"Our Care of Magical Creatures teacher will be delighted to take care of them," said Dumbledore, "the moment he has returned from dealing with a slight situation that has arisen with some of his other — er — charges."

"Skrewts," Ron muttered to Harry, grinning.

"My steeds require — er — forceful 'andling," said Madame Maxime, looking as though she doubted whether any Care of Magical Creatures teacher at Hogwarts could be up to the job. "Zey are very strong. . . ."

"I assure you that Hagrid will be well up to the job," said Dumbledore, smiling.

"Very well," said Madame Maxime, bowing slightly. "Will you please inform zis 'Agrid zat ze 'orses drink only single-malt whiskey?"

"It will be attended to," said Dumbledore, also bowing.

"Come," said Madame Maxime imperiously to her students, and the Hogwarts crowd parted to allow her and her students to pass up the stone steps.

"How big d'you reckon Durmstrang's horses are going to be?" Seamus Finnigan said, leaning around Lavender and Parvati to address Harry and Ron.

"Well, if they're any bigger than this lot, even Hagrid won't be able to handle them," said Harry. "That's if he hasn't been attacked by his skrewts. Wonder what's up with them?"

"Maybe they've escaped," said Ron hopefully.

"Oh don't say that," said Hermione with a shudder. "Imagine that lot loose on the grounds. . . ."

They stood, shivering slightly now, waiting for the Durmstrang party to arrive. Most people were gazing hopefully up at the sky.

For a few minutes, the silence was broken only by Madame Maxime's huge horses snorting and stamping. But then —

"Can you hear something?" said Ron suddenly.

Harry listened; a loud and oddly eerie noise was drifting toward them from out of the darkness: a muffled rumbling and sucking sound, as though an immense vacuum cleaner were moving along a riverbed. . . .

"The lake!" yelled Lee Jordan, pointing down at it. "Look at the lake!"

From their position at the top of the lawns overlooking the grounds, they had a clear view of the smooth black surface of the water — except that the surface was suddenly not smooth at all. Some disturbance was taking place deep in the center; great bubbles were forming on the surface, waves were now washing over the muddy banks — and then, out in the very middle of the lake, a whirlpool appeared, as if a giant plug had just been pulled out of the lake's floor. . . .

What seemed to be a long, black pole began to rise slowly out of the heart of the whirlpool . . . and then Harry saw the rigging. . . .

"It's a mast!" he said to Ron and Hermione.

Slowly, magnificently, the ship rose out of the water, gleaming in the moonlight. It had a strangely skeletal look about it, as though it were a resurrected wreck, and the dim, misty lights shimmering at its portholes looked like ghostly eyes. Finally, with a great sloshing noise, the ship emerged entirely, bobbing on the turbulent water, and began to glide toward the bank. A few moments later, they heard the splash of an anchor being thrown down in the shallows, and the thud of a plank being lowered onto the bank.

People were disembarking; they could see their silhouettes

passing the lights in the ship's portholes. All of them, Harry noticed, seemed to be built along the lines of Crabbe and Goyle . . . but then, as they drew nearer, walking up the lawns into the light streaming from the entrance hall, he saw that their bulk was really due to the fact that they were wearing cloaks of some kind of shaggy, matted fur. But the man who was leading them up to the castle was wearing furs of a different sort: sleek and silver, like his hair.

"Dumbledore!" he called heartily as he walked up the slope. "How are you, my dear fellow, how are you?"

"Blooming, thank you, Professor Karkaroff," Dumbledore replied.

Karkaroff had a fruity, unctuous voice; when he stepped into the light pouring from the front doors of the castle they saw that he was tall and thin like Dumbledore, but his white hair was short, and his goatee (finishing in a small curl) did not entirely hide his rather weak chin. When he reached Dumbledore, he shook hands with both of his own.

"Dear old Hogwarts," he said, looking up at the castle and smiling; his teeth were rather yellow, and Harry noticed that his smile did not extend to his eyes, which remained cold and shrewd. "How good it is to be here, how good. . . . Viktor, come along, into the warmth . . . you don't mind, Dumbledore? Viktor has a slight head cold. . . ."

Karkaroff beckoned forward one of his students. As the boy passed, Harry caught a glimpse of a prominent curved nose and thick black eyebrows. He didn't need the punch on the arm Ron gave him, or the hiss in his ear, to recognize that profile.

"Harry — *it's Krum!*"

# THE GOBLET OF FIRE

I don't believe it!" Ron said, in a stunned voice, as the Hogwarts students filed back up the steps behind the party from Durmstrang. "Krum, Harry! *Viktor Krum!*"

"For heaven's sake, Ron, he's only a Quidditch player," said Hermione.

*"Only a Quidditch player?"* Ron said, looking at her as though he couldn't believe his ears. "Hermione — he's one of the best Seekers in the world! I had no idea he was still at school!"

As they recrossed the entrance hall with the rest of the Hogwarts students heading for the Great Hall, Harry saw Lee Jordan jumping up and down on the soles of his feet to get a better look at the back of Krum's head. Several sixth-year girls were frantically searching their pockets as they walked —

"Oh I don't believe it, I haven't got a single quill on me —"

"D'you think he'd sign my hat in lipstick?"

"*Really,*" Hermione said loftily as they passed the girls, now squabbling over the lipstick.

"*I'm* getting his autograph if I can," said Ron. "You haven't got a quill, have you, Harry?"

"Nope, they're upstairs in my bag," said Harry.

They walked over to the Gryffindor table and sat down. Ron took care to sit on the side facing the doorway, because Krum and his fellow Durmstrang students were still gathered around it, apparently unsure about where they should sit. The students from Beauxbatons had chosen seats at the Ravenclaw table. They were looking around the Great Hall with glum expressions on their faces. Three of them were still clutching scarves and shawls around their heads.

"It's not *that* cold," said Hermione defensively. "Why didn't they bring cloaks?"

"Over here! Come and sit over here!" Ron hissed. "Over here! Hermione, budge up, make a space —"

"What?"

"Too late," said Ron bitterly.

Viktor Krum and his fellow Durmstrang students had settled themselves at the Slytherin table. Harry could see Malfoy, Crabbe, and Goyle looking very smug about this. As he watched, Malfoy bent forward to speak to Krum.

"Yeah, that's right, smarm up to him, Malfoy," said Ron scathingly. "I bet Krum can see right through him, though . . . bet he gets people fawning over him all the time. . . . Where d'you reckon they're going to sleep? We could offer him a space in our dormitory, Harry . . . I wouldn't mind giving him my bed, I could kip on a camp bed."

Hermione snorted.

"They look a lot happier than the Beauxbatons lot," said Harry.

The Durmstrang students were pulling off their heavy furs and looking up at the starry black ceiling with expressions of interest; a couple of them were picking up the golden plates and goblets and examining them, apparently impressed.

Up at the staff table, Filch, the caretaker, was adding chairs. He was wearing his moldy old tailcoat in honor of the occasion. Harry was surprised to see that he added four chairs, two on either side of Dumbledore's.

"But there are only two extra people," Harry said. "Why's Filch putting out four chairs, who else is coming?"

"Eh?" said Ron vaguely. He was still staring avidly at Krum.

When all the students had entered the Hall and settled down at their House tables, the staff entered, filing up to the top table and taking their seats. Last in line were Professor Dumbledore, Professor Karkaroff, and Madame Maxime. When their headmistress appeared, the pupils from Beauxbatons leapt to their feet. A few of the Hogwarts students laughed. The Beauxbatons party appeared quite unembarrassed, however, and did not resume their seats until Madame Maxime had sat down on Dumbledore's left-hand side. Dumbledore remained standing, and a silence fell over the Great Hall.

"Good evening, ladies and gentlemen, ghosts and — most particularly — guests," said Dumbledore, beaming around at the foreign students. "I have great pleasure in welcoming you all to Hogwarts. I hope and trust that your stay here will be both comfortable and enjoyable."

One of the Beauxbatons girls still clutching a muffler around her head gave what was unmistakably a derisive laugh.

"No one's making you stay!" Hermione whispered, bristling at her.

"The tournament will be officially opened at the end of the feast," said Dumbledore. "I now invite you all to eat, drink, and make yourselves at home!"

He sat down, and Harry saw Karkaroff lean forward at once and engage him in conversation.

The plates in front of them filled with food as usual. The house-elves in the kitchen seemed to have pulled out all the stops; there was a greater variety of dishes in front of them than Harry had ever seen, including several that were definitely foreign.

"What's *that*?" said Ron, pointing at a large dish of some sort of shellfish stew that stood beside a large steak-and-kidney pudding.

"Bouillabaisse," said Hermione.

"Bless you," said Ron.

"It's *French*," said Hermione, "I had it on holiday summer before last. It's very nice."

"I'll take your word for it," said Ron, helping himself to black pudding.

The Great Hall seemed somehow much more crowded than usual, even though there were barely twenty additional students there; perhaps it was because their differently colored uniforms stood out so clearly against the black of the Hogwarts robes. Now that they had removed their furs, the Durmstrang students were revealed to be wearing robes of a deep bloodred.

Hagrid sidled into the Hall through a door behind the staff table twenty minutes after the start of the feast. He slid into his seat at the end and waved at Harry, Ron, and Hermione with a very heavily bandaged hand.

"Skrewts doing all right, Hagrid?" Harry called.

"Thrivin'," Hagrid called back happily.

"Yeah, I'll just bet they are," said Ron quietly. "Looks like they've finally found a food they like, doesn't it? Hagrid's fingers."

At that moment, a voice said, "Excuse me, are you wanting ze bouillabaisse?"

It was the girl from Beauxbatons who had laughed during Dumbledore's speech. She had finally removed her muffler. A long sheet of silvery-blonde hair fell almost to her waist. She had large, deep blue eyes, and very white, even teeth.

Ron went purple. He stared up at her, opened his mouth to reply, but nothing came out except a faint gurgling noise.

"Yeah, have it," said Harry, pushing the dish toward the girl.

"You 'ave finished wiz it?"

"Yeah," Ron said breathlessly. "Yeah, it was excellent."

The girl picked up the dish and carried it carefully off to the Ravenclaw table. Ron was still goggling at the girl as though he had never seen one before. Harry started to laugh. The sound seemed to jog Ron back to his senses.

"She's a *veela*!" he said hoarsely to Harry.

"Of course she isn't!" said Hermione tartly. "I don't see anyone else gaping at her like an idiot!"

But she wasn't entirely right about that. As the girl crossed the Hall, many boys' heads turned, and some of them seemed to have become temporarily speechless, just like Ron.

"I'm telling you, that's not a normal girl!" said Ron, leaning sideways so he could keep a clear view of her. "They don't make them like that at Hogwarts!"

"They make them okay at Hogwarts," said Harry without thinking. Cho happened to be sitting only a few places away from the girl with the silvery hair.

"When you've both put your eyes back in," said Hermione briskly, "you'll be able to see who's just arrived."

She was pointing up at the staff table. The two remaining empty seats had just been filled. Ludo Bagman was now sitting on Professor Karkaroff's other side, while Mr. Crouch, Percy's boss, was next to Madame Maxime.

"What are *they* doing here?" said Harry in surprise.

"They organized the Triwizard Tournament, didn't they?" said Hermione. "I suppose they wanted to be here to see it start."

When the second course arrived they noticed a number of unfamiliar desserts too. Ron examined an odd sort of pale blancmange closely, then moved it carefully a few inches to his right, so that it would be clearly visible from the Ravenclaw table. The girl who looked like a veela appeared to have eaten enough, however, and did not come over to get it.

Once the golden plates had been wiped clean, Dumbledore stood up again. A pleasant sort of tension seemed to fill the Hall now. Harry felt a slight thrill of excitement, wondering what was coming. Several seats down from them, Fred and George were leaning forward, staring at Dumbledore with great concentration.

"The moment has come," said Dumbledore, smiling around at the sea of upturned faces. "The Triwizard Tournament is about to start. I would like to say a few words of explanation before we bring in the casket —"

"The what?" Harry muttered.

Ron shrugged.

"— just to clarify the procedure that we will be following this year. But first, let me introduce, for those who do not know them, Mr. Bartemius Crouch, Head of the Department of International Magical Cooperation" — there was a smattering of polite applause — "and Mr. Ludo Bagman, Head of the Department of Magical Games and Sports."

There was a much louder round of applause for Bagman than for Crouch, perhaps because of his fame as a Beater, or simply because he looked so much more likable. He acknowledged it with a jovial wave of his hand. Bartemius Crouch did not smile or wave when his name was announced. Remembering him in his neat suit at the Quidditch World Cup, Harry thought he looked strange in wizard's robes. His toothbrush mustache and severe parting looked very odd next to Dumbledore's long white hair and beard.

"Mr. Bagman and Mr. Crouch have worked tirelessly over the last few months on the arrangements for the Triwizard Tournament," Dumbledore continued, "and they will be joining myself, Professor Karkaroff, and Madame Maxime on the panel that will judge the champions' efforts."

At the mention of the word "champions," the attentiveness of the listening students seemed to sharpen. Perhaps Dumbledore had noticed their sudden stillness, for he smiled as he said, "The casket, then, if you please, Mr. Filch."

Filch, who had been lurking unnoticed in a far corner of the Hall, now approached Dumbledore carrying a great wooden chest encrusted with jewels. It looked extremely old. A murmur of excited interest rose from the watching students; Dennis Creevey actually stood on his chair to see it properly, but, being so tiny, his head hardly rose above anyone else's.

"The instructions for the tasks the champions will face this year have already been examined by Mr. Crouch and Mr. Bagman," said Dumbledore as Filch placed the chest carefully on the table before him, "and they have made the necessary arrangements for each challenge. There will be three tasks, spaced throughout the school year, and they will test the champions in many different ways . . . their magical prowess — their daring — their powers of deduction — and, of course, their ability to cope with danger."

At this last word, the Hall was filled with a silence so absolute that nobody seemed to be breathing.

"As you know, three champions compete in the tournament," Dumbledore went on calmly, "one from each of the participating schools. They will be marked on how well they perform each of the tournament tasks and the champion with the highest total after task three will win the Triwizard Cup. The champions will be chosen by an impartial selector: the Goblet of Fire."

Dumbledore now took out his wand and tapped three times upon the top of the casket. The lid creaked slowly open. Dumbledore reached inside it and pulled out a large, roughly hewn wooden cup. It would have been entirely unremarkable had it not been full to the brim with dancing blue-white flames.

Dumbledore closed the casket and placed the goblet carefully on top of it, where it would be clearly visible to everyone in the Hall.

"Anybody wishing to submit themselves as champion must write their name and school clearly upon a slip of parchment and drop it into the goblet," said Dumbledore. "Aspiring champions have twenty-four hours in which to put their names forward. Tomorrow night, Halloween, the goblet will return the names of the three it has judged most worthy to represent their schools. The goblet will be placed in the entrance hall tonight, where it will be freely accessible to all those wishing to compete.

"To ensure that no underage student yields to temptation," said Dumbledore, "I will be drawing an Age Line around the Goblet of Fire once it has been placed in the entrance hall. Nobody under the age of seventeen will be able to cross this line.

"Finally, I wish to impress upon any of you wishing to compete that this tournament is not to be entered into lightly. Once a champion has been selected by the Goblet of Fire, he or she is obliged to see the tournament through to the end. The placing of your name in the goblet constitutes a binding, magical contract. There can be no change of heart once you have become a champion. Please be very sure, therefore, that you are wholeheartedly prepared to play before you drop your name into the goblet. Now, I think it is time for bed. Good night to you all."

"An Age Line!" Fred Weasley said, his eyes glinting, as they all made their way across the Hall to the doors into the entrance hall. "Well, that should be fooled by an Aging Potion, shouldn't it? And once your name's in that goblet, you're laughing — it can't tell whether you're seventeen or not!"

"But I don't think anyone under seventeen will stand a chance," said Hermione, "we just haven't learned enough . . ."

"Speak for yourself," said George shortly. "You'll try and get in, won't you, Harry?"

Harry thought briefly of Dumbledore's insistence that nobody under seventeen should submit their name, but then the wonderful picture of himself winning the Triwizard Tournament filled his mind again. . . . He wondered how angry Dumbledore would be if someone younger than seventeen *did* find a way to get over the Age Line. . . .

"Where is he?" said Ron, who wasn't listening to a word of this conversation, but looking through the crowd to see what had become of Krum. "Dumbledore didn't say where the Durmstrang people are sleeping, did he?"

But this query was answered almost instantly; they were level with the Slytherin table now, and Karkaroff had just bustled up to his students.

"Back to the ship, then," he was saying. "Viktor, how are you feeling? Did you eat enough? Should I send for some mulled wine from the kitchens?"

Harry saw Krum shake his head as he pulled his furs back on.

"Professor, *I* vood like some vine," said one of the other Durmstrang boys hopefully.

"I wasn't offering it to *you*, Poliakoff," snapped Karkaroff, his warmly paternal air vanishing in an instant. "I notice you have dribbled food all down the front of your robes again, disgusting boy —"

Karkaroff turned and led his students toward the doors, reaching them at exactly the same moment as Harry, Ron, and Hermione. Harry stopped to let him walk through first.

"Thank you," said Karkaroff carelessly, glancing at him.

And then Karkaroff froze. He turned his head back to Harry and stared at him as though he couldn't believe his eyes. Behind their headmaster, the students from Durmstrang came to a halt too. Karkaroff's eyes moved slowly up Harry's face and fixed upon his scar. The Durmstrang students were staring curiously at Harry too.

Out of the corner of his eye, Harry saw comprehension dawn on a few of their faces. The boy with food all down his front nudged the girl next to him and pointed openly at Harry's forehead.

"Yeah, that's Harry Potter," said a growling voice from behind them.

Professor Karkaroff spun around. Mad-Eye Moody was standing there, leaning heavily on his staff, his magical eye glaring unblinkingly at the Durmstrang headmaster.

The color drained from Karkaroff's face as Harry watched. A terrible look of mingled fury and fear came over him.

"You!" he said, staring at Moody as though unsure he was really seeing him.

"Me," said Moody grimly. "And unless you've got anything to say to Potter, Karkaroff, you might want to move. You're blocking the doorway."

It was true; half the students in the Hall were now waiting behind them, looking over one another's shoulders to see what was causing the holdup.

Without another word, Professor Karkaroff swept his students away with him. Moody watched him until he was out of sight, his magical eye fixed upon his back, a look of intense dislike upon his mutilated face.

As the next day was Saturday, most students would normally have breakfasted late. Harry, Ron, and Hermione, however, were not alone in rising much earlier than they usually did on weekends. When they went down into the entrance hall, they saw about twenty people milling around it, some of them eating toast, all examining the Goblet of Fire. It had been placed in the center of the hall on the stool that normally bore the Sorting Hat. A thin golden line had been traced on the floor, forming a circle ten feet around it in every direction.

"Anyone put their name in yet?" Ron asked a third-year girl eagerly.

"All the Durmstrang lot," she replied. "But I haven't seen anyone from Hogwarts yet."

"Bet some of them put it in last night after we'd all gone to bed," said Harry. "I would've if it had been me . . . wouldn't have wanted everyone watching. What if the goblet just gobbed you right back out again?"

Someone laughed behind Harry. Turning, he saw Fred, George, and Lee Jordan hurrying down the staircase, all three of them looking extremely excited.

"Done it," Fred said in a triumphant whisper to Harry, Ron, and Hermione. "Just taken it."

"What?" said Ron.

"The Aging Potion, dung brains," said Fred.

"One drop each," said George, rubbing his hands together with glee. "We only need to be a few months older."

"We're going to split the thousand Galleons between the three of us if one of us wins," said Lee, grinning broadly.

"I'm not sure this is going to work, you know," said Hermione warningly. "I'm sure Dumbledore will have thought of this."

Fred, George, and Lee ignored her.

"Ready?" Fred said to the other two, quivering with excitement. "C'mon, then — I'll go first —"

Harry watched, fascinated, as Fred pulled a slip of parchment out of his pocket bearing the words *Fred Weasley — Hogwarts*. Fred walked right up to the edge of the line and stood there, rocking on his toes like a diver preparing for a fifty-foot drop. Then, with the eyes of every person in the entrance hall upon him, he took a great breath and stepped over the line.

For a split second Harry thought it had worked — George certainly thought so, for he let out a yell of triumph and leapt after Fred — but next moment, there was a loud sizzling sound, and both twins were hurled out of the golden circle as though they had been thrown by an invisible shot-putter. They landed painfully, ten feet away on the cold stone floor, and to add insult to injury, there was a loud popping noise, and both of them sprouted identical long white beards.

The entrance hall rang with laughter. Even Fred and George joined in, once they had gotten to their feet and taken a good look at each other's beards.

"I did warn you," said a deep, amused voice, and everyone turned to see Professor Dumbledore coming out of the Great Hall. He surveyed Fred and George, his eyes twinkling. "I suggest you both go up to Madam Pomfrey. She is already tending to Miss Fawcett, of Ravenclaw, and Mr. Summers, of Hufflepuff, both of whom decided to age themselves up a little too. Though I must say, neither of their beards is anything like as fine as yours."

Fred and George set off for the hospital wing, accompanied by Lee, who was howling with laughter, and Harry, Ron, and Hermione, also chortling, went in to breakfast.

The decorations in the Great Hall had changed this morning. As it was Halloween, a cloud of live bats was fluttering around the enchanted ceiling, while hundreds of carved pumpkins leered from every corner. Harry led the way over to Dean and Seamus, who were discussing those Hogwarts students of seventeen or over who might be entering.

"There's a rumor going around that Warrington got up early and put his name in," Dean told Harry. "That big bloke from Slytherin who looks like a sloth."

Harry, who had played Quidditch against Warrington, shook his head in disgust.

"We can't have a Slytherin champion!"

"And all the Hufflepuffs are talking about Diggory," said Seamus contemptuously. "But I wouldn't have thought he'd have wanted to risk his good looks."

"Listen!" said Hermione suddenly.

People were cheering out in the entrance hall. They all swiveled around in their seats and saw Angelina Johnson coming into the Hall, grinning in an embarrassed sort of way. A tall black girl who played Chaser on the Gryffindor Quidditch team, Angelina came over to them, sat down, and said, "Well, I've done it! Just put my name in!"

"You're kidding!" said Ron, looking impressed.

"Are you seventeen, then?" asked Harry.

"'Course she is, can't see a beard, can you?" said Ron.

"I had my birthday last week," said Angelina.

"Well, I'm glad someone from Gryffindor's entering," said Hermione. "I really hope you get it, Angelina!"

"Thanks, Hermione," said Angelina, smiling at her.

"Yeah, better you than Pretty-Boy Diggory," said Seamus, causing several Hufflepuffs passing their table to scowl heavily at him.

"What're we going to do today, then?" Ron asked Harry and Hermione when they had finished breakfast and were leaving the Great Hall.

"We haven't been down to visit Hagrid yet," said Harry.

"Okay," said Ron, "just as long as he doesn't ask us to donate a few fingers to the skrewts."

A look of great excitement suddenly dawned on Hermione's face.

"I've just realized — I haven't asked Hagrid to join S.P.E.W. yet!" she said brightly. "Wait for me, will you, while I nip upstairs and get the badges?"

"What is it with her?" said Ron, exasperated, as Hermione ran away up the marble staircase.

"Hey, Ron," said Harry suddenly. "It's your friend . . ."

The students from Beauxbatons were coming through the front doors from the grounds, among them, the veela-girl. Those gathered around the Goblet of Fire stood back to let them pass, watching eagerly.

Madame Maxime entered the hall behind her students and organized them into a line. One by one, the Beauxbatons students stepped across the Age Line and dropped their slips of parchment into the blue-white flames. As each name entered the fire, it turned briefly red and emitted sparks.

"What d'you reckon'll happen to the ones who aren't chosen?" Ron muttered to Harry as the veela-girl dropped her parchment into the Goblet of Fire. "Reckon they'll go back to school, or hang around to watch the tournament?"

"Dunno," said Harry. "Hang around, I suppose. . . . Madame Maxime's staying to judge, isn't she?"

When all the Beauxbatons students had submitted their names, Madame Maxime led them back out of the hall and out onto the grounds again.

"Where are *they* sleeping, then?" said Ron, moving toward the front doors and staring after them.

A loud rattling noise behind them announced Hermione's reappearance with the box of S.P.E.W. badges.

"Oh good, hurry up," said Ron, and he jumped down the stone steps, keeping his eyes on the back of the veela-girl, who was now halfway across the lawn with Madame Maxime.

As they neared Hagrid's cabin on the edge of the Forbidden Forest, the mystery of the Beauxbatons' sleeping quarters was solved. The gigantic powder-blue carriage in which they had arrived had been parked two hundred yards from Hagrid's front door, and the students were climbing back inside it. The elephantine flying horses that had pulled the carriage were now grazing in a makeshift paddock alongside it.

Harry knocked on Hagrid's door, and Fang's booming barks answered instantly.

"'Bout time!" said Hagrid, when he'd flung open the door. "Thought you lot'd forgotten where I live!"

"We've been really busy, Hag —" Hermione started to say, but then she stopped dead, looking up at Hagrid, apparently lost for words.

Hagrid was wearing his best (and very horrible) hairy brown suit, plus a checked yellow-and-orange tie. This wasn't the worst of it, though; he had evidently tried to tame his hair, using large quantities of what appeared to be axle grease. It was now slicked down into two bunches — perhaps he had tried a ponytail like

Bill's, but found he had too much hair. The look didn't really suit Hagrid at all. For a moment, Hermione goggled at him, then, obviously deciding not to comment, she said, "Erm — where are the skrewts?"

"Out by the pumpkin patch," said Hagrid happily. "They're gettin' massive, mus' be nearly three foot long now. On'y trouble is, they've started killin' each other."

"Oh no, really?" said Hermione, shooting a repressive look at Ron, who, staring at Hagrid's odd hairstyle, had just opened his mouth to say something about it.

"Yeah," said Hagrid sadly. "'S' okay, though, I've got 'em in separate boxes now. Still got abou' twenty."

"Well, that's lucky," said Ron. Hagrid missed the sarcasm.

Hagrid's cabin comprised a single room, in one corner of which was a gigantic bed covered in a patchwork quilt. A similarly enormous wooden table and chairs stood in front of the fire beneath the quantity of cured hams and dead birds hanging from the ceiling. They sat down at the table while Hagrid started to make tea, and were soon immersed in yet more discussion of the Triwizard Tournament. Hagrid seemed quite as excited about it as they were.

"You wait," he said, grinning. "You jus' wait. Yer going ter see some stuff yeh've never seen before. Firs' task . . . ah, but I'm not supposed ter say."

"Go on, Hagrid!" Harry, Ron, and Hermione urged him, but he just shook his head, grinning.

"I don' want ter spoil it fer yeh," said Hagrid. "But it's gonna be spectacular, I'll tell yeh that. Them champions're going ter have their work cut out. Never thought I'd live ter see the Triwizard Tournament played again!"

They ended up having lunch with Hagrid, though they didn't eat much — Hagrid had made what he said was a beef casserole, but after Hermione unearthed a large talon in hers, she, Harry, and Ron rather lost their appetites. However, they enjoyed themselves trying to make Hagrid tell them what the tasks in the tournament were going to be, speculating which of the entrants were likely to be selected as champions, and wondering whether Fred and George were beardless yet.

A light rain had started to fall by midafternoon; it was very cozy sitting by the fire, listening to the gentle patter of the drops on the window, watching Hagrid darning his socks and arguing with Hermione about house-elves — for he flatly refused to join S.P.E.W. when she showed him her badges.

"It'd be doin' 'em an unkindness, Hermione," he said gravely, threading a massive bone needle with thick yellow yarn. "It's in their nature ter look after humans, that's what they like, see? Yeh'd be makin' 'em unhappy ter take away their work, an' insultin' 'em if yeh tried ter pay 'em."

"But Harry set Dobby free, and he was over the moon about it!" said Hermione. "*And* we heard he's asking for wages now!"

"Yeah, well, yeh get weirdos in every breed. I'm not sayin' there isn't the odd elf who'd take freedom, but yeh'll never persuade most of 'em ter do it — no, nothin' doin', Hermione."

Hermione looked very cross indeed and stuffed her box of badges back into her cloak pocket.

By half past five it was growing dark, and Ron, Harry, and Hermione decided it was time to get back up to the castle for the Halloween feast — and, more important, the announcement of the school champions.

"I'll come with yeh," said Hagrid, putting away his darning. "Jus' give us a sec."

Hagrid got up, went across to the chest of drawers beside his bed, and began searching for something inside it. They didn't pay too much attention until a truly horrible smell reached their nostrils. Coughing, Ron said, "Hagrid, what's that?"

"Eh?" said Hagrid, turning around with a large bottle in his hand. "Don' yeh like it?"

"Is that aftershave?" said Hermione in a slightly choked voice.

"Er — eau de cologne," Hagrid muttered. He was blushing. "Maybe it's a bit much," he said gruffly. "I'll go take it off, hang on . . ."

He stumped out of the cabin, and they saw him washing himself vigorously in the water barrel outside the window.

"Eau de cologne?" said Hermione in amazement. *"Hagrid?"*

"And what's with the hair and the suit?" said Harry in an undertone.

"Look!" said Ron suddenly, pointing out of the window.

Hagrid had just straightened up and turned 'round. If he had been blushing before, it was nothing to what he was doing now. Getting to their feet very cautiously, so that Hagrid wouldn't spot them, Harry, Ron, and Hermione peered through the window and saw that Madame Maxime and the Beauxbatons students had just emerged from their carriage, clearly about to set off for the feast too. They couldn't hear what Hagrid was saying, but he was talking to Madame Maxime with a rapt, misty-eyed expression Harry had only ever seen him wear once before — when he had been looking at the baby dragon, Norbert.

"He's going up to the castle with her!" said Hermione indignantly. "I thought he was waiting for us!"

Without so much as a backward glance at his cabin, Hagrid was trudging off up the grounds with Madame Maxime, the Beauxbatons students following in their wake, jogging to keep up with their enormous strides.

"He fancies her!" said Ron incredulously. "Well, if they end up having children, they'll be setting a world record — bet any baby of theirs would weigh about a ton."

They let themselves out of the cabin and shut the door behind them. It was surprisingly dark outside. Drawing their cloaks more closely around themselves, they set off up the sloping lawns.

"Ooh it's them, look!" Hermione whispered.

The Durmstrang party was walking up toward the castle from the lake. Viktor Krum was walking side by side with Karkaroff, and the other Durmstrang students were straggling along behind them. Ron watched Krum excitedly, but Krum did not look around as he reached the front doors a little ahead of Hermione, Ron, and Harry and proceeded through them.

When they entered the candlelit Great Hall it was almost full. The Goblet of Fire had been moved; it was now standing in front of Dumbledore's empty chair at the teachers' table. Fred and George — clean-shaven again — seemed to have taken their disappointment fairly well.

"Hope it's Angelina," said Fred as Harry, Ron, and Hermione sat down.

"So do I!" said Hermione breathlessly. "Well, we'll soon know!"

The Halloween feast seemed to take much longer than usual.

Perhaps because it was their second feast in two days, Harry didn't seem to fancy the extravagantly prepared food as much as he would have normally. Like everyone else in the Hall, judging by the constantly craning necks, the impatient expressions on every face, the fidgeting, and the standing up to see whether Dumbledore had finished eating yet, Harry simply wanted the plates to clear, and to hear who had been selected as champions.

At long last, the golden plates returned to their original spotless state; there was a sharp upswing in the level of noise within the Hall, which died away almost instantly as Dumbledore got to his feet. On either side of him, Professor Karkaroff and Madame Maxime looked as tense and expectant as anyone. Ludo Bagman was beaming and winking at various students. Mr. Crouch, however, looked quite uninterested, almost bored.

"Well, the goblet is almost ready to make its decision," said Dumbledore. "I estimate that it requires one more minute. Now, when the champions' names are called, I would ask them please to come up to the top of the Hall, walk along the staff table, and go through into the next chamber" — he indicated the door behind the staff table — "where they will be receiving their first instructions."

He took out his wand and gave a great sweeping wave with it; at once, all the candles except those inside the carved pumpkins were extinguished, plunging them into a state of semidarkness. The Goblet of Fire now shone more brightly than anything in the whole Hall, the sparkling bright, bluey-whiteness of the flames almost painful on the eyes. Everyone watched, waiting. . . . A few people kept checking their watches. . . .

"Any second," Lee Jordan whispered, two seats away from Harry.

The flames inside the goblet turned suddenly red again. Sparks began to fly from it. Next moment, a tongue of flame shot into the air, a charred piece of parchment fluttered out of it — the whole room gasped.

Dumbledore caught the piece of parchment and held it at arm's length, so that he could read it by the light of the flames, which had turned back to blue-white.

"The champion for Durmstrang," he read, in a strong, clear voice, "will be Viktor Krum."

"No surprises there!" yelled Ron as a storm of applause and cheering swept the Hall. Harry saw Viktor Krum rise from the Slytherin table and slouch up toward Dumbledore; he turned right, walked along the staff table, and disappeared through the door into the next chamber.

"Bravo, Viktor!" boomed Karkaroff, so loudly that everyone could hear him, even over all the applause. "Knew you had it in you!"

The clapping and chatting died down. Now everyone's attention was focused again on the goblet, which, seconds later, turned red once more. A second piece of parchment shot out of it, propelled by the flames.

"The champion for Beauxbatons," said Dumbledore, "is Fleur Delacour!"

"It's her, Ron!" Harry shouted as the girl who so resembled a veela got gracefully to her feet, shook back her sheet of silvery blonde hair, and swept up between the Ravenclaw and Hufflepuff tables.

"Oh look, they're all disappointed," Hermione said over the noise, nodding toward the remainder of the Beauxbatons party.

"Disappointed" was a bit of an understatement, Harry thought. Two of the girls who had not been selected had dissolved into tears and were sobbing with their heads on their arms.

When Fleur Delacour too had vanished into the side chamber, silence fell again, but this time it was a silence so stiff with excitement you could almost taste it. The Hogwarts champion next . . .

And the Goblet of Fire turned red once more; sparks showered out of it; the tongue of flame shot high into the air, and from its tip Dumbledore pulled the third piece of parchment.

"The Hogwarts champion," he called, "is Cedric Diggory!"

"No!" said Ron loudly, but nobody heard him except Harry; the uproar from the next table was too great. Every single Hufflepuff had jumped to his or her feet, screaming and stamping, as Cedric made his way past them, grinning broadly, and headed off toward the chamber behind the teachers' table. Indeed, the applause for Cedric went on so long that it was some time before Dumbledore could make himself heard again.

"Excellent!" Dumbledore called happily as at last the tumult died down. "Well, we now have our three champions. I am sure I can count upon all of you, including the remaining students from Beauxbatons and Durmstrang, to give your champions every ounce of support you can muster. By cheering your champion on, you will contribute in a very real —"

But Dumbledore suddenly stopped speaking, and it was apparent to everybody what had distracted him.

The fire in the goblet had just turned red again. Sparks were flying out of it. A long flame shot suddenly into the air, and borne upon it was another piece of parchment.

Automatically, it seemed, Dumbledore reached out a long hand

and seized the parchment. He held it out and stared at the name written upon it. There was a long pause, during which Dumbledore stared at the slip in his hands, and everyone in the room stared at Dumbledore. And then Dumbledore cleared his throat and read out —

"*Harry Potter.*"

# THE FOUR CHAMPIONS

Harry sat there, aware that every head in the Great Hall had turned to look at him. He was stunned. He felt numb. He was surely dreaming. He had not heard correctly.

There was no applause. A buzzing, as though of angry bees, was starting to fill the Hall; some students were standing up to get a better look at Harry as he sat, frozen, in his seat.

Up at the top table, Professor McGonagall had got to her feet and swept past Ludo Bagman and Professor Karkaroff to whisper urgently to Professor Dumbledore, who bent his ear toward her, frowning slightly.

Harry turned to Ron and Hermione; beyond them, he saw the long Gryffindor table all watching him, openmouthed.

"I didn't put my name in," Harry said blankly. "You know I didn't."

Both of them stared just as blankly back.

At the top table, Professor Dumbledore had straightened up, nodding to Professor McGonagall.

"Harry Potter!" he called again. "Harry! Up here, if you please!"

"Go on," Hermione whispered, giving Harry a slight push.

Harry got to his feet, trod on the hem of his robes, and stumbled slightly. He set off up the gap between the Gryffindor and Hufflepuff tables. It felt like an immensely long walk; the top table didn't seem to be getting any nearer at all, and he could feel hundreds and hundreds of eyes upon him, as though each were a searchlight. The buzzing grew louder and louder. After what seemed like an hour, he was right in front of Dumbledore, feeling the stares of all the teachers upon him.

"Well . . . through the door, Harry," said Dumbledore. He wasn't smiling.

Harry moved off along the teachers' table. Hagrid was seated right at the end. He did not wink at Harry, or wave, or give any of his usual signs of greeting. He looked completely astonished and stared at Harry as he passed like everyone else. Harry went through the door out of the Great Hall and found himself in a smaller room, lined with paintings of witches and wizards. A handsome fire was roaring in the fireplace opposite him.

The faces in the portraits turned to look at him as he entered. He saw a wizened witch flit out of the frame of her picture and into the one next to it, which contained a wizard with a walrus mustache. The wizened witch started whispering in his ear.

Viktor Krum, Cedric Diggory, and Fleur Delacour were grouped around the fire. They looked strangely impressive, silhouetted against the flames. Krum, hunched-up and brooding, was leaning against the mantelpiece, slightly apart from the other two. Cedric was standing with his hands behind his back, staring into the fire. Fleur Delacour looked around when Harry walked in and threw back her sheet of long, silvery hair.

"What is it?" she said. "Do zey want us back in ze Hall?"

She thought he had come to deliver a message. Harry didn't know how to explain what had just happened. He just stood there, looking at the three champions. It struck him how very tall all of them were.

There was a sound of scurrying feet behind him, and Ludo Bagman entered the room. He took Harry by the arm and led him forward.

"Extraordinary!" he muttered, squeezing Harry's arm. "Absolutely extraordinary! Gentlemen . . . lady," he added, approaching the fireside and addressing the other three. "May I introduce — incredible though it may seem — the *fourth* Triwizard champion?"

Viktor Krum straightened up. His surly face darkened as he surveyed Harry. Cedric looked nonplussed. He looked from Bagman to Harry and back again as though sure he must have misheard what Bagman had said. Fleur Delacour, however, tossed her hair, smiling, and said, "Oh, vairy funny joke, Meester Bagman."

"Joke?" Bagman repeated, bewildered. "No, no, not at all! Harry's name just came out of the Goblet of Fire!"

Krum's thick eyebrows contracted slightly. Cedric was still looking politely bewildered. Fleur frowned.

"But evidently zair 'as been a mistake," she said contemptuously to Bagman. "'E cannot compete. 'E is too young."

"Well . . . it is amazing," said Bagman, rubbing his smooth chin and smiling down at Harry. "But, as you know, the age restriction was only imposed this year as an extra safety measure. And as his name's come out of the goblet . . . I mean, I don't think there can be any ducking out at this stage. . . . It's down in the rules, you're obliged . . . Harry will just have to do the best he —"

The door behind them opened again, and a large group of people came in: Professor Dumbledore, followed closely by Mr. Crouch, Professor Karkaroff, Madame Maxime, Professor McGonagall, and Professor Snape. Harry heard the buzzing of the hundreds of students on the other side of the wall, before Professor McGonagall closed the door.

"Madame Maxime!" said Fleur at once, striding over to her headmistress. "Zey are saying zat zis little boy is to compete also!"

Somewhere under Harry's numb disbelief he felt a ripple of anger. *Little boy?*

Madame Maxime had drawn herself up to her full, and considerable, height. The top of her handsome head brushed the candle-filled chandelier, and her gigantic black-satin bosom swelled.

"What is ze meaning of zis, Dumbly-dorr?" she said imperiously.

"I'd rather like to know that myself, Dumbledore," said Professor Karkaroff. He was wearing a steely smile, and his blue eyes were like chips of ice. "*Two* Hogwarts champions? I don't remember anyone telling me the host school is allowed two champions — or have I not read the rules carefully enough?"

He gave a short and nasty laugh.

"*C'est impossible,*" said Madame Maxime, whose enormous hand with its many superb opals was resting upon Fleur's shoulder. "'Ogwarts cannot 'ave two champions. It is most injust."

"We were under the impression that your Age Line would keep out younger contestants, Dumbledore," said Karkaroff, his steely smile still in place, though his eyes were colder than ever. "Otherwise, we would, of course, have brought along a wider selection of candidates from our own schools."

"It's no one's fault but Potter's, Karkaroff," said Snape softly. His black eyes were alight with malice. "Don't go blaming Dumbledore for Potter's determination to break rules. He has been crossing lines ever since he arrived here —"

"Thank you, Severus," said Dumbledore firmly, and Snape went quiet, though his eyes still glinted malevolently through his curtain of greasy black hair.

Professor Dumbledore was now looking down at Harry, who looked right back at him, trying to discern the expression of the eyes behind the half-moon spectacles.

"Did you put your name into the Goblet of Fire, Harry?" he asked calmly.

"No," said Harry. He was very aware of everybody watching him closely. Snape made a soft noise of impatient disbelief in the shadows.

"Did you ask an older student to put it into the Goblet of Fire for you?" said Professor Dumbledore, ignoring Snape.

*"No,"* said Harry vehemently.

"Ah, but of course 'e is lying!" cried Madame Maxime. Snape was now shaking his head, his lip curling.

"He could not have crossed the Age Line," said Professor McGonagall sharply. "I am sure we are all agreed on that —"

"Dumbly-dorr must 'ave made a mistake wiz ze line," said Madame Maxime, shrugging.

"It is possible, of course," said Dumbledore politely.

"Dumbledore, you know perfectly well you did not make a

mistake!" said Professor McGonagall angrily. "Really, what nonsense! Harry could not have crossed the line himself, and as Professor Dumbledore believes that he did not persuade an older student to do it for him, I'm sure that should be good enough for everybody else!"

She shot a very angry look at Professor Snape.

"Mr. Crouch . . . Mr. Bagman," said Karkaroff, his voice unctuous once more, "you are our — er — objective judges. Surely you will agree that this is most irregular?"

Bagman wiped his round, boyish face with his handkerchief and looked at Mr. Crouch, who was standing outside the circle of the firelight, his face half hidden in shadow. He looked slightly eerie, the half darkness making him look much older, giving him an almost skull-like appearance. When he spoke, however, it was in his usual curt voice.

"We must follow the rules, and the rules state clearly that those people whose names come out of the Goblet of Fire are bound to compete in the tournament."

"Well, Barty knows the rule book back to front," said Bagman, beaming and turning back to Karkaroff and Madame Maxime, as though the matter was now closed.

"I insist upon resubmitting the names of the rest of my students," said Karkaroff. He had dropped his unctuous tone and his smile now. His face wore a very ugly look indeed. "You will set up the Goblet of Fire once more, and we will continue adding names until each school has two champions. It's only fair, Dumbledore."

"But Karkaroff, it doesn't work like that," said Bagman. "The Goblet of Fire's just gone out — it won't reignite until the start of the next tournament —"

"— in which Durmstrang will most certainly not be competing!" exploded Karkaroff. "After all our meetings and negotiations and compromises, I little expected something of this nature to occur! I have half a mind to leave now!"

"Empty threat, Karkaroff," growled a voice from near the door. "You can't leave your champion now. He's got to compete. They've all got to compete. Binding magical contract, like Dumbledore said. Convenient, eh?"

Moody had just entered the room. He limped toward the fire, and with every right step he took, there was a loud *clunk.*

"Convenient?" said Karkaroff. "I'm afraid I don't understand you, Moody."

Harry could tell he was trying to sound disdainful, as though what Moody was saying was barely worth his notice, but his hands gave him away; they had balled themselves into fists.

"Don't you?" said Moody quietly. "It's very simple, Karkaroff. Someone put Potter's name in that goblet knowing he'd have to compete if it came out."

"Evidently, someone 'oo wished to give 'Ogwarts two bites at ze apple!" said Madame Maxime.

"I quite agree, Madame Maxime," said Karkaroff, bowing to her. "I shall be lodging complaints with the Ministry of Magic *and* the International Confederation of Wizards —"

"If anyone's got reason to complain, it's Potter," growled Moody, "but . . . funny thing . . . I don't hear *him* saying a word. . . ."

"Why should 'e complain?" burst out Fleur Delacour, stamping her foot. "'E 'as ze chance to compete, 'asn't 'e? We 'ave all been 'oping to be chosen for weeks and weeks! Ze honor for our schools!

A thousand Galleons in prize money — zis is a chance many would die for!"

"Maybe someone's hoping Potter *is* going to die for it," said Moody, with the merest trace of a growl.

An extremely tense silence followed these words. Ludo Bagman, who was looking very anxious indeed, bounced nervously up and down on his feet and said, "Moody, old man . . . what a thing to say!"

"We all know Professor Moody considers the morning wasted if he hasn't discovered six plots to murder him before lunchtime," said Karkaroff loudly. "Apparently he is now teaching his students to fear assassination too. An odd quality in a Defense Against the Dark Arts teacher, Dumbledore, but no doubt you had your reasons."

"Imagining things, am I?" growled Moody. "Seeing things, eh? It was a skilled witch or wizard who put the boy's name in that goblet. . . ."

"Ah, what evidence is zere of zat?" said Madame Maxime, throwing up her huge hands.

"Because they hoodwinked a very powerful magical object!" said Moody. "It would have needed an exceptionally strong Confundus Charm to bamboozle that goblet into forgetting that only three schools compete in the tournament. . . . I'm guessing they submitted Potter's name under a fourth school, to make sure he was the only one in his category. . . ."

"You seem to have given this a great deal of thought, Moody," said Karkaroff coldly, "and a very ingenious theory it is — though of course, I heard you recently got it into your head that one of your birthday presents contained a cunningly disguised basilisk egg, and smashed it to pieces before realizing it was a carriage clock. So you'll understand if we don't take you entirely seriously. . . ."

"There are those who'll turn innocent occasions to their advantage," Moody retorted in a menacing voice. "It's my job to think the way Dark wizards do, Karkaroff— as you ought to remember. . . ."

"Alastor!" said Dumbledore warningly. Harry wondered for a moment whom he was speaking to, but then realized "Mad-Eye" could hardly be Moody's real first name. Moody fell silent, though still surveying Karkaroff with satisfaction — Karkaroff's face was burning.

"How this situation arose, we do not know," said Dumbledore, speaking to everyone gathered in the room. "It seems to me, however, that we have no choice but to accept it. Both Cedric and Harry have been chosen to compete in the tournament. This, therefore, they will do. . . ."

"Ah, but Dumbly-dorr —"

"My dear Madame Maxime, if you have an alternative, I would be delighted to hear it."

Dumbledore waited, but Madame Maxime did not speak, she merely glared. She wasn't the only one either. Snape looked furious; Karkaroff livid; Bagman, however, looked rather excited.

"Well, shall we crack on, then?" he said, rubbing his hands together and smiling around the room. "Got to give our champions their instructions, haven't we? Barty, want to do the honors?"

Mr. Crouch seemed to come out of a deep reverie.

"Yes," he said, "instructions. Yes . . . the first task . . ."

He moved forward into the firelight. Close up, Harry thought he looked ill. There were dark shadows beneath his eyes and a thin, papery look about his wrinkled skin that had not been there at the Quidditch World Cup.

"The first task is designed to test your daring," he told Harry, Cedric, Fleur, and Viktor, "so we are not going to be telling you what it is. Courage in the face of the unknown is an important quality in a wizard . . . very important. . . .

"The first task will take place on November the twenty-fourth, in front of the other students and the panel of judges.

"The champions are not permitted to ask for or accept help of any kind from their teachers to complete the tasks in the tournament. The champions will face the first challenge armed only with their wands. They will receive information about the second task when the first is over. Owing to the demanding and time-consuming nature of the tournament, the champions are exempted from end-of-year tests."

Mr. Crouch turned to look at Dumbledore.

"I think that's all, is it, Albus?"

"I think so," said Dumbledore, who was looking at Mr. Crouch with mild concern. "Are you sure you wouldn't like to stay at Hogwarts tonight, Barty?"

"No, Dumbledore, I must get back to the Ministry," said Mr. Crouch. "It is a very busy, very difficult time at the moment. . . . I've left young Weatherby in charge. . . . Very enthusiastic . . . a little overenthusiastic, if truth be told. . . ."

"You'll come and have a drink before you go, at least?" said Dumbledore.

"Come on, Barty, I'm staying!" said Bagman brightly. "It's all happening at Hogwarts now, you know, much more exciting here than at the office!"

"I think not, Ludo," said Crouch with a touch of his old impatience.

"Professor Karkaroff— Madame Maxime — a nightcap?" said Dumbledore.

But Madame Maxime had already put her arm around Fleur's shoulders and was leading her swiftly out of the room. Harry could hear them both talking very fast in French as they went off into the Great Hall. Karkaroff beckoned to Krum, and they, too, exited, though in silence.

"Harry, Cedric, I suggest you go up to bed," said Dumbledore, smiling at both of them. "I am sure Gryffindor and Hufflepuff are waiting to celebrate with you, and it would be a shame to deprive them of this excellent excuse to make a great deal of mess and noise."

Harry glanced at Cedric, who nodded, and they left together.

The Great Hall was deserted now; the candles had burned low, giving the jagged smiles of the pumpkins an eerie, flickering quality.

"So," said Cedric, with a slight smile. "We're playing against each other again!"

"I s'pose," said Harry. He really couldn't think of anything to say. The inside of his head seemed to be in complete disarray, as though his brain had been ransacked.

"So . . . tell me . . ." said Cedric as they reached the entrance hall, which was now lit only by torches in the absence of the Goblet of Fire. "How *did* you get your name in?"

"I didn't," said Harry, staring up at him. "I didn't put it in. I was telling the truth."

"Ah . . . okay," said Cedric. Harry could tell Cedric didn't believe him. "Well . . . see you, then."

Instead of going up the marble staircase, Cedric headed for a door to its right. Harry stood listening to him going down the stone steps beyond it, then, slowly, he started to climb the marble ones.

Was anyone except Ron and Hermione going to believe him, or would they all think he'd put himself in for the tournament? Yet how could anyone think that, when he was facing competitors who'd had three years' more magical education than he had — when he was now facing tasks that not only sounded very dangerous, but which were to be performed in front of hundreds of people? Yes, he'd thought about it . . . he'd fantasized about it . . . but it had been a joke, really, an idle sort of dream . . . he'd never really, *seriously* considered entering. . . .

But someone else had considered it . . . someone else had wanted him in the tournament, and had made sure he was entered. Why? To give him a treat? He didn't think so, somehow. . . .

To see him make a fool of himself? Well, they were likely to get their wish. . . .

But to get him *killed*?

Was Moody just being his usual paranoid self? Couldn't someone have put Harry's name in the goblet as a trick, a practical joke? Did anyone really want him dead?

Harry was able to answer that at once. Yes, someone wanted him dead, someone had wanted him dead ever since he had been a year old . . . Lord Voldemort. But how could Voldemort have ensured that Harry's name got into the Goblet of Fire? Voldemort was supposed to be far away, in some distant country, in hiding, alone . . . feeble and powerless. . . .

Yet in that dream he had had, just before he had awoken with his scar hurting, Voldemort had not been alone . . . he had been talking to Wormtail . . . plotting Harry's murder. . . .

Harry got a shock to find himself facing the Fat Lady already. He had barely noticed where his feet were carrying him. It was also a surprise to see that she was not alone in her frame. The wizened witch who had flitted into her neighbor's painting when he had joined the champions downstairs was now sitting smugly beside the Fat Lady. She must have dashed through every picture lining seven staircases to reach here before him. Both she and the Fat Lady were looking down at him with the keenest interest.

"Well, well, well," said the Fat Lady, "Violet's just told me everything. Who's just been chosen as school champion, then?"

"Balderdash," said Harry dully.

"It most certainly isn't!" said the pale witch indignantly.

"No, no, Vi, it's the password," said the Fat Lady soothingly, and she swung forward on her hinges to let Harry into the common room.

The blast of noise that met Harry's ears when the portrait opened almost knocked him backward. Next thing he knew, he was being wrenched inside the common room by about a dozen pairs of hands, and was facing the whole of Gryffindor House, all of whom were screaming, applauding, and whistling.

"You should've told us you'd entered!" bellowed Fred; he looked half annoyed, half deeply impressed.

"How did you do it without getting a beard? Brilliant!" roared George.

"I didn't," Harry said. "I don't know how —"

But Angelina had now swooped down upon him; "Oh if it couldn't be me, at least it's a Gryffindor —"

"You'll be able to pay back Diggory for that last Quidditch match, Harry!" shrieked Katie Bell, another of the Gryffindor Chasers.

"We've got food, Harry, come and have some —"

"I'm not hungry, I had enough at the feast —"

But nobody wanted to hear that he wasn't hungry; nobody wanted to hear that he hadn't put his name in the goblet; not one single person seemed to have noticed that he wasn't at all in the mood to celebrate. . . . Lee Jordan had unearthed a Gryffindor banner from somewhere, and he insisted on draping it around Harry like a cloak. Harry couldn't get away; whenever he tried to sidle over to the staircase up to the dormitories, the crowd around him closed ranks, forcing another butterbeer on him, stuffing crisps and peanuts into his hands. . . . Everyone wanted to know how he had done it, how he had tricked Dumbledore's Age Line and managed to get his name into the goblet. . . .

"I didn't," he said, over and over again, "I don't know how it happened."

But for all the notice anyone took, he might just as well not have answered at all.

"I'm tired!" he bellowed finally, after nearly half an hour. "No, seriously, George — I'm going to bed —"

He wanted more than anything to find Ron and Hermione, to find a bit of sanity, but neither of them seemed to be in the common room. Insisting that he needed to sleep, and almost flattening the little Creevey brothers as they attempted to waylay him at the foot of the stairs, Harry managed to shake everyone off and climb up to the dormitory as fast as he could.

To his great relief, he found Ron was lying on his bed in the otherwise empty dormitory, still fully dressed. He looked up when Harry slammed the door behind him.

"Where've you been?" Harry said.

"Oh hello," said Ron.

He was grinning, but it was a very odd, strained sort of grin. Harry suddenly became aware that he was still wearing the scarlet Gryffindor banner that Lee had tied around him. He hastened to take it off, but it was knotted very tightly. Ron lay on the bed without moving, watching Harry struggle to remove it.

"So," he said, when Harry had finally removed the banner and thrown it into a corner. "Congratulations."

"What d'you mean, congratulations?" said Harry, staring at Ron. There was definitely something wrong with the way Ron was smiling: It was more like a grimace.

"Well . . . no one else got across the Age Line," said Ron. "Not even Fred and George. What did you use — the Invisibility Cloak?"

"The Invisibility Cloak wouldn't have got me over that line," said Harry slowly.

"Oh right," said Ron. "I thought you might've told me if it was the Cloak . . . because it would've covered both of us, wouldn't it? But you found another way, did you?"

"Listen," said Harry, "I didn't put my name in that goblet. Someone else must've done it."

Ron raised his eyebrows.

"What would they do that for?"

"I dunno," said Harry. He felt it would sound very melodramatic to say, "To kill me."

Ron's eyebrows rose so high that they were in danger of disappearing into his hair.

"It's okay, you know, you can tell *me* the truth," he said. "If you don't want everyone else to know, fine, but I don't know why you're bothering to lie, you didn't get into trouble for it, did you? That friend of the Fat Lady's, that Violet, she's already told us all Dumbledore's letting you enter. A thousand Galleons prize money, eh? And you don't have to do end-of-year tests either. . . ."

"I didn't put my name in that goblet!" said Harry, starting to feel angry.

"Yeah, okay," said Ron, in exactly the same skeptical tone as Cedric. "Only you said this morning you'd have done it last night, and no one would've seen you. . . . I'm not stupid, you know."

"You're doing a really good impression of it," Harry snapped.

"Yeah?" said Ron, and there was no trace of a grin, forced or otherwise, on his face now. "You want to get to bed, Harry. I expect you'll need to be up early tomorrow for a photo-call or something."

He wrenched the hangings shut around his four-poster, leaving Harry standing there by the door, staring at the dark red velvet curtains, now hiding one of the few people he had been sure would believe him.

# THE WEIGHING OF
# THE WANDS

When Harry woke up on Sunday morning, it took him a moment to remember why he felt so miserable and worried. Then the memory of the previous night rolled over him. He sat up and ripped back the curtains of his own four-poster, intending to talk to Ron, to force Ron to believe him — only to find that Ron's bed was empty; he had obviously gone down to breakfast.

Harry dressed and went down the spiral staircase into the common room. The moment he appeared, the people who had already finished breakfast broke into applause again. The prospect of going down into the Great Hall and facing the rest of the Gryffindors, all treating him like some sort of hero, was not inviting; it was that, however, or stay here and allow himself to be cornered by the Creevey brothers, who were both beckoning frantically to him to join them. He walked resolutely over to the portrait hole, pushed it open, climbed out of it, and found himself face-to-face with Hermione.

"Hello," she said, holding up a stack of toast, which she was carrying in a napkin. "I brought you this. . . . Want to go for a walk?"

"Good idea," said Harry gratefully.

They went downstairs, crossed the entrance hall quickly without looking in at the Great Hall, and were soon striding across the lawn toward the lake, where the Durmstrang ship was moored, reflected blackly in the water. It was a chilly morning, and they kept moving, munching their toast, as Harry told Hermione exactly what had happened after he had left the Gryffindor table the night before. To his immense relief, Hermione accepted his story without question.

"Well, of course I knew you hadn't entered yourself," she said when he'd finished telling her about the scene in the chamber off the Hall. "The look on your face when Dumbledore read out your name! But the question is, who *did* put it in? Because Moody's right, Harry . . . I don't think any student could have done it . . . they'd never be able to fool the goblet, or get over Dumbledore's —"

"Have you seen Ron?" Harry interrupted.

Hermione hesitated.

"Erm . . . yes . . . he was at breakfast," she said.

"Does he still think I entered myself?"

"Well . . . no, I don't think so . . . not *really*," said Hermione awkwardly.

"What's that supposed to mean, 'not *really*'?"

"Oh Harry, isn't it obvious?" Hermione said despairingly. "He's jealous!"

*"Jealous?"* Harry said incredulously. "Jealous of what? He wants to make a prat of himself in front of the whole school, does he?"

"Look," said Hermione patiently, "it's always you who gets all the attention, you know it is. I know it's not your fault," she added quickly, seeing Harry open his mouth furiously. "I know you don't ask for it . . . but — well — you know, Ron's got all those brothers to compete against at home, and you're his best friend, and you're really famous — he's always shunted to one side whenever people see you, and he puts up with it, and he never mentions it, but I suppose this is just one time too many. . . ."

"Great," said Harry bitterly. "Really great. Tell him from me I'll swap any time he wants. Tell him from me he's welcome to it. . . . People gawping at my forehead everywhere I go. . . ."

"I'm not telling him anything," Hermione said shortly. "Tell him yourself. It's the only way to sort this out."

"I'm not running around after him trying to make him grow up!" Harry said, so loudly that several owls in a nearby tree took flight in alarm. "Maybe he'll believe I'm not enjoying myself once I've got my neck broken or —"

"That's not funny," said Hermione quietly. "That's not funny at all." She looked extremely anxious. "Harry, I've been thinking — you know what we've got to do, don't you? Straight away, the moment we get back to the castle?"

"Yeah, give Ron a good kick up the —"

"*Write to Sirius.* You've got to tell him what's happened. He asked you to keep him posted on everything that's going on at Hogwarts. . . . It's almost as if he expected something like this to happen. I brought some parchment and a quill out with me —"

"Come off it," said Harry, looking around to check that they couldn't be overheard, but the grounds were quite deserted. "He came back to the country just because my scar twinged. He'll probably come bursting right into the castle if I tell him someone's entered me in the Triwizard Tournament —"

*"He'd want you to tell him,"* said Hermione sternly. "He's going to find out anyway —"

"How?"

"Harry, this isn't going to be kept quiet," said Hermione, very seriously. "This tournament's famous, and you're famous. I'll be really surprised if there isn't anything in the *Daily Prophet* about you competing. . . . You're already in half the books about You-Know-Who, you know . . . and Sirius would rather hear it from you, I know he would."

"Okay, okay, I'll write to him," said Harry, throwing his last piece of toast into the lake. They both stood and watched it floating there for a moment, before a large tentacle rose out of the water and scooped it beneath the surface. Then they returned to the castle.

"Whose owl am I going to use?" Harry said as they climbed the stairs. "He told me not to use Hedwig again."

"Ask Ron if you can borrow —"

"I'm not asking Ron for anything," Harry said flatly.

"Well, borrow one of the school owls, then, anyone can use them," said Hermione.

They went up to the Owlery. Hermione gave Harry a piece of parchment, a quill, and a bottle of ink, then strolled around the long lines of perches, looking at all the different owls, while Harry sat down against a wall and wrote his letter.

> *Dear Sirius,*
>
> *You told me to keep you posted on what's happening at Hog-warts, so here goes — I don't know if you've heard, but the Tri-wizard Tournament's happening this year and on Saturday night I got picked as a fourth champion. I don't know who put*

*my name in the Goblet of Fire, because I didn't. The other*
*Hogwarts champion is Cedric Diggory, from Hufflepuff.*

He paused at this point, thinking. He had an urge to say something about the large weight of anxiety that seemed to have settled inside his chest since last night, but he couldn't think how to translate this into words, so he simply dipped his quill back into the ink bottle and wrote,

*Hope you're okay, and Buckbeak —* Harry

"Finished," he told Hermione, getting to his feet and brushing straw off his robes. At this, Hedwig came fluttering down onto his shoulder and held out her leg.

"I can't use you," Harry told her, looking around for the school owls. "I've got to use one of these. . . ."

Hedwig gave a very loud hoot and took off so suddenly that her talons cut into his shoulder. She kept her back to Harry all the time he was tying his letter to the leg of a large barn owl. When the barn owl had flown off, Harry reached out to stroke Hedwig, but she clicked her beak furiously and soared up into the rafters out of reach.

"First Ron, then you," said Harry angrily. *"This isn't my fault."*

If Harry had thought that matters would improve once everyone got used to the idea of him being champion, the following day showed him how mistaken he was. He could no longer avoid the rest of the school once he was back at lessons — and it was clear that the rest of the school, just like the Gryffindors, thought Harry had entered himself for the tournament. Unlike the Gryffindors, however, they did not seem impressed.

The Hufflepuffs, who were usually on excellent terms with the Gryffindors, had turned remarkably cold toward the whole lot of them. One Herbology lesson was enough to demonstrate this. It was plain that the Hufflepuffs felt that Harry had stolen their champion's glory; a feeling exacerbated, perhaps, by the fact that Hufflepuff House very rarely got any glory, and that Cedric was one of the few who had ever given them any, having beaten Gryffindor once at Quidditch. Ernie Macmillan and Justin Finch-Fletchley, with whom Harry normally got on very well, did not talk to him even though they were repotting Bouncing Bulbs at the same tray — though they did laugh rather unpleasantly when one of the Bouncing Bulbs wriggled free from Harry's grip and smacked him hard in the face. Ron wasn't talking to Harry either. Hermione sat between them, making very forced conversation, but though both answered her normally, they avoided making eye contact with each other. Harry thought even Professor Sprout seemed distant with him — but then, she was Head of Hufflepuff House.

He would have been looking forward to seeing Hagrid under normal circumstances, but Care of Magical Creatures meant seeing the Slytherins too — the first time he would come face-to-face with them since becoming champion.

Predictably, Malfoy arrived at Hagrid's cabin with his familiar sneer firmly in place.

"Ah, look, boys, it's the champion," he said to Crabbe and Goyle the moment he got within earshot of Harry. "Got your autograph books? Better get a signature now, because I doubt he's going to be around much longer. . . . Half the Triwizard champions have died . . . how long d'you reckon you're going to last, Potter? Ten minutes into the first task's my bet."

Crabbe and Goyle guffawed sycophantically, but Malfoy had to stop there, because Hagrid emerged from the back of his cabin balancing a teetering tower of crates, each containing a very large Blast-Ended Skrewt. To the class's horror, Hagrid proceeded to explain that the reason the skrewts had been killing one another was an excess of pent-up energy, and that the solution would be for each student to fix a leash on a skrewt and take it for a short walk. The only good thing about this plan was that it distracted Malfoy completely.

"Take this thing for a walk?" he repeated in disgust, staring into one of the boxes. "And where exactly are we supposed to fix the leash? Around the sting, the blasting end, or the sucker?"

"Roun' the middle," said Hagrid, demonstrating. "Er — yeh might want ter put on yer dragon-hide gloves, jus' as an extra precaution, like. Harry — you come here an' help me with this big one. . . ."

Hagrid's real intention, however, was to talk to Harry away from the rest of the class. He waited until everyone else had set off with their skrewts, then turned to Harry and said, very seriously, "So — yer competin', Harry. In the tournament. School champion."

"One of the champions," Harry corrected him.

Hagrid's beetle-black eyes looked very anxious under his wild eyebrows.

"No idea who put yeh in fer it, Harry?"

"You believe I didn't do it, then?" said Harry, concealing with difficulty the rush of gratitude he felt at Hagrid's words.

"'Course I do," Hagrid grunted. "Yeh say it wasn' you, an' I believe yeh — an' Dumbledore believes yer, an' all."

"Wish I knew who *did* do it," said Harry bitterly.

The pair of them looked out over the lawn; the class was widely scattered now, and all in great difficulty. The skrewts were now over three feet long, and extremely powerful. No longer shell-less and colorless, they had developed a kind of thick, grayish, shiny armor. They looked like a cross between giant scorpions and elongated crabs — but still without recognizable heads or eyes. They had become immensely strong and very hard to control.

"Look like they're havin' fun, don' they?" Hagrid said happily. Harry assumed he was talking about the skrewts, because his classmates certainly weren't; every now and then, with an alarming *bang*, one of the skrewts' ends would explode, causing it to shoot forward several yards, and more than one person was being dragged along on their stomach, trying desperately to get back on their feet.

"Ah, I don' know, Harry," Hagrid sighed suddenly, looking back down at him with a worried expression on his face. "School champion . . . everythin' seems ter happen ter you, doesn' it?"

Harry didn't answer. Yes, everything did seem to happen to him . . . that was more or less what Hermione had said as they had walked around the lake, and that was the reason, according to her, that Ron was no longer talking to him.

The next few days were some of Harry's worst at Hogwarts. The closest he had ever come to feeling like this had been during those months, in his second year, when a large part of the school had suspected him of attacking his fellow students. But Ron had been on his side then. He thought he could have coped with the rest of the school's behavior if he could just have had Ron back as a friend, but he wasn't going to try and persuade Ron to talk to him if Ron didn't want to. Nevertheless, it was lonely with dislike pouring in on him from all sides.

He could understand the Hufflepuffs' attitude, even if he didn't like it; they had their own champion to support. He expected nothing less than vicious insults from the Slytherins — he was highly unpopular there and always had been, because he had helped Gryffindor beat them so often, both at Quidditch and in the Inter-House Championship. But he had hoped the Ravenclaws might have found it in their hearts to support him as much as Cedric. He was wrong, however. Most Ravenclaws seemed to think that he had been desperate to earn himself a bit more fame by tricking the goblet into accepting his name.

Then there was the fact that Cedric looked the part of a champion so much more than he did. Exceptionally handsome, with his straight nose, dark hair, and gray eyes, it was hard to say who was receiving more admiration these days, Cedric or Viktor Krum. Harry actually saw the same sixth-year girls who had been so keen to get Krum's autograph begging Cedric to sign their school bags one lunchtime.

Meanwhile there was no reply from Sirius, Hedwig was refusing to come anywhere near him, Professor Trelawney was predicting his death with even more certainty than usual, and he did so badly at Summoning Charms in Professor Flitwick's class that he was given extra homework — the only person to get any, apart from Neville.

"It's really not that difficult, Harry," Hermione tried to reassure him as they left Flitwick's class — she had been making objects zoom across the room to her all lesson, as though she were some sort of weird magnet for board dusters, wastepaper baskets, and lunascopes. "You just weren't concentrating properly —"

"Wonder why that was," said Harry darkly as Cedric Diggory walked past, surrounded by a large group of simpering girls, all of whom looked at Harry as though he were a particularly large Blast-Ended Skrewt. "Still — never mind, eh? Double Potions to look forward to this afternoon. . . ."

Double Potions was always a horrible experience, but these days it was nothing short of torture. Being shut in a dungeon for an hour and a half with Snape and the Slytherins, all of whom seemed determined to punish Harry as much as possible for daring to become school champion, was about the most unpleasant thing Harry could imagine. He had already struggled through one Friday's worth, with Hermione sitting next to him intoning "ignore them, ignore them, ignore them" under her breath, and he couldn't see why today should be any better.

When he and Hermione arrived at Snape's dungeon after lunch, they found the Slytherins waiting outside, each and every one of them wearing a large badge on the front of his or her robes. For one wild moment Harry thought they were S.P.E.W. badges — then he saw that they all bore the same message, in luminous red letters that burnt brightly in the dimly lit underground passage:

**SUPPORT CEDRIC DIGGORY—
THE REAL HOGWARTS CHAMPION!**

"Like them, Potter?" said Malfoy loudly as Harry approached. "And this isn't all they do — look!"

He pressed his badge into his chest, and the message upon it vanished, to be replaced by another one, which glowed green:

**POTTER STINKS**

The Slytherins howled with laughter. Each of them pressed their badges too, until the message *POTTER STINKS* was shining brightly all around Harry. He felt the heat rise in his face and neck.

"Oh *very* funny," Hermione said sarcastically to Pansy Parkinson and her gang of Slytherin girls, who were laughing harder than anyone, "really *witty*."

Ron was standing against the wall with Dean and Seamus. He wasn't laughing, but he wasn't sticking up for Harry either.

"Want one, Granger?" said Malfoy, holding out a badge to Hermione. "I've got loads. But don't touch my hand, now. I've just washed it, you see; don't want a Mudblood sliming it up."

Some of the anger Harry had been feeling for days and days seemed to burst through a dam in his chest. He had reached for his wand before he'd thought what he was doing. People all around them scrambled out of the way, backing down the corridor.

"Harry!" Hermione said warningly.

"Go on, then, Potter," Malfoy said quietly, drawing out his own wand. "Moody's not here to look after you now — do it, if you've got the guts —"

For a split second, they looked into each other's eyes, then, at exactly the same time, both acted.

"*Furnunculus!*" Harry yelled.

*"Densaugeo!"* screamed Malfoy.

Jets of light shot from both wands, hit each other in midair, and ricocheted off at angles — Harry's hit Goyle in the face, and Malfoy's hit Hermione. Goyle bellowed and put his hands to his nose, where great ugly boils were springing up — Hermione, whimpering in panic, was clutching her mouth.

"Hermione!"

Ron had hurried forward to see what was wrong with her; Harry turned and saw Ron dragging Hermione's hand away from her face. It wasn't a pretty sight. Hermione's front teeth — already larger than average — were now growing at an alarming rate; she was looking more and more like a beaver as her teeth elongated, past her bottom lip, toward her chin — panic-stricken, she felt them and let out a terrified cry.

"And what is all this noise about?" said a soft, deadly voice.

Snape had arrived. The Slytherins clamored to give their explanations; Snape pointed a long yellow finger at Malfoy and said, "Explain."

"Potter attacked me, sir —"

"We attacked each other at the same time!" Harry shouted.

"— and he hit Goyle — look —"

Snape examined Goyle, whose face now resembled something that would have been at home in a book on poisonous fungi.

"Hospital wing, Goyle," Snape said calmly.

"Malfoy got Hermione!" Ron said. *"Look!"*

He forced Hermione to show Snape her teeth — she was doing her best to hide them with her hands, though this was difficult as they had now grown down past her collar. Pansy Parkinson and the other Slytherin girls were doubled up with silent giggles, pointing at Hermione from behind Snape's back.

Snape looked coldly at Hermione, then said, "I see no difference."

Hermione let out a whimper; her eyes filled with tears, she turned on her heel and ran, ran all the way up the corridor and out of sight.

It was lucky, perhaps, that both Harry and Ron started shouting at Snape at the same time; lucky their voices echoed so much in the stone corridor, for in the confused din, it was impossible for him to hear exactly what they were calling him. He got the gist, however.

"Let's see," he said, in his silkiest voice. "Fifty points from Gryffindor and a detention each for Potter and Weasley. Now get inside, or it'll be a week's worth of detentions."

Harry's ears were ringing. The injustice of it made him want to curse Snape into a thousand slimy pieces. He passed Snape, walked with Ron to the back of the dungeon, and slammed his bag down onto the table. Ron was shaking with anger too — for a moment, it felt as though everything was back to normal between them, but then Ron turned and sat down with Dean and Seamus instead, leaving Harry alone at his table. On the other side of the dungeon, Malfoy turned his back on Snape and pressed his badge, smirking. *POTTER STINKS* flashed once more across the room.

Harry sat there staring at Snape as the lesson began, picturing horrific things happening to him. . . . If only he knew how to do the Cruciatus Curse . . . he'd have Snape flat on his back like that spider, jerking and twitching. . . .

"Antidotes!" said Snape, looking around at them all, his cold black eyes glittering unpleasantly. "You should all have prepared your recipes now. I want you to brew them carefully, and then, we will be selecting someone on whom to test one. . . ."

Snape's eyes met Harry's, and Harry knew what was coming. Snape was going to poison *him*. Harry imagined picking up his cauldron, and sprinting to the front of the class, and bringing it down on Snape's greasy head —

And then a knock on the dungeon door burst in on Harry's thoughts.

It was Colin Creevey; he edged into the room, beaming at Harry, and walked up to Snape's desk at the front of the room.

"Yes?" said Snape curtly.

"Please, sir, I'm supposed to take Harry Potter upstairs."

Snape stared down his hooked nose at Colin, whose smile faded from his eager face.

"Potter has another hour of Potions to complete," said Snape coldly. "He will come upstairs when this class is finished."

Colin went pink.

"Sir — sir, Mr. Bagman wants him," he said nervously. "All the champions have got to go, I think they want to take photographs. . . ."

Harry would have given anything he owned to have stopped Colin saying those last few words. He chanced half a glance at Ron, but Ron was staring determinedly at the ceiling.

"Very well, very well," Snape snapped. "Potter, leave your things here, I want you back down here later to test your antidote."

"Please, sir — he's got to take his things with him," squeaked Colin. "All the champions —"

"Very *well*!" said Snape. "Potter — take your bag and get out of my sight!"

Harry swung his bag over his shoulder, got up, and headed for the door. As he walked through the Slytherin desks, *POTTER STINKS* flashed at him from every direction.

"It's amazing, isn't it, Harry?" said Colin, starting to speak the moment Harry had closed the dungeon door behind him. "Isn't it, though? You being champion?"

"Yeah, really amazing," said Harry heavily as they set off toward the steps into the entrance hall. "What do they want photos for, Colin?"

"The *Daily Prophet,* I think!"

"Great," said Harry dully. "Exactly what I need. More publicity."

"Good luck!" said Colin when they had reached the right room. Harry knocked on the door and entered.

He was in a fairly small classroom; most of the desks had been pushed away to the back of the room, leaving a large space in the middle; three of them, however, had been placed end-to-end in front of the blackboard and covered with a long length of velvet. Five chairs had been set behind the velvet-covered desks, and Ludo Bagman was sitting in one of them, talking to a witch Harry had never seen before, who was wearing magenta robes.

Viktor Krum was standing moodily in a corner as usual and not talking to anybody. Cedric and Fleur were in conversation. Fleur looked a good deal happier than Harry had seen her so far; she kept throwing back her head so that her long silvery hair caught the light. A paunchy man, holding a large black camera that was smoking slightly, was watching Fleur out of the corner of his eye.

Bagman suddenly spotted Harry, got up quickly, and bounded forward.

"Ah, here he is! Champion number four! In you come, Harry, in you come . . . nothing to worry about, it's just the wand weighing ceremony, the rest of the judges will be here in a moment —"

"Wand weighing?" Harry repeated nervously.

"We have to check that your wands are fully functional, no problems, you know, as they're your most important tools in the tasks ahead," said Bagman. "The expert's upstairs now with Dumbledore. And then there's going to be a little photo shoot. This is Rita Skeeter," he added, gesturing toward the witch in magenta robes. "She's doing a small piece on the tournament for the *Daily Prophet*. . . ."

"Maybe not *that* small, Ludo," said Rita Skeeter, her eyes on Harry.

Her hair was set in elaborate and curiously rigid curls that contrasted oddly with her heavy-jawed face. She wore jeweled spectacles. The thick fingers clutching her crocodile-skin handbag ended in two-inch nails, painted crimson.

"I wonder if I could have a little word with Harry before we start?" she said to Bagman, but still gazing fixedly at Harry. "The youngest champion, you know . . . to add a bit of color?"

"Certainly!" cried Bagman. "That is — if Harry has no objection?"

"Er —" said Harry.

"Lovely," said Rita Skeeter, and in a second, her scarlet-taloned fingers had Harry's upper arm in a surprisingly strong grip, and she was steering him out of the room again and opening a nearby door.

"We don't want to be in there with all that noise," she said. "Let's see . . . ah, yes, this is nice and cozy."

It was a broom cupboard. Harry stared at her.

"Come along, dear — that's right — lovely," said Rita Skeeter again, perching herself precariously upon an upturned bucket, pushing Harry down onto a cardboard box, and closing the door, throwing them into darkness. "Let's see now . . ."

She unsnapped her crocodile-skin handbag and pulled out a handful of candles, which she lit with a wave of her wand and magicked into midair, so that they could see what they were doing.

"You won't mind, Harry, if I use a Quick-Quotes Quill? It leaves me free to talk to you normally. . . ."

"A what?" said Harry.

Rita Skeeter's smile widened. Harry counted three gold teeth. She reached again into her crocodile bag and drew out a long acid-green quill and a roll of parchment, which she stretched out between them on a crate of Mrs. Skower's All-Purpose Magical Mess Remover. She put the tip of the green quill into her mouth, sucked it for a moment with apparent relish, then placed it upright on the parchment, where it stood balanced on its point, quivering slightly.

"Testing . . . my name is Rita Skeeter, *Daily Prophet* reporter."

Harry looked down quickly at the quill. The moment Rita Skeeter had spoken, the green quill had started to scribble, skidding across the parchment:

*Attractive blonde Rita Skeeter, forty-three, whose savage quill has punctured many inflated reputations —*

"Lovely," said Rita Skeeter, yet again, and she ripped the top piece of parchment off, crumpled it up, and stuffed it into her handbag. Now she leaned toward Harry and said, "So, Harry . . . what made you decide to enter the Triwizard Tournament?"

"Er —" said Harry again, but he was distracted by the quill. Even though he wasn't speaking, it was dashing across the parchment, and in its wake he could make out a fresh sentence:

*An ugly scar, souvenir of a tragic past, disfigures the otherwise charming face of Harry Potter, whose eyes —*

"Ignore the quill, Harry," said Rita Skeeter firmly. Reluctantly, Harry looked up at her instead. "Now — why did you decide to enter the tournament, Harry?"

"I didn't," said Harry. "I don't know how my name got into the Goblet of Fire. I didn't put it in there."

Rita Skeeter raised one heavily penciled eyebrow.

"Come now, Harry, there's no need to be scared of getting into trouble. We all know you shouldn't really have entered at all. But don't worry about that. Our readers love a rebel."

"But I didn't enter," Harry repeated. "I don't know who —"

"How do you feel about the tasks ahead?" said Rita Skeeter. "Excited? Nervous?"

"I haven't really thought . . . yeah, nervous, I suppose," said Harry. His insides squirmed uncomfortably as he spoke.

"Champions have died in the past, haven't they?" said Rita Skeeter briskly. "Have you thought about that at all?"

"Well . . . they say it's going to be a lot safer this year," said Harry.

The quill whizzed across the parchment between them, back and forward as though it were skating.

"Of course, you've looked death in the face before, haven't you?" said Rita Skeeter, watching him closely. "How would you say that's affected you?"

"Er," said Harry, yet again.

"Do you think that the trauma in your past might have made you keen to prove yourself? To live up to your name? Do you think that perhaps you were tempted to enter the Triwizard Tournament because —"

*"I didn't enter,"* said Harry, starting to feel irritated.

"Can you remember your parents at all?" said Rita Skeeter, talking over him.

"No," said Harry.

"How do you think they'd feel if they knew you were competing in the Triwizard Tournament? Proud? Worried? Angry?"

Harry was feeling really annoyed now. How on earth was he to know how his parents would feel if they were alive? He could feel Rita Skeeter watching him very intently. Frowning, he avoided her gaze and looked down at words the quill had just written:

> *Tears fill those startlingly green eyes as our conversation turns to the parents he can barely remember.*

"I have NOT got tears in my eyes!" said Harry loudly.

Before Rita Skeeter could say a word, the door of the broom cupboard was pulled open. Harry looked around, blinking in the bright light. Albus Dumbledore stood there, looking down at both of them, squashed into the cupboard.

*"Dumbledore!"* cried Rita Skeeter, with every appearance of delight — but Harry noticed that her quill and the parchment had

suddenly vanished from the box of Magical Mess Remover, and Rita's clawed fingers were hastily snapping shut the clasp of her crocodile-skin bag. "How are you?" she said, standing up and holding out one of her large, mannish hands to Dumbledore. "I hope you saw my piece over the summer about the International Confederation of Wizards' Conference?"

"Enchantingly nasty," said Dumbledore, his eyes twinkling. "I particularly enjoyed your description of me as an obsolete dingbat."

Rita Skeeter didn't look remotely abashed.

"I was just making the point that some of your ideas are a little old-fashioned, Dumbledore, and that many wizards in the street —"

"I will be delighted to hear the reasoning behind the rudeness, Rita," said Dumbledore, with a courteous bow and a smile, "but I'm afraid we will have to discuss the matter later. The Weighing of the Wands is about to start, and it cannot take place if one of our champions is hidden in a broom cupboard."

Very glad to get away from Rita Skeeter, Harry hurried back into the room. The other champions were now sitting in chairs near the door, and he sat down quickly next to Cedric, looking up at the velvet-covered table, where four of the five judges were now sitting — Professor Karkaroff, Madame Maxime, Mr. Crouch, and Ludo Bagman. Rita Skeeter settled herself down in a corner; Harry saw her slip the parchment out of her bag again, spread it on her knee, suck the end of the Quick-Quotes Quill, and place it once more on the parchment.

"May I introduce Mr. Ollivander?" said Dumbledore, taking his place at the judges' table and talking to the champions. "He will be checking your wands to ensure that they are in good condition before the tournament."

Harry looked around, and with a jolt of surprise saw an old wizard with large, pale eyes standing quietly by the window. Harry had met Mr. Ollivander before — he was the wandmaker from whom Harry had bought his own wand over three years ago in Diagon Alley.

"Mademoiselle Delacour, could we have you first, please?" said Mr. Ollivander, stepping into the empty space in the middle of the room.

Fleur Delacour swept over to Mr. Ollivander and handed him her wand.

"Hmmm . . ." he said.

He twirled the wand between his long fingers like a baton and it emitted a number of pink and gold sparks. Then he held it close to his eyes and examined it carefully.

"Yes," he said quietly, "nine and a half inches . . . inflexible . . . rosewood . . . and containing . . . dear me . . ."

"An 'air from ze 'ead of a veela," said Fleur. "One of my grandmuzzer's."

So Fleur *was* part veela, thought Harry, making a mental note to tell Ron . . . then he remembered that Ron wasn't speaking to him.

"Yes," said Mr. Ollivander, "yes, I've never used veela hair myself, of course. I find it makes for rather temperamental wands . . . however, to each his own, and if this suits you . . ."

Mr. Ollivander ran his fingers along the wand, apparently checking for scratches or bumps; then he muttered, *"Orchideous!"* and a bunch of flowers burst from the wand-tip.

"Very well, very well, it's in fine working order," said Mr. Ollivander, scooping up the flowers and handing them to Fleur with her wand. "Mr. Diggory, you next."

Fleur glided back to her seat, smiling at Cedric as he passed her.

"Ah, now, this is one of mine, isn't it?" said Mr. Ollivander, with much more enthusiasm, as Cedric handed over his wand. "Yes, I remember it well. Containing a single hair from the tail of a particularly fine male unicorn . . . must have been seventeen hands; nearly gored me with his horn after I plucked his tail. Twelve and a quarter inches . . . ash . . . pleasantly springy. It's in fine condition. . . . You treat it regularly?"

"Polished it last night," said Cedric, grinning.

Harry looked down at his own wand. He could see finger marks all over it. He gathered a fistful of robe from his knee and tried to rub it clean surreptitiously. Several gold sparks shot out of the end of it. Fleur Delacour gave him a very patronizing look, and he desisted.

Mr. Ollivander sent a stream of silver smoke rings across the room from the tip of Cedric's wand, pronounced himself satisfied, and then said, "Mr. Krum, if you please."

Viktor Krum got up and slouched, round-shouldered and duck-footed, toward Mr. Ollivander. He thrust out his wand and stood scowling, with his hands in the pockets of his robes.

"Hmm," said Mr. Ollivander, "this is a Gregorovitch creation, unless I'm much mistaken? A fine wandmaker, though the styling is never quite what I . . . however . . ."

He lifted the wand and examined it minutely, turning it over and over before his eyes.

"Yes . . . hornbeam and dragon heartstring?" he shot at Krum, who nodded. "Rather thicker than one usually sees . . . quite rigid . . . ten and a quarter inches . . . *Avis!*"

The hornbeam wand let off a blast like a gun, and a number of small, twittering birds flew out of the end and through the open window into the watery sunlight.

"Good," said Mr. Ollivander, handing Krum back his wand. "Which leaves . . . Mr. Potter."

Harry got to his feet and walked past Krum to Mr. Ollivander. He handed over his wand.

"Aaaah, yes," said Mr. Ollivander, his pale eyes suddenly gleaming. "Yes, yes, yes. How well I remember."

Harry could remember too. He could remember it as though it had happened yesterday. . . .

Four summers ago, on his eleventh birthday, he had entered Mr. Ollivander's shop with Hagrid to buy a wand. Mr. Ollivander had taken his measurements and then started handing him wands to try. Harry had waved what felt like every wand in the shop, until at last he had found the one that suited him — this one, which was made of holly, eleven inches long, and contained a single feather from the tail of a phoenix. Mr. Ollivander had been very surprised that Harry had been so compatible with this wand. "Curious," he had said, "curious," and not until Harry asked what was curious had Mr. Ollivander explained that the phoenix feather in Harry's wand had come from the same bird that had supplied the core of Lord Voldemort's.

Harry had never shared this piece of information with anybody. He was very fond of his wand, and as far as he was concerned its relation to Voldemort's wand was something it couldn't help — rather as he couldn't help being related to Aunt Petunia. However, he really hoped that Mr. Ollivander wasn't about to tell the room about it. He had a funny feeling Rita Skeeter's Quick-Quotes Quill might just explode with excitement if he did.

Mr. Ollivander spent much longer examining Harry's wand than anyone else's. Eventually, however, he made a fountain of wine shoot out of it, and handed it back to Harry, announcing that it was still in perfect condition.

"Thank you all," said Dumbledore, standing up at the judges' table. "You may go back to your lessons now — or perhaps it would be quicker just to go down to dinner, as they are about to end —"

Feeling that at last something had gone right today, Harry got up to leave, but the man with the black camera jumped up and cleared his throat.

"Photos, Dumbledore, photos!" cried Bagman excitedly. "All the judges and champions, what do you think, Rita?"

"Er — yes, let's do those first," said Rita Skeeter, whose eyes were upon Harry again. "And then perhaps some individual shots."

The photographs took a long time. Madame Maxime cast everyone else into shadow wherever she stood, and the photographer couldn't stand far enough back to get her into the frame; eventually she had to sit while everyone else stood around her. Karkaroff kept twirling his goatee around his finger to give it an extra curl; Krum, whom Harry would have thought would have been used to this sort of thing, skulked, half-hidden, at the back of the group. The photographer seemed keenest to get Fleur at the front, but Rita Skeeter kept hurrying forward and dragging Harry into greater prominence. Then she insisted on separate shots of all the champions. At last, they were free to go.

Harry went down to dinner. Hermione wasn't there — he supposed she was still in the hospital wing having her teeth fixed. He ate alone at the end of the table, then returned to Gryffindor

Tower, thinking of all the extra work on Summoning Charms that he had to do. Up in the dormitory, he came across Ron.

"You've had an owl," said Ron brusquely the moment he walked in. He was pointing at Harry's pillow. The school barn owl was waiting for him there.

"Oh — right," said Harry.

"And we've got to do our detentions tomorrow night, Snape's dungeon," said Ron.

He then walked straight out of the room, not looking at Harry. For a moment, Harry considered going after him — he wasn't sure whether he wanted to talk to him or hit him, both seemed quite appealing — but the lure of Sirius's answer was too strong. Harry strode over to the barn owl, took the letter off its leg, and unrolled it.

*Harry —*

*I can't say everything I would like to in a letter, it's too risky in case the owl is intercepted — we need to talk face-to-face. Can you ensure that you are alone by the fire in Gryffindor Tower at one o'clock in the morning on the 22nd of November?*

*I know better than anyone that you can look after yourself, and while you're around Dumbledore and Moody I don't think anyone will be able to hurt you. However, someone seems to be having a good try. Entering you in that tournament would have been very risky, especially right under Dumbledore's nose.*

*Be on the watch, Harry. I still want to hear about anything unusual. Let me know about the 22nd of November as quickly as you can.*

*Sirius*

# THE HUNGARIAN
# HORNTAIL

The prospect of talking face-to-face with Sirius was all that sustained Harry over the next fortnight, the only bright spot on a horizon that had never looked darker. The shock of finding himself school champion had worn off slightly now, and the fear of what was facing him had started to sink in. The first task was drawing steadily nearer; he felt as though it were crouching ahead of him like some horrific monster, barring his path. He had never suffered nerves like these; they were way beyond anything he had experienced before a Quidditch match, not even his last one against Slytherin, which had decided who would win the Quidditch Cup. Harry was finding it hard to think about the future at all; he felt as though his whole life had been leading up to, and would finish with, the first task. . . .

Admittedly, he didn't see how Sirius was going to make him feel any better about having to perform an unknown piece of difficult and dangerous magic in front of hundreds of people, but the mere sight of a friendly face would be something at the moment. Harry wrote back to Sirius saying that he would be beside the common room fire at the time Sirius had suggested, and he and Hermione spent a long time going over plans for forcing any stragglers out of the common room on the night in question. If the worst came to the worst, they were going to drop a bag of Dungbombs, but they hoped they wouldn't have to resort to that — Filch would skin them alive.

In the meantime, life became even worse for Harry within the confines of the castle, for Rita Skeeter had published her piece about the Triwizard Tournament, and it had turned out to be not so much a report on the tournament as a highly colored life story of Harry. Much of the front page had been given over to a picture of Harry; the article (continuing on pages two, six, and seven) had been all about Harry, the names of the Beauxbatons and Durmstrang champions (misspelled) had been squashed into the last line of the article, and Cedric hadn't been mentioned at all.

The article had appeared ten days ago, and Harry still got a sick, burning feeling of shame in his stomach every time he thought about it. Rita Skeeter had reported him saying an awful lot of things that he couldn't remember ever saying in his life, let alone in that broom cupboard.

> I suppose I get my strength from my parents. I know they'd be very proud of me if they could see me now. . . . Yes, sometimes at night I still cry about them, I'm not ashamed to admit it. . . . I know nothing will hurt me during the tournament, because they're watching over me. . . .

But Rita Skeeter had gone even further than transforming his "er's" into long, sickly sentences: She had interviewed other people about him too.

> Harry has at last found love at Hogwarts. His close
> friend, Colin Creevey, says that Harry is rarely seen
> out of the company of one Hermione Granger, a
> stunningly pretty Muggle-born girl who, like Harry,
> is one of the top students in the school.

From the moment the article had appeared, Harry had had to endure people — Slytherins, mainly — quoting it at him as he passed and making sneering comments.

"Want a hanky, Potter, in case you start crying in Transfiguration?"

"Since when have you been one of the top students in the school, Potter? Or is this a school you and Longbottom have set up together?"

"Hey — Harry!"

"Yeah, that's right!" Harry found himself shouting as he wheeled around in the corridor, having had just about enough. "I've just been crying my eyes out over my dead mum, and I'm just off to do a bit more. . . ."

"No — it was just — you dropped your quill."

It was Cho. Harry felt the color rising in his face.

"Oh — right — sorry," he muttered, taking the quill back.

"Er . . . good luck on Tuesday," she said. "I really hope you do well."

Which left Harry feeling extremely stupid.

Hermione had come in for her fair share of unpleasantness too, but she hadn't yet started yelling at innocent bystanders; in fact, Harry was full of admiration for the way she was handling the situation.

*"Stunningly pretty? Her?"* Pansy Parkinson had shrieked the first time she had come face-to-face with Hermione after Rita's article had appeared. "What was she judging against — a chipmunk?"

"Ignore it," Hermione said in a dignified voice, holding her head in the air and stalking past the sniggering Slytherin girls as though she couldn't hear them. "Just ignore it, Harry."

But Harry couldn't ignore it. Ron hadn't spoken to him at all since he had told him about Snape's detentions. Harry had half hoped they would make things up during the two hours they were forced to pickle rats' brains in Snape's dungeon, but that had been the day Rita's article had appeared, which seemed to have confirmed Ron's belief that Harry was really enjoying all the attention.

Hermione was furious with the pair of them; she went from one to the other, trying to force them to talk to each other, but Harry was adamant: He would talk to Ron again only if Ron admitted that Harry hadn't put his name in the Goblet of Fire and apologized for calling him a liar.

"I didn't start this," Harry said stubbornly. "It's his problem."

"You miss him!" Hermione said impatiently. "And I *know* he misses you —"

*"Miss him?"* said Harry. "I don't *miss him.* . . . "

But this was a downright lie. Harry liked Hermione very much, but she just wasn't the same as Ron. There was much less laughter and a lot more hanging around in the library when Hermione was your best friend. Harry still hadn't mastered Summoning Charms, he seemed to have developed something of a block about them, and Hermione insisted that learning the theory would help. They consequently spent a lot of time poring over books during their lunchtimes.

Viktor Krum was in the library an awful lot too, and Harry wondered what he was up to. Was he studying, or was he looking for things to help him through the first task? Hermione often complained about Krum being there — not that he ever bothered them — but because groups of giggling girls often turned up to spy on him from behind bookshelves, and Hermione found the noise distracting.

"He's not even good-looking!" she muttered angrily, glaring at Krum's sharp profile. "They only like him because he's famous! They wouldn't look twice at him if he couldn't do that Wonky-Faint thing —"

"Wronski Feint," said Harry, through gritted teeth. Quite apart from liking to get Quidditch terms correct, it caused him another pang to imagine Ron's expression if he could have heard Hermione talking about Wonky-Faints.

It is a strange thing, but when you are dreading something, and would give anything to slow down time, it has a disobliging habit of speeding up. The days until the first task seemed to slip by as though someone had fixed the clocks to work at double speed. Harry's feeling of barely controlled panic was with him wherever he went, as ever-present as the snide comments about the *Daily Prophet* article.

On the Saturday before the first task, all students in the third year and above were permitted to visit the village of Hogsmeade. Hermione told Harry that it would do him good to get away from the castle for a bit, and Harry didn't need much persuasion.

"What about Ron, though?" he said. "Don't you want to go with him?"

"Oh . . . well . . ." Hermione went slightly pink. "I thought we might meet up with him in the Three Broomsticks. . . ."

"No," said Harry flatly.

"Oh Harry, this is so stupid —"

"I'll come, but I'm not meeting Ron, and I'm wearing my Invisibility Cloak."

"Oh all right then . . ." Hermione snapped, "but I hate talking to you in that Cloak, I never know if I'm looking at you or not."

So Harry put on his Invisibility Cloak in the dormitory, went back downstairs, and together he and Hermione set off for Hogsmeade.

Harry felt wonderfully free under the Cloak; he watched other students walking past them as they entered the village, most of them sporting *Support Cedric Diggory!* badges, but no horrible remarks came his way for a change, and nobody was quoting that stupid article.

"People keep looking at *me* now," said Hermione grumpily as they came out of Honeydukes Sweetshop later, eating large cream-filled chocolates. "They think I'm talking to myself."

"Don't move your lips so much then."

"Come *on,* please just take off your Cloak for a bit, no one's going to bother you here."

"Oh yeah?" said Harry. "Look behind you."

Rita Skeeter and her photographer friend had just emerged from the Three Broomsticks pub. Talking in low voices, they passed right by Hermione without looking at her. Harry backed into the wall of Honeydukes to stop Rita Skeeter from hitting him with her crocodile-skin handbag. When they were gone, Harry said, "She's staying in the village. I bet she's coming to watch the first task."

As he said it, his stomach flooded with a wave of molten panic. He didn't mention this; he and Hermione hadn't discussed what was coming in the first task much; he had the feeling she didn't want to think about it.

"She's gone," said Hermione, looking right through Harry toward the end of the street. "Why don't we go and have a butterbeer in the Three Broomsticks, it's a bit cold, isn't it? You don't have to talk to Ron!" she added irritably, correctly interpreting his silence.

The Three Broomsticks was packed, mainly with Hogwarts students enjoying their free afternoon, but also with a variety of magical people Harry rarely saw anywhere else. Harry supposed that as Hogsmeade was the only all-wizard village in Britain, it was a bit of a haven for creatures like hags, who were not as adept as wizards at disguising themselves.

It was very hard to move through crowds in the Invisibility Cloak, in case you accidentally trod on someone, which tended to lead to awkward questions. Harry edged slowly toward a spare table in the corner while Hermione went to buy drinks. On his way through the pub, Harry spotted Ron, who was sitting with Fred, George, and Lee Jordan. Resisting the urge to give Ron a good hard poke in the back of the head, he finally reached the table and sat down at it.

Hermione joined him a moment later and slipped him a butterbeer under his Cloak.

"I look like such an idiot, sitting here on my own," she muttered. "Lucky I brought something to do."

And she pulled out a notebook in which she had been keeping a record of S.P.E.W. members. Harry saw his and Ron's names at the top of the very short list. It seemed a long time ago that they had sat making up those predictions together, and Hermione had turned up and appointed them secretary and treasurer.

"You know, maybe I should try and get some of the villagers involved in S.P.E.W.," Hermione said thoughtfully, looking around the pub.

"Yeah, right," said Harry. He took a swig of butterbeer under his Cloak. "Hermione, when are you going to give up on this spew stuff?"

"When house-elves have decent wages and working conditions!" she hissed back. "You know, I'm starting to think it's time for more direct action. I wonder how you get into the school kitchens?"

"No idea, ask Fred and George," said Harry.

Hermione lapsed into thoughtful silence, while Harry drank his butterbeer, watching the people in the pub. All of them looked cheerful and relaxed. Ernie Macmillan and Hannah Abbott were swapping Chocolate Frog cards at a nearby table, both of them sporting *Support Cedric Diggory!* badges on their cloaks. Right over by the door he saw Cho and a large group of her Ravenclaw friends. She wasn't wearing a Cedric badge though. . . . This cheered up Harry very slightly. . . .

What wouldn't he have given to be one of these people, sitting around laughing and talking, with nothing to worry about but homework? He imagined how it would have felt to be here if his name *hadn't* come out of the Goblet of Fire. He wouldn't be wearing the Invisibility Cloak, for one thing. Ron would be sitting with him. The three of them would probably be happily imagining what deadly dangerous task the school champions would be facing on Tuesday. He'd have been really looking forward to it, watching them do whatever it was . . . cheering on Cedric with everyone else, safe in a seat at the back of the stands. . . .

He wondered how the other champions were feeling. Every time he had seen Cedric lately, he had been surrounded by admirers and looking nervous but excited. Harry glimpsed Fleur Delacour from time to time in the corridors; she looked exactly as she always did, haughty and unruffled. And Krum just sat in the library, poring over books.

Harry thought of Sirius, and the tight, tense knot in his chest seemed to ease slightly. He would be speaking to him in just over twelve hours, for tonight was the night they were meeting at the common room fire — assuming nothing went wrong, as everything else had done lately. . . .

"Look, it's Hagrid!" said Hermione.

The back of Hagrid's enormous shaggy head — he had mercifully abandoned his bunches — emerged over the crowd. Harry wondered why he hadn't spotted him at once, as Hagrid was so large, but standing up carefully, he saw that Hagrid had been leaning low, talking to Professor Moody. Hagrid had his usual enormous tankard in front of him, but Moody was drinking from his hip flask. Madam Rosmerta, the pretty landlady, didn't seem to think much of this; she was looking askance at Moody as she collected glasses from tables around them. Perhaps she thought it was an insult to her mulled mead, but Harry knew better. Moody had told them all during their last Defense Against the Dark Arts lesson that he preferred to prepare his own food and drink at all times, as it was so easy for Dark wizards to poison an unattended cup.

As Harry watched, he saw Hagrid and Moody get up to leave. He waved, then remembered that Hagrid couldn't see him. Moody, however, paused, his magical eye on the corner where Harry was standing. He tapped Hagrid in the small of the back (being unable to reach his shoulder), muttered something to him, and then the pair of them made their way back across the pub toward Harry and Hermione's table.

"All right, Hermione?" said Hagrid loudly.

"Hello," said Hermione, smiling back.

Moody limped around the table and bent down; Harry thought he was reading the S.P.E.W. notebook, until he muttered, "Nice Cloak, Potter."

Harry stared at him in amazement. The large chunk missing from Moody's nose was particularly obvious at a few inches' distance. Moody grinned.

"Can your eye — I mean, can you — ?"

"Yeah, it can see through Invisibility Cloaks," Moody said quietly. "And it's come in useful at times, I can tell you."

Hagrid was beaming down at Harry too. Harry knew Hagrid couldn't see him, but Moody had obviously told Hagrid he was there. Hagrid now bent down on the pretext of reading the S.P.E.W. notebook as well, and said in a whisper so low that only Harry could hear it, "Harry, meet me tonight at midnight at me cabin. Wear that Cloak."

Straightening up, Hagrid said loudly, "Nice ter see yeh, Hermione," winked, and departed. Moody followed him.

"Why does Hagrid want me to meet him at midnight?" Harry said, very surprised.

"Does he?" said Hermione, looking startled. "I wonder what he's up to? I don't know whether you should go, Harry. . . ." She looked nervously around and hissed, "It might make you late for Sirius."

It was true that going down to Hagrid's at midnight would mean cutting his meeting with Sirius very fine indeed; Hermione suggested sending Hedwig down to Hagrid's to tell him he couldn't go — always assuming she would consent to take the note, of course — Harry, however, thought it better just to be quick at whatever Hagrid wanted him for. He was very curious to know what this might be; Hagrid had never asked Harry to visit him so late at night.

At half past eleven that evening, Harry, who had pretended to go up to bed early, pulled the Invisibility Cloak back over himself and crept back downstairs through the common room. Quite a few people were still in there. The Creevey brothers had managed to get hold of a stack of *Support Cedric Diggory!* badges and were trying to bewitch them to make them say *Support Harry Potter!* instead. So far, however, all they had managed to do was get the badges stuck on *POTTER STINKS*. Harry crept past them to the portrait hole and waited for a minute or so, keeping an eye on his watch. Then Hermione opened the Fat Lady for him from outside as they had planned. He slipped past her with a whispered "Thanks!" and set off through the castle.

The grounds were very dark. Harry walked down the lawn toward the lights shining in Hagrid's cabin. The inside of the enormous Beauxbatons carriage was also lit up; Harry could hear Madame Maxime talking inside it as he knocked on Hagrid's front door.

"You there, Harry?" Hagrid whispered, opening the door and looking around.

"Yeah," said Harry, slipping inside the cabin and pulling the Cloak down off his head. "What's up?"

"Got summat ter show yeh," said Hagrid.

There was an air of enormous excitement about Hagrid. He was wearing a flower that resembled an oversized artichoke in his buttonhole. It looked as though he had abandoned the use of axle grease, but he had certainly attempted to comb his hair — Harry could see the comb's broken teeth tangled in it.

"What're you showing me?" Harry said warily, wondering if the skrewts had laid eggs, or Hagrid had managed to buy another giant three-headed dog off a stranger in a pub.

"Come with me, keep quiet, an' keep yerself covered with that Cloak," said Hagrid. "We won' take Fang, he won' like it. . . ."

"Listen, Hagrid, I can't stay long. . . . I've got to be back up at the castle by one o'clock —"

But Hagrid wasn't listening; he was opening the cabin door and striding off into the night. Harry hurried to follow and found, to his great surprise, that Hagrid was leading him to the Beauxbatons carriage.

"Hagrid, what — ?"

"Shhh!" said Hagrid, and he knocked three times on the door bearing the crossed golden wands.

Madame Maxime opened it. She was wearing a silk shawl wrapped around her massive shoulders. She smiled when she saw Hagrid.

"Ah, 'Agrid . . . it is time?"

"Bong-sewer," said Hagrid, beaming at her, and holding out a hand to help her down the golden steps.

Madame Maxime closed the door behind her, Hagrid offered her his arm, and they set off around the edge of the paddock containing Madame Maxime's giant winged horses, with Harry, totally bewildered, running to keep up with them. Had Hagrid wanted to show him Madame Maxime? He could see her any old time he wanted . . . she wasn't exactly hard to miss. . . .

But it seemed that Madame Maxime was in for the same treat as Harry, because after a while she said playfully, "Wair is it you are taking me, 'Agrid?"

"Yeh'll enjoy this," said Hagrid gruffly, "worth seein', trust me. On'y — don' go tellin' anyone I showed yeh, right? Yeh're not s'posed ter know."

"Of course not," said Madame Maxime, fluttering her long black eyelashes.

And still they walked, Harry getting more and more irritated as he jogged along in their wake, checking his watch every now and then. Hagrid had some harebrained scheme in hand, which might make him miss Sirius. If they didn't get there soon, he was going to turn around, go straight back to the castle, and leave Hagrid to enjoy his moonlit stroll with Madame Maxime. . . .

But then — when they had walked so far around the perimeter of the forest that the castle and the lake were out of sight — Harry heard something. Men were shouting up ahead . . . then came a deafening, earsplitting roar. . . .

Hagrid led Madame Maxime around a clump of trees and came to a halt. Harry hurried up alongside them — for a split second, he thought he was seeing bonfires, and men darting around them — and then his mouth fell open.

*Dragons.*

Four fully grown, enormous, vicious-looking dragons were rearing onto their hind legs inside an enclosure fenced with thick planks of wood, roaring and snorting — torrents of fire were shooting into the dark sky from their open, fanged mouths, fifty feet above the ground on their outstretched necks. There was a silvery-blue one with long, pointed horns, snapping and snarling at the wizards on the ground; a smooth-scaled green one, which was writhing and stamping with all its might; a red one with an odd fringe of fine gold spikes around its face, which was shooting mushroom-shaped fire clouds into the air; and a gigantic black one, more lizard-like than the others, which was nearest to them.

At least thirty wizards, seven or eight to each dragon, were attempting to control them, pulling on the chains connected to heavy leather straps around their necks and legs. Mesmerized, Harry looked up, high above him, and saw the eyes of the black dragon, with vertical pupils like a cat's, bulging with either fear or rage, he couldn't tell which. . . . It was making a horrible noise, a yowling, screeching scream. . . .

"Keep back there, Hagrid!" yelled a wizard near the fence, straining on the chain he was holding. "They can shoot fire at a range of twenty feet, you know! I've seen this Horntail do forty!"

"Is'n' it beautiful?" said Hagrid softly.

"It's no good!" yelled another wizard. "Stunning Spells, on the count of three!"

Harry saw each of the dragon keepers pull out his wand.

"*Stupefy!*" they shouted in unison, and the Stunning Spells shot into the darkness like fiery rockets, bursting in showers of stars on the dragons' scaly hides —

Harry watched the dragon nearest to them teeter dangerously on its back legs; its jaws stretched wide in a silent howl; its nostrils were suddenly devoid of flame, though still smoking — then, very slowly, it fell. Several tons of sinewy, scaly-black dragon hit the ground with a thud that Harry could have sworn made the trees behind him quake.

The dragon keepers lowered their wands and walked forward to their fallen charges, each of which was the size of a small hill. They hurried to tighten the chains and fasten them securely to iron pegs, which they forced deep into the ground with their wands.

"Wan' a closer look?" Hagrid asked Madame Maxime excitedly. The pair of them moved right up to the fence, and Harry followed. The wizard who had warned Hagrid not to come any closer turned, and Harry realized who it was: Charlie Weasley.

"All right, Hagrid?" he panted, coming over to talk. "They should be okay now — we put them out with a Sleeping Draught on the way here, thought it might be better for them to wake up in the dark and the quiet — but, like you saw, they weren't happy, not happy at all —"

"What breeds you got here, Charlie?" said Hagrid, gazing at the closest dragon, the black one, with something close to reverence. Its eyes were still just open. Harry could see a strip of gleaming yellow beneath its wrinkled black eyelid.

"This is a Hungarian Horntail," said Charlie. "There's a Common Welsh Green over there, the smaller one — a Swedish Short-Snout, that blue-gray — and a Chinese Fireball, that's the red."

Charlie looked around; Madame Maxime was strolling away around the edge of the enclosure, gazing at the Stunned dragons.

"I didn't know you were bringing her, Hagrid," Charlie said, frowning. "The champions aren't supposed to know what's coming — she's bound to tell her student, isn't she?"

"Jus' thought she'd like ter see 'em," shrugged Hagrid, still gazing, enraptured, at the dragons.

"Really romantic date, Hagrid," said Charlie, shaking his head.

"Four . . ." said Hagrid, "so it's one fer each o' the champions, is it? What've they gotta do — fight 'em?"

"Just get past them, I think," said Charlie. "We'll be on hand if it gets nasty, Extinguishing Spells at the ready. They wanted nesting mothers, I don't know why . . . but I tell you this, I don't envy the one who gets the Horntail. Vicious thing. Its back end's as dangerous as its front, look."

Charlie pointed toward the Horntail's tail, and Harry saw long, bronze-colored spikes protruding along it every few inches.

Five of Charlie's fellow keepers staggered up to the Horntail at that moment, carrying a clutch of huge granite-gray eggs between them in a blanket. They placed them carefully at the Horntail's side. Hagrid let out a moan of longing.

"I've got them counted, Hagrid," said Charlie sternly. Then he said, "How's Harry?"

"Fine," said Hagrid. He was still gazing at the eggs.

"Just hope he's still fine after he's faced this lot," said Charlie grimly, looking out over the dragons' enclosure. "I didn't dare tell Mum what he's got to do for the first task; she's already having kittens about him. . . ." Charlie imitated his mother's anxious voice. *"How could they let him enter that tournament, he's much too young! I thought they were all safe, I thought there was going to be an age limit!'* She was in floods after that *Daily Prophet* article about him. *'He still cries about his parents! Oh bless him, I never knew!'"*

Harry had had enough. Trusting to the fact that Hagrid wouldn't miss him, with the attractions of four dragons and Madame Maxime to occupy him, he turned silently and began to walk away, back to the castle.

He didn't know whether he was glad he'd seen what was coming or not. Perhaps this way was better. The first shock was over now. Maybe if he'd seen the dragons for the first time on Tuesday, he would have passed out cold in front of the whole school . . . but maybe he would anyway. . . . He was going to be armed with his wand — which, just now, felt like nothing more than a narrow strip of wood — against a fifty-foot-high, scaly, spike-ridden, fire-breathing dragon. And he had to get past it. With everyone watching. *How?*

Harry sped up, skirting the edge of the forest; he had just under fifteen minutes to get back to the fireside and talk to Sirius, and he couldn't remember, ever, wanting to talk to someone more than he did right now — when, without warning, he ran into something very solid.

Harry fell backward, his glasses askew, clutching the Cloak around him. A voice nearby said, "Ouch! Who's there?"

Harry hastily checked that the Cloak was covering him and lay very still, staring up at the dark outline of the wizard he had hit. He recognized the goatee . . . it was Karkaroff.

"Who's there?" said Karkaroff again, very suspiciously, looking around in the darkness. Harry remained still and silent. After a minute or so, Karkaroff seemed to decide that he had hit some sort of animal; he was looking around at waist height, as though expecting to see a dog. Then he crept back under the cover of the trees and started to edge forward toward the place where the dragons were.

Very slowly and very carefully, Harry got to his feet and set off again as fast as he could without making too much noise, hurrying through the darkness back toward Hogwarts.

He had no doubt whatsoever what Karkaroff was up to. He had sneaked off his ship to try and find out what the first task was going to be. He might even have spotted Hagrid and Madame Maxime heading off around the forest together — they were hardly difficult to spot at a distance . . . and now all Karkaroff had to do was follow the sound of voices, and he, like Madame Maxime, would know what was in store for the champions.

By the looks of it, the only champion who would be facing the unknown on Tuesday was Cedric.

Harry reached the castle, slipped in through the front doors, and began to climb the marble stairs; he was very out of breath, but he didn't dare slow down. . . . He had less than five minutes to get up to the fire. . . .

"Balderdash!" he gasped at the Fat Lady, who was snoozing in her frame in front of the portrait hole.

"If you say so," she muttered sleepily, without opening her eyes, and the picture swung forward to admit him. Harry climbed inside. The common room was deserted, and, judging by the fact that it smelled quite normal, Hermione had not needed to set off any Dungbombs to ensure that he and Sirius got privacy.

Harry pulled off the Invisibility Cloak and threw himself into an armchair in front of the fire. The room was in semidarkness; the flames were the only source of light. Nearby, on a table, the *Support Cedric Diggory!* badges the Creeveys had been trying to improve were glinting in the firelight. They now read *POTTER REALLY STINKS*. Harry looked back into the flames, and jumped.

Sirius's head was sitting in the fire. If Harry hadn't seen Mr. Diggory do exactly this back in the Weasleys' kitchen, it would have scared him out of his wits. Instead, his face breaking into the first smile he had worn for days, he scrambled out of his chair, crouched down by the hearth, and said, "Sirius — how're you doing?"

Sirius looked different from Harry's memory of him. When they had said good-bye, Sirius's face had been gaunt and sunken, surrounded by a quantity of long, black, matted hair — but the hair was short and clean now, Sirius's face was fuller, and he looked younger, much more like the only photograph Harry had of him, which had been taken at the Potters' wedding.

"Never mind me, how are you?" said Sirius seriously.

"I'm —" For a second, Harry tried to say "fine" — but he couldn't do it. Before he could stop himself, he was talking more than he'd talked in days — about how no one believed he hadn't entered the tournament of his own free will, how Rita Skeeter had lied about him in the *Daily Prophet,* how he couldn't walk down a corridor without being sneered at — and about Ron, Ron not believing him, Ron's jealousy . . .

". . . and now Hagrid's just shown me what's coming in the first task, and it's dragons, Sirius, and I'm a goner," he finished desperately.

Sirius looked at him, eyes full of concern, eyes that had not yet lost the look that Azkaban had given them — that deadened, haunted look. He had let Harry talk himself into silence without interruption, but now he said, "Dragons we can deal with, Harry, but we'll get to that in a minute — I haven't got long here . . . I've broken into a Wizarding house to use the fire, but they could be back at any time. There are things I need to warn you about."

"What?" said Harry, feeling his spirits slip a further few notches. . . . Surely there could be nothing worse than dragons coming?

"Karkaroff," said Sirius. "Harry, he was a Death Eater. You know what Death Eaters are, don't you?"

"Yes — he — what?"

"He was caught, he was in Azkaban with me, but he got released. I'd bet everything that's why Dumbledore wanted an Auror at Hogwarts this year — to keep an eye on him. Moody caught Karkaroff. Put him into Azkaban in the first place."

"Karkaroff got released?" Harry said slowly — his brain seemed to be struggling to absorb yet another piece of shocking information. "Why did they release him?"

"He did a deal with the Ministry of Magic," said Sirius bitterly. "He said he'd seen the error of his ways, and then he named names . . . he put a load of other people into Azkaban in his place. . . . He's not very popular in there, I can tell you. And since he got out, from what I can tell, he's been teaching the Dark Arts to every student who passes through that school of his. So watch out for the Durmstrang champion as well."

"Okay," said Harry slowly. "But . . . are you saying Karkaroff put my name in the goblet? Because if he did, he's a really good actor. He seemed furious about it. He wanted to stop me from competing."

"We know he's a good actor," said Sirius, "because he convinced the Ministry of Magic to set him free, didn't he? Now, I've been keeping an eye on the *Daily Prophet,* Harry —"

"— you and the rest of the world," said Harry bitterly.

"— and reading between the lines of that Skeeter woman's article last month, Moody was attacked the night before he started at Hogwarts. Yes, I know she says it was another false alarm," Sirius said hastily, seeing Harry about to speak, "but I don't think so, somehow. I think someone tried to stop him from getting to Hogwarts. I think someone knew their job would be a lot more difficult with him around. And no one's going to look into it too closely; Mad-Eye's heard intruders a bit too often. But that doesn't mean he can't still spot the real thing. Moody was the best Auror the Ministry ever had."

"So . . . what are you saying?" said Harry slowly. "Karkaroff's trying to kill me? But — why?"

Sirius hesitated.

"I've been hearing some very strange things," he said slowly. "The Death Eaters seem to be a bit more active than usual lately. They showed themselves at the Quidditch World Cup, didn't they? Someone set off the Dark Mark . . . and then — did you hear about that Ministry of Magic witch who's gone missing?"

"Bertha Jorkins?" said Harry.

"Exactly . . . she disappeared in Albania, and that's definitely where Voldemort was rumored to be last . . . and she would have known the Triwizard Tournament was coming up, wouldn't she?"

"Yeah, but . . . it's not very likely she'd have walked straight into Voldemort, is it?" said Harry.

"Listen, I knew Bertha Jorkins," said Sirius grimly. "She was at Hogwarts when I was, a few years above your dad and me. And she was an idiot. Very nosy, but no brains, none at all. It's not a good combination, Harry. I'd say she'd be very easy to lure into a trap."

"So . . . so Voldemort could have found out about the tournament?" said Harry. "Is that what you mean? You think Karkaroff might be here on his orders?"

"I don't know," said Sirius slowly, "I just don't know . . . Karkaroff doesn't strike me as the type who'd go back to Voldemort unless he knew Voldemort was powerful enough to protect him. But whoever put your name in that goblet did it for a reason, and I can't help thinking the tournament would be a very good way to attack you and make it look like an accident."

"Looks like a really good plan from where I'm standing," said Harry, grinning bleakly. "They'll just have to stand back and let the dragons do their stuff."

"Right — these dragons," said Sirius, speaking very quickly now. "There's a way, Harry. Don't be tempted to try a Stunning Spell — dragons are strong and too powerfully magical to be knocked out by a single Stunner, you need about half a dozen wizards at a time to overcome a dragon —"

"Yeah, I know, I just saw," said Harry.

"But you can do it alone," said Sirius. "There is a way, and a simple spell's all you need. Just —"

But Harry held up a hand to silence him, his heart suddenly pounding as though it would burst. He could hear footsteps coming down the spiral staircase behind him.

"Go!" he hissed at Sirius. "*Go!* There's someone coming!"

Harry scrambled to his feet, hiding the fire — if someone saw Sirius's face within the walls of Hogwarts, they would raise an almighty uproar — the Ministry would get dragged in — he, Harry, would be questioned about Sirius's whereabouts —

Harry heard a tiny *pop!* in the fire behind him and knew Sirius had gone. He watched the bottom of the spiral staircase. Who had decided to go for a stroll at one o'clock in the morning, and stopped Sirius from telling him how to get past a dragon?

It was Ron. Dressed in his maroon paisley pajamas, Ron stopped dead facing Harry across the room, and looked around.

"Who were you talking to?" he said.

"What's that got to do with you?" Harry snarled. "What are you doing down here at this time of night?"

"I just wondered where you —" Ron broke off, shrugging. "Nothing. I'm going back to bed."

"Just thought you'd come nosing around, did you?" Harry shouted. He knew that Ron had no idea what he'd walked in on, knew he hadn't done it on purpose, but he didn't care — at this moment he hated everything about Ron, right down to the several inches of bare ankle showing beneath his pajama trousers.

"Sorry about that," said Ron, his face reddening with anger. "Should've realized you didn't want to be disturbed. I'll let you get on with practicing for your next interview in peace."

Harry seized one of the *POTTER REALLY STINKS* badges off the table and chucked it, as hard as he could, across the room. It hit Ron on the forehead and bounced off.

"There you go," Harry said. "Something for you to wear on

Tuesday. You might even have a scar now, if you're lucky. . . . That's what you want, isn't it?"

He strode across the room toward the stairs; he half expected Ron to stop him, he would even have liked Ron to throw a punch at him, but Ron just stood there in his too-small pajamas, and Harry, having stormed upstairs, lay awake in bed fuming for a long time afterward and didn't hear him come up to bed.

# CHAPTER TWENTY

# THE FIRST TASK

Harry got up on Sunday morning and dressed so inattentively that it was a while before he realized he was trying to pull his hat onto his foot instead of his sock. When he'd finally got all his clothes on the right parts of his body, he hurried off to find Hermione, locating her at the Gryffindor table in the Great Hall, where she was eating breakfast with Ginny. Feeling too queasy to eat, Harry waited until Hermione had swallowed her last spoonful of porridge, then dragged her out onto the grounds. There, he told her all about the dragons, and about everything Sirius had said, while they took another long walk around the lake.

Alarmed as she was by Sirius's warnings about Karkaroff, Hermione still thought that the dragons were the more pressing problem.

"Let's just try and keep you alive until Tuesday evening," she said desperately, "and then we can worry about Karkaroff."

They walked three times around the lake, trying all the way to think of a simple spell that would subdue a dragon. Nothing whatsoever occurred to them, so they retired to the library instead. Here, Harry pulled down every book he could find on dragons, and both of them set to work searching through the large pile.

"*'Talon-clipping by charms . . . treating scale-rot . . .'* This is no good, this is for nutters like Hagrid who want to keep them healthy. . . ."

"*'Dragons are extremely difficult to slay, owing to the ancient magic that imbues their thick hides, which none but the most powerful spells can penetrate . . .'* But Sirius said a simple one would do it. . . ."

"Let's try some simple spellbooks, then," said Harry, throwing aside *Men Who Love Dragons Too Much.*

He returned to the table with a pile of spellbooks, set them down, and began to flick through each in turn, Hermione whispering nonstop at his elbow.

"Well, there are Switching Spells . . . but what's the point of Switching it? Unless you swapped its fangs for wine-gums or something that would make it less dangerous. . . . The trouble is, like that book said, not much is going to get through a dragon's hide. . . . I'd say Transfigure it, but something that big, you really haven't got a hope, I doubt even Professor McGonagall . . . unless you're supposed to put the spell on *yourself?* Maybe to give yourself extra powers? But *they're* not simple spells, I mean, we haven't done any of those in class, I only know about them because I've been doing O.W.L. practice papers. . . ."

"Hermione," Harry said, through gritted teeth, "will you shut up for a bit, please? I'm trying to concentrate."

But all that happened, when Hermione fell silent, was that

Harry's brain filled with a sort of blank buzzing, which didn't seem to allow room for concentration. He stared hopelessly down the index of *Basic Hexes for the Busy and Vexed. Instant scalping. . .* but dragons had no hair . . . *pepper breath. . .* that would probably increase a dragon's firepower . . . *horn tongue. . .* just what he needed, to give it an extra weapon . . .

"Oh no, he's back *again,* why can't he read on his stupid ship?" said Hermione irritably as Viktor Krum slouched in, cast a surly look over at the pair of them, and settled himself in a distant corner with a pile of books. "Come on, Harry, we'll go back to the common room . . . his fan club'll be here in a moment, twittering away. . . ."

And sure enough, as they left the library, a gang of girls tiptoed past them, one of them wearing a Bulgaria scarf tied around her waist.

Harry barely slept that night. When he awoke on Monday morning, he seriously considered for the first time ever just running away from Hogwarts. But as he looked around the Great Hall at breakfast time, and thought about what leaving the castle would mean, he knew he couldn't do it. It was the only place he had ever been happy . . . well, he supposed he must have been happy with his parents too, but he couldn't remember that.

Somehow, the knowledge that he would rather be here and facing a dragon than back on Privet Drive with Dudley was good to know; it made him feel slightly calmer. He finished his bacon with difficulty (his throat wasn't working too well), and as he and Hermione got up, he saw Cedric Diggory leaving the Hufflepuff table.

Cedric still didn't know about the dragons . . . the only champion who didn't, if Harry was right in thinking that Maxime and Karkaroff would have told Fleur and Krum. . . .

"Hermione, I'll see you in the greenhouses," Harry said, coming to his decision as he watched Cedric leaving the Hall. "Go on, I'll catch you up."

"Harry, you'll be late, the bell's about to ring —"

"I'll catch you up, okay?"

By the time Harry reached the bottom of the marble staircase, Cedric was at the top. He was with a load of sixth-year friends. Harry didn't want to talk to Cedric in front of them; they were among those who had been quoting Rita Skeeter's article at him every time he went near them. He followed Cedric at a distance and saw that he was heading toward the Charms corridor. This gave Harry an idea. Pausing at a distance from them, he pulled out his wand, and took careful aim.

"*Diffindo!*"

Cedric's bag split. Parchment, quills, and books spilled out of it onto the floor. Several bottles of ink smashed.

"Don't bother," said Cedric in an exasperated voice as his friends bent down to help him. "Tell Flitwick I'm coming, go on. . . ."

This was exactly what Harry had been hoping for. He slipped his wand back into his robes, waited until Cedric's friends had disappeared into their classroom, and hurried up the corridor, which was now empty of everyone but himself and Cedric.

"Hi," said Cedric, picking up a copy of *A Guide to Advanced Transfiguration* that was now splattered with ink. "My bag just split . . . brand-new and all . . ."

"Cedric," said Harry, "the first task is dragons."

"What?" said Cedric, looking up.

"Dragons," said Harry, speaking quickly, in case Professor Flitwick came out to see where Cedric had got to. "They've got four, one for each of us, and we've got to get past them."

Cedric stared at him. Harry saw some of the panic he'd been feeling since Saturday night flickering in Cedric's gray eyes.

"Are you sure?" Cedric said in a hushed voice.

"Dead sure," said Harry. "I've seen them."

"But how did you find out? We're not supposed to know. . . ."

"Never mind," said Harry quickly — he knew Hagrid would be in trouble if he told the truth. "But I'm not the only one who knows. Fleur and Krum will know by now — Maxime and Karkaroff both saw the dragons too."

Cedric straightened up, his arms full of inky quills, parchment, and books, his ripped bag dangling off one shoulder. He stared at Harry, and there was a puzzled, almost suspicious look in his eyes.

"Why are you telling me?" he asked.

Harry looked at him in disbelief. He was sure Cedric wouldn't have asked that if he had seen the dragons himself. Harry wouldn't have let his worst enemy face those monsters unprepared — well, perhaps Malfoy or Snape . . .

"It's just . . . fair, isn't it?" he said to Cedric. "We all know now . . . we're on an even footing, aren't we?"

Cedric was still looking at him in a slightly suspicious way when Harry heard a familiar clunking noise behind him. He turned around and saw Mad-Eye Moody emerging from a nearby classroom.

"Come with me, Potter," he growled. "Diggory, off you go."

Harry stared apprehensively at Moody. Had he overheard them?

"Er — Professor, I'm supposed to be in Herbology —"

"Never mind that, Potter. In my office, please. . . ."

Harry followed him, wondering what was going to happen to him now. What if Moody wanted to know how he'd found out about the dragons? Would Moody go to Dumbledore and tell on Hagrid, or just turn Harry into a ferret? Well, it might be easier to get past a dragon if he were a ferret, Harry thought dully, he'd be smaller, much less easy to see from a height of fifty feet . . . .

He followed Moody into his office. Moody closed the door behind them and turned to look at Harry, his magical eye fixed upon him as well as the normal one.

"That was a very decent thing you just did, Potter," Moody said quietly.

Harry didn't know what to say; this wasn't the reaction he had expected at all.

"Sit down," said Moody, and Harry sat, looking around.

He had visited this office under two of its previous occupants. In Professor Lockhart's day, the walls had been plastered with beaming, winking pictures of Professor Lockhart himself. When Lupin had lived here, you were more likely to come across a specimen of some fascinating new Dark creature he had procured for them to study in class. Now, however, the office was full of a number of exceptionally odd objects that Harry supposed Moody had used in the days when he had been an Auror.

On his desk stood what looked like a large, cracked, glass spinning top; Harry recognized it at once as a Sneakoscope, because he owned one himself, though it was much smaller than Moody's. In the corner on a small table stood an object that looked something like an extra-squiggly, golden television aerial. It was humming slightly. What appeared to be a mirror hung opposite Harry on the wall, but it was not reflecting the room. Shadowy figures were moving around inside it, none of them clearly in focus.

"Like my Dark Detectors, do you?" said Moody, who was watching Harry closely.

"What's that?" Harry asked, pointing at the squiggly golden aerial.

"Secrecy Sensor. Vibrates when it detects concealment and lies . . . no use here, of course, too much interference — students in every direction lying about why they haven't done their homework. Been humming ever since I got here. I had to disable my Sneakoscope because it wouldn't stop whistling. It's extra-sensitive, picks up stuff about a mile around. Of course, it could be picking up more than kid stuff," he added in a growl.

"And what's the mirror for?"

"Oh that's my Foe-Glass. See them out there, skulking around? I'm not really in trouble until I see the whites of their eyes. That's when I open my trunk."

He let out a short, harsh laugh, and pointed to the large trunk under the window. It had seven keyholes in a row. Harry wondered what was in there, until Moody's next question brought him sharply back to earth.

"So . . . found out about the dragons, have you?"

Harry hesitated. He'd been afraid of this — but he hadn't told Cedric, and he certainly wasn't going to tell Moody, that Hagrid had broken the rules.

"It's all right," said Moody, sitting down and stretching out his wooden leg with a groan. "Cheating's a traditional part of the Triwizard Tournament and always has been."

"I didn't cheat," said Harry sharply. "It was — a sort of accident that I found out."

Moody grinned. "I wasn't accusing you, laddie. I've been telling Dumbledore from the start, he can be as high-minded as he likes, but you can bet old Karkaroff and Maxime won't be. They'll have told their champions everything they can. They want to win. They want to beat Dumbledore. They'd like to prove he's only human."

Moody gave another harsh laugh, and his magical eye swiveled around so fast it made Harry feel queasy to watch it.

"So . . . got any ideas how you're going to get past your dragon yet?" said Moody.

"No," said Harry.

"Well, I'm not going to tell you," said Moody gruffly. "I don't show favoritism, me. I'm just going to give you some good, general advice. And the first bit is — *play to your strengths.*"

"I haven't got any," said Harry, before he could stop himself.

"Excuse me," growled Moody, "you've got strengths if I say you've got them. Think now. What are you best at?"

Harry tried to concentrate. What *was* he best at? Well, that was easy, really —

"Quidditch," he said dully, "and a fat lot of help —"

"That's right," said Moody, staring at him very hard, his magical eye barely moving at all. "You're a damn good flier from what I've heard."

"Yeah, but . . ." Harry stared at him. "I'm not allowed a broom, I've only got my wand —"

"My second piece of general advice," said Moody loudly, interrupting him, "is to use a nice, simple spell that will enable you to *get what you need.*"

Harry looked at him blankly. What did he need?

"Come on, boy . . ." whispered Moody. "Put them together . . . it's not that difficult. . . ."

And it clicked. He was best at flying. He needed to pass the dragon in the air. For that, he needed his Firebolt. And for his Firebolt, he needed —

"Hermione," Harry whispered, when he had sped into the greenhouse three minutes later, uttering a hurried apology to Professor Sprout as he passed her. "Hermione — I need you to help me."

"What d'you think I've been trying to do, Harry?" she whispered back, her eyes round with anxiety over the top of the quivering Flutterby Bush she was pruning.

"Hermione, I need to learn how to do a Summoning Charm properly by tomorrow afternoon."

And so they practiced. They didn't have lunch, but headed for a free classroom, where Harry tried with all his might to make various objects fly across the room toward him. He was still having problems. The books and quills kept losing heart halfway across the room and dropping like stones to the floor.

"Concentrate, Harry, *concentrate*. . . ."

"What d'you think I'm trying to do?" said Harry angrily. "A great big dragon keeps popping up in my head for some reason. . . . Okay, try again. . . ."

He wanted to skip Divination to keep practicing, but Hermione refused point-blank to skive off Arithmancy, and there was no point in staying without her. He therefore had to endure over an hour of Professor Trelawney, who spent half the lesson telling everyone that the position of Mars with relation to Saturn at that moment meant that people born in July were in great danger of sudden, violent deaths.

"Well, that's good," said Harry loudly, his temper getting the better of him, "just as long as it's not drawn-out. I don't want to suffer."

Ron looked for a moment as though he was going to laugh; he certainly caught Harry's eye for the first time in days, but Harry was still feeling too resentful toward Ron to care. He spent the rest of the lesson trying to attract small objects toward him under the table with his wand. He managed to make a fly zoom straight into his hand, though he wasn't entirely sure that was his prowess at Summoning Charms — perhaps the fly was just stupid.

He forced down some dinner after Divination, then returned to the empty classroom with Hermione, using the Invisibility Cloak to avoid the teachers. They kept practicing until past midnight. They would have stayed longer, but Peeves turned up and, pretending to think that Harry wanted things thrown at him, started chucking chairs across the room. Harry and Hermione left in a hurry before the noise attracted Filch, and went back to the Gryffindor common room, which was now mercifully empty.

At two o'clock in the morning, Harry stood near the fireplace, surrounded by heaps of objects: books, quills, several upturned chairs, an old set of Gobstones, and Neville's toad, Trevor. Only in the last hour had Harry really got the hang of the Summoning Charm.

"That's better, Harry, that's loads better," Hermione said, looking exhausted but very pleased.

"Well, now we know what to do next time I can't manage a

spell," Harry said, throwing a rune dictionary back to Hermione, so he could try again, "threaten me with a dragon. Right . . ." He raised his wand once more. *"Accio Dictionary!"*

The heavy book soared out of Hermione's hand, flew across the room, and Harry caught it.

"Harry, I really think you've got it!" said Hermione delightedly.

"Just as long as it works tomorrow," Harry said. "The Firebolt's going to be much farther away than the stuff in here, it's going to be in the castle, and I'm going to be out there on the grounds. . . ."

"That doesn't matter," said Hermione firmly. "Just as long as you're concentrating really, really hard on it, it'll come. Harry, we'd better get some sleep . . . you're going to need it."

Harry had been focusing so hard on learning the Summoning Charm that evening that some of his blind panic had left him. It returned in full measure, however, on the following morning. The atmosphere in the school was one of great tension and excitement. Lessons were to stop at midday, giving all the students time to get down to the dragons' enclosure — though of course, they didn't yet know what they would find there.

Harry felt oddly separate from everyone around him, whether they were wishing him good luck or hissing *"We'll have a box of tissues ready, Potter"* as he passed. It was a state of nervousness so advanced that he wondered whether he mightn't just lose his head when they tried to lead him out to his dragon, and start trying to curse everyone in sight. Time was behaving in a more peculiar fashion than ever, rushing past in great dollops, so that one moment he seemed to be sitting down in his first lesson, History of Magic, and the next, walking into lunch . . . and then (where had the morning gone? the last of the dragon-free hours?), Professor McGonagall was hurrying over to him in the Great Hall. Lots of people were watching.

"Potter, the champions have to come down onto the grounds now. . . . You have to get ready for your first task."

"Okay," said Harry, standing up, his fork falling onto his plate with a clatter.

"Good luck, Harry," Hermione whispered. "You'll be fine!"

"Yeah," said Harry in a voice that was most unlike his own.

He left the Great Hall with Professor McGonagall. She didn't seem herself either; in fact, she looked nearly as anxious as Hermione. As she walked him down the stone steps and out into the cold November afternoon, she put her hand on his shoulder.

"Now, don't panic," she said, "just keep a cool head. . . . We've got wizards standing by to control the situation if it gets out of hand. . . . The main thing is just to do your best, and nobody will think any the worse of you. . . . Are you all right?"

"Yes," Harry heard himself say. "Yes, I'm fine."

She was leading him toward the place where the dragons were, around the edge of the forest, but when they approached the clump of trees behind which the enclosure would be clearly visible, Harry saw that a tent had been erected, its entrance facing them, screening the dragons from view.

"You're to go in here with the other champions," said Professor McGonagall, in a rather shaky sort of voice, "and wait for your turn, Potter. Mr. Bagman is in there . . . he'll be telling you the — the procedure. . . . Good luck."

"Thanks," said Harry, in a flat, distant voice. She left him at the entrance of the tent. Harry went inside.

Fleur Delacour was sitting in a corner on a low wooden stool. She didn't look nearly as composed as usual, but rather pale and clammy. Viktor Krum looked even surlier than usual, which Harry supposed was his way of showing nerves. Cedric was pacing up and down. When Harry entered, Cedric gave him a small smile, which Harry returned, feeling the muscles in his face working rather hard, as though they had forgotten how to do it.

"Harry! Good-o!" said Bagman happily, looking around at him. "Come in, come in, make yourself at home!"

Bagman looked somehow like a slightly overblown cartoon figure, standing amid all the pale-faced champions. He was wearing his old Wasp robes again.

"Well, now we're all here — time to fill you in!" said Bagman brightly. "When the audience has assembled, I'm going to be offering each of you this bag" — he held up a small sack of purple silk and shook it at them — "from which you will each select a small model of the thing you are about to face! There are different — er — varieties, you see. And I have to tell you something else too . . . ah, yes . . . your task is to *collect the golden egg*!"

Harry glanced around. Cedric had nodded once, to show that he understood Bagman's words, and then started pacing around the tent again; he looked slightly green. Fleur Delacour and Krum hadn't reacted at all. Perhaps they thought they might be sick if they opened their mouths; that was certainly how Harry felt. But they, at least, had volunteered for this. . . .

And in no time at all, hundreds upon hundreds of pairs of feet could be heard passing the tent, their owners talking excitedly, laughing, joking. . . . Harry felt as separate from the crowd as though they were a different species. And then — it seemed like about a second later to Harry — Bagman was opening the neck of the purple silk sack.

"Ladies first," he said, offering it to Fleur Delacour.

She put a shaking hand inside the bag and drew out a tiny, perfect model of a dragon — a Welsh Green. It had the number two around its neck. And Harry knew, by the fact that Fleur showed no sign of surprise, but rather a determined resignation, that he had been right: Madame Maxime had told her what was coming.

The same held true for Krum. He pulled out the scarlet Chinese Fireball. It had a number three around its neck. He didn't even blink, just sat back down and stared at the ground.

Cedric put his hand into the bag, and out came the blueish-gray Swedish Short-Snout, the number one tied around its neck. Knowing what was left, Harry put his hand into the silk bag and pulled out the Hungarian Horntail, and the number four. It stretched its wings as he looked down at it, and bared its minuscule fangs.

"Well, there you are!" said Bagman. "You have each pulled out the dragon you will face, and the numbers refer to the order in which you are to take on the dragons, do you see? Now, I'm going to have to leave you in a moment, because I'm commentating. Mr. Diggory, you're first, just go out into the enclosure when you hear a whistle, all right? Now . . . Harry . . . could I have a quick word? Outside?"

"Er . . . yes," said Harry blankly, and he got up and went out of the tent with Bagman, who walked him a short distance away, into the trees, and then turned to him with a fatherly expression on his face.

"Feeling all right, Harry? Anything I can get you?"

"What?" said Harry. "I — no, nothing."

"Got a plan?" said Bagman, lowering his voice conspiratorially. "Because I don't mind sharing a few pointers, if you'd like them, you know. I mean," Bagman continued, lowering his voice still further, "you're the underdog here, Harry. . . . Anything I can do to help . . ."

"No," said Harry so quickly he knew he had sounded rude, "no — I — I know what I'm going to do, thanks."

"Nobody would *know*, Harry," said Bagman, winking at him.

"No, I'm fine," said Harry, wondering why he kept telling people this, and wondering whether he had ever been less fine. "I've got a plan worked out, I —"

A whistle had blown somewhere.

"Good lord, I've got to run!" said Bagman in alarm, and he hurried off.

Harry walked back to the tent and saw Cedric emerging from it, greener than ever. Harry tried to wish him luck as he walked past, but all that came out of his mouth was a sort of hoarse grunt.

Harry went back inside to Fleur and Krum. Seconds later, they heard the roar of the crowd, which meant Cedric had entered the enclosure and was now face-to-face with the living counterpart of his model. . . .

It was worse than Harry could ever have imagined, sitting there and listening. The crowd screamed . . . yelled . . . gasped like a single many-headed entity, as Cedric did whatever he was doing to get past the Swedish Short-Snout. Krum was still staring at the ground. Fleur had now taken to retracing Cedric's steps, around and around the tent. And Bagman's commentary made everything much, much worse. . . . Horrible pictures formed in Harry's mind as he heard: "Oooh, narrow miss there, very narrow". . . . "He's taking risks, this one!". . . "*Clever* move — pity it didn't work!"

And then, after about fifteen minutes, Harry heard the deafening roar that could mean only one thing: Cedric had gotten past his dragon and captured the golden egg.

"Very good indeed!" Bagman was shouting. "And now the marks from the judges!"

But he didn't shout out the marks; Harry supposed the judges were holding them up and showing them to the crowd.

"One down, three to go!" Bagman yelled as the whistle blew again. "Miss Delacour, if you please!"

Fleur was trembling from head to foot; Harry felt more warmly toward her than he had done so far as she left the tent with her head held high and her hand clutching her wand. He and Krum were left alone, at opposite sides of the tent, avoiding each other's gaze.

The same process started again. . . . "Oh I'm not sure that was wise!" they could hear Bagman shouting gleefully. "Oh . . . nearly! Careful now . . . good lord, I thought she'd had it then!"

Ten minutes later, Harry heard the crowd erupt into applause once more. . . . Fleur must have been successful too. A pause, while Fleur's marks were being shown . . . more clapping . . . then, for the third time, the whistle.

"And here comes Mr. Krum!" cried Bagman, and Krum slouched out, leaving Harry quite alone.

He felt much more aware of his body than usual; very aware of the way his heart was pumping fast, and his fingers tingling with fear . . . yet at the same time, he seemed to be outside himself, seeing the walls of the tent, and hearing the crowd, as though from far away. . . .

"Very daring!" Bagman was yelling, and Harry heard the Chinese Fireball emit a horrible, roaring shriek, while the crowd drew its collective breath. "That's some nerve he's showing — and — yes, he's got the egg!"

Applause shattered the wintery air like breaking glass; Krum had finished — it would be Harry's turn any moment.

He stood up, noticing dimly that his legs seemed to be made of marshmallow. He waited. And then he heard the whistle blow. He walked out through the entrance of the tent, the panic rising into a crescendo inside him. And now he was walking past the trees, through a gap in the enclosure fence.

He saw everything in front of him as though it was a very highly colored dream. There were hundreds and hundreds of faces staring down at him from stands that had been magicked there since he'd last stood on this spot. And there was the Horntail, at the other end of the enclosure, crouched low over her clutch of eggs, her wings half-furled, her evil, yellow eyes upon him, a monstrous, scaly, black lizard, thrashing her spiked tail, leaving yard-long gouge marks in the hard ground. The crowd was making a great deal of noise, but whether friendly or not, Harry didn't know or care. It was time to do what he had to do . . . to focus his mind, entirely and absolutely, upon the thing that was his only chance. . . .

He raised his wand.

*"Accio Firebolt!"* he shouted.

Harry waited, every fiber of him hoping, praying. . . . If it hadn't worked . . . if it wasn't coming . . . He seemed to be looking at everything around him through some sort of shimmering, transparent barrier, like a heat haze, which made the enclosure and the hundreds of faces around him swim strangely. . . .

And then he heard it, speeding through the air behind him; he turned and saw his Firebolt hurtling toward him around the edge of the woods, soaring into the enclosure, and stopping dead in midair beside him, waiting for him to mount. The crowd was making even more noise. . . . Bagman was shouting something . . . but Harry's ears were not working properly anymore . . . listening wasn't important. . . .

He swung his leg over the broom and kicked off from the ground. And a second later, something miraculous happened. . . .

As he soared upward, as the wind rushed through his hair, as the crowd's faces became mere flesh-colored pinpricks below, and the Horntail shrank to the size of a dog, he realized that he had left not only the ground behind, but also his fear. . . . He was back where he belonged. . . .

This was just another Quidditch match, that was all . . . just another Quidditch match, and that Horntail was just another ugly opposing team. . . .

He looked down at the clutch of eggs and spotted the gold one, gleaming against its cement-colored fellows, residing safely between the dragon's front legs. "Okay," Harry told himself, "diversionary tactics . . . let's go. . . ."

He dived. The Horntail's head followed him; he knew what it was going to do and pulled out of the dive just in time; a jet of fire had been released exactly where he would have been had he not swerved away . . . but Harry didn't care . . . that was no more than dodging a Bludger. . . .

"Great Scott, he can fly!" yelled Bagman as the crowd shrieked and gasped. "Are you watching this, Mr. Krum?"

Harry soared higher in a circle; the Horntail was still following his progress; its head revolving on its long neck — if he kept this up, it would be nicely dizzy — but better not push it too long, or it would be breathing fire again —

Harry plummeted just as the Horntail opened its mouth, but this time he was less lucky — he missed the flames, but the tail came whipping up to meet him instead, and as he swerved to the left, one of the long spikes grazed his shoulder, ripping his robes —

He could feel it stinging, he could hear screaming and groans from the crowd, but the cut didn't seem to be deep. . . . Now he zoomed around the back of the Horntail, and a possibility occurred to him. . . .

The Horntail didn't seem to want to take off, she was too protective of her eggs. Though she writhed and twisted, furling and unfurling her wings and keeping those fearsome yellow eyes on Harry, she was afraid to move too far from them . . . but he had to persuade her to do it, or he'd never get near them. . . . The trick was to do it carefully, gradually. . . .

He began to fly, first this way, then the other, not near enough to make her breathe fire to stave him off, but still posing a sufficient threat to ensure she kept her eyes on him. Her head swayed this way and that, watching him out of those vertical pupils, her fangs bared. . . .

He flew higher. The Horntail's head rose with him, her neck now stretched to its fullest extent, still swaying, like a snake before its charmer. . . .

Harry rose a few more feet, and she let out a roar of exasperation. He was like a fly to her, a fly she was longing to swat; her tail thrashed again, but he was too high to reach now. . . . She shot fire into the air, which he dodged. . . . Her jaws opened wide. . . .

"Come on," Harry hissed, swerving tantalizingly above her, "come on, come and get me . . . up you get now . . ."

And then she reared, spreading her great, black, leathery wings at last, as wide as those of a small airplane — and Harry dived. Before the dragon knew what he had done, or where he had disappeared to, he was speeding toward the ground as fast as he could go, toward the eggs now unprotected by her clawed front legs — he had taken his hands off his Firebolt — he had seized the golden egg —

And with a huge spurt of speed, he was off, he was soaring out over the stands, the heavy egg safely under his uninjured arm, and it was as though somebody had just turned the volume back up — for the first time, he became properly aware of the noise of the crowd, which was screaming and applauding as loudly as the Irish supporters at the World Cup —

"Look at that!" Bagman was yelling. "Will you look at that! Our youngest champion is quickest to get his egg! Well, this is going to shorten the odds on Mr. Potter!"

Harry saw the dragon keepers rushing forward to subdue the Horntail, and, over at the entrance to the enclosure, Professor McGonagall, Professor Moody, and Hagrid hurrying to meet him, all of them waving him toward them, their smiles evident even from this distance. He flew back over the stands, the noise of the crowd pounding his eardrums, and came in smoothly to land, his heart lighter than it had been in weeks. . . . He had got through the first task, he had survived. . . .

"That was excellent, Potter!" cried Professor McGonagall as he got off the Firebolt — which from her was extravagant praise. He noticed that her hand shook as she pointed at his shoulder. "You'll need to see Madam Pomfrey before the judges give out your score. . . . Over there, she's had to mop up Diggory already. . . ."

"Yeh did it, Harry!" said Hagrid hoarsely. "Yeh did it! An' agains' the Horntail an' all, an' yeh know Charlie said that was the wors' — "

"Thanks, Hagrid," said Harry loudly, so that Hagrid wouldn't blunder on and reveal that he had shown Harry the dragons beforehand.

Professor Moody looked very pleased too; his magical eye was dancing in its socket.

"Nice and easy does the trick, Potter," he growled.

"Right then, Potter, the first aid tent, please . . ." said Professor McGonagall.

Harry walked out of the enclosure, still panting, and saw Madam Pomfrey standing at the mouth of a second tent, looking worried.

"Dragons!" she said, in a disgusted tone, pulling Harry inside. The tent was divided into cubicles; he could make out Cedric's shadow through the canvas, but Cedric didn't seem to be badly injured; he was sitting up, at least. Madam Pomfrey examined Harry's shoulder, talking furiously all the while. "Last year dementors, this year dragons, what are they going to bring into this school next? You're very lucky . . . this is quite shallow . . . it'll need cleaning before I heal it up, though. . . ."

She cleaned the cut with a dab of some purple liquid that smoked and stung, but then poked his shoulder with her wand, and he felt it heal instantly.

"Now, just sit quietly for a minute — *sit*! And then you can go and get your score."

She bustled out of the tent and he heard her go next door and say, "How does it feel now, Diggory?"

Harry didn't want to sit still: He was too full of adrenaline. He got to his feet, wanting to see what was going on outside, but before he'd reached the mouth of the tent, two people had come darting inside — Hermione, followed closely by Ron.

"Harry, you were brilliant!" Hermione said squeakily. There were fingernail marks on her face where she had been clutching it in fear. "You were amazing! You really were!"

But Harry was looking at Ron, who was very white and staring at Harry as though he were a ghost.

"Harry," he said, very seriously, "whoever put your name in that goblet — I — I reckon they're trying to do you in!"

It was as though the last few weeks had never happened — as though Harry were meeting Ron for the first time, right after he'd been made champion.

"Caught on, have you?" said Harry coldly. "Took you long enough."

Hermione stood nervously between them, looking from one to the other. Ron opened his mouth uncertainly. Harry knew Ron was about to apologize and suddenly he found he didn't need to hear it.

"It's okay," he said, before Ron could get the words out. "Forget it."

"No," said Ron, "I shouldn't've —"

"*Forget it,*" Harry said.

Ron grinned nervously at him, and Harry grinned back.

Hermione burst into tears.

"There's nothing to cry about!" Harry told her, bewildered.

"You two are so *stupid*!" she shouted, stamping her foot on the ground, tears splashing down her front. Then, before either of them could stop her, she had given both of them a hug and dashed away, now positively howling.

"Barking mad," said Ron, shaking his head. "Harry, c'mon, they'll be putting up your scores. . . ."

Picking up the golden egg and his Firebolt, feeling more elated than he would have believed possible an hour ago, Harry ducked out of the tent, Ron by his side, talking fast.

"You were the best, you know, no competition. Cedric did this weird thing where he Transfigured a rock on the ground . . . turned it into a dog . . . he was trying to make the dragon go for the dog instead of him. Well, it was a pretty cool bit of Transfiguration, and it sort of worked, because he did get the egg, but he got burned as well — the dragon changed its mind halfway through and decided it would rather have him than the Labrador; he only just got away. And that Fleur girl tried this sort of charm, I think she was trying to put it into a trance — well, that kind of worked too, it went all sleepy, but then it snored, and this great jet of flame shot out, and her skirt caught fire — she put it out with a bit of water out of her wand. And Krum — you won't believe this, but he didn't even think of flying! He was probably the best after you, though. Hit it with some sort of spell right in the eye. Only thing is, it went trampling around in agony and squashed half the real eggs — they took marks off for that, he wasn't supposed to do any damage to them."

Ron drew breath as he and Harry reached the edge of the enclosure. Now that the Horntail had been taken away, Harry could see where the five judges were sitting — right at the other end, in raised seats draped in gold.

"It's marks out of ten from each one," Ron said, and Harry,

squinting up the field, saw the first judge — Madame Maxime — raise her wand in the air. What looked like a long silver ribbon shot out of it, which twisted itself into a large figure eight.

"Not bad!" said Ron as the crowd applauded. "I suppose she took marks off for your shoulder. . . ."

Mr. Crouch came next. He shot a number nine into the air.

"Looking good!" Ron yelled, thumping Harry on the back.

Next, Dumbledore. He too put up a nine. The crowd was cheering harder than ever.

Ludo Bagman — *ten.*

"Ten?" said Harry in disbelief. "But . . . I got hurt. . . . What's he playing at?"

"Harry, don't complain!" Ron yelled excitedly.

And now Karkaroff raised his wand. He paused for a moment, and then a number shot out of his wand too — four.

"*What?*" Ron bellowed furiously. "*Four?* You lousy, biased scumbag, you gave Krum ten!"

But Harry didn't care, he wouldn't have cared if Karkaroff had given him zero; Ron's indignation on his behalf was worth about a hundred points to him. He didn't tell Ron this, of course, but his heart felt lighter than air as he turned to leave the enclosure. And it wasn't just Ron . . . those weren't only Gryffindors cheering in the crowd. When it had come to it, when they had seen what he was facing, most of the school had been on his side as well as Cedric's. . . . He didn't care about the Slytherins, he could stand whatever they threw at him now.

"You're tied in first place, Harry! You and Krum!" said Charlie Weasley, hurrying to meet them as they set off back toward the school. "Listen, I've got to run, I've got to go and send Mum an owl, I swore I'd tell her what happened — but that was unbeliev-able! Oh yeah — and they told me to tell you you've got to hang around for a few more minutes. . . . Bagman wants a word, back in the champions' tent."

Ron said he would wait, so Harry reentered the tent, which somehow looked quite different now: friendly and welcoming. He thought back to how he'd felt while dodging the Horntail, and compared it to the long wait before he'd walked out to face it. . . . There was no comparison; the wait had been immeasurably worse.

Fleur, Cedric, and Krum all came in together. One side of Cedric's face was covered in a thick orange paste, which was presumably mending his burn. He grinned at Harry when he saw him.

"Good one, Harry."

"And you," said Harry, grinning back.

"Well done, *all* of you!" said Ludo Bagman, bouncing into the tent and looking as pleased as though he personally had just got past a dragon. "Now, just a quick few words. You've got a nice long break before the second task, which will take place at half past nine on the morning of February the twenty-fourth — but we're giving you something to think about in the meantime! If you look down at those golden eggs you're all holding, you will see that they open . . . see the hinges there? You need to solve the clue inside the egg — because it will tell you what the second task is, and enable you to prepare for it! All clear? Sure? Well, off you go, then!"

Harry left the tent, rejoined Ron, and they started to walk back around the edge of the forest, talking hard; Harry wanted to hear what the other champions had done in more detail. Then, as they rounded the clump of trees behind which Harry had first heard the dragons roar, a witch leapt out from behind them.

It was Rita Skeeter. She was wearing acid-green robes today; the Quick-Quotes Quill in her hand blended perfectly against them.

"Congratulations, Harry!" she said, beaming at him. "I wonder if you could give me a quick word? How you felt facing that dragon? How you feel *now*, about the fairness of the scoring?"

"Yeah, you can have a word," said Harry savagely. *"Good-bye."*

And he set off back to the castle with Ron.

# THE HOUSE-ELF
# LIBERATION FRONT

Harry, Ron, and Hermione went up to the Owlery that evening to find Pigwidgeon, so that Harry could send Sirius a letter telling him that he had managed to get past his dragon unscathed. On the way, Harry filled Ron in on everything Sirius had told him about Karkaroff. Though shocked at first to hear that Karkaroff had been a Death Eater, by the time they entered the Owlery Ron was saying that they ought to have suspected it all along.

"Fits, doesn't it?" he said. "Remember what Malfoy said on the train, about his dad being friends with Karkaroff? Now we know where they knew each other. They were probably running around in masks together at the World Cup. . . . I'll tell you one thing, though, Harry, if it *was* Karkaroff who put your name in the goblet, he's going to be feeling really stupid now, isn't he? Didn't work, did it? You only got a scratch! Come here — I'll do it —"

Pigwidgeon was so overexcited at the idea of a delivery he was flying around and around Harry's head, hooting incessantly. Ron snatched Pigwidgeon out of the air and held him still while Harry attached the letter to his leg.

"There's no way any of the other tasks are going to be that dangerous, how could they be?" Ron went on as he carried Pigwidgeon to the window. "You know what? I reckon you could win this tournament, Harry, I'm serious."

Harry knew that Ron was only saying this to make up for his behavior of the last few weeks, but he appreciated it all the same. Hermione, however, leaned against the Owlery wall, folded her arms, and frowned at Ron.

"Harry's got a long way to go before he finishes this tournament," she said seriously. "If that was the first task, I hate to think what's coming next."

"Right little ray of sunshine, aren't you?" said Ron. "You and Professor Trelawney should get together sometime."

He threw Pigwidgeon out of the window. Pigwidgeon plummeted twelve feet before managing to pull himself back up again; the letter attached to his leg was much longer and heavier than usual — Harry hadn't been able to resist giving Sirius a blow-by-blow account of exactly how he had swerved, circled, and dodged the Horntail. They watched Pigwidgeon disappear into the darkness, and then Ron said, "Well, we'd better get downstairs for your surprise party, Harry — Fred and George should have nicked enough food from the kitchens by now."

Sure enough, when they entered the Gryffindor common room it exploded with cheers and yells again. There were mountains of cakes and flagons of pumpkin juice and butterbeer on every surface; Lee Jordan had let off some Filibuster's Fireworks, so that the air was thick with stars and sparks; and Dean Thomas, who was very good at drawing, had put up some impressive new banners, most of which depicted Harry zooming around the Horntail's head on his Firebolt, though a couple showed Cedric with his head on fire.

Harry helped himself to food; he had almost forgotten what it was like to feel properly hungry, and sat down with Ron and Hermione. He couldn't believe how happy he felt; he had Ron back on his side, he'd gotten through the first task, and he wouldn't have to face the second one for three months.

"Blimey, this is heavy," said Lee Jordan, picking up the golden egg, which Harry had left on a table, and weighing it in his hands. "Open it, Harry, go on! Let's just see what's inside it!"

"He's supposed to work out the clue on his own," Hermione said swiftly. "It's in the tournament rules. . . ."

"I was supposed to work out how to get past the dragon on my own too," Harry muttered, so only Hermione could hear him, and she grinned rather guiltily.

"Yeah, go on, Harry, open it!" several people echoed.

Lee passed Harry the egg, and Harry dug his fingernails into the groove that ran all the way around it and prised it open.

It was hollow and completely empty — but the moment Harry opened it, the most horrible noise, a loud and screechy wailing, filled the room. The nearest thing to it Harry had ever heard was the ghost orchestra at Nearly Headless Nick's deathday party, who had all been playing the musical saw.

"Shut it!" Fred bellowed, his hands over his ears.

"What was that?" said Seamus Finnigan, staring at the egg as Harry slammed it shut again. "Sounded like a banshee. . . . Maybe you've got to get past one of those next, Harry!"

"It was someone being tortured!" said Neville, who had gone very white and spilled sausage rolls all over the floor. "You're going to have to fight the Cruciatus Curse!"

"Don't be a prat, Neville, that's illegal," said George. "They wouldn't use the Cruciatus Curse on the champions. I thought it sounded a bit like Percy singing . . . maybe you've got to attack him while he's in the shower, Harry."

"Want a jam tart, Hermione?" said Fred.

Hermione looked doubtfully at the plate he was offering her. Fred grinned.

"It's all right," he said. "I haven't done anything to them. It's the custard creams you've got to watch —"

Neville, who had just bitten into a custard cream, choked and spat it out. Fred laughed.

"Just my little joke, Neville. . . ."

Hermione took a jam tart. Then she said, "Did you get all this from the kitchens, Fred?"

"Yep," said Fred, grinning at her. He put on a high-pitched squeak and imitated a house-elf. "'Anything we can get you, sir, anything at all!' They're dead helpful . . . get me a roast ox if I said I was peckish."

"How do you get in there?" Hermione said in an innocently casual sort of voice.

"Easy," said Fred, "concealed door behind a painting of a bowl of fruit. Just tickle the pear, and it giggles and —" He stopped and looked suspiciously at her. "Why?"

"Nothing," said Hermione quickly.

"Going to try and lead the house-elves out on strike now, are you?" said George. "Going to give up all the leaflet stuff and try and stir them up into rebellion?"

Several people chortled. Hermione didn't answer.

"Don't you go upsetting them and telling them they've got to take clothes and salaries!" said Fred warningly. "You'll put them off their cooking!"

Just then, Neville caused a slight diversion by turning into a large canary.

"Oh — sorry, Neville!" Fred shouted over all the laughter. "I forgot — it *was* the custard creams we hexed —"

Within a minute, however, Neville had molted, and once his feathers had fallen off, he reappeared looking entirely normal. He even joined in laughing.

"Canary Creams!" Fred shouted to the excitable crowd. "George and I invented them — seven Sickles each, a bargain!"

It was nearly one in the morning when Harry finally went up to the dormitory with Ron, Neville, Seamus, and Dean. Before he pulled the curtains of his four-poster shut, Harry set his tiny model of the Hungarian Horntail on the table next to his bed, where it yawned, curled up, and closed its eyes. *Really,* Harry thought, as he pulled the hangings on his four-poster closed, *Hagrid had a point . . . they were all right, really, dragons. . . .*

The start of December brought wind and sleet to Hogwarts. Drafty though the castle always was in winter, Harry was glad of its fires and thick walls every time he passed the Durmstrang ship on the lake, which was pitching in the high winds, its black sails billowing against the dark skies. He thought the Beauxbatons caravan was likely to be pretty chilly too. Hagrid, he noticed, was keeping Madame Maxime's horses well provided with their preferred drink of single-malt whiskey; the fumes wafting from the trough in the corner of their paddock was enough to make the entire Care of Magical Creatures class light-headed. This was unhelpful, as they were still tending the horrible skrewts and needed their wits about them.

"I'm not sure whether they hibernate or not," Hagrid told the shivering class in the windy pumpkin patch next lesson. "Thought we'd jus' try an' see if they fancied a kip . . . we'll jus' settle 'em down in these boxes. . . ."

There were now only ten skrewts left; apparently their desire to kill one another had not been exercised out of them. Each of them was now approaching six feet in length. Their thick gray armor; their powerful, scuttling legs; their fire-blasting ends; their stings and their suckers, combined to make the skrewts the most repulsive things Harry had ever seen. The class looked dispiritedly at the enormous boxes Hagrid had brought out, all lined with pillows and fluffy blankets.

"We'll jus' lead 'em in here," Hagrid said, "an' put the lids on, and we'll see what happens."

But the skrewts, it transpired, did *not* hibernate, and did not appreciate being forced into pillow-lined boxes and nailed in. Hagrid was soon yelling, "Don' panic, now, don' panic!" while the skrewts rampaged around the pumpkin patch, now strewn with the smoldering wreckage of the boxes. Most of the class — Malfoy, Crabbe, and Goyle in the lead — had fled into Hagrid's cabin through the

back door and barricaded themselves in; Harry, Ron, and Hermione, however, were among those who remained outside trying to
help Hagrid. Together they managed to restrain and tie up nine of
the skrewts, though at the cost of numerous burns and cuts; finally,
only one skrewt was left.

"Don' frighten him, now!" Hagrid shouted as Ron and Harry
used their wands to shoot jets of fiery sparks at the skrewt, which
was advancing menacingly on them, its sting arched, quivering,
over its back. "Jus' try an' slip the rope 'round his sting, so he won'
hurt any o' the others!"

"Yeah, we wouldn't want that!" Ron shouted angrily as he and
Harry backed into the wall of Hagrid's cabin, still holding the
skrewt off with their sparks.

"Well, well, well . . . this *does* look like fun."

Rita Skeeter was leaning on Hagrid's garden fence, looking in at
the mayhem. She was wearing a thick magenta cloak with a furry
purple collar today, and her crocodile-skin handbag was over her
arm.

Hagrid launched himself forward on top of the skrewt that was
cornering Harry and Ron and flattened it; a blast of fire shot out of
its end, withering the pumpkin plants nearby.

"Who're you?" Hagrid asked Rita Skeeter as he slipped a loop of
rope around the skrewt's sting and tightened it.

"Rita Skeeter, *Daily Prophet* reporter," Rita replied, beaming at
him. Her gold teeth glinted.

"Thought Dumbledore said you weren' allowed inside the school
anymore," said Hagrid, frowning slightly as he got off the slightly
squashed skrewt and started tugging it over to its fellows.

Rita acted as though she hadn't heard what Hagrid had said.

"What are these fascinating creatures called?" she asked, beaming still more widely.

"Blast-Ended Skrewts," grunted Hagrid.

"Really?" said Rita, apparently full of lively interest. "I've never heard of them before . . . where do they come from?"

Harry noticed a dull red flush rising up out of Hagrid's wild black beard, and his heart sank. Where *had* Hagrid got the skrewts from? Hermione, who seemed to be thinking along these lines, said quickly, "They're very interesting, aren't they? Aren't they, Harry?"

"What? Oh yeah . . . ouch . . . interesting," said Harry as she stepped on his foot.

"Ah, *you're* here, Harry!" said Rita Skeeter as she looked around. "So you like Care of Magical Creatures, do you? One of your favorite lessons?"

"Yes," said Harry stoutly. Hagrid beamed at him.

"Lovely," said Rita. "Really lovely. Been teaching long?" she added to Hagrid.

Harry noticed her eyes travel over Dean (who had a nasty cut across one cheek), Lavender (whose robes were badly singed), Seamus (who was nursing several burnt fingers), and then to the cabin windows, where most of the class stood, their noses pressed against the glass waiting to see if the coast was clear.

"This is on'y me second year," said Hagrid.

"Lovely . . . I don't suppose you'd like to give an interview, would you? Share some of your experience of magical creatures? The *Prophet* does a zoological column every Wednesday, as I'm sure you know. We could feature these — er — Bang-Ended Scoots."

"Blast-Ended Skrewts," Hagrid said eagerly. "Er — yeah, why not?"

Harry had a very bad feeling about this, but there was no way of communicating it to Hagrid without Rita Skeeter seeing, so he had to stand and watch in silence as Hagrid and Rita Skeeter made arrangements to meet in the Three Broomsticks for a good long interview later that week. Then the bell rang up at the castle, signaling the end of the lesson.

"Well, good-bye, Harry!" Rita Skeeter called merrily to him as he set off with Ron and Hermione. "Until Friday night, then, Hagrid!"

"She'll twist everything he says," Harry said under his breath.

"Just as long as he didn't import those skrewts illegally or anything," said Hermione desperately. They looked at one another — it was exactly the sort of thing Hagrid might do.

"Hagrid's been in loads of trouble before, and Dumbledore's never sacked him," said Ron consolingly. "Worst that can happen is Hagrid'll have to get rid of the skrewts. Sorry . . . did I say worst? I meant best."

Harry and Hermione laughed, and, feeling slightly more cheerful, went off to lunch.

Harry thoroughly enjoyed double Divination that afternoon; they were still doing star charts and predictions, but now that he and Ron were friends once more, the whole thing seemed very funny again. Professor Trelawney, who had been so pleased with the pair of them when they had been predicting their own horrific deaths, quickly became irritated as they sniggered through her explanation of the various ways in which Pluto could disrupt everyday life.

"I would *think*," she said, in a mystical whisper that did not conceal her obvious annoyance, "that *some* of us" — she stared very meaningfully at Harry — "might be a little less *frivolous* had they seen what I have seen during my crystal gazing last night. As I sat here, absorbed in my needlework, the urge to consult the orb overpowered me. I arose, I settled myself before it, and I gazed into its crystalline depths . . . and what do you think I saw gazing back at me?"

"An ugly old bat in outsize specs?" Ron muttered under his breath.

Harry fought hard to keep his face straight.

"*Death,* my dears."

Parvati and Lavender both put their hands over their mouths, looking horrified.

"Yes," said Professor Trelawney, nodding impressively, "it comes, ever closer, it circles overhead like a vulture, ever lower . . . ever lower over the castle. . . ."

She stared pointedly at Harry, who yawned very widely and obviously.

"It'd be a bit more impressive if she hadn't done it about eighty times before," Harry said as they finally regained the fresh air of the staircase beneath Professor Trelawney's room. "But if I'd dropped dead every time she's told me I'm going to, I'd be a medical miracle."

"You'd be a sort of extra-concentrated ghost," said Ron, chortling, as they passed the Bloody Baron going in the opposite direction, his wide eyes staring sinisterly. "At least we didn't get homework. I hope Hermione got loads off Professor Vector, I love not working when she is. . . ."

But Hermione wasn't at dinner, nor was she in the library when they went to look for her afterward. The only person in there was Viktor Krum. Ron hovered behind the bookshelves for a while, watching Krum, debating in whispers with Harry whether he should ask for an autograph — but then Ron realized that six or seven girls were lurking in the next row of books, debating exactly the same thing, and he lost his enthusiasm for the idea.

"Wonder where she's got to?" Ron said as he and Harry went back to Gryffindor Tower.

"Dunno . . . balderdash."

But the Fat Lady had barely begun to swing forward when the sound of racing feet behind them announced Hermione's arrival.

"Harry!" she panted, skidding to a halt beside him (the Fat Lady stared down at her, eyebrows raised). "Harry, you've got to come — you've *got* to come, the most amazing thing's happened — please —"

She seized Harry's arm and started to try to drag him back along the corridor.

"What's the matter?" Harry said.

"I'll show you when we get there — oh come on, quick —"

Harry looked around at Ron; he looked back at Harry, intrigued.

"Okay," Harry said, starting off back down the corridor with Hermione, Ron hurrying to keep up.

"Oh don't mind me!" the Fat Lady called irritably after them. "Don't apologize for bothering me! I'll just hang here, wide open, until you get back, shall I?"

"Yeah, thanks!" Ron shouted over his shoulder.

"Hermione, where are we going?" Harry asked, after she had led them down through six floors, and started down the marble staircase into the entrance hall.

"You'll see, you'll see in a minute!" said Hermione excitedly.

She turned left at the bottom of the staircase and hurried toward the door through which Cedric Diggory had gone the night after the Goblet of Fire had regurgitated his and Harry's names. Harry had never been through here before. He and Ron followed Hermione down a flight of stone steps, but instead of ending up in a gloomy underground passage like the one that led to Snape's dungeon, they found themselves in a broad stone corridor, brightly lit with torches, and decorated with cheerful paintings that were mainly of food.

"Oh hang on . . ." said Harry slowly, halfway down the corridor. "Wait a minute, Hermione. . . ."

"What?" She turned around to look at him, anticipation all over her face.

"I know what this is about," said Harry.

He nudged Ron and pointed to the painting just behind Hermione. It showed a gigantic silver fruit bowl.

"Hermione!" said Ron, cottoning on. "You're trying to rope us into that spew stuff again!"

"No, no, I'm not!" she said hastily. "And it's not *spew*, Ron —"

"Changed the name, have you?" said Ron, frowning at her. "What are we now, then, the House-Elf Liberation Front? I'm not barging into that kitchen and trying to make them stop work, I'm not doing it —"

"I'm not asking you to!" Hermione said impatiently. "I came down here just now, to talk to them all, and I found — oh come *on*, Harry, I want to show you!"

She seized his arm again, pulled him in front of the picture of the giant fruit bowl, stretched out her forefinger, and tickled the huge green pear. It began to squirm, chuckling, and suddenly turned into a large green door handle. Hermione seized it, pulled the door open, and pushed Harry hard in the back, forcing him inside.

He had one brief glimpse of an enormous, high-ceilinged room, large as the Great Hall above it, with mounds of glittering brass pots and pans heaped around the stone walls, and a great brick fireplace at the other end, when something small hurtled toward him from the middle of the room, squealing, "Harry Potter, sir! *Harry Potter!*"

Next second all the wind had been knocked out of him as the squealing elf hit him hard in the midriff, hugging him so tightly he thought his ribs would break.

"D-Dobby?" Harry gasped.

"It *is* Dobby, sir, it is!" squealed the voice from somewhere around his navel. "Dobby has been hoping and hoping to see Harry Potter, sir, and Harry Potter has come to see him, sir!"

Dobby let go and stepped back a few paces, beaming up at Harry, his enormous, green, tennis-ball-shaped eyes brimming with tears of happiness. He looked almost exactly as Harry remembered him; the pencil-shaped nose, the batlike ears, the long fingers and feet — all except the clothes, which were very different.

When Dobby had worked for the Malfoys, he had always worn the same filthy old pillowcase. Now, however, he was wearing the strangest assortment of garments Harry had ever seen; he had done an even worse job of dressing himself than the wizards at the World Cup. He was wearing a tea cozy for a hat, on which he had pinned a number of bright badges; a tie patterned with horseshoes over a bare chest, a pair of what looked like children's soccer shorts, and odd socks. One of these, Harry saw, was the black one Harry had removed from his own foot and tricked Mr. Malfoy into giving Dobby, thereby setting Dobby free. The other was covered in pink and orange stripes.

"Dobby, what're you doing here?" Harry said in amazement.

"Dobby has come to work at Hogwarts, sir!" Dobby squealed excitedly. "Professor Dumbledore gave Dobby and Winky jobs, sir!"

"Winky?" said Harry. "She's here too?"

"Yes, sir, yes!" said Dobby, and he seized Harry's hand and pulled him off into the kitchen between the four long wooden tables that stood there. Each of these tables, Harry noticed as he passed them, was positioned exactly beneath the four House tables above, in the Great Hall. At the moment, they were clear of food, dinner having finished, but he supposed that an hour ago they had been laden with dishes that were then sent up through the ceiling to their counterparts above.

At least a hundred little elves were standing around the kitchen, beaming, bowing, and curtsying as Dobby led Harry past them. They were all wearing the same uniform: a tea towel stamped with the Hogwarts crest, and tied, as Winky's had been, like a toga.

Dobby stopped in front of the brick fireplace and pointed.

"Winky, sir!" he said.

Winky was sitting on a stool by the fire. Unlike Dobby, she had obviously not foraged for clothes. She was wearing a neat little skirt and blouse with a matching blue hat, which had holes in it for her large ears. However, while every one of Dobby's strange collection of garments was so clean and well cared for that it looked brand-new, Winky was plainly not taking care of her clothes at all. There were soup stains all down her blouse and a burn in her skirt.

"Hello, Winky," said Harry.

Winky's lip quivered. Then she burst into tears, which spilled out of her great brown eyes and splashed down her front, just as they had done at the Quidditch World Cup.

"Oh dear," said Hermione. She and Ron had followed Harry and Dobby to the end of the kitchen. "Winky, don't cry, please don't . . ."

But Winky cried harder than ever. Dobby, on the other hand, beamed up at Harry.

"Would Harry Potter like a cup of tea?" he squeaked loudly, over Winky's sobs.

"Er — yeah, okay," said Harry.

Instantly, about six house-elves came trotting up behind him, bearing a large silver tray laden with a teapot, cups for Harry, Ron, and Hermione, a milk jug, and a large plate of biscuits.

"Good service!" Ron said, in an impressed voice. Hermione frowned at him, but the elves all looked delighted; they bowed very low and retreated.

"How long have you been here, Dobby?" Harry asked as Dobby handed around the tea.

"Only a week, Harry Potter, sir!" said Dobby happily. "Dobby came to see Professor Dumbledore, sir. You see, sir, it is very diffi-cult for a house-elf who has been dismissed to get a new position, sir, very difficult indeed —"

At this, Winky howled even harder, her squashed-tomato of a nose dribbling all down her front, though she made no effort to stem the flow.

"Dobby has traveled the country for two whole years, sir, trying to find work!" Dobby squeaked. "But Dobby hasn't found work, sir, because Dobby wants paying now!"

The house-elves all around the kitchen, who had been listening and watching with interest, all looked away at these words, as though Dobby had said something rude and embarrassing. Hermione, however, said, "Good for you, Dobby!"

"Thank you, miss!" said Dobby, grinning toothily at her. "But most wizards doesn't want a house-elf who wants paying, miss. 'That's not the point of a house-elf,' they says, and they slammed the door in Dobby's face! Dobby likes work, but he wants to wear clothes and he wants to be paid, Harry Potter. . . . Dobby likes being free!"

The Hogwarts house-elves had now started edging away from Dobby, as though he were carrying something contagious. Winky, however, remained where she was, though there was a definite increase in the volume of her crying.

"And then, Harry Potter, Dobby goes to visit Winky, and finds out Winky has been freed too, sir!" said Dobby delightedly.

At this, Winky flung herself forward off her stool and lay facedown on the flagged stone floor, beating her tiny fists upon it and positively screaming with misery. Hermione hastily dropped down to her knees beside her and tried to comfort her, but nothing she said made the slightest difference. Dobby continued with his story, shouting shrilly over Winky's screeches.

"And then Dobby had the idea, Harry Potter, sir! 'Why doesn't

Dobby and Winky find work together?' Dobby says. 'Where is there enough work for two house-elves?' says Winky. And Dobby thinks, and it comes to him, sir! *Hogwarts!* So Dobby and Winky came to see Professor Dumbledore, sir, and Professor Dumbledore took us on!"

Dobby beamed very brightly, and happy tears welled in his eyes again.

"And Professor Dumbledore says he will pay Dobby, sir, if Dobby wants paying! And so Dobby is a free elf, sir, and Dobby gets a Galleon a week and one day off a month!"

"That's not very much!" Hermione shouted indignantly from the floor, over Winky's continued screaming and fist-beating.

"Professor Dumbledore offered Dobby ten Galleons a week, and weekends off," said Dobby, suddenly giving a little shiver, as though the prospect of so much leisure and riches were frightening, "but Dobby beat him down, miss. . . . Dobby likes freedom, miss, but he isn't wanting too much, miss, he likes work better."

"And how much is Professor Dumbledore paying *you*, Winky?" Hermione asked kindly.

If she had thought this would cheer up Winky, she was wildly mistaken. Winky did stop crying, but when she sat up she was glaring at Hermione through her massive brown eyes, her whole face sopping wet and suddenly furious.

"Winky is a disgraced elf, but Winky is not yet getting paid!" she squeaked. "Winky is not sunk so low as that! Winky is properly ashamed of being freed!"

"Ashamed?" said Hermione blankly. "But — Winky, come on! It's Mr. Crouch who should be ashamed, not you! You didn't do anything wrong, he was really horrible to you —"

But at these words, Winky clapped her hands over the holes in her hat, flattening her ears so that she couldn't hear a word, and screeched, "You is not insulting my master, miss! You is not insulting Mr. Crouch! Mr. Crouch is a good wizard, miss! Mr. Crouch is right to sack bad Winky!"

"Winky is having trouble adjusting, Harry Potter," squeaked Dobby confidentially. "Winky forgets she is not bound to Mr. Crouch anymore; she is allowed to speak her mind now, but she won't do it."

"Can't house-elves speak their minds about their masters, then?" Harry asked.

"Oh no, sir, no," said Dobby, looking suddenly serious. "'Tis part of the house-elf's enslavement, sir. We keeps their secrets and our silence, sir. We upholds the family's honor, and we never speaks ill of them — though Professor Dumbledore told Dobby he does not insist upon this. Professor Dumbledore said we is free to — to —"

Dobby looked suddenly nervous and beckoned Harry closer. Harry bent forward. Dobby whispered, "He said we is free to call him a — a barmy old codger if we likes, sir!"

Dobby gave a frightened sort of giggle.

"But Dobby is not wanting to, Harry Potter," he said, talking normally again, and shaking his head so that his ears flapped. "Dobby likes Professor Dumbledore very much, sir, and is proud to keep his secrets and our silence for him."

"But you can say what you like about the Malfoys now?" Harry asked him, grinning.

A slightly fearful look came into Dobby's immense eyes.

"Dobby — Dobby could," he said doubtfully. He squared his

small shoulders. "Dobby could tell Harry Potter that his old masters were — were — *bad Dark wizards*!"

Dobby stood for a moment, quivering all over, horror-struck by his own daring — then he rushed over to the nearest table and began banging his head on it very hard, squealing, *"Bad Dobby! Bad Dobby!"*

Harry seized Dobby by the back of his tie and pulled him away from the table.

"Thank you, Harry Potter, thank you," said Dobby breathlessly, rubbing his head.

"You just need a bit of practice," Harry said.

"Practice!" squealed Winky furiously. "You is ought to be ashamed of yourself, Dobby, talking that way about your masters!"

"They isn't my masters anymore, Winky!" said Dobby defiantly. "Dobby doesn't care what they think anymore!"

"Oh you is a bad elf, Dobby!" moaned Winky, tears leaking down her face once more. "My poor Mr. Crouch, what is he doing without Winky? He is needing me, he is needing my help! I is looking after the Crouches all my life, and my mother is doing it before me, and my grandmother is doing it before her . . . oh what is they saying if they knew Winky was freed? Oh the shame, the shame!" She buried her face in her skirt again and bawled.

"Winky," said Hermione firmly, "I'm quite sure Mr. Crouch is getting along perfectly well without you. We've seen him, you know —"

"You is seeing my master?" said Winky breathlessly, raising her tearstained face out of her skirt once more and goggling at Hermione. "You is seeing him here at Hogwarts?"

"Yes," said Hermione, "he and Mr. Bagman are judges in the Triwizard Tournament."

"Mr. Bagman comes too?" squeaked Winky, and to Harry's great surprise (and Ron's and Hermione's too, by the looks on their faces), she looked angry again. "Mr. Bagman is a bad wizard! A very bad wizard! My master isn't liking him, oh no, not at all!"

"Bagman — bad?" said Harry.

"Oh yes," Winky said, nodding her head furiously. "My master is telling Winky some things! But Winky is not saying . . . Winky — Winky keeps her master's secrets. . . ."

She dissolved yet again in tears; they could hear her sobbing into her skirt, "Poor master, poor master, no Winky to help him no more!"

They couldn't get another sensible word out of Winky. They left her to her crying and finished their tea, while Dobby chatted happily about his life as a free elf and his plans for his wages.

"Dobby is going to buy a sweater next, Harry Potter!" he said happily, pointing at his bare chest.

"Tell you what, Dobby," said Ron, who seemed to have taken a great liking to the elf, "I'll give you the one my mum knits me this Christmas, I always get one from her. You don't mind maroon, do you?"

Dobby was delighted.

"We might have to shrink it a bit to fit you," Ron told him, "but it'll go well with your tea cozy."

As they prepared to take their leave, many of the surrounding elves pressed in upon them, offering snacks to take back upstairs. Hermione refused, with a pained look at the way the elves kept bowing and curtsying, but Harry and Ron loaded their pockets with cream cakes and pies.

"Thanks a lot!" Harry said to the elves, who had all clustered around the door to say good night. "See you, Dobby!"

"Harry Potter . . . can Dobby come and see you sometimes, sir?" Dobby asked tentatively.

"'Course you can," said Harry, and Dobby beamed.

"You know what?" said Ron, once he, Hermione, and Harry had left the kitchens behind and were climbing the steps into the entrance hall again. "All these years I've been really impressed with Fred and George, nicking food from the kitchens — well, it's not exactly difficult, is it? They can't wait to give it away!"

"I think this is the best thing that could have happened to those elves, you know," said Hermione, leading the way back up the marble staircase. "Dobby coming to work here, I mean. The other elves will see how happy he is, being free, and slowly it'll dawn on them that they want that too!"

"Let's hope they don't look too closely at Winky," said Harry.

"Oh she'll cheer up," said Hermione, though she sounded a bit doubtful. "Once the shock's worn off, and she's got used to Hogwarts, she'll see how much better off she is without that Crouch man."

"She seems to love him," said Ron thickly (he had just started on a cream cake).

"Doesn't think much of Bagman, though, does she?" said Harry. "Wonder what Crouch says at home about him?"

"Probably says he's not a very good Head of Department," said Hermione, "and let's face it . . . he's got a point, hasn't he?"

"I'd still rather work for him than old Crouch," said Ron. "At least Bagman's got a sense of humor."

"Don't let Percy hear you saying that," Hermione said, smiling slightly.

"Yeah, well, Percy wouldn't want to work for anyone with a sense of humor, would he?" said Ron, now starting on a chocolate eclair. "Percy wouldn't recognize a joke if it danced naked in front of him wearing Dobby's tea cozy."

# THE UNEXPECTED TASK

"P otter! Weasley! *Will you pay attention?*"

Professor McGonagall's irritated voice cracked like a whip through the Transfiguration class on Thursday, and Harry and Ron both jumped and looked up.

It was the end of the lesson; they had finished their work; the guinea fowl they had been changing into guinea pigs had been shut away in a large cage on Professor McGonagall's desk (Neville's still had feathers); they had copied down their homework from the blackboard (*"Describe, with examples, the ways in which Transforming Spells must be adapted when performing Cross-Species Switches"*). The bell was due to ring at any moment, and Harry and Ron, who had been having a sword fight with a couple of Fred and George's fake wands at the back of the class, looked up, Ron holding a tin parrot and Harry, a rubber haddock.

"Now that Potter and Weasley have been kind enough to act

their age," said Professor McGonagall, with an angry look at the pair of them as the head of Harry's haddock drooped and fell silently to the floor — Ron's parrot's beak had severed it moments before — "I have something to say to you all.

"The Yule Ball is approaching — a traditional part of the Triwizard Tournament and an opportunity for us to socialize with our foreign guests. Now, the ball will be open only to fourth years and above — although you may invite a younger student if you wish —"

Lavender Brown let out a shrill giggle. Parvati Patil nudged her hard in the ribs, her face working furiously as she too fought not to giggle. They both looked around at Harry. Professor McGonagall ignored them, which Harry thought was distinctly unfair, as she had just told off him and Ron.

"Dress robes will be worn," Professor McGonagall continued, "and the ball will start at eight o'clock on Christmas Day, finishing at midnight in the Great Hall. Now then —"

Professor McGonagall stared deliberately around the class.

"The Yule Ball is of course a chance for us all to — er — let our hair down," she said, in a disapproving voice.

Lavender giggled harder than ever, with her hand pressed hard against her mouth to stifle the sound. Harry could see what was funny this time: Professor McGonagall, with her hair in a tight bun, looked as though she had never let her hair down in any sense.

"But that does NOT mean," Professor McGonagall went on, "that we will be relaxing the standards of behavior we expect from Hogwarts students. I will be most seriously displeased if a Gryffindor student embarrasses the school in any way."

The bell rang, and there was the usual scuffle of activity as everyone packed their bags and swung them onto their shoulders.

Professor McGonagall called above the noise, "Potter — a word, if you please."

Assuming this had something to do with his headless rubber haddock, Harry proceeded gloomily to the teacher's desk. Professor McGonagall waited until the rest of the class had gone, and then said, "Potter, the champions and their partners —"

"What partners?" said Harry.

Professor McGonagall looked suspiciously at him, as though she thought he was trying to be funny.

"Your partners for the Yule Ball, Potter," she said coldly. "Your *dance partners.*"

Harry's insides seemed to curl up and shrivel.

"Dance partners?" He felt himself going red. "I don't dance," he said quickly.

"Oh yes, you do," said Professor McGonagall irritably. "That's what I'm telling you. Traditionally, the champions and their partners open the ball."

Harry had a sudden mental image of himself in a top hat and tails, accompanied by a girl in the sort of frilly dress Aunt Petunia always wore to Uncle Vernon's work parties.

"I'm not dancing," he said.

"It is traditional," said Professor McGonagall firmly. "You are a Hogwarts champion, and you will do what is expected of you as a representative of the school. So make sure you get yourself a partner, Potter."

"But — I don't —"

"You heard me, Potter," said Professor McGonagall in a very final sort of way.

A week ago, Harry would have said finding a partner for a dance would be a cinch compared to taking on a Hungarian Horntail. But now that he had done the latter, and was facing the prospect of asking a girl to the ball, he thought he'd rather have another round with the dragon.

Harry had never known so many people to put their names down to stay at Hogwarts for Christmas; he always did, of course, because the alternative was usually going back to Privet Drive, but he had always been very much in the minority before now. This year, however, everyone in the fourth year and above seemed to be staying, and they all seemed to Harry to be obsessed with the coming ball — or at least all the girls were, and it was amazing how many girls Hogwarts suddenly seemed to hold; he had never quite noticed that before. Girls giggling and whispering in the corridors, girls shrieking with laughter as boys passed them, girls excitedly comparing notes on what they were going to wear on Christmas night. . . .

"Why do they have to move in packs?" Harry asked Ron as a dozen or so girls walked past them, sniggering and staring at Harry. "How're you supposed to get one on their own to ask them?"

"Lasso one?" Ron suggested. "Got any idea who you're going to try?"

Harry didn't answer. He knew perfectly well whom he'd *like* to ask, but working up the nerve was something else. . . . Cho was a year older than he was; she was very pretty; she was a very good Quidditch player, and she was also very popular.

Ron seemed to know what was going on inside Harry's head.

"Listen, you're not going to have any trouble. You're a champion. You've just beaten a Hungarian Horntail. I bet they'll be queuing up to go with you."

In tribute to their recently repaired friendship, Ron had kept the bitterness in his voice to a bare minimum. Moreover, to Harry's amazement, he turned out to be quite right.

A curly-haired third-year Hufflepuff girl to whom Harry had never spoken in his life asked him to go to the ball with her the very next day. Harry was so taken aback he said no before he'd even stopped to consider the matter. The girl walked off looking rather hurt, and Harry had to endure Dean's, Seamus's, and Ron's taunts about her all through History of Magic. The following day, two more girls asked him, a second year and (to his horror) a fifth year who looked as though she might knock him out if he refused.

"She was quite good-looking," said Ron fairly, after he'd stopped laughing.

"She was a foot taller than me," said Harry, still unnerved. "Imagine what I'd look like trying to dance with her."

Hermione's words about Krum kept coming back to him. "They only like him because he's famous!" Harry doubted very much if any of the girls who had asked to be his partner so far would have wanted to go to the ball with him if he hadn't been a school champion. Then he wondered if this would bother him if Cho asked him.

On the whole, Harry had to admit that even with the embarrassing prospect of opening the ball before him, life had definitely improved since he had got through the first task. He wasn't attracting nearly as much unpleasantness in the corridors anymore, which he suspected had a lot to do with Cedric — he had an idea Cedric might have told the Hufflepuffs to leave Harry alone, in gratitude for Harry's tip-off about the dragons. There seemed to be fewer *Support Cedric Diggory!* badges around too. Draco Malfoy, of course, was still quoting Rita Skeeter's article to him at every possible opportunity, but he was getting fewer and fewer laughs out of it — and just to heighten Harry's feeling of well-being, no story about Hagrid had appeared in the *Daily Prophet*.

"She didn' seem very int'rested in magical creatures, ter tell yeh the truth," Hagrid said, when Harry, Ron, and Hermione asked him how his interview with Rita Skeeter had gone during the last Care of Magical Creatures lesson of the term. To their very great relief, Hagrid had given up on direct contact with the skrewts now, and they were merely sheltering behind his cabin today, sitting at a trestle table and preparing a fresh selection of food with which to tempt the skrewts.

"She jus' wanted me ter talk about you, Harry," Hagrid continued in a low voice. "Well, I told her we'd been friends since I went ter fetch yeh from the Dursleys. 'Never had to tell him off in four years?' she said. 'Never played you up in lessons, has he?' I told her no, an' she didn' seem happy at all. Yeh'd think she wanted me to say yeh were horrible, Harry."

"'Course she did," said Harry, throwing lumps of dragon liver into a large metal bowl and picking up his knife to cut some more. "She can't keep writing about what a tragic little hero I am, it'll get boring."

"She wants a new angle, Hagrid," said Ron wisely as he shelled salamander eggs. "You were supposed to say Harry's a mad delinquent!"

"But he's not!" said Hagrid, looking genuinely shocked.

"She should've interviewed Snape," said Harry grimly. "He'd give her the goods on me any day. *Potter has been crossing lines ever since he first arrived at this school. . . .*"

"Said that, did he?" said Hagrid, while Ron and Hermione laughed. "Well, yeh might've bent a few rules, Harry, bu' yeh're all righ' really, aren' you?"

"Cheers, Hagrid," said Harry, grinning.

"You coming to this ball thing on Christmas Day, Hagrid?" said Ron.

"Though' I might look in on it, yeah," said Hagrid gruffly. "Should be a good do, I reckon. You'll be openin' the dancin', won' yeh, Harry? Who're you takin'?"

"No one, yet," said Harry, feeling himself going red again. Hagrid didn't pursue the subject.

The last week of term became increasingly boisterous as it progressed. Rumors about the Yule Ball were flying everywhere, though Harry didn't believe half of them — for instance, that Dumbledore had bought eight hundred barrels of mulled mead from Madam Rosmerta. It seemed to be fact, however, that he had booked the Weird Sisters. Exactly who or what the Weird Sisters were Harry didn't know, never having had access to a wizard's wireless, but he deduced from the wild excitement of those who had grown up listening to the WWN (Wizarding Wireless Network) that they were a very famous musical group.

Some of the teachers, like little Professor Flitwick, gave up trying to teach them much when their minds were so clearly elsewhere; he allowed them to play games in his lesson on Wednesday, and spent most of it talking to Harry about the perfect Summoning Charm

Harry had used during the first task of the Triwizard Tournament. Other teachers were not so generous. Nothing would ever deflect Professor Binns, for example, from plowing on through his notes on goblin rebellions — as Binns hadn't let his own death stand in the way of continuing to teach, they supposed a small thing like Christmas wasn't going to put him off. It was amazing how he could make even bloody and vicious goblin riots sound as boring as Percy's cauldron-bottom report. Professors McGonagall and Moody kept them working until the very last second of their classes too, and Snape, of course, would no sooner let them play games in class than adopt Harry. Staring nastily around at them all, he informed them that he would be testing them on poison antidotes during the last lesson of the term.

"Evil, he is," Ron said bitterly that night in the Gryffindor common room. "Springing a test on us on the last day. Ruining the last bit of term with a whole load of studying."

"Mmm . . . you're not exactly straining yourself, though, are you?" said Hermione, looking at him over the top of her Potions notes. Ron was busy building a card castle out of his Exploding Snap pack — a much more interesting pastime than with Muggle cards, because of the chance that the whole thing would blow up at any second.

"It's Christmas, Hermione," said Harry lazily; he was rereading *Flying with the Cannons* for the tenth time in an armchair near the fire.

Hermione looked severely over at him too. "I'd have thought you'd be doing something constructive, Harry, even if you don't want to learn your antidotes!"

"Like what?" Harry said as he watched Joey Jenkins of the Cannons belt a Bludger toward a Ballycastle Bats Chaser.

"That egg!" Hermione hissed.

"Come on, Hermione, I've got till February the twenty-fourth," Harry said.

He had put the golden egg upstairs in his trunk and hadn't opened it since the celebration party after the first task. There were still two and a half months to go until he needed to know what all the screechy wailing meant, after all.

"But it might take weeks to work it out!" said Hermione. "You're going to look a real idiot if everyone else knows what the next task is and you don't!"

"Leave him alone, Hermione, he's earned a bit of a break," said Ron, and he placed the last two cards on top of the castle and the whole lot blew up, singeing his eyebrows.

"Nice look, Ron . . . go well with your dress robes, that will."

It was Fred and George. They sat down at the table with Harry, Ron, and Hermione as Ron felt how much damage had been done.

"Ron, can we borrow Pigwidgeon?" George asked.

"No, he's off delivering a letter," said Ron. "Why?"

"Because George wants to invite him to the ball," said Fred sarcastically.

"Because *we* want to send a letter, you stupid great prat," said George.

"Who d'you two keep writing to, eh?" said Ron.

"Nose out, Ron, or I'll burn that for you too," said Fred, waving his wand threateningly. "So . . . you lot got dates for the ball yet?"

"Nope," said Ron.

"Well, you'd better hurry up, mate, or all the good ones will be gone," said Fred.

"Who're you going with, then?" said Ron.

"Angelina," said Fred promptly, without a trace of embarrassment.

"What?" said Ron, taken aback. "You've already asked her?"

"Good point," said Fred. He turned his head and called across the common room, "Oi! Angelina!"

Angelina, who had been chatting with Alicia Spinnet near the fire, looked over at him.

"What?" she called back.

"Want to come to the ball with me?"

Angelina gave Fred an appraising sort of look.

"All right, then," she said, and she turned back to Alicia and carried on chatting with a bit of a grin on her face.

"There you go," said Fred to Harry and Ron, "piece of cake."

He got to his feet, yawning, and said, "We'd better use a school owl then, George, come on. . . ."

They left. Ron stopped feeling his eyebrows and looked across the smoldering wreck of his card castle at Harry.

"We *should* get a move on, you know . . . ask someone. He's right. We don't want to end up with a pair of trolls."

Hermione let out a sputter of indignation.

"A pair of . . . *what,* excuse me?"

"Well — you know," said Ron, shrugging. "I'd rather go alone than with — with Eloise Midgen, say."

"Her acne's loads better lately — and she's really nice!"

"Her nose is off-center," said Ron.

"Oh I see," Hermione said, bristling. "So basically, you're going to take the best-looking girl who'll have you, even if she's com-pletely horrible?"

"Er — yeah, that sounds about right," said Ron.

"I'm going to bed," Hermione snapped, and she swept off toward the girls' staircase without another word.

The Hogwarts staff, demonstrating a continued desire to impress the visitors from Beauxbatons and Durmstrang, seemed deter-mined to show the castle at its best this Christmas. When the dec-orations went up, Harry noticed that they were the most stunning he had yet seen inside the school. Everlasting icicles had been at-tached to the banisters of the marble staircase; the usual twelve Christmas trees in the Great Hall were bedecked with everything from luminous holly berries to real, hooting, golden owls, and the suits of armor had all been bewitched to sing carols whenever any-one passed them. It was quite something to hear "O Come, All Ye Faithful" sung by an empty helmet that only knew half the words. Several times, Filch the caretaker had to extract Peeves from inside the armor, where he had taken to hiding, filling in the gaps in the songs with lyrics of his own invention, all of which were very rude.

And still, Harry hadn't asked Cho to the ball. He and Ron were getting very nervous now, though as Harry pointed out, Ron would look much less stupid than he would without a partner; Harry was supposed to be starting the dancing with the other champions.

"I suppose there's always Moaning Myrtle," he said gloomily, referring to the ghost who haunted the girls' toilets on the second floor.

"Harry — we've just got to grit our teeth and do it," said Ron on

Friday morning, in a tone that suggested they were planning the storming of an impregnable fortress. "When we get back to the common room tonight, we'll both have partners — agreed?"

"Er . . . okay," said Harry.

But every time he glimpsed Cho that day — during break, and then lunchtime, and once on the way to History of Magic — she was surrounded by friends. Didn't she *ever* go anywhere alone? Could he perhaps ambush her as she was going into a bathroom? But no — she even seemed to go there with an escort of four or five girls. Yet if he didn't do it soon, she was bound to have been asked by somebody else.

He found it hard to concentrate on Snape's Potions test, and consequently forgot to add the key ingredient — a bezoar — meaning that he received bottom marks. He didn't care, though; he was too busy screwing up his courage for what he was about to do. When the bell rang, he grabbed his bag, and hurried to the dungeon door.

"I'll meet you at dinner," he said to Ron and Hermione, and he dashed off upstairs.

He'd just have to ask Cho for a private word, that was all. . . . He hurried off through the packed corridors looking for her, and (rather sooner than he had expected) he found her, emerging from a Defense Against the Dark Arts lesson.

"Er — Cho? Could I have a word with you?"

Giggling should be made illegal, Harry thought furiously, as all the girls around Cho started doing it. She didn't, though. She said, "Okay," and followed him out of earshot of her classmates.

Harry turned to look at her and his stomach gave a weird lurch as though he had missed a step going downstairs.

"Er," he said.

He couldn't ask her. He couldn't. But he had to. Cho stood there looking puzzled, watching him.

The words came out before Harry had quite got his tongue around them.

"Wangoballwime?"

"Sorry?" said Cho.

"D'you — d'you want to go to the ball with me?" said Harry. Why did he have to go red now? *Why?*

"Oh!" said Cho, and she went red too. "Oh Harry, I'm really sorry," and she truly looked it. "I've already said I'll go with someone else."

"Oh," said Harry.

It was odd; a moment before his insides had been writhing like snakes, but suddenly he didn't seem to have any insides at all.

"Oh okay," he said, "no problem."

"I'm really sorry," she said again.

"That's okay," said Harry.

They stood there looking at each other, and then Cho said, "Well —"

"Yeah," said Harry.

"Well, 'bye," said Cho, still very red. She walked away.

Harry called after her, before he could stop himself.

"Who're you going with?"

"Oh — Cedric," she said. "Cedric Diggory."

"Oh right," said Harry.

His insides had come back again. It felt as though they had been filled with lead in their absence.

Completely forgetting about dinner, he walked slowly back up to Gryffindor Tower, Cho's voice echoing in his ears with every step he took. *"Cedric — Cedric Diggory."* He had been starting to quite like Cedric — prepared to overlook the fact that he had once beaten him at Quidditch, and was handsome, and popular, and nearly everyone's favorite champion. Now he suddenly realized that Cedric was in fact a useless pretty boy who didn't have enough brains to fill an eggcup.

"Fairy lights," he said dully to the Fat Lady — the password had been changed the previous day.

"Yes, indeed, dear!" she trilled, straightening her new tinsel hair band as she swung forward to admit him.

Entering the common room, Harry looked around, and to his surprise he saw Ron sitting ashen-faced in a distant corner. Ginny was sitting with him, talking to him in what seemed to be a low, soothing voice.

"What's up, Ron?" said Harry, joining them.

Ron looked up at Harry, a sort of blind horror in his face.

"Why did I do it?" he said wildly. "I don't know what made me do it!"

"What?" said Harry.

"He — er — just asked Fleur Delacour to go to the ball with him," said Ginny. She looked as though she was fighting back a smile, but she kept patting Ron's arm sympathetically.

"You *what*?" said Harry.

"I don't know what made me do it!" Ron gasped again. "What was I playing at? There were people — all around — I've gone mad — everyone watching! I was just walking past her in the entrance hall — she was standing there talking to Diggory — and it sort of came over me — and I asked her!"

Ron moaned and put his face in his hands. He kept talking, though the words were barely distinguishable.

"She looked at me like I was a sea slug or something. Didn't even answer. And then — I dunno — I just sort of came to my senses and ran for it."

"She's part veela," said Harry. "You were right — her grandmother was one. It wasn't your fault, I bet you just walked past when she was turning on the old charm for Diggory and got a blast of it — but she was wasting her time. He's going with Cho Chang."

Ron looked up.

"I asked her to go with me just now," Harry said dully, "and she told me."

Ginny had suddenly stopped smiling.

"This is mad," said Ron. "We're the only ones left who haven't got anyone — well, except Neville. Hey — guess who he asked? *Hermione!*"

"*What?*" said Harry, completely distracted by this startling news.

"Yeah, I know!" said Ron, some of the color coming back into his face as he started to laugh. "He told me after Potions! Said she's always been really nice, helping him out with work and stuff— but she told him she was already going with someone. Ha! As if! She just didn't want to go with Neville . . . I mean, who would?"

"Don't!" said Ginny, annoyed. "Don't laugh —"

Just then Hermione climbed in through the portrait hole.

"Why weren't you two at dinner?" she said, coming over to join them.

"Because — oh shut up laughing, you two — because they've both just been turned down by girls they asked to the ball!" said Ginny.

That shut Harry and Ron up.

"Thanks a bunch, Ginny," said Ron sourly.

"All the good-looking ones taken, Ron?" said Hermione loftily. "Eloise Midgen starting to look quite pretty now, is she? Well, I'm sure you'll find someone *somewhere* who'll have you."

But Ron was staring at Hermione as though suddenly seeing her in a whole new light.

"Hermione, Neville's right — you *are* a girl. . . ."

"Oh well spotted," she said acidly.

"Well — you can come with one of us!"

"No, I can't," snapped Hermione.

"Oh come on," he said impatiently, "we need partners, we're going to look really stupid if we haven't got any, everyone else has . . ."

"I can't come with you," said Hermione, now blushing, "because I'm already going with someone."

"No, you're not!" said Ron. "You just said that to get rid of Neville!"

"Oh *did* I?" said Hermione, and her eyes flashed dangerously. "Just because it's taken *you* three years to notice, Ron, doesn't mean no one *else* has spotted I'm a girl!"

Ron stared at her. Then he grinned again.

"Okay, okay, we know you're a girl," he said. "That do? Will you come now?"

"I've already told you!" Hermione said very angrily. "I'm going with someone else!"

And she stormed off toward the girls' dormitories again.

"She's lying," said Ron flatly, watching her go.

"She's not," said Ginny quietly.

"Who is it then?" said Ron sharply.

"I'm not telling you, it's her business," said Ginny.

"Right," said Ron, who looked extremely put out, "this is getting stupid. Ginny, *you* can go with Harry, and I'll just —"

"I can't," said Ginny, and she went scarlet too. "I'm going with — with Neville. He asked me when Hermione said no, and I thought . . . well . . . I'm not going to be able to go otherwise, I'm not in fourth year." She looked extremely miserable. "I think I'll go and have dinner," she said, and she got up and walked off to the portrait hole, her head bowed.

Ron goggled at Harry.

"What's got into them?" he demanded.

But Harry had just seen Parvati and Lavender come in through the portrait hole. The time had come for drastic action.

"Wait here," he said to Ron, and he stood up, walked straight up to Parvati, and said, "Parvati? Will you go to the ball with me?"

Parvati went into a fit of giggles. Harry waited for them to subside, his fingers crossed in the pocket of his robes.

"Yes, all right then," she said finally, blushing furiously.

"Thanks," said Harry, in relief. "Lavender — will you go with Ron?"

"She's going with Seamus," said Parvati, and the pair of them giggled harder than ever.

Harry sighed.

"Can't you think of anyone who'd go with Ron?" he said, lowering his voice so that Ron wouldn't hear.

"What about Hermione Granger?" said Parvati.

"She's going with someone else."

Parvati looked astonished.

"Ooooh — *who*?" she said keenly.

Harry shrugged. "No idea," he said. "So what about Ron?"

"Well . . ." said Parvati slowly, "I suppose my sister might . . . Padma, you know . . . in Ravenclaw. I'll ask her if you like."

"Yeah, that would be great," said Harry. "Let me know, will you?"

And he went back over to Ron, feeling that this ball was a lot more trouble than it was worth, and hoping very much that Padma Patil's nose was dead center.

# THE YULE BALL

Despite the very heavy load of homework that the fourth years had been given for the holidays, Harry was in no mood to work when term ended, and spent the week leading up to Christmas enjoying himself as fully as possible along with everyone else. Gryffindor Tower was hardly less crowded now than during term-time; it seemed to have shrunk slightly too, as its inhabitants were being so much rowdier than usual. Fred and George had had a great success with their Canary Creams, and for the first couple of days of the holidays, people kept bursting into feather all over the place. Before long, however, all the Gryffindors had learned to treat food anybody else offered them with extreme caution, in case it had a Canary Cream concealed in the center, and George confided to Harry that he and Fred were now working on developing something else. Harry made a mental note never to accept so much as a crisp from Fred and George in future. He still hadn't forgotten Dudley and the Ton-Tongue Toffee.

Snow was falling thickly upon the castle and its grounds now. The pale blue Beauxbatons carriage looked like a large, chilly, frosted pumpkin next to the iced gingerbread house that was Hagrid's cabin, while the Durmstrang ship's portholes were glazed with ice, the rigging white with frost. The house-elves down in the kitchen were outdoing themselves with a series of rich, warming stews and savory puddings, and only Fleur Delacour seemed to be able to find anything to complain about.

"It is too 'eavy, all zis 'Ogwarts food," they heard her saying grumpily as they left the Great Hall behind her one evening (Ron skulking behind Harry, keen not to be spotted by Fleur). "I will not fit into my dress robes!"

"Oooh there's a tragedy," Hermione snapped as Fleur went out into the entrance hall. "She really thinks a lot of herself, that one, doesn't she?"

"Hermione — who are you going to the ball with?" said Ron.

He kept springing this question on her, hoping to startle her into a response by asking it when she least expected it. However, Hermione merely frowned and said, "I'm not telling you, you'll just make fun of me."

"You're joking, Weasley!" said Malfoy, behind them. "You're not telling me someone's asked *that* to the ball? Not the long-molared Mudblood?"

Harry and Ron both whipped around, but Hermione said loudly, waving to somebody over Malfoy's shoulder, "Hello, Professor Moody!"

Malfoy went pale and jumped backward, looking wildly around for Moody, but he was still up at the staff table, finishing his stew.

"Twitchy little ferret, aren't you, Malfoy?" said Hermione

scathingly, and she, Harry, and Ron went up the marble staircase laughing heartily.

"Hermione," said Ron, looking sideways at her, suddenly frowning, "your teeth . . ."

"What about them?" she said.

"Well, they're different . . . I've just noticed. . . ."

"Of course they are — did you expect me to keep those fangs Malfoy gave me?"

"No, I mean, they're different to how they were before he put that hex on you. . . . They're all . . . straight and — and normalsized."

Hermione suddenly smiled very mischievously, and Harry noticed it too: It was a very different smile from the one he remembered.

"Well . . . when I went up to Madam Pomfrey to get them shrunk, she held up a mirror and told me to stop her when they were back to how they normally were," she said. "And I just . . . let her carry on a bit." She smiled even more widely. "Mum and Dad won't be too pleased. I've been trying to persuade them to let me shrink them for ages, but they wanted me to carry on with my braces. You know, they're dentists, they just don't think teeth and magic should — look! Pigwidgeon's back!"

Ron's tiny owl was twittering madly on the top of the icicle-laden banisters, a scroll of parchment tied to his leg. People passing him were pointing and laughing, and a group of third-year girls paused and said, "Oh look at the weeny owl! Isn't he *cute*?"

"Stupid little feathery git!" Ron hissed, hurrying up the stairs and snatching up Pigwidgeon. "You bring letters to the addressee! You don't hang around showing off!"

Pigwidgeon hooted happily, his head protruding over Ron's fist. The third-year girls all looked very shocked.

"Clear off!" Ron snapped at them, waving the fist holding Pigwidgeon, who hooted more happily than ever as he soared through the air. "Here — take it, Harry," Ron added in an undertone as the third-year girls scuttled away looking scandalized. He pulled Sirius's reply off Pigwidgeon's leg, Harry pocketed it, and they hurried back to Gryffindor Tower to read it.

Everyone in the common room was much too busy in letting off more holiday steam to observe what anyone else was up to. Ron, Harry, and Hermione sat apart from everyone else by a dark window that was gradually filling up with snow, and Harry read out:

> *Dear Harry,*
>
> *Congratulations on getting past the Horntail. Whoever put your name in that goblet shouldn't be feeling too happy right now! I was going to suggest a Conjunctivitis Curse, as a dragon's eyes are its weakest point —* "That's what Krum did!" Hermione whispered — *but your way was better, I'm impressed.*
>
> *Don't get complacent, though, Harry. You've only done one task; whoever put you in for the tournament's got plenty more opportunity if they're trying to hurt you. Keep your eyes open — particularly when the person we discussed is around — and concentrate on keeping yourself out of trouble.*
>
> *Keep in touch, I still want to hear about anything unusual.*
>
>

"He sounds exactly like Moody," said Harry quietly, tucking the letter away again inside his robes. "'Constant vigilance!' You'd think I walk around with my eyes shut, banging off the walls. . . ."

"But he's right, Harry," said Hermione, "you *have* still got two tasks to do. You really ought to have a look at that egg, you know, and start working out what it means. . . ."

"Hermione, he's got ages!" snapped Ron. "Want a game of chess, Harry?"

"Yeah, okay," said Harry. Then, spotting the look on Hermione's face, he said, "Come on, how'm I supposed to concentrate with all this noise going on? I won't even be able to hear the egg over this lot."

"Oh I suppose not," she sighed, and she sat down to watch their chess match, which culminated in an exciting checkmate of Ron's, involving a couple of recklessly brave pawns and a very violent bishop.

Harry awoke very suddenly on Christmas Day. Wondering what had caused his abrupt return to consciousness, he opened his eyes, and saw something with very large, round, green eyes staring back at him in the darkness, so close they were almost nose to nose.

*"Dobby!"* Harry yelled, scrambling away from the elf so fast he almost fell out of bed. "Don't *do* that!"

"Dobby is sorry, sir!" squeaked Dobby anxiously, jumping backward with his long fingers over his mouth. "Dobby is only wanting to wish Harry Potter 'Merry Christmas' and bring him a present, sir! Harry Potter did say Dobby could come and see him sometimes, sir!"

"It's okay," said Harry, still breathing rather faster than usual, while his heart rate returned to normal. "Just — just prod me or something in future, all right, don't bend over me like that. . . ."

Harry pulled back the curtains around his four-poster, took his glasses from his bedside table, and put them on. His yell had awoken Ron, Seamus, Dean, and Neville. All of them were peering through the gaps in their own hangings, heavy-eyed and tousle-haired.

"Someone attacking you, Harry?" Seamus asked sleepily.

"No, it's just Dobby," Harry muttered. "Go back to sleep."

"Nah . . . presents!" said Seamus, spotting the large pile at the foot of his bed. Ron, Dean, and Neville decided that now they were awake they might as well get down to some present-opening too. Harry turned back to Dobby, who was now standing nervously next to Harry's bed, still looking worried that he had upset Harry. There was a Christmas bauble tied to the loop on top of his tea cozy.

"Can Dobby give Harry Potter his present?" he squeaked tentatively.

"'Course you can," said Harry. "Er . . . I've got something for you too."

It was a lie; he hadn't bought anything for Dobby at all, but he quickly opened his trunk and pulled out a particularly knobbly rolled-up pair of socks. They were his oldest and foulest, mustard yellow, and had once belonged to Uncle Vernon. The reason they were extra-knobbly was that Harry had been using them to cushion his Sneakoscope for over a year now. He pulled out the Sneakoscope and handed the socks to Dobby, saying, "Sorry, I forgot to wrap them. . . ."

But Dobby was utterly delighted.

"Socks are Dobby's favorite, favorite clothes, sir!" he said, ripping off his odd ones and pulling on Uncle Vernon's. "I has seven now, sir. . . . But sir . . ." he said, his eyes widening, having pulled both socks up to their highest extent, so that they reached to the bottom of his shorts, "they has made a mistake in the shop, Harry Potter, they is giving you two the same!"

"Ah, no, Harry, how come you didn't spot that?" said Ron, grinning over from his own bed, which was now strewn with wrapping paper. "Tell you what, Dobby — here you go — take these two, and you can mix them up properly. And here's your sweater."

He threw Dobby a pair of violet socks he had just unwrapped, and the hand-knitted sweater Mrs. Weasley had sent. Dobby looked quite overwhelmed.

"Sir is very kind!" he squeaked, his eyes brimming with tears again, bowing deeply to Ron. "Dobby knew sir must be a great wizard, for he is Harry Potter's greatest friend, but Dobby did not know that he was also as generous of spirit, as noble, as selfless —"

"They're only socks," said Ron, who had gone slightly pink around the ears, though he looked rather pleased all the same. "Wow, Harry —" He had just opened Harry's present, a Chudley Cannon hat. "Cool!" He jammed it onto his head, where it clashed horribly with his hair.

Dobby now handed Harry a small package, which turned out to be — socks.

"Dobby is making them himself, sir!" the elf said happily. "He is buying the wool out of his wages, sir!"

The left sock was bright red and had a pattern of broomsticks upon it; the right sock was green with a pattern of Snitches.

"They're . . . they're really . . . well, thanks, Dobby," said Harry, and he pulled them on, causing Dobby's eyes to leak with happiness again.

"Dobby must go now, sir, we is already making Christmas dinner in the kitchens!" said Dobby, and he hurried out of the dormitory, waving good-bye to Ron and the others as he passed.

Harry's other presents were much more satisfactory than Dobby's odd socks — with the obvious exception of the Dursleys', which consisted of a single tissue, an all-time low — Harry supposed they too were remembering the Ton-Tongue Toffee. Hermione had given Harry a book called *Quidditch Teams of Britain and Ireland;* Ron, a bulging bag of Dungbombs; Sirius, a handy penknife with attachments to unlock any lock and undo any knot; and Hagrid, a vast box of sweets including all Harry's favorites: Bertie Bott's Every Flavor Beans, Chocolate Frogs, Drooble's Best Blowing Gum, and Fizzing Whizbees. There was also, of course, Mrs. Weasley's usual package, including a new sweater (green, with a picture of a dragon on it — Harry supposed Charlie had told her all about the Horntail), and a large quantity of homemade mince pies.

Harry and Ron met up with Hermione in the common room, and they went down to breakfast together. They spent most of the morning in Gryffindor Tower, where everyone was enjoying their presents, then returned to the Great Hall for a magnificent lunch, which included at least a hundred turkeys and Christmas puddings, and large piles of Cribbage's Wizarding Crackers.

They went out onto the grounds in the afternoon; the snow was untouched except for the deep channels made by the Durmstrang and Beauxbatons students on their way up to the castle. Hermione chose to watch Harry and the Weasleys' snowball fight rather than join in, and at five o'clock said she was going back upstairs to get ready for the ball.

"What, you need three hours?" said Ron, looking at her incredulously and paying for his lapse in concentration when a large snowball, thrown by George, hit him hard on the side of the head. "Who're you going with?" he yelled after Hermione, but she just waved and disappeared up the stone steps into the castle.

There was no Christmas tea today, as the ball included a feast, so at seven o'clock, when it had become hard to aim properly, the others abandoned their snowball fight and trooped back to the common room. The Fat Lady was sitting in her frame with her friend Violet from downstairs, both of them extremely tipsy, empty boxes of chocolate liqueurs littering the bottom of her picture.

"Lairy fights, that's the one!" she giggled when they gave the password, and she swung forward to let them inside.

Harry, Ron, Seamus, Dean, and Neville changed into their dress robes up in their dormitory, all of them looking very self-conscious, but none as much as Ron, who surveyed himself in the long mirror in the corner with an appalled look on his face. There was just no getting around the fact that his robes looked more like a dress than anything else. In a desperate attempt to make them look more manly, he used a Severing Charm on the ruff and cuffs. It worked fairly well; at least he was now lace-free, although he hadn't done a very neat job, and the edges still looked depressingly frayed as the boys set off downstairs.

"I still can't work out how you two got the best-looking girls in the year," muttered Dean.

"Animal magnetism," said Ron gloomily, pulling stray threads out of his cuffs.

The common room looked strange, full of people wearing different colors instead of the usual mass of black. Parvati was waiting for Harry at the foot of the stairs. She looked very pretty indeed, in robes of shocking pink, with her long dark plait braided with gold, and gold bracelets glimmering at her wrists. Harry was relieved to see that she wasn't giggling.

"You — er — look nice," he said awkwardly.

"Thanks," she said. "Padma's going to meet you in the entrance hall," she added to Ron.

"Right," said Ron, looking around. "Where's Hermione?"

Parvati shrugged. "Shall we go down then, Harry?"

"Okay," said Harry, wishing he could just stay in the common room. Fred winked at Harry as he passed him on the way out of the portrait hole.

The entrance hall was packed with students too, all milling around waiting for eight o'clock, when the doors to the Great Hall would be thrown open. Those people who were meeting partners from different Houses were edging through the crowd trying to find one another. Parvati found her sister, Padma, and led her over to Harry and Ron.

"Hi," said Padma, who was looking just as pretty as Parvati in robes of bright turquoise. She didn't look too enthusiastic about having Ron as a partner, though; her dark eyes lingered on the frayed neck and sleeves of his dress robes as she looked him up and down.

"Hi," said Ron, not looking at her, but staring around at the crowd. "Oh no . . ."

He bent his knees slightly to hide behind Harry, because Fleur Delacour was passing, looking stunning in robes of silver-gray satin, and accompanied by the Ravenclaw Quidditch Captain,

Roger Davies. When they had disappeared, Ron stood straight again and stared over the heads of the crowd.

"Where *is* Hermione?" he said again.

A group of Slytherins came up the steps from their dungeon common room. Malfoy was in front; he was wearing dress robes of black velvet with a high collar, which in Harry's opinion made him look like a vicar. Pansy Parkinson in very frilly robes of pale pink was clutching Malfoy's arm. Crabbe and Goyle were both wearing green; they resembled moss-colored boulders, and neither of them, Harry was pleased to see, had managed to find a partner.

The oak front doors opened, and everyone turned to look as the Durmstrang students entered with Professor Karkaroff. Krum was at the front of the party, accompanied by a pretty girl in blue robes Harry didn't know. Over their heads he saw that an area of lawn right in front of the castle had been transformed into a sort of grotto full of fairy lights — meaning hundreds of actual living fairies were sitting in the rosebushes that had been conjured there, and fluttering over the statues of what seemed to be Father Christmas and his reindeer.

Then Professor McGonagall's voice called, "Champions over here, please!"

Parvati readjusted her bangles, beaming; she and Harry said "See you in a minute" to Ron and Padma and walked forward, the chattering crowd parting to let them through. Professor McGonagall, who was wearing dress robes of red tartan and had arranged a rather ugly wreath of thistles around the brim of her hat, told them to wait on one side of the doors while everyone else went inside; they were to enter the Great Hall in procession when the rest of the students had sat down. Fleur Delacour and Roger Davies stationed themselves nearest the doors; Davies looked so stunned by his good fortune in having Fleur for a partner that he could hardly take his eyes off her. Cedric and Cho were close to Harry too; he looked away from them so he wouldn't have to talk to them. His eyes fell instead on the girl next to Krum. His jaw dropped.

It was Hermione.

But she didn't look like Hermione at all. She had done something with her hair; it was no longer bushy but sleek and shiny, and twisted up into an elegant knot at the back of her head. She was wearing robes made of a floaty, periwinkle-blue material, and she was holding herself differently, somehow — or maybe it was merely the absence of the twenty or so books she usually had slung over her back. She was also smiling — rather nervously, it was true — but the reduction in the size of her front teeth was more noticeable than ever; Harry couldn't understand how he hadn't spotted it before.

"Hi, Harry!" she said. "Hi, Parvati!"

Parvati was gazing at Hermione in unflattering disbelief. She wasn't the only one either; when the doors to the Great Hall opened, Krum's fan club from the library stalked past, throwing Hermione looks of deepest loathing. Pansy Parkinson gaped at her as she walked by with Malfoy, and even he didn't seem to be able to find an insult to throw at her. Ron, however, walked right past Hermione without looking at her.

Once everyone else was settled in the Hall, Professor McGonagall told the champions and their partners to get in line in pairs and to follow her. They did so, and everyone in the Great Hall applauded as they entered and started walking up toward a large round table at the top of the Hall, where the judges were sitting.

The walls of the Hall had all been covered in sparkling silver frost, with hundreds of garlands of mistletoe and ivy crossing the starry black ceiling. The House tables had vanished; instead, there were about a hundred smaller, lantern-lit ones, each seating about a dozen people.

Harry concentrated on not tripping over his feet. Parvati seemed to be enjoying herself; she was beaming around at everybody, steering Harry so forcefully that he felt as though he were a show dog she was putting through its paces. He caught sight of Ron and Padma as he neared the top table. Ron was watching Hermione pass with narrowed eyes. Padma was looking sulky.

Dumbledore smiled happily as the champions approached the top table, but Karkaroff wore an expression remarkably like Ron's as he watched Krum and Hermione draw nearer. Ludo Bagman, tonight in robes of bright purple with large yellow stars, was clapping as enthusiastically as any of the students; and Madame Maxime, who had changed her usual uniform of black satin for a flowing gown of lavender silk, was applauding them politely. But Mr. Crouch, Harry suddenly realized, was not there. The fifth seat at the table was occupied by Percy Weasley.

When the champions and their partners reached the table, Percy drew out the empty chair beside him, staring pointedly at Harry. Harry took the hint and sat down next to Percy, who was wearing brand-new, navy-blue dress robes and an expression of such smugness that Harry thought it ought to be fined.

"I've been promoted," Percy said before Harry could even ask, and from his tone, he might have been announcing his election as supreme ruler of the universe. "I'm now Mr. Crouch's personal assistant, and I'm here representing him."

"Why didn't he come?" Harry asked. He wasn't looking forward to being lectured on cauldron bottoms all through dinner.

"I'm afraid to say Mr. Crouch isn't well, not well at all. Hasn't been right since the World Cup. Hardly surprising — overwork. He's not as young as he was — though still quite brilliant, of course, the mind remains as great as it ever was. But the World Cup was a fiasco for the whole Ministry, and then, Mr. Crouch suffered a huge personal shock with the misbehavior of that house-elf of his, Blinky, or whatever she was called. Naturally, he dismissed her immediately afterward, but — well, as I say, he's getting on, he needs looking after, and I think he's found a definite drop in his home comforts since she left. And then we had the tournament to arrange, and the aftermath of the Cup to deal with — that revolting Skeeter woman buzzing around — no, poor man, he's having a well-earned, quiet Christmas. I'm just glad he knew he had someone he could rely upon to take his place."

Harry wanted very much to ask whether Mr. Crouch had stopped calling Percy "Weatherby" yet, but resisted the temptation.

There was no food as yet on the glittering golden plates, but small menus were lying in front of each of them. Harry picked his up uncertainly and looked around — there were no waiters. Dumbledore, however, looked carefully down at his own menu, then said very clearly to his plate, "Pork chops!"

And pork chops appeared. Getting the idea, the rest of the table placed their orders with their plates too. Harry glanced up at Hermione to see how she felt about this new and more complicated method of dining — surely it meant plenty of extra work for the house-elves? — but for once, Hermione didn't seem to be thinking about S.P.E.W. She was deep in talk with Viktor Krum and hardly seemed to notice what she was eating.

It now occurred to Harry that he had never actually heard Krum speak before, but he was certainly talking now, and very enthusiastically at that.

"Vell, ve have a castle also, not as big as this, nor as comfortable, I am thinking," he was telling Hermione. "Ve have just four floors, and the fires are lit only for magical purposes. But ve have grounds larger even than these — though in vinter, ve have very little daylight, so ve are not enjoying them. But in summer ve are flying every day, over the lakes and the mountains —"

"Now, now, Viktor!" said Karkaroff with a laugh that didn't reach his cold eyes, "don't go giving away anything else, now, or your charming friend will know exactly where to find us!"

Dumbledore smiled, his eyes twinkling. "Igor, all this secrecy . . . one would almost think you didn't want visitors."

"Well, Dumbledore," said Karkaroff, displaying his yellowing teeth to their fullest extent, "we are all protective of our private domains, are we not? Do we not jealously guard the halls of learning that have been entrusted to us? Are we not right to be proud that we alone know our school's secrets, and right to protect them?"

"Oh I would never dream of assuming I know all Hogwarts' secrets, Igor," said Dumbledore amicably. "Only this morning, for instance, I took a wrong turning on the way to the bathroom and found myself in a beautifully proportioned room I have never seen before, containing a really rather magnificent collection of chamber pots. When I went back to investigate more closely, I discovered that the room had vanished. But I must keep an eye out for it.

Possibly it is only accessible at five-thirty in the morning. Or it may only appear at the quarter moon — or when the seeker has an exceptionally full bladder."

Harry snorted into his plate of goulash. Percy frowned, but Harry could have sworn Dumbledore had given him a very small wink.

Meanwhile Fleur Delacour was criticizing the Hogwarts decorations to Roger Davies.

"Zis is nothing," she said dismissively, looking around at the sparkling walls of the Great Hall. "At ze Palace of Beauxbatons, we 'ave ice sculptures all around ze dining chamber at Chreestmas. Zey do not melt, of course . . . zey are like 'uge statues of diamond, glittering around ze place. And ze food is seemply superb. And we 'ave choirs of wood nymphs, 'oo serenade us as we eat. We 'ave none of zis ugly armor in ze 'alls, and eef a poltergeist ever entaired into Beauxbatons, 'e would be expelled like *zat*." She slapped her hand onto the table impatiently.

Roger Davies was watching her talk with a very dazed look on his face, and he kept missing his mouth with his fork. Harry had the impression that Davies was too busy staring at Fleur to take in a word she was saying.

"Absolutely right," he said quickly, slapping his own hand down on the table in imitation of Fleur. "Like *that*. Yeah."

Harry looked around the Hall. Hagrid was sitting at one of the other staff tables; he was back in his horrible hairy brown suit and gazing up at the top table. Harry saw him give a small wave, and looking around, saw Madame Maxime return it, her opals glittering in the candlelight.

Hermione was now teaching Krum to say her name properly; he kept calling her "Hermy-own."

"Her-my-oh-nee," she said slowly and clearly.

"Herm-own-ninny."

"Close enough," she said, catching Harry's eye and grinning.

When all the food had been consumed, Dumbledore stood up and asked the students to do the same. Then, with a wave of his wand, all the tables zoomed back along the walls leaving the floor clear, and then he conjured a raised platform into existence along the right wall. A set of drums, several guitars, a lute, a cello, and some bagpipes were set upon it.

The Weird Sisters now trooped up onto the stage to wildly enthusiastic applause; they were all extremely hairy and dressed in black robes that had been artfully ripped and torn. They picked up their instruments, and Harry, who had been so interested in watching them that he had almost forgotten what was coming, suddenly realized that the lanterns on all the other tables had gone out, and that the other champions and their partners were standing up.

"Come on!" Parvati hissed. "We're supposed to dance!"

Harry tripped over his dress robes as he stood up. The Weird Sisters struck up a slow, mournful tune; Harry walked onto the brightly lit dance floor, carefully avoiding catching anyone's eye (he could see Seamus and Dean waving at him and sniggering), and next moment, Parvati had seized his hands, placed one around her waist, and was holding the other tightly in hers.

It wasn't as bad as it could have been, Harry thought, revolving slowly on the spot (Parvati was steering). He kept his eyes fixed over the heads of the watching people, and very soon many of them too had come onto the dance floor, so that the champions were no longer the center of attention. Neville and Ginny were dancing nearby — he could see Ginny wincing frequently as Neville trod on her feet — and Dumbledore was waltzing with Madame Maxime. He was so dwarfed by her that the top of his pointed hat barely tickled her chin; however, she moved very gracefully for a woman so large. Mad-Eye Moody was doing an extremely ungainly two-step with Professor Sinistra, who was nervously avoiding his wooden leg.

"Nice socks, Potter," Moody growled as he passed, his magical eye staring through Harry's robes.

"Oh — yeah, Dobby the house-elf knitted them for me," said Harry, grinning.

"He is so *creepy*!" Parvati whispered as Moody clunked away. "I don't think that eye should be *allowed*!"

Harry heard the final, quavering note from the bagpipe with relief. The Weird Sisters stopped playing, applause filled the hall once more, and Harry let go of Parvati at once.

"Let's sit down, shall we?"

"Oh — but — this is a really good one!" Parvati said as the Weird Sisters struck up a new song, which was much faster.

"No, I don't like it," Harry lied, and he led her away from the dance floor, past Fred and Angelina, who were dancing so exuberantly that people around them were backing away in fear of injury, and over to the table where Ron and Padma were sitting.

"How's it going?" Harry asked Ron, sitting down and opening a bottle of butterbeer.

Ron didn't answer. He was glaring at Hermione and Krum, who were dancing nearby. Padma was sitting with her arms and legs crossed, one foot jiggling in time to the music. Every now and then she threw a disgruntled look at Ron, who was completely ignoring her. Parvati sat down on Harry's other side, crossed her arms and legs too, and within minutes was asked to dance by a boy from Beauxbatons.

"You don't mind, do you, Harry?" Parvati said.

"What?" said Harry, who was now watching Cho and Cedric.

"Oh never mind," snapped Parvati, and she went off with the boy from Beauxbatons. When the song ended, she did not return.

Hermione came over and sat down in Parvati's empty chair. She was a bit pink in the face from dancing.

"Hi," said Harry. Ron didn't say anything.

"It's hot, isn't it?" said Hermione, fanning herself with her hand. "Viktor's just gone to get some drinks."

Ron gave her a withering look. *Viktor?* he said. "Hasn't he asked you to call him *Vicky* yet?"

Hermione looked at him in surprise. "What's up with you?" she said.

"If you don't know," said Ron scathingly, "I'm not going to tell you."

Hermione stared at him, then at Harry, who shrugged.

"Ron, what — ?"

"He's from Durmstrang!" spat Ron. "He's competing against Harry! Against Hogwarts! You — you're —" Ron was obviously casting around for words strong enough to describe Hermione's crime, "*fraternizing with the enemy,* that's what you're doing!"

Hermione's mouth fell open.

"Don't be so stupid!" she said after a moment. "The *enemy*! Honestly — who was the one who was all excited when they saw him arrive? Who was the one who wanted his autograph? Who's got a model of him up in their dormitory?"

Ron chose to ignore this. "I s'pose he asked you to come with him while you were both in the library?"

"Yes, he did," said Hermione, the pink patches on her cheeks glowing more brightly. "So what?"

"What happened — trying to get him to join *spew*, were you?"

"No, I wasn't! If you *really* want to know, he — he said he'd been coming up to the library every day to try and talk to me, but he hadn't been able to pluck up the courage!"

Hermione said this very quickly, and blushed so deeply that she was the same color as Parvati's robes.

"Yeah, well — that's his story," said Ron nastily.

"And what's that supposed to mean?"

"Obvious, isn't it? He's Karkaroff's student, isn't he? He knows who you hang around with. . . . He's just trying to get closer to Harry — get inside information on him — or get near enough to jinx him —"

Hermione looked as though Ron had slapped her. When she spoke, her voice quivered.

"For your information, he hasn't asked me *one single thing* about Harry, not one —"

Ron changed tack at the speed of light.

"Then he's hoping you'll help him find out what his egg means! I suppose you've been putting your heads together during those cozy little library sessions —"

"I'd *never* help him work out that egg!" said Hermione, looking outraged. "*Never.* How could you say something like that — I want Harry to win the tournament, Harry knows that, don't you, Harry?"

"You've got a funny way of showing it," sneered Ron.

"This whole tournament's supposed to be about getting to know foreign wizards and making friends with them!" said Hermione hotly.

"No it isn't!" shouted Ron. "It's about winning!"

People were starting to stare at them.

"Ron," said Harry quietly, "I haven't got a problem with Hermione coming with Krum —"

But Ron ignored Harry too.

"Why don't you go and find Vicky, he'll be wondering where you are," said Ron.

*"Don't call him Vicky!"*

Hermione jumped to her feet and stormed off across the dance floor, disappearing into the crowd. Ron watched her go with a mixture of anger and satisfaction on his face.

"Are you going to ask me to dance at all?" Padma asked him.

"No," said Ron, still glaring after Hermione.

"Fine," snapped Padma, and she got up and went to join Parvati and the Beauxbatons boy, who conjured up one of his friends to join them so fast that Harry could have sworn he had zoomed him there by a Summoning Charm.

"Vare is Herm-own-ninny?" said a voice.

Krum had just arrived at their table clutching two butterbeers.

"No idea," said Ron mulishly, looking up at him. "Lost her, have you?"

Krum was looking surly again.

"Vell, if you see her, tell her I haff drinks," he said, and he slouched off.

"Made friends with Viktor Krum, have you, Ron?"

Percy had bustled over, rubbing his hands together and looking extremely pompous. "Excellent! That's the whole point, you know — international magical cooperation!"

To Harry's displeasure, Percy now took Padma's vacated seat. The top table was now empty; Professor Dumbledore was dancing with Professor Sprout, Ludo Bagman with Professor McGonagall; Madame Maxime and Hagrid were cutting a wide path around the dance floor as they waltzed through the students, and Karkaroff was nowhere to be seen. When the next song ended, everybody applauded once more, and Harry saw Ludo Bagman kiss Professor McGonagall's hand and make his way back through the crowds, at which point Fred and George accosted him.

"What do they think they're doing, annoying senior Ministry members?" Percy hissed, watching Fred and George suspiciously. "*No* respect . . ."

Ludo Bagman shook off Fred and George fairly quickly, however, and, spotting Harry, waved and came over to their table.

"I hope my brothers weren't bothering you, Mr. Bagman?" said Percy at once.

"What? Oh not at all, not at all!" said Bagman. "No, they were just telling me a bit more about those fake wands of theirs. Wondering if I could advise them on the marketing. I've promised to put them in touch with a couple of contacts of mine at Zonko's Joke Shop. . . ."

Percy didn't look happy about this at all, and Harry was prepared to bet he would be rushing to tell Mrs. Weasley about this the moment he got home. Apparently Fred and George's plans had grown even more ambitious lately, if they were hoping to sell to the public. Bagman opened his mouth to ask Harry something, but Percy diverted him.

"How do you feel the tournament's going, Mr. Bagman? *Our* department's quite satisfied — the hitch with the Goblet of Fire" — he glanced at Harry — "was a little unfortunate, of course, but it seems to have gone very smoothly since, don't you think?"

"Oh yes," Bagman said cheerfully, "it's all been enormous fun. How's old Barty doing? Shame he couldn't come."

"Oh I'm sure Mr. Crouch will be up and about in no time," said Percy importantly, "but in the meantime, I'm more than willing to take up the slack. Of course, it's not all attending balls" — he laughed airily — "oh no, I've had to deal with all sorts of things that have cropped up in his absence — you heard Ali Bashir was caught smuggling a consignment of flying carpets into the country? And then we've been trying to persuade the Transylvanians to sign the International Ban on Dueling. I've got a meeting with their Head of Magical Cooperation in the new year —"

"Let's go for a walk," Ron muttered to Harry, "get away from Percy. . . ."

Pretending they wanted more drinks, Harry and Ron left the table, edged around the dance floor, and slipped out into the entrance hall. The front doors stood open, and the fluttering fairy lights in the rose garden winked and twinkled as they went down the front steps, where they found themselves surrounded by bushes; winding, ornamental paths; and large stone statues. Harry could hear splashing water, which sounded like a fountain. Here and there, people were sitting on carved benches. He and Ron set off along one of the winding paths through the rosebushes, but they had gone only a short way when they heard an unpleasantly familiar voice.

". . . don't see what there is to fuss about, Igor."

"Severus, you cannot pretend this isn't happening!" Karkaroff's voice sounded anxious and hushed, as though keen not to be overheard. "It's been getting clearer and clearer for months. I am becoming seriously concerned, I can't deny it —"

"Then flee," said Snape's voice curtly. "Flee — I will make your excuses. I, however, am remaining at Hogwarts."

Snape and Karkaroff came around the corner. Snape had his wand out and was blasting rosebushes apart, his expression most ill-natured. Squeals issued from many of the bushes, and dark shapes emerged from them.

"Ten points from Ravenclaw, Fawcett!" Snape snarled as a girl ran past him. "And ten points from Hufflepuff too, Stebbins!" as a boy went rushing after her. "And what are you two doing?" he added, catching sight of Harry and Ron on the path ahead. Karkaroff, Harry saw, looked slightly discomposed to see them standing there. His hand went nervously to his goatee, and he began winding it around his finger.

"We're walking," Ron told Snape shortly. "Not against the law, is it?"

"Keep walking, then!" Snape snarled, and he brushed past them, his long black cloak billowing out behind him. Karkaroff hurried away after Snape. Harry and Ron continued down the path.

"What's got Karkaroff all worried?" Ron muttered.

"And since when have he and Snape been on first-name terms?" said Harry slowly.

They had reached a large stone reindeer now, over which they could see the sparkling jets of a tall fountain. The shadowy outlines of two enormous people were visible on a stone bench, watching the water in the moonlight. And then Harry heard Hagrid speak.

"Momen' I saw yeh, I knew," he was saying, in an oddly husky voice.

Harry and Ron froze. This didn't sound like the sort of scene they ought to walk in on, somehow. . . . Harry looked around, back up the path, and saw Fleur Delacour and Roger Davies standing half-concealed in a rosebush nearby. He tapped Ron on the shoulder and jerked his head toward them, meaning that they could easily sneak off that way without being noticed (Fleur and Davies looked very busy to Harry), but Ron, eyes widening in horror at the sight of Fleur, shook his head vigorously, and pulled Harry deeper into the shadows behind the reindeer.

"What did you know, 'Agrid?" said Madame Maxime, a purr in her low voice.

Harry definitely didn't want to listen to this; he knew Hagrid would hate to be overheard in a situation like this (he certainly would have) — if it had been possible he would have put his fingers in his ears and hummed loudly, but that wasn't really an option. Instead he tried to interest himself in a beetle crawling along the stone reindeer's back, but the beetle just wasn't interesting enough to block out Hagrid's next words.

"I jus' knew . . . knew you were like me. . . . Was it yer mother or yer father?"

"I — I don't know what you mean, 'Agrid. . . ."

"It was my mother," said Hagrid quietly. "She was one o' the las' ones in Britain. 'Course, I can' remember her too well . . . she left, see. When I was abou' three. She wasn' really the maternal sort.

Well . . . it's not in their natures, is it? Dunno what happened to her . . . might be dead fer all I know. . . ."

Madame Maxime didn't say anything. And Harry, in spite of himself, took his eyes off the beetle and looked over the top of the reindeer's antlers, listening. . . . He had never heard Hagrid talk about his childhood before.

"Me dad was broken-hearted when she wen'. Tiny little bloke, my dad was. By the time I was six I could lift him up an' put him on top o' the dresser if he annoyed me. Used ter make him laugh. . . ." Hagrid's deep voice broke. Madame Maxime was listening, motionless, apparently staring at the silvery fountain. "Dad raised me . . . but he died, o' course, jus' after I started school. Sorta had ter make me own way after that. Dumbledore was a real help, mind. Very kind ter me, he was. . . ."

Hagrid pulled out a large spotted silk handkerchief and blew his nose heavily.

"So . . . anyway . . . enough abou' me. What about you? Which side you got it on?"

But Madame Maxime had suddenly got to her feet.

"It is chilly," she said — but whatever the weather was doing, it was nowhere near as cold as her voice. "I think I will go in now."

"Eh?" said Hagrid blankly. "No, don' go! I've — I've never met another one before!"

"Anuzzer *what,* precisely?" said Madame Maxime, her tone icy.

Harry could have told Hagrid it was best not to answer; he stood there in the shadows gritting his teeth, hoping against hope he wouldn't — but it was no good.

"Another half-giant, o' course!" said Hagrid.

"'Ow dare you!" shrieked Madame Maxime. Her voice exploded

through the peaceful night air like a foghorn; behind him, Harry heard Fleur and Roger fall out of their rosebush. "I 'ave nevair been more insulted in my life! 'Alf-giant? *Moi?* I 'ave — I 'ave big bones!"

She stormed away; great multicolored swarms of fairies rose into the air as she passed, angrily pushing aside bushes. Hagrid was still sitting on the bench, staring after her. It was much too dark to make out his expression. Then, after about a minute, he stood up and strode away, not back to the castle, but off out into the dark grounds in the direction of his cabin.

"C'mon," Harry said, very quietly to Ron. "Let's go. . . ."

But Ron didn't move.

"What's up?" said Harry, looking at him.

Ron looked around at Harry, his expression very serious indeed.

"Did you know?" he whispered. "About Hagrid being half-giant?"

"No," Harry said, shrugging. "So what?"

He knew immediately, from the look Ron was giving him, that he was once again revealing his ignorance of the Wizarding world. Brought up by the Dursleys, there were many things that wizards took for granted that were revelations to Harry, but these surprises had become fewer with each successive year. Now, however, he could tell that most wizards would not have said "So what?" upon finding out that one of their friends had a giantess for a mother.

"I'll explain inside," said Ron quietly, "c'mon. . . ."

Fleur and Roger Davies had disappeared, probably into a more private clump of bushes. Harry and Ron returned to the Great Hall. Parvati and Padma were now sitting at a distant table with a whole crowd of Beauxbatons boys, and Hermione was once more dancing with Krum. Harry and Ron sat down at a table far removed from the dance floor.

"So?" Harry prompted Ron. "What's the problem with giants?"

"Well, they're . . . they're . . ." Ron struggled for words. ". . . not very nice," he finished lamely.

"Who cares?" Harry said. "There's nothing wrong with Hagrid!"

"I know there isn't, but . . . blimey, no wonder he keeps it quiet," Ron said, shaking his head. "I always thought he'd got in the way of a bad Engorgement Charm when he was a kid or something. Didn't like to mention it. . . ."

"But what's it matter if his mother was a giantess?" said Harry.

"Well . . . no one who knows him will care, 'cos they'll know he's not dangerous," said Ron slowly. "But . . . Harry, they're just vicious, giants. It's like Hagrid said, it's in their natures, they're like trolls . . . they just like killing, everyone knows that. There aren't any left in Britain now, though."

"What happened to them?"

"Well, they were dying out anyway, and then loads got themselves killed by Aurors. There're supposed to be giants abroad, though. . . . They hide out in mountains mostly. . . ."

"I don't know who Maxime thinks she's kidding," Harry said, watching Madame Maxime sitting alone at the judges' table, looking very somber. "If Hagrid's half-giant, she definitely is. Big bones . . . the only thing that's got bigger bones than her is a dinosaur."

Harry and Ron spent the rest of the ball discussing giants in their corner, neither of them having any inclination to dance. Harry tried not to watch Cho and Cedric too much; it gave him a strong desire to kick something.

When the Weird Sisters finished playing at midnight, everyone gave them a last, loud round of applause and started to wend their way into the entrance hall. Many people were expressing the wish that the ball could have gone on longer, but Harry was perfectly happy to be going to bed; as far as he was concerned, the evening hadn't been much fun.

Out in the entrance hall, Harry and Ron saw Hermione saying good night to Krum before he went back to the Durmstrang ship. She gave Ron a very cold look and swept past him up the marble staircase without speaking. Harry and Ron followed her, but halfway up the staircase Harry heard someone calling him.

"Hey — Harry!"

It was Cedric Diggory. Harry could see Cho waiting for him in the entrance hall below.

"Yeah?" said Harry coldly as Cedric ran up the stairs toward him.

Cedric looked as though he didn't want to say whatever it was in front of Ron, who shrugged, looking bad-tempered, and continued to climb the stairs.

"Listen . . ." Cedric lowered his voice as Ron disappeared. "I owe you one for telling me about the dragons. You know that golden egg? Does yours wail when you open it?"

"Yeah," said Harry.

"Well . . . take a bath, okay?"

"What?"

"Take a bath, and — er — take the egg with you, and — er — just mull things over in the hot water. It'll help you think. . . . Trust me."

Harry stared at him.

"Tell you what," Cedric said, "use the prefects' bathroom. Fourth door to the left of that statue of Boris the Bewildered on the fifth floor. Password's 'pine fresh.' Gotta go . . . want to say good night —"

He grinned at Harry again and hurried back down the stairs to Cho.

Harry walked back to Gryffindor Tower alone. That had been extremely strange advice. Why would a bath help him to work out what the wailing egg meant? Was Cedric pulling his leg? Was he trying to make Harry look like a fool, so Cho would like him even more by comparison?

The Fat Lady and her friend Vi were snoozing in the picture over the portrait hole. Harry had to yell "Fairy lights!" before he woke them up, and when he did, they were extremely irritated. He climbed into the common room and found Ron and Hermione having a blazing row. Standing ten feet apart, they were bellowing at each other, each scarlet in the face.

"Well, if you don't like it, you know what the solution is, don't you?" yelled Hermione; her hair was coming down out of its elegant bun now, and her face was screwed up in anger.

"Oh yeah?" Ron yelled back. "What's that?"

"Next time there's a ball, ask me before someone else does, and not as a last resort!"

Ron mouthed soundlessly like a goldfish out of water as Hermione turned on her heel and stormed up the girls' staircase to bed. Ron turned to look at Harry.

"Well," he sputtered, looking thunderstruck, "well — that just proves — completely missed the point —"

Harry didn't say anything. He liked being back on speaking terms with Ron too much to speak his mind right now — but he somehow thought that Hermione had gotten the point much better than Ron had.

# RITA SKEETER'S SCOOP

Everybody got up late on Boxing Day. The Gryffindor common room was much quieter than it had been lately, many yawns punctuating the lazy conversations. Hermione's hair was bushy again; she confessed to Harry that she had used liberal amounts of Sleekeazy's Hair Potion on it for the ball, "but it's way too much bother to do every day," she said matter-of-factly, scratching a purring Crookshanks behind the ears.

Ron and Hermione seemed to have reached an unspoken agreement not to discuss their argument. They were being quite friendly to each other, though oddly formal. Ron and Harry wasted no time in telling Hermione about the conversation they had overheard between Madame Maxime and Hagrid, but Hermione didn't seem to find the news that Hagrid was a half-giant nearly as shocking as Ron did.

"Well, I thought he must be," she said, shrugging. "I knew he couldn't be pure giant because they're about twenty feet tall.

But honestly, all this hysteria about giants. They can't *all* be horrible. . . . It's the same sort of prejudice that people have toward werewolves. . . . It's just bigotry, isn't it?"

Ron looked as though he would have liked to reply scathingly, but perhaps he didn't want another row, because he contented himself with shaking his head disbelievingly while Hermione wasn't looking.

It was time now to think of the homework they had neglected during the first week of the holidays. Everybody seemed to be feeling rather flat now that Christmas was over — everybody except Harry, that is, who was starting (once again) to feel slightly nervous.

The trouble was that February the twenty-fourth looked a lot closer from this side of Christmas, and he still hadn't done anything about working out the clue inside the golden egg. He therefore started taking the egg out of his trunk every time he went up to the dormitory, opening it, and listening intently, hoping that this time it would make some sense. He strained to think what the sound reminded him of, apart from thirty musical saws, but he had never heard anything else like it. He closed the egg, shook it vigorously, and opened it again to see if the sound had changed, but it hadn't. He tried asking the egg questions, shouting over all the wailing, but nothing happened. He even threw the egg across the room — though he hadn't really expected that to help.

Harry had not forgotten the hint that Cedric had given him, but his less-than-friendly feelings toward Cedric just now meant that he was keen not to take his help if he could avoid it. In any case, it seemed to him that if Cedric had really wanted to give Harry a hand, he would have been a lot more explicit. He, Harry, had told Cedric exactly what was coming in the first task — and Cedric's idea of a fair exchange had been to tell Harry to take a bath. Well, he didn't need that sort of rubbishy help — not from someone who kept walking down corridors hand in hand with Cho, anyway. And so the first day of the new term arrived, and Harry set off to lessons, weighed down with books, parchment, and quills as usual, but also with the lurking worry of the egg heavy in his stomach, as though he were carrying that around with him too.

Snow was still thick upon the grounds, and the greenhouse windows were covered in condensation so thick that they couldn't see out of them in Herbology. Nobody was looking forward to Care of Magical Creatures much in this weather, though as Ron said, the skrewts would probably warm them up nicely, either by chasing them, or blasting off so forcefully that Hagrid's cabin would catch fire.

When they arrived at Hagrid's cabin, however, they found an elderly witch with closely cropped gray hair and a very prominent chin standing before his front door.

"Hurry up, now, the bell rang five minutes ago," she barked at them as they struggled toward her through the snow.

"Who're you?" said Ron, staring at her. "Where's Hagrid?"

"My name is Professor Grubbly-Plank," she said briskly. "I am your temporary Care of Magical Creatures teacher."

"Where's Hagrid?" Harry repeated loudly.

"He is indisposed," said Professor Grubbly-Plank shortly.

Soft and unpleasant laughter reached Harry's ears. He turned; Draco Malfoy and the rest of the Slytherins were joining the class. All of them looked gleeful, and none of them looked surprised to see Professor Grubbly-Plank.

"This way, please," said Professor Grubbly-Plank, and she strode off around the paddock where the Beauxbatons horses were shivering. Harry, Ron, and Hermione followed her, looking back over their shoulders at Hagrid's cabin. All the curtains were closed. Was Hagrid in there, alone and ill?

"What's wrong with Hagrid?" Harry said, hurrying to catch up with Professor Grubbly-Plank.

"Never you mind," she said as though she thought he was being nosy.

"I do mind, though," said Harry hotly. "What's up with him?"

Professor Grubbly-Plank acted as though she couldn't hear him. She led them past the paddock where the huge Beauxbatons horses were standing, huddled against the cold, and toward a tree on the edge of the forest, where a large and beautiful unicorn was tethered.

Many of the girls "ooooohed!" at the sight of the unicorn.

"Oh it's so beautiful!" whispered Lavender Brown. "How did she get it? They're supposed to be really hard to catch!"

The unicorn was so brightly white it made the snow all around look gray. It was pawing the ground nervously with its golden hooves and throwing back its horned head.

"Boys keep back!" barked Professor Grubbly-Plank, throwing out an arm and catching Harry hard in the chest. "They prefer the woman's touch, unicorns. Girls to the front, and approach with care, come on, easy does it. . . ."

She and the girls walked slowly forward toward the unicorn, leaving the boys standing near the paddock fence, watching. The moment Professor Grubbly-Plank was out of earshot, Harry turned to Ron.

"What d'you reckon's wrong with him? You don't think a skrewt — ?"

"Oh he hasn't been attacked, Potter, if that's what you're thinking," said Malfoy softly. "No, he's just too ashamed to show his big, ugly face."

"What d'you mean?" said Harry sharply.

Malfoy put his hand inside the pocket of his robes and pulled out a folded page of newsprint.

"There you go," he said. "Hate to break it to you, Potter. . . ."

He smirked as Harry snatched the page, unfolded it, and read it, with Ron, Seamus, Dean, and Neville looking over his shoulder. It was an article topped with a picture of Hagrid looking extremely shifty.

### DUMBLEDORE'S GIANT MISTAKE

Albus Dumbledore, eccentric headmaster of Hogwarts School of Witchcraft and Wizardry, has never been afraid to make controversial staff appointments, *writes Rita Skeeter, Special Correspondent.* In September of this year, he hired Alastor "Mad-Eye" Moody, the notoriously jinx-happy ex-Auror, to teach Defense Against the Dark Arts, a decision that caused many raised eyebrows at the Ministry of Magic, given Moody's well-known habit of attacking anybody who makes a sudden movement in his presence. Mad-Eye Moody, however, looks responsible and kindly when set beside the part-human Dumbledore employs to teach Care of Magical Creatures.

Rubeus Hagrid, who admits to being expelled from Hogwarts in his third year, has enjoyed the position of gamekeeper at the school ever since, a job secured for him by Dumbledore. Last year, however, Hagrid used his mysterious influence over the headmaster to secure the additional post of Care of Magical Creatures teacher, over the heads of many better-qualified candidates.

An alarmingly large and ferocious-looking man, Hagrid has been using his newfound authority to terrify the students in his care with a succession of horrific creatures. While Dumbledore turns a blind eye, Hagrid has maimed several pupils during a series of lessons that many admit to being "very frightening."

"I was attacked by a hippogriff, and my friend Vincent Crabbe got a bad bite off a flobberworm," says Draco Malfoy, a fourth-year student. "We all hate Hagrid, but we're just too scared to say anything."

Hagrid has no intention of ceasing his campaign of intimidation, however. In conversation with a *Daily Prophet* reporter last month, he admitted breeding creatures he has dubbed "Blast-Ended Skrewts," highly dangerous crosses between manticores and fire-crabs. The creation of new breeds of magical creature is, of course, an activity usually closely observed by the Department for the Regulation and Control of Magical Creatures. Hagrid, however, considers himself to be above such petty restrictions.

"I was just having some fun," he says, before hastily changing the subject.

As if this were not enough, the *Daily Prophet* has now unearthed evidence that Hagrid is not — as he has always pretended — a pure-blood wizard. He is not, in fact, even pure human. His mother, we can exclusively reveal, is none other than the giantess Fridwulfa, whose whereabouts are currently unknown.

Bloodthirsty and brutal, the giants brought themselves to the point of extinction by warring amongst themselves during the last century. The handful that remained joined the ranks of He-Who-Must-Not-Be-Named, and were responsible for some of the worst mass Muggle killings of his reign of terror.

While many of the giants who served He-Who-Must-Not-Be-Named were killed by Aurors working against the Dark Side, Fridwulfa was not among them. It is possible she escaped to one of the giant communities still existing in foreign mountain ranges. If his antics during Care of Magical Creatures lessons are any guide, however, Fridwulfa's son appears to have inherited her brutal nature.

In a bizarre twist, Hagrid is reputed to have developed a close friendship with the boy who brought around You-Know-Who's fall from power — thereby driving Hagrid's own mother, like the rest of You-Know-Who's supporters, into hiding. Perhaps Harry Potter is unaware of the unpleasant truth about his large friend — but Albus Dumbledore surely has a duty to ensure that Harry Potter, along with his fellow students, is warned about the dangers of associating with part-giants.

Harry finished reading and looked up at Ron, whose mouth was hanging open.

"How did she find out?" he whispered.

But that wasn't what was bothering Harry.

"What d'you mean, 'we all hate Hagrid'?" Harry spat at Malfoy. "What's this rubbish about *him*"—he pointed at Crabbe — "getting a bad bite off a flobberworm? They haven't even got teeth!"

Crabbe was sniggering, apparently very pleased with himself.

"Well, I think this should put an end to the oaf's teaching career," said Malfoy, his eyes glinting. "Half-giant . . . and there was me thinking he'd just swallowed a bottle of Skele-Gro when he was young. . . . None of the mummies and daddies are going to like this at all. . . . They'll be worried he'll eat their kids, ha, ha. . . ."

"You —"

"Are you paying attention over there?"

Professor Grubbly-Plank's voice carried over to the boys; the girls were all clustered around the unicorn now, stroking it. Harry was so angry that the *Daily Prophet* article shook in his hands as he turned to stare unseeingly at the unicorn, whose many magical properties Professor Grubbly-Plank was now enumerating in a loud voice, so that the boys could hear too.

"I hope she stays, that woman!" said Parvati Patil when the lesson had ended and they were all heading back to the castle for lunch. "That's more what I thought Care of Magical Creatures would be like . . . proper creatures like unicorns, not monsters. . . ."

"What about Hagrid?" Harry said angrily as they went up the steps.

"What about him?" said Parvati in a hard voice. "He can still be gamekeeper, can't he?"

Parvati had been very cool toward Harry since the ball. He supposed that he ought to have paid her a bit more attention, but she seemed to have had a good time all the same. She was certainly telling anybody who would listen that she had made arrangements to meet the boy from Beauxbatons in Hogsmeade on the next weekend trip.

"That was a really good lesson," said Hermione as they entered the Great Hall. "I didn't know half the things Professor Grubbly-Plank told us about uni —"

"Look at this!" Harry snarled, and he shoved the *Daily Prophet* article under Hermione's nose.

Hermione's mouth fell open as she read. Her reaction was exactly the same as Ron's.

"How did that horrible Skeeter woman find out? You don't think Hagrid *told* her?"

"No," said Harry, leading the way over to the Gryffindor table and throwing himself into a chair, furious. "He never even told us, did he? I reckon she was so mad he wouldn't give her loads of horrible stuff about me, she went ferreting around to get him back."

"Maybe she heard him telling Madame Maxime at the ball," said Hermione quietly.

"We'd have seen her in the garden!" said Ron. "Anyway, she's not supposed to come into school anymore, Hagrid said Dumbledore banned her. . . ."

"Maybe she's got an Invisibility Cloak," said Harry, ladling chicken casserole onto his plate and splashing it everywhere in his anger. "Sort of thing she'd do, isn't it, hide in bushes listening to people."

"Like you and Ron did, you mean," said Hermione.

"We weren't trying to hear him!" said Ron indignantly. "We didn't have any choice! The stupid prat, talking about his giantess mother where anyone could have heard him!"

"We've got to go and see him," said Harry. "This evening, after Divination. Tell him we want him back . . . you *do* want him back?" he shot at Hermione.

"I — well, I'm not going to pretend it didn't make a nice change, having a proper Care of Magical Creatures lesson for once — but I do want Hagrid back, of course I do!" Hermione added hastily, quailing under Harry's furious stare.

So that evening after dinner, the three of them left the castle once more and went down through the frozen grounds to Hagrid's cabin. They knocked, and Fang's booming barks answered.

"Hagrid, it's us!" Harry shouted, pounding on the door. "Open up!"

Hagrid didn't answer. They could hear Fang scratching at the door, whining, but it didn't open. They hammered on it for ten more minutes; Ron even went and banged on one of the windows, but there was no response.

"What's he avoiding *us* for?" Hermione said when they had finally given up and were walking back to the school. "He surely doesn't think we'd care about him being half-giant?"

But it seemed that Hagrid did care. They didn't see a sign of him all week. He didn't appear at the staff table at mealtimes, they didn't see him going about his gamekeeper duties on the grounds, and Professor Grubbly-Plank continued to take the Care of Magical Creatures classes. Malfoy was gloating at every possible opportunity.

"Missing your half-breed pal?" he kept whispering to Harry whenever there was a teacher around, so that he was safe from Harry's retaliation. "Missing the elephant-man?"

There was a Hogsmeade visit halfway through January. Hermione was very surprised that Harry was going to go.

"I just thought you'd want to take advantage of the common room being quiet," she said. "Really get to work on that egg."

"Oh I — I reckon I've got a pretty good idea what it's about now," Harry lied.

"Have you really?" said Hermione, looking impressed. "Well done!"

Harry's insides gave a guilty squirm, but he ignored them. He still had five weeks to work out that egg clue, after all, and that was ages . . . whereas if he went into Hogsmeade, he might run into Hagrid, and get a chance to persuade him to come back.

He, Ron, and Hermione left the castle together on Saturday and set off through the cold, wet grounds toward the gates. As they passed the Durmstrang ship moored in the lake, they saw Viktor Krum emerge onto the deck, dressed in nothing but swimming trunks. He was very skinny indeed, but apparently a lot tougher than he looked, because he climbed up onto the side of the ship, stretched out his arms, and dived, right into the lake.

"He's mad!" said Harry, staring at Krum's dark head as it bobbed out into the middle of the lake. "It must be freezing, it's January!"

"It's a lot colder where he comes from," said Hermione. "I suppose it feels quite warm to him."

"Yeah, but there's still the giant squid," said Ron. He didn't sound anxious — if anything, he sounded hopeful. Hermione noticed his tone of voice and frowned.

"He's really nice, you know," she said. "He's not at all like you'd think, coming from Durmstrang. He likes it much better here, he told me."

Ron said nothing. He hadn't mentioned Viktor Krum since the ball, but Harry had found a miniature arm under his bed on Boxing Day, which had looked very much as though it had been snapped off a small model figure wearing Bulgarian Quidditch robes.

Harry kept his eyes skinned for a sign of Hagrid all the way down the slushy High Street, and suggested a visit to the Three Broomsticks once he had ascertained that Hagrid was not in any of the shops.

The pub was as crowded as ever, but one quick look around at all the tables told Harry that Hagrid wasn't there. Heart sinking, he went up to the bar with Ron and Hermione, ordered three butterbeers from Madam Rosmerta, and thought gloomily that he might just as well have stayed behind and listened to the egg wailing after all.

"Doesn't he *ever* go into the office?" Hermione whispered suddenly. "Look!"

She pointed into the mirror behind the bar, and Harry saw Ludo Bagman reflected there, sitting in a shadowy corner with a bunch of goblins. Bagman was talking very fast in a low voice to the goblins, all of whom had their arms crossed and were looking rather menacing.

It was indeed odd, Harry thought, that Bagman was here at the Three Broomsticks on a weekend when there was no Triwizard event, and therefore no judging to be done. He watched Bagman in the mirror. He was looking strained again, quite as strained as he had that night in the forest before the Dark Mark had appeared. But just then Bagman glanced over at the bar, saw Harry, and stood up.

"In a moment, in a moment!" Harry heard him say brusquely to the goblins, and Bagman hurried through the pub toward Harry, his boyish grin back in place.

"Harry!" he said. "How are you? Been hoping to run into you! Everything going all right?"

"Fine, thanks," said Harry.

"Wonder if I could have a quick, private word, Harry?" said Bagman eagerly. "You couldn't give us a moment, you two, could you?"

"Er — okay," said Ron, and he and Hermione went off to find a table.

Bagman led Harry along the bar to the end furthest from Madam Rosmerta.

"Well, I just thought I'd congratulate you again on your splendid performance against that Horntail, Harry," said Bagman. "Really superb."

"Thanks," said Harry, but he knew this couldn't be all that Bagman wanted to say, because he could have congratulated Harry in front of Ron and Hermione. Bagman didn't seem in any particular rush to spill the beans, though. Harry saw him glance into the mirror over the bar at the goblins, who were all watching him and Harry in silence through their dark, slanting eyes.

"Absolute nightmare," said Bagman to Harry in an undertone, noticing Harry watching the goblins too. "Their English isn't too good . . . it's like being back with all the Bulgarians at the Quidditch World Cup . . . but at least *they* used sign language another human could recognize. This lot keep gabbling in Gobbledegook . . . and I only know one word of Gobbledegook. *Bladvak*. It means 'pickax.' I don't like to use it in case they think I'm threatening them."

He gave a short, booming laugh.

"What do they want?" Harry said, noticing how the goblins were still watching Bagman very closely.

"Er — well . . ." said Bagman, looking suddenly nervous. "They . . . er . . . they're looking for Barty Crouch."

"Why are they looking for him here?" said Harry. "He's at the Ministry in London, isn't he?"

"Er . . . as a matter of fact, I've no idea where he is," said Bagman. "He's sort of . . . stopped coming to work. Been absent for a couple of weeks now. Young Percy, his assistant, says he's ill. Apparently he's just been sending instructions in by owl. But would you mind not mentioning that to anyone, Harry? Because Rita Skeeter's still poking around everywhere she can, and I'm willing to bet she'd work up Barty's illness into something sinister. Probably say he's gone missing like Bertha Jorkins."

"Have you heard anything about Bertha Jorkins?" Harry asked.

"No," said Bagman, looking strained again. "I've got people looking, of course . . ." (*About time,* thought Harry) "and it's all very strange. She definitely *arrived* in Albania, because she met her second cousin there. And then she left the cousin's house to go south and see an aunt . . . and she seems to have vanished without trace en route. Blowed if I can see where she's got to . . . she doesn't seem the type to elope, for instance . . . but still. . . . What are we doing, talking about goblins and Bertha Jorkins? I really wanted to ask you" — he lowered his voice — "how are you getting on with your golden egg?"

"Er . . . not bad," Harry said untruthfully.

Bagman seemed to know he wasn't being honest.

"Listen, Harry," he said (still in a very low voice), "I feel very bad about all this . . . you were thrown into this tournament, you didn't volunteer for it . . . and if . . ." (his voice was so quiet now, Harry had to lean closer to listen) "if I can help at all . . . a prod in the right direction . . . I've taken a liking to you . . . the way you got past that dragon! . . . well, just say the word."

Harry stared up into Bagman's round, rosy face and his wide, baby-blue eyes.

"We're supposed to work out the clues alone, aren't we?" he said, careful to keep his voice casual and not sound as though he was accusing the Head of the Department of Magical Games and Sports of breaking the rules.

"Well . . . well, yes," said Bagman impatiently, "but — come on, Harry — we all want a Hogwarts victory, don't we?"

"Have you offered Cedric help?" Harry said.

The smallest of frowns creased Bagman's smooth face. "No, I haven't," he said. "I — well, like I say, I've taken a liking to you. Just thought I'd offer . . ."

"Well, thanks," said Harry, "but I think I'm nearly there with the egg . . . couple more days should crack it."

He wasn't entirely sure why he was refusing Bagman's help, except that Bagman was almost a stranger to him, and accepting his assistance would feel somehow much more like cheating than asking advice from Ron, Hermione, or Sirius.

Bagman looked almost affronted, but couldn't say much more as Fred and George turned up at that point.

"Hello, Mr. Bagman," said Fred brightly. "Can we buy you a drink?"

"Er . . . no," said Bagman, with a last disappointed glance at Harry, "no, thank you, boys . . ."

Fred and George looked quite as disappointed as Bagman, who was surveying Harry as though he had let him down badly.

"Well, I must dash," he said. "Nice seeing you all. Good luck, Harry."

He hurried out of the pub. The goblins all slid off their chairs and exited after him. Harry went to rejoin Ron and Hermione.

"What did he want?" Ron said, the moment Harry had sat down.

"He offered to help me with the golden egg," said Harry.

"He shouldn't be doing that!" said Hermione, looking very shocked. "He's one of the judges! And anyway, you've already worked it out — haven't you?"

"Er . . . nearly," said Harry.

"Well, I don't think Dumbledore would like it if he knew Bagman was trying to persuade you to cheat!" said Hermione, still looking deeply disapproving. "I hope he's trying to help Cedric as much!"

"He's not, I asked," said Harry.

"Who cares if Diggory's getting help?" said Ron. Harry privately agreed.

"Those goblins didn't look very friendly," said Hermione, sipping her butterbeer. "What were they doing here?"

"Looking for Crouch, according to Bagman," said Harry. "He's still ill. Hasn't been into work."

"Maybe Percy's poisoning him," said Ron. "Probably thinks if Crouch snuffs it he'll be made Head of the Department of International Magical Cooperation."

Hermione gave Ron a don't-joke-about-things-like-that look, and said, "Funny, goblins looking for Mr. Crouch. . . . They'd normally deal with the Department for the Regulation and Control of Magical Creatures."

"Crouch can speak loads of different languages, though," said Harry. "Maybe they need an interpreter."

"Worrying about poor 'ickle goblins, now, are you?" Ron asked Hermione. "Thinking of starting up S.P.U.G. or something? Society for the Protection of Ugly Goblins?"

"Ha, ha, ha," said Hermione sarcastically. "Goblins don't need protection. Haven't you been listening to what Professor Binns has been telling us about goblin rebellions?"

"No," said Harry and Ron together.

"Well, they're quite capable of dealing with wizards," said Hermione, taking another sip of butterbeer. "They're very clever. They're not like house-elves, who never stick up for themselves."

"Uh-oh," said Ron, staring at the door.

Rita Skeeter had just entered. She was wearing banana-yellow robes today; her long nails were painted shocking pink, and she was accompanied by her paunchy photographer. She bought drinks, and she and the photographer made their way through the crowds to a table nearby, Harry, Ron, and Hermione glaring at her as she approached. She was talking fast and looking very satisfied about something.

". . . didn't seem very keen to talk to us, did he, Bozo? Now, why would that be, do you think? And what's he doing with a pack of goblins in tow anyway? Showing them the sights . . . what non-sense . . . he was always a bad liar. Reckon something's up? Think we should do a bit of digging? 'Disgraced Ex-Head of Magical Games and Sports, Ludo Bagman . . .' Snappy start to a sentence, Bozo — we just need to find a story to fit it —"

"Trying to ruin someone else's life?" said Harry loudly.

A few people looked around. Rita Skeeter's eyes widened behind her jeweled spectacles as she saw who had spoken.

"Harry!" she said, beaming. "How lovely! Why don't you come and join — ?"

"I wouldn't come near you with a ten-foot broomstick," said Harry furiously. "What did you do that to Hagrid for, eh?"

Rita Skeeter raised her heavily penciled eyebrows.

"Our readers have a right to the truth, Harry. I am merely doing my —"

"Who cares if he's half-giant?" Harry shouted. "There's nothing wrong with him!"

The whole pub had gone very quiet. Madam Rosmerta was star-ing over from behind the bar, apparently oblivious to the fact that the flagon she was filling with mead was overflowing.

Rita Skeeter's smile flickered very slightly, but she hitched it back almost at once; she snapped open her crocodile-skin handbag, pulled out her Quick-Quotes Quill, and said, "How about giving me an interview about the Hagrid *you* know, Harry? The man behind the muscles? Your unlikely friendship and the reasons behind it. Would you call him a father substitute?"

Hermione stood up very abruptly, her butterbeer clutched in her hand as though it were a grenade.

"You horrible woman," she said, through gritted teeth, "you don't care, do you, anything for a story, and anyone will do, won't they? Even Ludo Bagman —"

"Sit down, you silly little girl, and don't talk about things you don't understand," said Rita Skeeter coldly, her eyes hardening as they fell on Hermione. "I know things about Ludo Bagman that would make your hair curl . . . *not* that it needs it —" she added, eyeing Hermione's bushy hair.

"Let's go," said Hermione, "c'mon, Harry — Ron . . ."

They left; many people were staring at them as they went. Harry glanced back as they reached the door. Rita Skeeter's Quick-Quotes Quill was out; it was zooming backward and forward over a piece of parchment on the table.

"She'll be after you next, Hermione," said Ron in a low and worried voice as they walked quickly back up the street.

"Let her try!" said Hermione defiantly; she was shaking with rage. "I'll show her! Silly little girl, am I? Oh, I'll get her back for this. First Harry, then Hagrid . . ."

"You don't want to go upsetting Rita Skeeter," said Ron nervously. "I'm serious, Hermione, she'll dig up something on you —"

"My parents don't read the *Daily Prophet*. She can't scare me into hiding!" said Hermione, now striding along so fast that it was all Harry and Ron could do to keep up with her. The last time Harry had seen Hermione in a rage like this, she had hit Draco Malfoy around the face. "And Hagrid isn't hiding anymore! He should *never* have let that excuse for a human being upset him! Come *on*!"

Breaking into a run, she led them all the way back up the road, through the gates flanked by winged boars, and up through the grounds to Hagrid's cabin.

The curtains were still drawn, and they could hear Fang barking as they approached.

"Hagrid!" Hermione shouted, pounding on his front door. "Hagrid, that's enough! We know you're in there! Nobody cares if your mum was a giantess, Hagrid! You can't let that foul Skeeter woman do this to you! Hagrid, get out here, you're just being —"

The door opened. Hermione said, "About t —!" and then stopped, very suddenly, because she had found herself face-to-face, not with Hagrid, but with Albus Dumbledore.

"Good afternoon," he said pleasantly, smiling down at them.

"We — er — we wanted to see Hagrid," said Hermione in a rather small voice.

"Yes, I surmised as much," said Dumbledore, his eyes twinkling. "Why don't you come in?"

"Oh . . . um . . . okay," said Hermione.

She, Ron, and Harry went into the cabin; Fang launched himself upon Harry the moment he entered, barking madly and trying to lick his ears. Harry fended off Fang and looked around.

Hagrid was sitting at his table, where there were two large mugs of tea. He looked a real mess. His face was blotchy, his eyes swollen, and he had gone to the other extreme where his hair was concerned; far from trying to make it behave, it now looked like a wig of tangled wire.

"Hi, Hagrid," said Harry.

Hagrid looked up.

"'Lo," he said in a very hoarse voice.

"More tea, I think," said Dumbledore, closing the door behind Harry, Ron, and Hermione, drawing out his wand, and twiddling it; a revolving tea tray appeared in midair along with a plate of cakes. Dumbledore magicked the tray onto the table, and everybody sat down. There was a slight pause, and then Dumbledore said, "Did you by any chance hear what Miss Granger was shouting, Hagrid?"

Hermione went slightly pink, but Dumbledore smiled at her and continued, "Hermione, Harry, and Ron still seem to want to know you, judging by the way they were attempting to break down the door."

"Of course we still want to know you!" Harry said, staring at Hagrid. "You don't think anything that Skeeter cow — sorry, Professor," he added quickly, looking at Dumbledore.

"I have gone temporarily deaf and haven't any idea what you said, Harry," said Dumbledore, twiddling his thumbs and staring at the ceiling.

"Er — right," said Harry sheepishly. "I just meant — Hagrid, how could you think we'd care what that — woman — wrote about you?"

Two fat tears leaked out of Hagrid's beetle-black eyes and fell slowly into his tangled beard.

"Living proof of what I've been telling you, Hagrid," said Dumbledore, still looking carefully up at the ceiling. "I have shown you the letters from the countless parents who remember you from their own days here, telling me in no uncertain terms that if I sacked you, they would have something to say about it —"

"Not all of 'em," said Hagrid hoarsely. "Not all of 'em wan' me ter stay."

"Really, Hagrid, if you are holding out for universal popularity, I'm afraid you will be in this cabin for a very long time," said Dumbledore, now peering sternly over his half-moon spectacles. "Not a week has passed since I became headmaster of this school when I haven't had at least one owl complaining about the way I run it. But what should I do? Barricade myself in my study and refuse to talk to anybody?"

"Yeh — yeh're not half-giant!" said Hagrid croakily.

"Hagrid, look what I've got for relatives!" Harry said furiously. "Look at the Dursleys!"

"An excellent point," said Professor Dumbledore. "My own brother, Aberforth, was prosecuted for practicing inappropriate charms on a goat. It was all over the papers, but did Aberforth hide? No, he did not! He held his head high and went about his business as usual! Of course, I'm not entirely sure he can read, so that may not have been bravery. . . ."

"Come back and teach, Hagrid," said Hermione quietly, "please come back, we really miss you."

Hagrid gulped. More tears leaked out down his cheeks and into his tangled beard.

Dumbledore stood up. "I refuse to accept your resignation, Hagrid, and I expect you back at work on Monday," he said. "You will join me for breakfast at eight-thirty in the Great Hall. No excuses. Good afternoon to you all."

Dumbledore left the cabin, pausing only to scratch Fang's ears. When the door had shut behind him, Hagrid began to sob into his dustbin-lid-sized hands. Hermione kept patting his arm, and at last, Hagrid looked up, his eyes very red indeed, and said, "Great man, Dumbledore . . . great man . . ."

"Yeah, he is," said Ron. "Can I have one of these cakes, Hagrid?"

"Help yerself," said Hagrid, wiping his eyes on the back of his hand. "Ar, he's righ', o' course — yeh're all righ'. . . I bin stupid . . . my ol' dad woulda bin ashamed o' the way I've bin behavin'. . . ." More tears leaked out, but he wiped them away more forcefully, and said, "Never shown you a picture of my old dad, have I? Here . . ."

Hagrid got up, went over to his dresser, opened a drawer, and pulled out a picture of a short wizard with Hagrid's crinkled black eyes, beaming as he sat on top of Hagrid's shoulder. Hagrid was a good seven or eight feet tall, judging by the apple tree beside him, but his face was beardless, young, round, and smooth — he looked hardly older than eleven.

"Tha' was taken jus' after I got inter Hogwarts," Hagrid croaked. "Dad was dead chuffed . . . thought I migh' not be a wizard, see, 'cos me mum . . . well, anyway. 'Course, I never was great shakes at magic, really . . . but at least he never saw me expelled. Died, see, in me second year. . . .

"Dumbledore was the one who stuck up for me after Dad went. Got me the gamekeeper job . . . trusts people, he does. Gives 'em second chances . . . tha's what sets him apar' from other Heads, see. He'll accept anyone at Hogwarts, s'long as they've got the talent. Knows people can turn out okay even if their families weren'. . . well . . . all tha' respectable. But some don' understand that. There's some who'd always hold it against yeh . . . there's some who'd even pretend they just had big bones rather than stand up an' say — I am what I am, an' I'm not ashamed. 'Never be ashamed,' my ol' dad used ter say, 'there's some who'll hold it against you, but they're not worth botherin' with.' An' he was right. I've bin an idiot. I'm not botherin' with *her* no more, I promise yeh that. Big bones . . . I'll give her big bones."

Harry, Ron, and Hermione looked at one another nervously; Harry would rather have taken fifty Blast-Ended Skrewts for a walk than admit to Hagrid that he had overheard him talking to Madame Maxime, but Hagrid was still talking, apparently unaware that he had said anything odd.

"Yeh know wha', Harry?" he said, looking up from the photograph of his father, his eyes very bright, "when I firs' met you, you reminded me o' me a bit. Mum an' Dad gone, an' you was feelin' like yeh wouldn' fit in at Hogwarts, remember? Not sure yeh were really up to it . . . an' now look at yeh, Harry! School champion!"

He looked at Harry for a moment and then said, very seriously, "Yeh know what I'd love, Harry? I'd love yeh ter win, I really would. It'd show 'em all . . . yeh don' have ter be pureblood ter do it. Yeh don' have ter be ashamed of what yeh are. It'd show 'em Dumbledore's the one who's got it righ', lettin' anyone in as long as they can do magic. How you doin' with that egg, Harry?"

"Great," said Harry. "Really great."

Hagrid's miserable face broke into a wide, watery smile.

"Tha's my boy . . . you show 'em, Harry, you show 'em. Beat 'em all."

Lying to Hagrid wasn't quite like lying to anyone else. Harry went back to the castle later that afternoon with Ron and Hermione, unable to banish the image of the happy expression on

Hagrid's whiskery face as he had imagined Harry winning the tournament. The incomprehensible egg weighed more heavily than ever on Harry's conscience that evening, and by the time he had got into bed, he had made up his mind — it was time to shelve his pride and see if Cedric's hint was worth anything.

# THE EGG AND THE EYE

As Harry had no idea how long a bath he would need to work out the secret of the golden egg, he decided to do it at night, when he would be able to take as much time as he wanted. Reluctant though he was to accept more favors from Cedric, he also decided to use the prefects' bathroom; far fewer people were allowed in there, so it was much less likely that he would be disturbed.

Harry planned his excursion carefully, because he had been caught out of bed and out-of-bounds by Filch the caretaker in the middle of the night once before, and had no desire to repeat the experience. The Invisibility Cloak would, of course, be essential, and as an added precaution, Harry thought he would take the Marauder's Map, which, next to the Cloak, was the most useful aid to rule-breaking Harry owned. The map showed the whole of Hogwarts, including its many shortcuts and secret passageways and, most important of all, it revealed the people inside the castle as minuscule, labeled dots, moving around the corridors, so that Harry would be forewarned if somebody was approaching the bathroom.

On Thursday night, Harry sneaked up to bed, put on the Cloak, crept back downstairs, and, just as he had done on the night when Hagrid had shown him the dragons, waited for the portrait hole to open. This time it was Ron who waited outside to give the Fat Lady the password ("banana fritters"). "Good luck," Ron muttered, climbing into the room as Harry crept out past him.

It was awkward moving under the Cloak tonight, because Harry had the heavy egg under one arm and the map held in front of his nose with the other. However, the moonlit corridors were empty and silent, and by checking the map at strategic intervals, Harry was able to ensure that he wouldn't run into anyone he wanted to avoid. When he reached the statue of Boris the Bewildered, a lost-looking wizard with his gloves on the wrong hands, he located the right door, leaned close to it, and muttered the password, "Pine fresh," just as Cedric had told him.

The door creaked open. Harry slipped inside, bolted the door behind him, and pulled off the Invisibility Cloak, looking around.

His immediate reaction was that it would be worth becoming a prefect just to be able to use this bathroom. It was softly lit by a splendid candle-filled chandelier, and everything was made of white marble, including what looked like an empty, rectangular swimming pool sunk into the middle of the floor. About a hundred golden taps stood all around the pool's edges, each with a differently colored jewel set into its handle. There was also a diving board. Long white linen curtains hung at the windows; a large pile of fluffy white towels sat in a corner, and there was a single golden-framed painting on the wall. It featured a blonde mermaid who was fast asleep on a rock, her long hair over her face. It fluttered every time she snored.

Harry moved forward, looking around, his footsteps echoing off the walls. Magnificent though the bathroom was — and quite keen though he was to try out a few of those taps — now he was here he couldn't quite suppress the feeling that Cedric might have been having him on. How on earth was this supposed to help solve the mystery of the egg? Nevertheless, he put one of the fluffy towels, the Cloak, the map, and the egg at the side of the swimming-pool-sized bath, then knelt down and turned on a few of the taps.

He could tell at once that they carried different sorts of bubble bath mixed with the water, though it wasn't bubble bath as Harry had ever experienced it. One tap gushed pink and blue bubbles the size of footballs; another poured ice-white foam so thick that Harry thought it would have supported his weight if he'd cared to test it; a third sent heavily perfumed purple clouds hovering over the surface of the water. Harry amused himself for a while turning the taps on and off, particularly enjoying the effect of one whose jet bounced off the surface of the water in large arcs. Then, when the deep pool was full of hot water, foam, and bubbles, which took a very short time considering its size, Harry turned off all the taps, pulled off his pajamas, slippers, and dressing gown, and slid into the water.

It was so deep that his feet barely touched the bottom, and he actually did a couple of lengths before swimming back to the side and treading water, staring at the egg. Highly enjoyable though it was to swim in hot and foamy water with clouds of different-colored steam wafting all around him, no stroke of brilliance came to him, no sudden burst of understanding.

Harry stretched out his arms, lifted the egg in his wet hands, and opened it. The wailing, screeching sound filled the bathroom, echoing and reverberating off the marble walls, but it sounded just as incomprehensible as ever, if not more so with all the echoes. He snapped it shut again, worried that the sound would attract Filch, wondering whether that hadn't been Cedric's plan — and then, making him jump so badly that he dropped the egg, which clattered away across the bathroom floor, someone spoke.

"I'd try putting it *in* the water, if I were you."

Harry had swallowed a considerable amount of bubbles in shock. He stood up, sputtering, and saw the ghost of a very glum-looking girl sitting cross-legged on top of one of the taps. It was Moaning Myrtle, who was usually to be heard sobbing in the S-bend of a toilet three floors below.

"Myrtle!" Harry said in outrage, "I'm — I'm not wearing anything!"

The foam was so dense that this hardly mattered, but he had a nasty feeling that Myrtle had been spying on him from out of one of the taps ever since he had arrived.

"I closed my eyes when you got in," she said, blinking at him through her thick spectacles. "You haven't been to see me for *ages*."

"Yeah . . . well . . ." said Harry, bending his knees slightly, just to make absolutely sure Myrtle couldn't see anything but his head, "I'm not supposed to come into your bathroom, am I? It's a girls' one."

"You didn't used to care," said Myrtle miserably. "You used to be in there all the time."

This was true, though only because Harry, Ron, and Hermione had found Myrtle's out-of-order toilets a convenient place to brew

Polyjuice Potion in secret — a forbidden potion that had turned him and Ron into living replicas of Crabbe and Goyle for an hour, so that they could sneak into the Slytherin common room.

"I got told off for going in there," said Harry, which was half-true; Percy had once caught him coming out of Myrtle's bathroom. "I thought I'd better not come back after that."

"Oh . . . I see . . ." said Myrtle, picking at a spot on her chin in a morose sort of way. "Well . . . anyway . . . I'd try the egg in the water. That's what Cedric Diggory did."

"Have you been spying on him too?" said Harry indignantly. "What d'you do, sneak up here in the evenings to watch the prefects take baths?"

"Sometimes," said Myrtle, rather slyly, "but I've never come out to speak to anyone before."

"I'm honored," said Harry darkly. "You keep your eyes shut!"

He made sure Myrtle had her glasses well covered before hoisting himself out of the bath, wrapping the towel firmly around his waist, and going to retrieve the egg. Once he was back in the water, Myrtle peered through her fingers and said, "Go on, then . . . open it under the water!"

Harry lowered the egg beneath the foamy surface and opened it . . . and this time, it did not wail. A gurgling song was coming out of it, a song whose words he couldn't distinguish through the water.

"You need to put your head under too," said Myrtle, who seemed to be thoroughly enjoying bossing him around. "Go on!"

Harry took a great breath and slid under the surface — and now, sitting on the marble bottom of the bubble-filled bath, he heard a chorus of eerie voices singing to him from the open egg in his hands:

*"Come seek us where our voices sound,*
*We cannot sing above the ground,*
*And while you're searching, ponder this:*
*We've taken what you'll sorely miss,*
*An hour long you'll have to look,*
*And to recover what we took,*
*But past an hour — the prospect's black,*
*Too late, it's gone, it won't come back."*

Harry let himself float back upward and broke the bubbly surface, shaking his hair out of his eyes.

"Hear it?" said Myrtle.

"Yeah . . . 'Come seek us where our voices sound . . .' and if I need persuading . . . hang on, I need to listen again. . . ."

He sank back beneath the water. It took three more underwater renditions of the egg's song before Harry had it memorized; then he trod water for a while, thinking hard, while Myrtle sat and watched him.

"I've got to go and look for people who can't use their voices above the ground. . . ." he said slowly. "Er . . . who could that be?"

"Slow, aren't you?"

He had never seen Moaning Myrtle so cheerful, apart from the day when a dose of Polyjuice Potion had given Hermione the hairy face and tail of a cat. Harry stared around the bathroom, thinking . . . if the voices could only be heard underwater, then it made sense for them to belong to underwater creatures. He ran this theory past Myrtle, who smirked at him.

"Well, that's what Diggory thought," she said. "He lay there talking to himself for ages about it. Ages and ages . . . nearly all the bubbles had gone. . . ."

"Underwater . . ." Harry said slowly. "Myrtle . . . what lives in the lake, apart from the giant squid?"

"Oh all sorts," she said. "I sometimes go down there . . . sometimes don't have any choice, if someone flushes my toilet when I'm not expecting it. . . ."

Trying not to think about Moaning Myrtle zooming down a pipe to the lake with the contents of a toilet, Harry said, "Well, does anything in there have a human voice? Hang on —"

Harry's eyes had fallen on the picture of the snoozing mermaid on the wall.

"Myrtle, there aren't *merpeople* in there, are there?"

"Oooh, very good," she said, her thick glasses twinkling, "it took Diggory much longer than that! And that was with *her* awake too" — Myrtle jerked her head toward the mermaid with an expression of great dislike on her glum face — "giggling and showing off and flashing her fins. . . ."

"That's it, isn't it?" said Harry excitedly. "The second task's to go and find the merpeople in the lake and . . . and . . ."

But he suddenly realized what he was saying, and he felt the excitement drain out of him as though someone had just pulled a plug in his stomach. He wasn't a very good swimmer; he'd never had much practice. Dudley had had lessons in his youth, but Aunt Petunia and Uncle Vernon, no doubt hoping that Harry would drown one day, hadn't bothered to give him any. A couple of lengths of this bath were all very well, but that lake was very large, and very deep . . . and merpeople would surely live right at the bottom. . . .

"Myrtle," Harry said slowly, "how am I supposed to *breathe?*"

At this, Myrtle's eyes filled with sudden tears again.

"Tactless!" she muttered, groping in her robes for a handker-chief.

"What's tactless?" said Harry, bewildered.

"Talking about breathing in front of *me!*" she said shrilly, and her voice echoed loudly around the bathroom. "When I can't . . . when I haven't . . . not for ages . . ."

She buried her face in her handkerchief and sniffed loudly. Harry remembered how touchy Myrtle had always been about being dead, but none of the other ghosts he knew made such a fuss about it.

"Sorry," he said impatiently. "I didn't mean — I just forgot . . ."

"Oh yes, very easy to forget Myrtle's dead," said Myrtle, gulping, looking at him out of swollen eyes. "Nobody missed me even when I was alive. Took them hours and hours to find my body — I know, I was sitting there waiting for them. Olive Hornby came into the bathroom — 'Are you in here again, sulking, Myrtle?' she said, 'because Professor Dippet asked me to look for you —' And then she saw my body . . . ooooh, she didn't forget it until her dying day, I made sure of that . . . followed her around and reminded her, I did. I remember at her brother's wedding —"

But Harry wasn't listening; he was thinking about the merpeople's song again. *"We've taken what you'll sorely miss."* That sounded as though they were going to steal something of his, something he had to get back. What were they going to take?

"— and then, of course, she went to the Ministry of Magic to stop me stalking her, so I had to come back here and live in my toilet."

"Good," said Harry vaguely. "Well, I'm a lot further on than I was. . . . Shut your eyes again, will you? I'm getting out."

He retrieved the egg from the bottom of the bath, climbed out, dried himself, and pulled on his pajamas and dressing gown again.

"Will you come and visit me in my bathroom again sometime?" Moaning Myrtle asked mournfully as Harry picked up the Invisibility Cloak.

"Er . . . I'll try," Harry said, though privately thinking the only way he'd be visiting Myrtle's bathroom again was if every other toilet in the castle got blocked. "See you, Myrtle . . . thanks for your help."

" 'Bye, 'bye," she said gloomily, and as Harry put on the Invisibility Cloak he saw her zoom back up the tap.

Out in the dark corridor, Harry examined the Marauder's Map to check that the coast was still clear. Yes, the dots belonging to Filch and his cat, Mrs. Norris, were safely in their office . . . nothing else seemed to be moving apart from Peeves, though he was bouncing around the trophy room on the floor above. . . . Harry had taken his first step back toward Gryffindor Tower when something else on the map caught his eye . . . something distinctly odd.

Peeves was *not* the only thing that was moving. A single dot was flitting around a room in the bottom left-hand corner — Snape's office. But the dot wasn't labeled "Severus Snape". . . it was Bartemius Crouch.

Harry stared at the dot. Mr. Crouch was supposed to be too ill to go to work or to come to the Yule Ball — so what was he doing, sneaking into Hogwarts at one o'clock in the morning? Harry watched closely as the dot moved around and around the room, pausing here and there. . . .

Harry hesitated, thinking . . . and then his curiosity got the better of him. He turned and set off in the opposite direction toward the nearest staircase. He was going to see what Crouch was up to.

Harry walked down the stairs as quietly as possible, though the faces in some of the portraits still turned curiously at the squeak of a floorboard, the rustle of his pajamas. He crept along the corridor below, pushed aside a tapestry about halfway along, and proceeded down a narrower staircase, a shortcut that would take him down two floors. He kept glancing down at the map, wondering . . . It just didn't seem in character, somehow, for correct, law-abiding Mr. Crouch to be sneaking around somebody else's office this late at night. . . .

And then, halfway down the staircase, not thinking about what he was doing, not concentrating on anything but the peculiar behavior of Mr. Crouch, Harry's leg suddenly sank right through the trick step Neville always forgot to jump. He gave an ungainly wobble, and the golden egg, still damp from the bath, slipped from under his arm. He lurched forward to try and catch it, but too late; the egg fell down the long staircase with a bang as loud as a bass drum on every step — the Invisibility Cloak slipped — Harry snatched at it, and the Marauder's Map fluttered out of his hand and slid down six stairs, where, sunk in the step to above his knee, he couldn't reach it.

The golden egg fell through the tapestry at the bottom of the staircase, burst open, and began wailing loudly in the corridor below. Harry pulled out his wand and struggled to touch the Marauder's Map, to wipe it blank, but it was too far away to reach —

Pulling the Cloak back over himself, Harry straightened up, listening hard with his eyes screwed up with fear . . . and, almost immediately —

"PEEVES!"

It was the unmistakable hunting cry of Filch the caretaker. Harry could hear his rapid, shuffling footsteps coming nearer and nearer, his wheezy voice raised in fury.

"What's this racket? Wake up the whole castle, will you? I'll have you, Peeves, I'll have you, you'll . . . and what is this?"

Filch's footsteps halted; there was a clink of metal on metal and the wailing stopped — Filch had picked up the egg and closed it. Harry stood very still, one leg still jammed tightly in the magical step, listening. Any moment now, Filch was going to pull aside the tapestry, expecting to see Peeves . . . and there would be no Peeves . . . but if he came up the stairs, he would spot the Marauder's Map . . . and Invisibility Cloak or not, the map would show "Harry Potter" standing exactly where he was.

"Egg?" Filch said quietly at the foot of the stairs. "My sweet!" — Mrs. Norris was obviously with him — "This is a Triwizard clue! This belongs to a school champion!"

Harry felt sick; his heart was hammering very fast —

"PEEVES!" Filch roared gleefully. "You've been stealing!"

He ripped back the tapestry below, and Harry saw his horrible, pouchy face and bulging, pale eyes staring up the dark and (to Filch) deserted staircase.

"Hiding, are you?" he said softly. "I'm coming to get you, Peeves. . . . You've gone and stolen a Triwizard clue, Peeves. . . . Dumbledore'll have you out of here for this, you filthy, pilfering poltergeist. . . ."

Filch started to climb the stairs, his scrawny, dust-colored cat at his heels. Mrs. Norris's lamp-like eyes, so very like her master's, were fixed directly upon Harry. He had had occasion before now to wonder whether the Invisibility Cloak worked on cats. . . . Sick with apprehension, he watched Filch drawing nearer and nearer in his old flannel dressing gown — he tried desperately to pull his trapped leg free, but it merely sank a few more inches — any second now, Filch was going to spot the map or walk right into him —

"Filch? What's going on?"

Filch stopped a few steps below Harry and turned. At the foot of the stairs stood the only person who could make Harry's situation worse: Snape. He was wearing a long gray nightshirt and he looked livid.

"It's Peeves, Professor," Filch whispered malevolently. "He threw this egg down the stairs."

Snape climbed up the stairs quickly and stopped beside Filch. Harry gritted his teeth, convinced his loudly thumping heart would give him away at any second. . . .

"Peeves?" said Snape softly, staring at the egg in Filch's hands. "But Peeves couldn't get into my office. . . ."

"This egg was in your office, Professor?"

"Of course not," Snape snapped. "I heard banging and wailing —"

"Yes, Professor, that was the egg —"

"— I was coming to investigate —"

"— Peeves threw it, Professor —"

"— and when I passed my office, I saw that the torches were lit and a cupboard door was ajar! Somebody has been searching it!"

"But Peeves couldn't —"

"I know he couldn't, Filch!" Snape snapped again. "I seal my office with a spell none but a wizard could break!" Snape looked up the stairs, straight through Harry, and then down into the corridor below. "I want you to come and help me search for the intruder, Filch."

"I — yes, Professor — but —"

Filch looked yearningly up the stairs, right through Harry, who could see that he was very reluctant to forgo the chance of cornering Peeves. *Go,* Harry pleaded with him silently, *go with Snape . . . go . . .* Mrs. Norris was peering around Filch's legs. . . . Harry had the distinct impression that she could smell him. . . . Why had he filled that bath with so much perfumed foam?

"The thing is, Professor," said Filch plaintively, "the headmaster will have to listen to me this time. Peeves has been stealing from a student, it might be my chance to get him thrown out of the castle once and for all —"

"Filch, I don't give a damn about that wretched poltergeist; it's my office that's —"

*Clunk. Clunk. Clunk.*

Snape stopped talking very abruptly. He and Filch both looked down at the foot of the stairs. Harry saw Mad-Eye Moody limp into sight through the narrow gap between their heads. Moody was wearing his old traveling cloak over his nightshirt and leaning on his staff as usual.

"Pajama party, is it?" he growled up the stairs.

"Professor Snape and I heard noises, Professor," said Filch at once. "Peeves the Poltergeist, throwing things around as usual — and then Professor Snape discovered that someone had broken into his off —"

"Shut up!" Snape hissed to Filch.

Moody took a step closer to the foot of the stairs. Harry saw Moody's magical eye travel over Snape, and then, unmistakably, onto himself.

Harry's heart gave a horrible jolt. *Moody could see through Invisibility Cloaks. . .* he alone could see the full strangeness of the scene: Snape in his nightshirt, Filch clutching the egg, and he, Harry, trapped in the stairs behind them. Moody's lopsided gash of a mouth opened in surprise. For a few seconds, he and Harry stared straight into each other's eyes. Then Moody closed his mouth and turned his blue eye upon Snape again.

"Did I hear that correctly, Snape?" he asked slowly. "Someone broke into your office?"

"It is unimportant," said Snape coldly.

"On the contrary," growled Moody, "it is very important. Who'd want to break into your office?"

"A student, I daresay," said Snape. Harry could see a vein flickering horribly on Snape's greasy temple. "It has happened before. Potion ingredients have gone missing from my private store cupboard . . . students attempting illicit mixtures, no doubt. . . ."

"Reckon they were after potion ingredients, eh?" said Moody. "Not hiding anything else in your office, are you?"

Harry saw the edge of Snape's sallow face turn a nasty brick color, the vein in his temple pulsing more rapidly.

"You know I'm hiding nothing, Moody," he said in a soft and dangerous voice, "as you've searched my office pretty thoroughly yourself."

Moody's face twisted into a smile. "Auror's privilege, Snape. Dumbledore told me to keep an eye —"

"Dumbledore happens to trust me," said Snape through clenched teeth. "I refuse to believe that he gave you orders to search my office!"

"'Course Dumbledore trusts you," growled Moody. "He's a trusting man, isn't he? Believes in second chances. But me — I say there are spots that don't come off, Snape. Spots that never come off, d'you know what I mean?"

Snape suddenly did something very strange. He seized his left forearm convulsively with his right hand, as though something on it had hurt him.

Moody laughed. "Get back to bed, Snape."

"You don't have the authority to send me anywhere!" Snape hissed, letting go of his arm as though angry with himself. "I have as much right to prowl this school after dark as you do!"

"Prowl away," said Moody, but his voice was full of menace. "I look forward to meeting you in a dark corridor some time. . . . You've dropped something, by the way. . . ."

With a stab of horror, Harry saw Moody point at the Marauder's Map, still lying on the staircase six steps below him. As Snape and Filch both turned to look at it, Harry threw caution to the winds; he raised his arms under the Cloak and waved furiously at Moody to attract his attention, mouthing "It's mine! *Mine!*"

Snape had reached out for it, a horrible expression of dawning comprehension on his face —

*"Accio Parchment!"*

The map flew up into the air, slipped through Snape's outstretched fingers, and soared down the stairs into Moody's hand.

"My mistake," Moody said calmly. "It's mine — must've dropped it earlier —"

But Snape's black eyes were darting from the egg in Filch's arms to the map in Moody's hand, and Harry could tell he was putting two and two together, as only Snape could. . . .

"Potter," he said quietly.

"What's that?" said Moody calmly, folding up the map and pocketing it.

"Potter!" Snape snarled, and he actually turned his head and stared right at the place where Harry was, as though he could suddenly see him. "That egg is Potter's egg. That piece of parchment belongs to Potter. I have seen it before, I recognize it! Potter is here! Potter, in his Invisibility Cloak!"

Snape stretched out his hands like a blind man and began to move up the stairs; Harry could have sworn his over-large nostrils were dilating, trying to sniff Harry out — trapped, Harry leaned backward, trying to avoid Snape's fingertips, but any moment now —

"There's nothing there, Snape!" barked Moody, "but I'll be happy to tell the headmaster how quickly your mind jumped to Harry Potter!"

"Meaning what?" Snape turned again to look at Moody, his hands still outstretched, inches from Harry's chest.

"Meaning that Dumbledore's very interested to know who's got it in for that boy!" said Moody, limping nearer still to the foot of the stairs. "And so am I, Snape . . . very interested. . . ." The torchlight flickered across his mangled face, so that the scars, and the chunk missing from his nose, looked deeper and darker than ever.

Snape was looking down at Moody, and Harry couldn't see the expression on his face. For a moment, nobody moved or said anything. Then Snape slowly lowered his hands.

"I merely thought," said Snape, in a voice of forced calm, "that if Potter was wandering around after hours again . . . it's an unfortunate habit of his . . . he should be stopped. For — for his own safety."

"Ah, I see," said Moody softly. "Got Potter's best interests at heart, have you?"

There was a pause. Snape and Moody were still staring at each other. Mrs. Norris gave a loud meow, still peering around Filch's legs, looking for the source of Harry's bubble-bath smell.

"I think I will go back to bed," Snape said curtly.

"Best idea you've had all night," said Moody. "Now, Filch, if you'll just give me that egg —"

"No!" said Filch, clutching the egg as though it were his first-born son. "Professor Moody, this is evidence of Peeves' treachery!"

"It's the property of the champion he stole it from," said Moody. "Hand it over, now."

Snape swept downstairs and passed Moody without another word. Filch made a chirruping noise to Mrs. Norris, who stared blankly at Harry for a few more seconds before turning and following her master. Still breathing very fast, Harry heard Snape walking away down the corridor; Filch handed Moody the egg and disappeared from view too, muttering to Mrs. Norris. "Never mind, my sweet . . . we'll see Dumbledore in the morning . . . tell him what Peeves was up to. . . ."

A door slammed. Harry was left staring down at Moody, who placed his staff on the bottommost stair and started to climb laboriously toward him, a dull *clunk* on every other step.

"Close shave, Potter," he muttered.

"Yeah . . . I — er . . . thanks," said Harry weakly.

"What is this thing?" said Moody, drawing the Marauder's Map out of his pocket and unfolding it.

"Map of Hogwarts," said Harry, hoping Moody was going to pull him out of the staircase soon; his leg was really hurting him.

"Merlin's beard," Moody whispered, staring at the map, his magical eye going haywire. "This . . . this is some map, Potter!"

"Yeah, it's . . . quite useful," Harry said. His eyes were starting to water from the pain. "Er — Professor Moody, d'you think you could help me — ?"

"What? Oh! Yes . . . yes, of course . . ."

Moody took hold of Harry's arms and pulled; Harry's leg came free of the trick step, and he climbed onto the one above it. Moody was still gazing at the map.

"Potter . . ." he said slowly, "you didn't happen, by any chance, to see who broke into Snape's office, did you? On this map, I mean?"

"Er . . . yeah, I did . . ." Harry admitted. "It was Mr. Crouch."

Moody's magical eye whizzed over the entire surface of the map. He looked suddenly alarmed.

"Crouch?" he said. "You're — you're sure, Potter?"

"Positive," said Harry.

"Well, he's not here anymore," said Moody, his eye still whizzing over the map. "Crouch . . . that's very — very interesting. . . ."

He said nothing for almost a minute, still staring at the map. Harry could tell that this news meant something to Moody and very much wanted to know what it was. He wondered whether he dared ask. Moody scared him slightly . . . yet Moody had just helped him avoid an awful lot of trouble. . . .

"Er . . . Professor Moody . . . why d'you reckon Mr. Crouch wanted to look around Snape's office?"

Moody's magical eye left the map and fixed, quivering, upon Harry. It was a penetrating glare, and Harry had the impression that Moody was sizing him up, wondering whether to answer or not, or how much to tell him.

"Put it this way, Potter," Moody muttered finally, "they say old Mad-Eye's obsessed with catching Dark wizards . . . but I'm nothing — *nothing*—compared to Barty Crouch."

He continued to stare at the map. Harry was burning to know more.

"Professor Moody?" he said again. "D'you think . . . could this have anything to do with . . . maybe Mr. Crouch thinks there's something going on. . . ."

"Like what?" said Moody sharply.

Harry wondered how much he dare say. He didn't want Moody to guess that he had a source of information outside Hogwarts; that might lead to tricky questions about Sirius.

"I don't know," Harry muttered, "odd stuff's been happening lately, hasn't it? It's been in the *Daily Prophet*. . . the Dark Mark at the World Cup, and the Death Eaters and everything. . . ."

Both of Moody's mismatched eyes widened.

"You're a sharp boy, Potter," he said. His magical eye roved back to the Marauder's Map. "Crouch could be thinking along those lines," he said slowly. "Very possible . . . there have been some funny rumors flying around lately — helped along by Rita Skeeter, of course. It's making a lot of people nervous, I reckon." A grim smile twisted his lopsided mouth. "Oh if there's one thing I hate," he muttered, more to himself than to Harry, and his magical eye was fixed on the left-hand corner of the map, "it's a Death Eater who walked free. . . ."

Harry stared at him. Could Moody possibly mean what Harry thought he meant?

"And now I want to ask *you* a question, Potter," said Moody in a more businesslike tone.

Harry's heart sank; he had thought this was coming. Moody was going to ask where he had got this map, which was a very dubious magical object — and the story of how it had fallen into his hands incriminated not only him, but his own father, Fred and George Weasley, and Professor Lupin, their last Defense Against the Dark Arts teacher. Moody waved the map in front of Harry, who braced himself —

"Can I borrow this?"

"Oh!" said Harry.

He was very fond of his map, but on the other hand, he was extremely relieved that Moody wasn't asking where he'd got it, and there was no doubt that he owed Moody a favor.

"Yeah, okay."

"Good boy," growled Moody. "I can make good use of this . . . this might be *exactly* what I've been looking for. . . . Right, bed, Potter, come on, now. . . ."

They climbed to the top of the stairs together, Moody still examining the map as though it was a treasure the like of which he had never seen before. They walked in silence to the door of Moody's office, where he stopped and looked up at Harry.

"You ever thought of a career as an Auror, Potter?"

"No," said Harry, taken aback.

"You want to consider it," said Moody, nodding and looking

at Harry thoughtfully. "Yes, indeed . . . and incidentally . . . I'm guessing you weren't just taking that egg for a walk tonight?"

"Er — no," said Harry, grinning. "I've been working out the clue."

Moody winked at him, his magical eye going haywire again.

"Nothing like a nighttime stroll to give you ideas, Potter. . . . See you in the morning. . . ."

He went back into his office, staring down at the Marauder's Map again, and closed the door behind him.

Harry walked slowly back to Gryffindor Tower, lost in thought about Snape, and Crouch, and what it all meant. . . . Why was Crouch pretending to be ill, if he could manage to get to Hogwarts when he wanted to? What did he think Snape was concealing in his office?

And Moody thought he, Harry, ought to be an Auror! Interesting idea . . . but somehow, Harry thought, as he got quietly into his four-poster ten minutes later, the egg and the Cloak now safely back in his trunk, he thought he'd like to check how scarred the rest of them were before he chose it as a career.

# THE SECOND TASK

"Y ou said you'd already worked out that egg clue!" said
Hermione indignantly.

"Keep your voice down!" said Harry crossly. "I just need to —
sort of fine-tune it, all right?"

He, Ron, and Hermione were sitting at the very back of the
Charms class with a table to themselves. They were supposed to be
practicing the opposite of the Summoning Charm today — the
Banishing Charm. Owing to the potential for nasty accidents when
objects kept flying across the room, Professor Flitwick had given
each student a stack of cushions on which to practice, the theory
being that these wouldn't hurt anyone if they went off target. It was
a good theory, but it wasn't working very well. Neville's aim was so
poor that he kept accidentally sending much heavier things flying
across the room — Professor Flitwick, for instance.

"Just forget the egg for a minute, all right?" Harry hissed as Professor Flitwick went whizzing resignedly past them, landing on top

of a large cabinet. "I'm trying to tell you about Snape and Moody. . . ."

This class was an ideal cover for a private conversation, as everyone was having far too much fun to pay them any attention. Harry had been recounting his adventures of the previous night in whispered installments for the last half hour.

"Snape said Moody's searched his office as well?" Ron whispered, his eyes alight with interest as he Banished a cushion with a sweep of his wand (it soared into the air and knocked Parvati's hat off). "What . . . d'you reckon Moody's here to keep an eye on Snape as well as Karkaroff?"

"Well, I dunno if that's what Dumbledore asked him to do, but he's definitely doing it," said Harry, waving his wand without paying much attention, so that his cushion did an odd sort of belly flop off the desk. "Moody said Dumbledore only lets Snape stay here because he's giving him a second chance or something. . . ."

"What?" said Ron, his eyes widening, his next cushion spinning high into the air, ricocheting off the chandelier, and dropping heavily onto Flitwick's desk. "Harry . . . maybe Moody thinks *Snape* put your name in the Goblet of Fire!"

"Oh Ron," said Hermione, shaking her head skeptically, "we thought Snape was trying to kill Harry before, and it turned out he was saving Harry's life, remember?"

She Banished a cushion and it flew across the room and landed in the box they were all supposed to be aiming at. Harry looked at Hermione, thinking . . . it was true that Snape had saved his life once, but the odd thing was, Snape definitely loathed him, just as he'd loathed Harry's father when they had been at school together. Snape loved taking points from Harry, and had certainly never missed an opportunity to give him punishments, or even to suggest that he should be suspended from the school.

"I don't care what Moody says," Hermione went on. "Dumbledore's not stupid. He was right to trust Hagrid and Professor Lupin, even though loads of people wouldn't have given them jobs, so why shouldn't he be right about Snape, even if Snape is a bit —"

"— evil," said Ron promptly. "Come on, Hermione, why are all these Dark wizard catchers searching his office, then?"

"Why has Mr. Crouch been pretending to be ill?" said Hermione, ignoring Ron. "It's a bit funny, isn't it, that he can't manage to come to the Yule Ball, but he can get up here in the middle of the night when he wants to?"

"You just don't like Crouch because of that elf, Winky," said Ron, sending a cushion soaring into the window.

"*You* just want to think Snape's up to something," said Hermione, sending her cushion zooming neatly into the box.

"I just want to know what Snape did with his first chance, if he's on his second one," said Harry grimly, and his cushion, to his very great surprise, flew straight across the room and landed neatly on top of Hermione's.

Obedient to Sirius's wish of hearing about anything odd at Hogwarts, Harry sent him a letter by brown owl that night, explaining all about Mr. Crouch breaking into Snape's office, and Moody and Snape's conversation. Then Harry turned his attention in earnest to the most urgent problem facing him: how to survive underwater for an hour on the twenty-fourth of February.

Ron quite liked the idea of using the Summoning Charm again — Harry had explained about Aqua-Lungs, and Ron couldn't see why Harry shouldn't Summon one from the nearest Muggle town. Hermione squashed this plan by pointing out that, in the unlikely event that Harry managed to learn how to operate an Aqua-Lung within the set limit of an hour, he was sure to be disqualified for breaking the International Code of Wizarding Secrecy — it was too much to hope that no Muggles would spot an Aqua-Lung zooming across the countryside to Hogwarts.

"Of course, the ideal solution would be for you to Transfigure yourself into a submarine or something," Hermione said. "If only we'd done human Transfiguration already! But I don't think we start that until sixth year, and it can go badly wrong if you don't know what you're doing. . . ."

"Yeah, I don't fancy walking around with a periscope sticking out of my head," said Harry. "I s'pose I could always attack someone in front of Moody; he might do it for me. . . ."

"I don't think he'd let you choose what you wanted to be turned into, though," said Hermione seriously. "No, I think your best chance is some sort of charm."

So Harry, thinking that he would soon have had enough of the library to last him a lifetime, buried himself once more among the dusty volumes, looking for any spell that might enable a human to survive without oxygen. However, though he, Ron, and Hermione searched through their lunchtimes, evenings, and whole weekends — though Harry asked Professor McGonagall for a note of permission to use the Restricted Section, and even asked the irritable, vulture-like librarian, Madam Pince, for help — they found nothing whatsoever that would enable Harry to spend an hour underwater and live to tell the tale.

Familiar flutterings of panic were starting to disturb Harry now, and he was finding it difficult to concentrate in class again. The lake, which Harry had always taken for granted as just another feature of the grounds, drew his eyes whenever he was near a classroom window, a great, iron-gray mass of chilly water, whose dark and icy depths were starting to seem as distant as the moon.

Just as it had before he faced the Horntail, time was slipping away as though somebody had bewitched the clocks to go extra-fast. There was a week to go before February the twenty-fourth (there was still time) . . . there were five days to go (he was bound to find something soon) . . . three days to go (*please let me find something . . . please*) . . .

With two days left, Harry started to go off food again. The only good thing about breakfast on Monday was the return of the brown owl he had sent to Sirius. He pulled off the parchment, unrolled it, and saw the shortest letter Sirius had ever written to him.

*Send date of next Hogsmeade weekend by return owl.*

Harry turned the parchment over and looked at the back, hoping to see something else, but it was blank.

"Weekend after next," whispered Hermione, who had read the note over Harry's shoulder. "Here — take my quill and send this owl back straight away."

Harry scribbled the dates down on the back of Sirius's letter, tied it onto the brown owl's leg, and watched it take flight again. What had he expected? Advice on how to survive underwater? He had been so intent on telling Sirius all about Snape and Moody he had completely forgotten to mention the egg's clue.

"What's he want to know about the next Hogsmeade weekend for?" said Ron.

"Dunno," said Harry dully. The momentary happiness that had flared inside him at the sight of the owl had died. "Come on . . . Care of Magical Creatures."

Whether Hagrid was trying to make up for the Blast-Ended Skrewts, or because there were now only two skrewts left, or because he was trying to prove he could do anything that Professor Grubbly-Plank could, Harry didn't know, but Hagrid had been continuing her lessons on unicorns ever since he'd returned to work. It turned out that Hagrid knew quite as much about unicorns as he did about monsters, though it was clear that he found their lack of poisonous fangs disappointing.

Today he had managed to capture two unicorn foals. Unlike full-grown unicorns, they were pure gold. Parvati and Lavender went into transports of delight at the sight of them, and even Pansy Parkinson had to work hard to conceal how much she liked them.

"Easier ter spot than the adults," Hagrid told the class. "They turn silver when they're abou' two years old, an' they grow horns at aroun' four. Don' go pure white till they're full grown, 'round about seven. They're a bit more trustin' when they're babies . . . don' mind boys so much. . . . C'mon, move in a bit, yeh can pat 'em if yeh want . . . give 'em a few o' these sugar lumps. . . ."

"You okay, Harry?" Hagrid muttered, moving aside slightly, while most of the others swarmed around the baby unicorns.

"Yeah," said Harry.

"Jus' nervous, eh?" said Hagrid.

"Bit," said Harry.

"Harry," said Hagrid, clapping a massive hand on his shoulder, so that Harry's knees buckled under its weight, "I'd've bin worried before I saw yeh take on tha' Horntail, but I know now yeh can do anythin' yeh set yer mind ter. I'm not worried at all. Yeh're goin' ter be fine. Got yer clue worked out, haven' yeh?"

Harry nodded, but even as he did so, an insane urge to confess that he didn't have any idea how to survive at the bottom of the lake for an hour came over him. He looked up at Hagrid — perhaps he had to go into the lake sometimes, to deal with the creatures in it? He looked after everything else on the grounds, after all —

"Yeh're goin' ter win," Hagrid growled, patting Harry's shoulder again, so that Harry actually felt himself sink a couple of inches into the soft ground. "I know it. I can feel it. *Yeh're goin' ter win, Harry.*"

Harry just couldn't bring himself to wipe the happy, confident smile off Hagrid's face. Pretending he was interested in the young unicorns, he forced a smile in return, and moved forward to pat them with the others.

By the evening before the second task, Harry felt as though he were trapped in a nightmare. He was fully aware that even if, by some miracle, he managed to find a suitable spell, he'd have a real job mastering it overnight. How could he have let this happen? Why hadn't he got to work on the egg's clue sooner? Why had he ever let his mind wander in class — what if a teacher had once mentioned how to breathe underwater?

He sat with Hermione and Ron in the library as the sun set outside, tearing feverishly through page after page of spells, hidden from one another by the massive piles of books on the desk in front of each of them. Harry's heart gave a huge leap every time he saw the word "water" on a page, but more often than not it was merely "Take two pints of water, half a pound of shredded mandrake leaves, and a newt . . ."

"I don't reckon it can be done," said Ron's voice flatly from the other side of the table. "There's nothing. *Nothing.* Closest was that thing to dry up puddles and ponds, that Drought Charm, but that was nowhere near powerful enough to drain the lake."

"There must be something," Hermione muttered, moving a candle closer to her. Her eyes were so tired she was poring over the tiny print of *Olde and Forgotten Bewitchments and Charmes* with her nose about an inch from the page. "They'd never have set a task that was undoable."

"They have," said Ron. "Harry, just go down to the lake tomorrow, right, stick your head in, yell at the merpeople to give back whatever they've nicked, and see if they chuck it out. Best you can do, mate."

"There's a way of doing it!" Hermione said crossly. "There just has to be!"

She seemed to be taking the library's lack of useful information on the subject as a personal insult; it had never failed her before.

"I know what I should have done," said Harry, resting, face-down, on *Saucy Tricks for Tricky Sorts.* "I should've learned to be an Animagus like Sirius."

An Animagus was a wizard who could transform into an animal.

"Yeah, you could've turned into a goldfish any time you wanted!" said Ron.

"Or a frog," yawned Harry. He was exhausted.

"It takes years to become an Animagus, and then you have to

register yourself and everything," said Hermione vaguely, now squinting down the index of *Weird Wizarding Dilemmas and Their Solutions.* "Professor McGonagall told us, remember . . . you've got to register yourself with the Improper Use of Magic Office . . . what animal you become, and your markings, so you can't abuse it. . . ."

"Hermione, I was joking," said Harry wearily. "I know I haven't got a chance of turning into a frog by tomorrow morning. . . ."

"Oh this is no use," Hermione said, snapping shut *Weird Wizarding Dilemmas.* "Who on earth wants to make their nose hair grow into ringlets?"

"I wouldn't mind," said Fred Weasley's voice. "Be a talking point, wouldn't it?"

Harry, Ron, and Hermione looked up. Fred and George had just emerged from behind some bookshelves.

"What're you two doing here?" Ron asked.

"Looking for you," said George. "McGonagall wants you, Ron. And you, Hermione."

"Why?" said Hermione, looking surprised.

"Dunno . . . she was looking a bit grim, though," said Fred.

"We're supposed to take you down to her office," said George.

Ron and Hermione stared at Harry, who felt his stomach drop. Was Professor McGonagall about to tell Ron and Hermione off? Perhaps she'd noticed how much they were helping him, when he ought to be working out how to do the task alone?

"We'll meet you back in the common room," Hermione told Harry as she got up to go with Ron — both of them looked very anxious. "Bring as many of these books as you can, okay?"

"Right," said Harry uneasily.

By eight o'clock, Madam Pince had extinguished all the lamps and came to chivvy Harry out of the library. Staggering under the weight of as many books as he could carry, Harry returned to the Gryffindor common room, pulled a table into a corner, and continued to search. There was nothing in *Madcap Magic for Wacky Warlocks* . . . nothing in *A Guide to Medieval Sorcery* . . . not one mention of underwater exploits in *An Anthology of Eighteenth-Century Charms,* or in *Dreadful Denizens of the Deep,* or *Powers You Never Knew You Had and What to Do with Them Now You've Wised Up.*

Crookshanks crawled into Harry's lap and curled up, purring deeply. The common room emptied slowly around Harry. People kept wishing him luck for the next morning in cheery, confident voices like Hagrid's, all of them apparently convinced that he was about to pull off another stunning performance like the one he had managed in the first task. Harry couldn't answer them, he just nodded, feeling as though there were a golf ball stuck in his throat. By ten to midnight, he was alone in the room with Crookshanks. He had searched all the remaining books, and Ron and Hermione had not come back.

It's over, he told himself. You can't do it. You'll just have to go down to the lake in the morning and tell the judges. . . .

He imagined himself explaining that he couldn't do the task. He pictured Bagman's look of round-eyed surprise, Karkaroff's satisfied, yellow-toothed smile. He could almost hear Fleur Delacour saying *"I knew it . . . 'e is too young, 'e is only a little boy."* He saw Malfoy flashing his *POTTER STINKS* badge at the front of the crowd, saw Hagrid's crestfallen, disbelieving face. . . .

Forgetting that Crookshanks was on his lap, Harry stood up

very suddenly; Crookshanks hissed angrily as he landed on the floor, gave Harry a disgusted look, and stalked away with his bottlebrush tail in the air, but Harry was already hurrying up the spiral staircase to his dormitory. . . . He would grab the Invisibility Cloak and go back to the library, he'd stay there all night if he had to. . . .

"*Lumos,*" Harry whispered fifteen minutes later as he opened the library door.

Wand-tip alight, he crept along the bookshelves, pulling down more books — books of hexes and charms, books on merpeople and water monsters, books on famous witches and wizards, on magical inventions, on anything at all that might include one passing reference to underwater survival. He carried them over to a table, then set to work, searching them by the narrow beam of his wand, occasionally checking his watch. . . .

One in the morning . . . two in the morning . . . the only way he could keep going was to tell himself, over and over again, *next book . . . in the next one . . . the next one . . .*

The mermaid in the painting in the prefects' bathroom was laughing. Harry was bobbing like a cork in bubbly water next to her rock, while she held his Firebolt over his head.

"Come and get it!" she giggled maliciously. "Come on, jump!"

"I can't," Harry panted, snatching at the Firebolt, and struggling not to sink. "Give it to me!"

But she just poked him painfully in the side with the end of the broomstick, laughing at him.

"That hurts — get off — ouch —"

"Harry Potter must wake up, sir!"

"Stop poking me —"

"Dobby must poke Harry Potter, sir, he must wake up!"

Harry opened his eyes. He was still in the library; the Invisibility Cloak had slipped off his head as he'd slept, and the side of his face was stuck to the pages of *Where There's a Wand, There's a Way*. He sat up, straightening his glasses, blinking in the bright daylight.

"Harry Potter needs to hurry!" squeaked Dobby. "The second task starts in ten minutes, and Harry Potter —"

"Ten minutes?" Harry croaked. "Ten — *ten minutes?*"

He looked down at his watch. Dobby was right. It was twenty past nine. A large, dead weight seemed to fall through Harry's chest into his stomach.

"Hurry, Harry Potter!" squeaked Dobby, plucking at Harry's sleeve. "You is supposed to be down by the lake with the other champions, sir!"

"It's too late, Dobby," Harry said hopelessly. "I'm not doing the task, I don't know how —"

"Harry Potter *will* do the task!" squeaked the elf. "Dobby knew Harry had not found the right book, so Dobby did it for him!"

"What?" said Harry. "But *you* don't know what the second task is —"

"Dobby knows, sir! Harry Potter has to go into the lake and find his Wheezy —"

"Find my what?"

"— and take his Wheezy back from the merpeople!"

"What's a Wheezy?"

"Your Wheezy, sir, your Wheezy — Wheezy who is giving Dobby his sweater!"

Dobby plucked at the shrunken maroon sweater he was now wearing over his shorts.

"*What?*" Harry gasped. "They've got . . . they've got *Ron?*"

"The thing Harry Potter will miss most, sir!" squeaked Dobby. "'*But past an hour* —'"

"— '*the prospect's black,*'" Harry recited, staring, horror-struck, at the elf. "'*Too late, it's gone, it won't come back.*' Dobby — what've I got to do?"

"You has to eat this, sir!" squeaked the elf, and he put his hand in the pocket of his shorts and drew out a ball of what looked like slimy, grayish-green rat tails. "Right before you go into the lake, sir — gillyweed!"

"What's it do?" said Harry, staring at the gillyweed.

"It will make Harry Potter breathe underwater, sir!"

"Dobby," said Harry frantically, "listen — are you sure about this?"

He couldn't quite forget that the last time Dobby had tried to "help" him, he had ended up with no bones in his right arm.

"Dobby is quite sure, sir!" said the elf earnestly. "Dobby hears things, sir, he is a house-elf, he goes all over the castle as he lights the fires and mops the floors. Dobby heard Professor McGonagall and Professor Moody in the staffroom, talking about the next task. . . . Dobby cannot let Harry Potter lose his Wheezy!"

Harry's doubts vanished. Jumping to his feet he pulled off the Invisibility Cloak, stuffed it into his bag, grabbed the gillyweed, and put it into his pocket, then tore out of the library with Dobby at his heels.

"Dobby is supposed to be in the kitchens, sir!" Dobby squealed as they burst into the corridor. "Dobby will be missed — good luck, Harry Potter, sir, good luck!"

"See you later, Dobby!" Harry shouted, and he sprinted along the corridor and down the stairs, three at a time.

The entrance hall contained a few last-minute stragglers, all leaving the Great Hall after breakfast and heading through the double oak doors to watch the second task. They stared as Harry flashed past, sending Colin and Dennis Creevey flying as he leapt down the stone steps and out onto the bright, chilly grounds.

As he pounded down the lawn he saw that the seats that had encircled the dragons' enclosure in November were now ranged along the opposite bank, rising in stands that were packed to the bursting point and reflected in the lake below. The excited babble of the crowd echoed strangely across the water as Harry ran flat-out around the other side of the lake toward the judges, who were sitting at another gold-draped table at the water's edge. Cedric, Fleur, and Krum were beside the judges' table, watching Harry sprint toward them.

"I'm . . . here . . ." Harry panted, skidding to a halt in the mud and accidentally splattering Fleur's robes.

"Where have you been?" said a bossy, disapproving voice. "The task's about to start!"

Harry looked around. Percy Weasley was sitting at the judges' table — Mr. Crouch had failed to turn up again.

"Now, now, Percy!" said Ludo Bagman, who was looking intensely relieved to see Harry. "Let him catch his breath!"

Dumbledore smiled at Harry, but Karkaroff and Madame Maxime didn't look at all pleased to see him. . . . It was obvious from the looks on their faces that they had thought he wasn't going to turn up.

Harry bent over, hands on his knees, gasping for breath; he had a stitch in his side that felt as though he had a knife between his ribs, but there was no time to get rid of it; Ludo Bagman was now moving among the champions, spacing them along the bank at intervals of ten feet. Harry was on the very end of the line, next to Krum, who was wearing swimming trunks and was holding his wand ready.

"All right, Harry?" Bagman whispered as he moved Harry a few feet farther away from Krum. "Know what you're going to do?"

"Yeah," Harry panted, massaging his ribs.

Bagman gave Harry's shoulder a quick squeeze and returned to the judges' table; he pointed his wand at his throat as he had done at the World Cup, said, *"Sonorus!"* and his voice boomed out across the dark water toward the stands.

"Well, all our champions are ready for the second task, which will start on my whistle. They have precisely an hour to recover what has been taken from them. On the count of three, then. One . . . two . . . *three!*"

The whistle echoed shrilly in the cold, still air; the stands erupted with cheers and applause; without looking to see what the other champions were doing, Harry pulled off his shoes and socks, pulled the handful of gillyweed out of his pocket, stuffed it into his mouth, and waded out into the lake.

It was so cold he felt the skin on his legs searing as though this were fire, not icy water. His sodden robes weighed him down as he walked in deeper; now the water was over his knees, and his rapidly numbing feet were slipping over silt and flat, slimy stones. He was chewing the gillyweed as hard and fast as he could; it felt unpleasantly slimy and rubbery, like octopus tentacles. Waist-deep in the freezing water he stopped, swallowed, and waited for something to happen.

He could hear laughter in the crowd and knew he must look stupid, walking into the lake without showing any sign of magical power. The part of him that was still dry was covered in goose pimples; half immersed in the icy water, a cruel breeze lifting his hair, Harry started to shiver violently. He avoided looking at the stands; the laughter was becoming louder, and there were catcalls and jeering from the Slytherins. . . .

Then, quite suddenly, Harry felt as though an invisible pillow had been pressed over his mouth and nose. He tried to draw breath, but it made his head spin; his lungs were empty, and he suddenly felt a piercing pain on either side of his neck —

Harry clapped his hands around his throat and felt two large slits just below his ears, flapping in the cold air. . . . *He had gills.* Without pausing to think, he did the only thing that made sense — he flung himself forward into the water.

The first gulp of icy lake water felt like the breath of life. His head had stopped spinning; he took another great gulp of water and felt it pass smoothly through his gills, sending oxygen back to his brain. He stretched out his hands in front of him and stared at them. They looked green and ghostly under the water, and they had become webbed. He twisted around and looked at his bare feet — they had become elongated and the toes were webbed too: It looked as though he had sprouted flippers.

The water didn't feel icy anymore either . . . on the contrary, he felt pleasantly cool and very light. . . . Harry struck out once more, marveling at how far and fast his flipper-like feet propelled him through the water, and noticing how clearly he could see, and how he no longer seemed to need to blink. He had soon swum so far into the lake that he could no longer see the bottom. He flipped over and dived into its depths.

Silence pressed upon his ears as he soared over a strange, dark, foggy landscape. He could only see ten feet around him, so that as he sped through the water new scenes seemed to loom suddenly out of the oncoming darkness: forests of rippling, tangled black weed, wide plains of mud littered with dull, glimmering stones. He swam deeper and deeper, out toward the middle of the lake, his eyes wide, staring through the eerily gray-lit water around him to the shadows beyond, where the water became opaque.

Small fish flickered past him like silver darts. Once or twice he thought he saw something larger moving ahead of him, but when he got nearer, he discovered it to be nothing but a large, black-ened log, or a dense clump of weed. There was no sign of any of the other champions, merpeople, Ron — nor, thankfully, the giant squid.

Light green weed stretched ahead of him as far as he could see, two feet deep, like a meadow of very overgrown grass. Harry was staring unblinkingly ahead of him, trying to discern shapes through the gloom . . . and then, without warning, something grabbed hold of his ankle.

Harry twisted his body around and saw a grindylow, a small, horned water demon, poking out of the weed, its long fingers clutched tightly around Harry's leg, its pointed fangs bared — Harry stuck his webbed hand quickly inside his robes and fumbled for his wand. By the time he had grasped it, two more grindylows had risen out of the weed, had seized handfuls of Harry's robes, and were attempting to drag him down.

*"Relashio!"* Harry shouted, except that no sound came out. . . . A large bubble issued from his mouth, and his wand, instead of sending sparks at the grindylows, pelted them with what seemed to be a jet of boiling water, for where it struck them, angry red patches appeared on their green skin. Harry pulled his ankle out of the grindylow's grip and swam, as fast as he could, occasionally sending more jets of hot water over his shoulder at random; every now and then he felt one of the grindylows snatch at his foot again, and he kicked out, hard; finally, he felt his foot connect with a horned skull, and looking back, saw the dazed grindylow floating away, cross-eyed, while its fellows shook their fists at Harry and sank back into the weed.

Harry slowed down a little, slipped his wand back inside his robes, and looked around, listening again. He turned full circle in the water, the silence pressing harder than ever against his eardrums. He knew he must be even deeper in the lake now, but nothing was moving but the rippling weed.

"How are you getting on?"

Harry thought he was having a heart attack. He whipped around and saw Moaning Myrtle floating hazily in front of him, gazing at him through her thick, pearly glasses.

"Myrtle!" Harry tried to shout — but once again, nothing came out of his mouth but a very large bubble. Moaning Myrtle actually giggled.

"You want to try over there!" she said, pointing. "I won't come with you. . . . I don't like them much, they always chase me when I get too close. . . ."

Harry gave her the thumbs-up to show his thanks and set off once more, careful to swim a bit higher over the weed to avoid any more grindylows that might be lurking there.

He swam on for what felt like at least twenty minutes. He was passing over vast expanses of black mud now, which swirled murkily as he disturbed the water. Then, at long last, he heard a snatch of haunting mersong.

> *"An hour long you'll have to look,*
> *And to recover what we took . . ."*

Harry swam faster and soon saw a large rock emerge out of the muddy water ahead. It had paintings of merpeople on it; they were carrying spears and chasing what looked like the giant squid. Harry swam on past the rock, following the mersong.

> *". . . your time's half gone, so tarry not*
> *Lest what you seek stays here to rot. . . ."*

A cluster of crude stone dwellings stained with algae loomed suddenly out of the gloom on all sides. Here and there at the dark windows, Harry saw faces . . . faces that bore no resemblance at all to the painting of the mermaid in the prefects' bathroom. . . .

The merpeople had grayish skin and long, wild, dark green hair. Their eyes were yellow, as were their broken teeth, and they wore thick ropes of pebbles around their necks. They leered at Harry as he swam past; one or two of them emerged from their caves to watch him better, their powerful, silver fish tails beating the water, spears clutched in their hands.

Harry sped on, staring around, and soon the dwellings became more numerous; there were gardens of weed around some of them, and he even saw a pet grindylow tied to a stake outside one door. Merpeople were emerging on all sides now, watching him eagerly, pointing at his webbed hands and gills, talking behind their hands to one another. Harry sped around a corner and a very strange sight met his eyes.

A whole crowd of merpeople was floating in front of the houses that lined what looked like a mer-version of a village square. A choir of merpeople was singing in the middle, calling the champions toward them, and behind them rose a crude sort of statue; a gigantic merperson hewn from a boulder. Four people were bound tightly to the tail of the stone merperson.

Ron was tied between Hermione and Cho Chang. There was also a girl who looked no older than eight, whose clouds of silvery hair made Harry feel sure that she was Fleur Delacour's sister. All four of them appeared to be in a very deep sleep. Their heads were lolling onto their shoulders, and fine streams of bubbles kept issuing from their mouths.

Harry sped toward the hostages, half expecting the merpeople to lower their spears and charge at him, but they did nothing. The ropes of weed tying the hostages to the statue were thick, slimy, and very strong. For a fleeting second he thought of the knife Sirius had bought him for Christmas — locked in his trunk in the castle a quarter of a mile away, no use to him whatsoever.

He looked around. Many of the merpeople surrounding them

were carrying spears. He swam swiftly toward a seven-foot-tall merman with a long green beard and a choker of shark fangs and tried to mime a request to borrow the spear. The merman laughed and shook his head.

"We do not help," he said in a harsh, croaky voice.

"Come ON!" Harry said fiercely (but only bubbles issued from his mouth), and he tried to pull the spear away from the merman, but the merman yanked it back, still shaking his head and laughing.

Harry swirled around, staring about. Something sharp . . . anything . . .

There were rocks littering the lake bottom. He dived and snatched up a particularly jagged one and returned to the statue. He began to hack at the ropes binding Ron, and after several minutes' hard work, they broke apart. Ron floated, unconscious, a few inches above the lake bottom, drifting a little in the ebb of the water.

Harry looked around. There was no sign of any of the other champions. What were they playing at? Why didn't they hurry up? He turned back to Hermione, raised the jagged rock, and began to hack at her bindings too —

At once, several pairs of strong gray hands seized him. Half a dozen mermen were pulling him away from Hermione, shaking their green-haired heads, and laughing.

"You take your own hostage," one of them said to him. "Leave the others . . ."

"No way!" said Harry furiously — but only two large bubbles came out.

"Your task is to retrieve your own friend . . . leave the others . . ."

"She's my friend too!" Harry yelled, gesturing toward Hermione, an enormous silver bubble emerging soundlessly from his lips. "And I don't want *them* to die either!"

Cho's head was on Hermione's shoulder; the small silver-haired girl was ghostly green and pale. Harry struggled to fight off the mermen, but they laughed harder than ever, holding him back. Harry looked wildly around. Where were the other champions? Would he have time to take Ron to the surface and come back down for Hermione and the others? Would he be able to find them again? He looked down at his watch to see how much time was left — it had stopped working.

But then the merpeople around him started pointing excitedly over his head. Harry looked up and saw Cedric swimming toward them. There was an enormous bubble around his head, which made his features look oddly wide and stretched.

"Got lost!" he mouthed, looking panic-stricken. "Fleur and Krum're coming now!"

Feeling enormously relieved, Harry watched Cedric pull a knife out of his pocket and cut Cho free. He pulled her upward and out of sight.

Harry looked around, waiting. Where were Fleur and Krum? Time was getting short, and according to the song, the hostages would be lost after an hour. . . .

The merpeople started screeching animatedly. Those holding Harry loosened their grip, staring behind them. Harry turned and saw something monstrous cutting through the water toward them: a human body in swimming trunks with the head of a shark. . . . It was Krum. He appeared to have transfigured himself — but badly.

The shark-man swam straight to Hermione and began snapping and biting at her ropes; the trouble was that Krum's new teeth were positioned very awkwardly for biting anything smaller than a dolphin, and Harry was quite sure that if Krum wasn't careful, he was going to rip Hermione in half. Darting forward, Harry hit Krum hard on the shoulder and held up the jagged stone. Krum seized it and began to cut Hermione free. Within seconds, he had done it; he grabbed Hermione around the waist, and without a backward glance, began to rise rapidly with her toward the surface.

*Now what?* Harry thought desperately. If he could be sure that Fleur was coming. . . . But still no sign. There was nothing to be done except . . .

He snatched up the stone, which Krum had dropped, but the mermen now closed in around Ron and the little girl, shaking their heads at him. Harry pulled out his wand.

"Get out of the way!"

Only bubbles flew out of his mouth, but he had the distinct impression that the mermen had understood him, because they suddenly stopped laughing. Their yellowish eyes were fixed upon Harry's wand, and they looked scared. There might be a lot more of them than there were of him, but Harry could tell, by the looks on their faces, that they knew no more magic than the giant squid did.

"You've got until three!" Harry shouted; a great stream of bubbles burst from him, but he held up three fingers to make sure they got the message. "One . . ." (he put down a finger) "two . . ." (he put down a second one) —

They scattered. Harry darted forward and began to hack at the ropes binding the small girl to the statue, and at last she was free. He seized the little girl around the waist, grabbed the neck of Ron's robes, and kicked off from the bottom.

It was very slow work. He could no longer use his webbed hands to propel himself forward; he worked his flippers furiously, but Ron and Fleur's sister were like potato-filled sacks dragging him back down. . . . He fixed his eyes skyward, though he knew he must still be very deep, the water above him was so dark. . . .

Merpeople were rising with him. He could see them swirling around him with ease, watching him struggle through the water. . . . Would they pull him back down to the depths when the time was up? Did they perhaps eat humans? Harry's legs were seizing up with the effort to keep swimming; his shoulders were aching horribly with the effort of dragging Ron and the girl. . . .

He was drawing breath with extreme difficulty. He could feel pain on the sides of his neck again . . . he was becoming very aware of how wet the water was in his mouth . . . yet the darkness was definitely thinning now . . . he could see daylight above him. . . .

He kicked hard with his flippers and discovered that they were nothing more than feet . . . water was flooding through his mouth into his lungs . . . he was starting to feel dizzy, but he knew light and air were only ten feet above him . . . he had to get there . . . he had to . . .

Harry kicked his legs so hard and fast it felt as though his muscles were screaming in protest; his very brain felt waterlogged, he couldn't breathe, he needed oxygen, he had to keep going, he could not stop —

And then he felt his head break the surface of the lake; wonderful, cold, clear air was making his wet face sting; he gulped it down, feeling as though he had never breathed properly before, and, panting, pulled Ron and the little girl up with him. All around him, wild, green-haired heads were emerging out of the water with him, but they were smiling at him.

The crowd in the stands was making a great deal of noise; shouting and screaming, they all seemed to be on their feet; Harry had the impression they thought that Ron and the little girl might be dead, but they were wrong . . . both of them had opened their eyes; the girl looked scared and confused, but Ron merely expelled a great spout of water, blinked in the bright light, turned to Harry, and said, "Wet, this, isn't it?" Then he spotted Fleur's sister. "What did you bring her for?"

"Fleur didn't turn up, I couldn't leave her," Harry panted.

"Harry, you prat," said Ron, "you didn't take that song thing seriously, did you? Dumbledore wouldn't have let any of us drown!"

"The song said —"

"It was only to make sure you got back inside the time limit!" said Ron. "I hope you didn't waste time down there acting the hero!"

Harry felt both stupid and annoyed. It was all very well for Ron; *he'd* been asleep, he hadn't felt how eerie it was down in the lake, surrounded by spear-carrying merpeople who'd looked more than capable of murder.

"C'mon," Harry said shortly, "help me with her, I don't think she can swim very well."

They pulled Fleur's sister through the water, back toward the bank where the judges stood watching, twenty merpeople accompanying them like a guard of honor, singing their horrible screechy songs.

Harry could see Madam Pomfrey fussing over Hermione, Krum, Cedric, and Cho, all of whom were wrapped in thick blankets.

Dumbledore and Ludo Bagman stood beaming at Harry and Ron from the bank as they swam nearer, but Percy, who looked very white and somehow much younger than usual, came splashing out to meet them. Meanwhile Madame Maxime was trying to restrain Fleur Delacour, who was quite hysterical, fighting tooth and nail to return to the water.

"Gabrielle! *Gabrielle! Is she alive? Is she 'urt?*"

"She's fine!" Harry tried to tell her, but he was so exhausted he could hardly talk, let alone shout.

Percy seized Ron and was dragging him back to the bank ("Gerroff, Percy, I'm all right!"); Dumbledore and Bagman were pulling Harry upright; Fleur had broken free of Madame Maxime and was hugging her sister.

"It was ze grindylows . . . zey attacked me . . . oh Gabrielle, I thought . . . I thought . . ."

"Come here, you," said Madam Pomfrey. She seized Harry and pulled him over to Hermione and the others, wrapped him so tightly in a blanket that he felt as though he were in a straitjacket, and forced a measure of very hot potion down his throat. Steam gushed out of his ears.

"Harry, well done!" Hermione cried. "You did it, you found out how all by yourself!"

"Well —" said Harry. He would have told her about Dobby, but he had just noticed Karkaroff watching him. He was the only judge who had not left the table; the only judge not showing signs of pleasure and relief that Harry, Ron, and Fleur's sister had got back safely. "Yeah, that's right," said Harry, raising his voice slightly so that Karkaroff could hear him.

"You haff a water beetle in your hair, Herm-own-ninny," said

Krum. Harry had the impression that Krum was drawing her attention back onto himself; perhaps to remind her that he had just rescued her from the lake, but Hermione brushed away the beetle impatiently and said, "You're well outside the time limit, though, Harry. . . . Did it take you ages to find us?"

"No . . . I found you okay. . . ."

Harry's feeling of stupidity was growing. Now he was out of the water, it seemed perfectly clear that Dumbledore's safety precautions wouldn't have permitted the death of a hostage just because their champion hadn't turned up. Why hadn't he just grabbed Ron and gone? He would have been first back. . . . Cedric and Krum hadn't wasted time worrying about anyone else; they hadn't taken the mersong seriously. . . .

Dumbledore was crouching at the water's edge, deep in conversation with what seemed to be the chief merperson, a particularly wild and ferocious-looking female. He was making the same sort of screechy noises that the merpeople made when they were above water; clearly, Dumbledore could speak Mermish. Finally he straightened up, turned to his fellow judges, and said, "A conference before we give the marks, I think."

The judges went into a huddle. Madam Pomfrey had gone to rescue Ron from Percy's clutches; she led him over to Harry and the others, gave him a blanket and some Pepperup Potion, then went to fetch Fleur and her sister. Fleur had many cuts on her face and arms and her robes were torn, but she didn't seem to care, nor would she allow Madam Pomfrey to clean them.

"Look after Gabrielle," she told her, and then she turned to Harry. "You saved 'er," she said breathlessly. "Even though she was not your 'ostage."

"Yeah," said Harry, who was now heartily wishing he'd left all three girls tied to the statue.

Fleur bent down, kissed Harry twice on each cheek (he felt his face burn and wouldn't have been surprised if steam was coming out of his ears again), then said to Ron, "And you too — you 'elped —"

"Yeah," said Ron, looking extremely hopeful, "yeah, a bit —"

Fleur swooped down on him too and kissed him. Hermione looked simply furious, but just then, Ludo Bagman's magically magnified voice boomed out beside them, making them all jump, and causing the crowd in the stands to go very quiet.

"Ladies and gentlemen, we have reached our decision. Merchieftainess Murcus has told us exactly what happened at the bottom of the lake, and we have therefore decided to award marks out of fifty for each of the champions, as follows. . . .

"Fleur Delacour, though she demonstrated excellent use of the Bubble-Head Charm, was attacked by grindylows as she approached her goal, and failed to retrieve her hostage. We award her twenty-five points."

Applause from the stands.

"I deserved zero," said Fleur throatily, shaking her magnificent head.

"Cedric Diggory, who also used the Bubble-Head Charm, was first to return with his hostage, though he returned one minute outside the time limit of an hour." Enormous cheers from the Hufflepuffs in the crowd; Harry saw Cho give Cedric a glowing look. "We therefore award him forty-seven points."

Harry's heart sank. If Cedric had been outside the time limit, he most certainly had been.

"Viktor Krum used an incomplete form of Transfiguration, which was nevertheless effective, and was second to return with his hostage. We award him forty points."

Karkaroff clapped particularly hard, looking very superior.

"Harry Potter used gillyweed to great effect," Bagman continued. "He returned last, and well outside the time limit of an hour. However, the Merchieftainess informs us that Mr. Potter was first to reach the hostages, and that the delay in his return was due to his determination to return all hostages to safety, not merely his own."

Ron and Hermione both gave Harry half-exasperated, half-commiserating looks.

"Most of the judges," and here, Bagman gave Karkaroff a very nasty look, "feel that this shows moral fiber and merits full marks. However . . . Mr. Potter's score is forty-five points."

Harry's stomach leapt — he was now tying for first place with *Cedric*. Ron and Hermione, caught by surprise, stared at Harry, then laughed and started applauding hard with the rest of the crowd.

"There you go, Harry!" Ron shouted over the noise. "You weren't being thick after all — you were showing moral fiber!"

Fleur was clapping very hard too, but Krum didn't look happy at all. He attempted to engage Hermione in conversation again, but she was too busy cheering Harry to listen.

"The third and final task will take place at dusk on the twenty-fourth of June," continued Bagman. "The champions will be notified of what is coming precisely one month beforehand. Thank you all for your support of the champions."

It was over, Harry thought dazedly, as Madam Pomfrey began herding the champions and hostages back to the castle to get into dry clothes . . . it was over, he had got through . . . he didn't have to worry about anything now until June the twenty-fourth. . . .

Next time he was in Hogsmeade, Harry decided as he walked back up the stone steps into the castle, he was going to buy Dobby a pair of socks for every day of the year.

# PADFOOT RETURNS

One of the best things about the aftermath of the second task was that everybody was very keen to hear details of what had happened down in the lake, which meant that Ron was getting to share Harry's limelight for once. Harry noticed that Ron's version of events changed subtly with every retelling. At first, he gave what seemed to be the truth; it tallied with Hermione's story, anyway — Dumbledore had put all the hostages into a bewitched sleep in Professor McGonagall's office, first assuring them that they would be quite safe, and would awake when they were back above the water. One week later, however, Ron was telling a thrilling tale of kidnap in which he struggled single-handedly against fifty heavily armed merpeople who had to beat him into submission before tying him up.

"But I had my wand hidden up my sleeve," he assured Padma Patil, who seemed to be a lot keener on Ron now that he was getting so much attention and was making a point of talking to him every time they passed in the corridors. "I could've taken those mer-idiots any time I wanted."

"What were you going to do, snore at them?" said Hermione waspishly. People had been teasing her so much about being the thing that Viktor Krum would most miss that she was in a rather tetchy mood.

Ron's ears went red, and thereafter, he reverted to the bewitched sleep version of events.

As they entered March the weather became drier, but cruel winds skinned their hands and faces every time they went out onto the grounds. There were delays in the post because the owls kept being blown off course. The brown owl that Harry had sent to Sirius with the dates of the Hogsmeade weekend turned up at breakfast on Friday morning with half its feathers sticking up the wrong way; Harry had no sooner torn off Sirius's reply than it took flight, clearly afraid it was going to be sent outside again.

Sirius's letter was almost as short as the previous one.

> *Be at stile at end of road out of Hogsmeade (past Dervish and Banges) at two o'clock on Saturday afternoon. Bring as much food as you can.*

"He hasn't come back to Hogsmeade?" said Ron incredulously.

"It looks like it, doesn't it?" said Hermione.

"I can't believe him," said Harry tensely, "if he's caught . . ."

"Made it so far, though, hasn't he?" said Ron. "And it's not like the place is swarming with dementors anymore."

Harry folded up the letter, thinking. If he was honest with himself, he really wanted to see Sirius again. He therefore approached the final lesson of the afternoon — double Potions — feeling considerably more cheerful than he usually did when descending the steps to the dungeons.

Malfoy, Crabbe, and Goyle were standing in a huddle outside the classroom door with Pansy Parkinson's gang of Slytherin girls. All of them were looking at something Harry couldn't see and sniggering heartily. Pansy's pug-like face peered excitedly around Goyle's broad back as Harry, Ron, and Hermione approached.

"There they are, there they are!" she giggled, and the knot of Slytherins broke apart. Harry saw that Pansy had a magazine in her hands — *Witch Weekly*. The moving picture on the front showed a curly-haired witch who was smiling toothily and pointing at a large sponge cake with her wand.

"You might find something to interest you in there, Granger!" Pansy said loudly, and she threw the magazine at Hermione, who caught it, looking startled. At that moment, the dungeon door opened, and Snape beckoned them all inside.

Hermione, Harry, and Ron headed for a table at the back of the dungeon as usual. Once Snape had turned his back on them to write up the ingredients of today's potion on the blackboard, Hermione hastily rifled through the magazine under the desk. At last, in the center pages, Hermione found what they were looking for. Harry and Ron leaned in closer. A color photograph of Harry headed a short piece entitled:

### Harry Potter's Secret Heartache

A boy like no other, perhaps — yet a boy suffering all the usual pangs of adolescence, *writes Rita Skeeter*. Deprived of love since the tragic demise of his parents, fourteen-year-old Harry Potter thought he had found solace in his steady girlfriend at Hogwarts, Muggle-born Hermione Granger. Little did he know that he would shortly be suffering yet another emotional blow in a life already littered with personal loss.

Miss Granger, a plain but ambitious girl, seems to have a taste for famous wizards that Harry alone cannot satisfy. Since the arrival at Hogwarts of Viktor Krum, Bulgarian Seeker and hero of the last World Quidditch Cup, Miss Granger has been toying with both boys' affections. Krum, who is openly smitten with the devious Miss Granger, has already invited her to visit him in Bulgaria over the summer holidays, and insists that he has "never felt this way about any other girl."

However, it might not be Miss Granger's doubtful natural charms that have captured these unfortunate boys' interest.

"She's really ugly," says Pansy Parkinson, a pretty and vivacious fourth-year student, "but she'd be well up to making a Love Potion, she's quite brainy. I think that's how she's doing it."

Love Potions are, of course, banned at Hogwarts, and no doubt Albus Dumbledore will want to investigate these claims. In the meantime, Harry Potter's well-wishers must hope that, next time, he bestows his heart on a worthier candidate.

"I told you!" Ron hissed at Hermione as she stared down at the article. "I *told* you not to annoy Rita Skeeter! She's made you out to be some sort of — of scarlet woman!"

Hermione stopped looking astonished and snorted with laughter. *"Scarlet woman?"* she repeated, shaking with suppressed giggles as she looked around at Ron.

"It's what my mum calls them," Ron muttered, his ears going red.

"If that's the best Rita can do, she's losing her touch," said Hermione, still giggling, as she threw *Witch Weekly* onto the empty chair beside her. "What a pile of old rubbish."

She looked over at the Slytherins, who were all watching her and Harry closely across the room to see if they had been upset by the article. Hermione gave them a sarcastic smile and a wave, and she, Harry, and Ron started unpacking the ingredients they would need for their Wit-Sharpening Potion.

"There's something funny, though," said Hermione ten minutes later, holding her pestle suspended over a bowl of scarab beetles. "How could Rita Skeeter have known . . . ?"

"Known what?" said Ron quickly. "You *haven't* been mixing up Love Potions, have you?"

"Don't be stupid," Hermione snapped, starting to pound up her beetles again. "No, it's just . . . how did she know Viktor asked me to visit him over the summer?"

Hermione blushed scarlet as she said this and determinedly avoided Ron's eyes.

"What?" said Ron, dropping his pestle with a loud clunk.

"He asked me right after he'd pulled me out of the lake,"

Hermione muttered. "After he'd got rid of his shark's head. Madam Pomfrey gave us both blankets and then he sort of pulled me away from the judges so they wouldn't hear, and he said, if I wasn't doing anything over the summer, would I like to —"

"And what did you say?" said Ron, who had picked up his pestle and was grinding it on the desk, a good six inches from his bowl, because he was looking at Hermione.

"And he *did* say he'd never felt the same way about anyone else," Hermione went on, going so red now that Harry could almost feel the heat coming from her, "but how could Rita Skeeter have heard him? She wasn't there . . . or was she? Maybe she *has* got an Invisibility Cloak; maybe she sneaked onto the grounds to watch the second task. . . ."

"And what did you say?" Ron repeated, pounding his pestle down so hard that it dented the desk.

"Well, I was too busy seeing whether you and Harry were okay to —"

"Fascinating though your social life undoubtedly is, Miss Granger," said an icy voice right behind them, and all three of them jumped, "I must ask you not to discuss it in my class. Ten points from Gryffindor."

Snape had glided over to their desk while they were talking. The whole class was now looking around at them; Malfoy took the opportunity to flash *POTTER STINKS* across the dungeon at Harry.

"Ah . . . reading magazines under the table as well?" Snape added, snatching up the copy of *Witch Weekly*. "A further ten points from Gryffindor . . . oh but of course . . ." Snape's black eyes glittered as they fell on Rita Skeeter's article. "Potter has to keep up with his press cuttings. . . ."

The dungeon rang with the Slytherins' laughter, and an unpleasant smile curled Snape's thin mouth. To Harry's fury, he began to read the article aloud.

"*'Harry Potter's Secret Heartache'.* . . dear, dear, Potter, what's ailing you now? *'A boy like no other, perhaps . . .'*"

Harry could feel his face burning. Snape was pausing at the end of every sentence to allow the Slytherins a hearty laugh. The article sounded ten times worse when read by Snape. Even Hermione was blushing scarlet now.

"'. . . *Harry Potter's well-wishers must hope that, next time, he bestows his heart upon a worthier candidate.'* How very touching," sneered Snape, rolling up the magazine to continued gales of laughter from the Slytherins. "Well, I think I had better separate the three of you, so you can keep your minds on your potions rather than on your tangled love lives. Weasley, you stay here. Miss Granger, over there, beside Miss Parkinson. Potter — that table in front of my desk. Move. Now."

Furious, Harry threw his ingredients and his bag into his cauldron and dragged it up to the front of the dungeon to the empty table. Snape followed, sat down at his desk and watched Harry unload his cauldron. Determined not to look at Snape, Harry resumed the mashing of his scarab beetles, imagining each one to have Snape's face.

"All this press attention seems to have inflated your already overlarge head, Potter," said Snape quietly, once the rest of the class had settled down again.

Harry didn't answer. He knew Snape was trying to provoke him; he had done this before. No doubt he was hoping for an excuse to take a round fifty points from Gryffindor before the end of the class.

"You might be laboring under the delusion that the entire Wizarding world is impressed with you," Snape went on, so quietly that no one else could hear him (Harry continued to pound his scarab beetles, even though he had already reduced them to a very fine powder), "but I don't care how many times your picture appears in the papers. To me, Potter, you are nothing but a nasty little boy who considers rules to be beneath him."

Harry tipped the powdered beetles into his cauldron and started cutting up his ginger roots. His hands were shaking slightly out of anger, but he kept his eyes down, as though he couldn't hear what Snape was saying to him.

"So I give you fair warning, Potter," Snape continued in a softer and more dangerous voice, "pint-sized celebrity or not — if I catch you breaking into my office one more time —"

"I haven't been anywhere near your office!" said Harry angrily, forgetting his feigned deafness.

"Don't lie to me," Snape hissed, his fathomless black eyes boring into Harry's. "Boomslang skin. Gillyweed. Both come from my private stores, and I know who stole them."

Harry stared back at Snape, determined not to blink or to look guilty. In truth, he hadn't stolen either of these things from Snape. Hermione had taken the boomslang skin back in their second year — they had needed it for the Polyjuice Potion — and while Snape had suspected Harry at the time, he had never been able to prove it. Dobby, of course, had stolen the gillyweed.

"I don't know what you're talking about," Harry lied coldly.

"You were out of bed on the night my office was broken into!" Snape hissed. "I know it, Potter! Now, Mad-Eye Moody might have joined your fan club, but I will not tolerate your behavior!

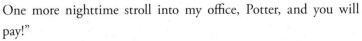

One more nighttime stroll into my office, Potter, and you will pay!"

"Right," said Harry coolly, turning back to his ginger roots. "I'll bear that in mind if I ever get the urge to go in there."

Snape's eyes flashed. He plunged a hand into the inside of his black robes. For one wild moment, Harry thought Snape was about to pull out his wand and curse him — then he saw that Snape had drawn out a small crystal bottle of a completely clear potion. Harry stared at it.

"Do you know what this is, Potter?" Snape said, his eyes glittering dangerously again.

"No," said Harry, with complete honesty this time.

"It is Veritaserum — a Truth Potion so powerful that three drops would have you spilling your innermost secrets for this entire class to hear," said Snape viciously. "Now, the use of this potion is controlled by very strict Ministry guidelines. But unless you watch your step, you might just find that my hand *slips*"— he shook the crystal bottle slightly — "right over your evening pumpkin juice. And then, Potter . . . then we'll find out whether you've been in my office or not."

Harry said nothing. He turned back to his ginger roots once more, picked up his knife, and started slicing them again. He didn't like the sound of that Truth Potion at all, nor would he put it past Snape to slip him some. He repressed a shudder at the thought of what might come spilling out of his mouth if Snape did it . . . quite apart from landing a whole lot of people in trouble — Hermione and Dobby for a start — there were all the other things he was concealing . . . like the fact that he was in contact with Sirius . . . and — his insides squirmed at the thought — how he felt about

Cho. . . . . He tipped his ginger roots into the cauldron too, and wondered whether he ought to take a leaf out of Moody's book and start drinking only from a private hip flask.

There was a knock on the dungeon door.

"Enter," said Snape in his usual voice.

The class looked around as the door opened. Professor Karkaroff came in. Everyone watched him as he walked up toward Snape's desk. He was twisting his finger around his goatee and looking agitated.

"We need to talk," said Karkaroff abruptly when he had reached Snape. He seemed so determined that nobody should hear what he was saying that he was barely opening his lips; it was as though he were a rather poor ventriloquist. Harry kept his eyes on his ginger roots, listening hard.

"I'll talk to you after my lesson, Karkaroff," Snape muttered, but Karkaroff interrupted him.

"I want to talk now, while you can't slip off, Severus. You've been avoiding me."

"After the lesson," Snape snapped.

Under the pretext of holding up a measuring cup to see if he'd poured out enough armadillo bile, Harry sneaked a sidelong glance at the pair of them. Karkaroff looked extremely worried, and Snape looked angry.

Karkaroff hovered behind Snape's desk for the rest of the double period. He seemed intent on preventing Snape from slipping away at the end of class. Keen to hear what Karkaroff wanted to say, Harry deliberately knocked over his bottle of armadillo bile with two minutes to go to the bell, which gave him an excuse to duck down behind his cauldron and mop up while the rest of the class moved noisily toward the door.

"What's so urgent?" he heard Snape hiss at Karkaroff.

*"This,"* said Karkaroff, and Harry, peering around the edge of his cauldron, saw Karkaroff pull up the left-hand sleeve of his robe and show Snape something on his inner forearm.

"Well?" said Karkaroff, still making every effort not to move his lips. "Do you see? It's never been this clear, never since —"

"Put it away!" snarled Snape, his black eyes sweeping the classroom.

"But you must have noticed —" Karkaroff began in an agitated voice.

"We can talk later, Karkaroff!" spat Snape. "Potter! What are you doing?"

"Clearing up my armadillo bile, Professor," said Harry innocently, straightening up and showing Snape the sodden rag he was holding.

Karkaroff turned on his heel and strode out of the dungeon. He looked both worried and angry. Not wanting to remain alone with an exceptionally angry Snape, Harry threw his books and ingredients back into his bag and left at top speed to tell Ron and Hermione what he had just witnessed.

They left the castle at noon the next day to find a weak silver sun shining down upon the grounds. The weather was milder than it had been all year, and by the time they arrived in Hogsmeade, all three of them had taken off their cloaks and thrown them over their shoulders. The food Sirius had told them to bring was in

Harry's bag; they had sneaked a dozen chicken legs, a loaf of bread, and a flask of pumpkin juice from the lunch table.

They went into Gladrags Wizardwear to buy a present for Dobby, where they had fun selecting the most lurid socks they could find, including a pair patterned with flashing gold and silver stars, and another that screamed loudly when they became too smelly. Then, at half past one, they made their way up the High Street, past Dervish and Banges, and out toward the edge of the village.

Harry had never been in this direction before. The winding lane was leading them out into the wild countryside around Hogsmeade. The cottages were fewer here, and their gardens larger; they were walking toward the foot of the mountain in whose shadow Hogsmeade lay. Then they turned a corner and saw a stile at the end of the lane. Waiting for them, its front paws on the topmost bar, was a very large, shaggy black dog, which was carrying some newspapers in its mouth and looking very familiar. . . .

"Hello, Sirius," said Harry when they had reached him.

The black dog sniffed Harry's bag eagerly, wagged its tail once, then turned and began to trot away from them across the scrubby patch of ground that rose to meet the rocky foot of the mountain. Harry, Ron, and Hermione climbed over the stile and followed.

Sirius led them to the very foot of the mountain, where the ground was covered with boulders and rocks. It was easy for him, with his four paws, but Harry, Ron, and Hermione were soon out of breath. They followed Sirius higher, up onto the mountain itself. For nearly half an hour they climbed a steep, winding, and stony path, following Sirius's wagging tail, sweating in the sun, the shoulder straps of Harry's bag cutting into his shoulders.

Then, at last, Sirius slipped out of sight, and when they reached the place where he had vanished, they saw a narrow fissure in the rock. They squeezed into it and found themselves in a cool, dimly lit cave. Tethered at the end of it, one end of his rope around a large rock, was Buckbeak the hippogriff. Half gray horse, half giant eagle, Buckbeak's fierce orange eye flashed at the sight of them. All three of them bowed low to him, and after regarding them imperiously for a moment, Buckbeak bent his scaly front knees and allowed Hermione to rush forward and stroke his feathery neck. Harry, however, was looking at the black dog, which had just turned into his godfather.

Sirius was wearing ragged gray robes; the same ones he had been wearing when he had left Azkaban. His black hair was longer than it had been when he had appeared in the fire, and it was untidy and matted once more. He looked very thin.

"Chicken!" he said hoarsely after removing the old *Daily Prophet*s from his mouth and throwing them down onto the cave floor.

Harry pulled open his bag and handed over the bundle of chicken legs and bread.

"Thanks," said Sirius, opening it, grabbing a drumstick, sitting down on the cave floor, and tearing off a large chunk with his teeth. "I've been living off rats mostly. Can't steal too much food from Hogsmeade; I'd draw attention to myself."

He grinned up at Harry, but Harry returned the grin only reluctantly.

"What're you doing here, Sirius?" he said.

"Fulfilling my duty as godfather," said Sirius, gnawing on the chicken bone in a very doglike way. "Don't worry about it, I'm pretending to be a lovable stray."

He was still grinning, but seeing the anxiety in Harry's face, said more seriously, "I want to be on the spot. Your last letter . . . well, let's just say things are getting fishier. I've been stealing the paper every time someone throws one out, and by the looks of things, I'm not the only one who's getting worried."

He nodded at the yellowing *Daily Prophets* on the cave floor, and Ron picked them up and unfolded them. Harry, however, continued to stare at Sirius.

"What if they catch you? What if you're seen?"

"You three and Dumbledore are the only ones around here who know I'm an Animagus," said Sirius, shrugging, and continuing to devour the chicken leg.

Ron nudged Harry and passed him the *Daily Prophets*. There were two: The first bore the headline *Mystery Illness of Bartemius Crouch*, the second, *Ministry Witch Still Missing — Minister of Magic Now Personally Involved*.

Harry scanned the story about Crouch. Phrases jumped out at him: *hasn't been seen in public since November . . . house appears deserted . . . St. Mungo's Hospital for Magical Maladies and Injuries decline comment . . . Ministry refuses to confirm rumors of critical illness. . . .*

"They're making it sound like he's dying," said Harry slowly. "But he can't be that ill if he managed to get up here. . . ."

"My brother's Crouch's personal assistant," Ron informed Sirius. "He says Crouch is suffering from overwork."

"Mind you, he *did* look ill, last time I saw him up close," said Harry slowly, still reading the story. "The night my name came out of the goblet. . . ."

"Getting his comeuppance for sacking Winky, isn't he?" said Hermione, an edge to her voice. She was stroking Buckbeak, who was crunching up Sirius's chicken bones. "I bet he wishes he hadn't done it now — bet he feels the difference now she's not there to look after him."

"Hermione's obsessed with house-elves," Ron muttered to Sirius, casting Hermione a dark look. Sirius, however, looked interested.

"Crouch sacked his house-elf?"

"Yeah, at the Quidditch World Cup," said Harry, and he launched into the story of the Dark Mark's appearance, and Winky being found with Harry's wand clutched in her hand, and Mr. Crouch's fury. When Harry had finished, Sirius was on his feet again and had started pacing up and down the cave.

"Let me get this straight," he said after a while, brandishing a fresh chicken leg. "You first saw the elf in the Top Box. She was saving Crouch a seat, right?"

"Right," said Harry, Ron, and Hermione together.

"But Crouch didn't turn up for the match?"

"No," said Harry. "I think he said he'd been too busy."

Sirius paced all around the cave in silence. Then he said, "Harry, did you check your pockets for your wand after you'd left the Top Box?"

"Erm . . ." Harry thought hard. "No," he said finally. "I didn't need to use it before we got in the forest. And then I put my hand in my pocket, and all that was in there were my Omnioculars." He stared at Sirius. "Are you saying whoever conjured the Mark stole my wand in the Top Box?"

"It's possible," said Sirius.

"Winky didn't steal that wand!" Hermione insisted.

"The elf wasn't the only one in that box," said Sirius, his brow furrowed as he continued to pace. "Who else was sitting behind you?"

"Loads of people," said Harry. "Some Bulgarian ministers . . . Cornelius Fudge . . . the Malfoys . . ."

"The Malfoys!" said Ron suddenly, so loudly that his voice echoed all around the cave, and Buckbeak tossed his head nervously. "I bet it was Lucius Malfoy!"

"Anyone else?" said Sirius.

"No one," said Harry.

"Yes, there was, there was Ludo Bagman," Hermione reminded him.

"Oh yeah . . ."

"I don't know anything about Bagman except that he used to be Beater for the Wimbourne Wasps," said Sirius, still pacing. "What's he like?"

"He's okay," said Harry. "He keeps offering to help me with the Triwizard Tournament."

"Does he, now?" said Sirius, frowning more deeply. "I wonder why he'd do that?"

"Says he's taken a liking to me," said Harry.

"Hmm," said Sirius, looking thoughtful.

"We saw him in the forest just before the Dark Mark appeared," Hermione told Sirius. "Remember?" she said to Harry and Ron.

"Yeah, but he didn't stay in the forest, did he?" said Ron. "The moment we told him about the riot, he went off to the campsite."

"How d'you know?" Hermione shot back. "How d'you know where he Disapparated to?"

"Come off it," said Ron incredulously. "Are you saying you reckon Ludo Bagman conjured the Dark Mark?"

"It's more likely he did it than Winky," said Hermione stubbornly.

"Told you," said Ron, looking meaningfully at Sirius, "told you she's obsessed with house —"

But Sirius held up a hand to silence Ron.

"When the Dark Mark had been conjured, and the elf had been discovered holding Harry's wand, what did Crouch do?"

"Went to look in the bushes," said Harry, "but there wasn't anyone else there."

"Of course," Sirius muttered, pacing up and down, "of course, he'd want to pin it on anyone but his own elf . . . and then he sacked her?"

"Yes," said Hermione in a heated voice, "he sacked her, just because she hadn't stayed in her tent and let herself get trampled —"

"Hermione, will you give it a rest with the elf!" said Ron.

Sirius shook his head and said, "She's got the measure of Crouch better than you have, Ron. If you want to know what a man's like, take a good look at how he treats his inferiors, not his equals."

He ran a hand over his unshaven face, evidently thinking hard.

"All these absences of Barty Crouch's . . . he goes to the trouble of making sure his house-elf saves him a seat at the Quidditch World Cup, but doesn't bother to turn up and watch. He works very hard to reinstate the Triwizard Tournament, and then stops coming to that too. . . . It's not like Crouch. If he's ever taken a day off work because of illness before this, I'll eat Buckbeak."

"D'you know Crouch, then?" said Harry.

Sirius's face darkened. He suddenly looked as menacing as he had the night when Harry first met him, the night when Harry still believed Sirius to be a murderer.

"Oh I know Crouch all right," he said quietly. "He was the one who gave the order for me to be sent to Azkaban — without a trial."

"*What?*" said Ron and Hermione together.

"You're kidding!" said Harry.

"No, I'm not," said Sirius, taking another great bite of chicken. "Crouch used to be Head of the Department of Magical Law Enforcement, didn't you know?"

Harry, Ron, and Hermione shook their heads.

"He was tipped for the next Minister of Magic," said Sirius. "He's a great wizard, Barty Crouch, powerfully magical — and power-hungry. Oh never a Voldemort supporter," he said, reading the look on Harry's face. "No, Barty Crouch was always very outspoken against the Dark Side. But then a lot of people who were against the Dark Side . . . well, you wouldn't understand . . . you're too young. . . ."

"That's what my dad said at the World Cup," said Ron, with a trace of irritation in his voice. "Try us, why don't you?"

A grin flashed across Sirius's thin face.

"All right, I'll try you. . . ." He walked once up the cave, back again, and then said, "Imagine that Voldemort's powerful now. You don't know who his supporters are, you don't know who's working for him and who isn't; you know he can control people so that they do terrible things without being able to stop themselves. You're scared for yourself, and your family, and your friends. Every week, news comes of more deaths, more disappearances, more torturing . . . the Ministry of Magic's in disarray, they don't know what to do, they're trying to keep everything hidden from the Muggles, but meanwhile, Muggles are dying too. Terror everywhere . . . panic . . . confusion . . . that's how it used to be.

"Well, times like that bring out the best in some people and the worst in others. Crouch's principles might've been good in the beginning — I wouldn't know. He rose quickly through the Ministry, and he started ordering very harsh measures against Voldemort's supporters. The Aurors were given new powers — powers to kill rather than capture, for instance. And I wasn't the only one who was handed straight to the dementors without trial. Crouch fought violence with violence, and authorized the use of the Unforgivable Curses against suspects. I would say he became as ruthless and cruel as many on the Dark Side. He had his supporters, mind you — plenty of people thought he was going about things the right way, and there were a lot of witches and wizards clamoring for him to take over as Minister of Magic. When Voldemort disappeared, it looked like only a matter of time until Crouch got the top job. But then something rather unfortunate happened. . . ." Sirius smiled grimly. "Crouch's own son was caught with a group of Death Eaters who'd managed to talk their way out of Azkaban. Apparently they were trying to find Voldemort and return him to power."

"Crouch's *son* was caught?" gasped Hermione.

"Yep," said Sirius, throwing his chicken bone to Buckbeak, flinging himself back down on the ground beside the loaf of bread, and tearing it in half. "Nasty little shock for old Barty, I'd imagine. Should have spent a bit more time at home with his family, shouldn't he? Ought to have left the office early once in a while . . . gotten to know his own son."

He began to wolf down large pieces of bread.

"*Was* his son a Death Eater?" said Harry.

"No idea," said Sirius, still stuffing down bread. "I was in Azkaban myself when he was brought in. This is mostly stuff I've found out since I got out. The boy was definitely caught in the company of people I'd bet my life were Death Eaters — but he might have been in the wrong place at the wrong time, just like the house-elf."

"Did Crouch try and get his son off?" Hermione whispered.

Sirius let out a laugh that was much more like a bark.

"Crouch let his son off? I thought you had the measure of him, Hermione! Anything that threatened to tarnish his reputation had to go; he had dedicated his whole life to becoming Minister of Magic. You saw him dismiss a devoted house-elf because she associated him with the Dark Mark again — doesn't that tell you what he's like? Crouch's fatherly affection stretched just far enough to give his son a trial, and by all accounts, it wasn't much more than an excuse for Crouch to show how much he hated the boy . . . then he sent him straight to Azkaban."

"He gave his own son to the dementors?" asked Harry quietly.

"That's right," said Sirius, and he didn't look remotely amused now. "I saw the dementors bringing him in, watched them through the bars in my cell door. He can't have been more than nineteen. They took him into a cell near mine. He was screaming for his mother by nightfall. He went quiet after a few days, though . . .

they all went quiet in the end . . . . except when they shrieked in their sleep. . . ."

For a moment, the deadened look in Sirius's eyes became more pronounced than ever, as though shutters had closed behind them.

"So he's still in Azkaban?" Harry said.

"No," said Sirius dully. "No, he's not in there anymore. He died about a year after they brought him in."

"He *died*?"

"He wasn't the only one," said Sirius bitterly. "Most go mad in there, and plenty stop eating in the end. They lose the will to live. You could always tell when a death was coming, because the dementors could sense it, they got excited. That boy looked pretty sickly when he arrived. Crouch being an important Ministry member, he and his wife were allowed a deathbed visit. That was the last time I saw Barty Crouch, half carrying his wife past my cell. She died herself, apparently, shortly afterward. Grief. Wasted away just like the boy. Crouch never came for his son's body. The dementors buried him outside the fortress; I watched them do it."

Sirius threw aside the bread he had just lifted to his mouth and instead picked up the flask of pumpkin juice and drained it.

"So old Crouch lost it all, just when he thought he had it made," he continued, wiping his mouth with the back of his hand. "One moment, a hero, poised to become Minister of Magic . . . next, his son dead, his wife dead, the family name dishonored, and, so I've heard since I escaped, a big drop in popularity. Once the boy had died, people started feeling a bit more sympathetic toward the son and started asking how a nice young lad from a good family had gone so badly astray. The conclusion was that his father never cared much for him. So Cornelius Fudge got the top job, and Crouch was shunted sideways into the Department of International Magical Cooperation."

There was a long silence. Harry was thinking of the way Crouch's eyes had bulged as he'd looked down at his disobedient house-elf back in the wood at the Quidditch World Cup. This, then, must have been why Crouch had overreacted to Winky being found beneath the Dark Mark. It had brought back memories of his son, and the old scandal, and his fall from grace at the Ministry.

"Moody says Crouch is obsessed with catching Dark wizards," Harry told Sirius.

"Yeah, I've heard it's become a bit of a mania with him," said Sirius, nodding. "If you ask me, he still thinks he can bring back the old popularity by catching one more Death Eater."

"And he sneaked up here to search Snape's office!" said Ron triumphantly, looking at Hermione.

"Yes, and that doesn't make sense at all," said Sirius.

"Yeah, it does!" said Ron excitedly, but Sirius shook his head.

"Listen, if Crouch wants to investigate Snape, why hasn't he been coming to judge the tournament? It would be an ideal excuse to make regular visits to Hogwarts and keep an eye on him."

"So you think Snape could be up to something, then?" asked Harry, but Hermione broke in.

"Look, I don't care what you say, Dumbledore trusts Snape —"

"Oh give it a rest, Hermione," said Ron impatiently. "I know Dumbledore's brilliant and everything, but that doesn't mean a really clever Dark wizard couldn't fool him —"

"Why did Snape save Harry's life in the first year, then? Why didn't he just let him die?"

"I dunno — maybe he thought Dumbledore would kick him out —"

"What d'you think, Sirius?" Harry said loudly, and Ron and Hermione stopped bickering to listen.

"I think they've both got a point," said Sirius, looking thoughtfully at Ron and Hermione. "Ever since I found out Snape was teaching here, I've wondered why Dumbledore hired him. Snape's always been fascinated by the Dark Arts, he was famous for it at school. Slimy, oily, greasy-haired kid, he was," Sirius added, and Harry and Ron grinned at each other. "Snape knew more curses when he arrived at school than half the kids in seventh year, and he was part of a gang of Slytherins who nearly all turned out to be Death Eaters."

Sirius held up his fingers and began ticking off names.

"Rosier and Wilkes — they were both killed by Aurors the year before Voldemort fell. The Lestranges — they're a married couple — they're in Azkaban. Avery — from what I've heard he wormed his way out of trouble by saying he'd been acting under the Imperius Curse — he's still at large. But as far as I know, Snape was never even accused of being a Death Eater — not that that means much. Plenty of them were never caught. And Snape's certainly clever and cunning enough to keep himself out of trouble."

"Snape knows Karkaroff pretty well, but he wants to keep that quiet," said Ron.

"Yeah, you should've seen Snape's face when Karkaroff turned up in Potions yesterday!" said Harry quickly. "Karkaroff wanted to talk to Snape, he says Snape's been avoiding him. Karkaroff looked really worried. He showed Snape something on his arm, but I couldn't see what it was."

"He showed Snape something on his arm?" said Sirius, looking frankly bewildered. He ran his fingers distractedly through his filthy hair, then shrugged again. "Well, I've no idea what that's about . . . but if Karkaroff's genuinely worried, and he's going to Snape for answers . . ."

Sirius stared at the cave wall, then made a grimace of frustration.

"There's still the fact that Dumbledore trusts Snape, and I know Dumbledore trusts where a lot of other people wouldn't, but I just can't see him letting Snape teach at Hogwarts if he'd ever worked for Voldemort."

"Why are Moody and Crouch so keen to get into Snape's office then?" said Ron stubbornly.

"Well," said Sirius slowly, "I wouldn't put it past Mad-Eye to have searched every single teacher's office when he got to Hogwarts. He takes his Defense Against the Dark Arts seriously, Moody. I'm not sure *he* trusts anyone at all, and after the things he's seen, it's not surprising. I'll say this for Moody, though, he never killed if he could help it. Always brought people in alive where possible. He was tough, but he never descended to the level of the Death Eaters. Crouch, though . . . he's a different matter . . . is he really ill? If he is, why did he make the effort to drag himself up to Snape's office? And if he's not . . . what's he up to? What was he doing at the World Cup that was so important he didn't turn up in the Top Box? What's he been doing while he should have been judging the tournament?"

Sirius lapsed into silence, still staring at the cave wall. Buckbeak was ferreting around on the rocky floor, looking for bones he might have overlooked. Finally, Sirius looked up at Ron.

"You say your brother's Crouch's personal assistant? Any chance you could ask him if he's seen Crouch lately?"

"I can try," said Ron doubtfully. "Better not make it sound like I reckon Crouch is up to anything dodgy, though. Percy loves Crouch."

"And you might try and find out whether they've got any leads on Bertha Jorkins while you're at it," said Sirius, gesturing to the second copy of the *Daily Prophet*.

"Bagman told me they hadn't," said Harry.

"Yes, he's quoted in the article in there," said Sirius, nodding at the paper. "Blustering on about how bad Bertha's memory is. Well, maybe she's changed since I knew her, but the Bertha I knew wasn't forgetful at all — quite the reverse. She was a bit dim, but she had an excellent memory for gossip. It used to get her into a lot of trouble; she never knew when to keep her mouth shut. I can see her being a bit of a liability at the Ministry of Magic . . . maybe that's why Bagman didn't bother to look for her for so long. . . ."

Sirius heaved an enormous sigh and rubbed his shadowed eyes.

"What's the time?"

Harry checked his watch, then remembered it hadn't been working since it had spent over an hour in the lake.

"It's half past three," said Hermione.

"You'd better get back to school," Sirius said, getting to his feet. "Now listen . . ." He looked particularly hard at Harry. "I don't want you lot sneaking out of school to see me, all right? Just send notes to me here. I still want to hear about anything odd. But you're not to go leaving Hogwarts without permission; it would be an ideal opportunity for someone to attack you."

"No one's tried to attack me so far, except a dragon and a couple of grindylows," Harry said, but Sirius scowled at him.

"I don't care . . . I'll breathe freely again when this tournament's over, and that's not until June. And don't forget, if you're talking about me among yourselves, call me Snuffles, okay?"

He handed Harry the empty napkin and flask and went to pat Buckbeak good-bye. "I'll walk to the edge of the village with you," said Sirius, "see if I can scrounge another paper."

He transformed into the great black dog before they left the cave, and they walked back down the mountainside with him, across the boulder-strewn ground, and back to the stile. Here he allowed each of them to pat him on the head, before turning and setting off at a run around the outskirts of the village. Harry, Ron, and Hermione made their way back into Hogsmeade and up toward Hogwarts.

"Wonder if Percy knows all that stuff about Crouch?" Ron said as they walked up the drive to the castle. "But maybe he doesn't care . . . it'd probably just make him admire Crouch even more. Yeah, Percy loves rules. He'd just say Crouch was refusing to break them for his own son."

"Percy would never throw any of his family to the dementors," said Hermione severely.

"I don't know," said Ron. "If he thought we were standing in the way of his career . . . Percy's really ambitious, you know. . . ."

They walked up the stone steps into the entrance hall, where the delicious smells of dinner wafted toward them from the Great Hall.

"Poor old Snuffles," said Ron, breathing deeply. "He must really like you, Harry. . . . Imagine having to live off rats."

# THE MADNESS OF
# MR. CROUCH

Harry, Ron, and Hermione went up to the Owlery after breakfast on Sunday to send a letter to Percy, asking, as Sirius had suggested, whether he had seen Mr. Crouch lately. They used Hedwig, because it had been so long since she'd had a job. When they had watched her fly out of sight through the Owlery window, they proceeded down to the kitchen to give Dobby his new socks.

The house-elves gave them a very cheery welcome, bowing and curtsying and bustling around making tea again. Dobby was ecstatic about his present.

"Harry Potter is too good to Dobby!" he squeaked, wiping large tears out of his enormous eyes.

"You saved my life with that gillyweed, Dobby, you really did," said Harry.

"No chance of more of those eclairs, is there?" said Ron, who was looking around at the beaming and bowing house-elves.

"You've just had breakfast!" said Hermione irritably, but a great silver platter of eclairs was already zooming toward them, supported by four elves.

"We should get some stuff to send up to Snuffles," Harry muttered.

"Good idea," said Ron. "Give Pig something to do. You couldn't give us a bit of extra food, could you?" he said to the surrounding elves, and they bowed delightedly and hurried off to get some more.

"Dobby, where's Winky?" said Hermione, who was looking around.

"Winky is over there by the fire, miss," said Dobby quietly, his ears drooping slightly.

"Oh dear," said Hermione as she spotted Winky.

Harry looked over at the fireplace too. Winky was sitting on the same stool as last time, but she had allowed herself to become so filthy that she was not immediately distinguishable from the smoke-blackened brick behind her. Her clothes were ragged and unwashed. She was clutching a bottle of butterbeer and swaying slightly on her stool, staring into the fire. As they watched her, she gave an enormous hiccup.

"Winky is getting through six bottles a day now," Dobby whispered to Harry.

"Well, it's not strong, that stuff," Harry said.

But Dobby shook his head. "'Tis strong for a house-elf, sir," he said.

Winky hiccuped again. The elves who had brought the eclairs gave her disapproving looks as they returned to work.

"Winky is pining, Harry Potter," Dobby whispered sadly.

"Winky wants to go home. Winky still thinks Mr. Crouch is her master, sir, and nothing Dobby says will persuade her that Professor Dumbledore is her master now."

"Hey, Winky," said Harry, struck by a sudden inspiration, walking over to her, and bending down, "you don't know what Mr. Crouch might be up to, do you? Because he's stopped turning up to judge the Triwizard Tournament."

Winky's eyes flickered. Her enormous pupils focused on Harry. She swayed slightly again and then said, "M — Master is stopped — *hic* — coming?"

"Yeah," said Harry, "we haven't seen him since the first task. The *Daily Prophet*'s saying he's ill."

Winky swayed some more, staring blurrily at Harry.

"Master — *hic*—ill?"

Her bottom lip began to tremble.

"But we're not sure if that's true," said Hermione quickly.

"Master is needing his — *hic* — Winky!" whimpered the elf. "Master cannot — *hic* — manage — *hic* — all by himself. . . ."

"Other people manage to do their own housework, you know, Winky," Hermione said severely.

"Winky — *hic* — is not only — *hic* — doing housework for Mr. Crouch!" Winky squeaked indignantly, swaying worse than ever and slopping butterbeer down her already heavily stained blouse. "Master is — *hic* — trusting Winky with — *hic* — the most important — *hic* — the most secret —"

"What?" said Harry.

But Winky shook her head very hard, spilling more butterbeer down herself.

"Winky keeps — *hic* — her master's secrets," she said muti-
nously, swaying very heavily now, frowning up at Harry with her
eyes crossed. "You is — *hic* — nosing, you is."

"Winky must not talk like that to Harry Potter!" said Dobby
angrily. "Harry Potter is brave and noble and Harry Potter is not
nosy!"

"He is nosing — *hic* — into my master's — *hic* — private and
secret — *hic* — Winky is a good house-elf — *hic* — Winky keeps
her silence — *hic* — people trying to — *hic* — pry and poke —
*hic* —"

Winky's eyelids drooped and suddenly, without warning, she
slid off her stool into the hearth, snoring loudly. The empty bottle of butterbeer rolled away across the stone-flagged floor. Half a
dozen house-elves came hurrying forward, looking disgusted. One
of them picked up the bottle; the others covered Winky with a
large checked tablecloth and tucked the ends in neatly, hiding her
from view.

"We is sorry you had to see that, sirs and miss!" squeaked a
nearby elf, shaking his head and looking very ashamed. "We is hoping you will not judge us all by Winky, sirs and miss!"

"She's unhappy!" said Hermione, exasperated. "Why don't you
try and cheer her up instead of covering her up?"

"Begging your pardon, miss," said the house-elf, bowing deeply
again, "but house-elves has no right to be unhappy when there is
work to be done and masters to be served."

"Oh for heaven's sake!" Hermione cried. "Listen to me, all of
you! You've got just as much right as wizards to be unhappy! You've
got the right to wages and holidays and proper clothes, you don't
have to do everything you're told — look at Dobby!"

"Miss will please keep Dobby out of this," Dobby mumbled, looking scared. The cheery smiles had vanished from the faces of the house-elves around the kitchen. They were suddenly looking at Hermione as though she were mad and dangerous.

"We has your extra food!" squeaked an elf at Harry's elbow, and he shoved a large ham, a dozen cakes, and some fruit into Harry's arms. "Good-bye!"

The house-elves crowded around Harry, Ron, and Hermione and began shunting them out of the kitchen, many little hands pushing in the smalls of their backs.

"Thank you for the socks, Harry Potter!" Dobby called miserably from the hearth, where he was standing next to the lumpy tablecloth that was Winky.

"You couldn't keep your mouth shut, could you, Hermione?" said Ron angrily as the kitchen door slammed shut behind them. "They won't want us visiting them now! We could've tried to get more stuff out of Winky about Crouch!"

"Oh as if you care about that!" scoffed Hermione. "You only like coming down here for the food!"

It was an irritable sort of day after that. Harry got so tired of Ron and Hermione sniping at each other over their homework in the common room that he took Sirius's food up to the Owlery that evening on his own.

Pigwidgeon was much too small to carry an entire ham up to the mountain by himself, so Harry enlisted the help of two school screech owls as well. When they had set off into the dusk, looking extremely odd carrying the large package between them, Harry leaned on the windowsill, looking out at the grounds, at the dark, rustling treetops of the Forbidden Forest, and the rippling sails of the Durmstrang ship. An eagle owl flew through the coil of smoke rising from Hagrid's chimney; it soared toward the castle, around the Owlery, and out of sight. Looking down, Harry saw Hagrid digging energetically in front of his cabin. Harry wondered what he was doing; it looked as though he were making a new vegetable patch. As he watched, Madame Maxime emerged from the Beauxbatons carriage and walked over to Hagrid. She appeared to be trying to engage him in conversation. Hagrid leaned upon his spade, but did not seem keen to prolong their talk, because Madame Maxime returned to the carriage shortly afterward.

Unwilling to go back to Gryffindor Tower and listen to Ron and Hermione snarling at each other, Harry watched Hagrid digging until the darkness swallowed him and the owls around Harry began to awake, swooshing past him into the night.

By breakfast the next day Ron's and Hermione's bad moods had burnt out, and to Harry's relief, Ron's dark predictions that the house-elves would send substandard food up to the Gryffindor table because Hermione had insulted them proved false; the bacon, eggs, and kippers were quite as good as usual.

When the post owls arrived, Hermione looked up eagerly; she seemed to be expecting something.

"Percy won't've had time to answer yet," said Ron. "We only sent Hedwig yesterday."

"No, it's not that," said Hermione. "I've taken out a subscription to the *Daily Prophet*. I'm getting sick of finding everything out from the Slytherins."

"Good thinking!" said Harry, also looking up at the owls. "Hey, Hermione, I think you're in luck —"

A gray owl was soaring down toward Hermione.

"It hasn't got a newspaper, though," she said, looking disappointed. "It's —"

But to her bewilderment, the gray owl landed in front of her plate, closely followed by four barn owls, a brown owl, and a tawny.

"How many subscriptions did you take out?" said Harry, seizing Hermione's goblet before it was knocked over by the cluster of owls, all of whom were jostling close to her, trying to deliver their own letter first.

"What on earth — ?" Hermione said, taking the letter from the gray owl, opening it, and starting to read. "Oh really!" she sputtered, going rather red.

"What's up?" said Ron.

"It's — oh how ridiculous —"

She thrust the letter at Harry, who saw that it was not handwritten, but composed from pasted letters that seemed to have been cut out of the *Daily Prophet*.

> You are a WickEd giRL. HarRy PotTER deSErVes BeTteR. GO back wherE you cAMe from mUGgle.

"They're all like it!" said Hermione desperately, opening one letter after another. "'*Harry Potter can do much better than the likes of you. . . .*' '*You deserve to be boiled in frog spawn. . . .*' Ouch!"

She had opened the last envelope, and yellowish-green liquid smelling strongly of petrol gushed over her hands, which began to erupt in large yellow boils.

"Undiluted bubotuber pus!" said Ron, picking up the envelope gingerly and sniffing it.

"Ow!" said Hermione, tears starting in her eyes as she tried to rub the pus off her hands with a napkin, but her fingers were now so thickly covered in painful sores that it looked as though she were wearing a pair of thick, knobbly gloves.

"You'd better get up to the hospital wing," said Harry as the owls around Hermione took flight. "We'll tell Professor Sprout where you've gone. . . ."

"I warned her!" said Ron as Hermione hurried out of the Great Hall, cradling her hands. "I warned her not to annoy Rita Skeeter! Look at this one . . ." He read out one of the letters Hermione had left behind: "*I read in* Witch Weekly *about how you are playing Harry Potter false and that boy has had enough hardship and I will be sending you a curse by next post as soon as I can find a big enough envelope.*' Blimey, she'd better watch out for herself."

Hermione didn't turn up for Herbology. As Harry and Ron left the greenhouse for their Care of Magical Creatures class, they saw Malfoy, Crabbe, and Goyle descending the stone steps of the castle. Pansy Parkinson was whispering and giggling behind them with her gang of Slytherin girls. Catching sight of Harry, Pansy called, "Potter, have you split up with your girlfriend? Why was she so upset at breakfast?"

Harry ignored her; he didn't want to give her the satisfaction of knowing how much trouble the *Witch Weekly* article had caused.

Hagrid, who had told them last lesson that they had finished with unicorns, was waiting for them outside his cabin with a fresh supply of open crates at his feet. Harry's heart sank at the sight of the crates — surely not another skrewt hatching? — but when he got near enough to see inside, he found himself looking at a number of fluffy black creatures with long snouts. Their front paws were curiously flat, like spades, and they were blinking up at the class, looking politely puzzled at all the attention.

"These're nifflers," said Hagrid, when the class had gathered around. "Yeh find 'em down mines mostly. They like sparkly stuff. . . . There yeh go, look."

One of the nifflers had suddenly leapt up and attempted to bite Pansy Parkinson's watch off her wrist. She shrieked and jumped backward.

"Useful little treasure detectors," said Hagrid happily. "Thought we'd have some fun with 'em today. See over there?" He pointed at the large patch of freshly turned earth Harry had watched him digging from the Owlery window. "I've buried some gold coins. I've got a prize fer whoever picks the niffler that digs up most. Jus' take off all yer valuables, an' choose a niffler, an' get ready ter set 'em loose."

Harry took off his watch, which he was only wearing out of habit, as it didn't work anymore, and stuffed it into his pocket. Then he picked up a niffler. It put its long snout in Harry's ear and sniffed enthusiastically. It was really quite cuddly.

"Hang on," said Hagrid, looking down into the crate, "there's a spare niffler here . . . who's missin'? Where's Hermione?"

"She had to go to the hospital wing," said Ron.

"We'll explain later," Harry muttered; Pansy Parkinson was listening.

It was easily the most fun they had ever had in Care of Magical Creatures. The nifflers dived in and out of the patch of earth as though it were water, each scurrying back to the student who had released it and spitting gold into their hands. Ron's was particularly efficient; it had soon filled his lap with coins.

"Can you buy these as pets, Hagrid?" he asked excitedly as his niffler dived back into the soil, splattering his robes.

"Yer mum wouldn' be happy, Ron," said Hagrid, grinning. "They wreck houses, nifflers. I reckon they've nearly got the lot, now," he added, pacing around the patch of earth while the nifflers continued to dive. "I on'y buried a hundred coins. Oh there y'are, Hermione!"

Hermione was walking toward them across the lawn. Her hands were very heavily bandaged and she looked miserable. Pansy Parkinson was watching her beadily.

"Well, let's check how yeh've done!" said Hagrid. "Count yer coins! An' there's no point tryin' ter steal any, Goyle," he added, his beetle-black eyes narrowed. "It's leprechaun gold. Vanishes after a few hours."

Goyle emptied his pockets, looking extremely sulky. It turned out that Ron's niffler had been most successful, so Hagrid gave him an enormous slab of Honeydukes chocolate for a prize. The bell rang across the grounds for lunch; the rest of the class set off back to the castle, but Harry, Ron, and Hermione stayed behind to help Hagrid put the nifflers back in their boxes. Harry noticed Madame Maxime watching them out of her carriage window.

"What yeh done ter your hands, Hermione?" said Hagrid, looking concerned.

Hermione told him about the hate mail she had received that morning, and the envelope full of bubotuber pus.

"Aaah, don' worry," said Hagrid gently, looking down at her. "I got some o' those letters an' all, after Rita Skeeter wrote abou' me mum. *'Yeh're a monster an' yeh should be put down.' 'Yer mother killed innocent people an' if you had any decency you'd jump in a lake.'*"

"No!" said Hermione, looking shocked.

"Yeah," said Hagrid, heaving the niffler crates over by his cabin wall. "They're jus' nutters, Hermione. Don' open 'em if yeh get any more. Chuck 'em straigh' in the fire."

"You missed a really good lesson," Harry told Hermione as they headed back toward the castle. "They're good, nifflers, aren't they, Ron?"

Ron, however, was frowning at the chocolate Hagrid had given him. He looked thoroughly put out about something.

"What's the matter?" said Harry. "Wrong flavor?"

"No," said Ron shortly. "Why didn't you tell me about the gold?"

"What gold?" said Harry.

"The gold I gave you at the Quidditch World Cup," said Ron. "The leprechaun gold I gave you for my Omnioculars. In the Top Box. Why didn't you tell me it disappeared?"

Harry had to think for a moment before he realized what Ron was talking about.

"Oh . . ." he said, the memory coming back to him at last. "I dunno . . . I never noticed it had gone. I was more worried about my wand, wasn't I?"

They climbed the steps into the entrance hall and went into the Great Hall for lunch.

"Must be nice," Ron said abruptly, when they had sat down and started serving themselves roast beef and Yorkshire puddings. "To have so much money you don't notice if a pocketful of Galleons goes missing."

"Listen, I had other stuff on my mind that night!" said Harry impatiently. "We all did, remember?"

"I didn't know leprechaun gold vanishes," Ron muttered. "I thought I was paying you back. You shouldn't've given me that Chudley Cannon hat for Christmas."

"Forget it, all right?" said Harry.

Ron speared a roast potato on the end of his fork, glaring at it. Then he said, "I hate being poor."

Harry and Hermione looked at each other. Neither of them really knew what to say.

"It's rubbish," said Ron, still glaring down at his potato. "I don't blame Fred and George for trying to make some extra money. Wish I could. Wish I had a niffler."

"Well, we know what to get you next Christmas," said Hermione brightly. Then, when Ron continued to look gloomy, she said, "Come on, Ron, it could be worse. At least your fingers aren't full of pus." Hermione was having a lot of difficulty managing her knife and fork, her fingers were so stiff and swollen. "I *hate* that Skeeter woman!" she burst out savagely. "I'll get her back for this if it's the last thing I do!"

Hate mail continued to arrive for Hermione over the following week, and although she followed Hagrid's advice and stopped opening it, several of her ill-wishers sent Howlers, which exploded at the Gryffindor table and shrieked insults at her for the whole Hall to hear. Even those people who didn't read *Witch Weekly* knew all about the supposed Harry–Krum–Hermione triangle now. Harry was getting sick of telling people that Hermione wasn't his girlfriend.

"It'll die down, though," he told Hermione, "if we just ignore it. . . . People got bored with that stuff she wrote about me last time —"

"I want to know how she's listening into private conversations when she's supposed to be banned from the grounds!" said Hermione angrily.

Hermione hung back in their next Defense Against the Dark Arts lesson to ask Professor Moody something. The rest of the class was very eager to leave; Moody had given them such a rigorous test of hex-deflection that many of them were nursing small injuries. Harry had such a bad case of Twitchy Ears, he had to hold his hands clamped over them as he walked away from the class.

"Well, Rita's definitely not using an Invisibility Cloak!" Hermione panted five minutes later, catching up with Harry and Ron in the entrance hall and pulling Harry's hand away from one of his wiggling ears so that he could hear her. "Moody says he didn't see her anywhere near the judges' table at the second task, or anywhere near the lake!"

"Hermione, is there any point in telling you to drop this?" said Ron.

"No!" said Hermione stubbornly. "I want to know how she heard me talking to Viktor! *And* how she found out about Hagrid's mum!"

"Maybe she had you bugged," said Harry.

"Bugged?" said Ron blankly. "What . . . put fleas on her or something?"

Harry started explaining about hidden microphones and recording equipment. Ron was fascinated, but Hermione interrupted them.

"Aren't you two *ever* going to read *Hogwarts: A History*?"

"What's the point?" said Ron. "You know it by heart, we can just ask you."

"All those substitutes for magic Muggles use — electricity, computers, and radar, and all those things — they all go haywire around Hogwarts, there's too much magic in the air. No, Rita's using magic to eavesdrop, she must be. . . . If I could just find out what it is . . . ooh, if it's illegal, I'll have her . . ."

"Haven't we got enough to worry about?" Ron asked her. "Do we have to start a vendetta against Rita Skeeter as well?"

"I'm not asking you to help!" Hermione snapped. "I'll do it on my own!"

She marched back up the marble staircase without a backward glance. Harry was quite sure she was going to the library.

"What's the betting she comes back with a box of *I Hate Rita Skeeter* badges?" said Ron.

Hermione, however, did not ask Harry and Ron to help her pursue vengeance against Rita Skeeter, for which they were both grateful, because their workload was mounting ever higher in the days before the Easter holidays. Harry frankly marveled at the fact that Hermione could research magical methods of eavesdropping as well as everything else they had to do. He was working flat-out just to get through all their homework, though he made a point of sending regular food packages up to the cave in the mountain for Sirius; after last summer, Harry had not forgotten what it felt like to be continually hungry. He enclosed notes to Sirius, telling him that nothing out of the ordinary had happened, and that they were still waiting for an answer from Percy.

Hedwig didn't return until the end of the Easter holidays. Percy's letter was enclosed in a package of Easter eggs that Mrs. Weasley had sent. Both Harry's and Ron's were the size of dragon eggs and full of homemade toffee. Hermione's, however, was smaller than a chicken egg. Her face fell when she saw it.

"Your mum doesn't read *Witch Weekly*, by any chance, does she, Ron?" she asked quietly.

"Yeah," said Ron, whose mouth was full of toffee. "Gets it for the recipes."

Hermione looked sadly at her tiny egg.

"Don't you want to see what Percy's written?" Harry asked her hastily.

Percy's letter was short and irritated.

*As I am constantly telling the* Daily Prophet, *Mr. Crouch is taking a well-deserved break. He is sending in regular owls with instructions. No, I haven't actually seen him, but I think I can be trusted to know my own superior's handwriting. I have quite enough to do at the moment without trying to quash these ridiculous rumors. Please don't bother me again unless it's something important. Happy Easter.*

The start of the summer term would normally have meant that Harry was training hard for the last Quidditch match of the season. This year, however, it was the third and final task in the Triwizard Tournament for which he needed to prepare, but he still didn't know what he would have to do. Finally, in the last week of May, Professor McGonagall held him back in Transfiguration.

"You are to go down to the Quidditch field tonight at nine o'clock, Potter," she told him. "Mr. Bagman will be there to tell the champions about the third task."

So at half past eight that night, Harry left Ron and Hermione in Gryffindor Tower and went downstairs. As he crossed the entrance hall, Cedric came up from the Hufflepuff common room.

"What d'you reckon it's going to be?" he asked Harry as they went together down the stone steps, out into the cloudy night. "Fleur keeps going on about underground tunnels; she reckons we've got to find treasure."

"That wouldn't be too bad," said Harry, thinking that he would simply ask Hagrid for a niffler to do the job for him.

They walked down the dark lawn to the Quidditch stadium, turned through a gap in the stands, and walked out onto the field.

"What've they done to it?" Cedric said indignantly, stopping dead.

The Quidditch field was no longer smooth and flat. It looked as though somebody had been building long, low walls all over it that twisted and crisscrossed in every direction.

"They're hedges!" said Harry, bending to examine the nearest one.

"Hello there!" called a cheery voice.

Ludo Bagman was standing in the middle of the field with Krum and Fleur. Harry and Cedric made their way toward them, climbing over the hedges. Fleur beamed at Harry as he came nearer. Her attitude toward him had changed completely since he had saved her sister from the lake.

"Well, what d'you think?" said Bagman happily as Harry and Cedric climbed over the last hedge. "Growing nicely, aren't they?

Give them a month and Hagrid'll have them twenty feet high. Don't worry," he added, grinning, spotting the less-than-happy expressions on Harry's and Cedric's faces, "you'll have your Quidditch field back to normal once the task is over! Now, I imagine you can guess what we're making here?"

No one spoke for a moment. Then —

"Maze," grunted Krum.

"That's right!" said Bagman. "A maze. The third task's really very straightforward. The Triwizard Cup will be placed in the center of the maze. The first champion to touch it will receive full marks."

"We seemply 'ave to get through the maze?" said Fleur.

"There will be obstacles," said Bagman happily, bouncing on the balls of his feet. "Hagrid is providing a number of creatures . . . then there will be spells that must be broken . . . all that sort of thing, you know. Now, the champions who are leading on points will get a head start into the maze." Bagman grinned at Harry and Cedric. "Then Mr. Krum will enter . . . then Miss Delacour. But you'll all be in with a fighting chance, depending how well you get past the obstacles. Should be fun, eh?"

Harry, who knew only too well the kind of creatures that Hagrid was likely to provide for an event like this, thought it was unlikely to be any fun at all. However, he nodded politely like the other champions.

"Very well . . . if you haven't got any questions, we'll go back up to the castle, shall we, it's a bit chilly. . . ."

Bagman hurried alongside Harry as they began to wend their way out of the growing maze. Harry had the feeling that Bagman was going to start offering to help him again, but just then, Krum tapped Harry on the shoulder.

"Could I haff a vord?"

"Yeah, all right," said Harry, slightly surprised.

"Vill you valk vith me?"

"Okay," said Harry curiously.

Bagman looked slightly perturbed.

"I'll wait for you, Harry, shall I?"

"No, it's okay, Mr. Bagman," said Harry, suppressing a smile, "I think I can find the castle on my own, thanks."

Harry and Krum left the stadium together, but Krum did not set a course for the Durmstrang ship. Instead, he walked toward the forest.

"What're we going this way for?" said Harry as they passed Hagrid's cabin and the illuminated Beauxbatons carriage.

"Don't vont to be overheard," said Krum shortly.

When at last they had reached a quiet stretch of ground a short way from the Beauxbatons horses' paddock, Krum stopped in the shade of the trees and turned to face Harry.

"I vant to know," he said, glowering, "vot there is between you and Hermy-own-ninny."

Harry, who from Krum's secretive manner had expected something much more serious than this, stared up at Krum in amazement.

"Nothing," he said. But Krum glowered at him, and Harry, somehow struck anew by how tall Krum was, elaborated. "We're friends. She's not my girlfriend and she never has been. It's just that Skeeter woman making things up."

"Hermy-own-ninny talks about you very often," said Krum, looking suspiciously at Harry.

"Yeah," said Harry, "because we're *friends*."

He couldn't quite believe he was having this conversation with Viktor Krum, the famous International Quidditch player. It was as though the eighteen-year-old Krum thought he, Harry, was an equal — a real rival —

"You haff never . . . you haff not . . ."

"No," said Harry very firmly.

Krum looked slightly happier. He stared at Harry for a few seconds, then said, "You fly very vell. I vos votching at the first task."

"Thanks," said Harry, grinning broadly and suddenly feeling much taller himself. "I saw you at the Quidditch World Cup. The Wronski Feint, you really —"

But something moved behind Krum in the trees, and Harry, who had some experience of the sort of thing that lurked in the forest, instinctively grabbed Krum's arm and pulled him around.

"Vot is it?"

Harry shook his head, staring at the place where he'd seen movement. He slipped his hand inside his robes, reaching for his wand.

Suddenly a man staggered out from behind a tall oak. For a moment, Harry didn't recognize him . . . then he realized it was Mr. Crouch.

He looked as though he had been traveling for days. The knees of his robes were ripped and bloody, his face scratched; he was unshaven and gray with exhaustion. His neat hair and mustache were both in need of a wash and a trim. His strange appearance, however, was nothing to the way he was behaving. Muttering and gesticulating, Mr. Crouch appeared to be talking to someone that he alone could see. He reminded Harry vividly of an old tramp he had seen once when out shopping with the Dursleys. That man too had been conversing wildly with thin air; Aunt Petunia had seized

Dudley's hand and pulled him across the road to avoid him; Uncle Vernon had then treated the family to a long rant about what he would like to do with beggars and vagrants.

"Vosn't he a judge?" said Krum, staring at Mr. Crouch. "Isn't he vith your Ministry?"

Harry nodded, hesitated for a moment, then walked slowly toward Mr. Crouch, who did not look at him, but continued to talk to a nearby tree.

". . . and when you've done that, Weatherby, send an owl to Dumbledore confirming the number of Durmstrang students who will be attending the tournament, Karkaroff has just sent word there will be twelve. . . ."

"Mr. Crouch?" said Harry cautiously.

". . . and then send another owl to Madame Maxime, because she might want to up the number of students she's bringing, now Karkaroff's made it a round dozen . . . do that, Weatherby, will you? Will you? Will . . ."

Mr. Crouch's eyes were bulging. He stood staring at the tree, muttering soundlessly at it. Then he staggered sideways and fell to his knees.

"Mr. Crouch?" Harry said loudly. "Are you all right?"

Crouch's eyes were rolling in his head. Harry looked around at Krum, who had followed him into the trees, and was looking down at Crouch in alarm.

"Vot is wrong with him?"

"No idea," Harry muttered. "Listen, you'd better go and get someone —"

"Dumbledore!" gasped Mr. Crouch. He reached out and seized a handful of Harry's robes, dragging him closer, though his eyes were staring over Harry's head. "I need . . . see . . . Dumbledore. . . ."

"Okay," said Harry, "if you get up, Mr. Crouch, we can go up to the —"

"I've done . . . stupid . . . thing . . ." Mr. Crouch breathed. He looked utterly mad. His eyes were rolling and bulging, and a trickle of spittle was sliding down his chin. Every word he spoke seemed to cost him a terrible effort. "Must . . . tell . . . Dumbledore . . ."

"Get up, Mr. Crouch," said Harry loudly and clearly. "Get up, I'll take you to Dumbledore!"

Mr. Crouch's eyes rolled forward onto Harry.

"Who . . . you?" he whispered.

"I'm a student at the school," said Harry, looking around at Krum for some help, but Krum was hanging back, looking extremely nervous.

"You're not . . . *his?*" whispered Crouch, his mouth sagging.

"No," said Harry, without the faintest idea what Crouch was talking about.

"Dumbledore's?"

"That's right," said Harry.

Crouch was pulling him closer; Harry tried to loosen Crouch's grip on his robes, but it was too powerful.

"Warn . . . Dumbledore . . ."

"I'll get Dumbledore if you let go of me," said Harry. "Just let go, Mr. Crouch, and I'll get him. . . ."

"Thank you, Weatherby, and when you have done that, I would like a cup of tea. My wife and son will be arriving shortly, we are attending a concert tonight with Mr. and Mrs. Fudge."

Crouch was now talking fluently to a tree again, and seemed

completely unaware that Harry was there, which surprised Harry so much he didn't notice that Crouch had released him.

"Yes, my son has recently gained twelve O.W.L.s, most satisfactory, yes, thank you, yes, very proud indeed. Now, if you could bring me that memo from the Andorran Minister of Magic, I think I will have time to draft a response. . . ."

"You stay here with him!" Harry said to Krum. "I'll get Dumbledore, I'll be quicker, I know where his office is —"

"He is mad," said Krum doubtfully, staring down at Crouch, who was still gabbling to the tree, apparently convinced it was Percy.

"Just stay with him," said Harry, starting to get up, but his movement seemed to trigger another abrupt change in Mr. Crouch, who seized him hard around the knees and pulled Harry back to the ground.

"Don't . . . leave . . . me!" he whispered, his eyes bulging again. "I . . . escaped . . . must warn . . . must tell . . . see Dumbledore . . . my fault . . . all my fault . . . Bertha . . . dead . . . all my fault . . . my son . . . my fault . . . tell Dumbledore . . . Harry Potter . . . the Dark Lord . . . stronger . . . Harry Potter . . ."

"I'll get Dumbledore if you let me go, Mr. Crouch!" said Harry. He looked furiously around at Krum. "Help me, will you?"

Looking extremely apprehensive, Krum moved forward and squatted down next to Mr. Crouch.

"Just keep him here," said Harry, pulling himself free of Mr. Crouch. "I'll be back with Dumbledore."

"Hurry, von't you?" Krum called after him as Harry sprinted away from the forest and up through the dark grounds. They were deserted; Bagman, Cedric, and Fleur had disappeared. Harry tore up the stone steps, through the oak front doors, and off up the marble staircase, toward the second floor.

Five minutes later he was hurtling toward a stone gargoyle standing halfway along an empty corridor.

"Lem — lemon drop!" he panted at it.

This was the password to the hidden staircase to Dumbledore's office — or at least, it had been two years ago. The password had evidently changed, however, for the stone gargoyle did not spring to life and jump aside, but stood frozen, glaring at Harry malevolently.

"Move!" Harry shouted at it. "C'mon!"

But nothing at Hogwarts had ever moved just because he shouted at it; he knew it was no good. He looked up and down the dark corridor. Perhaps Dumbledore was in the staffroom? He started running as fast as he could toward the staircase —

"POTTER!"

Harry skidded to a halt and looked around. Snape had just emerged from the hidden staircase behind the stone gargoyle. The wall was sliding shut behind him even as he beckoned Harry back toward him.

"What are you doing here, Potter?"

"I need to see Professor Dumbledore!" said Harry, running back up the corridor and skidding to a standstill in front of Snape instead. "It's Mr. Crouch . . . he's just turned up . . . he's in the forest . . . he's asking —"

"What is this rubbish?" said Snape, his black eyes glittering. "What are you talking about?"

"Mr. Crouch!" Harry shouted. "From the Ministry! He's ill or something — he's in the forest, he wants to see Dumbledore! Just give me the password up to —"

"The headmaster is busy, Potter," said Snape, his thin mouth curling into an unpleasant smile.

"I've got to tell Dumbledore!" Harry yelled.

"Didn't you hear me, Potter?"

Harry could tell Snape was thoroughly enjoying himself, denying Harry the thing he wanted when he was so panicky.

"Look," said Harry angrily, "Crouch isn't right — he's — he's out of his mind — he says he wants to warn —"

The stone wall behind Snape slid open. Dumbledore was standing there, wearing long green robes and a mildly curious expression. "Is there a problem?" he said, looking between Harry and Snape.

"Professor!" Harry said, sidestepping Snape before Snape could speak, "Mr. Crouch is here — he's down in the forest, he wants to speak to you!"

Harry expected Dumbledore to ask questions, but to his relief, Dumbledore did nothing of the sort.

"Lead the way," he said promptly, and he swept off along the corridor behind Harry, leaving Snape standing next to the gargoyle and looking twice as ugly.

"What did Mr. Crouch say, Harry?" said Dumbledore as they walked swiftly down the marble staircase.

"Said he wants to warn you . . . said he's done something terrible . . . he mentioned his son . . . and Bertha Jorkins . . . and — and Voldemort . . . something about Voldemort getting stronger. . . ."

"Indeed," said Dumbledore, and he quickened his pace as they hurried out into the pitch-darkness.

"He's not acting normally," Harry said, hurrying along beside Dumbledore. "He doesn't seem to know where he is. He keeps talking like he thinks Percy Weasley's there, and then he changes, and says he needs to see you. . . . I left him with Viktor Krum."

"You did?" said Dumbledore sharply, and he began to take longer strides still, so that Harry was running to keep up. "Do you know if anybody else saw Mr. Crouch?"

"No," said Harry. "Krum and I were talking, Mr. Bagman had just finished telling us about the third task, we stayed behind, and then we saw Mr. Crouch coming out of the forest —"

"Where are they?" said Dumbledore as the Beauxbatons carriage emerged from the darkness.

"Over here," said Harry, moving in front of Dumbledore, leading the way through the trees. He couldn't hear Crouch's voice anymore, but he knew where he was going; it hadn't been much past the Beauxbatons carriage . . . somewhere around here. . . .

"Viktor?" Harry shouted.

No one answered.

"They were here," Harry said to Dumbledore. "They were definitely somewhere around here. . . ."

"*Lumos,*" Dumbledore said, lighting his wand and holding it up.

Its narrow beam traveled from black trunk to black trunk, illuminating the ground. And then it fell upon a pair of feet.

Harry and Dumbledore hurried forward. Krum was sprawled on the forest floor. He seemed to be unconscious. There was no sign at all of Mr. Crouch. Dumbledore bent over Krum and gently lifted one of his eyelids.

"Stunned," he said softly. His half-moon glasses glittered in the wandlight as he peered around at the surrounding trees.

"Should I go and get someone?" said Harry. "Madam Pomfrey?"

"No," said Dumbledore swiftly. "Stay here."

He raised his wand into the air and pointed it in the direction of Hagrid's cabin. Harry saw something silvery dart out of it and streak away through the trees like a ghostly bird. Then Dumbledore bent over Krum again, pointed his wand at him, and muttered, *"Rennervate."*

Krum opened his eyes. He looked dazed. When he saw Dumbledore, he tried to sit up, but Dumbledore put a hand on his shoulder and made him lie still.

"He attacked me!" Krum muttered, putting a hand up to his head. "The old madman attacked me! I vos looking around to see vare Potter had gone and he attacked from behind!"

"Lie still for a moment," Dumbledore said.

The sound of thunderous footfalls reached them, and Hagrid came panting into sight with Fang at his heels. He was carrying his crossbow.

"Professor Dumbledore!" he said, his eyes widening. "Harry — what the — ?"

"Hagrid, I need you to fetch Professor Karkaroff," said Dumbledore. "His student has been attacked. When you've done that, kindly alert Professor Moody —"

"No need, Dumbledore," said a wheezy growl. "I'm here."

Moody was limping toward them, leaning on his staff, his wand lit.

"Damn leg," he said furiously. "Would've been here quicker . . . what's happened? Snape said something about Crouch —"

"Crouch?" said Hagrid blankly.

"Karkaroff, please, Hagrid!" said Dumbledore sharply.

"Oh yeah . . . right y'are, Professor . . ." said Hagrid, and he turned and disappeared into the dark trees, Fang trotting after him.

"I don't know where Barty Crouch is," Dumbledore told Moody, "but it is essential that we find him."

"I'm onto it," growled Moody, and he raised his wand and limped off into the forest.

Neither Dumbledore nor Harry spoke again until they heard the unmistakable sounds of Hagrid and Fang returning. Karkaroff was hurrying along behind them. He was wearing his sleek silver furs, and he looked pale and agitated.

"What is this?" he cried when he saw Krum on the ground and Dumbledore and Harry beside him. "What's going on?"

"I vos attacked!" said Krum, sitting up now and rubbing his head. "Mr. Crouch or votever his name —"

"Crouch attacked you? *Crouch* attacked you? The Triwizard judge?"

"Igor," Dumbledore began, but Karkaroff had drawn himself up, clutching his furs around him, looking livid.

"Treachery!" he bellowed, pointing at Dumbledore. "It is a plot! You and your Ministry of Magic have lured me here under false pretenses, Dumbledore! This is not an equal competition! First you sneak Potter into the tournament, though he is underage! Now one of your Ministry friends attempts to put *my* champion out of action! I smell double-dealing and corruption in this whole affair, and you, Dumbledore, you, with your talk of closer international

Wizarding links, of rebuilding old ties, of forgetting old differences — here's what I think of *you*!"

Karkaroff spat onto the ground at Dumbledore's feet. In one swift movement, Hagrid seized the front of Karkaroff's furs, lifted him into the air, and slammed him against a nearby tree.

"Apologize!" Hagrid snarled as Karkaroff gasped for breath, Hagrid's massive fist at his throat, his feet dangling in midair.

"Hagrid, *no*!" Dumbledore shouted, his eyes flashing.

Hagrid removed the hand pinning Karkaroff to the tree, and Karkaroff slid all the way down the trunk and slumped in a huddle at its roots; a few twigs and leaves showered down upon his head.

"Kindly escort Harry back up to the castle, Hagrid," said Dumbledore sharply.

Breathing heavily, Hagrid gave Karkaroff a glowering look.

"Maybe I'd better stay here, Headmaster. . . ."

"You will take Harry back to school, Hagrid," Dumbledore repeated firmly. "Take him right up to Gryffindor Tower. And Harry — I want you to stay there. Anything you might want to do — any owls you might want to send — they can wait until morning, do you understand me?"

"Er — yes," said Harry, staring at him. How had Dumbledore known that, at that very moment, he had been thinking about sending Pigwidgeon straight to Sirius, to tell him what had happened?

"I'll leave Fang with yeh, Headmaster," Hagrid said, staring menacingly at Karkaroff, who was still sprawled at the foot of the tree, tangled in furs and tree roots. "Stay, Fang. C'mon, Harry."

They marched in silence past the Beauxbatons carriage and up toward the castle.

"How dare he," Hagrid growled as they strode past the lake. "How dare he accuse Dumbledore. Like Dumbledore'd do anythin' like that. Like Dumbledore wanted *you* in the tournament in the firs' place. Worried! I dunno when I seen Dumbledore more worried than he's bin lately. An' you!" Hagrid suddenly said angrily to Harry, who looked up at him, taken aback. "What were yeh doin', wanderin' off with ruddy Krum? He's from Durmstrang, Harry! Coulda jinxed yeh right there, couldn' he? Hasn' Moody taught yeh nothin'? 'Magine lettin' him lure yeh off on yer own —"

"Krum's all right!" said Harry as they climbed the steps into the entrance hall. "He wasn't trying to jinx me, he just wanted to talk about Hermione —"

"I'll be havin' a few words with her, an' all," said Hagrid grimly, stomping up the stairs. "The less you lot 'ave ter do with these foreigners, the happier yeh'll be. Yeh can' trust any of 'em."

"You were getting on all right with Madame Maxime," Harry said, annoyed.

"Don' you talk ter me abou' her!" said Hagrid, and he looked quite frightening for a moment. "I've got her number now! Tryin' ter get back in me good books, tryin' ter get me ter tell her what's comin' in the third task. Ha! You can' trust any of 'em!"

Hagrid was in such a bad mood, Harry was quite glad to say good-bye to him in front of the Fat Lady. He clambered through the portrait hole into the common room and hurried straight for the corner where Ron and Hermione were sitting, to tell them what had happened.

# THE DREAM

I t comes down to this," said Hermione, rubbing her forehead. "Either Mr. Crouch attacked Viktor, or somebody else attacked both of them when Viktor wasn't looking."

"It must've been Crouch," said Ron at once. "That's why he was gone when Harry and Dumbledore got there. He'd done a runner."

"I don't think so," said Harry, shaking his head. "He seemed really weak — I don't reckon he was up to Disapparating or anything."

"You *can't* Disapparate on the Hogwarts grounds, haven't I told you enough times?" said Hermione.

"Okay . . . how's this for a theory," said Ron excitedly. "Krum attacked Crouch — no, wait for it — and then Stunned himself!"

"And Mr. Crouch evaporated, did he?" said Hermione coldly.

"Oh yeah . . ."

It was daybreak. Harry, Ron, and Hermione had crept out of their dormitories very early and hurried up to the Owlery together to send a note to Sirius. Now they were standing looking out at the misty grounds. All three of them were puffy-eyed and pale because they had been talking late into the night about Mr. Crouch.

"Just go through it again, Harry," said Hermione. "What did Mr. Crouch actually say?"

"I've told you, he wasn't making much sense," said Harry. "He said he wanted to warn Dumbledore about something. He definitely mentioned Bertha Jorkins, and he seemed to think she was dead. He kept saying stuff was his fault. . . . He mentioned his son."

"Well, that *was* his fault," said Hermione testily.

"He was out of his mind," said Harry. "Half the time he seemed to think his wife and son were still alive, and he kept talking to Percy about work and giving him instructions."

"And . . . remind me what he said about You-Know-Who?" said Ron tentatively.

"I've told you," Harry repeated dully. "He said he's getting stronger."

There was a pause. Then Ron said in a falsely confident voice, "But he was out of his mind, like you said, so half of it was probably just raving. . . ."

"He was sanest when he was trying to talk about Voldemort," said Harry, and Ron winced at the sound of the name. "He was having real trouble stringing two words together, but that was when he seemed to know where he was, and know what he wanted to do. He just kept saying he had to see Dumbledore."

Harry turned away from the window and stared up into the

rafters. The many perches were half-empty; every now and then, another owl would swoop in through one of the windows, returning from its night's hunting with a mouse in its beak.

"If Snape hadn't held me up," Harry said bitterly, "we might've got there in time. 'The headmaster is busy, Potter . . . what's this rubbish, Potter?' Why couldn't he have just got out of the way?"

"Maybe he didn't want you to get there!" said Ron quickly. "Maybe — hang on — how fast d'you reckon he could've gotten down to the forest? D'you reckon he could've beaten you and Dumbledore there?"

"Not unless he can turn himself into a bat or something," said Harry.

"Wouldn't put it past him," Ron muttered.

"We need to see Professor Moody," said Hermione. "We need to find out whether he found Mr. Crouch."

"If he had the Marauder's Map on him, it would've been easy," said Harry.

"Unless Crouch was already outside the grounds," said Ron, "because it only shows up to the boundaries, doesn't —"

"Shh!" said Hermione suddenly.

Somebody was climbing the steps up to the Owlery. Harry could hear two voices arguing, coming closer and closer.

"— that's blackmail, that is, we could get into a lot of trouble for that —"

"— we've tried being polite; it's time to play dirty, like him. He wouldn't like the Ministry of Magic knowing what he did —"

"I'm telling you, if you put that in writing, it's blackmail!"

"Yeah, and you won't be complaining if we get a nice fat payoff, will you?"

The Owlery door banged open. Fred and George came over the threshold, then froze at the sight of Harry, Ron, and Hermione.

"What're you doing here?" Ron and Fred said at the same time.

"Sending a letter," said Harry and George in unison.

"What, at this time?" said Hermione and Fred.

Fred grinned.

"Fine — we won't ask you what you're doing, if you don't ask us," he said.

He was holding a sealed envelope in his hands. Harry glanced at it, but Fred, whether accidentally or on purpose, shifted his hand so that the name on it was covered.

"Well, don't let us hold you up," Fred said, making a mock bow and pointing at the door.

Ron didn't move. "Who're you blackmailing?" he said.

The grin vanished from Fred's face. Harry saw George half glance at Fred, before smiling at Ron.

"Don't be stupid, I was only joking," he said easily.

"Didn't sound like that," said Ron.

Fred and George looked at each other. Then Fred said abruptly, "I've told you before, Ron, keep your nose out if you like it the shape it is. Can't see why you would, but —"

"It's my business if you're blackmailing someone," said Ron. "George's right, you could end up in serious trouble for that."

"Told you, I was joking," said George. He walked over to Fred, pulled the letter out of his hands, and began attaching it to the leg of the nearest barn owl. "You're starting to sound a bit like our dear older brother, you are, Ron. Carry on like this and you'll be made a prefect."

"No, I won't!" said Ron hotly.

George carried the barn owl over to the window and it took off. George turned around and grinned at Ron.

"Well, stop telling people what to do then. See you later."

He and Fred left the Owlery. Harry, Ron, and Hermione stared at one another.

"You don't think they know something about all this, do you?" Hermione whispered. "About Crouch and everything?"

"No," said Harry. "If it was something that serious, they'd tell someone. They'd tell Dumbledore."

Ron, however, was looking uncomfortable.

"What's the matter?" Hermione asked him.

"Well . . ." said Ron slowly, "I dunno if they would. They're . . . they're obsessed with making money lately, I noticed it when I was hanging around with them — when — you know —"

"We weren't talking." Harry finished the sentence for him. "Yeah, but blackmail . . ."

"It's this joke shop idea they've got," said Ron. "I thought they were only saying it to annoy Mum, but they really mean it, they want to start one. They've only got a year left at Hogwarts, they keep going on about how it's time to think about their future, and Dad can't help them, and they need gold to get started."

Hermione was looking uncomfortable now.

"Yes, but . . . they wouldn't do anything against the law to get gold."

"Wouldn't they?" said Ron, looking skeptical. "I dunno . . . they don't exactly mind breaking rules, do they?"

"Yes, but this is the *law*," said Hermione, looking scared. "This isn't some silly school rule. . . . They'll get a lot more than detention for blackmail! Ron . . . maybe you'd better tell Percy. . . ."

"Are you mad?" said Ron. "Tell Percy? He'd probably do a Crouch and turn them in." He stared at the window through which Fred and George's owl had departed, then said, "Come on, let's get some breakfast."

"D'you think it's too early to go and see Professor Moody?" Hermione said as they went down the spiral staircase.

"Yes," said Harry. "He'd probably blast us through the door if we wake him at the crack of dawn; he'll think we're trying to attack him while he's asleep. Let's give it till break."

History of Magic had rarely gone so slowly. Harry kept checking Ron's watch, having finally discarded his own, but Ron's was moving so slowly he could have sworn it had stopped working too. All three of them were so tired they could happily have put their heads down on the desks and slept; even Hermione wasn't taking her usual notes, but was sitting with her head on her hand, gazing at Professor Binns with her eyes out of focus.

When the bell finally rang, they hurried out into the corridors toward the Dark Arts classroom and found Professor Moody leaving it. He looked as tired as they felt. The eyelid of his normal eye was drooping, giving his face an even more lopsided appearance than usual.

"Professor Moody?" Harry called as they made their way toward him through the crowd.

"Hello, Potter," growled Moody. His magical eye followed a couple of passing first years, who sped up, looking nervous; it rolled into the back of Moody's head and watched them around the corner before he spoke again.

"Come in here."

He stood back to let them into his empty classroom, limped in after them, and closed the door.

"Did you find him?" Harry asked without preamble. "Mr. Crouch?"

"No," said Moody. He moved over to his desk, sat down, stretched out his wooden leg with a slight groan, and pulled out his hip flask.

"Did you use the map?" Harry said.

"Of course," said Moody, taking a swig from his flask. "Took a leaf out of your book, Potter. Summoned it from my office into the forest. He wasn't anywhere on there."

"So he *did* Disapparate?" said Ron.

*"You can't Disapparate on the grounds, Ron!"* said Hermione. "There are other ways he could have disappeared, aren't there, Professor?"

Moody's magical eye quivered as it rested on Hermione. "You're another one who might think about a career as an Auror," he told her. "Mind works the right way, Granger."

Hermione flushed pink with pleasure.

"Well, he wasn't invisible," said Harry. "The map shows invisible people. He must've left the grounds, then."

"But under his own steam?" said Hermione eagerly, "or because someone made him?"

"Yeah, someone could've — could've pulled him onto a broom and flown off with him, couldn't they?" said Ron quickly, looking hopefully at Moody as if he too wanted to be told he had the makings of an Auror.

"We can't rule out kidnap," growled Moody.

"So," said Ron, "d'you reckon he's somewhere in Hogsmeade?"

"Could be anywhere," said Moody, shaking his head. "Only thing we know for sure is that he's not here."

He yawned widely, so that his scars stretched, and his lopsided mouth revealed a number of missing teeth. Then he said, "Now, Dumbledore's told me you three fancy yourselves as investigators, but there's nothing you can do for Crouch. The Ministry'll be looking for him now, Dumbledore's notified them. Potter, you just keep your mind on the third task."

"What?" said Harry. "Oh yeah . . ."

He hadn't given the maze a single thought since he'd left it with Krum the previous night.

"Should be right up your street, this one," said Moody, looking up at Harry and scratching his scarred and stubbly chin. "From what Dumbledore's said, you've managed to get through stuff like this plenty of times. Broke your way through a series of obstacles guarding the Sorcerer's Stone in your first year, didn't you?"

"We helped," Ron said quickly. "Me and Hermione helped."

Moody grinned.

"Well, help him practice for this one, and I'll be very surprised if he doesn't win," said Moody. "In the meantime . . . constant vigilance, Potter. Constant vigilance." He took another long draw from his hip flask, and his magical eye swiveled onto the window. The topmost sail of the Durmstrang ship was visible through it.

"You two," counseled Moody, his normal eye on Ron and Hermione, "you stick close to Potter, all right? I'm keeping an eye on things, but all the same . . . you can never have too many eyes out."

*　*　*

Sirius sent their owl back the very next morning. It fluttered down beside Harry at the same moment that a tawny owl landed in front of Hermione, clutching a copy of the *Daily Prophet* in its beak. She took the newspaper, scanned the first few pages, said, "Ha! She hasn't got wind of Crouch!" then joined Ron and Harry in reading what Sirius had to say on the mysterious events of the night before last.

> *Harry — what do you think you are playing at, walking off into the forest with Viktor Krum? I want you to swear, by return owl, that you are not going to go walking with anyone else at night. There is somebody highly dangerous at Hogwarts. It is clear to me that they wanted to stop Crouch from seeing Dumbledore and you were probably feet away from them in the dark. You could have been killed.*
>
> *Your name didn't get into the Goblet of Fire by accident. If someone's trying to attack you, they're on their last chance. Stay close to Ron and Hermione, do not leave Gryffindor Tower after hours, and arm yourself for the third task. Practice Stunning and Disarming. A few hexes wouldn't go amiss either. There's nothing you can do about Crouch. Keep your head down and look after yourself. I'm waiting for your letter giving me your word you won't stray out-of-bounds again.*
>
> *Sirius*

"Who's he, to lecture me about being out-of-bounds?" said Harry in mild indignation as he folded up Sirius's letter and put it inside his robes. "After all the stuff he did at school!"

"He's worried about you!" said Hermione sharply. "Just like Moody and Hagrid! So listen to them!"

"No one's tried to attack me all year," said Harry. "No one's done anything to me at all —"

"Except put your name in the Goblet of Fire," said Hermione. "And they must've done that for a reason, Harry. Snuffles is right. Maybe they've been biding their time. Maybe this is the task they're going to get you."

"Look," said Harry impatiently, "let's say Sirius is right, and someone Stunned Krum to kidnap Crouch. Well, they *would've* been in the trees near us, wouldn't they? But they waited till I was out of the way until they acted, didn't they? So it doesn't look like I'm their target, does it?"

"They couldn't have made it look like an accident if they'd murdered you in the forest!" said Hermione. "But if you die during a task —"

"They didn't care about attacking Krum, did they?" said Harry. "Why didn't they just polish me off at the same time? They could've made it look like Krum and I had a duel or something."

"Harry, I don't understand it either," said Hermione desperately. "I just know there are a lot of odd things going on, and I don't like it. . . . Moody's right — Sirius is right — you've got to get in training for the third task, straight away. And you make sure you write back to Sirius and promise him you're not going to go sneaking off alone again."

The Hogwarts grounds never looked more inviting than when Harry had to stay indoors. For the next few days he spent all of his

free time either in the library with Hermione and Ron, looking
up hexes, or else in empty classrooms, which they sneaked into to
practice. Harry was concentrating on the Stunning Spell, which he
had never used before. The trouble was that practicing it involved
certain sacrifices on Ron's and Hermione's part.

"Can't we kidnap Mrs. Norris?" Ron suggested on Monday
lunchtime as he lay flat on his back in the middle of their Charms
classroom, having just been Stunned and reawoken by Harry for
the fifth time in a row. "Let's Stun her for a bit. Or you could use
Dobby, Harry, I bet he'd do anything to help you. I'm not complaining or anything" — he got gingerly to his feet, rubbing his
backside — "but I'm aching all over. . . ."

"Well, you keep missing the cushions, don't you!" said Hermione impatiently, rearranging the pile of cushions they had used for
the Banishing Spell, which Flitwick had left in a cabinet. "Just try
and fall backward!"

"Once you're Stunned, you can't aim too well, Hermione!" said
Ron angrily. "Why don't you take a turn?"

"Well, I think Harry's got it now, anyway," said Hermione hastily. "And we don't have to worry about Disarming, because he's
been able to do that for ages. . . . I think we ought to start on some
of these hexes this evening."

She looked down the list they had made in the library.

"I like the look of this one," she said, "this Impediment Curse.
Should slow down anything that's trying to attack you, Harry.
We'll start with that one."

The bell rang. They hastily shoved the cushions back into Flitwick's cupboard and slipped out of the classroom.

"See you at dinner!" said Hermione, and she set off for Arithmancy, while Harry and Ron headed toward North Tower, and Divination. Broad strips of dazzling gold sunlight fell across the corridor from the high windows. The sky outside was so brightly blue it looked as though it had been enameled.

"It's going to be boiling in Trelawney's room, she never puts out that fire," said Ron as they started up the staircase toward the silver ladder and the trapdoor.

He was quite right. The dimly lit room was swelteringly hot. The fumes from the perfumed fire were heavier than ever. Harry's head swam as he made his way over to one of the curtained windows. While Professor Trelawney was looking the other way, disentangling her shawl from a lamp, he opened it an inch or so and settled back in his chintz armchair, so that a soft breeze played across his face. It was extremely comfortable.

"My dears," said Professor Trelawney, sitting down in her winged armchair in front of the class and peering around at them all with her strangely enlarged eyes, "we have almost finished our work on planetary divination. Today, however, will be an excellent opportunity to examine the effects of Mars, for he is placed most interestingly at the present time. If you will all look this way, I will dim the lights. . . ."

She waved her wand and the lamps went out. The fire was the only source of light now. Professor Trelawney bent down and lifted, from under her chair, a miniature model of the solar system, contained within a glass dome. It was a beautiful thing; each of the moons glimmered in place around the nine planets and the fiery sun, all of them hanging in thin air beneath the glass. Harry watched lazily as Professor Trelawney began to point out the fascinating angle Mars was making to Neptune. The heavily perfumed fumes washed over him, and the breeze from the window played across his face. He could hear an insect humming gently somewhere behind the curtain. His eyelids began to droop. . . .

He was riding on the back of an eagle owl, soaring through the clear blue sky toward an old, ivy-covered house set high on a hillside. Lower and lower they flew, the wind blowing pleasantly in Harry's face, until they reached a dark and broken window in the upper story of the house and entered. Now they were flying along a gloomy passageway, to a room at the very end . . . through the door they went, into a dark room whose windows were boarded up. . . .

Harry had left the owl's back . . . he was watching, now, as it fluttered across the room, into a chair with its back to him. . . . There were two dark shapes on the floor beside the chair . . . both of them were stirring. . . .

One was a huge snake . . . the other was a man . . . a short, balding man, a man with watery eyes and a pointed nose . . . he was wheezing and sobbing on the hearth rug. . . .

"You are in luck, Wormtail," said a cold, high-pitched voice from the depths of the chair in which the owl had landed. "You are very fortunate indeed. Your blunder has not ruined everything. He is dead."

"My Lord!" gasped the man on the floor. "My Lord, I am . . . I am so pleased . . . and so sorry. . . ."

"Nagini," said the cold voice, "you are out of luck. I will not be feeding Wormtail to you, after all . . . but never mind, never mind . . . there is still Harry Potter. . . ."

The snake hissed. Harry could see its tongue fluttering.

"Now, Wormtail," said the cold voice, "perhaps one more little reminder why I will not tolerate another blunder from you. . . ."

"My Lord . . . no . . . I beg you . . ."

The tip of a wand emerged from around the back of the chair. It was pointing at Wormtail.

"*Crucio!*" said the cold voice.

Wormtail screamed, screamed as though every nerve in his body were on fire, the screaming filled Harry's ears as the scar on his forehead seared with pain; he was yelling too. . . . Voldemort would hear him, would know he was there. . . .

"Harry! *Harry!*"

Harry opened his eyes. He was lying on the floor of Professor Trelawney's room with his hands over his face. His scar was still burning so badly that his eyes were watering. The pain had been real. The whole class was standing around him, and Ron was kneeling next to him, looking terrified.

"You all right?" he said.

"Of course he isn't!" said Professor Trelawney, looking thoroughly excited. Her great eyes loomed over Harry, gazing at him. "What was it, Potter? A premonition? An apparition? What did you see?"

"Nothing," Harry lied. He sat up. He could feel himself shaking. He couldn't stop himself from looking around, into the shadows behind him; Voldemort's voice had sounded so close. . . .

"You were clutching your scar!" said Professor Trelawney. "You were rolling on the floor, clutching your scar! Come now, Potter, I have experience in these matters!"

Harry looked up at her.

"I need to go to the hospital wing, I think," he said. "Bad headache."

"My dear, you were undoubtedly stimulated by the extraordinary clairvoyant vibrations of my room!" said Professor Trelawney. "If you leave now, you may lose the opportunity to see further than you have ever —"

"I don't want to see anything except a headache cure," said Harry.

He stood up. The class backed away. They all looked unnerved.

"See you later," Harry muttered to Ron, and he picked up his bag and headed for the trapdoor, ignoring Professor Trelawney, who was wearing an expression of great frustration, as though she had just been denied a real treat.

When Harry reached the bottom of her stepladder, however, he did not set off for the hospital wing. He had no intention whatsoever of going there. Sirius had told him what to do if his scar hurt him again, and Harry was going to follow his advice: He was going straight to Dumbledore's office. He marched down the corridors, thinking about what he had seen in the dream . . . it had been as vivid as the one that had awoken him on Privet Drive. . . . He ran over the details in his mind, trying to make sure he could remember them. . . . He had heard Voldemort accusing Wormtail of making a blunder . . . but the owl had brought good news, the blunder had been repaired, somebody was dead . . . so Wormtail was not going to be fed to the snake . . . he, Harry, was going to be fed to it instead. . . .

Harry had walked right past the stone gargoyle guarding the entrance to Dumbledore's office without noticing. He blinked, looked around, realized what he had done, and retraced his steps, stopping in front of it. Then he remembered that he didn't know the password.

"Lemon drop?" he tried tentatively.

The gargoyle did not move.

"Okay," said Harry, staring at it, "Pear Drop. Er — Licorice Wand. Fizzing Whizbee. Drooble's Best Blowing Gum. Bertie Bott's Every Flavor Beans . . . oh no, he doesn't like them, does he? . . . oh just open, can't you?" he said angrily. "I really need to see him, it's urgent!"

The gargoyle remained immovable.

Harry kicked it, achieving nothing but an excruciating pain in his big toe.

"Chocolate Frog!" he yelled angrily, standing on one leg. "Sugar Quill! Cockroach Cluster!"

The gargoyle sprang to life and jumped aside. Harry blinked.

"Cockroach Cluster?" he said, amazed. "I was only joking. . . ."

He hurried through the gap in the walls and stepped onto the foot of a spiral stone staircase, which moved slowly upward as the doors closed behind him, taking him up to a polished oak door with a brass door knocker.

He could hear voices from inside the office. He stepped off the moving staircase and hesitated, listening.

"Dumbledore, I'm afraid I don't see the connection, don't see it at all!" It was the voice of the Minister of Magic, Cornelius Fudge. "Ludo says Bertha's perfectly capable of getting herself lost. I agree we would have expected to have found her by now, but all the same, we've no evidence of foul play, Dumbledore, none at all. As for her disappearance being linked with Barty Crouch's!"

"And what do you think's happened to Barty Crouch, Minister?" said Moody's growling voice.

"I see two possibilities, Alastor," said Fudge. "Either Crouch has finally cracked — more than likely, I'm sure you'll agree, given his personal history — lost his mind, and gone wandering off somewhere —"

"He wandered extremely quickly, if that is the case, Cornelius," said Dumbledore calmly.

"Or else — well . . ." Fudge sounded embarrassed. "Well, I'll reserve judgment until after I've seen the place where he was found, but you say it was just past the Beauxbatons carriage? Dumbledore, you know what that woman *is*?"

"I consider her to be a very able headmistress — and an excellent dancer," said Dumbledore quietly.

"Dumbledore, come!" said Fudge angrily. "Don't you think you might be prejudiced in her favor because of Hagrid? They don't all turn out harmless — if, indeed, you can call Hagrid harmless, with that monster fixation he's got —"

"I no more suspect Madame Maxime than Hagrid," said Dumbledore, just as calmly. "I think it possible that it is you who are prejudiced, Cornelius."

"Can we wrap up this discussion?" growled Moody.

"Yes, yes, let's go down to the grounds, then," said Fudge impatiently.

"No, it's not that," said Moody, "it's just that Potter wants a word with you, Dumbledore. He's just outside the door."

# CHAPTER THIRTY

# THE PENSIEVE

The door of the office opened.

"Hello, Potter," said Moody. "Come in, then."

Harry walked inside. He had been inside Dumbledore's office once before; it was a very beautiful, circular room, lined with pictures of previous headmasters and headmistresses of Hogwarts, all of whom were fast asleep, their chests rising and falling gently.

Cornelius Fudge was standing beside Dumbledore's desk, wearing his usual pinstriped cloak and holding his lime-green bowler hat.

"Harry!" said Fudge jovially, moving forward. "How are you?"

"Fine," Harry lied.

"We were just talking about the night when Mr. Crouch turned up on the grounds," said Fudge. "It was you who found him, was it not?"

"Yes," said Harry. Then, feeling it was pointless to pretend that he hadn't overheard what they had been saying, he added, "I didn't see Madame Maxime anywhere, though, and she'd have a job hiding, wouldn't she?"

Dumbledore smiled at Harry behind Fudge's back, his eyes twinkling.

"Yes, well," said Fudge, looking embarrassed, "we're about to go for a short walk on the grounds, Harry, if you'll excuse us . . . perhaps if you just go back to your class —"

"I wanted to talk to you, Professor," Harry said quickly, looking at Dumbledore, who gave him a swift, searching look.

"Wait here for me, Harry," he said. "Our examination of the grounds will not take long."

They trooped out in silence past him and closed the door. After a minute or so, Harry heard the clunks of Moody's wooden leg growing fainter in the corridor below. He looked around.

"Hello, Fawkes," he said.

Fawkes, Professor Dumbledore's phoenix, was standing on his golden perch beside the door. The size of a swan, with magnificent scarlet-and-gold plumage, he swished his long tail and blinked benignly at Harry.

Harry sat down in a chair in front of Dumbledore's desk. For several minutes, he sat and watched the old headmasters and headmistresses snoozing in their frames, thinking about what he had just heard, and running his fingers over his scar. It had stopped hurting now.

He felt much calmer, somehow, now that he was in Dumbledore's office, knowing he would shortly be telling him about the dream. Harry looked up at the walls behind the desk. The patched and ragged Sorting Hat was standing on a shelf. A glass case next to it held a magnificent silver sword with large rubies set into the hilt, which Harry recognized as the one he himself had pulled out of the Sorting Hat in his second year. The sword had once belonged to Godric Gryffindor, founder of Harry's House. He was gazing at it, remembering how it had come to his aid when he had thought all hope was lost, when he noticed a patch of silvery light, dancing and shimmering on the glass case. He looked around for the source of the light and saw a sliver of silver-white shining brightly from within a black cabinet behind him, whose door had not been closed properly. Harry hesitated, glanced at Fawkes, then got up, walked across the office, and pulled open the cabinet door.

A shallow stone basin lay there, with odd carvings around the edge: runes and symbols that Harry did not recognize. The silvery light was coming from the basin's contents, which were like nothing Harry had ever seen before. He could not tell whether the substance was liquid or gas. It was a bright, whitish silver, and it was moving ceaselessly; the surface of it became ruffled like water beneath wind, and then, like clouds, separated and swirled smoothly. It looked like light made liquid — or like wind made solid — Harry couldn't make up his mind.

He wanted to touch it, to find out what it felt like, but nearly four years' experience of the magical world told him that sticking his hand into a bowl full of some unknown substance was a very stupid thing to do. He therefore pulled his wand out of the inside of his robes, cast a nervous look around the office, looked back at the contents of the basin, and prodded them.

The surface of the silvery stuff inside the basin began to swirl very fast.

Harry bent closer, his head right inside the cabinet. The silvery substance had become transparent; it looked like glass. He looked down into it, expecting to see the stone bottom of the basin — and saw instead an enormous room below the surface of the mysterious substance, a room into which he seemed to be looking through a circular window in the ceiling.

The room was dimly lit; he thought it might even be underground, for there were no windows, merely torches in brackets such as the ones that illuminated the walls of Hogwarts. Lowering his face so that his nose was a mere inch away from the glassy substance, Harry saw that rows and rows of witches and wizards were seated around every wall on what seemed to be benches rising in levels. An empty chair stood in the very center of the room. There was something about the chair that gave Harry an ominous feeling. Chains encircled the arms of it, as though its occupants were usually tied to it.

Where was this place? It surely wasn't Hogwarts; he had never seen a room like that here in the castle. Moreover, the crowd in the mysterious room at the bottom of the basin was comprised of adults, and Harry knew there were not nearly that many teachers at Hogwarts. They seemed, he thought, to be waiting for something; even though he could only see the tops of their hats, all of their faces seemed to be pointing in one direction, and none of them were talking to one another.

The basin being circular, and the room he was observing square, Harry could not make out what was going on in the corners of it. He leaned even closer, tilting his head, trying to see . . .

The tip of his nose touched the strange substance into which he was staring.

Dumbledore's office gave an almighty lurch — Harry was

thrown forward and pitched headfirst into the substance inside the basin —

But his head did not hit the stone bottom. He was falling through something icy-cold and black; it was like being sucked into a dark whirlpool —

And suddenly, Harry found himself sitting on a bench at the end of the room inside the basin, a bench raised high above the others. He looked up at the high stone ceiling, expecting to see the circular window through which he had just been staring, but there was nothing there but dark, solid stone.

Breathing hard and fast, Harry looked around him. Not one of the witches and wizards in the room (and there were at least two hundred of them) was looking at him. Not one of them seemed to have noticed that a fourteen-year-old boy had just dropped from the ceiling into their midst. Harry turned to the wizard next to him on the bench and uttered a loud cry of surprise that reverberated around the silent room.

He was sitting right next to Albus Dumbledore.

"Professor!" Harry said in a kind of strangled whisper. "I'm sorry — I didn't mean to — I was just looking at that basin in your cabinet — I — where are we?"

But Dumbledore didn't move or speak. He ignored Harry completely. Like every other wizard on the benches, he was staring into the far corner of the room, where there was a door.

Harry gazed, nonplussed, at Dumbledore, then around at the silently watchful crowd, then back at Dumbledore. And then it dawned on him. . . .

Once before, Harry had found himself somewhere that nobody

could see or hear him. That time, he had fallen through a page in an enchanted diary, right into somebody else's memory . . . and unless he was very much mistaken, something of the sort had happened again. . . .

Harry raised his right hand, hesitated, and then waved it energetically in front of Dumbledore's face. Dumbledore did not blink, look around at Harry, or indeed move at all. And that, in Harry's opinion, settled the matter. Dumbledore wouldn't ignore him like that. He was inside a memory, and this was not the present-day Dumbledore. Yet it couldn't be that long ago . . . the Dumbledore sitting next to him now was silver-haired, just like the present-day Dumbledore. But what was this place? What were all these wizards waiting for?

Harry looked around more carefully. The room, as he had suspected when observing it from above, was almost certainly underground — more of a dungeon than a room, he thought. There was a bleak and forbidding air about the place; there were no pictures on the walls, no decorations at all; just these serried rows of benches, rising in levels all around the room, all positioned so that they had a clear view of that chair with the chains on its arms.

Before Harry could reach any conclusions about the place in which they were, he heard footsteps. The door in the corner of the dungeon opened and three people entered — or at least one man, flanked by two dementors.

Harry's insides went cold. The dementors — tall, hooded creatures whose faces were concealed — were gliding slowly toward the chair in the center of the room, each grasping one of the man's arms with their dead and rotten-looking hands. The man between them looked as though he was about to faint, and Harry couldn't blame him . . . he knew the dementors could not touch him inside a memory, but he remembered their power only too well. The watching crowd recoiled slightly as the dementors placed the man in the chained chair and glided back out of the room. The door swung shut behind them.

Harry looked down at the man now sitting in the chair and saw that it was Karkaroff.

Unlike Dumbledore, Karkaroff looked much younger; his hair and goatee were black. He was not dressed in sleek furs, but in thin and ragged robes. He was shaking. Even as Harry watched, the chains on the arms of the chair glowed suddenly gold and snaked their way up Karkaroff's arms, binding him there.

"Igor Karkaroff," said a curt voice to Harry's left. Harry looked around and saw Mr. Crouch standing up in the middle of the bench beside him. Crouch's hair was dark, his face was much less lined, he looked fit and alert. "You have been brought from Azkaban to present evidence to the Ministry of Magic. You have given us to understand that you have important information for us."

Karkaroff straightened himself as best he could, tightly bound to the chair.

"I have, sir," he said, and although his voice was very scared, Harry could still hear the familiar unctuous note in it. "I wish to be of use to the Ministry. I wish to help. I — I know that the Ministry is trying to — to round up the last of the Dark Lord's supporters. I am eager to assist in any way I can. . . ."

There was a murmur around the benches. Some of the wizards and witches were surveying Karkaroff with interest, others with pronounced mistrust. Then Harry heard, quite distinctly, from Dumbledore's other side, a familiar, growling voice saying, "Filth."

Harry leaned forward so that he could see past Dumbledore. Mad-Eye Moody was sitting there — except that there was a very noticeable difference in his appearance. He did not have his magical eye, but two normal ones. Both were looking down upon Karkaroff, and both were narrowed in intense dislike.

"Crouch is going to let him out," Moody breathed quietly to Dumbledore. "He's done a deal with him. Took me six months to track him down, and Crouch is going to let him go if he's got enough new names. Let's hear his information, I say, and throw him straight back to the dementors."

Dumbledore made a small noise of dissent through his long, crooked nose.

"Ah, I was forgetting . . . you don't like the dementors, do you, Albus?" said Moody with a sardonic smile.

"No," said Dumbledore calmly, "I'm afraid I don't. I have long felt the Ministry is wrong to ally itself with such creatures."

"But for filth like this . . ." Moody said softly.

"You say you have names for us, Karkaroff," said Mr. Crouch. "Let us hear them, please."

"You must understand," said Karkaroff hurriedly, "that He-Who-Must-Not-Be-Named operated always in the greatest secrecy. . . . He preferred that we — I mean to say, his supporters — and I regret now, very deeply, that I ever counted myself among them —"

"Get on with it," sneered Moody.

"— we never knew the names of every one of our fellows — He alone knew exactly who we all were —"

"Which was a wise move, wasn't it, as it prevented someone like you, Karkaroff, from turning all of them in," muttered Moody.

"Yet you say you have *some* names for us?" said Mr. Crouch.

"I — I do," said Karkaroff breathlessly. "And these were important supporters, mark you. People I saw with my own eyes doing his
bidding. I give this information as a sign that I fully and totally renounce him, and am filled with a remorse so deep I can barely —"

"These names are?" said Mr. Crouch sharply.

Karkaroff drew a deep breath.

"There was Antonin Dolohov," he said. "I — I saw him torture
countless Muggles and — and non-supporters of the Dark Lord."

"And helped him do it," murmured Moody.

"We have already apprehended Dolohov," said Crouch. "He was
caught shortly after yourself."

"Indeed?" said Karkaroff, his eyes widening. "I — I am delighted to hear it!"

But he didn't look it. Harry could tell that this news had come
as a real blow to him. One of his names was worthless.

"Any others?" said Crouch coldly.

"Why, yes . . . there was Rosier," said Karkaroff hurriedly. "Evan
Rosier."

"Rosier is dead," said Crouch. "He was caught shortly after you
were too. He preferred to fight rather than come quietly and was
killed in the struggle."

"Took a bit of me with him, though," whispered Moody to
Harry's right. Harry looked around at him once more, and saw
him indicating the large chunk out of his nose to Dumbledore.

"No — no more than Rosier deserved!" said Karkaroff, a real
note of panic in his voice now. Harry could see that he was starting
to worry that none of his information would be of any use to the
Ministry. Karkaroff's eyes darted toward the door in the corner,
behind which the dementors undoubtedly still stood, waiting.

"Any more?" said Crouch.

"Yes!" said Karkaroff. "There was Travers — he helped murder the McKinnons! Mulciber — he specialized in the Imperius Curse, forced countless people to do horrific things! Rookwood, who was a spy, and passed He-Who-Must-Not-Be-Named useful information from inside the Ministry itself!"

Harry could tell that, this time, Karkaroff had struck gold. The watching crowd was all murmuring together.

"Rookwood?" said Mr. Crouch, nodding to a witch sitting in front of him, who began scribbling upon her piece of parchment. "Augustus Rookwood of the Department of Mysteries?"

"The very same," said Karkaroff eagerly. "I believe he used a network of well-placed wizards, both inside the Ministry and out, to collect information —"

"But Travers and Mulciber we have," said Mr. Crouch. "Very well, Karkaroff, if that is all, you will be returned to Azkaban while we decide —"

"Not yet!" cried Karkaroff, looking quite desperate. "Wait, I have more!"

Harry could see him sweating in the torchlight, his white skin contrasting strongly with the black of his hair and beard.

"Snape!" he shouted. "Severus Snape!"

"Snape has been cleared by this council," said Crouch disdainfully. "He has been vouched for by Albus Dumbledore."

"No!" shouted Karkaroff, straining at the chains that bound him to the chair. "I assure you! Severus Snape is a Death Eater!"

Dumbledore had gotten to his feet.

"I have given evidence already on this matter," he said calmly. "Severus Snape was indeed a Death Eater. However, he rejoined our side before Lord Voldemort's downfall and turned spy for us, at great personal risk. He is now no more a Death Eater than I am."

Harry turned to look at Mad-Eye Moody. He was wearing a look of deep skepticism behind Dumbledore's back.

"Very well, Karkaroff," Crouch said coldly, "you have been of assistance. I shall review your case. You will return to Azkaban in the meantime. . . ."

Mr. Crouch's voice faded. Harry looked around; the dungeon was dissolving as though it were made of smoke; everything was fading; he could see only his own body — all else was swirling darkness. . . .

And then, the dungeon returned. Harry was sitting in a different seat, still on the highest bench, but now to the left side of Mr. Crouch. The atmosphere seemed quite different: relaxed, even cheerful. The witches and wizards all around the walls were talking to one another, almost as though they were at some sort of sporting event. Harry noticed a witch halfway up the rows of benches opposite. She had short blonde hair, was wearing magenta robes, and was sucking the end of an acid-green quill. It was, unmistakably, a younger Rita Skeeter. Harry looked around; Dumbledore was sitting beside him again, wearing different robes. Mr. Crouch looked more tired and somehow fiercer, gaunter. . . . Harry understood. It was a different memory, a different day . . . a different trial.

The door in the corner opened, and Ludo Bagman walked into the room.

This was not, however, a Ludo Bagman gone to seed, but a Ludo Bagman who was clearly at the height of his Quidditch-playing fitness. His nose wasn't broken now; he was tall and lean and muscular. Bagman looked nervous as he sat down in the chained chair, but it did not bind him there as it had bound Karkaroff, and Bagman, perhaps taking heart from this, glanced around at the watching crowd, waved at a couple of them, and managed a small smile.

"Ludo Bagman, you have been brought here in front of the Council of Magical Law to answer charges relating to the activities of the Death Eaters," said Mr. Crouch. "We have heard the evidence against you, and are about to reach our verdict. Do you have anything to add to your testimony before we pronounce judgment?"

Harry couldn't believe his ears. *Ludo Bagman, a Death Eater?*

"Only," said Bagman, smiling awkwardly, "well — I know I've been a bit of an idiot —"

One or two wizards and witches in the surrounding seats smiled indulgently. Mr. Crouch did not appear to share their feelings. He was staring down at Ludo Bagman with an expression of the utmost severity and dislike.

"You never spoke a truer word, boy," someone muttered dryly to Dumbledore behind Harry. He looked around and saw Moody sitting there again. "If I didn't know he'd always been dim, I'd have said some of those Bludgers had permanently affected his brain. . . ."

"Ludovic Bagman, you were caught passing information to Lord Voldemort's supporters," said Mr. Crouch. "For this, I suggest a term of imprisonment in Azkaban lasting no less than —"

But there was an angry outcry from the surrounding benches. Several of the witches and wizards around the walls stood up, shaking their heads, and even their fists, at Mr. Crouch.

"But I've told you, I had no idea!" Bagman called earnestly over the crowd's babble, his round blue eyes widening. "None at all! Old Rookwood was a friend of my dad's . . . never crossed my mind he was in with You-Know-Who! I thought I was collecting information for our side! And Rookwood kept talking about getting me a job in the Ministry later on . . . once my Quidditch days are over, you know . . . I mean, I can't keep getting hit by Bludgers for the rest of my life, can I?"

There were titters from the crowd.

"It will be put to the vote," said Mr. Crouch coldly. He turned to the right-hand side of the dungeon. "The jury will please raise their hands . . . those in favor of imprisonment . . ."

Harry looked toward the right-hand side of the dungeon. Not one person raised their hand. Many of the witches and wizards around the walls began to clap. One of the witches on the jury stood up.

"Yes?" barked Crouch.

"We'd just like to congratulate Mr. Bagman on his splendid performance for England in the Quidditch match against Turkey last Saturday," the witch said breathlessly.

Mr. Crouch looked furious. The dungeon was ringing with applause now. Bagman got to his feet and bowed, beaming.

"Despicable," Mr. Crouch spat at Dumbledore, sitting down as Bagman walked out of the dungeon. "Rookwood get him a job indeed. . . . The day Ludo Bagman joins us will be a sad day indeed for the Ministry. . . ."

And the dungeon dissolved again. When it had returned, Harry looked around. He and Dumbledore were still sitting beside Mr. Crouch, but the atmosphere could not have been more different. There was total silence, broken only by the dry sobs of a frail, wispy-looking witch in the seat next to Mr. Crouch. She was clutching a handkerchief to her mouth with trembling hands.

Harry looked up at Crouch and saw that he looked gaunter and grayer than ever before. A nerve was twitching in his temple.

"Bring them in," he said, and his voice echoed through the silent dungeon.

The door in the corner opened yet again. Six dementors entered this time, flanking a group of four people. Harry saw the people in the crowd turn to look up at Mr. Crouch. A few of them whispered to one another.

The dementors placed each of the four people in the four chairs with chained arms that now stood on the dungeon floor. There was a thickset man who stared blankly up at Crouch; a thinner and more nervous-looking man, whose eyes were darting around the crowd; a woman with thick, shining dark hair and heavily hooded eyes, who was sitting in the chained chair as though it were a throne; and a boy in his late teens, who looked nothing short of petrified. He was shivering, his straw-colored hair all over his face, his freckled skin milk-white. The wispy little witch beside Crouch began to rock backward and forward in her seat, whimpering into her handkerchief.

Crouch stood up. He looked down upon the four in front of him, and there was pure hatred in his face.

"You have been brought here before the Council of Magical Law," he said clearly, "so that we may pass judgment on you, for a crime so heinous —"

"Father," said the boy with the straw-colored hair. "Father . . . please . . ."

"— that we have rarely heard the like of it within this court," said Crouch, speaking more loudly, drowning out his son's voice.

"We have heard the evidence against you. The four of you stand accused of capturing an Auror — Frank Longbottom — and subjecting him to the Cruciatus Curse, believing him to have knowledge of the present whereabouts of your exiled master, He-Who-Must-Not-Be-Named —"

"Father, I didn't!" shrieked the boy in chains below. "I didn't, I swear it, Father, don't send me back to the dementors —"

"You are further accused," bellowed Mr. Crouch, "of using the Cruciatus Curse on Frank Longbottom's wife, when he would not give you information. You planned to restore He-Who-Must-Not-Be-Named to power, and to resume the lives of violence you presumably led while he was strong. I now ask the jury —"

"Mother!" screamed the boy below, and the wispy little witch beside Crouch began to sob, rocking backward and forward. "Mother, stop him, Mother, I didn't do it, it wasn't me!"

"I now ask the jury," shouted Mr. Crouch, "to raise their hands if they believe, as I do, that these crimes deserve a life sentence in Azkaban!"

In unison, the witches and wizards along the right-hand side of the dungeon raised their hands. The crowd around the walls began to clap as it had for Bagman, their faces full of savage triumph. The boy began to scream.

"No! Mother, no! I didn't do it, I didn't do it, I didn't know! Don't send me there, don't let him!"

The dementors were gliding back into the room. The boys' three companions rose quietly from their seats; the woman with the heavy-lidded eyes looked up at Crouch and called, "The Dark Lord will rise again, Crouch! Throw us into Azkaban; we will wait! He will rise again and will come for us, he will reward us beyond any of his other supporters! We alone were faithful! We alone tried to find him!"

But the boy was trying to fight off the dementors, even though Harry could see their cold, draining power starting to affect him. The crowd was jeering, some of them on their feet, as the woman swept out of the dungeon, and the boy continued to struggle.

"I'm your son!" he screamed up at Crouch. "I'm your son!"

"You are no son of mine!" bellowed Mr. Crouch, his eyes bulging suddenly. "I have no son!"

The wispy witch beside him gave a great gasp and slumped in her seat. She had fainted. Crouch appeared not to have noticed.

"Take them away!" Crouch roared at the dementors, spit flying from his mouth. "Take them away, and may they rot there!"

"Father! Father, I wasn't involved! No! No! Father, please!"

"I think, Harry, it is time to return to my office," said a quiet voice in Harry's ear.

Harry started. He looked around. Then he looked on his other side.

There was an Albus Dumbledore sitting on his right, watching Crouch's son being dragged away by the dementors — and there was an Albus Dumbledore on his left, looking right at him.

"Come," said the Dumbledore on his left, and he put his hand under Harry's elbow. Harry felt himself rising into the air; the dungeon dissolved around him; for a moment, all was blackness, and then he felt as though he had done a slow-motion somersault, suddenly landing flat on his feet, in what seemed like the dazzling light of Dumbledore's sunlit office. The stone basin was shimmering in the cabinet in front of him, and Albus Dumbledore was standing beside him.

"Professor," Harry gasped, "I know I shouldn't've — I didn't mean — the cabinet door was sort of open and —"

"I quite understand," said Dumbledore. He lifted the basin, carried it over to his desk, placed it upon the polished top, and sat down in the chair behind it. He motioned for Harry to sit down opposite him.

Harry did so, staring at the stone basin. The contents had returned to their original, silvery-white state, swirling and rippling beneath his gaze.

"What is it?" Harry asked shakily.

"This? It is called a Pensieve," said Dumbledore. "I sometimes find, and I am sure you know the feeling, that I simply have too many thoughts and memories crammed into my mind."

"Er," said Harry, who couldn't truthfully say that he had ever felt anything of the sort.

"At these times," said Dumbledore, indicating the stone basin, "I use the Pensieve. One simply siphons the excess thoughts from one's mind, pours them into the basin, and examines them at one's leisure. It becomes easier to spot patterns and links, you understand, when they are in this form."

"You mean . . . that stuff's your *thoughts*?" Harry said, staring at the swirling white substance in the basin.

"Certainly," said Dumbledore. "Let me show you."

Dumbledore drew his wand out of the inside of his robes and placed the tip into his own silvery hair, near his temple. When he took the wand away, hair seemed to be clinging to it — but then

Harry saw that it was in fact a glistening strand of the same strange silvery-white substance that filled the Pensieve. Dumbledore added this fresh thought to the basin, and Harry, astonished, saw his own face swimming around the surface of the bowl. Dumbledore placed his long hands on either side of the Pensieve and swirled it, rather as a gold prospector would pan for fragments of gold . . . and Harry saw his own face change smoothly into Snape's, who opened his mouth and spoke to the ceiling, his voice echoing slightly.

"It's coming back . . . Karkaroff's too . . . stronger and clearer than ever . . ."

"A connection I could have made without assistance," Dumbledore sighed, "but never mind." He peered over the top of his half-moon spectacles at Harry, who was gaping at Snape's face, which was continuing to swirl around the bowl. "I was using the Pensieve when Mr. Fudge arrived for our meeting and put it away rather hastily. Undoubtedly I did not fasten the cabinet door properly. Naturally, it would have attracted your attention."

"I'm sorry," Harry mumbled.

Dumbledore shook his head. "Curiosity is not a sin," he said. "But we should exercise caution with our curiosity . . . yes, indeed . . ."

Frowning slightly, he prodded the thoughts within the basin with the tip of his wand. Instantly, a figure rose out of it, a plump, scowling girl of about sixteen, who began to revolve slowly, with her feet still in the basin. She took no notice whatsoever of Harry or Professor Dumbledore. When she spoke, her voice echoed as Snape's had done, as though it were coming from the depths of the stone basin. "He put a hex on me, Professor Dumbledore, and I was only teasing him, sir, I only said I'd seen him kissing Florence behind the greenhouses last Thursday. . . ."

"But why, Bertha," said Dumbledore sadly, looking up at the now silently revolving girl, "why did you have to follow him in the first place?"

"Bertha?" Harry whispered, looking up at her. "Is that — was that Bertha Jorkins?"

"Yes," said Dumbledore, prodding the thoughts in the basin again; Bertha sank back into them, and they became silvery and opaque once more. "That was Bertha as I remember her at school."

The silvery light from the Pensieve illuminated Dumbledore's face, and it struck Harry suddenly how very old he was looking. He knew, of course, that Dumbledore was getting on in years, but somehow he never really thought of Dumbledore as an old man.

"So, Harry," said Dumbledore quietly. "Before you got lost in my thoughts, you wanted to tell me something."

"Yes," said Harry. "Professor — I was in Divination just now, and — er — I fell asleep."

He hesitated here, wondering if a reprimand was coming, but Dumbledore merely said, "Quite understandable. Continue."

"Well, I had a dream," said Harry. "A dream about Lord Voldemort. He was torturing Wormtail . . . you know who Wormtail —"

"I do know," said Dumbledore promptly. "Please continue."

"Voldemort got a letter from an owl. He said something like, Wormtail's blunder had been repaired. He said someone was dead. Then he said, Wormtail wouldn't be fed to the snake — there was a snake beside his chair. He said — he said he'd be feeding me to it, instead. Then he did the Cruciatus Curse on Wormtail — and my scar hurt," Harry said. "It woke me up, it hurt so badly."

Dumbledore merely looked at him.

"Er — that's all," said Harry.

"I see," said Dumbledore quietly. "I see. Now, has your scar hurt at any other time this year, excepting the time it woke you up over the summer?"

"No, I — how did you know it woke me up over the summer?" said Harry, astonished.

"You are not Sirius's only correspondent," said Dumbledore. "I have also been in contact with him ever since he left Hogwarts last year. It was I who suggested the mountainside cave as the safest place for him to stay."

Dumbledore got up and began walking up and down behind his desk. Every now and then, he placed his wand-tip to his temple, removed another shining silver thought, and added it to the Pensieve. The thoughts inside began to swirl so fast that Harry couldn't make out anything clearly: It was merely a blur of color.

"Professor?" he said quietly, after a couple of minutes.

Dumbledore stopped pacing and looked at Harry.

"My apologies," he said quietly. He sat back down at his desk.

"D'you — d'you know why my scar's hurting me?"

Dumbledore looked very intently at Harry for a moment, and then said, "I have a theory, no more than that. . . . It is my belief that your scar hurts both when Lord Voldemort is near you, and when he is feeling a particularly strong surge of hatred."

"But . . . why?"

"Because you and he are connected by the curse that failed," said Dumbledore. "That is no ordinary scar."

"So you think . . . that dream . . . did it really happen?"

"It is possible," said Dumbledore. "I would say — probable. Harry — did you see Voldemort?"

"No," said Harry. "Just the back of his chair. But — there wouldn't have been anything to see, would there? I mean, he hasn't got a body, has he? But . . . but then how could he have held the wand?" Harry said slowly.

"How indeed?" muttered Dumbledore. "How indeed . . ."

Neither Dumbledore nor Harry spoke for a while. Dumbledore was gazing across the room, and, every now and then, placing his wand-tip to his temple and adding another shining silver thought to the seething mass within the Pensieve.

"Professor," Harry said at last, "do you think he's getting stronger?"

"Voldemort?" said Dumbledore, looking at Harry over the Pensieve. It was the characteristic, piercing look Dumbledore had given him on other occasions, and always made Harry feel as though Dumbledore were seeing right through him in a way that even Moody's magical eye could not. "Once again, Harry, I can only give you my suspicions."

Dumbledore sighed again, and he looked older, and wearier, than ever.

"The years of Voldemort's ascent to power," he said, "were marked with disappearances. Bertha Jorkins has vanished without a trace in the place where Voldemort was certainly known to be last. Mr. Crouch too has disappeared . . . within these very grounds. And there was a third disappearance, one which the Ministry, I regret to say, do not consider of any importance, for it concerns a Muggle. His name was Frank Bryce, he lived in the village where

Voldemort's father grew up, and he has not been seen since last August. You see, I read the Muggle newspapers, unlike most of my Ministry friends."

Dumbledore looked very seriously at Harry.

"These disappearances seem to me to be linked. The Ministry disagrees — as you may have heard, while waiting outside my office."

Harry nodded. Silence fell between them again, Dumbledore extracting thoughts every now and then. Harry felt as though he ought to go, but his curiosity held him in his chair.

"Professor?" he said again.

"Yes, Harry?" said Dumbledore.

"Er . . . could I ask you about . . . that court thing I was in . . . in the Pensieve?"

"You could," said Dumbledore heavily. "I attended it many times, but some trials come back to me more clearly than others . . . particularly now. . . ."

"You know — you know the trial you found me in? The one with Crouch's son? Well . . . were they talking about Neville's parents?"

Dumbledore gave Harry a very sharp look. "Has Neville never told you why he has been brought up by his grandmother?" he said.

Harry shook his head, wondering, as he did so, how he could have failed to ask Neville this, in almost four years of knowing him.

"Yes, they were talking about Neville's parents," said Dumbledore. "His father, Frank, was an Auror just like Professor Moody. He and his wife were tortured for information about Voldemort's whereabouts after he lost his powers, as you heard."

"So they're dead?" said Harry quietly.

"No," said Dumbledore, his voice full of a bitterness Harry had never heard there before. "They are insane. They are both in St. Mungo's Hospital for Magical Maladies and Injuries. I believe Neville visits them, with his grandmother, during the holidays. They do not recognize him."

Harry sat there, horror-struck. He had never known . . . never, in four years, bothered to find out . . .

"The Longbottoms were very popular," said Dumbledore. "The attacks on them came after Voldemort's fall from power, just when everyone thought they were safe. Those attacks caused a wave of fury such as I have never known. The Ministry was under great pressure to catch those who had done it. Unfortunately, the Longbottoms' evidence was — given their condition — none too reliable."

"Then Mr. Crouch's son might not have been involved?" said Harry slowly.

Dumbledore shook his head.

"As to that, I have no idea."

Harry sat in silence once more, watching the contents of the Pensieve swirl. There were two more questions he was burning to ask . . . but they concerned the guilt of living people. . . .

"Er," he said, "Mr. Bagman . . ."

". . . has never been accused of any Dark activity since," said Dumbledore calmly.

"Right," said Harry hastily, staring at the contents of the Pensieve again, which were swirling more slowly now that Dumbledore had stopped adding thoughts. "And . . . er . . ."

But the Pensieve seemed to be asking his question for him.

Snape's face was swimming on the surface again. Dumbledore glanced down into it, and then up at Harry.

"No more has Professor Snape," he said.

Harry looked into Dumbledore's light blue eyes, and the thing he really wanted to know spilled out of his mouth before he could stop it.

"What made you think he'd really stopped supporting Voldemort, Professor?"

Dumbledore held Harry's gaze for a few seconds, and then said, "That, Harry, is a matter between Professor Snape and myself."

Harry knew that the interview was over; Dumbledore did not look angry, yet there was a finality in his tone that told Harry it was time to go. He stood up, and so did Dumbledore.

"Harry," he said as Harry reached the door. "Please do not speak about Neville's parents to anybody else. He has the right to let people know, when he is ready."

"Yes, Professor," said Harry, turning to go.

"And —"

Harry looked back. Dumbledore was standing over the Pensieve, his face lit from beneath by its silvery spots of light, looking older than ever. He stared at Harry for a moment, and then said, "Good luck with the third task."

# THE THIRD TASK

D umbledore reckons You-Know-Who's getting stronger again as well?" Ron whispered.

Everything Harry had seen in the Pensieve, nearly everything Dumbledore had told and shown him afterward, he had now shared with Ron and Hermione — and, of course, with Sirius, to whom Harry had sent an owl the moment he had left Dumbledore's office. Harry, Ron, and Hermione sat up late in the common room once again that night, talking it all over until Harry's mind was reeling, until he understood what Dumbledore had meant about a head becoming so full of thoughts that it would have been a relief to siphon them off.

Ron stared into the common room fire. Harry thought he saw Ron shiver slightly, even though the evening was warm.

"And he trusts Snape?" Ron said. "He really trusts Snape, even though he knows he was a Death Eater?"

"Yes," said Harry.

Hermione had not spoken for ten minutes. She was sitting with her forehead in her hands, staring at her knees. Harry thought she too looked as though she could have done with a Pensieve.

"Rita Skeeter," she muttered finally.

"How can you be worrying about her now?" said Ron, in utter disbelief.

"I'm not worrying about her," Hermione said to her knees. "I'm just thinking . . . remember what she said to me in the Three Broomsticks? 'I know things about Ludo Bagman that would make your hair curl.' This is what she meant, isn't it? She reported his trial, she knew he'd passed information to the Death Eaters. And Winky too, remember . . . 'Ludo Bagman's a bad wizard.' Mr. Crouch would have been furious he got off, he would have talked about it at home."

"Yeah, but Bagman didn't pass information on purpose, did he?"

Hermione shrugged.

"And Fudge reckons *Madame Maxime* attacked Crouch?" Ron said, turning back to Harry.

"Yeah," said Harry, "but he's only saying that because Crouch disappeared near the Beauxbatons carriage."

"We never thought of her, did we?" said Ron slowly. "Mind you, she's definitely got giant blood, and she doesn't want to admit it —"

"Of course she doesn't," said Hermione sharply, looking up. "Look what happened to Hagrid when Rita found out about his mother. Look at Fudge, jumping to conclusions about her, just because she's part giant. Who needs that sort of prejudice? I'd probably say I had big bones if I knew that's what I'd get for telling the truth."

Hermione looked at her watch. "We haven't done any practicing!" she said, looking shocked. "We were going to do the Impediment Curse! We'll have to really get down to it tomorrow! Come on, Harry, you need to get some sleep."

Harry and Ron went slowly upstairs to their dormitory. As Harry pulled on his pajamas, he looked over at Neville's bed. True to his word to Dumbledore, he had not told Ron and Hermione about Neville's parents. As Harry took off his glasses and climbed into his four-poster, he imagined how it must feel to have parents still living but unable to recognize you. He often got sympathy from strangers for being an orphan, but as he listened to Neville's snores, he thought that Neville deserved it more than he did. Lying in the darkness, Harry felt a rush of anger and hate toward the people who had tortured Mr. and Mrs. Longbottom. . . . He remembered the jeers of the crowd as Crouch's son and his companions had been dragged from the court by the dementors. . . . He understood how they had felt. . . . Then he remembered the milk-white face of the screaming boy and realized with a jolt that he had died a year later. . . .

It was Voldemort, Harry thought, staring up at the canopy of his bed in the darkness, it all came back to Voldemort. . . . He was the one who had torn these families apart, who had ruined all these lives. . . .

Ron and Hermione were supposed to be studying for their exams, which would finish on the day of the third task, but they were putting most of their efforts into helping Harry prepare.

"Don't worry about it," Hermione said shortly when Harry pointed this out to them and said he didn't mind practicing on his own for a while, "at least we'll get top marks in Defense Against the Dark Arts. We'd never have found out about all these hexes in class."

"Good training for when we're all Aurors," said Ron excitedly, attempting the Impediment Curse on a wasp that had buzzed into the room and making it stop dead in midair.

The mood in the castle as they entered June became excited and tense again. Everyone was looking forward to the third task, which would take place a week before the end of term. Harry was practicing hexes at every available moment. He felt more confident about this task than either of the others. Difficult and dangerous though it would undoubtedly be, Moody was right: Harry had managed to find his way past monstrous creatures and enchanted barriers before now, and this time he had some notice, some chance to prepare himself for what lay ahead.

Tired of walking in on Harry, Hermione, and Ron all over the school, Professor McGonagall had given them permission to use the empty Transfiguration classroom at lunchtimes. Harry had soon mastered the Impediment Curse, a spell to slow down and obstruct attackers; the Reductor Curse, which would enable him to blast solid objects out of his way; and the Four-Point Spell, a useful discovery of Hermione's that would make his wand point due north, therefore enabling him to check whether he was going in the right direction within the maze. He was still having trouble with the Shield Charm, though. This was supposed to cast a temporary, invisible wall around himself that deflected minor curses; Hermione managed to shatter it with a well-placed Jelly-Legs Jinx, and Harry wobbled around the room for ten minutes afterward before she had looked up the counter-jinx.

"You're still doing really well, though," Hermione said encouragingly, looking down her list and crossing off those spells they had already learned. "Some of these are bound to come in handy."

"Come and look at this," said Ron, who was standing by the window. He was staring down onto the grounds. "What's Malfoy doing?"

Harry and Hermione went to see. Malfoy, Crabbe, and Goyle were standing in the shadow of a tree below. Crabbe and Goyle seemed to be keeping a lookout; both were smirking. Malfoy was holding his hand up to his mouth and speaking into it.

"He looks like he's using a walkie-talkie," said Harry curiously.

"He can't be," said Hermione, "I've told you, those sorts of things don't work around Hogwarts. Come on, Harry," she added briskly, turning away from the window and moving back into the middle of the room, "let's try that Shield Charm again."

Sirius was sending daily owls now. Like Hermione, he seemed to want to concentrate on getting Harry through the last task before they concerned themselves with anything else. He reminded Harry in every letter that whatever might be going on outside the walls of Hogwarts was not Harry's responsibility, nor was it within his power to influence it.

*If Voldemort is really getting stronger again,* he wrote, *my priority is to ensure your safety. He cannot hope to lay hands on you while you are under Dumbledore's protection, but all the same, take no risks: Concentrate on getting through that maze safely, and then we can turn our attention to other matters.*

Harry's nerves mounted as June the twenty-fourth drew closer, but they were not as bad as those he had felt before the first and second tasks. For one thing, he was confident that, this time, he had done everything in his power to prepare for the task. For another, this was the final hurdle, and however well or badly he did, the tournament would at last be over, which would be an enormous relief.

Breakfast was a very noisy affair at the Gryffindor table on the morning of the third task. The post owls appeared, bringing Harry a good-luck card from Sirius. It was only a piece of parchment, folded over and bearing a muddy paw print on its front, but Harry appreciated it all the same. A screech owl arrived for Hermione, carrying her morning copy of the *Daily Prophet* as usual. She unfolded the paper, glanced at the front page, and spat out a mouthful of pumpkin juice all over it.

"What?" said Harry and Ron together, staring at her.

"Nothing," said Hermione quickly, trying to shove the paper out of sight, but Ron grabbed it. He stared at the headline and said, "No way. Not today. That old *cow*."

"What?" said Harry. "Rita Skeeter again?"

"No," said Ron, and just like Hermione, he attempted to push the paper out of sight.

"It's about me, isn't it?" said Harry.

"No," said Ron, in an entirely unconvincing tone.

But before Harry could demand to see the paper, Draco Malfoy shouted across the Great Hall from the Slytherin table.

"Hey, Potter! *Potter!* How's your head? You feeling all right? Sure you're not going to go berserk on us?"

Malfoy was holding a copy of the *Daily Prophet* too. Slytherins

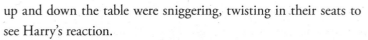

up and down the table were sniggering, twisting in their seats to see Harry's reaction.

"Let me see it," Harry said to Ron. "Give it here."

Very reluctantly, Ron handed over the newspaper. Harry turned it over and found himself staring at his own picture, beneath the banner headline:

### HARRY POTTER
### "DISTURBED AND DANGEROUS"

The boy who defeated He-Who-Must-Not-Be-Named is unstable and possibly dangerous, *writes Rita Skeeter, Special Correspondent.* Alarming evidence has recently come to light about Harry Potter's strange behavior, which casts doubts upon his suitability to compete in a demanding competition like the Triwizard Tournament, or even to attend Hogwarts School.

Potter, the *Daily Prophet* can exclusively reveal, regularly collapses at school, and is often heard to complain of pain in the scar on his forehead (relic of the curse with which You-Know-Who attempted to kill him). On Monday last, midway through a Divination lesson, your *Daily Prophet* reporter witnessed Potter storming from the class, claiming that his scar was hurting too badly to continue studying.

It is possible, say top experts at St. Mungo's Hospital for Magical Maladies and Injuries, that Potter's brain was affected by the attack inflicted upon him by You-Know-Who, and that his insistence that the scar is still hurting is an expression of his deep-seated confusion.

"He might even be pretending," said one specialist. "This could be a plea for attention."

The *Daily Prophet,* however, has unearthed worrying facts about Harry Potter that Albus Dumbledore, headmaster of Hogwarts, has carefully concealed from the Wizarding public.

"Potter can speak Parseltongue," reveals Draco Malfoy, a Hogwarts fourth year. "There were a lot of attacks on students a couple of years ago, and most people thought Potter was behind them after they saw him lose his temper at a dueling club and set a snake on another boy. It was all hushed up, though. But he's made friends with werewolves and giants too. We think he'd do anything for a bit of power."

Parseltongue, the ability to converse with snakes, has long been considered a Dark Art. Indeed, the most famous Parselmouth of our times is none other than You-Know-Who himself. A member of the Dark Force Defense League, who wished to remain unnamed, stated that he would regard any wizard who could speak Parseltongue "as worthy of investigation. Personally, I would be highly suspicious of anybody who could converse with snakes, as serpents are often used in the worst kinds of Dark Magic, and are historically associated with evildoers." Similarly, "anyone who seeks out the company of such vicious creatures as werewolves and giants would appear to have a fondness for violence."

Albus Dumbledore should surely consider whether a boy such as this should be allowed to compete in the Triwizard Tournament. Some fear that Potter might resort to the Dark Arts in his desperation to win the tournament, the third task of which takes place this evening.

"Gone off me a bit, hasn't she?" said Harry lightly, folding up the paper.

Over at the Slytherin table, Malfoy, Crabbe, and Goyle were laughing at him, tapping their heads with their fingers, pulling grotesquely mad faces, and waggling their tongues like snakes.

"How did she know your scar hurt in Divination?" Ron said. "There's no way she was there, there's no way she could've heard —"

"The window was open," said Harry. "I opened it to breathe."

"You were at the top of North Tower!" Hermione said. "Your voice couldn't have carried all the way down to the grounds!"

"Well, you're the one who's supposed to be researching magical methods of bugging!" said Harry. "You tell me how she did it!"

"I've been trying!" said Hermione. "But I . . . but . . ."

An odd, dreamy expression suddenly came over Hermione's face. She slowly raised a hand and ran her fingers through her hair.

"Are you all right?" said Ron, frowning at her.

"Yes," said Hermione breathlessly. She ran her fingers through her hair again, and then held her hand up to her mouth, as though speaking into an invisible walkie-talkie. Harry and Ron stared at each other.

"I've had an idea," Hermione said, gazing into space. "I think I know . . . because then no one would be able to see . . . even Moody . . . and she'd have been able to get onto the window ledge . . . but she's not allowed . . . she's *definitely* not allowed . . . I think we've got her! Just give me two seconds in the library — just to make sure!"

With that, Hermione seized her school bag and dashed out of the Great Hall.

"Oi!" Ron called after her. "We've got our History of Magic exam in ten minutes! Blimey," he said, turning back to Harry, "she must really hate that Skeeter woman to risk missing the start of an exam. What're you going to do in Binns's class — read again?"

Exempt from the end-of-term tests as a Triwizard champion, Harry had been sitting in the back of every exam class so far, looking up fresh hexes for the third task.

"S'pose so," Harry said to Ron; but just then, Professor McGonagall came walking alongside the Gryffindor table toward him.

"Potter, the champions are congregating in the chamber off the Hall after breakfast," she said.

"But the task's not till tonight!" said Harry, accidentally spilling scrambled eggs down his front, afraid he had mistaken the time.

"I'm aware of that, Potter," she said. "The champions' families are invited to watch the final task, you know. This is simply a chance for you to greet them."

She moved away. Harry gaped after her.

"She doesn't expect the Dursleys to turn up, does she?" he asked Ron blankly.

"Dunno," said Ron. "Harry, I'd better hurry, I'm going to be late for Binns. See you later."

Harry finished his breakfast in the emptying Great Hall. He saw Fleur Delacour get up from the Ravenclaw table and join Cedric as he crossed to the side chamber and entered. Krum slouched off to join them shortly afterward. Harry stayed where he was. He really didn't want to go into the chamber. He had no family — no family who would turn up to see him risk his life, anyway. But just as he was getting up, thinking that he might as well go up to the library and do a spot more hex research, the door of the side chamber opened, and Cedric stuck his head out.

"Harry, come on, they're waiting for you!"

Utterly perplexed, Harry got up. The Dursleys couldn't possibly be here, could they? He walked across the Hall and opened the door into the chamber.

Cedric and his parents were just inside the door. Viktor Krum was over in a corner, conversing with his dark-haired mother and father in rapid Bulgarian. He had inherited his father's hooked nose. On the other side of the room, Fleur was jabbering away in French to her mother. Fleur's little sister, Gabrielle, was holding her mother's hand. She waved at Harry, who waved back, grinning. Then he saw Mrs. Weasley and Bill standing in front of the fireplace, beaming at him.

"Surprise!" Mrs. Weasley said excitedly as he smiled broadly and walked over to them. "Thought we'd come and watch you, Harry!" She bent down and kissed him on the cheek.

"You all right?" said Bill, grinning at Harry and shaking his hand. "Charlie wanted to come, but he couldn't get time off. He said you were incredible against the Horntail."

Fleur Delacour, Harry noticed, was eyeing Bill with great interest over her mother's shoulder. Harry could tell she had no objection whatsoever to long hair or earrings with fangs on them.

"This is really nice of you," Harry muttered to Mrs. Weasley. "I thought for a moment — the Dursleys —"

"Hmm," said Mrs. Weasley, pursing her lips. She had always refrained from criticizing the Dursleys in front of Harry, but her eyes flashed every time they were mentioned.

"It's great being back here," said Bill, looking around the chamber (Violet, the Fat Lady's friend, winked at him from her frame). "Haven't seen this place for five years. Is that picture of the mad knight still around? Sir Cadogan?"

"Oh yeah," said Harry, who had met Sir Cadogan the previous year.

"And the Fat Lady?" said Bill.

"She was here in my time," said Mrs. Weasley. "She gave me such a telling off one night when I got back to the dormitory at four in the morning —"

"What were you doing out of your dormitory at four in the morning?" said Bill, surveying his mother with amazement.

Mrs. Weasley grinned, her eyes twinkling.

"Your father and I had been for a nighttime stroll," she said. "He got caught by Apollyon Pringle — he was the caretaker in those days — your father's still got the marks."

"Fancy giving us a tour, Harry?" said Bill.

"Yeah, okay," said Harry, and they made their way back toward the door into the Great Hall. As they passed Amos Diggory, he looked around.

"There you are, are you?" he said, looking Harry up and down.

"Bet you're not feeling quite as full of yourself now Cedric's caught you up on points, are you?"

"What?" said Harry.

"Ignore him," said Cedric in a low voice to Harry, frowning after his father. "He's been angry ever since Rita Skeeter's article about the Triwizard Tournament — you know, when she made out you were the only Hogwarts champion."

"Didn't bother to correct her, though, did he?" said Amos Diggory, loudly enough for Harry to hear as he started to walk out of the door with Mrs. Weasley and Bill. "Still . . . you'll show him, Ced. Beaten him once before, haven't you?"

"Rita Skeeter goes out of her way to cause trouble, Amos!" Mrs. Weasley said angrily. "I would have thought you'd know that, working at the Ministry!"

Mr. Diggory looked as though he was going to say something angry, but his wife laid a hand on his arm, and he merely shrugged and turned away.

Harry had a very enjoyable morning walking over the sunny grounds with Bill and Mrs. Weasley, showing them the Beauxbatons carriage and the Durmstrang ship. Mrs. Weasley was intrigued by the Whomping Willow, which had been planted after she had left school, and reminisced at length about the gamekeeper before Hagrid, a man called Ogg.

"How's Percy?" Harry asked as they walked around the greenhouses.

"Not good," said Bill.

"He's very upset," said Mrs. Weasley, lowering her voice and glancing around. "The Ministry wants to keep Mr. Crouch's disappearance quiet, but Percy's been hauled in for questioning about the instructions Mr. Crouch has been sending in. They seem to think there's a chance they weren't genuinely written by him. Percy's been under a lot of strain. They're not letting him fill in for Mr. Crouch as the fifth judge tonight. Cornelius Fudge is going to be doing it."

They returned to the castle for lunch.

"Mum — Bill!" said Ron, looking stunned, as he joined the Gryffindor table. "What're you doing here?"

"Come to watch Harry in the last task!" said Mrs. Weasley brightly. "I must say, it makes a lovely change, not having to cook. How was your exam?"

"Oh . . . okay," said Ron. "Couldn't remember all the goblin rebels' names, so I invented a few. It's all right," he said, helping himself to a Cornish pasty, while Mrs. Weasley looked stern, "they're all called stuff like Bodrod the Bearded and Urg the Unclean; it wasn't hard."

Fred, George, and Ginny came to sit next to them too, and Harry was having such a good time he felt almost as though he were back at the Burrow; he had forgotten to worry about that evening's task, and not until Hermione turned up, halfway through lunch, did he remember that she had had a brainwave about Rita Skeeter.

"Are you going to tell us — ?"

Hermione shook her head warningly and glanced at Mrs. Weasley.

"Hello, Hermione," said Mrs. Weasley, much more stiffly than usual.

"Hello," said Hermione, her smile faltering at the cold expression on Mrs. Weasley's face.

Harry looked between them, then said, "Mrs. Weasley, you didn't believe that rubbish Rita Skeeter wrote in *Witch Weekly,* did you? Because Hermione's not my girlfriend."

"Oh!" said Mrs. Weasley. "No — of course I didn't!"

But she became considerably warmer toward Hermione after that.

Harry, Bill, and Mrs. Weasley whiled away the afternoon with a long walk around the castle, and then returned to the Great Hall for the evening feast. Ludo Bagman and Cornelius Fudge had joined the staff table now. Bagman looked quite cheerful, but Cornelius Fudge, who was sitting next to Madame Maxime, looked stern and was not talking. Madame Maxime was concentrating on her plate, and Harry thought her eyes looked red. Hagrid kept glancing along the table at her.

There were more courses than usual, but Harry, who was starting to feel really nervous now, didn't eat much. As the enchanted ceiling overhead began to fade from blue to a dusky purple, Dumbledore rose to his feet at the staff table, and silence fell.

"Ladies and gentlemen, in five minutes' time, I will be asking you to make your way down to the Quidditch field for the third and final task of the Triwizard Tournament. Will the champions please follow Mr. Bagman down to the stadium now."

Harry got up. The Gryffindors all along the table were applauding him; the Weasleys and Hermione all wished him good luck, and he headed off out of the Great Hall with Cedric, Fleur, and Viktor.

"Feeling all right, Harry?" Bagman asked as they went down the stone steps onto the grounds. "Confident?"

"I'm okay," said Harry. It was sort of true; he was nervous, but he kept running over all the hexes and spells he had been practicing in his mind as they walked, and the knowledge that he could remember them all made him feel better.

They walked onto the Quidditch field, which was now completely unrecognizable. A twenty-foot-high hedge ran all the way around the edge of it. There was a gap right in front of them: the entrance to the vast maze. The passage beyond it looked dark and creepy.

Five minutes later, the stands had begun to fill; the air was full of excited voices and the rumbling of feet as the hundreds of students filed into their seats. The sky was a deep, clear blue now, and the first stars were starting to appear. Hagrid, Professor Moody, Professor McGonagall, and Professor Flitwick came walking into the stadium and approached Bagman and the champions. They were wearing large, red, luminous stars on their hats, all except Hagrid, who had his on the back of his moleskin vest.

"We are going to be patrolling the outside of the maze," said Professor McGonagall to the champions. "If you get into difficulty, and wish to be rescued, send red sparks into the air, and one of us will come and get you, do you understand?"

The champions nodded.

"Off you go, then!" said Bagman brightly to the four patrollers.

"Good luck, Harry," Hagrid whispered, and the four of them walked away in different directions, to station themselves around the maze. Bagman now pointed his wand at his throat, muttered, *"Sonorus,"* and his magically magnified voice echoed into the stands.

"Ladies and gentlemen, the third and final task of the Triwizard

Tournament is about to begin! Let me remind you how the points currently stand! Tied in first place, with eighty-five points each — Mr. Cedric Diggory and Mr. Harry Potter, both of Hogwarts School!" The cheers and applause sent birds from the Forbidden Forest fluttering into the darkening sky. "In second place, with eighty points — Mr. Viktor Krum, of Durmstrang Institute!" More applause. "And in third place — Miss Fleur Delacour, of Beauxbatons Academy!"

Harry could just make out Mrs. Weasley, Bill, Ron, and Hermione applauding Fleur politely, halfway up the stands. He waved up at them, and they waved back, beaming at him.

"So . . . on my whistle, Harry and Cedric!" said Bagman. "Three — two — one —"

He gave a short blast on his whistle, and Harry and Cedric hurried forward into the maze.

The towering hedges cast black shadows across the path, and, whether because they were so tall and thick or because they had been enchanted, the sound of the surrounding crowd was silenced the moment they entered the maze. Harry felt almost as though he were underwater again. He pulled out his wand, muttered, *"Lumos,"* and heard Cedric do the same just behind him.

After about fifty yards, they reached a fork. They looked at each other.

"See you," Harry said, and he took the left one, while Cedric took the right.

Harry heard Bagman's whistle for the second time. Krum had entered the maze. Harry sped up. His chosen path seemed completely deserted. He turned right, and hurried on, holding his wand high over his head, trying to see as far ahead as possible. Still, there was nothing in sight.

Bagman's whistle blew in the distance for the third time. All of the champions were now inside.

Harry kept looking behind him. The old feeling that he was being watched was upon him. The maze was growing darker with every passing minute as the sky overhead deepened to navy. He reached a second fork.

"*Point Me,*" he whispered to his wand, holding it flat in his palm.

The wand spun around once and pointed toward his right, into solid hedge. That way was north, and he knew that he needed to go northwest for the center of the maze. The best he could do was to take the left fork and go right again as soon as possible.

The path ahead was empty too, and when Harry reached a right turn and took it, he again found his way unblocked. Harry didn't know why, but the lack of obstacles was unnerving him. Surely he should have met something by now? It felt as though the maze were luring him into a false sense of security. Then he heard movement right behind him. He held out his wand, ready to attack, but its beam fell only upon Cedric, who had just hurried out of a path on the right-hand side. Cedric looked severely shaken. The sleeve of his robe was smoking.

"Hagrid's Blast-Ended Skrewts!" he hissed. "They're enormous — I only just got away!"

He shook his head and dived out of sight, along another path. Keen to put plenty of distance between himself and the skrewts, Harry hurried off again. Then, as he turned a corner, he saw . . . a dementor gliding toward him. Twelve feet tall, its face hidden by its hood, its rotting, scabbed hands outstretched, it advanced, sensing its way blindly toward him. Harry could hear its rattling breath; he felt clammy coldness stealing over him, but knew what he had to do. . . .

He summoned the happiest thought he could, concentrated with all his might on the thought of getting out of the maze and celebrating with Ron and Hermione, raised his wand, and cried, *"Expecto Patronum!"*

A silver stag erupted from the end of Harry's wand and galloped toward the dementor, which fell back and tripped over the hem of its robes. . . . Harry had never seen a dementor stumble.

"Hang on!" he shouted, advancing in the wake of his silver Patronus. "You're a boggart! *Riddikulus!*"

There was a loud crack, and the shape-shifter exploded in a wisp of smoke. The silver stag faded from sight. Harry wished it could have stayed, he could have used some company . . . but he moved on, quickly and quietly as possible, listening hard, his wand held high once more.

Left . . . right . . . left again . . . Twice he found himself facing dead ends. He did the Four-Point Spell again and found that he was going too far east. He turned back, took a right turn, and saw an odd golden mist floating ahead of him.

Harry approached it cautiously, pointing the wand's beam at it. This looked like some kind of enchantment. He wondered whether he might be able to blast it out of the way.

*"Reducto!"* he said.

The spell shot straight through the mist, leaving it intact. He supposed he should have known better; the Reductor Curse was for solid objects. What would happen if he walked through the mist? Was it worth chancing it, or should he double back?

He was still hesitating when a scream shattered the silence.

"Fleur?" Harry yelled.

There was silence. He stared all around him. What had happened to her? Her scream seemed to have come from somewhere ahead. He took a deep breath and ran through the enchanted mist.

The world turned upside down. Harry was hanging from the ground, with his hair on end, his glasses dangling off his nose, threatening to fall into the bottomless sky. He clutched them to the end of his nose and hung there, terrified. It felt as though his feet were glued to the grass, which had now become the ceiling. Below him the dark, star-spangled heavens stretched endlessly. He felt as though if he tried to move one of his feet, he would fall away from the earth completely.

*Think,* he told himself, as all the blood rushed to his head, *think . . .*

But not one of the spells he had practiced had been designed to combat a sudden reversal of ground and sky. Did he dare move his foot? He could hear the blood pounding in his ears. He had two choices — try and move, or send up red sparks, and get rescued and disqualified from the task.

He shut his eyes, so he wouldn't be able to see the view of endless space below him, and pulled his right foot as hard as he could away from the grassy ceiling.

Immediately, the world righted itself. Harry fell forward onto his knees onto the wonderfully solid ground. He felt temporarily limp with shock. He took a deep, steadying breath, then got up again and hurried forward, looking back over his shoulder as he ran away from the golden mist, which twinkled innocently at him in the moonlight.

He paused at a junction of two paths and looked around for some sign of Fleur. He was sure it had been she who had screamed. What had she met? Was she all right? There was no sign of red sparks — did that mean she had got herself out of trouble, or was she in such trouble that she couldn't reach her wand? Harry took the right fork with a feeling of increasing unease . . . but at the same time, he couldn't help thinking, *One champion down . . .*

The Cup was somewhere close by, and it sounded as though Fleur was no longer in the running. He'd got this far, hadn't he? What if he actually managed to win? Fleetingly, and for the first time since he'd found himself champion, he saw again that image of himself, raising the Triwizard Cup in front of the rest of the school. . . .

He met nothing for ten minutes, but kept running into dead ends. Twice he took the same wrong turning. Finally, he found a new route and started to jog along it, his wandlight waving, making his shadow flicker and distort on the hedge walls. Then he rounded another corner and found himself facing a Blast-Ended Skrewt.

Cedric was right — it *was* enormous. Ten feet long, it looked more like a giant scorpion than anything. Its long sting was curled over its back. Its thick armor glinted in the light from Harry's wand, which he pointed at it.

"*Stupefy!*"

The spell hit the skrewt's armor and rebounded; Harry ducked just in time, but could smell burning hair; it had singed the top of his head. The skrewt issued a blast of fire from its end and flew forward toward him.

"*Impedimenta!*" Harry yelled. The spell hit the skrewt's armor again and ricocheted off; Harry staggered back a few paces and fell over. "*IMPEDIMENTA!*"

The skrewt was inches from him when it froze — he had managed to hit it on its fleshy, shell-less underside. Panting, Harry pushed himself away from it and ran, hard, in the opposite direction — the Impediment Curse was not permanent; the skrewt would be regaining the use of its legs at any moment.

He took a left path and hit a dead end, a right, and hit another; forcing himself to stop, heart hammering, he performed the Four-Point Spell again, backtracked, and chose a path that would take him northwest.

He had been hurrying along the new path for a few minutes, when he heard something in the path running parallel to his own that made him stop dead.

"What are you doing?" yelled Cedric's voice. "What the hell d'you think you're doing?"

And then Harry heard Krum's voice.

"*Crucio!*"

The air was suddenly full of Cedric's yells. Horrified, Harry began sprinting up his path, trying to find a way into Cedric's. When none appeared, he tried the Reductor Curse again. It wasn't very effective, but it burned a small hole in the hedge through which Harry forced his leg, kicking at the thick brambles and branches until they broke and made an opening; he struggled through it, tearing his robes, and looking to his right, saw Cedric jerking and twitching on the ground, Krum standing over him.

Harry pulled himself up and pointed his wand at Krum just as Krum looked up. Krum turned and began to run.

"*Stupefy!*" Harry yelled.

The spell hit Krum in the back; he stopped dead in his tracks, fell forward, and lay motionless, facedown in the grass. Harry dashed over to Cedric, who had stopped twitching and was lying there panting, his hands over his face.

"Are you all right?" Harry said roughly, grabbing Cedric's arm.

"Yeah," panted Cedric. "Yeah . . . I don't believe it . . . he crept up behind me. . . . I heard him, I turned around, and he had his wand on me. . . ."

Cedric got up. He was still shaking. He and Harry looked down at Krum.

"I can't believe this . . . I thought he was all right," Harry said, staring at Krum.

"So did I," said Cedric.

"Did you hear Fleur scream earlier?" said Harry.

"Yeah," said Cedric. "You don't think Krum got her too?"

"I don't know," said Harry slowly.

"Should we leave him here?" Cedric muttered.

"No," said Harry. "I reckon we should send up red sparks. Someone'll come and collect him . . . otherwise he'll probably be eaten by a skrewt."

"He'd deserve it," Cedric muttered, but all the same, he raised his wand and shot a shower of red sparks into the air, which hovered high above Krum, marking the spot where he lay.

Harry and Cedric stood there in the darkness for a moment, looking around them. Then Cedric said, "Well . . . I s'pose we'd better go on. . . ."

"What?" said Harry. "Oh . . . yeah . . . right . . ."

It was an odd moment. He and Cedric had been briefly united against Krum — now the fact that they were opponents came back to Harry. The two of them proceeded up the dark path without speaking, then Harry turned left, and Cedric right. Cedric's footsteps soon died away.

Harry moved on, continuing to use the Four-Point Spell, making sure he was moving in the right direction. It was between him and Cedric now. His desire to reach the cup first was now burning stronger than ever, but he could hardly believe what he'd just seen Krum do. The use of an Unforgivable Curse on a fellow human being meant a life term in Azkaban, that was what Moody had told them. Krum surely couldn't have wanted the Triwizard Cup that badly. . . . Harry sped up.

Every so often he hit more dead ends, but the increasing darkness made him feel sure he was getting near the heart of the maze. Then, as he strode down a long, straight path, he saw movement once again, and his beam of wandlight hit an extraordinary creature, one which he had only seen in picture form, in his *Monster Book of Monsters*.

It was a sphinx. It had the body of an over-large lion: great clawed paws and a long yellowish tail ending in a brown tuft. Its head, however, was that of a woman. She turned her long, almond-shaped eyes upon Harry as he approached. He raised his wand, hesitating. She was not crouching as if to spring, but pacing from side to side of the path, blocking his progress. Then she spoke, in a deep, hoarse voice.

"You are very near your goal. The quickest way is past me."

"So . . . so will you move, please?" said Harry, knowing what the answer was going to be.

"No," she said, continuing to pace. "Not unless you can answer my riddle. Answer on your first guess — I let you pass. Answer wrongly — I attack. Remain silent — I will let you walk away from me unscathed."

Harry's stomach slipped several notches. It was Hermione who was good at this sort of thing, not him. He weighed his chances. If the riddle was too hard, he could keep silent, get away from the sphinx unharmed, and try and find an alternative route to the center.

"Okay," he said. "Can I hear the riddle?"

The sphinx sat down upon her hind legs, in the very middle of the path, and recited:

> *"First think of the person who lives in disguise,*
> *Who deals in secrets and tells naught but lies.*
> *Next, tell me what's always the last thing to mend,*
> *The middle of middle and end of the end?*
> *And finally give me the sound often heard*
> *During the search for a hard-to-find word.*
> *Now string them together, and answer me this,*
> *Which creature would you be unwilling to kiss?"*

Harry gaped at her.

"Could I have it again . . . more slowly?" he asked tentatively.

She blinked at him, smiled, and repeated the poem.

"All the clues add up to a creature I wouldn't want to kiss?" Harry asked.

She merely smiled her mysterious smile. Harry took that for a "yes." Harry cast his mind around. There were plenty of animals he wouldn't want to kiss; his immediate thought was a Blast-Ended Skrewt, but something told him that wasn't the answer. He'd have to try and work out the clues. . . .

"A person in disguise," Harry muttered, staring at her, "who lies . . . er . . . that'd be a — an imposter. No, that's not my guess! A — a spy? I'll come back to that . . . could you give me the next clue again, please?"

She repeated the next lines of the poem.

"'The last thing to mend,'" Harry repeated. "Er . . . no idea . . . 'middle of middle'. . . could I have the last bit again?"

She gave him the last four lines.

"'The sound often heard during the search for a hard-to-find word,'" said Harry. "Er . . . that'd be . . . er . . . hang on — 'er'! Er's a sound!"

The sphinx smiled at him.

"Spy . . . er . . . spy . . . er . . ." said Harry, pacing up and down. "A creature I wouldn't want to kiss . . . *a spider!*"

The sphinx smiled more broadly. She got up, stretched her front legs, and then moved aside for him to pass.

"Thanks!" said Harry, and, amazed at his own brilliance, he dashed forward.

He had to be close now, he had to be. . . . His wand was telling him he was bang on course; as long as he didn't meet anything too horrible, he might have a chance. . . .

Harry broke into a run. He had a choice of paths up ahead. *"Point Me!"* he whispered again to his wand, and it spun around and pointed him to the right-hand one. He dashed up this one and saw light ahead.

The Triwizard Cup was gleaming on a plinth a hundred yards away. Suddenly a dark figure hurtled out onto the path in front of him.

Cedric was going to get there first. Cedric was sprinting as fast as he could toward the cup, and Harry knew he would never catch up, Cedric was much taller, had much longer legs —

Then Harry saw something immense over a hedge to his left, moving quickly along a path that intersected with his own; it was moving so fast Cedric was about to run into it, and Cedric, his eyes on the cup, had not seen it —

"Cedric!" Harry bellowed. "On your left!"

Cedric looked around just in time to hurl himself past the thing and avoid colliding with it, but in his haste, he tripped. Harry saw Cedric's wand fly out of his hand as a gigantic spider stepped into the path and began to bear down upon Cedric.

"*Stupefy!*" Harry yelled; the spell hit the spider's gigantic, hairy black body, but for all the good it did, he might as well have thrown a stone at it; the spider jerked, scuttled around, and ran at Harry instead.

"*Stupefy! Impedimenta! Stupefy!*"

But it was no use — the spider was either so large, or so magical, that the spells were doing no more than aggravating it. Harry had one horrifying glimpse of eight shining black eyes and razor-sharp pincers before it was upon him.

He was lifted into the air in its front legs; struggling madly, he tried to kick it; his leg connected with the pincers and next moment he was in excruciating pain. He could hear Cedric yelling *"Stupefy!"* too, but his spell had no more effect than Harry's — Harry raised his wand as the spider opened its pincers once more and shouted *"Expelliarmus!"*

It worked — the Disarming Spell made the spider drop him, but that meant that Harry fell twelve feet onto his already injured leg, which crumpled beneath him. Without pausing to think, he aimed high at the spider's underbelly, as he had done with the skrewt, and shouted *"Stupefy!"* just as Cedric yelled the same thing.

The two spells combined did what one alone had not: The spider keeled over sideways, flattening a nearby hedge, and strewing the path with a tangle of hairy legs.

"Harry!" he heard Cedric shouting. "You all right? Did it fall on you?"

"No," Harry called back, panting. He looked down at his leg. It was bleeding freely. He could see some sort of thick, gluey secretion from the spider's pincers on his torn robes. He tried to get up, but his leg was shaking badly and did not want to support his weight. He leaned against the hedge, gasping for breath, and looked around.

Cedric was standing feet from the Triwizard Cup, which was gleaming behind him.

"Take it, then," Harry panted to Cedric. "Go on, take it. You're there."

But Cedric didn't move. He merely stood there, looking at Harry. Then he turned to stare at the cup. Harry saw the longing expression on his face in its golden light. Cedric looked around at Harry again, who was now holding onto the hedge to support himself. Cedric took a deep breath.

"You take it. You should win. That's twice you've saved my neck in here."

"That's not how it's supposed to work," Harry said. He felt angry; his leg was very painful, he was aching all over from trying to throw off the spider, and after all his efforts, Cedric had beaten him to it, just as he'd beaten Harry to ask Cho to the ball. "The one who reaches the cup first gets the points. That's you. I'm telling you, I'm not going to win any races on this leg."

Cedric took a few paces nearer to the Stunned spider, away from the cup, shaking his head.

"No," he said.

"Stop being noble," said Harry irritably. "Just take it, then we can get out of here."

Cedric watched Harry steadying himself, holding tight to the hedge.

"You told me about the dragons," Cedric said. "I would've gone down in the first task if you hadn't told me what was coming."

"I had help on that too," Harry snapped, trying to mop up his bloody leg with his robes. "You helped me with the egg — we're square."

"I had help on the egg in the first place," said Cedric.

"We're still square," said Harry, testing his leg gingerly; it shook violently as he put weight on it; he had sprained his ankle when the spider had dropped him.

"You should've got more points on the second task," said Cedric mulishly. "You stayed behind to get all the hostages. I should've done that."

"I was the only one who was thick enough to take that song seriously!" said Harry bitterly. "Just take the cup!"

"No," said Cedric.

He stepped over the spider's tangled legs to join Harry, who stared at him. Cedric was serious. He was walking away from the sort of glory Hufflepuff House hadn't had in centuries.

"Go on," Cedric said. He looked as though this was costing him every ounce of resolution he had, but his face was set, his arms were folded, he seemed decided.

Harry looked from Cedric to the cup. For one shining moment, he saw himself emerging from the maze, holding it. He saw himself holding the Triwizard Cup aloft, heard the roar of the crowd, saw Cho's face shining with admiration, more clearly than he had ever seen it before . . . and then the picture faded, and he found himself staring at Cedric's shadowy, stubborn face.

"Both of us," Harry said.

"What?"

"We'll take it at the same time. It's still a Hogwarts victory. We'll tie for it."

Cedric stared at Harry. He unfolded his arms.

"You — you sure?"

"Yeah," said Harry. "Yeah . . . we've helped each other out, haven't we? We both got here. Let's just take it together."

For a moment, Cedric looked as though he couldn't believe his ears; then his face split in a grin.

"You're on," he said. "Come here."

He grabbed Harry's arm below the shoulder and helped Harry limp toward the plinth where the cup stood. When they had reached it, they both held a hand out over one of the cup's gleaming handles.

"On three, right?" said Harry. "One — two — three —"

He and Cedric both grasped a handle.

Instantly, Harry felt a jerk somewhere behind his navel. His feet had left the ground. He could not unclench the hand holding the Triwizard Cup; it was pulling him onward in a howl of wind and swirling color, Cedric at his side.

# FLESH, BLOOD, AND BONE

Harry felt his feet slam into the ground; his injured leg gave way, and he fell forward; his hand let go of the Triwizard Cup at last. He raised his head.

"Where are we?" he said.

Cedric shook his head. He got up, pulled Harry to his feet, and they looked around.

They had left the Hogwarts grounds completely; they had obviously traveled miles — perhaps hundreds of miles — for even the mountains surrounding the castle were gone. They were standing instead in a dark and overgrown graveyard; the black outline of a small church was visible beyond a large yew tree to their right. A hill rose above them to their left. Harry could just make out the outline of a fine old house on the hillside.

Cedric looked down at the Triwizard Cup and then up at Harry.

"Did anyone tell *you* the Cup was a Portkey?" he asked.

"Nope," said Harry. He was looking around the graveyard. It was completely silent and slightly eerie. "Is this supposed to be part of the task?"

"I dunno," said Cedric. He sounded slightly nervous. "Wands out, d'you reckon?"

"Yeah," said Harry, glad that Cedric had made the suggestion rather than him.

They pulled out their wands. Harry kept looking around him. He had, yet again, the strange feeling that they were being watched.

"Someone's coming," he said suddenly.

Squinting tensely through the darkness, they watched the figure drawing nearer, walking steadily toward them between the graves. Harry couldn't make out a face, but from the way it was walking and holding its arms, he could tell that it was carrying something. Whoever it was, he was short, and wearing a hooded cloak pulled up over his head to obscure his face. And — several paces nearer, the gap between them closing all the time — Harry saw that the thing in the person's arms looked like a baby . . . or was it merely a bundle of robes?

Harry lowered his wand slightly and glanced sideways at Cedric. Cedric shot him a quizzical look. They both turned back to watch the approaching figure.

It stopped beside a towering marble headstone, only six feet from them. For a second, Harry and Cedric and the short figure simply looked at one another.

And then, without warning, Harry's scar exploded with pain. It was agony such as he had never felt in all his life; his wand slipped

from his fingers as he put his hands over his face; his knees buckled; he was on the ground and he could see nothing at all; his head
was about to split open.

From far away, above his head, he heard a high, cold voice say,
*"Kill the spare."*

A swishing noise and a second voice, which screeched the words
to the night: *"Avada Kedavra!"*

A blast of green light blazed through Harry's eyelids, and he
heard something heavy fall to the ground beside him; the pain in
his scar reached such a pitch that he retched, and then it diminished; terrified of what he was about to see, he opened his stinging
eyes.

Cedric was lying spread-eagled on the ground beside him. He
was dead.

For a second that contained an eternity, Harry stared into
Cedric's face, at his open gray eyes, blank and expressionless as
the windows of a deserted house, at his half-open mouth, which
looked slightly surprised. And then, before Harry's mind had accepted what he was seeing, before he could feel anything but numb
disbelief, he felt himself being pulled to his feet.

The short man in the cloak had put down his bundle, lit his
wand, and was dragging Harry toward the marble headstone.
Harry saw the name upon it flickering in the wandlight before he
was forced around and slammed against it.

## TOM RIDDLE

The cloaked man was now conjuring tight cords around Harry,
tying him from neck to ankles to the headstone. Harry could hear

shallow, fast breathing from the depths of the hood; he struggled, and the man hit him — hit him with a hand that had a finger missing. And Harry realized who was under the hood. It was Wormtail.

"You!" he gasped.

But Wormtail, who had finished conjuring the ropes, did not reply; he was busy checking the tightness of the cords, his fingers trembling uncontrollably, fumbling over the knots. Once sure that Harry was bound so tightly to the headstone that he couldn't move an inch, Wormtail drew a length of some black material from the inside of his cloak and stuffed it roughly into Harry's mouth; then, without a word, he turned from Harry and hurried away. Harry couldn't make a sound, nor could he see where Wormtail had gone; he couldn't turn his head to see beyond the headstone; he could see only what was right in front of him.

Cedric's body was lying some twenty feet away. Some way beyond him, glinting in the starlight, lay the Triwizard Cup. Harry's wand was on the ground at Cedric's feet. The bundle of robes that Harry had thought was a baby was close by, at the foot of the grave. It seemed to be stirring fretfully. Harry watched it, and his scar seared with pain again . . . and he suddenly knew that he didn't want to see what was in those robes . . . he didn't want that bundle opened. . . .

He could hear noises at his feet. He looked down and saw a gigantic snake slithering through the grass, circling the headstone where he was tied. Wormtail's fast, wheezy breathing was growing louder again. It sounded as though he was forcing something heavy across the ground. Then he came back within Harry's range of vision, and Harry saw him pushing a stone cauldron to the foot of the grave. It was full of what seemed to be water — Harry could hear it slopping around — and it was larger than any cauldron Harry had ever used; a great stone belly large enough for a full-grown man to sit in.

The thing inside the bundle of robes on the ground was stirring more persistently, as though it was trying to free itself. Now Wormtail was busying himself at the bottom of the cauldron with a wand. Suddenly there were crackling flames beneath it. The large snake slithered away into the darkness.

The liquid in the cauldron seemed to heat very fast. The surface began not only to bubble, but to send out fiery sparks, as though it were on fire. Steam was thickening, blurring the outline of Wormtail tending the fire. The movements beneath the robes became more agitated. And Harry heard the high, cold voice again.

*"Hurry!"*

The whole surface of the water was alight with sparks now. It might have been encrusted with diamonds.

"It is ready, Master."

*"Now . . ."* said the cold voice.

Wormtail pulled open the robes on the ground, revealing what was inside them, and Harry let out a yell that was strangled in the wad of material blocking his mouth.

It was as though Wormtail had flipped over a stone and revealed something ugly, slimy, and blind — but worse, a hundred times worse. The thing Wormtail had been carrying had the shape of a crouched human child, except that Harry had never seen anything less like a child. It was hairless and scaly-looking, a dark, raw, reddish black. Its arms and legs were thin and feeble, and its face — no child alive ever had a face like that — flat and snakelike, with gleaming red eyes.

The thing seemed almost helpless; it raised its thin arms, put them around Wormtail's neck, and Wormtail lifted it. As he did so, his hood fell back, and Harry saw the look of revulsion on Wormtail's weak, pale face in the firelight as he carried the creature to the rim of the cauldron. For one moment, Harry saw the evil, flat face illuminated in the sparks dancing on the surface of the potion. And then Wormtail lowered the creature into the cauldron; there was a hiss, and it vanished below the surface; Harry heard its frail body hit the bottom with a soft thud.

*Let it drown,* Harry thought, his scar burning almost past endurance, *please . . . let it drown. . . .*

Wormtail was speaking. His voice shook; he seemed frightened beyond his wits. He raised his wand, closed his eyes, and spoke to the night.

*"Bone of the father, unknowingly given, you will renew your son!"*

The surface of the grave at Harry's feet cracked. Horrified, Harry watched as a fine trickle of dust rose into the air at Wormtail's command and fell softly into the cauldron. The diamond surface of the water broke and hissed; it sent sparks in all directions and turned a vivid, poisonous-looking blue.

And now Wormtail was whimpering. He pulled a long, thin, shining silver dagger from inside his cloak. His voice broke into petrified sobs.

*"Flesh — of the servant — w-willingly given — you will — revive — your master."*

He stretched his right hand out in front of him — the hand with the missing finger. He gripped the dagger very tightly in his left hand and swung it upward.

Harry realized what Wormtail was about to do a second before it happened — he closed his eyes as tightly as he could, but he could not block the scream that pierced the night, that went through Harry as though he had been stabbed with the dagger too. He heard something fall to the ground, heard Wormtail's anguished panting, then a sickening splash, as something was dropped into the cauldron. Harry couldn't stand to look . . . but the potion had turned a burning red; the light of it shone through Harry's closed eyelids. . . .

Wormtail was gasping and moaning with agony. Not until Harry felt Wormtail's anguished breath on his face did he realize that Wormtail was right in front of him.

*"B-blood of the enemy . . . forcibly taken . . . you will . . . resurrect your foe."*

Harry could do nothing to prevent it, he was tied too tightly. . . . Squinting down, struggling hopelessly at the ropes binding him, he saw the shining silver dagger shaking in Wormtail's remaining hand. He felt its point penetrate the crook of his right arm and blood seeping down the sleeve of his torn robes. Wormtail, still panting with pain, fumbled in his pocket for a glass vial and held it to Harry's cut, so that a dribble of blood fell into it.

He staggered back to the cauldron with Harry's blood. He poured it inside. The liquid within turned, instantly, a blinding white. Wormtail, his job done, dropped to his knees beside the cauldron, then slumped sideways and lay on the ground, cradling the bleeding stump of his arm, gasping and sobbing.

The cauldron was simmering, sending its diamond sparks in all directions, so blindingly bright that it turned all else to velvety blackness. Nothing happened. . . .

*Let it have drowned,* Harry thought, *let it have gone wrong. . . .*

And then, suddenly, the sparks emanating from the cauldron were extinguished. A surge of white steam billowed thickly from the cauldron instead, obliterating everything in front of Harry, so that he couldn't see Wormtail or Cedric or anything but vapor hanging in the air. . . . *It's gone wrong,* he thought . . . *it's drowned. . . please. . . please let it be dead. . . .*

But then, through the mist in front of him, he saw, with an icy surge of terror, the dark outline of a man, tall and skeletally thin, rising slowly from inside the cauldron.

"Robe me," said the high, cold voice from behind the steam, and Wormtail, sobbing and moaning, still cradling his mutilated arm, scrambled to pick up the black robes from the ground, got to his feet, reached up, and pulled them one-handed over his master's head.

The thin man stepped out of the cauldron, staring at Harry . . . and Harry stared back into the face that had haunted his nightmares for three years. Whiter than a skull, with wide, livid scarlet eyes and a nose that was flat as a snake's with slits for nostrils . . .

Lord Voldemort had risen again.

# THE DEATH EATERS

Voldemort looked away from Harry and began examining his own body. His hands were like large, pale spiders; his long white fingers caressed his own chest, his arms, his face; the red eyes, whose pupils were slits, like a cat's, gleamed still more brightly through the darkness. He held up his hands and flexed the fingers, his expression rapt and exultant. He took not the slightest notice of Wormtail, who lay twitching and bleeding on the ground, nor of the great snake, which had slithered back into sight and was circling Harry again, hissing. Voldemort slipped one of those unnaturally long-fingered hands into a deep pocket and drew out a wand. He caressed it gently too; and then he raised it, and pointed it at Wormtail, who was lifted off the ground and thrown against the headstone where Harry was tied; he fell to the foot of it and lay there, crumpled up and crying. Voldemort turned his scarlet eyes upon Harry, laughing a high, cold, mirthless laugh.

Wormtail's robes were shining with blood now; he had wrapped the stump of his arm in them.

"My Lord . . ." he choked, "my Lord . . . you promised . . . you did promise . . ."

"Hold out your arm," said Voldemort lazily.

"Oh Master . . . thank you, Master . . ."

He extended the bleeding stump, but Voldemort laughed again.

"The other arm, Wormtail."

"Master, please . . . *please. . .*"

Voldemort bent down and pulled out Wormtail's left arm; he forced the sleeve of Wormtail's robes up past his elbow, and Harry saw something upon the skin there, something like a vivid red tattoo — a skull with a snake protruding from its mouth — the image that had appeared in the sky at the Quidditch World Cup: the Dark Mark. Voldemort examined it carefully, ignoring Wormtail's uncontrollable weeping.

"It is back," he said softly, "they will all have noticed it . . . and now, we shall see . . . now we shall know . . ."

He pressed his long white forefinger to the brand on Wormtail's arm.

The scar on Harry's forehead seared with a sharp pain again, and Wormtail let out a fresh howl; Voldemort removed his fingers from Wormtail's mark, and Harry saw that it had turned jet black.

A look of cruel satisfaction on his face, Voldemort straightened up, threw back his head, and stared around at the dark graveyard.

"How many will be brave enough to return when they feel it?" he whispered, his gleaming red eyes fixed upon the stars. "And how many will be foolish enough to stay away?"

He began to pace up and down before Harry and Wormtail, eyes sweeping the graveyard all the while. After a minute or so, he looked down at Harry again, a cruel smile twisting his snakelike face.

"You stand, Harry Potter, upon the remains of my late father," he hissed softly. "A Muggle and a fool . . . very like your dear mother. But they both had their uses, did they not? Your mother died to defend you as a child . . . and I killed my father, and see how useful he has proved himself, in death. . . ."

Voldemort laughed again. Up and down he paced, looking all around him as he walked, and the snake continued to circle in the grass.

"You see that house upon the hillside, Potter? My father lived there. My mother, a witch who lived here in this village, fell in love with him. But he abandoned her when she told him what she was. . . . He didn't like magic, my father . . .

"He left her and returned to his Muggle parents before I was even born, Potter, and she died giving birth to me, leaving me to be raised in a Muggle orphanage . . . but I vowed to find him . . . I revenged myself upon him, that fool who gave me his name . . . *Tom Riddle.* . . ."

Still he paced, his red eyes darting from grave to grave.

"Listen to me, reliving family history . . ." he said quietly, "why, I am growing quite sentimental. . . . But look, Harry! My *true* family returns. . . ."

The air was suddenly full of the swishing of cloaks. Between graves, behind the yew tree, in every shadowy space, wizards were Apparating. All of them were hooded and masked. And one by one they moved forward . . . slowly, cautiously, as though they could hardly believe their eyes. Voldemort stood in silence, waiting for them. Then one of the Death Eaters fell to his knees, crawled toward Voldemort, and kissed the hem of his black robes.

"Master . . . Master . . ." he murmured.

The Death Eaters behind him did the same; each of them approaching Voldemort on his knees and kissing his robes, before backing away and standing up, forming a silent circle, which enclosed Tom Riddle's grave, Harry, Voldemort, and the sobbing and twitching heap that was Wormtail. Yet they left gaps in the circle, as though waiting for more people. Voldemort, however, did not seem to expect more. He looked around at the hooded faces, and though there was no wind, a rustling seemed to run around the circle, as though it had shivered.

"Welcome, Death Eaters," said Voldemort quietly. "Thirteen years . . . thirteen years since last we met. Yet you answer my call as though it were yesterday. . . . We are still united under the Dark Mark, then! *Or are we?*"

He put back his terrible face and sniffed, his slit-like nostrils widening.

"I smell guilt," he said. "There is a stench of guilt upon the air."

A second shiver ran around the circle, as though each member of it longed, but did not dare, to step back from him.

"I see you all, whole and healthy, with your powers intact — such prompt appearances! — and I ask myself . . . why did this band of wizards never come to the aid of their master, to whom they swore eternal loyalty?"

No one spoke. No one moved except Wormtail, who was upon the ground, still sobbing over his bleeding arm.

"And I answer myself," whispered Voldemort, "they must have

believed me broken, they thought I was gone. They slipped back among my enemies, and they pleaded innocence, and ignorance, and bewitchment. . . .

"And then I ask myself, but how could they have believed I would not rise again? They, who knew the steps I took, long ago, to guard myself against mortal death? They, who had seen proofs of the immensity of my power in the times when I was mightier than any wizard living?

"And I answer myself, perhaps they believed a still greater power could exist, one that could vanquish even Lord Voldemort . . . perhaps they now pay allegiance to another . . . perhaps that champion of commoners, of Mudbloods and Muggles, Albus Dumbledore?"

At the mention of Dumbledore's name, the members of the circle stirred, and some muttered and shook their heads. Voldemort ignored them.

"It is a disappointment to me . . . I confess myself disappointed. . . ."

One of the men suddenly flung himself forward, breaking the circle. Trembling from head to foot, he collapsed at Voldemort's feet.

"Master!" he shrieked, "Master, forgive me! Forgive us all!"

Voldemort began to laugh. He raised his wand.

*"Crucio!"*

The Death Eater on the ground writhed and shrieked; Harry was sure the sound must carry to the houses around. . . . *Let the police come,* he thought desperately . . . *anyone. . . anything. . .*

Voldemort raised his wand. The tortured Death Eater lay flat upon the ground, gasping.

"Get up, Avery," said Voldemort softly. "Stand up. You ask for forgiveness? I do not forgive. I do not forget. Thirteen long years . . . I want thirteen years' repayment before I forgive you. Wormtail here has paid some of his debt already, have you not, Wormtail?"

He looked down at Wormtail, who continued to sob.

"You returned to me, not out of loyalty, but out of fear of your old friends. You deserve this pain, Wormtail. You know that, don't you?"

"Yes, Master," moaned Wormtail, "please, Master . . . please . . ."

"Yet you helped return me to my body," said Voldemort coolly, watching Wormtail sob on the ground. "Worthless and traitorous as you are, you helped me . . . and Lord Voldemort rewards his helpers. . . ."

Voldemort raised his wand again and whirled it through the air. A streak of what looked like molten silver hung shining in the wand's wake. Momentarily shapeless, it writhed and then formed itself into a gleaming replica of a human hand, bright as moonlight, which soared downward and fixed itself upon Wormtail's bleeding wrist.

Wormtail's sobbing stopped abruptly. His breathing harsh and ragged, he raised his head and stared in disbelief at the silver hand, now attached seamlessly to his arm, as though he were wearing a dazzling glove. He flexed the shining fingers, then, trembling, picked up a small twig on the ground and crushed it into powder.

"My Lord," he whispered. "Master . . . it is beautiful . . . thank you . . . *thank you. . . .*"

He scrambled forward on his knees and kissed the hem of Voldemort's robes.

"May your loyalty never waver again, Wormtail," said Voldemort.

"No, my Lord . . . never, my Lord . . ."

Wormtail stood up and took his place in the circle, staring at his powerful new hand, his face still shining with tears. Voldemort now approached the man on Wormtail's right.

"Lucius, my slippery friend," he whispered, halting before him. "I am told that you have not renounced the old ways, though to the world you present a respectable face. You are still ready to take the lead in a spot of Muggle-torture, I believe? Yet you never tried to find me, Lucius. . . . Your exploits at the Quidditch World Cup were fun, I daresay . . . but might not your energies have been better directed toward finding and aiding your master?"

"My Lord, I was constantly on the alert," came Lucius Malfoy's voice swiftly from beneath the hood. "Had there been any sign from you, any whisper of your whereabouts, I would have been at your side immediately, nothing could have prevented me —"

"And yet you ran from my Mark, when a faithful Death Eater sent it into the sky last summer?" said Voldemort lazily, and Mr. Malfoy stopped talking abruptly. "Yes, I know all about that, Lucius. . . . You have disappointed me. . . . I expect more faithful service in the future."

"Of course, my Lord, of course. . . . You are merciful, thank you. . . ."

Voldemort moved on, and stopped, staring at the space — large enough for two people — that separated Malfoy and the next man.

"The Lestranges should stand here," said Voldemort quietly. "But they are entombed in Azkaban. They were faithful. They went to Azkaban rather than renounce me. . . . When Azkaban is broken open, the Lestranges will be honored beyond their dreams. The dementors will join us . . . they are our natural allies . . . we will recall the banished giants . . . I shall have all my devoted servants returned to me, and an army of creatures whom all fear. . . ."

He walked on. Some of the Death Eaters he passed in silence, but he paused before others and spoke to them.

"Macnair . . . destroying dangerous beasts for the Ministry of Magic now, Wormtail tells me? You shall have better victims than that soon, Macnair. Lord Voldemort will provide. . . ."

"Thank you, Master . . . thank you," murmured Macnair.

"And here" — Voldemort moved on to the two largest hooded figures — "we have Crabbe . . . you will do better this time, will you not, Crabbe? And you, Goyle?"

They bowed clumsily, muttering dully.

"Yes, Master . . ."

"We will, Master. . . ."

"The same goes for you, Nott," said Voldemort quietly as he walked past a stooped figure in Mr. Goyle's shadow.

"My Lord, I prostrate myself before you, I am your most faithful —"

"That will do," said Voldemort.

He had reached the largest gap of all, and he stood surveying it with his blank, red eyes, as though he could see people standing there.

"And here we have six missing Death Eaters . . . three dead in my service. One, too cowardly to return . . . he will pay. One, who I believe has left me forever . . . he will be killed, of course . . . and one, who remains my most faithful servant, and who has already reentered my service."

The Death Eaters stirred, and Harry saw their eyes dart sideways at one another through their masks.

"He is at Hogwarts, that faithful servant, and it was through his efforts that our young friend arrived here tonight. . . ."

"Yes," said Voldemort, a grin curling his lipless mouth as the eyes of the circle flashed in Harry's direction. "Harry Potter has kindly joined us for my rebirthing party. One might go so far as to call him my guest of honor."

There was a silence. Then the Death Eater to the right of Wormtail stepped forward, and Lucius Malfoy's voice spoke from under the mask.

"Master, we crave to know . . . we beg you to tell us . . . how you have achieved this . . . this miracle . . . how you managed to return to us. . . ."

"Ah, what a story it is, Lucius," said Voldemort. "And it begins — and ends — with my young friend here."

He walked lazily over to stand next to Harry, so that the eyes of the whole circle were upon the two of them. The snake continued to circle.

"You know, of course, that they have called this boy my downfall?" Voldemort said softly, his red eyes upon Harry, whose scar began to burn so fiercely that he almost screamed in agony. "You all know that on the night I lost my powers and my body, I tried to kill him. His mother died in the attempt to save him — and unwittingly provided him with a protection I admit I had not foreseen. . . . I could not touch the boy."

Voldemort raised one of his long white fingers and put it very close to Harry's cheek.

"His mother left upon him the traces of her sacrifice. . . . This is old magic, I should have remembered it, I was foolish to overlook it . . . but no matter. I can touch him now."

Harry felt the cold tip of the long white finger touch him, and thought his head would burst with the pain. Voldemort laughed softly in his ear, then took the finger away and continued addressing the Death Eaters.

"I miscalculated, my friends, I admit it. My curse was deflected by the woman's foolish sacrifice, and it rebounded upon myself. Aaah . . . pain beyond pain, my friends; nothing could have prepared me for it. I was ripped from my body, I was less than spirit, less than the meanest ghost . . . but still, I was alive. What I was, even I do not know . . . I, who have gone further than anybody along the path that leads to immortality. You know my goal — to conquer death. And now, I was tested, and it appeared that one or more of my experiments had worked . . . for I had not been killed, though the curse should have done it. Nevertheless, I was as powerless as the weakest creature alive, and without the means to help myself . . . for I had no body, and every spell that might have helped me required the use of a wand. . . .

"I remember only forcing myself, sleeplessly, endlessly, second by second, to exist. . . . I settled in a faraway place, in a forest, and I waited. . . . Surely, one of my faithful Death Eaters would try and find me . . . one of them would come and perform the magic I could not, to restore me to a body . . . but I waited in vain. . . ."

The shiver ran once more around the circle of listening Death Eaters. Voldemort let the silence spiral horribly before continuing.

"Only one power remained to me. I could possess the bodies of others. But I dared not go where other humans were plentiful, for I knew that the Aurors were still abroad and searching for me.

I sometimes inhabited animals — snakes, of course, being my preference — but I was little better off inside them than as pure spirit, for their bodies were ill adapted to perform magic . . . and my possession of them shortened their lives; none of them lasted long. . . .

"Then . . . four years ago . . . the means for my return seemed assured. A wizard — young, foolish, and gullible — wandered across my path in the forest I had made my home. Oh, he seemed the very chance I had been dreaming of . . . for he was a teacher at Dumbledore's school . . . he was easy to bend to my will . . . he brought me back to this country, and after a while, I took possession of his body, to supervise him closely as he carried out my orders. But my plan failed. I did not manage to steal the Sorcerer's Stone. I was not to be assured immortal life. I was thwarted . . . thwarted, once again, by Harry Potter. . . ."

Silence once more; nothing was stirring, not even the leaves on the yew tree. The Death Eaters were quite motionless, the glittering eyes in their masks fixed upon Voldemort, and upon Harry.

"The servant died when I left his body, and I was left as weak as ever I had been," Voldemort continued. "I returned to my hiding place far away, and I will not pretend to you that I didn't then fear that I might never regain my powers. . . . Yes, that was perhaps my darkest hour . . . I could not hope that I would be sent another wizard to possess . . . and I had given up hope, now, that any of my Death Eaters cared what had become of me. . . ."

One or two of the masked wizards in the circle moved uncomfortably, but Voldemort took no notice.

"And then, not even a year ago, when I had almost abandoned hope, it happened at last . . . a servant returned to me. Wormtail here, who had faked his own death to escape justice, was driven out

of hiding by those he had once counted friends, and decided to return to his master. He sought me in the country where it had long
been rumored I was hiding . . . helped, of course, by the rats he
met along the way. Wormtail has a curious affinity with rats, do
you not, Wormtail? His filthy little friends told him there was a
place, deep in an Albanian forest, that they avoided, where small
animals like themselves had met their deaths by a dark shadow that
possessed them. . . .

"But his journey back to me was not smooth, was it, Wormtail?
For, hungry one night, on the edge of the very forest where he had
hoped to find me, he foolishly stopped at an inn for some food . . .
and who should he meet there, but one Bertha Jorkins, a witch
from the Ministry of Magic.

"Now see the way that fate favors Lord Voldemort. This might
have been the end of Wormtail, and of my last hope for regenera-
tion. But Wormtail — displaying a presence of mind I would never
have expected from him — convinced Bertha Jorkins to accompany him on a nighttime stroll. He overpowered her . . . he brought
her to me. And Bertha Jorkins, who might have ruined all, proved
instead to be a gift beyond my wildest dreams . . . for — with a
little persuasion — she became a veritable mine of information.

"She told me that the Triwizard Tournament would be played at
Hogwarts this year. She told me that she knew of a faithful Death
Eater who would be only too willing to help me, if I could only
contact him. She told me many things . . . but the means I used
to break the Memory Charm upon her were powerful, and when I
had extracted all useful information from her, her mind and body
were both damaged beyond repair. She had now served her purpose. I could not possess her. I disposed of her."

Voldemort smiled his terrible smile, his red eyes blank and pitiless.

"Wormtail's body, of course, was ill adapted for possession, as all assumed him dead, and would attract far too much attention if noticed. However, he was the able-bodied servant I needed, and, poor wizard though he is, Wormtail was able to follow the instructions I gave him, which would return me to a rudimentary, weak body of my own, a body I would be able to inhabit while awaiting the essential ingredients for true rebirth . . . a spell or two of my own invention . . . a little help from my dear Nagini," Voldemort's red eyes fell upon the continually circling snake, "a potion concocted from unicorn blood, and the snake venom Nagini provided . . . I was soon returned to an almost human form, and strong enough to travel.

"There was no hope of stealing the Sorcerer's Stone anymore, for I knew that Dumbledore would have seen to it that it was destroyed. But I was willing to embrace mortal life again, before chasing immortality. I set my sights lower . . . I would settle for my old body back again, and my old strength.

"I knew that to achieve this — it is an old piece of Dark Magic, the potion that revived me tonight — I would need three powerful ingredients. Well, one of them was already at hand, was it not, Wormtail? Flesh given by a servant. . . .

"My father's bone, naturally, meant that we would have to come here, where he was buried. But the blood of a foe . . . Wormtail would have had me use any wizard, would you not, Wormtail? Any wizard who had hated me . . . as so many of them still do. But I knew the one I must use, if I was to rise again, more powerful than I had been when I had fallen. I wanted Harry Potter's blood.

I wanted the blood of the one who had stripped me of power thirteen years ago . . . for the lingering protection his mother once gave him would then reside in my veins too. . . .

"But how to get at Harry Potter? For he has been better protected than I think even he knows, protected in ways devised by Dumbledore long ago, when it fell to him to arrange the boy's future. Dumbledore invoked an ancient magic, to ensure the boy's protection as long as he is in his relations' care. Not even I can touch him there. . . . Then, of course, there was the Quidditch World Cup. . . . I thought his protection might be weaker there, away from his relations and Dumbledore, but I was not yet strong enough to attempt kidnap in the midst of a horde of Ministry wizards. And then, the boy would return to Hogwarts, where he is under the crooked nose of that Muggle-loving fool from morning until night. So how could I take him?

"Why . . . by using Bertha Jorkins's information, of course. Use my one faithful Death Eater, stationed at Hogwarts, to ensure that the boy's name was entered into the Goblet of Fire. Use my Death Eater to ensure that the boy won the tournament — that he touched the Triwizard Cup first — the Cup which my Death Eater had turned into a Portkey, which would bring him here, beyond the reach of Dumbledore's help and protection, and into my waiting arms. And here he is . . . the boy you all believed had been my downfall. . . ."

Voldemort moved slowly forward and turned to face Harry. He raised his wand.

*"Crucio!"*

It was pain beyond anything Harry had ever experienced; his very bones were on fire; his head was surely splitting along his scar;

his eyes were rolling madly in his head; he wanted it to end . . . to black out . . . to die . . .

And then it was gone. He was hanging limply in the ropes binding him to the headstone of Voldemort's father, looking up into those bright red eyes through a kind of mist. The night was ringing with the sound of the Death Eaters' laughter.

"You see, I think, how foolish it was to suppose that this boy could ever have been stronger than me," said Voldemort. "But I want there to be no mistake in anybody's mind. Harry Potter escaped me by a lucky chance. And I am now going to prove my power by killing him, here and now, in front of you all, when there is no Dumbledore to help him, and no mother to die for him. I will give him his chance. He will be allowed to fight, and you will be left in no doubt which of us is the stronger. Just a little longer, Nagini," he whispered, and the snake glided away through the grass to where the Death Eaters stood watching.

"Now untie him, Wormtail, and give him back his wand."

# PRIORI INCANTATEM

Wormtail approached Harry, who scrambled to find his feet, to support his own weight before the ropes were untied. Wormtail raised his new silver hand, pulled out the wad of material gagging Harry, and then, with one swipe, cut through the bonds tying Harry to the gravestone.

There was a split second, perhaps, when Harry might have considered running for it, but his injured leg shook under him as he stood on the overgrown grave, as the Death Eaters closed ranks, forming a tighter circle around him and Voldemort, so that the gaps where the missing Death Eaters should have stood were filled. Wormtail walked out of the circle to the place where Cedric's body lay and returned with Harry's wand, which he thrust roughly into Harry's hand without looking at him. Then Wormtail resumed his place in the circle of watching Death Eaters.

"You have been taught how to duel, Harry Potter?" said Voldemort softly, his red eyes glinting through the darkness.

At these words Harry remembered, as though from a former life, the dueling club at Hogwarts he had attended briefly two years ago. . . . All he had learned there was the Disarming Spell, *"Expelliarmus"* . . . and what use would it be to deprive Voldemort of his wand, even if he could, when he was surrounded by Death Eaters, outnumbered by at least thirty to one? He had never learned anything that could possibly fit him for this. He knew he was facing the thing against which Moody had always warned . . . the unblockable *Avada Kedavra* curse — and Voldemort was right — his mother was not here to die for him this time. : . . He was quite unprotected. . . .

"We bow to each other, Harry," said Voldemort, bending a little, but keeping his snakelike face upturned to Harry. "Come, the niceties must be observed. . . . Dumbledore would like you to show manners. . . . Bow to death, Harry. . . ."

The Death Eaters were laughing again. Voldemort's lipless mouth was smiling. Harry did not bow. He was not going to let Voldemort play with him before killing him . . . he was not going to give him that satisfaction. . . .

"I said, *bow,*" Voldemort said, raising his wand — and Harry felt his spine curve as though a huge, invisible hand were bending him ruthlessly forward, and the Death Eaters laughed harder than ever.

"Very good," said Voldemort softly, and as he raised his wand the pressure bearing down upon Harry lifted too. "And now you face me, like a man . . . straight-backed and proud, the way your father died. . . .

"And now — we duel."

Voldemort raised his wand, and before Harry could do anything to defend himself, before he could even move, he had been hit again by the Cruciatus Curse. The pain was so intense, so all-consuming, that he no longer knew where he was. . . . White-hot knives were piercing every inch of his skin, his head was surely going to burst with pain, he was screaming more loudly than he'd ever screamed in his life —

And then it stopped. Harry rolled over and scrambled to his feet; he was shaking as uncontrollably as Wormtail had done when his hand had been cut off; he staggered sideways into the wall of watching Death Eaters, and they pushed him away, back toward Voldemort.

"A little break," said Voldemort, the slit-like nostrils dilating with excitement, "a little pause . . . That hurt, didn't it, Harry? You don't want me to do that again, do you?"

Harry didn't answer. He was going to die like Cedric, those pitiless red eyes were telling him so . . . he was going to die, and there was nothing he could do about it . . . but he wasn't going to play along. He wasn't going to obey Voldemort . . . he wasn't going to beg. . . .

"I asked you whether you want me to do that again," said Voldemort softly. "Answer me! *Imperio!*"

And Harry felt, for the third time in his life, the sensation that his mind had been wiped of all thought. . . . Ah, it was bliss, not to think, it was as though he were floating, dreaming . . . *just answer no . . . say no . . . just answer no. . . .*

I will not, said a stronger voice, in the back of his head, I won't answer. . . .

*Just answer no. . . .*

I won't do it, I won't say it. . . .

*Just answer no. . . .*

"I WON'T!"

And these words burst from Harry's mouth; they echoed through the graveyard, and the dream state was lifted as suddenly as though cold water had been thrown over him — back rushed the aches that the Cruciatus Curse had left all over his body — back rushed the realization of where he was, and what he was facing. . . .

"You won't?" said Voldemort quietly, and the Death Eaters were not laughing now. "You won't say no? Harry, obedience is a virtue I need to teach you before you die. . . . Perhaps another little dose of pain?"

Voldemort raised his wand, but this time Harry was ready; with the reflexes born of his Quidditch training, he flung himself sideways onto the ground; he rolled behind the marble headstone of Voldemort's father, and he heard it crack as the curse missed him.

"We are not playing hide-and-seek, Harry," said Voldemort's soft, cold voice, drawing nearer, as the Death Eaters laughed. "You cannot hide from me. Does this mean you are tired of our duel? Does this mean that you would prefer me to finish it now, Harry? Come out, Harry . . . come out and play, then . . . it will be quick . . . it might even be painless . . . I would not know . . . I have never died. . . ."

Harry crouched behind the headstone and knew the end had come. There was no hope . . . no help to be had. And as he heard Voldemort draw nearer still, he knew one thing only, and it was beyond fear or reason: He was not going to die crouching here like a child playing hide-and-seek; he was not going to die kneeling at Voldemort's feet . . . he was going to die upright like his father, and he was going to die trying to defend himself, even if no defense was possible. . . .

Before Voldemort could stick his snakelike face around the headstone, Harry stood up . . . he gripped his wand tightly in his hand, thrust it out in front of him, and threw himself around the headstone, facing Voldemort.

Voldemort was ready. As Harry shouted, *"Expelliarmus!"* Voldemort cried, *"Avada Kedavra!"*

A jet of green light issued from Voldemort's wand just as a jet of red light blasted from Harry's — they met in midair — and suddenly Harry's wand was vibrating as though an electric charge were surging through it; his hand seized up around it; he couldn't have released it if he'd wanted to — and a narrow beam of light connected the two wands, neither red nor green, but bright, deep gold. Harry, following the beam with his astonished gaze, saw that Voldemort's long white fingers too were gripping a wand that was shaking and vibrating.

And then — nothing could have prepared Harry for this — he felt his feet lift from the ground. He and Voldemort were both being raised into the air, their wands still connected by that thread of shimmering golden light. They glided away from the tombstone of Voldemort's father and then came to rest on a patch of ground that was clear and free of graves. . . . The Death Eaters were shouting; they were asking Voldemort for instructions; they were closing in, reforming the circle around Harry and Voldemort, the snake slithering at their heels, some of them drawing their wands —

The golden thread connecting Harry and Voldemort splintered; though the wands remained connected, a thousand more beams arced high over Harry and Voldemort, crisscrossing all around them, until they were enclosed in a golden, dome-shaped web, a cage of light, beyond which the Death Eaters circled like jackals, their cries strangely muffled now. . . .

"Do nothing!" Voldemort shrieked to the Death Eaters, and Harry saw his red eyes wide with astonishment at what was happening, saw him fighting to break the thread of light still connecting his wand with Harry's; Harry held onto his wand more tightly, with both hands, and the golden thread remained unbroken. "Do nothing unless I command you!" Voldemort shouted to the Death Eaters.

And then an unearthly and beautiful sound filled the air. . . . It was coming from every thread of the light-spun web vibrating around Harry and Voldemort. It was a sound Harry recognized, though he had heard it only once before in his life: phoenix song.

It was the sound of hope to Harry . . . the most beautiful and welcome thing he had ever heard in his life. . . . He felt as though the song were inside him instead of just around him. . . . It was the sound he connected with Dumbledore, and it was almost as though a friend were speaking in his ear. . . .

*Don't break the connection.*

I know, Harry told the music, I know I mustn't . . . but no sooner had he thought it, than the thing became much harder to do. His wand began to vibrate more powerfully than ever . . . and now the beam between him and Voldemort changed too . . . it was as though large beads of light were sliding up and down the thread connecting the wands — Harry felt his wand give a shudder under his hand as the light beads began to slide slowly and steadily his way. . . . The direction of the beam's movement was now toward him, from Voldemort, and he felt his wand shudder angrily. . . .

As the closest bead of light moved nearer to Harry's wand-tip, the wood beneath his fingers grew so hot he feared it would burst into flame. The closer that bead moved, the harder Harry's wand vibrated; he was sure his wand would not survive contact with it; it felt as though it was about to shatter under his fingers —

He concentrated every last particle of his mind upon forcing the bead back toward Voldemort, his ears full of phoenix song, his eyes furious, fixed . . . and slowly, very slowly, the beads quivered to a halt, and then, just as slowly, they began to move the other way . . . and it was Voldemort's wand that was vibrating extra-hard now . . . Voldemort who looked astonished, and almost fearful. . . .

One of the beads of light was quivering, inches from the tip of Voldemort's wand. Harry didn't understand why he was doing it, didn't know what it might achieve . . . but he now concentrated as he had never done in his life on forcing that bead of light right back into Voldemort's wand . . . and slowly . . . very slowly . . . it moved along the golden thread . . . it trembled for a moment . . . and then it connected. . . .

At once, Voldemort's wand began to emit echoing screams of pain . . . then — Voldemort's red eyes widened with shock — a dense, smoky hand flew out of the tip of it and vanished . . . the ghost of the hand he had made Wormtail . . . more shouts of pain . . . and then something much larger began to blossom from Voldemort's wand-tip, a great, grayish something, that looked as though it were made of the solidest, densest smoke. . . . It was a head . . . now a chest and arms . . . the torso of Cedric Diggory.

If ever Harry might have released his wand from shock, it would have been then, but instinct kept him clutching his wand tightly, so that the thread of golden light remained unbroken, even though the thick gray ghost of Cedric Diggory (*was* it a ghost? it looked so solid) emerged in its entirety from the end of Voldemort's wand, as though it were squeezing itself out of a very narrow tunnel . . . and this shade of Cedric stood up, and looked up and down the golden thread of light, and spoke.

"Hold on, Harry," it said.

Its voice was distant and echoing. Harry looked at Voldemort . . . his wide red eyes were still shocked . . . he had no more expected this than Harry had . . . and, very dimly, Harry heard the frightened yells of the Death Eaters, prowling around the edges of the golden dome. . . .

More screams of pain from the wand . . . and then something else emerged from its tip . . . the dense shadow of a second head, quickly followed by arms and torso . . . an old man Harry had seen only in a dream was now pushing himself out of the end of the wand just as Cedric had done . . . and his ghost, or his shadow, or whatever it was, fell next to Cedric's, and surveyed Harry and Voldemort, and the golden web, and the connected wands, with mild surprise, leaning on his walking stick. . . .

"He was a real wizard, then?" the old man said, his eyes on Voldemort. "Killed me, that one did. . . . You fight him, boy. . . ."

But already, yet another head was emerging . . . and this head, gray as a smoky statue, was a woman's. . . . Harry, both arms shaking now as he fought to keep his wand still, saw her drop to the ground and straighten up like the others, staring. . . .

The shadow of Bertha Jorkins surveyed the battle before her with wide eyes.

"Don't let go, now!" she cried, and her voice echoed like Cedric's as though from very far away. "Don't let him get you, Harry — don't let go!"

She and the other two shadowy figures began to pace around the inner walls of the golden web, while the Death Eaters flitted around the outside of it . . . and Voldemort's dead victims whispered as they circled the duelers, whispered words of encouragement to Harry, and hissed words Harry couldn't hear to Voldemort.

And now another head was emerging from the tip of Voldemort's wand . . . and Harry knew when he saw it who it would be . . . he knew, as though he had expected it from the moment when Cedric had appeared from the wand . . . knew, because the woman appearing was the one he'd thought of more than any other tonight. . . .

The smoky shadow of a young woman with long hair fell to the ground as Bertha had done, straightened up, and looked at him . . . and Harry, his arms shaking madly now, looked back into the ghostly face of his mother.

"Your father's coming. . . ." she said quietly. "Hold on for your father. . . . It will be all right. . . . Hold on. . . ."

And he came . . . first his head, then his body . . . tall and untidy-haired like Harry, the smoky, shadowy form of James Potter blossomed from the end of Voldemort's wand, fell to the ground, and straightened like his wife. He walked close to Harry, looking down at him, and he spoke in the same distant, echoing voice as the others, but quietly, so that Voldemort, his face now livid with fear as his victims prowled around him, could not hear. . . .

"When the connection is broken, we will linger for only moments . . . but we will give you time . . . you must get to the Portkey, it will return you to Hogwarts . . . do you understand, Harry?"

"Yes," Harry gasped, fighting now to keep a hold on his wand, which was slipping and sliding beneath his fingers.

"Harry . . ." whispered the figure of Cedric, "take my body back, will you? Take my body back to my parents. . . ."

"I will," said Harry, his face screwed up with the effort of holding the wand.

"Do it now," whispered his father's voice, "be ready to run . . . do it now. . . ."

"NOW!" Harry yelled; he didn't think he could have held on for another moment anyway — he pulled his wand upward with an almighty wrench, and the golden thread broke; the cage of light vanished, the phoenix song died — but the shadowy figures of Voldemort's victims did not disappear — they were closing in upon Voldemort, shielding Harry from his gaze —

And Harry ran as he had never run in his life, knocking two stunned Death Eaters aside as he passed; he zigzagged behind headstones, feeling their curses following him, hearing them hit the headstones — he was dodging curses and graves, pelting toward Cedric's body, no longer aware of the pain in his leg, his whole being concentrated on what he had to do —

"Stun him!" he heard Voldemort scream.

Ten feet from Cedric, Harry dived behind a marble angel to avoid the jets of red light and saw the tip of its wing shatter as the spells hit it. Gripping his wand more tightly, he dashed out from behind the angel —

"Impedimenta!" he bellowed, pointing his wand wildly over his shoulder at the Death Eaters running at him.

From a muffled yell, he thought he had stopped at least one of them, but there was no time to stop and look; he jumped over the

Cup and dived as he heard more wand blasts behind him; more jets of light flew over his head as he fell, stretching out his hand to grab Cedric's arm —

"Stand aside! I will kill him! He is mine!" shrieked Voldemort.

Harry's hand had closed on Cedric's wrist; one tombstone stood between him and Voldemort, but Cedric was too heavy to carry, and the Cup was out of reach —

Voldemort's red eyes flamed in the darkness. Harry saw his mouth curl into a smile, saw him raise his wand.

"*Accio!*" Harry yelled, pointing his wand at the Triwizard Cup.

It flew into the air and soared toward him. Harry caught it by the handle —

He heard Voldemort's scream of fury at the same moment that he felt the jerk behind his navel that meant the Portkey had worked — it was speeding him away in a whirl of wind and color, and Cedric along with him. . . . They were going back.

# VERITASERUM

Harry felt himself slam flat into the ground; his face was pressed into grass; the smell of it filled his nostrils. He had closed his eyes while the Portkey transported him, and he kept them closed now. He did not move. All the breath seemed to have been knocked out of him; his head was swimming so badly he felt as though the ground beneath him were swaying like the deck of a ship. To hold himself steady, he tightened his hold on the two things he was still clutching: the smooth, cold handle of the Triwizard Cup and Cedric's body. He felt as though he would slide away into the blackness gathering at the edges of his brain if he let go of either of them. Shock and exhaustion kept him on the ground, breathing in the smell of the grass, waiting . . . waiting for someone to do something . . . something to happen . . . and all the while, his scar burned dully on his forehead. . . .

A torrent of sound deafened and confused him; there were voices everywhere, footsteps, screams. . . . He remained where he was, his face screwed up against the noise, as though it were a nightmare that would pass. . . .

Then a pair of hands seized him roughly and turned him over. "Harry! *Harry!*"

He opened his eyes.

He was looking up at the starry sky, and Albus Dumbledore was crouched over him. The dark shadows of a crowd of people pressed in around them, pushing nearer; Harry felt the ground beneath his head reverberating with their footsteps.

He had come back to the edge of the maze. He could see the stands rising above him, the shapes of people moving in them, the stars above.

Harry let go of the Cup, but he clutched Cedric to him even more tightly. He raised his free hand and seized Dumbledore's wrist, while Dumbledore's face swam in and out of focus.

"He's back," Harry whispered. "He's back. Voldemort."

"What's going on? What's happened?"

The face of Cornelius Fudge appeared upside down over Harry; it looked white, appalled.

"My God — Diggory!" it whispered. "Dumbledore — he's dead!"

The words were repeated, the shadowy figures pressing in on them gasped it to those around them . . . and then others shouted it — screeched it — into the night — "He's dead!" "He's *dead!*" "Cedric Diggory! *Dead!*"

"Harry, let go of him," he heard Fudge's voice say, and he felt fingers trying to pry him from Cedric's limp body, but Harry wouldn't let him go. Then Dumbledore's face, which was still blurred and misted, came closer.

"Harry, you can't help him now. It's over. Let go."

"He wanted me to bring him back," Harry muttered — it seemed important to explain this. "He wanted me to bring him back to his parents. . . ."

"That's right, Harry . . . just let go now. . . ."

Dumbledore bent down, and with extraordinary strength for a man so old and thin, raised Harry from the ground and set him on his feet. Harry swayed. His head was pounding. His injured leg would no longer support his weight. The crowd around them jostled, fighting to get closer, pressing darkly in on him — "What's happened?" "What's wrong with him?" "Diggory's dead!"

"He'll need to go to the hospital wing!" Fudge was saying loudly. "He's ill, he's injured — Dumbledore, Diggory's parents, they're here, they're in the stands. . . ."

"I'll take Harry, Dumbledore, I'll take him —"

"No, I would prefer —"

"Dumbledore, Amos Diggory's running . . . he's coming over. . . . Don't you think you should tell him — before he sees — ?"

"Harry, stay here —"

Girls were screaming, sobbing hysterically. . . . The scene flickered oddly before Harry's eyes. . . .

"It's all right, son, I've got you . . . come on . . . hospital wing . . ."

"Dumbledore said stay," said Harry thickly, the pounding in his scar making him feel as though he was about to throw up; his vision was blurring worse than ever.

"You need to lie down. . . . Come on now. . . ."

Someone larger and stronger than he was was half pulling, half carrying him through the frightened crowd. Harry heard people gasping, screaming, and shouting as the man supporting him pushed a path through them, taking him back to the castle. Across the lawn, past the lake and the Durmstrang ship, Harry heard nothing but the heavy breathing of the man helping him walk.

"What happened, Harry?" the man asked at last as he lifted Harry up the stone steps. *Clunk. Clunk. Clunk.* It was Mad-Eye Moody.

"Cup was a Portkey," said Harry as they crossed the entrance hall. "Took me and Cedric to a graveyard . . . and Voldemort was there . . . Lord Voldemort . . ."

*Clunk. Clunk. Clunk.* Up the marble stairs . . .

"The Dark Lord was there? What happened then?"

"Killed Cedric . . . they killed Cedric. . . ."

"And then?"

*Clunk. Clunk. Clunk.* Along the corridor . . .

"Made a potion . . . got his body back. . . ."

"The Dark Lord got his body back? He's returned?"

"And the Death Eaters came . . . and then we dueled. . . ."

"You dueled with the Dark Lord?"

"Got away . . . my wand . . . did something funny. . . . I saw my mum and dad . . . they came out of his wand. . . ."

"In here, Harry . . . in here, and sit down. . . . You'll be all right now . . . drink this. . . ."

Harry heard a key scrape in a lock and felt a cup being pushed into his hands.

"Drink it . . . you'll feel better . . . come on, now, Harry, I need to know exactly what happened. . . ."

Moody helped tip the stuff down Harry's throat; he coughed, a peppery taste burning his throat. Moody's office came into sharper

focus, and so did Moody himself. . . . He looked as white as Fudge
had looked, and both eyes were fixed unblinkingly upon Harry's
face.

"Voldemort's back, Harry? You're sure he's back? How did he
do it?"

"He took stuff from his father's grave, and from Wormtail, and
me," said Harry. His head felt clearer; his scar wasn't hurting so
badly; he could now see Moody's face distinctly, even though the
office was dark. He could still hear screaming and shouting from
the distant Quidditch field.

"What did the Dark Lord take from you?" said Moody.

"Blood," said Harry, raising his arm. His sleeve was ripped
where Wormtail's dagger had torn it.

Moody let out his breath in a long, low hiss.

"And the Death Eaters? They returned?"

"Yes," said Harry. "Loads of them . . ."

"How did he treat them?" Moody asked quietly. "Did he forgive
them?"

But Harry had suddenly remembered. He should have told
Dumbledore, he should have said it straightaway —

"There's a Death Eater at Hogwarts! There's a Death Eater
here — they put my name in the Goblet of Fire, they made sure I
got through to the end —"

Harry tried to get up, but Moody pushed him back down.

"I know who the Death Eater is," he said quietly.

"Karkaroff?" said Harry wildly. "Where is he? Have you got
him? Is he locked up?"

"Karkaroff?" said Moody with an odd laugh. "Karkaroff fled
tonight, when he felt the Dark Mark burn upon his arm. He

betrayed too many faithful supporters of the Dark Lord to wish to meet them . . . but I doubt he will get far. The Dark Lord has ways of tracking his enemies."

"Karkaroff's *gone*? He ran away? But then — he didn't put my name in the goblet?"

"No," said Moody slowly. "No, he didn't. It was I who did that."

Harry heard, but didn't believe.

"No, you didn't," he said. "You didn't do that . . . you can't have done . . ."

"I assure you I did," said Moody, and his magical eye swung around and fixed upon the door, and Harry knew he was making sure that there was no one outside it. At the same time, Moody drew out his wand and pointed it at Harry.

"He forgave them, then?" he said. "The Death Eaters who went free? The ones who escaped Azkaban?"

"What?" said Harry.

He was looking at the wand Moody was pointing at him. This was a bad joke, it had to be.

"I asked you," said Moody quietly, "whether he forgave the scum who never even went to look for him. Those treacherous cowards who wouldn't even brave Azkaban for him. The faithless, worthless bits of filth who were brave enough to cavort in masks at the Quidditch World Cup, but fled at the sight of the Dark Mark when I fired it into the sky."

"*You* fired . . . What are you talking about . . . ?"

"I told you, Harry . . . I told you. If there's one thing I hate more than any other, it's a Death Eater who walked free. They turned their backs on my master when he needed them most. I expected him to punish them. I expected him to torture them. Tell me he hurt them, Harry.... ." Moody's face was suddenly lit with an insane smile. "Tell me he told them that I, I alone remained faithful . . . prepared to risk everything to deliver to him the one thing he wanted above all . . . *you.*"

"You didn't . . . it — it can't be you. . . ."

"Who put your name in the Goblet of Fire, under the name of a different school? I did. Who frightened off every person I thought might try to hurt you or prevent you from winning the tournament? I did. Who nudged Hagrid into showing you the dragons? I did. Who helped you see the only way you could beat the dragon? *I did.*"

Moody's magical eye had now left the door. It was fixed upon Harry. His lopsided mouth leered more widely than ever.

"It hasn't been easy, Harry, guiding you through these tasks without arousing suspicion. I have had to use every ounce of cunning I possess, so that my hand would not be detectable in your success. Dumbledore would have been very suspicious if you had managed everything too easily. As long as you got into that maze, preferably with a decent head start — then, I knew, I would have a chance of getting rid of the other champions and leaving your way clear. But I also had to contend with your stupidity. The second task . . . that was when I was most afraid we would fail. I was keeping watch on you, Potter. I knew you hadn't worked out the egg's clue, so I had to give you another hint —"

"You didn't," Harry said hoarsely. "Cedric gave me the clue —"

"Who told Cedric to open it underwater? I did. I trusted that he would pass the information on to you. Decent people are so easy to manipulate, Potter. I was sure Cedric would want to repay you for telling him about the dragons, and so he did. But even then,

Potter, even then you seemed likely to fail. I was watching all the time . . . all those hours in the library. Didn't you realize that the book you needed was in your dormitory all along? I planted it there early on, I gave it to the Longbottom boy, don't you remember? *Magical Water Plants of the Mediterranean.* It would have told you all you needed to know about gillyweed. I expected you to ask everyone and anyone you could for help. Longbottom would have told you in an instant. But you did not . . . you did not. . . . You have a streak of pride and independence that might have ruined all.

"So what could I do? Feed you information from another innocent source. You told me at the Yule Ball a house-elf called Dobby had given you a Christmas present. I called the elf to the staffroom to collect some robes for cleaning. I staged a loud conversation with Professor McGonagall about the hostages who had been taken, and whether Potter would think to use gillyweed. And your little elf friend ran straight to Snape's office and then hurried to find you. . . ."

Moody's wand was still pointing directly at Harry's heart. Over his shoulder, foggy shapes were moving in the Foe-Glass on the wall.

"You were so long in that lake, Potter, I thought you had drowned. But luckily, Dumbledore took your idiocy for nobility, and marked you high for it. I breathed again.

"You had an easier time of it than you should have in that maze tonight, of course," said Moody. "I was patrolling around it, able to see through the outer hedges, able to curse many obstacles out of your way. I Stunned Fleur Delacour as she passed. I put the Imperius Curse on Krum, so that he would finish Diggory and leave your path to the Cup clear."

Harry stared at Moody. He just didn't see how this could be. . . . Dumbledore's friend, the famous Auror . . . the one who had caught so many Death Eaters . . . It made no sense . . . no sense at all. . . .

The foggy shapes in the Foe-Glass were sharpening, had become more distinct. Harry could see the outlines of three people over Moody's shoulder, moving closer and closer. But Moody wasn't watching them. His magical eye was upon Harry.

"The Dark Lord didn't manage to kill you, Potter, and he *so* wanted to," whispered Moody. "Imagine how he will reward me when he finds I have done it for him. I gave you to him — the thing he needed above all to regenerate — and then I killed you for him. I will be honored beyond all other Death Eaters. I will be his dearest, his closest supporter . . . closer than a son. . . ."

Moody's normal eye was bulging, the magical eye fixed upon Harry. The door was barred, and Harry knew he would never reach his own wand in time. . . .

"The Dark Lord and I," said Moody, and he looked completely insane now, towering over Harry, leering down at him, "have much in common. Both of us, for instance, had very disappointing fathers . . . very disappointing indeed. Both of us suffered the indignity, Harry, of being named after those fathers. And both of us had the pleasure . . . the very great pleasure . . . of killing our fathers to ensure the continued rise of the Dark Order!"

"You're mad," Harry said — he couldn't stop himself — "you're mad!"

"Mad, am I?" said Moody, his voice rising uncontrollably. "We'll see! We'll see who's mad, now that the Dark Lord has returned, with me at his side! He is back, Harry Potter, you did not conquer him — and now — I conquer you!"

Moody raised his wand, he opened his mouth; Harry plunged his own hand into his robes —

"*Stupefy!*" There was a blinding flash of red light, and with a great splintering and crashing, the door of Moody's office was blasted apart —

Moody was thrown backward onto the office floor. Harry, still staring at the place where Moody's face had been, saw Albus Dumbledore, Professor Snape, and Professor McGonagall looking back at him out of the Foe-Glass. He looked around and saw the three of them standing in the doorway, Dumbledore in front, his wand outstretched.

At that moment, Harry fully understood for the first time why people said Dumbledore was the only wizard Voldemort had ever feared. The look upon Dumbledore's face as he stared down at the unconscious form of Mad-Eye Moody was more terrible than Harry could have ever imagined. There was no benign smile upon Dumbledore's face, no twinkle in the eyes behind the spectacles. There was cold fury in every line of the ancient face; a sense of power radiated from Dumbledore as though he were giving off burning heat.

He stepped into the office, placed a foot underneath Moody's unconscious body, and kicked him over onto his back, so that his face was visible. Snape followed him, looking into the Foe-Glass, where his own face was still visible, glaring into the room. Professor McGonagall went straight to Harry.

"Come along, Potter," she whispered. The thin line of her

mouth was twitching as though she was about to cry. "Come along . . . hospital wing . . ."

"No," said Dumbledore sharply.

"Dumbledore, he ought to — look at him — he's been through enough tonight —"

"He will stay, Minerva, because he needs to understand," said Dumbledore curtly. "Understanding is the first step to acceptance, and only with acceptance can there be recovery. He needs to know who has put him through the ordeal he has suffered tonight, and why."

"Moody," Harry said. He was still in a state of complete disbelief. "How can it have been Moody?"

"This is not Alastor Moody," said Dumbledore quietly. "You have never known Alastor Moody. The real Moody would not have removed you from my sight after what happened tonight. The moment he took you, I knew — and I followed."

Dumbledore bent down over Moody's limp form and put a hand inside his robes. He pulled out Moody's hip flask and a set of keys on a ring. Then he turned to Professors McGonagall and Snape.

"Severus, please fetch me the strongest Truth Potion you possess, and then go down to the kitchens and bring up the house-elf called Winky. Minerva, kindly go down to Hagrid's house, where you will find a large black dog sitting in the pumpkin patch. Take the dog up to my office, tell him I will be with him shortly, then come back here."

If either Snape or McGonagall found these instructions peculiar, they hid their confusion. Both turned at once and left the office. Dumbledore walked over to the trunk with seven locks, fitted the first key in the lock, and opened it. It contained a mass of spell-books. Dumbledore closed the trunk, placed a second key in the second lock, and opened the trunk again. The spellbooks had vanished; this time it contained an assortment of broken Sneakoscopes, some parchment and quills, and what looked like a silvery Invisibility Cloak. Harry watched, astounded, as Dumbledore placed the third, fourth, fifth, and sixth keys in their respective locks, reopening the trunk, and each time revealing different contents. Then he placed the seventh key in the lock, threw open the lid, and Harry let out a cry of amazement.

He was looking down into a kind of pit, an underground room, and lying on the floor some ten feet below, apparently fast asleep, thin and starved in appearance, was the real Mad-Eye Moody. His wooden leg was gone, the socket that should have held the magical eye looked empty beneath its lid, and chunks of his grizzled hair were missing. Harry stared, thunderstruck, between the sleeping Moody in the trunk and the unconscious Moody lying on the floor of the office.

Dumbledore climbed into the trunk, lowered himself, and fell lightly onto the floor beside the sleeping Moody. He bent over him.

"Stunned — controlled by the Imperius Curse — very weak," he said. "Of course, they would have needed to keep him alive. Harry, throw down the imposter's cloak — he's freezing. Madam Pomfrey will need to see him, but he seems in no immediate danger."

Harry did as he was told; Dumbledore covered Moody in the cloak, tucked it around him, and clambered out of the trunk again. Then he picked up the hip flask that stood upon the desk, unscrewed it, and turned it over. A thick glutinous liquid splattered onto the office floor.

"Polyjuice Potion, Harry," said Dumbledore. "You see the simplicity of it, and the brilliance. For Moody never *does* drink except from his hip flask, he's well known for it. The imposter needed, of course, to keep the real Moody close by, so that he could continue making the potion. You see his hair . . ." Dumbledore looked down on the Moody in the trunk. "The imposter has been cutting it off all year, see where it is uneven? But I think, in the excitement of tonight, our fake Moody might have forgotten to take it as frequently as he should have done . . . on the hour . . . every hour. . . . We shall see."

Dumbledore pulled out the chair at the desk and sat down upon it, his eyes fixed upon the unconscious Moody on the floor. Harry stared at him too. Minutes passed in silence. . . .

Then, before Harry's very eyes, the face of the man on the floor began to change. The scars were disappearing, the skin was becoming smooth; the mangled nose became whole and started to shrink. The long mane of grizzled gray hair was withdrawing into the scalp and turning the color of straw. Suddenly, with a loud *clunk,* the wooden leg fell away as a normal leg regrew in its place; next moment, the magical eyeball had popped out of the man's face as a real eye replaced it; it rolled away across the floor and continued to swivel in every direction.

Harry saw a man lying before him, pale-skinned, slightly freckled, with a mop of fair hair. He knew who he was. He had seen him in Dumbledore's Pensieve, had watched him being led away from court by the dementors, trying to convince Mr. Crouch that he was innocent . . . but he was lined around the eyes now and looked much older. . . .

There were hurried footsteps outside in the corridor. Snape had returned with Winky at his heels. Professor McGonagall was right behind them.

"Crouch!" Snape said, stopping dead in the doorway. "Barty Crouch!"

"Good heavens," said Professor McGonagall, stopping dead and staring down at the man on the floor.

Filthy, disheveled, Winky peered around Snape's legs. Her mouth opened wide and she let out a piercing shriek.

"Master Barty, Master Barty, what is you doing here?"

She flung herself forward onto the young man's chest.

"You is killed him! You is killed him! You is killed Master's son!"

"He is simply Stunned, Winky," said Dumbledore. "Step aside, please. Severus, you have the potion?"

Snape handed Dumbledore a small glass bottle of completely clear liquid: the Veritaserum with which he had threatened Harry in class. Dumbledore got up, bent over the man on the floor, and pulled him into a sitting position against the wall beneath the Foe-Glass, in which the reflections of Dumbledore, Snape, and McGonagall were still glaring down upon them all. Winky remained on her knees, trembling, her hands over her face. Dumbledore forced the man's mouth open and poured three drops inside it. Then he pointed his wand at the man's chest and said, *"Rennervate."*

Crouch's son opened his eyes. His face was slack, his gaze unfocused. Dumbledore knelt before him, so that their faces were level.

"Can you hear me?" Dumbledore asked quietly.

The man's eyelids flickered.

"Yes," he muttered.

"I would like you to tell us," said Dumbledore softly, "how you came to be here. How did you escape from Azkaban?"

Crouch took a deep, shuddering breath, then began to speak in a flat, expressionless voice.

"My mother saved me. She knew she was dying. She persuaded my father to rescue me as a last favor to her. He loved her as he had never loved me. He agreed. They came to visit me. They gave me a draught of Polyjuice Potion containing one of my mother's hairs. She took a draught of Polyjuice Potion containing one of my hairs. We took on each other's appearance."

Winky was shaking her head, trembling.

"Say no more, Master Barty, say no more, you is getting your father into trouble!"

But Crouch took another deep breath and continued in the same flat voice.

"The dementors are blind. They sensed one healthy, one dying person entering Azkaban. They sensed one healthy, one dying person leaving it. My father smuggled me out, disguised as my mother, in case any prisoners were watching through their doors.

"My mother died a short while afterward in Azkaban. She was careful to drink Polyjuice Potion until the end. She was buried under my name and bearing my appearance. Everyone believed her to be me."

The man's eyelids flickered.

"And what did your father do with you, when he had got you home?" said Dumbledore quietly.

"Staged my mother's death. A quiet, private funeral. That grave is empty. The house-elf nursed me back to health. Then I had to be concealed. I had to be controlled. My father had to use a number of spells to subdue me. When I had recovered my strength, I thought only of finding my master . . . of returning to his service."

"How did your father subdue you?" said Dumbledore.

"The Imperius Curse," Crouch said. "I was under my father's control. I was forced to wear an Invisibility Cloak day and night. I was always with the house-elf. She was my keeper and caretaker. She pitied me. She persuaded my father to give me occasional treats. Rewards for my good behavior."

"Master Barty, Master Barty," sobbed Winky through her hands. "You isn't ought to tell them, we is getting in trouble. . . ."

"Did anybody ever discover that you were still alive?" said Dumbledore softly. "Did anyone know except your father and the house-elf?"

"Yes," said Crouch, his eyelids flickering again. "A witch in my father's office. Bertha Jorkins. She came to the house with papers for my father's signature. He was not at home. Winky showed her inside and returned to the kitchen, to me. But Bertha Jorkins heard Winky talking to me. She came to investigate. She heard enough to guess who was hiding under the Invisibility Cloak. My father arrived home. She confronted him. He put a very powerful Memory Charm on her to make her forget what she'd found out. Too powerful. He said it damaged her memory permanently."

"Why is she coming to nose into my master's private business?" sobbed Winky. "Why isn't she leaving us be?"

"Tell me about the Quidditch World Cup," said Dumbledore.

"Winky talked my father into it," said Crouch, still in the same monotonous voice. "She spent months persuading him. I had not left the house for years. I had loved Quidditch. Let him go, she said. He will be in his Invisibility Cloak. He can watch. Let him smell fresh air for once. She said my mother would have wanted it. She told my father that my mother had died to give me freedom. She had not saved me for a life of imprisonment. He agreed in the end.

"It was carefully planned. My father led me and Winky up to the Top Box early in the day. Winky was to say that she was saving a seat for my father. I was to sit there, invisible. When everyone had left the box, we would emerge. Winky would appear to be alone. Nobody would ever know.

"But Winky didn't know that I was growing stronger. I was starting to fight my father's Imperius Curse. There were times when I was almost myself again. There were brief periods when I seemed outside his control. It happened, there, in the Top Box. It was like waking from a deep sleep. I found myself out in public, in the middle of the match, and I saw, in front of me, a wand sticking out of a boy's pocket. I had not been allowed a wand since before Azkaban. I stole it. Winky didn't know. Winky is frightened of heights. She had her face hidden."

"Master Barty, you bad boy!" whispered Winky, tears trickling between her fingers.

"So you took the wand," said Dumbledore, "and what did you do with it?"

"We went back to the tent," said Crouch. "Then we heard them. We heard the Death Eaters. The ones who had never been to Azkaban. The ones who had never suffered for my master. They had turned their backs on him. They were not enslaved, as I was. They were free to seek him, but they did not. They were merely making sport of Muggles. The sound of their voices awoke me. My mind was clearer than it had been in years. I was angry. I had the wand.

I wanted to attack them for their disloyalty to my master. My father had left the tent; he had gone to free the Muggles. Winky was afraid to see me so angry. She used her own brand of magic to bind me to her. She pulled me from the tent, pulled me into the forest, away from the Death Eaters. I tried to hold her back. I wanted to return to the campsite. I wanted to show those Death Eaters what loyalty to the Dark Lord meant, and to punish them for their lack of it. I used the stolen wand to cast the Dark Mark into the sky.

"Ministry wizards arrived. They shot Stunning Spells everywhere. One of the spells came through the trees where Winky and I stood. The bond connecting us was broken. We were both Stunned.

"When Winky was discovered, my father knew I must be nearby. He searched the bushes where she had been found and felt me lying there. He waited until the other Ministry members had left the forest. He put me back under the Imperius Curse and took me home. He dismissed Winky. She had failed him. She had let me acquire a wand. She had almost let me escape."

Winky let out a wail of despair.

"Now it was just Father and I, alone in the house. And then . . . and then . . ." Crouch's head rolled on his neck, and an insane grin spread across his face. "My master came for me.

"He arrived at our house late one night in the arms of his servant Wormtail. My master had found out that I was still alive. He had captured Bertha Jorkins in Albania. He had tortured her. She told him a great deal. She told him about the Triwizard Tournament. She told him the old Auror, Moody, was going to teach at Hogwarts. He tortured her until he broke through the Memory Charm my father had placed upon her. She told him I had escaped from Azkaban. She told him my father kept me imprisoned to prevent me from seeking my master. And so my master knew that I was still his faithful servant — perhaps the most faithful of all. My master conceived a plan, based upon the information Bertha had given him. He needed me. He arrived at our house near midnight. My father answered the door."

The smile spread wider over Crouch's face, as though recalling the sweetest memory of his life. Winky's petrified brown eyes were visible through her fingers. She seemed too appalled to speak.

"It was very quick. My father was placed under the Imperius Curse by my master. Now my father was the one imprisoned, controlled. My master forced him to go about his business as usual, to act as though nothing was wrong. And I was released. I awoke. I was myself again, alive as I hadn't been in years."

"And what did Lord Voldemort ask you to do?" said Dumbledore.

"He asked me whether I was ready to risk everything for him. I was ready. It was my dream, my greatest ambition, to serve him, to prove myself to him. He told me he needed to place a faithful servant at Hogwarts. A servant who would guide Harry Potter through the Triwizard Tournament without appearing to do so. A servant who would watch over Harry Potter. Ensure he reached the Triwizard Cup. Turn the Cup into a Portkey, which would take the first person to touch it to my master. But first —"

"You needed Alastor Moody," said Dumbledore. His blue eyes were blazing, though his voice remained calm.

"Wormtail and I did it. We had prepared the Polyjuice Potion beforehand. We journeyed to his house. Moody put up a struggle.

There was a commotion. We managed to subdue him just in time. Forced him into a compartment of his own magical trunk. Took some of his hair and added it to the potion. I drank it; I became Moody's double. I took his leg and his eye. I was ready to face Arthur Weasley when he arrived to sort out the Muggles who had heard a disturbance. I made the dustbins move around the yard. I told Arthur Weasley I had heard intruders in my yard, who had set off the dustbins. Then I packed up Moody's clothes and Dark Detectors, put them in the trunk with Moody, and set off for Hogwarts. I kept him alive, under the Imperius Curse. I wanted to be able to question him. To find out about his past, learn his habits, so that I could fool even Dumbledore. I also needed his hair to make the Polyjuice Potion. The other ingredients were easy. I stole boomslang skin from the dungeons. When the Potions master found me in his office, I said I was under orders to search it."

"And what became of Wormtail after you attacked Moody?" said Dumbledore.

"Wormtail returned to care for my master, in my father's house, and to keep watch over my father."

"But your father escaped," said Dumbledore.

"Yes. After a while he began to fight the Imperius Curse just as I had done. There were periods when he knew what was happening. My master decided it was no longer safe for my father to leave the house. He forced him to send letters to the Ministry instead. He made him write and say he was ill. But Wormtail neglected his duty. He was not watchful enough. My father escaped. My master guessed that he was heading for Hogwarts. My father was going to tell Dumbledore everything, to confess. He was going to admit that he had smuggled me from Azkaban.

"My master sent me word of my father's escape. He told me to stop him at all costs. So I waited and watched. I used the map I had taken from Harry Potter. The map that had almost ruined everything."

"Map?" said Dumbledore quickly. "What map is this?"

"Potter's map of Hogwarts. Potter saw me on it. Potter saw me stealing more ingredients for the Polyjuice Potion from Snape's office one night. He thought I was my father. We have the same first name. I took the map from Potter that night. I told him my father hated Dark wizards. Potter believed my father was after Snape.

"For a week I waited for my father to arrive at Hogwarts. At last, one evening, the map showed my father entering the grounds. I pulled on my Invisibility Cloak and went down to meet him. He was walking around the edge of the forest. Then Potter came, and Krum. I waited. I could not hurt Potter; my master needed him. Potter ran to get Dumbledore. I Stunned Krum. I killed my father."

*"Noooo!"* wailed Winky. "Master Barty, Master Barty, what is you saying?"

"You killed your father," Dumbledore said, in the same soft voice. "What did you do with the body?"

"Carried it into the forest. Covered it with the Invisibility Cloak. I had the map with me. I watched Potter run into the castle. He met Snape. Dumbledore joined them. I watched Potter bringing Dumbledore out of the castle. I walked back out of the forest, doubled around behind them, went to meet them. I told Dumbledore Snape had told me where to come.

"Dumbledore told me to go and look for my father. I went back to my father's body. Watched the map. When everyone was gone, I Transfigured my father's body. He became a bone . . . I buried it, while wearing the Invisibility Cloak, in the freshly dug earth in front of Hagrid's cabin."

There was complete silence now, except for Winky's continued sobs. Then Dumbledore said, "And tonight . . ."

"I offered to carry the Triwizard Cup into the maze before dinner," whispered Barty Crouch. "Turned it into a Portkey. My master's plan worked. He is returned to power and I will be honored by him beyond the dreams of wizards."

The insane smile lit his features once more, and his head drooped onto his shoulder as Winky wailed and sobbed at his side.

# THE PARTING OF
# THE WAYS

Dumbledore stood up. He stared down at Barty Crouch for a moment with disgust on his face. Then he raised his wand once more and ropes flew out of it, ropes that twisted themselves around Barty Crouch, binding him tightly. He turned to Professor McGonagall.

"Minerva, could I ask you to stand guard here while I take Harry upstairs?"

"Of course," said Professor McGonagall. She looked slightly nauseous, as though she had just watched someone being sick. However, when she drew out her wand and pointed it at Barty Crouch, her hand was quite steady.

"Severus" — Dumbledore turned to Snape — "please tell Madam Pomfrey to come down here; we need to get Alastor Moody into the hospital wing. Then go down into the grounds, find Cornelius Fudge, and bring him up to this office. He will undoubtedly want to question Crouch himself. Tell him I will be in the hospital wing in half an hour's time if he needs me."

Snape nodded silently and swept out of the room.

"Harry?" Dumbledore said gently.

Harry got up and swayed again; the pain in his leg, which he had not noticed all the time he had been listening to Crouch, now returned in full measure. He also realized that he was shaking. Dumbledore gripped his arm and helped him out into the dark corridor.

"I want you to come up to my office first, Harry," he said quietly as they headed up the passageway. "Sirius is waiting for us there."

Harry nodded. A kind of numbness and a sense of complete unreality were upon him, but he did not care; he was even glad of it. He didn't want to have to think about anything that had happened since he had first touched the Triwizard Cup. He didn't want to have to examine the memories, fresh and sharp as photographs, which kept flashing across his mind. Mad-Eye Moody, inside the trunk. Wormtail, slumped on the ground, cradling his stump of an arm. Voldemort, rising from the steaming cauldron. Cedric . . . dead . . . Cedric, asking to be returned to his parents. . . .

"Professor," Harry mumbled, "where are Mr. and Mrs. Diggory?"

"They are with Professor Sprout," said Dumbledore. His voice, which had been so calm throughout the interrogation of Barty Crouch, shook very slightly for the first time. "She was Head of Cedric's House, and knew him best."

They had reached the stone gargoyle. Dumbledore gave the password, it sprang aside, and he and Harry went up the moving spiral staircase to the oak door. Dumbledore pushed it open. Sirius was standing there. His face was white and gaunt as it had been when he had escaped Azkaban. In one swift moment, he had crossed the room.

"Harry, are you all right? I knew it — I knew something like this — what happened?"

His hands shook as he helped Harry into a chair in front of the desk.

"What happened?" he asked more urgently.

Dumbledore began to tell Sirius everything Barty Crouch had said. Harry was only half listening. So tired every bone in his body was aching, he wanted nothing more than to sit here, undisturbed, for hours and hours, until he fell asleep and didn't have to think or feel anymore.

There was a soft rush of wings. Fawkes the phoenix had left his perch, flown across the office, and landed on Harry's knee.

"'Lo, Fawkes," said Harry quietly. He stroked the phoenix's beautiful scarlet-and-gold plumage. Fawkes blinked peacefully up at him. There was something comforting about his warm weight.

Dumbledore stopped talking. He sat down opposite Harry, behind his desk. He was looking at Harry, who avoided his eyes. Dumbledore was going to question him. He was going to make Harry relive everything.

"I need to know what happened after you touched the Portkey in the maze, Harry," said Dumbledore.

"We can leave that till morning, can't we, Dumbledore?" said Sirius harshly. He had put a hand on Harry's shoulder. "Let him have a sleep. Let him rest."

Harry felt a rush of gratitude toward Sirius, but Dumbledore took no notice of Sirius's words. He leaned forward toward Harry.

Very unwillingly, Harry raised his head and looked into those blue eyes.

"If I thought I could help you," Dumbledore said gently, "by putting you into an enchanted sleep and allowing you to postpone the moment when you would have to think about what has happened tonight, I would do it. But I know better. Numbing the pain for a while will make it worse when you finally feel it. You have shown bravery beyond anything I could have expected of you. I ask you to demonstrate your courage one more time. I ask you to tell us what happened."

The phoenix let out one soft, quavering note. It shivered in the air, and Harry felt as though a drop of hot liquid had slipped down his throat into his stomach, warming him, and strengthening him.

He took a deep breath and began to tell them. As he spoke, visions of everything that had passed that night seemed to rise before his eyes; he saw the sparkling surface of the potion that had revived Voldemort; he saw the Death Eaters Apparating between the graves around them; he saw Cedric's body, lying on the ground beside the cup.

Once or twice, Sirius made a noise as though about to say something, his hand still tight on Harry's shoulder, but Dumbledore raised his hand to stop him, and Harry was glad of this, because it was easier to keep going now he had started. It was even a relief; he felt almost as though something poisonous were being extracted from him. It was costing him every bit of determination he had to keep talking, yet he sensed that once he had finished, he would feel better.

When Harry told of Wormtail piercing his arm with the dagger, however, Sirius let out a vehement exclamation and Dumbledore stood up so quickly that Harry started. Dumbledore walked around the desk and told Harry to stretch out his arm. Harry showed them both the place where his robes were torn and the cut beneath them.

"He said my blood would make him stronger than if he'd used someone else's," Harry told Dumbledore. "He said the protection my — my mother left in me — he'd have it too. And he was right — he could touch me without hurting himself, he touched my face."

For a fleeting instant, Harry thought he saw a gleam of something like triumph in Dumbledore's eyes. But next second, Harry was sure he had imagined it, for when Dumbledore had returned to his seat behind the desk, he looked as old and weary as Harry had ever seen him.

"Very well," he said, sitting down again. "Voldemort has overcome that particular barrier. Harry, continue, please."

Harry went on; he explained how Voldemort had emerged from the cauldron, and told them all he could remember of Voldemort's speech to the Death Eaters. Then he told how Voldemort had untied him, returned his wand to him, and prepared to duel.

But when he reached the part where the golden beam of light had connected his and Voldemort's wands, he found his throat obstructed. He tried to keep talking, but the memories of what had come out of Voldemort's wand were flooding into his mind. He could see Cedric emerging, see the old man, Bertha Jorkins . . . his father . . . his mother . . .

He was glad when Sirius broke the silence.

"The wands connected?" he said, looking from Harry to Dumbledore. "Why?"

Harry looked up at Dumbledore again, on whose face there was an arrested look.

"*Priori Incantatem,*" he muttered.

His eyes gazed into Harry's and it was almost as though an invisible beam of understanding shot between them.

"The Reverse Spell effect?" said Sirius sharply.

"Exactly," said Dumbledore. "Harry's wand and Voldemort's wand share cores. Each of them contains a feather from the tail of the same phoenix. *This* phoenix, in fact," he added, and he pointed at the scarlet-and-gold bird, perching peacefully on Harry's knee.

"My wand's feather came from Fawkes?" Harry said, amazed.

"Yes," said Dumbledore. "Mr. Ollivander wrote to tell me you had bought the second wand, the moment you left his shop four years ago."

"So what happens when a wand meets its brother?" said Sirius.

"They will not work properly against each other," said Dumbledore. "If, however, the owners of the wands force the wands to do battle . . . a very rare effect will take place. One of the wands will force the other to regurgitate spells it has performed — in reverse. The most recent first . . . and then those which preceded it. . . ."

He looked interrogatively at Harry, and Harry nodded.

"Which means," said Dumbledore slowly, his eyes upon Harry's face, "that some form of Cedric must have reappeared."

Harry nodded again.

"Diggory came back to life?" said Sirius sharply.

"No spell can reawaken the dead," said Dumbledore heavily. "All that would have happened is a kind of reverse echo. A shadow of the living Cedric would have emerged from the wand . . . am I correct, Harry?"

"He spoke to me," Harry said. He was suddenly shaking again. "The . . . the ghost Cedric, or whatever he was, spoke."

"An echo," said Dumbledore, "which retained Cedric's appearance and character. I am guessing other such forms appeared . . . less recent victims of Voldemort's wand. . . ."

"An old man," Harry said, his throat still constricted. "Bertha Jorkins. And . . ."

"Your parents?" said Dumbledore quietly.

"Yes," said Harry.

Sirius's grip on Harry's shoulder was now so tight it was painful.

"The last murders the wand performed," said Dumbledore, nodding. "In reverse order. More would have appeared, of course, had you maintained the connection. Very well, Harry, these echoes, these shadows . . . what did they do?"

Harry described how the figures that had emerged from the wand had prowled the edges of the golden web, how Voldemort had seemed to fear them, how the shadow of Harry's father had told him what to do, how Cedric's had made its final request.

At this point, Harry found he could not continue. He looked around at Sirius and saw that he had his face in his hands.

Harry suddenly became aware that Fawkes had left his knee. The phoenix had fluttered to the floor. It was resting its beautiful head against Harry's injured leg, and thick, pearly tears were falling from its eyes onto the wound left by the spider. The pain vanished. The skin mended. His leg was repaired.

"I will say it again," said Dumbledore as the phoenix rose into the air and resettled itself upon the perch beside the door. "You have shown bravery beyond anything I could have expected of you tonight, Harry. You have shown bravery equal to those who died fighting Voldemort at the height of his powers. You have shouldered a grown wizard's burden and found yourself equal to it — and you have now given us all that we have a right to expect. You will come with me to the hospital wing. I do not want you returning to the dormitory tonight. A Sleeping Potion, and some peace . . . Sirius, would you like to stay with him?"

Sirius nodded and stood up. He transformed back into the great black dog and walked with Harry and Dumbledore out of the office, accompanying them down a flight of stairs to the hospital wing.

When Dumbledore pushed open the door, Harry saw Mrs. Weasley, Bill, Ron, and Hermione grouped around a harassed-looking Madam Pomfrey. They appeared to be demanding to know where Harry was and what had happened to him. All of them whipped around as Harry, Dumbledore, and the black dog entered, and Mrs. Weasley let out a kind of muffled scream.

"Harry! Oh Harry!"

She started to hurry toward him, but Dumbledore moved between them.

"Molly," he said, holding up a hand, "please listen to me for a moment. Harry has been through a terrible ordeal tonight. He has just had to relive it for me. What he needs now is sleep, and peace, and quiet. If he would like you all to stay with him," he added, looking around at Ron, Hermione, and Bill too, "you may do so. But I do not want you questioning him until he is ready to answer, and certainly not this evening."

Mrs. Weasley nodded. She was very white. She rounded on Ron,

Hermione, and Bill as though they were being noisy, and hissed, "Did you hear? He needs quiet!"

"Headmaster," said Madam Pomfrey, staring at the great black dog that was Sirius, "may I ask what — ?"

"This dog will be remaining with Harry for a while," said Dumbledore simply. "I assure you, he is extremely well trained. Harry — I will wait while you get into bed."

Harry felt an inexpressible sense of gratitude to Dumbledore for asking the others not to question him. It wasn't as though he didn't want them there; but the thought of explaining it all over again, the idea of reliving it one more time, was more than he could stand.

"I will be back to see you as soon as I have met with Fudge, Harry," said Dumbledore. "I would like you to remain here tomorrow until I have spoken to the school." He left.

As Madam Pomfrey led Harry to a nearby bed, he caught sight of the real Moody lying motionless in a bed at the far end of the room. His wooden leg and magical eye were lying on the bedside table.

"Is he okay?" Harry asked.

"He'll be fine," said Madam Pomfrey, giving Harry some pajamas and pulling screens around him. He took off his robes, pulled on the pajamas, and got into bed. Ron, Hermione, Bill, Mrs. Weasley, and the black dog came around the screen and settled themselves in chairs on either side of him. Ron and Hermione were looking at him almost cautiously, as though scared of him.

"I'm all right," he told them. "Just tired."

Mrs. Weasley's eyes filled with tears as she smoothed his bedcovers unnecessarily.

Madam Pomfrey, who had bustled off to her office, returned holding a small bottle of some purple potion and a goblet.

"You'll need to drink all of this, Harry," she said. "It's a potion for dreamless sleep."

Harry took the goblet and drank a few mouthfuls. He felt himself becoming drowsy at once. Everything around him became hazy; the lamps around the hospital wing seemed to be winking at him in a friendly way through the screen around his bed; his body felt as though it was sinking deeper into the warmth of the feather mattress. Before he could finish the potion, before he could say another word, his exhaustion had carried him off to sleep.

Harry woke up, so warm, so very sleepy, that he didn't open his eyes, wanting to drop off again. The room was still dimly lit; he was sure it was still nighttime and had a feeling that he couldn't have been asleep very long.

Then he heard whispering around him.

"They'll wake him if they don't shut up!"

"What are they shouting about? Nothing else can have happened, can it?"

Harry opened his eyes blearily. Someone had removed his glasses. He could see the fuzzy outlines of Mrs. Weasley and Bill close by. Mrs. Weasley was on her feet.

"That's Fudge's voice," she whispered. "And that's Minerva McGonagall's, isn't it? But what are they arguing about?"

Now Harry could hear them too: people shouting and running toward the hospital wing.

"Regrettable, but all the same, Minerva —" Cornelius Fudge was saying loudly.

"You should never have brought it inside the castle!" yelled Professor McGonagall. "When Dumbledore finds out —"

Harry heard the hospital doors burst open. Unnoticed by any of the people around his bed, all of whom were staring at the door as Bill pulled back the screens, Harry sat up and put his glasses back on.

Fudge came striding up the ward. Professors McGonagall and Snape were at his heels.

"Where's Dumbledore?" Fudge demanded of Mrs. Weasley.

"He's not here," said Mrs. Weasley angrily. "This is a hospital wing, Minister, don't you think you'd do better to —"

But the door opened, and Dumbledore came sweeping up the ward.

"What has happened?" said Dumbledore sharply, looking from Fudge to Professor McGonagall. "Why are you disturbing these people? Minerva, I'm surprised at you — I asked you to stand guard over Barty Crouch —"

"There is no need to stand guard over him anymore, Dumbledore!" she shrieked. "The Minister has seen to that!"

Harry had never seen Professor McGonagall lose control like this. There were angry blotches of color in her cheeks, and her hands were balled into fists; she was trembling with fury.

"When we told Mr. Fudge that we had caught the Death Eater responsible for tonight's events," said Snape, in a low voice, "he seemed to feel his personal safety was in question. He insisted on summoning a dementor to accompany him into the castle. He brought it up to the office where Barty Crouch —"

"I told him you would not agree, Dumbledore!" Professor McGonagall fumed. "I told him you would never allow dementors to set foot inside the castle, but —"

"My dear woman!" roared Fudge, who likewise looked angrier than Harry had ever seen him, "as Minister of Magic, it is my decision whether I wish to bring protection with me when interviewing a possibly dangerous —"

But Professor McGonagall's voice drowned Fudge's.

"The moment that — that thing entered the room," she screamed, pointing at Fudge, trembling all over, "it swooped down on Crouch and — and —"

Harry felt a chill in his stomach as Professor McGonagall struggled to find words to describe what had happened. He did not need her to finish her sentence. He knew what the dementor must have done. It had administered its fatal Kiss to Barty Crouch. It had sucked his soul out through his mouth. He was worse than dead.

"By all accounts, he is no loss!" blustered Fudge. "It seems he has been responsible for several deaths!"

"But he cannot now give testimony, Cornelius," said Dumbledore. He was staring hard at Fudge, as though seeing him plainly for the first time. "He cannot give evidence about why he killed those people."

"Why he killed them? Well, that's no mystery, is it?" blustered Fudge. "He was a raving lunatic! From what Minerva and Severus have told me, he seems to have thought he was doing it all on You-Know-Who's instructions!"

"Lord Voldemort *was* giving him instructions, Cornelius," Dumbledore said. "Those people's deaths were mere by-products of a plan to restore Voldemort to full strength again. The plan succeeded. Voldemort has been restored to his body."

Fudge looked as though someone had just swung a heavy weight into his face. Dazed and blinking, he stared back at Dumbledore as if he couldn't quite believe what he had just heard. He began to sputter, still goggling at Dumbledore.

"You-Know-Who . . . returned? Preposterous. Come now, Dumbledore . . ."

"As Minerva and Severus have doubtless told you," said Dumbledore, "we heard Barty Crouch confess. Under the influence of Veritaserum, he told us how he was smuggled out of Azkaban, and how Voldemort — learning of his continued existence from Bertha Jorkins — went to free him from his father and used him to capture Harry. The plan worked, I tell you. Crouch has helped Voldemort to return."

"See here, Dumbledore," said Fudge, and Harry was astonished to see a slight smile dawning on his face, "you — you can't seriously believe that. You-Know-Who — back? Come now, come now . . . certainly, Crouch may have *believed* himself to be acting upon You-Know-Who's orders — but to take the word of a lunatic like that, Dumbledore . . ."

"When Harry touched the Triwizard Cup tonight, he was transported straight to Voldemort," said Dumbledore steadily. "He witnessed Lord Voldemort's rebirth. I will explain it all to you if you will step up to my office."

Dumbledore glanced around at Harry and saw that he was awake, but shook his head and said, "I am afraid I cannot permit you to question Harry tonight."

Fudge's curious smile lingered. He too glanced at Harry, then looked back at Dumbledore, and said, "You are — er — prepared to take Harry's word on this, are you, Dumbledore?"

There was a moment's silence, which was broken by Sirius

growling. His hackles were raised, and he was baring his teeth at Fudge.

"Certainly, I believe Harry," said Dumbledore. His eyes were blazing now. "I heard Crouch's confession, and I heard Harry's account of what happened after he touched the Triwizard Cup; the two stories make sense, they explain everything that has happened since Bertha Jorkins disappeared last summer."

Fudge still had that strange smile on his face. Once again, he glanced at Harry before answering.

"You are prepared to believe that Lord Voldemort has returned, on the word of a lunatic murderer, and a boy who . . . well . . ."

Fudge shot Harry another look, and Harry suddenly understood.

"You've been reading Rita Skeeter, Mr. Fudge," he said quietly.

Ron, Hermione, Mrs. Weasley, and Bill all jumped. None of them had realized that Harry was awake.

Fudge reddened slightly, but a defiant and obstinate look came over his face.

"And if I have?" he said, looking at Dumbledore. "If I have discovered that you've been keeping certain facts about the boy very quiet? A Parselmouth, eh? And having funny turns all over the place —"

"I assume that you are referring to the pains Harry has been experiencing in his scar?" said Dumbledore coolly.

"You admit that he has been having these pains, then?" said Fudge quickly. "Headaches? Nightmares? Possibly — hallucinations?"

"Listen to me, Cornelius," said Dumbledore, taking a step toward Fudge, and once again, he seemed to radiate that indefinable sense of power that Harry had felt after Dumbledore had Stunned young Crouch. "Harry is as sane as you or I. That scar upon his forehead has not addled his brains. I believe it hurts him when Lord Voldemort is close by, or feeling particularly murderous."

Fudge had taken half a step back from Dumbledore, but he looked no less stubborn.

"You'll forgive me, Dumbledore, but I've never heard of a curse scar acting as an alarm bell before. . . ."

"Look, I saw Voldemort come back!" Harry shouted. He tried to get out of bed again, but Mrs. Weasley forced him back. "I saw the Death Eaters! I can give you their names! Lucius Malfoy —"

Snape made a sudden movement, but as Harry looked at him, Snape's eyes flew back to Fudge.

"Malfoy was cleared!" said Fudge, visibly affronted. "A very old family — donations to excellent causes —"

"Macnair!" Harry continued.

"Also cleared! Now working for the Ministry!"

"Avery — Nott — Crabbe — Goyle —"

"You are merely repeating the names of those who were acquitted of being Death Eaters thirteen years ago!" said Fudge angrily. "You could have found those names in old reports of the trials! For heaven's sake, Dumbledore — the boy was full of some crackpot story at the end of last year too — his tales are getting taller, and you're still swallowing them — the boy can talk to snakes, Dumbledore, and you still think he's trustworthy?"

"You fool!" Professor McGonagall cried. "Cedric Diggory! Mr. Crouch! These deaths were not the random work of a lunatic!"

"I see no evidence to the contrary!" shouted Fudge, now matching her anger, his face purpling. "It seems to me that you are all determined to start a panic that will destabilize everything we have worked for these last thirteen years!"

Harry couldn't believe what he was hearing. He had always thought of Fudge as a kindly figure, a little blustering, a little pompous, but essentially good-natured. But now a short, angry wizard stood before him, refusing, point-blank, to accept the prospect of disruption in his comfortable and ordered world — to believe that Voldemort could have risen.

"Voldemort has returned," Dumbledore repeated. "If you accept that fact straightaway, Fudge, and take the necessary measures, we may still be able to save the situation. The first and most essential step is to remove Azkaban from the control of the dementors —"

"Preposterous!" shouted Fudge again. "Remove the dementors? I'd be kicked out of office for suggesting it! Half of us only feel safe in our beds at night because we know the dementors are standing guard at Azkaban!"

"The rest of us sleep less soundly in our beds, Cornelius, knowing that you have put Lord Voldemort's most dangerous supporters in the care of creatures who will join him the instant he asks them!" said Dumbledore. "They will not remain loyal to you, Fudge! Voldemort can offer them much more scope for their powers and their pleasures than you can! With the dementors behind him, and his old supporters returned to him, you will be hard-pressed to stop him regaining the sort of power he had thirteen years ago!"

Fudge was opening and closing his mouth as though no words could express his outrage.

"The second step you must take — and at once," Dumbledore pressed on, "is to send envoys to the giants."

"Envoys to the giants?" Fudge shrieked, finding his tongue again. "What madness is this?"

"Extend them the hand of friendship, now, before it is too late," said Dumbledore, "or Voldemort will persuade them, as he did before, that he alone among wizards will give them their rights and their freedom!"

"You — you cannot be serious!" Fudge gasped, shaking his head and retreating further from Dumbledore. "If the magical community got wind that I had approached the giants — people hate them, Dumbledore — end of my career —"

"You are blinded," said Dumbledore, his voice rising now, the aura of power around him palpable, his eyes blazing once more, "by the love of the office you hold, Cornelius! You place too much importance, and you always have done, on the so-called purity of blood! You fail to recognize that it matters not what someone is born, but what they grow to be! Your dementor has just destroyed the last remaining member of a pure-blood family as old as any — and see what that man chose to make of his life! I tell you now — take the steps I have suggested, and you will be remembered, in office or out, as one of the bravest and greatest Ministers of Magic we have ever known. Fail to act — and history will remember you as the man who stepped aside and allowed Voldemort a second chance to destroy the world we have tried to rebuild!"

"Insane," whispered Fudge, still backing away. "Mad . . ."

And then there was silence. Madam Pomfrey was standing frozen at the foot of Harry's bed, her hands over her mouth. Mrs.

Weasley was still standing over Harry, her hand on his shoulder to prevent him from rising. Bill, Ron, and Hermione were staring at Fudge.

"If your determination to shut your eyes will carry you as far as this, Cornelius," said Dumbledore, "we have reached a parting of the ways. You must act as you see fit. And I — I shall act as I see fit."

Dumbledore's voice carried no hint of a threat; it sounded like a mere statement, but Fudge bristled as though Dumbledore were advancing upon him with a wand.

"Now, see here, Dumbledore," he said, waving a threatening finger. "I've given you free rein, always. I've had a lot of respect for you. I might not have agreed with some of your decisions, but I've kept quiet. There aren't many who'd have let you hire werewolves, or keep Hagrid, or decide what to teach your students without reference to the Ministry. But if you're going to work against me —"

"The only one against whom I intend to work," said Dumbledore, "is Lord Voldemort. If you are against him, then we remain, Cornelius, on the same side."

It seemed Fudge could think of no answer to this. He rocked backward and forward on his small feet for a moment and spun his bowler hat in his hands. Finally, he said, with a hint of a plea in his voice, "He can't be back, Dumbledore, he just can't be . . ."

Snape strode forward, past Dumbledore, pulling up the left sleeve of his robes as he went. He stuck out his forearm and showed it to Fudge, who recoiled.

"There," said Snape harshly. "There. The Dark Mark. It is not as clear as it was an hour or so ago, when it burned black, but you can still see it. Every Death Eater had the sign burned into him by the Dark Lord. It was a means of distinguishing one another, and his means of summoning us to him. When he touched the Mark of any Death Eater, we were to Disapparate, and Apparate, instantly, at his side. This Mark has been growing clearer all year. Karkaroff's too. Why do you think Karkaroff fled tonight? We both felt the Mark burn. We both knew he had returned. Karkaroff fears the Dark Lord's vengeance. He betrayed too many of his fellow Death Eaters to be sure of a welcome back into the fold."

Fudge stepped back from Snape too. He was shaking his head. He did not seem to have taken in a word Snape had said. He stared, apparently repelled by the ugly mark on Snape's arm, then looked up at Dumbledore and whispered, "I don't know what you and your staff are playing at, Dumbledore, but I have heard enough. I have no more to add. I will be in touch with you tomorrow, Dumbledore, to discuss the running of this school. I must return to the Ministry."

He had almost reached the door when he paused. He turned around, strode back down the dormitory, and stopped at Harry's bed.

"Your winnings," he said shortly, taking a large bag of gold out of his pocket and dropping it onto Harry's bedside table. "One thousand Galleons. There should have been a presentation ceremony, but under the circumstances . . ."

He crammed his bowler hat onto his head and walked out of the room, slamming the door behind him. The moment he had disappeared, Dumbledore turned to look at the group around Harry's bed.

"There is work to be done," he said. "Molly . . . am I right in thinking that I can count on you and Arthur?"

"Of course you can," said Mrs. Weasley. She was white to the lips, but she looked resolute. "We know what Fudge is. It's Arthur's fondness for Muggles that has held him back at the Ministry all these years. Fudge thinks he lacks proper Wizarding pride."

"Then I need to send a message to Arthur," said Dumbledore. "All those that we can persuade of the truth must be notified immediately, and he is well placed to contact those at the Ministry who are not as shortsighted as Cornelius."

"I'll go to Dad," said Bill, standing up. "I'll go now."

"Excellent," said Dumbledore. "Tell him what has happened. Tell him I will be in direct contact with him shortly. He will need to be discreet, however. If Fudge thinks I am interfering at the Ministry —"

"Leave it to me," said Bill.

He clapped a hand on Harry's shoulder, kissed his mother on the cheek, pulled on his cloak, and strode quickly from the room.

"Minerva," said Dumbledore, turning to Professor McGonagall, "I want to see Hagrid in my office as soon as possible. Also — if she will consent to come — Madame Maxime."

Professor McGonagall nodded and left without a word.

"Poppy," Dumbledore said to Madam Pomfrey, "would you be very kind and go down to Professor Moody's office, where I think you will find a house-elf called Winky in considerable distress? Do what you can for her, and take her back to the kitchens. I think Dobby will look after her for us."

"Very — very well," said Madam Pomfrey, looking startled, and she too left.

Dumbledore made sure that the door was closed, and that Madam Pomfrey's footsteps had died away, before he spoke again.

"And now," he said, "it is time for two of our number to recognize each other for what they are. Sirius . . . if you could resume your usual form."

The great black dog looked up at Dumbledore, then, in an instant, turned back into a man.

Mrs. Weasley screamed and leapt back from the bed.

"Sirius Black!" she shrieked, pointing at him.

"Mum, shut up!" Ron yelled. "It's okay!"

Snape had not yelled or jumped backward, but the look on his face was one of mingled fury and horror.

"Him!" he snarled, staring at Sirius, whose face showed equal dislike. "What is he doing here?"

"He is here at my invitation," said Dumbledore, looking between them, "as are you, Severus. I trust you both. It is time for you to lay aside your old differences and trust each other."

Harry thought Dumbledore was asking for a near miracle. Sirius and Snape were eyeing each other with the utmost loathing.

"I will settle, in the short term," said Dumbledore, with a bite of impatience in his voice, "for a lack of open hostility. You will shake hands. You are on the same side now. Time is short, and unless the few of us who know the truth stand united, there is no hope for any of us."

Very slowly — but still glaring at each other as though each wished the other nothing but ill — Sirius and Snape moved toward each other and shook hands. They let go extremely quickly.

"That will do to be going on with," said Dumbledore, stepping between them once more. "Now I have work for each of you. Fudge's attitude, though not unexpected, changes everything. Sirius, I need you to set off at once. You are to alert Remus Lupin, Arabella Figg, Mundungus Fletcher — the old crowd. Lie low at Lupin's for a while; I will contact you there."

"But —" said Harry.

He wanted Sirius to stay. He did not want to have to say goodbye again so quickly.

"You'll see me very soon, Harry," said Sirius, turning to him. "I promise you. But I must do what I can, you understand, don't you?"

"Yeah," said Harry. "Yeah . . . of course I do."

Sirius grasped his hand briefly, nodded to Dumbledore, transformed again into the black dog, and ran the length of the room to the door, whose handle he turned with a paw. Then he was gone.

"Severus," said Dumbledore, turning to Snape, "you know what I must ask you to do. If you are ready . . . if you are prepared . . ."

"I am," said Snape.

He looked slightly paler than usual, and his cold, black eyes glittered strangely.

"Then good luck," said Dumbledore, and he watched, with a trace of apprehension on his face, as Snape swept wordlessly after Sirius.

It was several minutes before Dumbledore spoke again.

"I must go downstairs," he said finally. "I must see the Diggorys. Harry — take the rest of your potion. I will see all of you later."

Harry slumped back against his pillows as Dumbledore

disappeared. Hermione, Ron, and Mrs. Weasley were all looking at him. None of them spoke for a very long time.

"You've got to take the rest of your potion, Harry," Mrs. Weasley said at last. Her hand nudged the sack of gold on his bedside cabinet as she reached for the bottle and the goblet. "You have a good long sleep. Try and think about something else for a while . . . think about what you're going to buy with your winnings!"

"I don't want that gold," said Harry in an expressionless voice. "You have it. Anyone can have it. I shouldn't have won it. It should've been Cedric's."

The thing against which he had been fighting on and off ever since he had come out of the maze was threatening to overpower him. He could feel a burning, prickling feeling in the inner corners of his eyes. He blinked and stared up at the ceiling.

"It wasn't your fault, Harry," Mrs. Weasley whispered.

"I told him to take the Cup with me," said Harry.

Now the burning feeling was in his throat too. He wished Ron would look away.

Mrs. Weasley set the potion down on the bedside cabinet, bent down, and put her arms around Harry. He had no memory of ever being hugged like this, as though by a mother. The full weight of everything he had seen that night seemed to fall in upon him as Mrs. Weasley held him to her. His mother's face, his father's voice, the sight of Cedric, dead on the ground all started spinning in his head until he could hardly bear it, until he was screwing up his face against the howl of misery fighting to get out of him.

There was a loud slamming noise, and Mrs. Weasley and Harry broke apart. Hermione was standing by the window. She was holding something tight in her hand.

"Sorry," she whispered.

"Your potion, Harry," said Mrs. Weasley quickly, wiping her eyes on the back of her hand.

Harry drank it in one gulp. The effect was instantaneous. Heavy, irresistible waves of dreamless sleep broke over him; he fell back onto his pillows and thought no more.

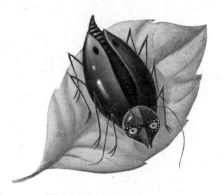

# THE BEGINNING

When he looked back, even a month later, Harry found he had only scattered memories of the next few days. It was as though he had been through too much to take in any more. The recollections he did have were very painful. The worst, perhaps, was the meeting with the Diggorys that took place the following morning.

They did not blame him for what had happened; on the contrary, both thanked him for returning Cedric's body to them. Mr. Diggory sobbed through most of the interview. Mrs. Diggory's grief seemed to be beyond tears.

"He suffered very little then," she said, when Harry had told her how Cedric had died. "And after all, Amos . . . he died just when he'd won the tournament. He must have been happy."

When they got to their feet, she looked down at Harry and said, "You look after yourself, now."

Harry seized the sack of gold on the bedside table.

"You take this," he muttered to her. "It should've been Cedric's, he got there first, you take it —"

But she backed away from him.

"Oh no, it's yours, dear, I couldn't . . . you keep it."

Harry returned to Gryffindor Tower the following evening. From what Hermione and Ron told him, Dumbledore had spoken to the school that morning at breakfast. He had merely requested that they leave Harry alone, that nobody ask him questions or badger him to tell the story of what had happened in the maze. Most people, he noticed, were skirting him in the corridors, avoiding his eyes. Some whispered behind their hands as he passed. He guessed that many of them had believed Rita Skeeter's article about how disturbed and possibly dangerous he was. Perhaps they were formulating their own theories about how Cedric had died. He found he didn't care very much. He liked it best when he was with Ron and Hermione and they were talking about other things, or else letting him sit in silence while they played chess. He felt as though all three of them had reached an understanding they didn't need to put into words; that each was waiting for some sign, some word, of what was going on outside Hogwarts — and that it was useless to speculate about what might be coming until they knew anything for certain. The only time they touched upon the subject was when Ron told Harry about a meeting Mrs. Weasley had had with Dumbledore before going home.

"She went to ask him if you could come straight to us this summer," he said. "But he wants you to go back to the Dursleys, at least at first."

"Why?" said Harry.

"She said Dumbledore's got his reasons," said Ron, shaking his head darkly. "I suppose we've got to trust him, haven't we?"

The only person apart from Ron and Hermione that Harry felt able to talk to was Hagrid. As there was no longer a Defense Against the Dark Arts teacher, they had those lessons free. They used the one on Thursday afternoon to go down and visit Hagrid in his cabin. It was a bright and sunny day; Fang bounded out of the open door as they approached, barking and wagging his tail madly.

"Who's that?" called Hagrid, coming to the door. *"Harry!"*

He strode out to meet them, pulled Harry into a one-armed hug, ruffled his hair, and said, "Good ter see yeh, mate. Good ter see yeh."

They saw two bucket-size cups and saucers on the wooden table in front of the fireplace when they entered Hagrid's cabin.

"Bin havin' a cuppa with Olympe," Hagrid said. "She's jus' left."

"Who?" said Ron curiously.

"Madame Maxime, o' course!" said Hagrid.

"You two made up, have you?" said Ron.

"Dunno what yeh're talkin' about," said Hagrid airily, fetching more cups from the dresser. When he had made tea and offered around a plate of doughy cookies, he leaned back in his chair and surveyed Harry closely through his beetle-black eyes.

"You all righ'?" he said gruffly.

"Yeah," said Harry.

"No, yeh're not," said Hagrid. "'Course yeh're not. But yeh will be."

Harry said nothing.

"Knew he was goin' ter come back," said Hagrid, and Harry,

Ron, and Hermione looked up at him, shocked. "Known it fer years, Harry. Knew he was out there, bidin' his time. It had ter happen. Well, now it has, an' we'll jus' have ter get on with it. We'll fight. Migh' be able ter stop him before he gets a good hold. That's Dumbledore's plan, anyway. Great man, Dumbledore. 'S long as we've got him, I'm not too worried."

Hagrid raised his bushy eyebrows at the disbelieving expressions on their faces.

"No good sittin' worryin' abou' it," he said. "What's comin' will come, an' we'll meet it when it does. Dumbledore told me wha' you did, Harry."

Hagrid's chest swelled as he looked at Harry.

"Yeh did as much as yer father would've done, an' I can' give yeh no higher praise than that."

Harry smiled back at him. It was the first time he'd smiled in days. "What's Dumbledore asked you to do, Hagrid?" he asked. "He sent Professor McGonagall to ask you and Madame Maxime to meet him — that night."

"Got a little job fer me over the summer," said Hagrid. "Secret, though. I'm not s'pposed ter talk abou' it, no, not even ter you lot. Olympe — Madame Maxime ter you — might be comin' with me. I think she will. Think I got her persuaded."

"Is it to do with Voldemort?"

Hagrid flinched at the sound of the name.

"Migh' be," he said evasively. "Now . . . who'd like ter come an' visit the las' skrewt with me? I was jokin' — jokin'!" he added hastily, seeing the looks on their faces.

*   *   *

It was with a heavy heart that Harry packed his trunk up in the dormitory on the night before his return to Privet Drive. He was dreading the Leaving Feast, which was usually a cause for celebration, when the winner of the Inter-House Championship would be announced. He had avoided being in the Great Hall when it was full ever since he had left the hospital wing, preferring to eat when it was nearly empty to avoid the stares of his fellow students.

When he, Ron, and Hermione entered the Hall, they saw at once that the usual decorations were missing. The Great Hall was normally decorated with the winning House's colors for the Leaving Feast. Tonight, however, there were black drapes on the wall behind the teachers' table. Harry knew instantly that they were there as a mark of respect to Cedric.

The real Mad-Eye Moody was at the staff table now, his wooden leg and his magical eye back in place. He was extremely twitchy, jumping every time someone spoke to him. Harry couldn't blame him; Moody's fear of attack was bound to have been increased by his ten-month imprisonment in his own trunk. Professor Karkaroff's chair was empty. Harry wondered, as he sat down with the other Gryffindors, where Karkaroff was now, and whether Voldemort had caught up with him.

Madame Maxime was still there. She was sitting next to Hagrid. They were talking quietly together. Further along the table, sitting next to Professor McGonagall, was Snape. His eyes lingered on Harry for a moment as Harry looked at him. His expression was difficult to read. He looked as sour and unpleasant as ever. Harry continued to watch him, long after Snape had looked away.

What was it that Snape had done on Dumbledore's orders, the night that Voldemort had returned? And why . . . *why* . . . was

Dumbledore so convinced that Snape was truly on their side? He had been their spy, Dumbledore had said so in the Pensieve. Snape had turned spy against Voldemort, "at great personal risk." Was that the job he had taken up again? Had he made contact with the Death Eaters, perhaps? Pretended that he had never really gone over to Dumbledore, that he had been, like Voldemort himself, biding his time?

Harry's musings were ended by Professor Dumbledore, who stood up at the staff table. The Great Hall, which in any case had been less noisy than it usually was at the Leaving Feast, became very quiet.

"The end," said Dumbledore, looking around at them all, "of another year."

He paused, and his eyes fell upon the Hufflepuff table. Theirs had been the most subdued table before he had gotten to his feet, and theirs were still the saddest and palest faces in the Hall.

"There is much that I would like to say to you all tonight," said Dumbledore, "but I must first acknowledge the loss of a very fine person, who should be sitting here," he gestured toward the Hufflepuffs, "enjoying our feast with us. I would like you all, please, to stand, and raise your glasses, to Cedric Diggory."

They did it, all of them; the benches scraped as everyone in the Hall stood, and raised their goblets, and echoed, in one loud, low, rumbling voice, "Cedric Diggory."

Harry caught a glimpse of Cho through the crowd. There were tears pouring silently down her face. He looked down at the table as they all sat down again.

"Cedric was a person who exemplified many of the qualities that distinguish Hufflepuff House," Dumbledore continued. "He was a good and loyal friend, a hard worker, he valued fair play. His death has affected you all, whether you knew him well or not. I think that you have the right, therefore, to know exactly how it came about."

Harry raised his head and stared at Dumbledore.

"Cedric Diggory was murdered by Lord Voldemort."

A panicked whisper swept the Great Hall. People were staring at Dumbledore in disbelief, in horror. He looked perfectly calm as he watched them mutter themselves into silence.

"The Ministry of Magic," Dumbledore continued, "does not wish me to tell you this. It is possible that some of your parents will be horrified that I have done so — either because they will not believe that Lord Voldemort has returned, or because they think I should not tell you so, young as you are. It is my belief, however, that the truth is generally preferable to lies, and that any attempt to pretend that Cedric died as the result of an accident, or some sort of blunder of his own, is an insult to his memory."

Stunned and frightened, every face in the Hall was turned toward Dumbledore now . . . or almost every face. Over at the Slytherin table, Harry saw Draco Malfoy muttering something to Crabbe and Goyle. Harry felt a hot, sick swoop of anger in his stomach. He forced himself to look back at Dumbledore.

"There is somebody else who must be mentioned in connection with Cedric's death," Dumbledore went on. "I am talking, of course, about Harry Potter."

A kind of ripple crossed the Great Hall as a few heads turned in Harry's direction before flicking back to face Dumbledore.

"Harry Potter managed to escape Lord Voldemort," said Dumbledore. "He risked his own life to return Cedric's body to Hogwarts. He showed, in every respect, the sort of bravery that few wizards have ever shown in facing Lord Voldemort, and for this, I honor him."

Dumbledore turned gravely to Harry and raised his goblet once more. Nearly everyone in the Great Hall followed suit. They murmured his name, as they had murmured Cedric's, and drank to him. But through a gap in the standing figures, Harry saw that Malfoy, Crabbe, Goyle, and many of the other Slytherins had remained defiantly in their seats, their goblets untouched. Dumbledore, who after all possessed no magical eye, did not see them.

When everyone had once again resumed their seats, Dumbledore continued, "The Triwizard Tournament's aim was to further and promote magical understanding. In the light of what has happened — of Lord Voldemort's return — such ties are more important than ever before."

Dumbledore looked from Madame Maxime and Hagrid, to Fleur Delacour and her fellow Beauxbatons students, to Viktor Krum and the Durmstrangs at the Slytherin table. Krum, Harry saw, looked wary, almost frightened, as though he expected Dumbledore to say something harsh.

"Every guest in this Hall," said Dumbledore, and his eyes lingered upon the Durmstrang students, "will be welcomed back here at any time, should they wish to come. I say to you all, once again — in the light of Lord Voldemort's return, we are only as strong as we are united, as weak as we are divided. Lord Voldemort's gift for spreading discord and enmity is very great. We can fight it only by showing an equally strong bond of friendship and trust. Differences of habit and language are nothing at all if our aims are identical and our hearts are open.

"It is my belief — and never have I so hoped that I am

mistaken — that we are all facing dark and difficult times. Some of you in this Hall have already suffered directly at the hands of Lord Voldemort. Many of your families have been torn asunder. A week ago, a student was taken from our midst.

"Remember Cedric. Remember, if the time should come when you have to make a choice between what is right and what is easy, remember what happened to a boy who was good, and kind, and brave, because he strayed across the path of Lord Voldemort. Remember Cedric Diggory."

Harry's trunk was packed; Hedwig was back in her cage on top of it. He, Ron, and Hermione were waiting in the crowded entrance hall with the rest of the fourth years for the carriages that would take them back to Hogsmeade station. It was another beautiful summer's day. He supposed that Privet Drive would be hot and leafy, its flower beds a riot of color, when he arrived there that evening. The thought gave him no pleasure at all.

"'Arry!"

He looked around. Fleur Delacour was hurrying up the stone steps into the castle. Beyond her, far across the grounds, Harry could see Hagrid helping Madame Maxime to back two of the giant horses into their harness. The Beauxbatons carriage was about to take off.

"We will see each uzzer again, I 'ope," said Fleur as she reached him, holding out her hand. "I am 'oping to get a job 'ere, to improve my Eenglish."

"It's very good already," said Ron in a strangled sort of voice. Fleur smiled at him; Hermione scowled.

"Good-bye, 'Arry," said Fleur, turning to go. "It 'az been a plea-sure meeting you!"

Harry's spirits couldn't help but lift slightly as he watched Fleur hurry back across the lawns to Madame Maxime, her silvery hair rippling in the sunlight.

"Wonder how the Durmstrang students are getting back," said Ron. "D'you reckon they can steer that ship without Karkaroff?"

"Karkaroff did not steer," said a gruff voice. "He stayed in his cabin and let us do the vork."

Krum had come to say good-bye to Hermione.

"Could I have a vord?" he asked her.

"Oh . . . yes . . . all right," said Hermione, looking slightly flus-tered, and following Krum through the crowd and out of sight.

"You'd better hurry up!" Ron called loudly after her. "The carriages'll be here in a minute!"

He let Harry keep a watch for the carriages, however, and spent the next few minutes craning his neck over the crowd to try and see what Krum and Hermione might be up to. They returned quite soon. Ron stared at Hermione, but her face was quite impassive.

"I liked Diggory," said Krum abruptly to Harry. "He vos alvays polite to me. Alvays. Even though I vos from Durmstrang — with Karkaroff," he added, scowling.

"Have you got a new headmaster yet?" said Harry.

Krum shrugged. He held out his hand as Fleur had done, shook Harry's hand, and then Ron's. Ron looked as though he was suffer-ing some sort of painful internal struggle. Krum had already started walking away when Ron burst out, "Can I have your autograph?"

Hermione turned away, smiling at the horseless carriages that were now trundling toward them up the drive, as Krum, looking surprised but gratified, signed a fragment of parchment for Ron.

The weather could not have been more different on the journey back to King's Cross than it had been on their way to Hogwarts the previous September. There wasn't a single cloud in the sky. Harry, Ron, and Hermione had managed to get a compartment to themselves. Pigwidgeon was once again hidden under Ron's dress robes to stop him from hooting continually; Hedwig was dozing, her head under her wing, and Crookshanks was curled up in a spare seat like a large, furry ginger cushion. Harry, Ron, and Hermione talked more fully and freely than they had all week as the train sped them southward. Harry felt as though Dumbledore's speech at the Leaving Feast had unblocked him, somehow. It was less painful to discuss what had happened now. They broke off their conversation about what action Dumbledore might be taking, even now, to stop Voldemort only when the lunch trolley arrived.

When Hermione returned from the trolley and put her money back into her schoolbag, she dislodged a copy of the *Daily Prophet* that she had been carrying in there. Harry looked at it, unsure whether he really wanted to know what it might say, but Hermione, seeing him looking at it, said calmly, "There's nothing in there. You can look for yourself, but there's nothing at all. I've been checking every day. Just a small piece the day after the third task saying you won the tournament. They didn't even mention Cedric. Nothing about any of it. If you ask me, Fudge is forcing them to keep quiet."

"He'll never keep Rita quiet," said Harry. "Not on a story like this."

"Oh, Rita hasn't written anything at all since the third task," said Hermione in an oddly constrained voice. "As a matter of fact," she added, her voice now trembling slightly, "Rita Skeeter isn't going to be writing anything at all for a while. Not unless she wants me to spill the beans on *her*."

"What are you talking about?" said Ron.

"I found out how she was listening in on private conversations when she wasn't supposed to be coming onto the grounds," said Hermione in a rush.

Harry had the impression that Hermione had been dying to tell them this for days, but that she had restrained herself in light of everything else that had happened.

"How was she doing it?" said Harry at once.

"How did you find out?" said Ron, staring at her.

"Well, it was you, really, who gave me the idea, Harry," she said.

"Did I?" said Harry, perplexed. "How?"

*"Bugging,"* said Hermione happily.

"But you said they didn't work —"

"Oh not *electronic* bugs," said Hermione. "No, you see . . . Rita Skeeter" — Hermione's voice trembled with quiet triumph — "is an unregistered Animagus. She can turn —"

Hermione pulled a small sealed glass jar out of her bag.

"— into a beetle."

"You're kidding," said Ron. "You haven't . . . she's not . . ."

"Oh yes she is," said Hermione happily, brandishing the jar at them.

Inside were a few twigs and leaves and one large, fat beetle.

"That's never — you're kidding —" Ron whispered, lifting the jar to his eyes.

"No, I'm not," said Hermione, beaming. "I caught her on the windowsill in the hospital wing. Look very closely, and you'll notice the markings around her antennae are exactly like those foul glasses she wears."

Harry looked and saw that she was quite right. He also remembered something.

"There was a beetle on the statue the night we heard Hagrid telling Madame Maxime about his mum!"

"Exactly," said Hermione. "And Viktor pulled a beetle out of my hair after we'd had our conversation by the lake. And unless I'm very much mistaken, Rita was perched on the windowsill of the Divination class the day your scar hurt. She's been buzzing around for stories all year."

"When we saw Malfoy under that tree . . ." said Ron slowly.

"He was talking to her, in his hand," said Hermione. "He knew, of course. That's how she's been getting all those nice little interviews with the Slytherins. They wouldn't care that she was doing something illegal, as long as they were giving her horrible stuff about us and Hagrid."

Hermione took the glass jar back from Ron and smiled at the beetle, which buzzed angrily against the glass.

"I've told her I'll let her out when we get back to London," said Hermione. "I've put an Unbreakable Charm on the jar, you see, so she can't transform. And I've told her she's to keep her quill to herself for a whole year. See if she can't break the habit of writing horrible lies about people."

Smiling serenely, Hermione placed the beetle back inside her schoolbag.

The door of the compartment slid open.

"Very clever, Granger," said Draco Malfoy.

Crabbe and Goyle were standing behind him. All three of them looked more pleased with themselves, more arrogant and more menacing, than Harry had ever seen them.

"So," said Malfoy slowly, advancing slightly into the compartment and looking slowly around at them, a smirk quivering on his lips. "You caught some pathetic reporter, and Potter's Dumbledore's favorite boy again. Big deal."

His smirk widened. Crabbe and Goyle leered.

"Trying not to think about it, are we?" said Malfoy softly, looking around at all three of them. "Trying to pretend it hasn't happened?"

"Get out," said Harry.

He had not been this close to Malfoy since he had watched him muttering to Crabbe and Goyle during Dumbledore's speech about Cedric. He could feel a kind of ringing in his ears. His hand gripped his wand under his robes.

"You've picked the losing side, Potter! I warned you! I told you you ought to choose your company more carefully, remember? When we met on the train, first day at Hogwarts? I told you not to hang around with riffraff like this!" He jerked his head at Ron and Hermione. "Too late now, Potter! They'll be the first to go, now the Dark Lord's back! Mudbloods and Muggle-lovers first! Well — second — Diggory was the f —"

It was as though someone had exploded a box of fireworks within the compartment. Blinded by the blaze of the spells that had blasted from every direction, deafened by a series of bangs, Harry blinked and looked down at the floor.

Malfoy, Crabbe, and Goyle were all lying unconscious in the

doorway. He, Ron, and Hermione were on their feet, all three of them having used a different hex. Nor were they the only ones to have done so.

"Thought we'd see what those three were up to," said Fred matter-of-factly, stepping onto Goyle and into the compartment. He had his wand out, and so did George, who was careful to tread on Malfoy as he followed Fred inside.

"Interesting effect," said George, looking down at Crabbe. "Who used the Furnunculus Curse?"

"Me," said Harry.

"Odd," said George lightly. "I used Jelly-Legs. Looks as though those two shouldn't be mixed. He seems to have sprouted little tentacles all over his face. Well, let's not leave them here, they don't add much to the decor."

Ron, Harry, and George kicked, rolled, and pushed the unconscious Malfoy, Crabbe, and Goyle — each of whom looked distinctly the worse for the jumble of jinxes with which they had been hit — out into the corridor, then came back into the compartment and rolled the door shut.

"Exploding Snap, anyone?" said Fred, pulling out a pack of cards.

They were halfway through their fifth game when Harry decided to ask them.

"You going to tell us, then?" he said to George. "Who you were blackmailing?"

"Oh," said George darkly. "*That.*"

"It doesn't matter," said Fred, shaking his head impatiently. "It wasn't anything important. Not now, anyway."

"We've given up," said George, shrugging.

But Harry, Ron, and Hermione kept on asking, and finally, Fred said, "All right, all right, if you really want to know . . . it was Ludo Bagman."

"Bagman?" said Harry sharply. "Are you saying he was involved in —"

"Nah," said George gloomily. "Nothing like that. Stupid git. He wouldn't have the brains."

"Well, what, then?" said Ron.

Fred hesitated, then said, "You remember that bet we had with him at the Quidditch World Cup? About how Ireland would win, but Krum would get the Snitch?"

"Yeah," said Harry and Ron slowly.

"Well, the git paid us in leprechaun gold he'd caught from the Irish mascots."

"So?"

"So," said Fred impatiently, "it vanished, didn't it? By next morning, it had gone!"

"But — it must've been an accident, mustn't it?" said Hermione.

George laughed very bitterly.

"Yeah, that's what we thought, at first. We thought if we just wrote to him, and told him he'd made a mistake, he'd cough up. But nothing doing. Ignored our letter. We kept trying to talk to him about it at Hogwarts, but he was always making some excuse to get away from us."

"In the end, he turned pretty nasty," said Fred. "Told us we were too young to gamble, and he wasn't giving us anything."

"So we asked for our money back," said George, glowering.

"He didn't refuse!" gasped Hermione.

"Right in one," said Fred.

"But that was all your savings!" said Ron.

"Tell me about it," said George. "'Course, we found out what was going on in the end. Lee Jordan's dad had had a bit of trouble getting money off Bagman as well. Turns out he's in big trouble with the goblins. Borrowed loads of gold off them. A gang of them cornered him in the woods after the World Cup and took all the gold he had, and it still wasn't enough to cover all his debts. They followed him all the way to Hogwarts to keep an eye on him. He's lost everything gambling. Hasn't got two Galleons to rub together. And you know how the idiot tried to pay the goblins back?"

"How?" said Harry.

"He put a bet on you, mate," said Fred. "Put a big bet on you to win the tournament. Bet against the goblins."

"So *that's* why he kept trying to help me win!" said Harry. "Well — I did win, didn't I? So he can pay you your gold!"

"Nope," said George, shaking his head. "The goblins play as dirty as him. They say you drew with Diggory, and Bagman was betting you'd win outright. So Bagman had to run for it. He did run for it right after the third task."

George sighed deeply and started dealing out the cards again.

The rest of the journey passed pleasantly enough; Harry wished it could have gone on all summer, in fact, and that he would never arrive at King's Cross . . . but as he had learned the hard way that year, time will not slow down when something unpleasant lies ahead, and all too soon, the Hogwarts Express was pulling in at platform nine and three-quarters. The usual confusion and noise filled the corridors as the students began to disembark. Ron and Hermione struggled out past Malfoy, Crabbe, and Goyle, carrying their trunks. Harry, however, stayed put.

"Fred — George — wait a moment."

The twins turned. Harry pulled open his trunk and drew out his Triwizard winnings.

"Take it," he said, and he thrust the sack into George's hands.

"What?" said Fred, looking flabbergasted.

"Take it," Harry repeated firmly. "I don't want it."

"You're mental," said George, trying to push it back at Harry.

"No, I'm not," said Harry. "You take it, and get inventing. It's for the joke shop."

"He *is* mental," Fred said in an almost awed voice.

"Listen," said Harry firmly. "If you don't take it, I'm throwing it down the drain. I don't want it and I don't need it. But I could do with a few laughs. We could all do with a few laughs. I've got a feeling we're going to need them more than usual before long."

"Harry," said George weakly, weighing the money bag in his hands, "there's got to be a thousand Galleons in here."

"Yeah," said Harry, grinning. "Think how many Canary Creams that is."

The twins stared at him.

"Just don't tell your mum where you got it . . . although she might not be so keen for you to join the Ministry anymore, come to think of it. . . ."

"Harry," Fred began, but Harry pulled out his wand.

"Look," he said flatly, "take it, or I'll hex you. I know some good ones now. Just do me one favor, okay? Buy Ron some different dress robes and say they're from you."

He left the compartment before they could say another word, stepping over Malfoy, Crabbe, and Goyle, who were still lying on the floor, covered in hex marks.

Uncle Vernon was waiting beyond the barrier. Mrs. Weasley was close by him. She hugged Harry very tightly when she saw him and whispered in his ear, "I think Dumbledore will let you come to us later in the summer. Keep in touch, Harry."

"See you, Harry," said Ron, clapping him on the back.

"'Bye, Harry!" said Hermione, and she did something she had never done before, and kissed him on the cheek.

"Harry — thanks," George muttered, while Fred nodded fervently at his side.

Harry winked at them, turned to Uncle Vernon, and followed him silently from the station. There was no point worrying yet, he told himself, as he got into the back of the Dursleys' car.

As Hagrid had said, what would come, would come . . . and he would have to meet it when it did.

HARRY POTTER'S

ADVENTURES CONTINUE IN

# HARRY POTTER

## AND THE ORDER OF THE PHOENIX

TURN THE PAGE FOR

A SNEAK PREVIEW!

# DUDLEY DEMENTED

The hottest day of the summer so far was drawing to a close and a drowsy silence lay over the large, square houses of Privet Drive. Cars that were usually gleaming stood dusty in their drives and lawns that were once emerald green lay parched and yellowing; the use of hosepipes had been banned due to drought. Deprived of their usual car-washing and lawn-mowing pursuits, the inhabitants of Privet Drive had retreated into the shade of their cool houses, windows thrown wide in the hope of tempting in a nonexistent breeze. The only person left outdoors was a teenage boy who was lying flat on his back in a flower bed outside number four.

He was a skinny, black-haired, bespectacled boy who had the pinched, slightly unhealthy look of someone who has grown a lot in a short space of time. His jeans were torn and dirty, his T-shirt baggy and faded, and the soles of his trainers were peeling away from the uppers. Harry Potter's appearance did not endear him to the neighbors, who were the sort of people who thought scruffiness ought to be punishable by law, but as he had hidden himself behind a large hydrangea bush this evening he was quite invisible to passersby. In fact, the only way he would be spotted was if his Uncle Vernon or Aunt Petunia stuck their heads out of the living room window and looked straight down into the flower bed below.

On the whole, Harry thought he was to be congratulated on his idea of hiding here. He was not, perhaps, very comfortable lying on the hot, hard earth, but on the other hand, nobody was glaring at him, grinding their teeth so loudly that he could not hear the news, or shooting nasty questions at him, as had happened every time he had tried sitting down in the living room and watching television with his aunt and uncle.

Almost as though this thought had fluttered through the open window, Vernon Dursley, Harry's uncle, suddenly spoke. "Glad to see the boy's stopped trying to butt in. Where is he anyway?"

"I don't know," said Aunt Petunia unconcernedly. "Not in the house."

Uncle Vernon grunted.

*"Watching the news . . ."* he said scathingly. "I'd like to know what he's really up to. As if a normal boy cares what's on the news — Dudley hasn't got a clue what's going on, doubt he knows who the Prime Minister is! Anyway, it's not as if there'd be anything about *his lot* on *our* news —"

"Vernon, *shh!*" said Aunt Petunia. "The window's open!"

"Oh — yes — sorry, dear . . ."

The Dursleys fell silent. Harry listened to a jingle about Fruit 'N Bran breakfast cereal while he watched Mrs. Figg, a batty, cat-loving old lady from nearby Wisteria Walk, amble slowly past. She was frowning and muttering to herself. Harry was very pleased that he was concealed behind the bush; Mrs. Figg had recently taken to asking him around for tea whenever she met him in the street. She had rounded the corner and vanished from view before Uncle Vernon's voice floated out of the window again.

"Dudders out for tea?"

"At the Polkisses'," said Aunt Petunia fondly. "He's got so many little friends, he's so popular . . ."

Harry repressed a snort with difficulty. The Dursleys really were astonishingly stupid about their son, Dudley; they had swallowed all his dim-witted lies about having tea with a different member of his gang every night of the summer holidays. Harry knew perfectly well that Dudley had not been to tea anywhere; he and his gang spent every evening vandalizing the play park, smoking on street corners, and throwing stones at passing cars and children. Harry had seen them at it during his evening walks around Little Whinging; he had spent most of the holidays wandering the streets, scavenging newspapers from bins along the way.

The opening notes of the music that heralded the seven o'clock news reached Harry's ears and his stomach turned over. Perhaps tonight — after a month of waiting — would be the night —

"Record numbers of stranded holidaymakers fill airports as the Spanish baggage-handlers' strike reaches its second week —"

"Give 'em a lifelong siesta, I would," snarled Uncle Vernon over the end of the newsreader's sentence, but no matter: Outside in the flower bed, Harry's stomach seemed to unclench. If anything had happened, it would surely have been the first item on the news; death and destruction were more important than stranded holidaymakers. . . .

He let out a long, slow breath and stared up at the brilliant blue sky. Every day this summer had been the same: the tension, the expectation, the temporary relief, and then mounting tension again . . . and always, growing more insistent all the time, the question of *why* nothing had happened yet. . . .

He kept listening, just in case there was some small clue, not recognized for what it really was by the Muggles — an unexplained disappearance, perhaps, or some strange accident . . . but the baggage-handlers' strike was followed by news on the drought in the Southeast ("I hope he's listening next door!" bellowed Uncle Vernon, "with his sprinklers on at three in the morning!"); then a helicopter that had almost crashed in a field in Surrey, then a famous actress's divorce from her famous husband ("as if we're interested in their sordid affairs," sniffed Aunt Petunia, who had followed the case obsessively in every magazine she could lay her bony hands on).

Harry closed his eyes against the now blazing evening sky as the newsreader said, "And finally, Bungy the budgie has found a novel way of keeping cool this summer. Bungy, who lives at the Five Feathers in Barnsley, has learned to water-ski! Mary Dorkins went to find out more. . . ."

Harry opened his eyes again. If they had reached water-skiing budgerigars, there was nothing else worth hearing. He rolled cautiously onto his front and raised himself onto his knees and elbows, preparing to crawl out from under the window.

He had moved about two inches when several things happened in very quick succession.

A loud, echoing *crack* broke the sleepy silence like a gunshot; a cat streaked out from under a parked car and flew out of sight; a shriek, a bellowed oath, and the sound of breaking china came from the Dursleys' living room, and as though Harry had been waiting for this signal, he jumped to his feet, at the same time pulling from the waistband of his jeans a thin wooden wand as if he were unsheathing a sword. But before he could draw himself up to full height, the top of his head collided with the Dursleys' open window, and the resultant crash made Aunt Petunia scream even louder.

Harry felt as if his head had been split in two; eyes streaming, he swayed, trying to focus on the street and spot the source of the noise, but he had barely staggered upright again when two large purple hands reached through the open window and closed tightly around his throat.

"*Put — it — away!*" Uncle Vernon snarled into Harry's ear. "*Now! Before — anyone — sees!*"

"Get — off — me!" Harry gasped; for a few seconds they struggled, Harry pulling at his uncle's sausage-like fingers with his left hand, his right maintaining a firm grip on his raised wand. Then, as the pain in the top of Harry's head gave a particularly nasty throb, Uncle Vernon yelped and released Harry as though he had received an electric shock — some invisible force seemed to have surged through his nephew, making him impossible to hold.

Panting, Harry fell forward over the hydrangea bush, straightened up, and stared around. There was no sign of what had caused the loud cracking noise, but there were several faces peering through various nearby windows. Harry stuffed his wand hastily back into his jeans and tried to look innocent.

"Lovely evening!" shouted Uncle Vernon, waving at Mrs. Number Seven, who was glaring from behind her net curtains. "Did you hear that car backfire just now? Gave Petunia and me quite a turn!"

He continued to grin in a horrible, manic way until all the curious neighbors had disappeared from their various windows, then the grin became a grimace of rage as he beckoned Harry back toward him.

Harry moved a few steps closer, taking care to stop just short of the point at which Uncle Vernon's outstretched hands could resume their strangling.

"What the *devil* do you mean by it, boy?" asked Uncle Vernon in a croaky voice that trembled with fury.

"What do I mean by what?" said Harry coldly. He kept looking left and right up the street, still hoping to see the person who had made the cracking noise.

"Making a racket like a starting pistol right outside our —"

"I didn't make that noise," said Harry firmly.

Aunt Petunia's thin, horsey face now appeared beside Uncle Vernon's wide, purple one. She looked livid.

"Why were you lurking under our window?"

"Yes — yes, good point, Petunia! *What were you doing under our window, boy?*"

"Listening to the news," said Harry in a resigned voice.

His aunt and uncle exchanged looks of outrage.

"Listening to the news! *Again?*"

"Well, it changes every day, you see," said Harry.

"Don't you be clever with me, boy! I want to know what you're really up to — and don't give me any more of this *listening to the news* tosh! You know perfectly well that *your lot* . . ."

"Careful, Vernon!" breathed Aunt Petunia, and Uncle Vernon lowered his voice so that Harry could barely hear him, ". . . that *your lot* don't get on *our* news!"

"That's all you know," said Harry.

The Dursleys goggled at him for a few seconds, then Aunt Petunia said, "You're a nasty little liar. What are all those —" she too lowered her voice so that Harry had to lip-read the next word, "— *owls* — doing if they're not bringing you news?"

"Aha!" said Uncle Vernon in a triumphant whisper. "Get out of that one, boy! As if we didn't know you get all your news from those pestilential birds!"

Harry hesitated for a moment. It cost him something to tell the truth this time, even though his aunt and uncle could not possibly know how bad Harry felt at admitting it.

"The owls . . . aren't bringing me news," said Harry tonelessly.

"I don't believe it," said Aunt Petunia at once.

"No more do I," said Uncle Vernon forcefully.

"We know you're up to something funny," said Aunt Petunia.

"We're not stupid, you know," said Uncle Vernon.

"Well, *that's* news to me," said Harry, his temper rising, and before the Dursleys could call him back, he had wheeled about, crossed the front lawn, stepped over the low garden wall, and was striding off up the street.

He was in trouble now and he knew it. He would have to face his aunt and uncle later and pay the price for his rudeness, but he did not care very much just at the moment; he had much more pressing matters on his mind.

Harry was sure that the cracking noise had been made by someone Apparating or Disapparating. It was exactly the sound Dobby the house-elf made when he vanished into thin air. Was it possible that Dobby was here in Privet Drive? Could Dobby be following him right at this very moment? As this thought occurred he wheeled around and stared back down Privet Drive, but it appeared to be completely deserted again and Harry was sure that Dobby did not know how to become invisible. . . .

He walked on, hardly aware of the route he was taking, for he had pounded these streets so often lately that his feet carried him to his favorite haunts automatically. Every few steps he glanced back over his shoulder. Someone magical had been near him as he lay among Aunt Petunia's dying begonias, he was sure of it. Why hadn't they spoken to him, why hadn't they made contact, why were they hiding now?

And then, as his feeling of frustration peaked, his certainty leaked away.

Perhaps it hadn't been a magical sound after all. Perhaps he was so desperate for the tiniest sign of contact from the world to which he belonged that he was simply overreacting to perfectly ordinary noises. Could he be *sure* it hadn't been the sound of something breaking inside a neighbor's house?

Harry felt a dull, sinking sensation in his stomach and, before he knew it, the feeling of hopelessness that had plagued him all summer rolled over him once again. . . .

Tomorrow morning he would be awoken by the alarm at five

o'clock so that he could pay the owl that delivered the *Daily Prophet* —
but was there any point in continuing to take it? Harry merely glanced
at the front page before throwing it aside these days; when the idiots
who ran the paper finally realized that Voldemort was back it would
be headline news, and that was the only kind Harry cared about.

If he was lucky, there would also be owls carrying letters from his
best friends, Ron and Hermione, though any expectation he had had
that their letters would bring him news had long since been dashed.

*"We can't say much about you-know-what, obviously. . . ." "We've been
told not to say anything important in case our letters go astray. . . ."
"We're quite busy but I can't give you details here. . . ." "There's a fair
amount going on, we'll tell you everything when we see you. . . ."*

But when were they going to see him? Nobody seemed too bothered with a precise date. Hermione had scribbled, *"I expect we'll be
seeing you quite soon"* inside his birthday card, but how soon was soon?
As far as Harry could tell from the vague hints in their letters, Hermione and Ron were in the same place, presumably at Ron's parents'
house. He could hardly bear to think of the pair of them having fun
at the Burrow when he was stuck in Privet Drive. In fact, he was so
angry at them that he had thrown both their birthday presents of
Honeydukes chocolates away unopened, though he had regretted this
after eating the wilting salad Aunt Petunia had provided for dinner
that night.

And what were Ron and Hermione busy with? Why wasn't he,
Harry, busy? Hadn't he proved himself capable of handling much
more than they? Had they all forgotten what he had done? Hadn't it
been *he* who had entered that graveyard and watched Cedric being
murdered and been tied to that tombstone and nearly killed . . . ?

*Don't think about that,* Harry told himself sternly for the hundredth
time that summer. It was bad enough that he kept revisiting the graveyard in his nightmares, without dwelling on it in his waking moments
too.

He turned a corner into Magnolia Crescent; halfway along he passed the narrow alleyway down the side of a garage where he had first clapped eyes on his godfather. Sirius, at least, seemed to understand how Harry was feeling; admittedly his letters were just as empty of proper news as Ron and Hermione's, but at least they contained words of caution and consolation instead of tantalizing hints:

*"I know this must be frustrating for you. . . ." "Keep your nose clean and everything will be okay. . . ." "Be careful and don't do anything rash. . . ."*

Well, thought Harry, as he crossed Magnolia Crescent, turned into Magnolia Road, and headed toward the darkening play park, he had (by and large) done as Sirius advised; he had at least resisted the temptation to tie his trunk to his broomstick and set off for the Burrow by himself. In fact Harry thought his behavior had been very good considering how frustrated and angry he felt at being stuck in Privet Drive this long, reduced to hiding in flower beds in the hope of hearing something that might point to what Lord Voldemort was doing. Nevertheless, it was quite galling to be told not to be rash by a man who had served twelve years in the wizard prison, Azkaban, escaped, attempted to commit the murder he had been convicted for in the first place, then gone on the run with a stolen hippogriff. . . .

Harry vaulted over the locked park gate and set off across the parched grass. The park was as empty as the surrounding streets. When he reached the swings he sank onto the only one that Dudley and his friends had not yet managed to break, coiled one arm around the chain, and stared moodily at the ground. He would not be able to hide in the Dursleys' flower bed again. Tomorrow he would have to think of some fresh way of listening to the news. In the meantime, he had nothing to look forward to but another restless, disturbed night, because even when he escaped nightmares about Cedric he had unsettling dreams about long dark corridors, all finishing in dead ends and locked doors, which he supposed had something to do with the trapped feeling he had when he was awake. Often the old scar on his forehead prickled uncomfortably, but he did not fool himself that Ron or Hermione or Sirius would find that very interesting anymore. . . . In the past his scar hurting had warned that Voldemort was getting stronger again, but now that Voldemort was back they would probably remind him that its regular irritation was only to be expected. . . . Nothing to worry about . . . old news . . .

The injustice of it all welled up inside him so that he wanted to yell with fury. If it hadn't been for him, nobody would even have known Voldemort was back! And his reward was to be stuck in Little Whinging for four solid weeks, completely cut off from the magical world, reduced to squatting among dying begonias so that he could hear about water-skiing budgerigars! How could Dumbledore have forgotten him so easily? Why had Ron and Hermione got together without inviting him along too? How much longer was he supposed to endure Sirius telling him to sit tight and be a good boy; or resist the temptation to write to the stupid *Daily Prophet* and point out that Voldemort had returned? These furious thoughts whirled around in Harry's head, and his insides writhed with anger as a sultry, velvety night fell around him, the air full of the smell of warm, dry grass and the only sound that of the low grumble of traffic on the road beyond the park railings.

He did not know how long he had sat on the swing before the sound of voices interrupted his musings and he looked up. The streetlamps from the surrounding roads were casting a misty glow strong enough to silhouette a group of people making their way across the park. One of them was singing a loud, crude song. The others were laughing. A soft ticking noise came from several expensive racing bikes that they were wheeling along.

Harry knew who those people were. The figure in front was unmistakably his cousin, Dudley Dursley, wending his way home, accompanied by his faithful gang.

Dudley was as vast as ever, but a year's hard dieting and the discovery of a new talent had wrought quite a change in his physique. As Uncle Vernon delightedly told anyone who would listen, Dudley had recently become the Junior Heavyweight Inter-School Boxing Champion of the Southeast. "The noble sport," as Uncle Vernon called it, had made Dudley even more formidable than he had seemed to Harry in the primary school days when he had served as Dudley's first punching bag. Harry was not remotely afraid of his cousin anymore but he still didn't think that Dudley learning to punch harder and more accurately was cause for celebration. Neighborhood children all around were terrified of him — even more terrified than they were of "that Potter boy," who, they had been warned, was a hardened hooligan who attended St. Brutus's Secure Center for Incurably Criminal Boys.

Harry watched the dark figures crossing the grass and wondered whom they had been beating up tonight. *Look round,* Harry found himself thinking as he watched them. *Come on . . . look round . . . I'm sitting here all alone. . . . Come and have a go. . . .*

If Dudley's friends saw him sitting here, they would be sure to make a beeline for him, and what would Dudley do then? He wouldn't want to lose face in front of the gang, but he'd be terrified of provoking Harry. . . . It would be really fun to watch Dudley's dilemma; to taunt him, watch him, with him powerless to respond . . . and if any of the others tried hitting Harry, Harry was ready — he had his wand . . . let them try . . . He'd love to vent some of his frustration on the boys who had once made his life hell —

But they did not turn around, they did not see him, they were almost at the railings. Harry mastered the impulse to call after them. . . . Seeking a fight was not a smart move. . . . He must not use magic. . . . He would be risking expulsion again. . . .

Dudley's gang's voices died; they were out of sight, heading along Magnolia Road.

*There you go, Sirius,* Harry thought dully. *Nothing rash. Kept my nose clean. Exactly the opposite of what you'd have done . . .*

He got to his feet and stretched. Aunt Petunia and Uncle Vernon seemed to feel that whenever Dudley turned up was the right time to be home, and anytime after that was much too late. Uncle Vernon had threatened to lock Harry in the shed if he came home after Dudley again, so, stifling a yawn, still scowling, Harry set off toward the park gate.

Magnolia Road, like Privet Drive, was full of large, square houses with perfectly manicured lawns, all owned by large, square owners who drove very clean cars similar to Uncle Vernon's. Harry preferred Little Whinging by night, when the curtained windows made patches of jewel-bright colors in the darkness and he ran no danger of hearing disapproving mutters about his "delinquent" appearance when he passed the householders. He walked quickly, so that halfway along Magnolia Road Dudley's gang came into view again; they were saying their farewells at the entrance to Magnolia Crescent. Harry stepped into the shadow of a large lilac tree and waited.

". . . squealed like a pig, didn't he?" Malcolm was saying, to guffaws from the others.

"Nice right hook, Big D," said Piers.

"Same time tomorrow?" said Dudley.

"Round at my place, my parents are out," said Gordon.

"See you then," said Dudley.

"'Bye Dud!"

"See ya, Big D!"

Harry waited for the rest of the gang to move on before setting off again. When their voices had faded once more he headed around the corner into Magnolia Crescent and by walking very quickly he soon came within hailing distance of Dudley, who was strolling along at his ease, humming tunelessly.

"Hey, Big D!"

Dudley turned.

"Oh," he grunted. "It's you."

"How long have you been 'Big D' then?" said Harry.

"Shut it," snarled Dudley, turning away again.

"Cool name," said Harry, grinning and falling into step beside his cousin. "But you'll always be Ickle Diddykins to me."

"I said; SHUT IT!" said Dudley, whose ham-like hands had curled into fists.

"Don't the boys know that's what your mum calls you?"

"Shut your face."

"You don't tell *her* to shut her face. What about 'popkin' and 'Dinky Diddydums,' can I use them then?"

Dudley said nothing. The effort of keeping himself from hitting Harry seemed to be demanding all his self-control.

"So who've you been beating up tonight?" Harry asked, his grin fading. "Another ten-year-old? I know you did Mark Evans two nights ago —"

"He was asking for it," snarled Dudley.

"Oh yeah?"

"He cheeked me."

"Yeah? Did he say you look like a pig that's been taught to walk on its hind legs? 'Cause that's not cheek, Dud, that's true . . ."

A muscle was twitching in Dudley's jaw. It gave Harry enormous satisfaction to know how furious he was making Dudley; he felt as though he was siphoning off his own frustration into his cousin, the only outlet he had.

They turned right down the narrow alleyway where Harry had first seen Sirius and which formed a shortcut between Magnolia Crescent and Wisteria Walk. It was empty and much darker than the streets it linked because there were no streetlamps. Their footsteps were muffled between garage walls on one side and a high fence on the other.

"Think you're a big man carrying that thing, don't you?" Dudley said after a few seconds.

"What thing?"

"That — that thing you're hiding."

Harry grinned again.

"Not as stupid as you look, are you, Dud? But I s'pose if you were, you wouldn't be able to walk and talk at the same time. . . ."

Harry pulled out his wand. He saw Dudley look sideways at it.

"You're not allowed," Dudley said at once. "I know you're not. You'd get expelled from that freak school you go to."

"How d'you know they haven't changed the rules, Big D?"

"They haven't," said Dudley, though he didn't sound completely convinced. Harry laughed softly.

"You haven't got the guts to take me on without that thing, have you?" Dudley snarled.

"Whereas you just need four mates behind you before you can beat up a ten-year-old. You know that boxing title you keep banging on about? How old was your opponent? Seven? Eight?"

"He was sixteen for your information," snarled Dudley, "and he was out cold for twenty minutes after I'd finished with him and he was twice as heavy as you. You just wait till I tell Dad you had that thing out —"

"Running to Daddy now, are you? Is his ickle boxing champ frightened of nasty Harry's wand?"

"Not this brave at night, are you?" sneered Dudley.

"This *is* night, Diddykins. That's what we call it when it goes all dark like this."

"I mean when you're in bed!" Dudley snarled.

He had stopped walking. Harry stopped too, staring at his cousin. From the little he could see of Dudley's large face, he was wearing a strangely triumphant look.

"What d'you mean, I'm not brave in bed?" said Harry, completely nonplussed. "What — am I supposed to be frightened of pillows or something?"

"I heard you last night," said Dudley breathlessly. "Talking in your sleep. *Moaning.*"

"What d'you mean?" Harry said again, but there was a cold, plunging sensation in his stomach. He had revisited the graveyard last night in his dreams.

Dudley gave a harsh bark of laughter then adopted a high-pitched, whimpering voice. "'Don't kill Cedric! Don't kill Cedric!' Who's Cedric — your boyfriend?"

"I — you're lying —" said Harry automatically. But his mouth had gone dry. He knew Dudley wasn't lying — how else would he know about Cedric?

"'Dad! Help me, Dad! He's going to kill me, Dad! Boo-hoo!'"

"Shut up," said Harry quietly. "Shut up, Dudley, I'm warning you!"

"'Come and help me, Dad! Mum, come and help me! He's killed Cedric! Dad, help me! He's going to —' *Don't you point that thing at me!*"

Dudley backed into the alley wall. Harry was pointing the wand directly at Dudley's heart. Harry could feel fourteen years' hatred of Dudley pounding in his veins — what wouldn't he give to strike now, to jinx Dudley so thoroughly he'd have to crawl home like an insect, struck dumb, sprouting feelers —

"Don't ever talk about that again," Harry snarled. "D'you understand me?"

"Point that thing somewhere else!"

"I said, *do you understand me?*"

"*Point it somewhere else!*"

"DO YOU UNDERSTAND ME?"

"GET THAT THING AWAY FROM —"

Dudley gave an odd, shuddering gasp, as though he had been doused in icy water.

Something had happened to the night. The star-strewn indigo sky was suddenly pitch-black and lightless — the stars, the moon, the misty streetlamps at either end of the alley had vanished. The distant grumble of cars and the whisper of trees had gone. The balmy evening was suddenly piercingly, bitingly cold. They were surrounded by total, impenetrable, silent darkness, as though some giant hand had dropped a thick, icy mantle over the entire alleyway, blinding them.

For a split second Harry thought he had done magic without meaning to, despite the fact that he'd been resisting as hard as he could — then his reason caught up with his senses — he didn't have the power to turn off the stars. He turned his head this way and that, trying to see something, but the darkness pressed on his eyes like a weightless veil.

Dudley's terrified voice broke in Harry's ear.

"W-what are you d-doing? St-stop it!"

"I'm not doing anything! Shut up and don't move!"

"I c-can't see! I've g-gone blind! I —"

"I said shut up!"

Harry stood stock-still, turning his sightless eyes left and right. The cold was so intense that he was shivering all over; goose bumps had erupted up his arms, and the hairs on the back of his neck were standing up — he opened his eyes to their fullest extent, staring blankly around, unseeing . . .

It was impossible. . . . They couldn't be here. . . . Not in Little Whinging . . . He strained his ears. . . . He would hear them before he saw them. . . .

"I'll t-tell Dad!" Dudley whimpered. "W-where are you? What are you d-do — ?"

"Will you shut up?" Harry hissed, "I'm trying to lis —"

But he fell silent. He had heard just the thing he had been dreading.

J.K. ROWLING is the author of the record-breaking, multi-award-winning Harry Potter novels. Loved by fans around the world, the series has sold over 500 million copies, been translated into over 80 languages, and made into eight blockbuster films. She has written three companion volumes in aid of charity: *Quidditch Through the Ages* and *Fantastic Beasts and Where to Find Them* (in aid of Comic Relief UK and Lumos), and *The Tales of Beedle the Bard* (in aid of Lumos), as well as a screenplay inspired by *Fantastic Beasts and Where to Find Them*, which marked the start of a five-film series to be written by the author. She has also collaborated on a stage play, *Harry Potter and the Cursed Child Parts One and Two*, which opened in London's West End in the summer of 2016 and on Broadway in the spring of 2018. In 2012, J.K. Rowling's digital company Pottermore was launched, where fans can enjoy news, features, and articles, as well as original content from J.K. Rowling. She is also the author of *The Casual Vacancy*, a novel for adult readers, and the Strike crime series, written under the pseudonym Robert Galbraith. She has received many awards and honors, including an OBE and Companion of Honour, France's Légion d'honneur, and the Hans Christian Andersen Award.

BRIAN SELZNICK is the Caldecott Medal–winning creator of the #1 *New York Times* bestsellers *The Invention of Hugo Cabret*, adapted into Martin Scorsese's Oscar-winning movie *Hugo*, and *Wonderstruck*, adapted by celebrated filmmaker Todd Haynes with a screenplay by Selznick, as well as *The Marvels* and *Baby Monkey, Private Eye* (cowritten with Dr. David Serlin). His books have garnered countless accolades worldwide and have been translated into more than 35 languages. Selznick divides his time between Brooklyn, New York, and San Diego, California.

MARY GRANDPRÉ has illustrated more than twenty beautiful books, including *The Noisy Paint Box*, which received a Caldecott Honor; *Cleonardo, the Little Inventor*, of which she is also the author; and the original American editions of all seven Harry Potter novels. Her work has also appeared in the *New Yorker*, the *Atlantic Monthly*, and the *Wall Street Journal*, and her paintings and pastels have been shown in galleries across the United States. Ms. GrandPré lives in Sarasota, Florida, with her family.